FOUL LIVES!

"You are mine!"

The voice was that of Lord Foul the Despiser, gloating over his triumph. Thomas Covenant, leper and pariah in his own world, was back in the Land, high up on Kevin's Watch, again listening to the evil promises of Foul. And beside him lay Dr. Linden Avery, whose efforts to save him had doomed her to share his summons.

Ten quiet, undisturbed years had passed for Covenant since he was last called to the Land where magic and Earthpower worked. At that time, as ur-Lord Thomas Covenant the Unbeliever, he had used the wild magic of his white gold ring to defeat the evil plans of Lord Foul and seemingly destroy that ancient enemy of the Land. He had believed that Foul was banished forever.

THE WOUNDED LAND is a stunning achievement, pitting the devilish legions of Lord Foul against two exiles who struggle mightily to revive a dying world.

Also by Stephen R. Donaldson
Published by Ballantine Books:

LORD FOUL'S BANE

THE ILLEARTH WAR

THE POWER THAT PRESERVES

Book One of The Second Chronicles of Thomas Covenant

The Wounded Land

STEPHEN R. DONALDSON

A Del Rey Book

BALLANTINE BOOKS • **NEW YORK**

A Del Rey Book
Published by Ballantine Books

Library of Congress Catalog Card Number: 79-20644

ISBN 0-345-27831-3

Manufactured in the United States of America

First Ballantine Books Edition: June 1980

Paperback format
First Edition: May 1981

Cover art by Darrell K. Sweet

Contents

Contents

PART III: Purpose

What Has Gone Before

AFTER AN INFECTION causes the amputation of two fingers, Thomas Covenant learns he has leprosy. Once a popular author, he is now a pariah to his community. His wife Joan divorces him.

Lonely and bitter, he meets an old beggar who tells him to "be true." Confused by the odd encounter, he stumbles in front of a car and revives on a high mountain in a strange world. After an evil voice of one called Lord Foul gives him a message of doom for the Lords of the Land, he is led down to the village of Mithil Stonedown by Lena. There Covenant is considered the reincarnation of the legendary Berek Halfhand, the first High Lord, and his white gold wedding ring is regarded as a talisman of great power, capable of wild magic.

Lena heals him with hurtloam mud. His sudden recovery is more than he can bear, and he rapes Lena. Despite this, Lena's mother Atiaran agrees to guide Covenant to Revelstone, home of the Lords. Covenant calls himself the Unbeliever because he cannot believe in the magic of the Land. He fears it is merely a delirious escape from reality.

A friendly Giant, Saltheart Foamfollower, takes Covenant to Revelstone, where he is greeted as ur-Lord. The Lords are shocked at Foul's message that an evil Cavewight holds the powerful Staff of Law, without which they cannot overcome Foul's plot to ruin the Land. They must rescue the Staff from the Cavewight caverns under Mount Thunder. Covenant goes with them, guarded by Bannor, one of the Bloodguard who have taken an ancient vow to protect the Lords.

After many encounters with Foul's evil creatures, they rescue the Staff from the Cavewights. The Lords escape when Covenant—without knowing how—somehow uses the wild magic of his ring. But Covenant begins to fade and wakes in a hospital a few hours after his accident—though months passed in the Land.

A few weeks later, Covenant rushes to answer a call from Joan, only to stumble and knock himself out. He again finds himself in the Land—where forty years have passed. The Lords are desperate. Foul has found the Illearth Stone, a source of evil power, and prepares to attack. The weaker army of the Lords is commanded by Hile Troy, who also comes from the "real" Earth. The High Lord is now Elena, Covenant's daughter by Lena. She greets him as a savior.

A force of Bloodguard and Lords is sent to *Coercri* to ask help of the Giants. But there Foul has possessed three Giants to house the spirits of his ancient Raver lieutenants. The other Giants are monstrously murdered. The surviving Lord destroys one Giant-Raver, and the Bloodguard seize a piece of the Illearth Stone to return it to Revelstone. But the Lord dies before he can warn them of its danger.

Hile Troy takes his army south, accompanied by Lord Mhoram, Covenant's friend. Foul's army is commanded by another Giant-Raver, and Troy is forced to flee to Garroting Deep, a forest protected by an ancient, mysterious Forestal, Caerroil Wildwood. The Forestal saves Troy's army but demands that Troy become an apprentice Forestal.

Elena has taken Covenant and Bannor to *Melenkurion* Skyweir, a mountain near Garroting Deep. Inside the mountain, Elena drinks from the water called the EarthBlood, and thus gains the Power of Command. She summons the spirit of Kevin, an ancient Lord, and orders him to destroy Foul. But Foul overcomes Kevin and sends him back to drag Elena and the Staff to their doom within the mountain.

Covenant and Bannor escape down a river, to meet with Mhoram. But again Covenant fades, to come to in his own living room.

Filled with guilt, he neglects himself and wanders the country at night. Then he encounters a little girl endangered by a snake. He saves her, but is bitten. Again, he returns to the Land—to Kevin's Watch where he first appeared in the Land. He has been summoned by a surviving Foamfollower and Triock, Lena's former lover, who has overcome his hatred of Covenant for the good of the Land. In Mithil Stonedown, Covenant again meets Lena—a crazed woman who claims to have kept herself young for love of Covenant, though she is old now.

During the seven years since the Staff was lost, things have grown worse for the Land. Mhoram is about to be besieged in Revelstone, and no place is safe. Only Covenant can destroy Foul with the power of the ring, they believe. Finally, Covenant sets out for Foul's Creche in the far east, accompanied by Foamfollower, Triock and Lena. They seek help from the Ramen, a people who serve the great Ranyhyn, the wild horses of the plains. But the Ramen are betrayed. Lena gives her life to save Covenant, but he is seriously wounded.

He is saved by an Unfettered One and healed. He meets Foamfollower and Triock—but they are captured by a Raver and brought to the Colossus that guards the Upper Land. There the ghost of Elena tries to destroy them, since she has been enslaved by Foul. With his ring, Covenant overcomes her and destroys the Staff she holds.

He and Foamfollower continue down into the Lower Land toward Foul's Creche. They are helped by the *jheherrin*, pitiful creatures of living mud, and finally penetrate the stronghold of Foul. There, with the courage of Foamfollower to help, Covenant discovers how to tap the power of the ring—though still without really understanding it. Whereupon he overcomes Foul and destroys the Illearth Stone.

He seems to be destroyed also. But the Creator of this world—the old beggar who first told him to "be true"—saves him. After showing Covenant that Mhoram has also triumphed against the forces of evil—by using the *krill*, a sword activated by Covenant's presence in the Land—the Creator sends him back to his own world.

Satisfied that the Land will survive, Covenant willingly faces the challenge of making his way as a leper in his own time and place. And for some ten years, he does face that challenge, with no further summons from the Land.

And now to begin The Second Chronicles of Thomas Covenant . . .

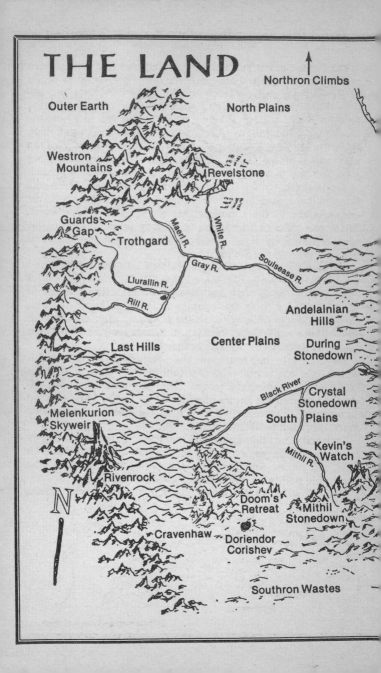

From a map by Lynn K. Plagge

Gallow-fells

PROLOGUE

Choice

ONE: Daughter

WHEN Linden Avery heard the knock at her door, she groaned aloud. She was in a black mood, and did not want visitors. She wanted a cold shower and privacy—a chance to accustom herself to the deliberate austerity of her surroundings.

She had spent most of the afternoon of an unnaturally muggy day in the middle of spring moving herself into this apartment which the Hospital had rented for her, lugging her sparse wardrobe, her inadequate furniture, and a back-breaking series of cardboard boxes containing textbooks from her middle-aged sedan up the outside stairs to the second floor of the old wooden house. The house squatted among its weeds like a crippled toad, spavined by antiquity; and when she had unlocked her apartment for the first time, she had been greeted by three rooms and a bath with grubby yellow walls, floorboards covered only by chipped beige paint, an atmosphere of desuetude bordering on indignity—and by a piece of paper which must have been slipped under the door. Thick red lines like lipstick or fresh blood marked the paper—a large crude triangle with two words inside it:

JESUS SAVES

She had glared at the paper for a moment, then had crumpled it in her pocket. She had no use for offers of salvation. She wanted nothing she did not earn.

3

But the note, combined with the turgid air, the long exertion of heaving her belongings up the stairs, and the apartment itself, left her feeling capable of murder. The rooms reminded her of her parents' house. That was why she hated the apartment. But it was condign, and she chose to accept it. She both loathed and approved the aptness of her state. Its personal stringency was appropriate.

She was a doctor newly out of residency, and she had purposely sought a job which would bring her to a small half-rural, half-stagnant town like this one—a town like the one near which she had been born and her parents had died. Though she was only thirty, she felt old, unlovely, and severe. This was just; she had lived an unlovely and severe life. Her father had died when she was eight; her mother, when she was fifteen. After three empty years in a foster home, she had put herself through college, then medical school, internship, and residency, specializing in Family Practice. She had been lonely ever since she could remember, and her isolation had largely become ingrained. Her two or three love affairs had been like hygienic exercises or experiments in physiology; they had left her untouched. So now when she looked at herself, she saw severity, and the consequences of violence.

Hard work and clenched emotions had not hurt the gratuitous womanliness of her body, or dulled the essential luster of her shoulder-length wheaten hair, or harmed the structural beauty of her face. Her driven and self-contained life had not changed the way her eyes misted and ran almost without provocation. But lines had already marked her face, leaving her with a perpetual frown of concentration above the bridge of her straight, delicate nose, and gullies like the implications of pain on either side of her mouth—a mouth which had originally been formed for something more generous than the life which had befallen her. And her voice had become flat, so that it sounded more like a diagnostic tool, a way of eliciting pertinent data, than a vehicle for communication.

But the way she had lived her life had given her something more than loneliness and a liability to black moods. It had taught her to believe in her own strength. She was a physician; she had held life and death in her hands, and had learned how to grasp them effectively. She trusted her ability to carry burdens. When she heard the knock at her door, she groaned aloud. But then she straightened her sweat-marked clothes as if she were tugging her emotions into order, and went to open the door.

She recognized the short, wry man who stood on the landing. He was Julius Berenford, Chief of Staff of the County Hospital. He was the man who had hired her to run his Outpatient Clinic and Emergency Room. In a more metropolitan hospital, the hiring of a Family Practitioner for such a position would have been unusual. But the County Hospital served a region composed largely of farmers and hill people. This town, the county seat, had been calcifying steadily for twenty years. Dr. Berenford needed a generalist.

The top of his head was level with her eyes, and he was twice her age. The round bulge of his stomach belied the thinness of his limbs. He gave an impression of dyspeptic affection, as if he found human behavior both incomprehensible and endearing. When he smiled below his white moustache, the pouches under his eyes tightened ironically.

"Dr. Avery," he said, wheezing faintly after the exertion of the stairs.

"Dr. Berenford." She wanted to protest the intrusion; so she stepped aside and said tightly, "Come in."

He entered the apartment, glancing around as he wandered toward a chair. "You've already moved in," he observed. "Good. I hope you had help getting everything up here."

She took a chair near his, seated herself squarely, as if she were on duty. "No." Who could she have asked for help?

Dr. Berenford started to expostulate. She stopped him with a gesture of dismissal. "No problem. I'm used to it."

"Well, you shouldn't be." His gaze on her was complex. "You just finished your residency at a highly respected hospital, and your work was excellent. The least you should be able to expect in life is help carrying your furniture upstairs."

His tone was only half humorous; but she understood the seriousness behind it because the question had come up more than once during their interviews. He had asked repeatedly why someone with her credentials wanted a job in a poor county hospital. He had not accepted the glib answers she had prepared for him; eventually, she had been forced to offer him at least an approximation of the facts. "Both my parents died near a town like this," she had said. "They were hardly middle-aged. If they'd been under the care of a good Family Practitioner, they would be alive today."

This was both true and false, and it lay at the root of the ambivalence which made her feel old. If her mother's melanoma had been properly diagnosed in time, it could have been treated surgically with a ninety per cent chance of success. And if her father's depression had been observed by anybody with any knowledge or insight, his suicide might have been prevented. But the reverse was true as well; nothing could have saved her parents. They had died because they were simply too ineffectual to go on living. Whenever she thought about such things, she seemed to feel her bones growing more brittle by the hour.

She had come to this town because she wanted to try to help people like her parents. And because she wanted to prove that she could be effective under such circumstances—that she was not like her parents. And because she wanted to die.

When she did not speak, Dr. Berenford said, "However, that's neither here nor there." The humorlessness of her silence appeared to discomfit him. "I'm glad you're here. Is there anything I can do? Help you get settled?"

Linden was about to refuse his offer, out of habit if not conviction, when she remembered the piece of paper in her pocket. On an impulse, she dug it out, handed it to him. "This came under the door. Maybe you ought to tell me what I'm getting into."

He peered at the triangle and the writing, muttered, "Jesus saves," under his breath, then sighed. "Occupational hazard. I've been going to church faithfully in this town for forty years. But since I'm a trained professional who earns a decent living, some of our good people"—he grimaced wryly—"are always trying to convert me. Ignorance is the only form of innocence they understand." He shrugged, returned the note to her. "This area has been depressed for a long time. After a while, depressed people do strange things. They try to turn depression into a virtue—they need something to make themselves feel less helpless. What they usually do around here is become evangelical. I'm afraid you're just going to have to put up with people who worry about your soul. Nobody gets much privacy in a small town."

Linden nodded; but she hardly heard her visitor. She was trapped in a sudden memory of her mother, weeping with poignant self-pity. She had blamed Linden for her father's death—

With a scowl, she drove back the recollection. Her revulsion was so strong that she might have consented to having the memories physically cut out of her brain. But Dr. Berenford was watching her as if her abhorrence showed on her face. To avoid exposing herself, she pulled discipline over her features like a surgical mask. "What can I do for you, doctor?"

"Well, for one thing," he said, forcing himself to sound genial in spite of her tone, "you can call me Julius. I'm going to call you Linden, so you might as well."

She acquiesced with a shrug. "Julius."

"Linden." He smiled; but his smile did not soften his discomfort. After a moment, he said hurriedly, as if he were trying to outrun the difficulty of his purpose, "Actually, I came over for two reasons. Of course, I wanted to welcome you to town. But I could have done that later. The truth is, I want to put you to work."

Work? she thought. The word sparked an involuntary protest. I just got here. I'm tired and angry, and I don't know how I'm going to stand this apartment. Carefully, she said, "It's Friday. I'm not supposed to start until Monday."

"This doesn't have anything to do with the Hospital. It should, but it doesn't." His gaze brushed her face like a touch of need. "It's a personal favor. I'm in over my head. I've spent so many years getting involved in the lives of my patients that I can't seem to make objective decisions anymore. Or maybe I'm just out of date—don't have enough medical knowledge. Seems to me that what I need is a second opinion."

"About what?" she asked, striving to sound noncommittal. But she was groaning inwardly. She already knew that she would attempt to provide whatever he asked of her. He was appealing to a part of her that had never learned how to refuse.

He frowned sourly. "Unfortunately, I can't tell you. It's in confidence."

"Oh, come on." She was in no mood for guessing games. "I took the same oath you did."

"I know." He raised his hands as if to ward off her vexation. "I know. But it isn't exactly that kind of confidence."

She stared at him, momentarily nonplussed. Wasn't he talking about a medical problem? "This sounds like it's going to be quite a favor."

"Could be. That's up to you." Before she could muster the

words to ask him what he was talking about, Dr. Berenford said abruptly, "Have you ever heard of Thomas Covenant? He writes novels."

She felt him watching her while she groped mentally. But she had no way of following his line of thought. She had not read a novel since she had finished her literature requirement in college. She had had so little time. Striving for detachment, she shook her head.

"He lives around here," the doctor said. "Has a house outside town on an old property called Haven Farm. You turn right on Main." He gestured vaguely toward the intersection. "Go through the middle of town, and about two miles later you'll come to it. On the right. He's a leper."

At the word *leper*, her mind bifurcated. This was the result of her training—dedication which had made her a physician without resolving her attitude toward herself. She murmured inwardly, Hansen's disease, and began reviewing information.

Mycobacterium lepra. Leprosy. It progressed by killing nerve tissue, typically in the extremities and in the cornea of the eye. In most cases, the disease could be arrested by means of a comprehensive treatment program pivoting around DDS: diamino-diphenyl-sulfone. If not arrested, the degeneration could produce muscular atrophy and deformation, changes in skin pigmentation, blindness. It also left the victim subject to a host of secondary afflictions, the most common of which was infection that destroyed other tissues, leaving the victim with the appearance—and consequences—of having been eaten alive. Incidence was extremely rare; leprosy was not contagious in any usual sense. Perhaps the only statistically significant way to contract it was to suffer prolonged exposure as a child in the tropics under crowded and unsanitary living conditions.

But while one part of her brain unwound its skein of knowledge, another was tangled in questions and emotions. A leper? Here? Why tell me? She was torn between visceral distaste and empathy. The disease itself attracted and repelled her because it was incurable—as immedicable as death. She had to take a deep breath before she could ask, "What do you want me to do about it?"

"Well—" He was studying her as if he thought there were indeed something she could do about it. "Nothing. That isn't why I brought it up." Abruptly, he got to his feet, began measuring out his unease on the chipped floorboards. Though he was not heavy, they squeaked vaguely under him. "He was diagnosed early enough—only lost two fingers. One of our better lab technicians caught it, right here at County Hospital. He's been stable for more than nine years now. The only reason I told you is to find out if you're—squeamish. About lepers." He spoke with a twisted expression. "I used to be. But I've had time to get over it."

He did not give her a chance to reply. He went on as if he were confessing. "I've reached the point now where I don't think of him as leprosy personified. But I never forget he's a leper." He was talking about something for which he had not been able to forgive himself. "Part of that's his fault," he said defensively. "He never forgets, either. He doesn't think of himself as Thomas Covenant the writer—the man—the human being. He thinks of himself as Thomas Covenant the leper."

When she continued to stare at him flatly, he dropped his gaze. "But that's not the point. The point is, would it bother you to go see him?"

"No," she said severely; but her severity was for herself rather than for him. I'm a doctor. Sick people are my business. "But I still don't understand why you want me to go out there."

The pouches under his eyes shook as if he were pleading with her. "I can't tell you."

"You can't tell me." The quietness of her tone belied the blackness of her mood. "What good do you think I can possibly do if I don't even know why I'm talking to him?"

"You could get *him* to tell you." Dr. Berenford's voice sounded like the misery of an ineffectual old man. "That's what I want. I want him to accept you—tell you what's going on himself. So I won't have to break any promises."

"Let me get this straight." She made no more effort to conceal her anger. "You want me to go out there, and ask him outright to tell me his secrets. A total stranger arrives at his door, and wants to know what's bothering him—for no other reason than because Dr. Berenford would like a second opinion. I'll be lucky if he doesn't have me arrested for trespassing."

For a moment, the doctor faced her sarcasm and indignation. Then he sighed. "I know. He's like that—he'd never tell you. He's been locked into himself so long——" The next instant, his voice became sharp with pain. "But I think he's *wrong*."

"Then tell me what it is," insisted Linden.

His mouth opened and shut; his hands made supplicating gestures. But then he recovered himself. "No. That's backward. First I need to know which one of us is wrong. I owe him that. Mrs. Roman is no help. This is a medical decision. But I can't make it. I've tried, and I can't."

The simplicity with which he admitted his inadequacy snared her. She was tired, dirty, and bitter, and her mind searched for an escape. But his need for assistance struck too close to the driving compulsions of her life. Her hands were knotted together like certainty. After a moment, she looked up at him. His features had sagged as if the muscles were exhausted by the weight of his mortality. In her flat professional voice, she said, "Give me some excuse I can use to go out there."

She could hardly bear the sight of his relief. "That I can do," he said with a show of briskness. Reaching into a jacket pocket, he pulled out a paperback and handed it to her. The lettering across the drab cover said:

Or I Will Sell My Soul for Guilt
a novel by
THOMAS COVENANT

"Ask for his autograph." The older man had regained his sense of irony. "Try to get him talking. If you can get inside his defenses, something will happen."

Silently, she cursed herself. She knew nothing about novels, had never learned how to talk to strangers about anything except their symptoms. Anticipations of embarrassment filled her like shame. But she had been mortifying herself for so long that she had no respect left for the parts of her which could still feel shame. "After I see him," she said dully, "I'll want to talk to you. I don't have a phone yet. Where do you live?"

Her acceptance restored his earlier manner; he became wry and solicitous again. He gave her directions to his house, repeated his offer of help, thanked her for her willingness to involve herself in Thomas Covenant's affairs. When he left, she felt dimly astonished that he did not appear to resent the need which had forced him to display his futility in front of her.

And yet the sound of his feet descending the stairs gave her a sense of abandonment, as if she had been left to carry alone a burden that she would never be able to understand.

Foreboding nagged at her, but she ignored it. She had no acceptable alternatives. She sat where she was for a moment, glaring around the blind yellow walls, then went to take a shower.

After she had washed away as much of the blackness as she could reach with soap and water, she donned a dull gray dress that had the effect of minimizing her femininity, then spent a few minutes checking the contents of her medical bag. They always seemed insufficient—there were so many things she might conceivably need which she could not carry with her—and now they appeared to be a particularly improvident arsenal against the unknown. But she knew from experience that she would have felt naked without her bag. With a sigh of fatigue, she locked the apartment and went down the stairs to her car.

Driving slowly to give herself time to learn landmarks, she followed Dr. Berenford's directions and soon found herself moving through the center of town.

The late afternoon sun and the thickness of the air made the buildings look as if they were sweating. The businesses seemed to lean away from the hot sidewalks, as if they had forgotten the enthusiasm, even the accessibility, that they needed to survive; and the courthouse, with its dull white marble and its roof supported by stone giant heads atop ersatz Greek columns, looked altogether unequal to its responsibilities.

The sidewalks were relatively busy—people were going home from work—but one small group in front of the courthouse caught Linden's eye. A faded woman with three small children stood on the steps. She wore a shapeless shift which appeared to have been made from burlap; and the children were dressed in gunny sacks. Her face was gray and blank, as if she were inured by poverty and weariness to the emaciation of her children. All four of them held short wooden sticks bearing crude signs.

The signs were marked with red triangles. Inside each triangle was written one word: REPENT.

The woman and her children ignored the passersby. They stood dumbly on the steps as if they were engaged in a penance which stupefied them. Linden's heart ached uselessly at the sight of their moral and physical penury. There was nothing she could do for such people.

Three minutes later, she was outside the municipal limits.

There the road began to run through tilled valleys, between wooded hills. Beyond the town, the unseasonable heat and humidity were kinder to what they touched; they made the air lambent, so that it lay like immanence across the new crops, up the tangled weed-and-grass hillsides, among the budding trees; and her mood lifted at the way the landscape glowed in the approach of evening. She had spent so much of her life in cities. She continued to drive slowly; she wanted to savor the faint hope that she had found something she would be able to enjoy.

After a couple of miles, she came to a wide field on her right, thickly overgrown with milkweed and wild mustard. Across the field, a quarter of a mile away against a wall of trees, stood a white frame house. Two or three other houses bordered the field, closer to the highway; but the white one drew her attention as if it were the only habitable structure in the area.

A dirt road ran into the field. Branches went to the other houses, but the main track led straight to the white one.

Beside the entrance stood a wooden sign. Despite faded paint and several old splintered holes like bullet scars, the lettering was still legible: Haven Farm.

Gripping her courage, Linden turned onto the dirt road.

Without warning, the periphery of her gaze caught a flick of ochre. A robed figure stood beside the sign.

What—?

He stood there as if he had just appeared out of the air. An instant ago, she had seen nothing except the sign.

Taken by surprise, she instinctively twitched the wheel, trying to evade a hazard she had already passed. At once, she righted the sedan, stepped on the brakes. Her eyes jumped to the rearview mirror.

She saw an old man in an ochre robe. He was tall and lean,

barefoot, dirty. His long gray beard and thin hair flared about his head like frenzy.

He took one step into the road toward her, then clutched at his chest convulsively, and collapsed.

She barked a warning, though there was no one to hear it. Moving with a celerity that felt like slow-motion, she cut the ignition, grabbed for her bag, pushed open the door. Apprehension roiled in her, fear of death, of failure; but her training controlled it. In a moment, she was at the old man's side.

He looked strangely out of place in the road, out of time in the world she knew. The robe was his only garment; it looked as if he had been living in it for years. His features were sharp, made fierce by destitution or fanaticism. The declining sunlight colored his withered skin like dead gold.

He was not breathing.

Her discipline made her move. She knelt beside him, felt for his pulse. But within her she wailed. He bore a sickening resemblance to her father. If her father had lived to become old and mad, he might have been this stricken, preterite figure.

He had no pulse.

He revolted her. Her father had committed suicide. People who killed themselves deserved to die. The old man's appearance brought back memories of her own screaming which echoed in her ears as if it could never be silenced.

But he was dying. Already, his muscles had slackened, relaxing the pain of his seizure. And she was a doctor.

With the sureness of hard training, self-abnegation which mastered revulsion, her hands snapped open her bag. She took out her penlight, checked his pupils.

They were equal and reactive.

It was still possible to save him.

Quickly, she adjusted his head, tilted it back to clear his throat. Then she folded her hands together over his sternum, leaned her weight on her arms, and began to apply CPR.

The rhythm of cardiopulmonary resuscitation was so deeply ingrained in her that she followed it automatically: fifteen firm heels of her hands to his sternum; then two deep exhalations into his mouth, blocking his nose as she did so. But his mouth was foul—carious and vile, as if his teeth were rotten, or his palate gangrenous. She almost faltered. Instantly, her revulsion became an acute physical nausea, as if she

were tasting the exudation of a boil. But she was a doctor; this
was her work.

Fifteen. Two.

Fifteen. Two.

She did not permit herself to miss a beat.

But fear surged through her nausea. Exhaustion. Failure.
CPR was so demanding that no one person could sustain it
alone for more than a few minutes. If he did not come back
to life soon—

Breathe, damn you, she muttered along the beats. Fifteen.
Two. Damn you. Breathe. There was still no pulse.

Her own breathing became ragged; giddiness welled up in
her like a tide of darkness. The air seemed to resist her lungs.
Heat and the approach of sunset dimmed the old man. He
had lost all muscle-tone, all appearance of life.

Breathe!

Abruptly, she stopped her rhythm, snatched at her bag. Her
arms trembled; she clenched them still as she broke open a
disposable syringe, a vial of adrenaline, a cardiac needle.
Fighting for steadiness, she filled the syringe, cleared out the
air. In spite of her urgency, she took a moment to swab
clean a patch of the man's thin chest with alcohol. Then she
slid the needle delicately past his ribs, injected adrenaline into
his heart.

Setting aside the syringe, she risked pounding her fist once
against his sternum. But the blow had no effect.

Cursing, she resumed her CPR.

She needed help. But she could not do anything about that.
If she stopped to take him into town, or to go in search of a
phone, he would die. Yet if she exhausted herself alone he
would still die.

Breathe!

He did not breathe. His heart did not beat. His mouth was
as foetid as the maw of a corpse. The whole ordeal was
hopeless.

She did not relent.

All the blackness of her life was in her. She had spent too
many years teaching herself to be effective against death; she
could not surrender now. She had been too young, weak, and
ignorant to save her father, could not have saved her mother;
now that she knew what to do and could do it, she would
never quit, never falsify her life by quitting.

Dark motes began to dance across her vision; the air swarmed with moisture and inadequacy. Her arms felt leaden; her lungs cried out every time she forced breath down the old man's throat. He lay inert. Tears of rage and need ran hotly down her face. Yet she did not relent.

She was still half conscious when a tremor ran through him, and he took a hoarse gulp of air.

At once, her will snapped. Blood rushed to her head. She did not feel herself fall away to the side.

When she regained enough self-command to raise her head, her sight was a smear of pain and her face was slick with sweat. The old man was standing over her. His eyes were on her; the intense blue of his gaze held her like a hand of compassion. He looked impossibly tall and healthy; his very posture seemed to deny that he had ever been close to death. Gently, he reached down to her, drew her to her feet. As he put his arms around her, she slumped against him, unable to resist his embrace.

"Ah, my daughter, do not fear."

His voice was husky with regret and tenderness.

"You will not fail, however he may assail you. There is also love in the world."

Then he released her, stepped back. His eyes became commandments.

"Be true."

She watched him dumbly as he turned, walked away from her into the field. Milkweed and wild mustard whipped against his robe for a moment. She could hardly see him through the blurring of her vision. A musky breeze stirred his hair, made it a nimbus around his head as the sun began to set. Then he faded into the humidity, and was gone.

She wanted to call out after him, but the memory of his eyes stopped her.

Be true.

Deep in her chest, her heart began to tremble.

TWO: Something Broken

AFTER a moment, the trembling spread to her limbs. The surface of her skin felt fiery, as if the rays of the sun were concentrated on her. The muscles of her abdomen knotted.

The old man had vanished. He had put his arms around her as if he had the right, and then he had vanished.

She feared that her guts were going to rebel.

But then her gaze lurched toward the dirt where the old man had lain. There she saw the used hypodermic, the sterile wrappings, the empty vial. The dust bore the faint imprint of a body.

A shudder ran through her, and she began to relax.

So he had been real. He had only appeared to vanish. Her eyes had tricked her.

She scanned the area for him. He should not be walking around; he needed care, observation, until his condition stabilized. But she saw no sign of him. Fighting an odd reluctance, she waded out into the wild mustard after him. But when she reached the place where her eyes had lost him, she found nothing.

Baffled, she returned to the roadway. She did not like to give him up; but she appeared to have no choice in the matter. Muttering under her breath, she went to retrieve her bag.

The debris of her treatment she stuffed into one of the plastic specimen sacks she carried. Then she returned to her car. As she slid into the front seat, she gripped the steering wheel with both hands to steady herself on its hard actuality.

She did not remember why she had come to Haven Farm until the book on the seat beside her caught her attention.

Oh, damn!

She felt intensely unready to confront Thomas Covenant.

For a moment, she considered simply abandoning the favor she had promised Dr. Berenford. She started the engine, began to turn the wheel. But the exigency of the old man's eyes held her. That blue would not approve the breaking of promises. And she had saved him. She had set a precedent for

16

herself which was more important than any question of difficulty or mortification. When she put the sedan into motion, she sent it straight down the dirt road toward the white frame house, with the dust and the sunset at her back.

The light cast a tinge of red over the house, as if it were in the process of being transformed into something else. As she parked her car, she had to fight another surge of reluctance. She did not want to have anything to do with Thomas Covenant—not because he was a leper, but because he was something unknown and fierce, something so extravagant that even Dr. Berenford was afraid of him.

But she had already made her commitment. Picking up the book, she left her car and went to the front door of the house, hoping to be able to finish this task before the light failed.

She spent a moment straightening her hair. Then she knocked.

The house was silent.

Her shoulders throbbed with the consequences of strain. Fatigue and embarrassment made her arms feel too heavy to lift. She had to grit her teeth to make herself knock again.

Abruptly, she heard the sound of feet. They came stamping through the house toward her. She could hear anger in them.

The front door was snatched open, and a man confronted her, a lean figure in old jeans and a T-shirt, a few inches taller than herself. About forty years old. He had an intense face. His mouth was as strict as a stone tablet; his cheeks were lined with difficulties; his eyes were like embers, capable of fire. His hair above his forehead was raddled with gray, as if he had been aged more by his thoughts than by time.

He was exhausted. Almost automatically, she noted the redness of his orbs and eyelids, the pallor of his skin, the febrile rawness of his movements. He was either ill or under extreme stress.

She opened her mouth to speak, got no further. He registered her presence for a second, then snapped, "Goddamn it, if I wanted visitors I'd post a sign!" and clapped the door shut in her face.

She blinked after him momentarily while darkness gathered at her back, and her uncertainty turned to anger. Then she hit the door so hard that the wood rattled in its frame.

He came back almost at once. His voice hurled acid at her. "Maybe you don't speak English. I—"

She met his glare with a mordant smile. "Aren't you sup-posed to ring a bell, or something?"

That stopped him. His eyes narrowed as he reconsidered her. When he spoke again, his words came more slowly, as if he were trying to measure the danger she represented.

"If you know that, you don't need any warning."

She nodded. "My name is Linden Avery. I'm a doctor."

"And you're not afraid of lepers."

His sarcasm was as heavy as a bludgeon; but she matched it. "If I were afraid of sick people, I wouldn't be a doctor."

His glower expressed his disbelief. But he said curtly, "I don't need a doctor," and started to swing the door shut again.

"So actually," she rasped, "you're the one who's afraid."

His face darkened. Enunciating each word as if it were a dagger, he said, "What do you want, doctor?"

To her dismay, his controlled vehemence made her falter. For the second time in the course of the sunset, she was held by eyes that were too potent for her. His gaze shamed her. The book—her excuse for being there—was in her hand; but her hand was behind her back. She could not tell the lie Dr. Berenford had suggested to her. And she had no other answer. She could see vividly that Covenant needed help. Yet if he did not ask for it, what recourse did she have?

But then a leap of intuition crossed her mind. Speaking before she could question herself, she said, "That old man told me to 'Be true.' "

His reaction startled her. Surprise and fear flared in his eyes. His shoulders winced; his jaw dropped. Then abruptly he had closed the door behind him. He stood before her with his face thrust hotly forward. "What old man?"

She met his fire squarely. "He was out at the end of your driveway—an old man in an ochre robe. As soon as I saw him, he went into cardiac arrest." For an instant, a cold hand of doubt touched her heart. He had recovered too easily. Had he staged the whole situation? Impossible! His heart had stopped. "I had to work like hell to save him. Then he just walked away."

Covenant's belligerence collapsed. His gaze clung to her as if he were drowning. His hands gaped in front of him. For the first time, she observed that the last two fingers of his right hand were missing. He wore a wedding band of white gold on

what had once been the middle finger of that hand. His voice
was a scraping of pain in his throat. "He's gone?"

"Yes."

"An old man in an ochre robe?"

"Yes."

"You saved him?" His features were fading into night as
the sun dropped below the horizon.

"Yes."

"What did he say?"

"I already told you." Her uncertainty made her impatient.
"He said, 'Be true.' "

"He said that to you?"

"Yes!"

Covenant's eyes left her face. "Hellfire." He sagged as if he
carried a weight of cruelty on his back. "Have mercy on me. I
can't bear it." Turning, he slumped back to the door, opened
it. But there he stopped.

"Why *you?*"

Then he had reentered his house, the door was closed, and
Linden stood alone in the evening as if she had been bereft.

She did not move until the need to do something, take some
kind of action to restore the familiarity of her world, impelled
her to her car. Sitting behind the wheel as if she were stunned,
she tried to think.

Why you?

What kind of question was that? She was a doctor, and the
old man had needed help. It was that simple. What was Covenant talking about?

But *Be true* was not all the old man had said. He had also
said, *You will not fail, however he may assail you.*

He? Was that a reference to Covenant? Was the old man
trying to warn her of something? Or did it imply some other
kind of connection between him and the writer? What did
they have to do with each other? Or with her?

Nobody could fake cardiac arrest!

She took a harsh grip on her scrambled thoughts. The
whole situation made no sense. All she could say for certain
was that Covenant had recognized her description of the old
man. And Covenant's mental stability was clearly open to
question.

Clenching the wheel, she started her car, backed up in
order to turn around. She was convinced now that Covenant's

problem was serious; but that conviction only made her more angry at Dr. Berenford's refusal to tell her what the problem was. The dirt road was obscure in the twilight; she slapped on her headlights as she put the sedan in gear to complete her turn.

A scream like a mouthful of broken glass snatched her to a halt. It pierced the mutter of her sedan. Slivers of sound cut at her hearing. A woman screaming in agony or madness.

It had come from Covenant's house.

In an instant, Linden stood beside the car, waiting for the cry to be repeated.

She heard nothing. Lights shone from some of the windows; but no shadows moved. No sounds of violence betrayed the night. She stood poised to race to the house. Her ears searched the air. But the dark held its breath. The scream did not come again.

For a long moment, indecision held her. Confront Covenant—demand answers? Or leave? She had met his hostility. What right did she have—? Every right, if he were torturing some woman. But how could she be sure? Dr. Berenford had called it a medical problem.

Dr. Berenford—

Spitting curses, she jumped back into her car, stamped down on the accelerator, and sped away in a rattle of dust and gravel.

Two minutes later, she was back in town. But then she had to slow down so that she could watch for street signs.

When she arrived at the Chief of Staff's house, all she could see was an outline against the night sky. Its front frowned as if this, too, were a place where secrets were kept. But she did not hesitate. Striding up the steps, she pounded on the front door.

That door led to a screened veranda like a neutral zone between the dwelling itself and the outside world. As she knocked, the porch lights came on. Dr. Berenford opened the inner door, closed it behind him, then crossed the veranda to admit her.

He smiled a welcome; but his eyes evaded hers as if he had reason to be frightened; and she could see his pulse beating in the pouches below their sockets.

"Dr. Berenford," she said grimly.

"Please." He made a gesture of appeal. "Julius."

"Dr. Berenford." She was not sure that she wanted this man's friendship. "Who is she?"

His gaze flinched. "She?"

"The woman who screamed."

He seemed unable to lift his eyes to her face. In a tired voice, he murmured, "He didn't tell you anything."

"No."

Dr. Berenford considered for a moment, then motioned her toward two rocking chairs at one end of the veranda. "Please sit down. It's cooler out here." His attention seemed to wander. "This heat wave can't last forever."

"Doctor!" she lashed at him. "He's torturing that woman."

"No, he isn't." Suddenly, the older man was angry. "You get that out of your head right now. He's doing everything he can for her. Whatever's torturing her, it isn't him."

Linden held his glare, measuring his candor until she felt sure that he was Thomas Covenant's friend, whether or not he was hers. Then she said flatly, "Tell me."

By degrees, his expression recovered its habitual irony. "Won't you sit down?"

Brusquely, she moved down the porch, seated herself in one of the rockers. At once, he turned off the lights, and darkness came pouring through the screens. "I think better in the dark." Before her eyes adjusted, she heard the chair beside her squeak as he sat down.

For a time, the only sounds were the soft protest of his chair and the stridulation of the crickets. Then he said abruptly, "Some things I'm not going to tell you. Some I can't—some I won't. But I got you into this. I owe you a few answers."

After that, he spoke like the voice of the night; and she listened in a state of suspension—half concentrating, as she would have concentrated on a patient describing symptoms, half musing on the image of the gaunt vivid man who had said with such astonishment and pain, *Why you?*

"Eleven years ago, Thomas Covenant was a writer with one bestseller, a lovely wife named Joan, and an infant son, Roger. He hates that novel—calls it inane—but his wife and son he still loves. Or thinks he does. Personally, I doubt it. He's an intensely loyal man. What he calls love, I call being loyal to his own pain.

"Eleven years ago, an infection on his right hand turned

out to be leprosy, and those two fingers were amputated. He was sent down to the leprosarium in Louisiana, and Joan divorced him. To protect Roger from being raised in close proximity to a leper. The way Covenant tells it, her decision was perfectly reasonable. A mother's natural concern for a child. I think he's rationalizing. I think she was just afraid. I think the idea of what Hansen's disease could do to him—not to mention to her and Roger—just terrified her. She ran away."

His tone conveyed a shrug. "But I'm just guessing. The fact is, she divorced him, and he didn't contest it. After a few months, his illness was arrested, and he came back to Haven Farm. Alone. That was not a good time for him. All his neighbors moved away. Some people in this fair town tried to force him to leave. He was in the Hospital a couple times, and the second time he was half dead—" Dr. Berenford seemed to wince at the memory. "His disease was active again. We sent him back to the leprosarium.

"When he came home again, everything was different. He seemed to have recovered his sanity. For ten years now he's been stable. A little grim, maybe—not exactly what you might call diffident—but accessible, reasonable, compassionate. Every year he foots the bill for several of our indigent patients."

The older man sighed. "You know, it's strange. The same people who try to convert me seem to think *he* needs saving, too. He's a leper who doesn't go to church, and he's got money. Some of our evangelicals consider that an insult to the Almighty."

The professional part of Linden absorbed the facts Dr. Berenford gave, and discounted his subjective reactions. But her musing raised Covenant's visage before her in the darkness. Gradually, that needy face became more real to her. She saw the lines of loneliness and gall on his mien. She responded to the strictness of his countenance as if she had recognized a comrade. After all, she was familiar with bitterness, loss, isolation.

But the doctor's speech also filled her with questions. She wanted to know where Covenant had learned his stability. What had changed him? Where had he found an answer potent enough to preserve him against the poverty of his life? And what had happened recently to take it away from him?

"Since then," the Chief of Staff continued, "he's published seven novels, and that's where you can really see the difference. Oh, he's mentioned something about three or four other manuscripts, but I don't know anything about them. The point is, if you didn't know better, you wouldn't be able to believe his bestseller and the other seven were written by the same man. He's right about the first one. It's fluff—self-indulgent melodrama. But the others—

"If you had a chance to read *Or I Will Sell My Soul for Guilt*, you'd find him arguing that innocence is a wonderful thing except for the fact that it's impotent. Guilt is power. All effective people are guilty because the use of power is guilt, and only guilty people can be effective. Effective for *good*, mind you. Only the damned can be saved."

Linden was squirming. She understood at least one kind of relationship between guilt and effectiveness. She had committed murder, and had become a doctor because she had committed murder. She knew that people like herself were driven to power by the need to assoil their guilt. But she had found nothing—no anodyne or restitution—to verify the claim that the damned could be saved. Perhaps Covenant had fooled Dr. Berenford: perhaps he *was* crazy, a madman wearing a clever mask of stability. Or perhaps he knew something she did not.

Something she needed.

That thought gave her a pang of fear. She was suddenly conscious of the night, the rungs of the rocker pressing against her back, the crickets. She ached to retreat from the necessity of confronting Covenant again. Possibilities of harm crowded the darkness. But she needed to understand her peril. When Dr. Berenford stopped, she bore the silence as long as she could, then, faintly, repeated her initial question.

"Who is she?"

The doctor sighed. His chair left a few splinters of agitation in the air. But he became completely still before he said, "His ex-wife. Joan."

Linden flinched. That piece of information gave a world of explanation to Covenant's haggard, febrile appearance. But it was not enough. "Why did she come back? What's wrong with her?"

The older man began rocking again. "Now we're back to where we were this afternoon. I can't tell you. I can't tell you why she came back because he told me in confidence. *If* he's right—" His voice trailed away, then resumed. "I can't tell you what's wrong with her because I don't know."

She stared at his unseen face. "That's why you got me into this."

"Yes." His reply sounded like a recognition of mortality.

"There are other doctors around. Or you could call in a specialist." Her throat closed suddenly; she had to swallow heavily in order to say, "Why me?"

"Well, I suppose—" Now his tone conveyed a wry smile. "I could say it's because you're well trained. But the fact is, I thought of you because you seem to fit. You and Covenant could talk to each other—if you gave yourselves a chance."

"I see." In the silence, she was groaning, Is it that obvious? After everything I've done to hide it, make up for it, does it still show? To defend herself, she got to her feet. Old bitterness made her sound querulous. "I hope you like playing God."

He paused for a long moment before he replied quietly, "If that's what I'm doing—no, I don't. But I don't look at it that way. I'm just in over my head. So I asked you for help."

Help, Linden snarled inwardly. Jesus Christ! But she did not speak her indignation aloud. Dr. Berenford had touched her again, placed his finger on the nerves which compelled her. Because she did not want to utter her weakness, or her anger, or her lack of choice, she moved past him to the outer door of the veranda. "Goodnight," she said in a flat tone.

"Goodnight, Linden." He did not ask her what she was going to do. Perhaps he understood her. Or perhaps he had no courage.

She got into her car and headed back toward Haven Farm.

She drove slowly, trying to regain a sense of perspective. True, she had no choice now; but that was not because she was helpless. Rather, it was because she had already made the choice—made it long ago, when she had decided to be a doctor. She had elected deliberately to be who she was now. If some of the implications of that choice gave her pain—well, there was pain everywhere. She deserved whatever pain she had to bear.

She had not realized until she reached the dirt road that she had forgotten to ask Dr. Berenford about the old man.

She could see lights from Covenant's house. The building

lay flickering against a line of dark trees like a gleam about to be swallowed by the woods and the night. The moon only confirmed this impression; its nearly-full light made the field a lake of silver, eldritch and fathomless, but could not touch the black trees, or the house which lay in their shadow. Linden shivered at the damp air, and drove with her hands tight on the wheel and her senses taut, as if she were approaching a crisis.

Twenty yards from the house, she stopped, parked her car so that it stood in the open moonlight.

Be true.

She did not know how.

The approach of her headlights must have warned him. An outside lamp came on as she neared the front door. He stepped out to meet her. His stance was erect and forbidding, silhouetted by the yellow light at his back. She could not read his face.

"Dr. Avery." His voice rasped like a saw. "Go away."

"No." The uncertainty of her respiration made her speak abruptly, one piece at a time. "Not until I see her."

"Her?" he demanded.

"Your ex-wife."

For a moment, he was silent. Then he grated, "What else did that bastard tell you?"

She ignored his anger. "You need help."

His shoulders hunched as if he were strangling retorts. "He's mistaken. I don't need help. I don't need you. Go away."

"No." She did not falter. "He's right. You're exhausted. Taking care of her alone is wearing you out. I can help."

"You can't," he whispered, denying her fiercely. "She doesn't need a doctor. She needs to be left alone."

"I'll believe that when I see it."

He tensed as if she had moved, tried to get past him. "You're trespassing. If you don't go away, I'll call the Sheriff."

The falseness of her position infuriated her. "Goddamn it!" she snapped. "What are you afraid of?"

"You." His voice was gravid, cold.

"Me? You don't even know me."

"And you don't know me. You don't know what's going on here. You couldn't possibly understand it. And you didn't choose it." He brandished words at her like blades. "Berenford got you into this. That old man——" He swallowed, then barked, "You saved him, and he chose you, and you don't have any idea what that *means*. You haven't got the faintest idea what he chose you for. By hell, I'm not going to stand for it! *Go away*."

"What does it have to do with you?" She groped to understand him. "What makes you think it has anything to do with you?"

"Because I *do* know."

"Know what?" She could not tolerate the condescension of his refusal. "What's so special about you? Leprosy? Do you think being a leper gives you some kind of private claim on loneliness or pain? Don't be arrogant. There are other people in the world who suffer, and it doesn't take being a leper to understand them. What's so goddamn special about you?"

Her anger stopped him. She could not see his face; but his posture seemed to twist, reconsidering her. After a moment, he said carefully, "Nothing about me. But I'm on the inside of this thing, and you aren't. I know it. You don't. It can't be explained. You don't understand what you're doing."

"Then tell me. Make me understand. So I can make the right choice."

"Dr. Avery." His voice was sudden and harsh. "Maybe suffering isn't private. Maybe sickness and harm are in the public domain. But *this* is private."

His intensity silenced her. She wrestled with him in her thoughts, and could find no way to take hold of him. He knew more than she did—had endured more, purchased more, learned more. Yet she could not let go. She needed some kind of explanation. The night air was thick and humid, blurring the meaning of the stars. Because she had no other argument, she challenged him with her incomprehension itself. " 'Be true,' " she articulated, "isn't the only thing he said."

Covenant recoiled. She held herself still until the suspense drove him to ask in a muffled tone, "What else?"

"He said, 'Do not fear. You will not fail, however he may assail you.' " There she halted, unwilling to say the rest. Covenant's shoulders began to shake. Grimly, she pursued her advantage. "Who was he talking about? You?"

He did not respond. His hands were pressed to his face, stifling his emotion.

"Or was it somebody else? Did somebody hurt Joan?"

A shard of pain slipped past his teeth before he could lock them against himself.

"Or is something going to happen to me? What does that old man have to do with me? Why do you say he chose me?"

"He's using you." Covenant's hands occluded his voice. But he had mastered himself. When he dropped his arms, his tone was dull and faint, like the falling of ashes. "He's like Berenford. Thinks I need help. Thinks I can't handle it this time." He should have sounded bitter; but he had momentarily lost even that resource. "The only difference is, he knows—what I know."

"Then tell me," Linden urged again. "Let me try."

By force of will, Covenant straightened so that he stood upright against the light. "No. Maybe I can't stop you, but I as sure as hell don't have to let you. I'm not going to contribute to this. If you're dead set on getting involved, you're going to have to find some way to do it behind my back." He stopped as if he were finished. But then he raged at her, "And tell that bastard Berenford he ought to try trusting me for a change!"

Retorts jumped into her throat. She wanted to yell back, Why should he? You don't trust anybody else! But as she gathered force into her lungs, a scream stung the air.

A woman screaming, raw and heinous. Impossible that anybody could feel such virulent terror and stay sane. It shrilled like the heart-shriek of the night.

Before it ended, Linden was on her way past Covenant toward the front door.

He caught her arm: she broke the grip of his half-hand, flung him off. "I'm a *doctor*." Leaving him no time for permission or denial, she jerked open the door, strode into the house.

The door admitted her to the living room. It looked bare, in spite of its carpeting and bookcases; there were no pictures, no ornaments; and the only furniture was a long overstuffed sofa with a coffee table in front of it. They occupied the center of the floor, as if to make the space around them navigable.

She gave the room a glance, then marched down a short

passage to the kitchen. There, too, a table and two straight-backed wooden chairs occupied the center of the space. She went past them, turned to enter another hall. Covenant hurried after her as she by-passed two open doors—the bathroom, his bedroom—to reach the one at the end of the hall.

It was closed.

At once, she took hold of the knob.

He snatched at her wrist. "Listen." His voice must have held emotion—urgency, anguish, something—but she did not hear it. "This you have to understand. There's only one way to hurt a man who's lost everything. Give him back something broken."

She gripped the knob with her free hand. He let her go.

She opened the door, went into the room.

All the lights were on.

Joan sat on an iron-frame bed in the middle of the room. Her ankles and wrists were tied with cloth bonds which allowed her to sit up or lie down but did not permit her to bring her hands together. The long cotton nightgown covering her thin limbs had been twisted around her by her distress.

A white gold wedding ring hung from a silver chain around her neck.

She did not look at Covenant. Her gaze sprang at Linden, and a mad fury clenched her face. She had rabid eyes, the eyes of a demented lioness. Whimpers moaned in her throat. Her pallid skin stretched tightly over her bones.

Intuitive revulsion appalled Linden. She could not think. She was not accustomed to such savagery. It violated all her conceptions of illness or harm, paralyzed her responses. This was not ordinary human ineffectuality or pain raised to the level of despair; this was pure ferocity, concentrated and murderous. She had to force herself forward. But when she drew near the woman and stretched out a tentative hand, Joan bit at her like a baited cat. Involuntarily, Linden recoiled.

"Dear God!" she panted. "What's wrong with her?"

Joan raised her head, let out a scream like the anguish of the damned.

Covenant could not speak. Grief contorted his features. He went to Joan's side. Fumbling over the knot, he untied her left wrist, released her arm. Instantly, she clawed at him, straining her whole body to reach him. He evaded her, caught her forearm.

Linden watched with a silent wail as he let Joan's nails rake the back of his right hand. Blood welled from the cuts.

Joan smeared her fingers in his blood. Then her hand jumped to her mouth, and she sucked it eagerly, greedily.

The taste of blood seemed to restore her self-awareness. Almost immediately, the madness faded from her face. Her eyes softened, turned to tears; her mouth trembled. "Oh, Tom," she quavered weakly. "I'm so sorry. I can't— He's in my mind, and I can't get him out. He hates you. He makes— makes me—" She was sobbing brokenly. Her lucidity was acutely cruel to her.

He sat on the bed beside her, put his arms around her. "I know." His voice ached in the room. "I understand."

"Tom," she wept. "Tom. Help me."

"I will." His tone promised that he would face any ordeal, make any sacrifice, commit any violence. "As soon as he's ready, I'll get you free."

Slowly, her frail limbs relaxed. Her sobs grew quieter. She was exhausted. When he stretched her out on the bed, she closed her eyes, went to sleep with her fingers in her mouth like a child.

He took a tissue from a box on a table near the bed, pressed it to the back of his hand. Then, tenderly, he pulled Joan's fingers from her mouth and retied her wrist. Only then did he look at Linden.

"It doesn't hurt," he said. "The backs of my hands have been numb for years." The torment was gone from his face; it held nothing now except the long weariness of a pain he could not heal.

Watching his blood soak into the tissue, she knew she should do something to treat that injury. But an essential part of her had failed, proved itself inadequate to Joan; she could not bear to touch him. She had no answer to what she had seen. For a moment, her eyes were helpless with tears. Only the old habit of severity kept her from weeping. Only her need kept her from fleeing into the night. It drove her to say grimly, "Now you're going to tell me what's wrong with her."

"Yes," he murmured. "I suppose I am."

THREE: Plight

HE guided her back to the living room in silence. His hand on her arm was reluctant, as if he dreaded that mere human contact. When she sat on the sofa, he gestured toward his injury, and left her alone. She was glad to be alone. She was stunned by her failure; she needed time to regain possession of herself.

What had happened to her? She understood nothing about evil, did not even believe in it as an idea; but she had seen it in Joan's feral hunger. She was trained to perceive the world in terms of dysfunction and disease, medication and treatment, success or death. Words like *good* or *evil* meant nothing to her. But Joan—! Where did such malignant ferocity come from? And how—?

When Covenant returned, with his right hand wrapped in a white bandage, she stared at him, demanding explanations.

He stood before her, did not meet her gaze. The slouch of his posture gave him a look of abandonment; the skin at the corners of his eyes crumpled like dismay pinching his flesh. But his mouth had learned the habit of defiance; it was twisted with refusals. After a moment, he muttered, "So you see why I didn't want you to know about her," and began to pace.

"Nobody knows"—the words came as if he were dredging them out of the privacy of his heart—"except Berenford and Roman. The law doesn't exactly smile on people who keep other people prisoner—even in her condition. I don't have any legal rights at all as far as she's concerned. What I'm supposed to do is turn her over to the authorities. But I've been living without the benefit of law so long now I don't give a damn."

"But what's wrong with her?" Linden could not keep her voice from twitching; she was too tightly clenched to sound steady.

He sighed. "She needs to hurt me. She's starving for it—that's what makes her so violent. It's the best way she can think of to punish herself."

With a wrench, Linden's analytical instinct began to func-

30

tion again. Paranoiac, she winced to herself. He's paranoiac. But aloud she insisted, "But why? What's happened to her?"

He stopped, looked at her as if he were trying to gauge her capacity for the truth, then went back to his pacing.

"Of course," he murmured, "that isn't how Berenford sees it. He thinks it's a psychiatric problem. The only reason he hasn't tried to get her away from me is because he understands why I want to take care of her. Or part of it. His wife is a paraplegic, and he would never consider dumping the problem off on anyone else. I haven't told him about her taste for blood."

He was evading her question. She struggled for patience. "*Isn't* it a psychiatric problem? Hasn't Dr. Berenford been able to rule out physical causes? What else could it be?"

Covenant hesitated, then said distantly, "He doesn't know what's going on."

"You keep saying that. It's too convenient."

"No," he retorted, "it's not convenient. It's the truth. You don't have the background to understand it."

"How can you be so goddamn sure?" The clench of her self-command made her voice raw. "I've spent half my life coping with other people's pain." She wanted to add, Can't you get it through your head that I'm a doctor? But her throat locked on those words. She had failed—

For an instant, his gaze winced as if he were distressed by the idea that she did in fact have the necessary background. But then he shook his head sharply. When he resumed, she could not tell what kind of answer he had decided to give her.

"I wouldn't know about it myself," he said, "if her parents hadn't called me. About a month ago. They don't have much use for me, but they were frantic. They told me everything they knew.

"I suppose it's an old story. The only thing that makes it new is the way it hurts. Joan divorced me when we found out I had leprosy. Eleven years ago. Took Roger and went back to her family. She thought she was justified—ah, hell, for years *I* thought she was justified. Kids are more susceptible to leprosy than adults. So she divorced me. For Roger's sake.

"But it didn't work. Deep inside her, she believed she'd betrayed me. It's hard to forgive yourself for deserting someone you love—someone who needs you. It erodes your self-respect. Like leprosy. It gnaws away at you. Before long, you're a moral cripple. She stood it for a while. Then she started hunting for cures."

His voice, and the information he was giving her, steadied Linden. As he paced, she became conscious of the way he carried himself, the care and specificity of all his movements. He navigated past the coffee table as if it were a danger to him. And repeatedly he scanned himself with his eyes, checking in turn each hand, each arm, his legs, his chest, as if he expected to find that he had injured himself without knowing it.

She had read about such things. His self-inspection was called VSE—visual surveillance of extremities. Like the care with which he moved, it was part of the discipline he needed to keep his illness arrested. Because of the damage leprosy had done to his nerves, the largest single threat to his health was the possibility that he might bump, burn, scrape, cut, or bruise himself without realizing it. Then infection would set in because the wound was not tended. So he moved with all the caution he could muster. The furniture in his house was arranged to minimize the risk of protruding corners, obstacles, accidents. And he scanned himself regularly, looking for signs of danger.

Watching him in this objective, professional way helped restore her sense of who she was. Slowly, she became better able to listen to his indirect explanation without impatience.

He had not paused; he was saying, "First she tried psychology. She wanted to believe it was all in her mind—and minds can be fixed, like broken arms. She started going through psychological fads the way some people trade in cars, a new one every year. As if her problem really was mental instead of spiritual.

"None of it made sense to her parents, but they tried to be tolerant, just did what they could to give Roger a stable home.

"So they thought she was finally going to be all right when she suddenly gave that up and went churchy. They believed all along that religion was the answer. Well, it's good enough for most people, but it didn't give her what she needed. It was too easy. Her disease was progressing all the time. A year ago, she became a fanatic. Took Roger and went to join a commune. One of those places where people learn the ecstasy of humiliation, and the leader preaches love and mass suicide.

"She must have been so desperate— For most of her life, the only thing she really wanted to believe was that she was perfectly all right. But after all those years of failure, she didn't have any defenses left. What did she have to lose?"

Linden was not wholly convinced. She had no more use for God than for conceptions of good and evil. But Covenant's passion held her. His eyes were wet with violence and grief; his mouth was as sharp as a blade. He believed what he was saying.

Her expression must have betrayed some of her doubt; his voice took on an echo of Joan's ferocity. "You don't have to believe in God to grasp what she was going through. She was suffering from an affliction for which there's no mortal cure. She couldn't even arrest the way it rotted her. Maybe she didn't know what it was she was trying to cure. She was looking for magic, some power that could reach into her and heal— When you've tried all the salves in the world and they don't work, you start thinking about fire. Burn out the pain. She wanted to punish herself, find some kind of abnegation to match her personal rot."

His voice broke; but he controlled it instantly. "I know all about it. But she didn't have any defenses. She opened the door for him, and he saw she was the perfect tool, and he's been using her—*using* her, when she's too damaged to even understand what he's using her for."

Using her? Linden did not comprehend. He?

Slowly, Covenant suppressed his anger. "Of course, her parents didn't know anything about that. How could they? All they knew was that about six weeks ago she woke them up in the middle of the night and started babbling. She was a prophet, she'd had a vision, the Lord had given her a mission. Woe and retribution to the wicked, death to the sick and the unbelieving. The only sense they could make out of it was that she wanted them to take care of Roger. Then she was gone. They haven't seen her since.

"After a couple weeks, they called me. I hadn't seen her— that was the first I'd heard about it. But about two weeks ago she showed up here. Sneaked into my room during the night and tried to tear my face off. If she hadn't been so weak, she would have succeeded. She must have come all the way on foot."

He seemed too exhausted himself to go on pacing. His red-rimmed eyes made him look ill, and his hands trembled. How long had he been without decent sleep or peace? Two weeks? When he sat down on the opposite end of the sofa, Linden turned so that she could continue to study him. In the back of her mind, she began trying to conceive some way to give him a sedative.

"Since then," he sighed, "Berenford and I have been taking care of her. I got him into this because he's the only doctor I know. He thinks I'm wrong about her, but he's helping me. Or he was. Until he got you into this." He was too tired to sound bitter. "I'm trying to reach her any way I can, and he's giving her drugs that are supposed to clear her mind. Or at least calm her so I can feed her. I leave the lights on in there all the time. Something happens to her when she's alone in the dark. She goes berserk—I'm afraid she'll break an arm or something."

He fell silent. Apparently, he had reached the end of his story—or of his strength. Linden felt that his explanation was incomplete, but she held her questions in abeyance. He needed aid, a relief from strain. Carefully she said, "Maybe she really should be in a hospital. I'm sure Dr. Berenford's doing what he can. But there are all kinds of diagnostic procedures he can't use here. If she were in a hospital—"

"If she were in a hospital"— he swung toward her so roughly that she recoiled—"they'd keep her in a straitjacket, and force-feed her three times a day, and turn her brain into jelly with electroshock, and fill her up with drugs until she couldn't recognize her own name if God Himself were calling for her, and it wouldn't do any good! Goddamn it, she was my *wife*!" He brandished his right fist. "I'm still wearing the bloody ring!"

"Is that what you think doctors do?" She was suddenly livid; her failure made her defensive. "Brutalize sick people?"

He strove to contain his ire. "Doctors try to cure problems whether they understand them or not. It doesn't always work. This isn't something a doctor can cure."

"Is that a fact?" She did not want to taunt him; but her own compulsions drove her. "Tell me what good *you're* doing her."

He flinched. Rage and pain struggled in him; but he fought them down. Then he said simply, "She came to me."

"She didn't know what she was doing."

"But I do." His grimness defied her. "I understand it well enough. I'm the only one who can help her."

Frustration boiled up in her. "Understand *what*?"

He jerked to his feet. He was a figure of passion, held erect and potent in spite of weakness by the intensity of his heart. His eyes were chisels; when he spoke, each word fell distinctly, like a chip of granite.

"She is possessed."

Linden blinked at him. "Possessed?" He had staggered her. He did not seem to be talking a language she could comprehend. This was the twentieth century; medical science had not taken *possession* seriously for at least a hundred years. She was on her feet. "Are you out of your mind?"

She expected him to retreat. But he still had resources she had not plumbed. He held her glare, and his visage—charged and purified by some kind of sustaining conviction—made her acutely aware of her own moral poverty. When he looked away, he did not do so because he was abashed or beaten; he looked away in order to spare her the implications of his knowledge.

"You see?" he murmured. "It's a question of experience. You're just not equipped to understand."

"By God!" she fumed defensively, "that's the most arrogant thing I've ever heard. You stand there spouting the most egregious nonsense, and when I question you, you just naturally assume there must be something wrong with me. Where do you get the gall to—?"

"Dr. Avery." His voice was low, dangerous. "I didn't say there was anything wrong with you."

She did not listen to him. "You're suffering from classic paranoia, Mr. Covenant." She bit each word mordantly. "You think that everybody who doubts you isn't quite right in the head. You're a textbook case."

Seething irrationally, she turned on her heel, stamped toward the door—fleeing from him, and fighting furiously to believe that she was not fleeing. But he came after her, caught hold of her shoulders. She whirled on him as if he had assaulted her.

He had not. His hands dropped to his sides, and twitched as if they ached to make gestures of supplication. His face was open and vulnerable; she saw intuitively that at that moment she could have asked him anything, and he would have done his best to answer. "Please," he breathed. "You're in an impossible situation, and I haven't made it any easier. But please. At least consider the chance that I know what I'm doing."

A retort coiled in her mouth, then frayed and fell apart. She was furious, not because she had any right to be, but because his attitude showed her how far she had fallen into the wrong. She swallowed to stifle a groan, almost reached out toward him to apologize. But he deserved something better than an apology. Carefully, she said, "I'll consider it." She could not meet his eyes. "I won't do anything until I talk to you again."

Then she left the house, frankly escaping from the exigency of his incomprehensible convictions. Her hands fumbled like traitors as she opened the door of her car, slid behind the wheel.

With failure in her mouth like the taste of sickness, she drove back to her apartment.

She needed to be comforted; but there was no comfort in those grubby walls, in the chipped and peeling floorboards which moaned like victims under her feet. She had accepted that apartment precisely because it offered her no comfort; but the woman who had made that decision was a woman who had never watched herself buckle under the demands of her profession. Now, for the first time since that moment of murder fifteen years ago, when her hands had accepted the burden of blood, she yearned for solace. She lived in a world where there was no solace.

Because she could think of no other recourse, she went to bed.

Tension and muggy sheets kept her awake for a long time; and when she finally slept, her dreams were sweat and fear in the hot night. The old man, Covenant, Joan—all babbled of *He*, trying to warn her. *He* who possessed Joan for purposes too cruel to be answered. *He* who intended to harm them all. But at last she sank into a deeper slumber, and the evil went back into hiding.

She was awakened by a knocking at her door.

Her head felt swollen with nightmares, and the knocking had a tentative sound, as if the knocker believed the apartment to be dangerous. But it was imperative. She was a doctor.

When she unclosed her eyes, the light of midmorning pierced her brain.

Groaning, she climbed out of bed, shrugged her arms into a bathrobe, then went to open the door.

A short timid woman with hands that fluttered and eyes

that shied stood on the landing. Timorously, she asked, "Dr. Avery? Dr. Linden Avery?"

With an effort, Linden cleared her throat. "Yes."

"Dr. Berenford called." The woman seemed to have no idea what she was saying. "I'm his secretary. You don't have a phone. I don't work on Saturdays, but he called me at home. He wants you to meet him. He's supposed to be on rounds."

"Meet him?" A pang of apprehension went through her. "Where?"

"He said you'd know where." Insistently, the woman went on, "I'm his secretary. I don't work on Saturdays, but I'm always glad to help him. He's a fine man—a fine doctor. His wife had polio. He really should be on rounds."

Linden shut her eyes. If she could have summoned any strength, she would have cried out, Why are you doing this to me? But she felt drained by bad dreams and doubt. Muttering, "Thank you," she closed the door.

For a moment, she did not move; she leaned against the door as if to hold it shut, wanting to scream. But Dr. Berenford would not have gone to such trouble to send for her if the situation were not urgent. She had to go.

As she dressed in the clothes she had worn the previous day and ran a comb through her hair, she realized that she had made a choice. Sometime during the night, she had given her allegiance to Covenant. She did not understand what was wrong with Joan, or what he thought he could do about it; but she was attracted to him. The same intransigence which had so infuriated her had also touched her deeply; she was vulnerable to the strange appeal of his anger, his extremity, his paradoxically savage and compassionate determination to stand loyal to his ex-wife.

She drank a quick glass of orange juice to clear her head, then went down to her car.

The day was already unnaturally hot; the sunlight hurt her eyes. She felt oddly giddy and detached, as if she were experiencing a hallucination, as she entered the dirt roadway and approached Covenant's house. At first, she was not sure of her vision when she descried the dark stain on the wall.

She parked beside Dr. Berenford's car, jumped out to look.

Near the doorway, a tall, crude triangle violated the white wall. It was reddish-black, the color of dried blood. The vehemence of its intent convinced her that it was blood.

She began to run.

Springing into the living room, she saw that it, too, had been desecrated. All the furnishings were intact; but everything was splotched and soaked with blood. Buckets of blood had been thrown into the room. A sickly-sweet smell clogged the air.

On the floor near the coffee table lay a shotgun.

Her stomach writhed. She slapped her hands to her mouth to keep herself from crying out. All this blood could not have come from one ordinary human body. Some atrocity . . .

Then she saw Dr. Berenford. He sat in the kitchen at the table, with a cup between his hands. He was looking at her.

She strode toward him, started to demand, "What the hell—?"

He stopped her with a warning gesture. "Keep it down," he said softly. "He's sleeping."

For a moment, she gaped at the Chief of Staff. But she was accustomed to emergencies; her self-command quickly reasserted itself. Moving as if to prove to him that she could be calm, she found a cup, poured herself some coffee from the pot on the stove, sat down in the other chair at the old enamel-topped table. In a flat tone, she asked, "What happened?"

He sipped his own coffee. All the humor was gone out of him, and his hands shook. "I guess he was right all along." He did not meet her stare. "She's gone."

"Gone?" For an instant, her control slipped. *Gone?* She could hardly breathe past the thudding of her heart. "Is anybody looking for her?"

"The police," he replied. "Mrs. Roman—did I tell you about her? She's his lawyer. She went back to town after I got here—a couple hours ago. To light a fire under the Sheriff. Right now, every able-bodied cop in the county is probably out looking. The only reason you don't see cars is because our Sheriff—bless his warm little heart—won't let his men park this close to a leper."

"All right." Linden mustered her training, gripped it in both hands. "Tell me what happened."

He made a gesture of helplessness. "I don't really know. I only know what he told Mrs. Roman—what he told me. It doesn't make any sense." He sighed. "Well, this is what he says. Sometime after midnight, he heard people at his door. He'd spent most of the evening trying to bathe her, but after that he fell asleep. He didn't wake up until these people began acting like they wanted to tear the door down.

"He didn't have to ask them what they wanted. I guess he's been expecting something like this ever since Joan showed up. He went and got his shotgun—did you know he had a shotgun? Had Mrs. Roman buy it for him last week. For self-defense—as if being a leper wasn't more defense than he ever had any use for." Seeing Linden's impatience, he went back to his story. "Anyway, he got his gun, and turned on all the lights. Then he opened the door.

"They came in—maybe half a dozen of them. He says they wore sackcloth and ashes." Dr. Berenford grimaced. "If he recognized any of them, he won't admit it. He waved the shotgun at them and told them they couldn't have her.

"But they acted as if they wanted to be shot. And when it came right down to it, he couldn't. Not even to save his ex-wife." He shook his head. "He tried to fight them off by main strength, but one against six, he didn't have much chance.

"Sometime early this morning, he came to long enough to call Mrs. Roman. He was incoherent—kept telling her to start a search, only he couldn't explain why—but at least he had sense enough to know he needed help. Then he passed out again. When she got here, she found him unconscious on the floor. There was blood everywhere. Whoever they were, they must have bled an entire cow." He gulped coffee as if it were an antidote for the reek in the air. "Well, she got him on his feet, and he took her to check on Joan. She was gone. Restraints had been cut."

"They didn't kill her?" interjected Linden.

He glanced at her. "He says no. How he knows—your guess is as good as mine." After a moment, he resumed, "Anyway, Mrs. Roman called me. When I got here, she left to see what she could do about finding Joan. I've examined him, and he seems to be all right. Suffering from exhaustion as much as anything else."

Linden shrugged aside her doubts about Covenant's condition. "I'll watch him."

He nodded. "That was why I called for you."

She drank some of her coffee to steady herself, then inquired carefully, "Do you know who they were?"

"I asked him that," Dr. Berenford replied with a frown. "He said, 'How the hell should I know?' "

"Well, then, what do they want with her?"

He thought for a moment, then said, "You know, the worst part about the whole thing is—I think he knows."

Frustration made her querulous. "So why won't he tell us?"

"Hard to say," said the doctor slowly. "I think *he* thinks if we knew what was going on we'd try to stop him."

Linden did not respond. She was no longer prepared to try to prevent Thomas Covenant from doing anything. But she was equally determined to learn the truth about Joan, about him—and, yes, about the old man in the ochre robe. For her own sake. And for Covenant's. In spite of his fierce independence, she could not shake the conviction that he was desperately in need of help.

"Which is another reason for you to stay," the older man muttered as he rose to his feet. "I've got to go. But somebody has to prevent him from doing anything crazy. Some days—" His voice trailed away, then came back in sudden vexation. "My God, some days I think that man needs a keeper, not a doctor." For the first time since her arrival, he faced her squarely. "Will you keep him?"

She could see he wanted reassurance that she shared his sense of responsibility for Covenant and Joan. She could not make such a promise. But she could offer him something similar. "Well, at any rate," she said severely, "I won't let go of him."

He nodded vaguely. He was no longer looking at her. As he moved toward the door, he murmured, "Be patient with him. It's been so long since he met somebody who isn't afraid of him, he doesn't know what to do about it. When he wakes up, make him eat something." Then he left the house, went out to his car.

Linden watched until he disappeared in dust toward the highway. Then she turned back to the living room.

What to do about it? Like Covenant, she did not know. But she meant to find out. The smell of blood made her feel unclean; but she suppressed the sensation long enough to fix a breakfast for herself. Then she tackled the living room.

With a scrub brush and a bucket of soapy water, she attacked the stains as if they were an affront to her. Deep within her, where her guilt and coercion had their roots, she felt that blood was life—a thing of value, too precious to be squandered and denied, as her parents had squandered and denied it. Grimly, she scrubbed at the madness or malice which had violated this room, trying to eradicate it.

Whenever she needed a break, she went quietly to look at Covenant. His bruises gave his face a misshapen look. His sleep seemed agitated, but he showed no sign of drifting into coma. Occasionally, the movements of his eyes betrayed that he was dreaming. He slept with his mouth open like a silent cry; and once his cheeks were wet with tears. Her heart went out to him as he lay stretched there, disconsolate and vulnerable. He had so little respect for his own mortality.

Shortly after noon, while she was still at work, he came out of his bedroom. He moved groggily, his gait blurred with sleep. He peered at her across the room as if he were summoning anger; but his voice held nothing except resignation. "You can't help her now. You might as well go home."

She stood up to face him. "I want to help you."

"I can handle it."

Linden swallowed bile, tried not to sound acerbic. "Somehow, you don't look that tough. You couldn't stop them from taking her. How are you going to make them give her back?"

His eyes widened; her guess had struck home. But he did not waver. He seemed almost inhumanly calm—or doomed. "They don't want her. She's just a way for them to get at me."

"You?" Was he paranoiac after all? "Are you trying to tell me that this whole thing happened to her because of you? Why?"

"I haven't found that out yet."

"No. I mean, why do you think this has anything to do with you? If they wanted you, why didn't they just take you? You couldn't have stopped them."

"Because it has to be voluntary." His voice had the flat timbre of over-stressed cable in a high wind. He should have snapped long ago. But he did not sound like a man who snapped. "He can't just force me. I have to choose to do it. Joan—" A surge of darkness occluded his eyes. "She's just his way of exerting pressure. He has to take the chance that I might refuse."

He. Linden's breathing came heavily. "You keep saying *he.* Who is *he*?"

His frown made his face seem even more malformed.

"Leave it alone." He was trying to warn her. "You don't believe in possession. How can I make you believe in possessors?"

She took his warning, but not in the way he intended. Hints of purpose—half guesswork, half determination—unexpectedly lit her thoughts. A way to learn the truth. He had said, *You're going to have to find some way to do it behind my back.* Well, by God, if that was what she had to do, she would do it.

"All right," she said, glaring at him to conceal her intentions. "I can't make you make sense. Just tell me one thing. Who was that old man? You knew him."

Covenant returned her stare as if he did not mean to answer. But then he relented stiffly. "A harbinger. Or a warning. When he shows up, you've only got two choices. Give up everything you ever understood, and take your chances. Or run for your life. The problem is"— his tone took on a peculiar resonance, as if he were trying to say more than he could put into words—"he doesn't usually waste his time talking to the kind of people who run away. And you can't possibly know what you're getting into."

She winced inwardly, fearing that he had guessed her intent. But she held herself firm. "Why don't you tell me?"

"I can't." His intensity was gone, transformed back into resignation. "It's like signing a blank check. That kind of trust, foolhardiness, wealth, whatever, doesn't mean anything if you know how much the check is going to be for. You either sign or you don't. How much do you think you can afford?"

"Well, in any case"— she shrugged —"I don't plan to sign any blank checks. I've done about all I can stand to clean up this place. I'm going home." She could not meet his scrutiny. "Dr. Berenford wants you to eat. Are you going to do it, or do I have to send him back out here?"

He did not answer her question. "Goodby, Dr. Avery."

"Oh, dear God," she protested in a sudden rush of dismay at his loneliness. "I'm probably going to spend the rest of the day worrying about you. At least call me Linden."

"Linden." His voice denied all emotion. "I can handle it."

"I know," she murmured, half to herself. She went out into the thick afternoon. *I'm the one who needs help.*

On her way back to her apartment, she noticed that the woman and children who advised repentance were nowhere to be seen.

Several hours later, as sunset dwindled into twilight, streaking the streets with muggy orange and pink, she was driving again. She had showered and rested; she had dressed herself in a checked flannel shirt, tough jeans, and a pair of sturdy hiking shoes. She drove slowly, giving the evening time to darken. Half a mile before she reached Haven Farm, she turned off her headlights.

Leaving the highway, she took the first side road to one of the abandoned houses on the Farm. There she parked her car and locked it to protect her medical bag and purse.

On foot, she approached Covenant's house. As much as possible, she hid herself among the trees along that side of the Farm. She was gambling that she was not too late, that the people who had taken Joan would not have done anything during the afternoon. From the trees, she hastened stealthily to the wall of the house. There, she found a window which gave her a view of the living room without exposing her to the door.

The lights were on. With all her caution, she looked in on Thomas Covenant.

He slouched in the center of the sofa with his head bowed and his hands in his pockets, as if he were waiting for something. His bruises had darkened, giving him the visage of a man who had already been beaten. The muscles along his jaw bunched, relaxed, bunched again. He strove to possess himself in patience; but after a moment the tension impelled him to his feet. He began to walk in circles around the sofa and coffee table. His movements were rigid, denying the mortality of his heart.

So that she would not have to watch him, Linden lowered herself to the ground and sat against the wall. Hidden by the darkness, she waited with him.

She did not like what she was doing. It was a violation of his privacy, completely unprofessional. But her ignorance and his stubbornness were intolerable. She had an absolute need to understand what had made her quail when she had faced Joan.

She did not have to wait long. Scant minutes after she had settled herself, abrupt feet approached the house.

The lurching of her heart almost daunted her. But she resisted it. Carefully, she raised her head to the window just as a fist hammered at the door.

Covenant flinched at the sound. Dread knurled his face.

The sight of his reaction stung Linden. He was such a potent individual, seemed to have so many strengths which she lacked. How had he been brought to this?

But an instant later he crushed his fear as if he were stamping on the neck of a viper. Defying his own weakness, he strode toward the door.

It opened before he reached it. A lone man stepped uninvited out of the dark. Linden could see him clearly. He wore burlap wound around him like cerements. Ash had been rubbed unevenly into his hair, smeared thickly over his cheeks. It emphasized the deadness of his eyes, so that he looked like a ghoul in masque.

"Covenant?" Like his mien, his voice was ashen, dead.

Covenant faced the man. He seemed suddenly taller, as if he were elevated by his own hard grasp on life. "Yes."

"Thomas Covenant?"

The writer nodded impatiently. "What do you want?"

"The hour of judgment is at hand." The man stared into the room as if he were blind. "The Master calls for your soul. Will you come?"

Covenant's mouth twisted into a snarl. "Your master knows what I can do to him."

The man did not react. He went on as if his speech had already been arrayed for burial. "The woman will be sacrificed at the rising of the full moon. Expiation must be made for sin. She will pay if you do not. This is the commandment of the Master of life and death. Will you come?"

Sacrificed? Linden gaped. Expiation? A flush of indignation burned her skin. What the hell—?

Covenant's shoulders knotted. His eyes flamed with extreme promises, threats. "I'll come."

No flicker of consciousness animated the man's gray features. He turned like a marionette and retreated into the night.

For a moment, Covenant stood still. His arms hugged his chest as if to stifle an outcry; his head stretched back in anguish. The bruises marked his face like a bereavement.

But then he moved. With a violence that startled Linden, appalled her, he struck himself across the cheek with his half-hand. Abruptly, he threw himself into the darkness after his summoner.

Linden almost lost her chance to follow. She felt stunned by dismay. The Master—? Sacrificed? Dreads and doubts crawled her skin like vermin. The man in burlap had looked so insentient—soulless more than any animal. Drugs? Or—?

However he may assail—

Was Covenant right? About the old man, about possession? About the purpose—? *She's just a way for them to get at me.*

Sacrificed?

Oh, dear God! The man in burlap appeared insane enough, lost enough, to be dangerous. And Covenant—? Covenant was capable of anything.

Her guess at what he was doing galvanized her. Fear for him broke through her personal apprehension, sent her hurrying around the corner of the house in pursuit.

His summoner had led him away from the highway, away from the house into the woods. Linden could hear them in the brush; without light, they were unable to move quietly. As her eyes adjusted, she glimpsed them ahead of her, flickering like shadows in and out of the variegated dark. She followed them.

They traveled blindly through the woods, over hills and along valleys. They used no path; Linden had the impression that they were cutting as straight as a plumb line toward their destination. And as they moved, the night seemed to mount around her, growing steadily more hostile as her trepidation increased. The trees and brush became malevolent, as if she were passing into another wood altogether, a place of hazard and cruel intent.

Then a hill lay across their way. Covenant and his summoner ascended, disappeared over the crest in a strange flare of orange light. It picked them out of the dark, then quenched them like an instant of translation. Warned by that brief gleam, Linden climbed slowly. The keening of her nerves seemed loud in the blackness. The last few yards she crossed on her hands and knees, keeping herself within the cover of the underbrush.

As her head crested the hill, she was struck by a blaze of light. Fire invisible a foot away burst in her face as if she had just penetrated the boundary of dreams. For an instant, she was blinded by the light, paralyzed by the silence. The night swallowed all sound, leaving the air empty of life.

Blinking furiously, she peered past the hillcrest.

Beyond her lay a deep barren hollow. Its slopes were devoid of grass, brush, trees, as if the soil had been scoured by acid.

A bonfire burned at the bottom of the hollow. Its flames sprang upward like lust, writhed like madness; but it made no noise. Seeing it, Linden felt that she had been stricken deaf. Impossible that such a fire could blaze in silence.

Near the fire stretched a rough plane of native rock, perhaps ten feet across. A large triangle had been painted on it in red—color as crimson as fresh blood.

Joan lay on her back within the triangle. She did not move, appeared to be unconscious; only the slow lifting of her chest against her nightgown showed that she was alive.

People clustered around her, twenty or thirty of them. Men, women, children—all dressed in habiliments of burlap; all masked with gray as if they had been wallowing in ashes. They were as gaunt as icons of hunger. They gazed out of eyes as dead as if the minds behind their orbs had been extirpated—eyes which had been dispossessed of every vestige of will or spirit. Even the children stood like puppets and made no sound.

Their faces were turned toward a place on Linden's left.

Toward Thomas Covenant.

He stood halfway down the hillside, confronting the fire across the barrenness of the hollow. His shoulders hunched; his hands were fists at his sides, and his head was thrust combatively forward. His chest heaved as if he were full of denunciations.

Nobody moved, spoke, blinked. The air was intense with silence like concentrated coercion.

Abruptly, Covenant grated through his teeth, "I'm here." The clench of his throat made each word sound like a self-inflicted wound. "Let her go."

A movement snatched Linden's attention back to the bottom of the hollow. A man brawnier than the rest changed positions, took a stance on the rock at the point of the triangle, above Joan's head. He raised his arms, revealing a long, curved dagger gripped in his right fist. In a shrill voice like a man on the verge of ecstasy, he shouted, "It is time! We are the will of the Master of life and death! This is the hour of retribution and cleansing and blood! Let us open the way for the Master's presence!"

The night sucked his voice out of the air, left in its place a stillness as sharp as a cut. For a moment, nothing happened.

Covenant took a step downward, then jerked to a halt.

A woman near the fire shambled forward. Linden nearly gasped aloud as she recognized the woman who had stood on the steps of the courthouse, warning people to repent. With her three children behind her, she approached the blaze.

She bowed to it like a dead woman.

Blankly, she put her right hand into the flames.

A shriek of pain rent the night. She recoiled from the fire, fell in agony to the bare ground.

A red quivering ran through the flames like a spasm of desire. The fire seemed to mount as if it fed on the woman's pain.

Linden's muscles bunched, ached to hurl her to her feet. She wanted to shout her horror, stop this atrocity. But her limbs were locked. Images of desperation or evil froze her where she crouched. All these people were like Joan.

Then the woman regained her feet and stood as dumbly as if the nerves to her burned hand had been severed. Her gaze returned to Covenant like a compulsion, exerting its demand against him.

The oldest of her children took her place at the bonfire.

No! Linden cried, striving uselessly to break the silence.

The young boy bowed, thrust his emaciated arm into the blaze.

His wail broke Linden's will, left her panting in helpless abomination. She could not move, could not look away. Loathings for which she had no name mastered her.

The boy's younger sister did what he had done, as if his agony meant nothing to her. And the third waif followed in turn, surrendering her flesh to harm like lifeless tissue animated solely for immolation.

Then Linden would have moved. The rigid abhorrence of Covenant's stance showed that he would have moved. But the fire stopped them, held them. At every taste of flesh, lust flared through it; flames raged higher.

A figure began to take shape in the heart of the blaze.

More people moved to sacrifice their hands. As they did so, the figure solidified. It was indistinct in the flames; but the glaring red outlined a man in a flowing robe. He stood blood-limned with his arms folded across his powerful chest—created by pain out of fire and self-abandonment.

The worshipper with the knife sank to his knees, cried out in exaltation, "Master!"

The figure's eyes were like fangs, carious and yellow; and they raged venomously out of the flames. Their malignance cowed Linden like a personal assault on her sanity, her conception of life. They were rabid and deliberate, like voluntary disease, telic corruption. Nothing in all her life had readied her to witness such palpable hate.

Across the stillness, she heard Covenant gasp in fury, "Foul! Even children?" But his wrath could not penetrate the dread which paralyzed her. For her, the fiery silence was punctuated only by the screaming of the burned.

Then the moon began to rise opposite her. A rim as white as bone crested the hill, looked down into the hollow like a leer.

The man with the knife came to his feet. Again he raised his arms, brandished his dagger. His personal transport was approaching its climax. In a shout like a moan, he cried, "Now is the hour of apocalypse! The Master has come! Doom is at hand for those who seek to thwart His will. Now we will witness vengeance against sin and life, we who have watched and waited and suffered in His name. Here we fulfill the vision that was given to us. We have touched the fire, and we have been redeemed!" His voice rose until he was shrieking like the burned. "Now we will bring all wickedness to blood and eternal torment!"

He's mad. Linden clung to that thought, fought to think of these people as fanatics, driven wild by destitution and fear. They're all crazy. This is impossible. But she could not move.

And Covenant did not move. She yearned for him to do something, break the trance somehow, rescue Joan, save Linden herself from her extremity. But he remained motionless, watching the fire as if he were trapped between savagery and helplessness.

The figure in the blaze stirred. His eyes focused the flames like twin scars of malice, searing everything with his contempt. His right arm made a gesture as final as a sentence of execution.

At once, the brawny man dropped to his knees. Bending over Joan, he bared her throat. She lay limp under him, frail and lost. The skin of her neck seemed to gleam in the firelight like a plea for help.

Trembling as if he were rapturous or terrified, the man set his blade against Joan's white throat.

Now the people in the hollow stared emptily at his hands. They appeared to have lost all interest in Covenant. Their silence was appalling. The man's hands shook.

"Stop!"

Covenant's shout scourged the air.

"You've done enough! Let her go!"

The baleful eyes in the fire swung at him, nailed him with denigration. The worshipper at Joan's throat stared whitely upward. "Release her?" he croaked. "Why?"

"Because you don't have to do this!" Anger and supplication thickened Covenant's tone. "I don't know how you were driven to this. I don't know what went wrong with your life. But you don't have to do it."

The man did not blink, the eyes in the fire clenched him. Deliberately, he knotted his free hand in Joan's hair.

"All right!" Covenant barked immediately. "All right. I accept. I'll trade you. Me for her."

"No." Linden strove to shout aloud, but her cry was barely a whisper. *"No."*

The worshippers were as silent as gravestones.

Slowly, the man with the knife rose to his feet. He alone seemed to have the capacity to feel triumph; he was grinning ferally as he said, "It is as the Master promised."

He stepped back. At the same time, a quiver ran through Joan. She raised her head, gaped around her. Her face was free of possession. Moving awkwardly, she climbed to her feet. Bewildered and afraid, she searched for an escape, for anything she could understand.

She saw Covenant.

"Tom!" Springing from the rock, she fled toward him and threw herself into his arms.

He hugged her, strained his arms around her as if he could not bear to lose her. But then, roughly, he pushed her away. "Go home," he ordered. "It's over. You'll be safe now." He faced her in the right direction, urged her into motion.

She stopped and looked at him, imploring him to go with her.

"Don't worry about me." A difficult tenderness softened his tone. "You're safe now—that's the important thing. I'll be all right." Somehow, he managed to smile. His eyes betrayed his pain. The light from the fire cast shadows of self-defiance across his bruised mien. And yet his smile expressed so much valor and rue that the sight of it tore Linden's heart.

Kneeling with her head bowed and hot tears on her cheeks, she sensed rather than saw Joan leave the hollow. She could not bear to watch as Covenant moved down the hillside. *I'm the only one who can help her.* He was committing a kind of suicide.

Suicide. Linden's father had killed himself. Her mother had begged for death. Her revulsion toward such things was a compelling obsession.

But Thomas Covenant had chosen to die. And he had smiled.

For Joan's sake.

Linden had never seen one person do so much for another. She could not endure it. She already had too much blood on her hands. Dashing the tears from her eyes, she looked up.

Covenant moved among the people as if he were beyond hope. The man with the knife guided him into the triangle of blood. The carious eyes in the fire blazed avidly.

It was too much. With a passionate wrench, Linden broke the hold of her dismay, jumped upright.

"Over here!" she yelled. "Police! Hurry! They're over here!" She flailed her arms as if she were signalling to people behind her.

The eyes of the fire whipped at her, hit her with withering force. In that instant, she felt completely vulnerable, felt all her secrets exposed and devoured. But she ignored the eyes. She sped downward, daring the worshippers to believe she was alone.

Covenant whirled in the triangle. Every line of his stance howled, *No!*

People cried out. Her charge seemed to shatter the trance of the fire. The worshippers were thrown into confusion. They fled in all directions, scattered as if she had unpent a vast pressure of repugnance. For an instant, she was wild with hope.

But the man with the knife did not flee. The rage of the bonfire exalted him. He slapped his arms around Covenant, threw him to the stone, kicked him so that he lay flat.

The knife—! Covenant was too stunned to move.

Linden hurled herself at the man, grappled for his arms. He was slick with ashes, and strong. She lost her grip.

Covenant struggled to roll over. Swiftly, the man stooped to him, pinned him with one hand, raised the knife in the other.

Linden attacked again, blocked the knife. Her fingernails gouged the man's face.

Yowling, he dealt her a blow which stretched her on the rock.

Everything reeled. Darkness spun at her from all sides.

She saw the knife flash.

Then the eyes of the fire blazed at her, and she was lost in a yellow triumph that roared like the furnace of the sun.

PART I

Need

FOUR: "You Are Mine"

RED agony spiked the center of Thomas Covenant's chest. He felt that he was screaming. But the fire was too bright; he could not hear himself. From the wound, flame writhed through him, mapping his nerves like a territory of pain. He could not fight it.

He did not want to fight it. He had saved Joan. Saved Joan. That thought iterated through him, consoling him for the unanswerable violence of the wound. For the first time in eleven years, he was at peace with his ex-wife. He had repaid the old debt between them to the limit of his mortality; he had given everything he possessed to make restitution for the blameless crime of his leprosy. Nothing more could be asked of him.

But the fire had a voice. At first, it was too loud to be understood. It retorted in his ears like the crushing of boulders. He inhaled it with every failing breath; it echoed along the conflagration in his chest. But gradually it became clear. It uttered words as heavy as stones.

"Your will is mine—
You have no hope of life without me,
Have no life or hope without me.
All is mine.

"Your heart is mine—
There is no love or peace within you,
Is no peace or love within you.
All is mine.

55

> "Your soul is mine—
> You cannot dream of your salvation,
> Cannot plead for your salvation.
> You are mine."

The arrogance of the words filled him with repudiation. He knew that voice. He had spent ten years strengthening himself against it, tightening his grip on the truth of love and rage which had enabled him to master it. And still it had the power to appall him. It thronged with relish for the misery of lepers. It claimed him and would not let him go.

Now he wanted to fight. He wanted to live. He could not bear to let that voice have its way with him.

But the knife had struck too deeply; the wound was complete. A numbness crept through him, and the red fire faded toward mist. He had no pulse, could not remember breathing. Could not—

Out of the mist, he remembered Linden Avery.

Hellfire!

She had followed him, even though he had warned her— warned her in spite of the fact that she had obviously been chosen to fulfill some essential role. He had been so torn— She had given an excruciating twist to his dilemma, had dismayed and infuriated him with her determination to meddle in matters she could not comprehend. And yet she was the first woman he had met in ten years who was not afraid of him.

And she had fallen beside him, trying to save his life. The man had struck her; the fire had covered her as it reached for him. If she were being taken to the Land—!

Of course she was. Why else had the old man accosted her?

But she had neither knowledge nor power with which to defend herself, had no way to understand what was happening to her.

Blindly, Covenant struggled against the numbness, resisted the voice. Linden had tried to save his life. He could not leave her to face such a doom alone. Wrath at the brutality of her plight crowded his heart. By hell! he raged. You can't do this!

Suddenly, a resurgence of fire burned out of him—pure white flame, the fire of his need. It concentrated in the knife wound, screamed through his chest like an apotheosis or cautery. Heat hammered at his heart, his lungs, his half-hand. His body arched in ire and pain.

The next instant, the crisis broke. Palpable relief poured through him. The pain receded, leaving him limp and gasping on the stone. The mist swirled with malice, but did not touch him.

"Ah, you are stubborn yet," the voice sneered, so personal in its contempt that it might have come from within his mind rather than from the attar-laden air. "Stubborn beyond my fondest desires. In one stroke you have ensured your own defeat. My will commands now, and you are lost. Groveler!"

Covenant flinched at the virulence of the sound.

Lord Foul.

"Do you mislike the title I have given you?" The Despiser spoke softly, hardly above a whisper; but his quietness only emphasized his sharp hate. "You will merit it absolutely. Never have you been more truly mine. You believe that you have been near unto death. That is false, groveler! I would not permit you to die. I will obtain far better service from your life."

Covenant wanted to strike out at the mist, flail it away from him. But he was too weak. He lay on the stone as if his limbs had been bled dry. He needed all his will to dredge his voice back to life. "I don't believe it," he panted hoarsely. "You can't be stupid enough to try this again."

"Ah, you do not believe," jeered Lord Foul. "Misdoubt it, then. Disbelieve, and I will rend your very soul from your bones!"

No! Covenant rasped in silence. I've had ten years to understand what happened the last time. You can't do that to me again.

"You will grovel before me," the Despiser went on, "and call it joy. Your victory over me was nothing. It serves me well. Plans which I planted in my anguish have come to fruit. Time is altered. The world is not what it was. You are changed, Unbeliever." The mist made that word, *Unbeliever*, into a name of sovereign scorn. "You are no longer free. You have sold yourself for that paltry woman who loathes you. When you accepted her life from me, you became my tool. A tool does not choose. Did not my Enemy expound to you the necessity of freedom? Your very presence here empowers me to master you."

Covenant flinched. Lord Foul spoke the truth; he was not

free. In trading himself for Joan, he had committed himself to something he could neither measure nor recall. He wanted to cry out; but he was too angry to show that much weakness.

"We are foemen, you and I," continued Lord Foul, "enemies to the end. But the end will be yours, Unbeliever, not mine. That you will learn to believe. For a score of centuries I lay entombed in the Land which I abhor, capable of naught but revulsion. But in time I was restored to myself. For nearly as many centuries more, I have been preparing retribution. When last comes to last, you will be the instrument of my victory."

Bloody hell! Covenant gagged on the thickness of the mist and Lord Foul's vitriol. But his passion was clear. *I won't let you do this!*

"Now hear me, groveler. Hear my prophecy. It is for your ears alone—for behold! there are none left in the Land to whom you could deliver it."

That hurt him. None? What had happened to the Lords?

But the Despiser went on remorselessly, mocking Covenant by his very softness. "No, to you alone I say it: tremble in your heart, for the ill that you deem most terrible is upon you! Your former victory accomplished naught but to prepare the way for this moment. I am Lord Foul the Despiser, and I speak the one word of truth. To you I say it: the wild magic is no longer potent against me! It cannot serve you now. No power will suffice.

"Unbeliever, you cannot oppose me. At the last there will be but one choice for you, and you will make it in all despair. Of your own volition you will give the white gold into my hand."

No! Covenant shouted. *No!* But he could not penetrate Lord Foul's certitude.

"Knowing that I will make use of that power to destroy the Earth, you will place it into my hand, and no hope or chance under all the Arch of Time can prevent you!

"Yes, tremble, groveler! There is despair laid up for you here beyond anything your petty mortal heart can bear!"

The passionate whisper threatened to crush Covenant against the stone. He wailed refusals and curses, but they had no force, could not drive the attar from his throat.

Then Lord Foul began to chuckle. The corruption of death clogged the air. For a long moment, Covenant retched as if the muscles of his chest were breaking.

But as he gagged, the jeering drifted away from him. Wind sifted through it, pulling the mist apart. The wind was cold, as if a chill of laughter rode it, echoing soundlessly; but the atmosphere grew bright as the mist frayed and vanished.

Covenant lay on his back under a brilliant azure sky and a strange sun.

The sun was well up in the heavens. The central glare of its light was familiar, comforting. But it wore a blue corona like a ring of sapphire; and its radiance deepened the rest of the sky to the texture of sendaline.

He squinted at it dumbly, too stunned to move or react. *Of your own volition—* The sun's aurora disturbed him in a way he could not define. *Plans which I planted in my anguish—* Shifting as if it had a mind of its own, his right hand slowly probed toward the spot where the knife had struck him.

His fingers were too numb to tell him anything. But he could feel their pressure on his chest. He could feel their touch when they slipped through the slit in the center of his T-shirt.

There was no pain.

He withdrew his hand, took his gaze out of the sky to look at his fingers.

There was no blood.

He sat up with a jerk that made his head reel. For a moment, he had to prop himself up with his arms. Blinking against the sun-dazzle, he forced his eyes into focus on his chest.

His shirt had been cut—a slash the width of his hand just below his sternum. Under it lay the white line of a new scar.

He gaped at it. How—?

You are stubborn yet. Had he healed himself? With wild magic?

He did not know. He had not been conscious of wielding any power. Could he have done such a thing unconsciously? High Lord Mhoram had once said to him, *You are the white gold.* Did that mean he was capable of using power without knowing it? Without being in control of it? Hellfire!

Long moments passed before he realized that he was facing a parapet. He was sitting on one side of a round stone slab encircled by a low wall, chest-high on him in this position.

A jolt of recognition brought him out of his stupor. He knew this place.

Kevin's Watch.

For an instant, he asked himself, Why here? But then a chain of connections jumped taut in him, and he whirled, to find Linden stretched unconscious behind him.

He almost panicked. She lay completely still. Her eyes were open, but she saw nothing. The muscles of her limbs hung slack against the bones. Her hair was tangled across her face. Blood seeped in slow drops from behind her left ear.

You are mine.

Suddenly, Covenant was sweating in the cool air.

He gripped her shoulders, shook her, then snatched up her left hand, started to slap her wrist. Her head rolled in protest. A whimper tightened her lips. She began to writhe. He dropped her arm, clamped his hands to the sides of her face to keep her from hurting herself against the stone.

Abruptly, her gaze sprang outward. She drew a harsh gasp of air and screamed. Her cry sounded like destitution under the immense sky and the strange blue-ringed sun.

"Linden!" he shouted. She sucked air to howl again. "Linden!"

Her eyes lurched into focus on him, flared in horror or rage as if he had threatened her with leprosy.

Fiercely, she struck him across the cheek.

He recoiled, more in surprise than in pain.

"You bastard," she panted, surging to her knees. "Haven't you even got the guts to go on living?" She inhaled deeply to yell at him. But before she could release her ire, dismay knotted her features. Her hands leaped to her mouth, then covered her face. She gave a muffled groan. "Oh my God."

He stared at her in confusion. What had happened to her? He wanted to challenge her at once, demand an answer. But the situation was too complex. And she was totally unprepared for it. He remembered vividly his first appearance here. If Lena had not extended her hand to him, he would have died in vertigo and madness. It was too much for any mind to accept. If only she had listened to him, stayed out of danger—

But she had not listened. She was here, and in need. She did not yet know the extent of her need. For her sake, he forced a semblance of gentleness into his voice. "You wanted to understand, and I kept telling you you weren't equipped. Now I think you're going to understand whether you want to or not."

"Covenant," she moaned through her hands. "Covenant."

"Linden." Carefully, he touched her wrists, urged her to lower her arms.

"Covenant—" She bared her face to him. Her eyes were brown, deep and moist, and dark with the repercussions of fear. They shied from his, then returned. "I must have been dreaming." Her voice quavered. "I thought you were my father."

He smiled for her, though the strain made his battered bones ache. Father? He wanted to pursue that, but did not. Other questions were more immediate.

But before he could frame an inquiry, she began to recollect herself. She ran her hands through her hair, winced when she touched the injury behind her ear. For a moment, she looked at the trace of blood on her fingers. Then other memories returned. She gasped sharply. Her eyes jerked to his chest. "The knife—" Her urgency was almost an attack. "I saw—" She grabbed for him, yanked up his shirt, gaped at the new scar under his sternum. It appalled her. Her hands reached toward it, flinched away. Her voice was a hoarse whisper. "That's not possible."

"Listen." He raised her head with his left hand, made her meet his gaze. He wanted to distract her, prepare her. "What happened to you? That man hit you. The fire was all over us. What happened after that?"

"What happened to you?"

"One thing at a time." The exertion of keeping himself steady made him sound grim. "There are too many other things you have to understand first. Please give me a chance. Tell me what happened."

She pulled away. Her whole body rejected his question. One trembling finger pointed at his chest. "That's impossible."

Impossible. At that moment, he could have overwhelmed her with impossibilities. But he refrained, permitted himself to say only, "So is possession."

She met his gaze miserably. Then her eyes closed. In a low voice, she said, "I must have been unconscious. I was dreaming about my parents."

"You didn't hear anything? A voice making threats?"

Her eyes snapped open in surprise. "No. Why would I?"

He bowed his head to hide his turmoil. Foul hadn't spoken to her? The implications both relieved and frightened him. Was she somehow independent of him? Free of his control? Or was he already that sure of her?

When Covenant looked up again, Linden's attention had slipped away to the parapet, the sun, the wide sky. Slowly, her face froze. She started to her feet. "*Where are we?*"

He caught her arms, held her sitting in front of him. "Look at me." Her head winced from side to side in frantic denial. Exigencies thronged about him; questions were everywhere. But at this moment the stark need in her face dominated all other issues. "Dr. Avery." There was insanity in the air; he knew that from experience. If he did not help her now, she might never be within reach of help again. "*Look* at me."

His demand brought her wild stare back to him.

"I can explain it. Just give me a chance."

Her voice knifed at him. "Explain it."

He flinched in shame; it was his fault that she was here— and that she was so unready. But he forced himself to face her squarely. "I couldn't tell you about it before." The difficulty of what he had to say roughened his tone. "There was no way you could have believed it. And now it's so complicated—"

Her eyes clung to him like claws.

"There are two completely different explanations," he said as evenly as he could. "Outside and inside. The outside explanation might be easier to accept. It goes like this." He took a deep breath. "You and I are still lying in that triangle." A grimace strained his bruises. "We're unconscious. And while we're unconscious, we're dreaming. We're sharing a dream."

Her mien was tight with disbelief. He hastened to add, "It's not as farfetched as you think. Deep down in their minds— down where dreams come from—most people have a lot in common. That's why so many of our dreams fall into patterns that other people can recognize.

"It's happening to us." He kept pouring words at her, not because he wanted to convince her, but because he knew she needed time, needed any answer, however improbable, to help her survive the first shock of her situation. "We're sharing a dream. And we're not the only ones," he went on, denying her a chance to put her incredulity into words. "Joan had fragments of the same dream. And that old man—the one you saved. We're all tied into the same unconscious process."

Her gaze wavered. He snapped, "Keep looking at me! I have to tell you what kind of dream it is. It's dangerous. It can hurt you. The things buried in us are powerful and violent, and they are going to come out. The darkness in us—the destructive side, the side we keep locked up all our lives—is alive here. Everybody has some self-hate inside. Here it's personified—externalized, the way things happen in dreams. He calls himself Lord Foul the Despiser, and he wants to destroy us.

"That's what Joan kept talking about. Lord Foul. And that's what the old man meant. 'However he may assail you. Be true.' Be true to yourself, don't serve the Despiser, don't let him destroy you. That's what we have to do." He pleaded with her to accept the consequences of what he was saying, even if she chose not to believe the explanation itself. "We have to stay sane, hang onto ourselves, defend what we are and what we believe and what we want. Until it's over. Until we regain consciousness."

He stopped, forced himself to give her time.

Her eyes dropped to his chest, as if that scar were a test of what he said. Shadows of fear passed across her countenance. Covenant felt suddenly sure that she was familiar with self-hate.

Tightly, she said, "This has happened to you before."

He nodded.

She did not raise her head. "And you believe it?"

He wanted to say, Partially. If you put the two explanations together, they come close to what I believe. But in her present straits he could not trouble her with disclaimers. Instead, he got to his feet, drew her with him to look out from the Watch.

She stiffened against him in shock.

They were on a slab like a platform that appeared to hang suspended in the air. An expanse of sky as huge as if they were perched on a mountaintop covered them. The weird halo of the sun gave a disturbing hue to the roiling gray sea of clouds two hundred feet below them. The clouds thrashed like thunderheads, concealing the earth from horizon to horizon.

A spasm of vertigo wrenched Covenant; he remembered acutely that he was four thousand feet above the foothills. But he ignored the imminent reel and panic around him and concentrated on Linden.

She was stunned, rigid. This leap without transition from

night in the woods to morning on such an eminence staggered
her. He wanted to put his arms around her, hide her face
against his chest to protect her; but he knew he could not do
so, could not give her the strength to bear things which once
had almost shattered him. She had to achieve her own survival. Grimly, he turned her to look in the opposite direction.

The mountains rising dramatically there seemed to strike
her a blow. They sprang upward out of the clouds a stone's
throw from the Watch. Their peaks were rugged and dour.
From the cliff behind the Watch, they withdrew on both sides
like a wedge, piling higher into the distance. But off to the
right a spur of the range marched back across the clouds
before falling away again.

Linden gaped at the cliff as if it were about to fall on her.
Covenant could feel her ribs straining; she was caught in the
predicament of the mad and could not find enough air in all
the open sky to enable her to cry out. Fearing that she might
break away from him, lose herself over the parapet, he tugged
her back down to the safety of the floor. She crumpled to her
knees, gagging silently. Her eyes had a terrible glazed and
empty look.

"Linden!" Because he did not know what else to do, he
barked, "Haven't you even got the guts to go on living?"

She gasped, inhaled. Her eyes swept into focus on him like
swords leaping from their scabbards. The odd sunlight gave
her face an aspect of dark fury.

"I'm sorry," he said thickly. Her reaction made him ache as
badly as helplessness. "You were so—" Unwittingly, he had
trespassed on something which he had no right to touch. "I
never wanted this to happen to you."

She rejected his regret with a violent shake of her head.
"Now," she panted, "you're going to tell me the other explanation."

He nodded. Slowly, he released her, withdrew to sit with his
back against the parapet. He did not understand her strange
combination of strength and weakness; but at the moment his
incomprehension was unimportant. "The inside explanation."

A deep weariness ran through him. He fought it for the
words he needed. "We're in a place called the Land. It's a
different world—like being on a completely different planet.
These mountains are the Southron Range, the southern edge.
All the rest of the Land is west and north and east from us.

This place is Kevin's Watch. Below us, and a bit to the west, there used to be a village called Mithil Stonedown. Revelstone is—" But the thought of Revelstone recalled the Lords; he shied away from it. "I've been here before.

"Most of what I can tell you about it won't make much sense until you see it for yourself. But there's one thing that's important right now. The Land has an enemy. Lord Foul." He studied her, trying to read her response. But her eyes brandished darkness at him, nothing else. "For thousands of years," he went on, "Foul has been trying to destroy the Land. It's—sort of a prison for him. He wants to break out." He groaned inwardly at the impossibility of making what he had to say acceptable to someone who had never had the experience. "He translated us out of our world. Brought us here. He wants us to serve him. He thinks he can manipulate us into helping him destroy the Land.

"We have power here." He prayed he was speaking the truth. "Since we come from outside, we aren't bound by the Law, the natural order that holds everything together. That's why Foul wants us, wants to use us. We can do things nobody else here can."

To spare himself the burden of her incredulity, he leaned his head against the parapet and gazed up at the mountains. "The necessity of freedom," he breathed. "As long as we aren't bound by any Law, or anybody or any explanation," he said to ease his conscience, "we're powerful." But I'm not free. I've already chosen. "That's what it comes down to. Power. The power that healed me.

"That old man— Somehow, he knows what's going on in the Land. And he's no friend of Foul's. He chose you for something—I don't know what. Or maybe he wanted to reassure himself. Find out if you're the kind of person Foul can manipulate.

"As for Joan, she was Foul's way of getting at me. She was vulnerable to him. After what happened the last time I was here, I wasn't. He used her to get me to step into that triangle by my own choice. So he could summon me here." What I don't understand, he sighed, is why he had to do it that way. It wasn't like that before. "Maybe it's an accident that you're here, too. But I don't think so."

Linden glanced down at the stone as if to verify that it was substantial, then touched the bruise behind her ear. Frowning, she shifted into a sitting position. Now she did not look at him. "I don't understand," she said stiffly. "First you tell me this is a dream—then you say it's real. First you're dying back there in the woods—then you're healed by some kind of—some kind of magic. First Lord Foul is a figment—then he's real." In spite of her control, her voice trembled slightly. "Which is it? You can't have it both ways." Her fist clenched. "You could be dying."

Ah, I have to have it both ways, Covenant murmured. It's like vertigo. The answer is in the contradiction—in the eye of the paradox. But he did not utter his thought aloud.

Yet Linden's question relieved him. Already, her restless mind—that need which had rejected his efforts to warn her, had driven her to follow him to his doom—was beginning to grapple with her situation. If she had the strength to challenge him, then her crisis was past, at least for the moment. He found himself smiling in spite of his fear.

"It doesn't matter," he replied. "Maybe this is real—maybe it isn't. You can believe whatever you want. I'm just offering you a frame of reference, so you'll have some place to start."

Her hands kept moving, touching herself, the stone, as if she needed tactile sensation to assure her of her own existence. After a moment, she said, "You've been here before." Her anger had turned to pain. "It's your life. Tell me how to understand."

"Face it," he said without hesitation. "Go forward. Find out what happens—what's at stake. What matters to you." He knew from experience that there was no other defense against insanity; the Land's reality and its unreality could not be reconciled. "Give yourself a chance to find out who you are."

"I know who I am." Her jaw was stubborn. The lines of her nose seemed precise rather than fragile; her mouth was severe by habit. "I'm a doctor." But she was facing something she did not know how to grasp. "I don't even have my bag." She scrutinized her hands as if she wondered what they were good for. When she met his gaze, her question was a demand as well as an appeal. "What do you believe?"

"I believe"— he made no effort to muffle his hardness —"that we've got to find some way to stop Foul. That's more important than anything. He's trying to destroy the Land. I'm not going to let him get away with that. That's who *I* am."

She stared at his affirmation. "Why? What does it have to

do with you? If this is a dream, it doesn't matter. And if it's—" She had difficulty saying the words. "If it's real, it's not your problem. You can ignore it."

Covenant tasted old rage. "Foul laughs at lepers."

At that, a glare of comprehension touched her eyes. Her scowl said plainly, Nobody has the right to laugh at illness.

In a tight voice, she asked, "What do we do now?"

"Now?" He was weak with fatigue; but her question galvanized him. She had reasons, strengths, possibilities. The old man had not risked her gratuitously. "Now," he said grimly, "if I can hold off my vertigo, we get down from here, and go find out what kind of trouble we're in."

"Down?" She blinked at him. "I don't know how we got up."

To answer her, he nodded toward the mountains. When she turned, she noticed the gap in the curve of the parapet facing the cliff. He watched as she crawled to the gap, saw what he already knew was there.

The parapet circled the tip of a long spire of stone which angled toward the cliff under the Watch. There were rude stairs cut into the upper surface of the shaft.

He joined her. One glance told him that his dizziness would not be easily overcome. Two hundred feet below him, the stairs vanished in the clouds like a fall into darkness.

FIVE: Thunder and Lightning

"I'LL go first." Covenant was trembling deep in his bones. He did not look at Linden. "This stair joins the cliff— but if we fall, it's four thousand feet down. I'm no good at heights. If I slip, I don't want to take you with me." Deliberately, he set himself at the gap, feet first so that he could back through it.

There he paused, tried to resist the vertigo which unmoored his mind by giving himself a VSE. But the exercise aroused a pang of leper's anxiety. Under the blue-tinged sun, his skin had a dim purple cast, as if his leprosy had already spread up his arms, affecting the pigmentation, killing the nerves.

A sudden weakness yearned in his muscles, making his shoulders quiver. The particular numbness of his dead nerves had not altered, for better or worse. But the diseased hue of his flesh looked fatal and prophetic; it struck him like a leap of intuition. One of his questions answered itself. Why was Linden here? Why had the old man spoken to her rather than to him? Because she was necessary. To save the Land when he failed.

The wild magic is no longer potent. So much for power. He had already abandoned himself to Lord Foul's machinations. A groan escaped him before he could lock his teeth on it.

"Covenant?" Concern sharpened Linden's voice. "Are you all right?"

He could not reply. The simple fact that she was worried about him, was capable of worrying about him when she was under so much stress, multiplied the dismay in his bones. His eyes clung to the stone, searching for strength.

"Covenant!" Her demand was like a slap in the face. "I don't know how to help you. Tell me what to do."

What to do. None of this was her fault. She deserved an answer. He pulled himself down into the center of his fatigue and dizziness. Had he really doomed himself by taking Joan's place? Surely he did not have to fail? Surely the power for which he had paid such a price was not so easily discounted? Without raising his head, he gritted, "At the bottom of the stairs, to my left, there's a ledge in the cliff. Be careful."

Coercing himself into motion, he backed through the gap.

As his head passed below the level of the Watch, he heard her whisper fiercely, "Damn you, why do you have to act so impervious? All I want to do is help." She sounded as if her sanity depended on her ability to be of help.

But he could not afford to think about her; the peril of the stairs consumed his attention. He worked his way down them as if they were a ladder, clutching them with his hands, kicking each foot into them to be sure it was secure before he trusted it. His gaze never left his hands. They strained on the steps until the sinews stood out like desperation.

The void around him seemed fathomless. He could hear the emptiness of the wind. And the swift seething of the clouds below him had a hypnotic power, sucking at his concentration. Long plunges yawned all around him.

But he knew this fear. Holding his breath, he lowered himself into the clouds—into the still center of his vertigo.

Abruptly, the sun faded and went out. Gray gloom thickened toward midnight at every step of the descent.

A pale flash ran through the dank sea, followed almost at once by thunder. The wind mounted, rushed wetly at him as if it sought to lift him off the spire. The stone became slick. His numb fingers could not tell the difference, but the nerves in his wrists and elbows registered every slippage of his grasp.

Again, a bolt of lightning thrashed past him, illuminating the mad boil and speed of the clouds. The sky shattered. Instinctively, he flattened himself against the stone. Something in him howled, but he could not tell whether it howled aloud.

Crawling painfully through the brutal impact of the storm, he went on downward.

He marked his progress in the intensifying weight of the rain. The fine cold sting of spray against his sore face became a pelting of heavy drops like a shower of pebbles. Soon he was drenched and battered. Lightning and thunder shouted across him, articulating savagery. But the promise of the ledge drew him on.

At last, his feet found it. Thrusting away from the spire, he pressed his back to the wall of the cliff, gaping upward.

A flail of blue-white fire rendered Linden out of the darkness. She was just above the level of his head.

When she reached the ledge, he caught her so that she would not stumble over the precipice. She gripped him urgently. "Covenant!" The wind ripped her shout away; he could barely hear her. "Are you all right?"

He put his mouth to her ear. "Stay against the cliff! We've got to find shelter!"

She nodded sharply.

Clenching her right hand in his left, he turned his back on the fall and began to shuttle west along the ledge.

Lightning burned overhead, to give him a glimpse of his situation. The ledge was two or three feet wide and ran roughly level across the cliff face. From its edge, the mountain disappeared into the abyss of the clouds.

Thunder hammered at him like the voice of his vertigo, commanding him to lose his balance. Wind and rain as shrill as chaos lashed his back. But Linden's hand anchored him. He squeezed himself like yearning against the cliff and crept slowly forward.

At every lightning blast, he peered ahead through the rain, trying to see the end of the ledge.

There: a vertical line like a scar in the cliff face.

He reached it, pulled Linden past the corner, up a slope of mud and scree which gushed water as if it were a stream bed. At once, the wind became a constricted yowl. The next blue glare revealed that they had entered a narrow ravine sluicing upward through the mountainside. Water frothed like rapids past the boulders which cramped the floor of the ravine.

He struggled ahead until he and Linden were above a boulder that appeared large enough to be secure. There he halted and sat down in the current with his back braced on the wall. She joined him. Water flooded over their legs; rain blinded their faces. He did not care. He had to rest.

After a few moments, she shifted, put her face to his ear. "Now what?"

Now what? He did not know. Exhaustion numbed his mind. But she was right; they could not remain where they were. He mustered a wan shout. "There's a path somewhere!"

"You don't know the way? You said you've been here before!"

"Ten years ago!" And he had been unconscious the second time; Saltheart Foamfollower had carried him.

Lightning lit her face for an instant. Her visage was smeared with rain. "What are we going to do?"

The thought of Foamfollower, the Giant who had been his friend, gave him what he needed. "Try!" Bracing himself on her shoulder, he lurched to his feet. She seemed to support his weight easily. "Maybe I'll remember!"

She stood up beside him, leaned close to yell, "I don't like this storm! It doesn't feel right!"

Doesn't feel—? He blinked at her. For a moment, he did not understand. To him, it was just a storm, natural violence like any other. But then he caught her meaning. To her, the storm felt *un*natural. It offended some instinctive sensitivity in her.

Already, she was ahead of him; her senses were growing attuned to the Land, while his remained flat and dull, blind to the spirit of what he perceived. Ten years ago, he had been able to do what she had just done: identify the rightness or wrongness, the health or corruption, of physical things and processes, of wind, rain, stone, wood, flesh. But now he could feel nothing except the storm's vehemence, as if such force had no meaning, no implications. No soul.

He muttered tired curses at himself. Were his senses merely slow in making the adjustment? Or had he lost the ability to be in harmony with the Land? Had leprosy and time bereft him entirely of that sensitivity? Hell and blood! he rasped weakly, bitterly. If Linden could see where he was blind—

Aching at the old grief of his insufficiency, he tried to master himself. He expected Linden to ask him what was wrong. And that thought, too, was bitter; he did not want his frailties and fears, his innate wrongness, to be visible to her. But she did not question him. She was rigid with surprise or apprehension.

Her face was turned up the ravine.

He jerked around and tried to penetrate the downpour.

At once, he saw it—a faint yellow light in the distance.

It flickered toward them slowly, picked its way with care down the spine of the ravine. As it neared, a long blast of lightning revealed that it was a torch in the hand of a man. Then blackness and thunder crashed over them, and Covenant could see nothing but the strange flame. It burned bravely, impossibly, in spite of the deluge and battery of the storm.

It approached until it was close enough to light the man who held it. He was a short, stooped figure wearing a sodden robe. Rain gushed through his sparse hair and tangled beard, streamed in runnels down the creases of his old face, giving him a look of lunacy. He squinted at Covenant and Linden as if they had been incarnated out of nightmares to appall him.

Covenant held himself still, returned the old man's stare mutely.

Linden touched his arm as if she wanted to warn him of something.

Suddenly, the old man jerked up his right hand, raised it with the palm forward, and spread his fingers.

Covenant copied the gesture. He did not know whether or not Lord Foul had prepared this encounter for him. But he needed shelter, food, information. And he was prepared to acknowledge anyone who could keep a brand alight in this rain. As he lifted his half-hand into the light, his ring gleamed dully on the second finger.

The sight shocked the old man. He winced, mumbled to

himself, retreated a step as if in fear. Then he pointed tremu-
lously at Covenant's ring. "White gold?" he cried. His voice
shook.

"Yes!" Covenant replied.

"Halfhand?"

"Yes!"

"How are you named?" the man quavered.

Covenant struggled to drive each word through the storm.
"Ur-Lord Thomas Covenant, Unbeliever and white gold
wielder!"

"Illender?" gasped the man as if the rain were suffocating
him. "Prover of Life?"

"Yes!"

The old man retreated another step. The torchlight gave his
visage a dismayed look. Abruptly, he turned, started scrambling frailly upward through the water and muck.

Over his shoulder, he wailed, "Come!"

"Who is that?" Linden asked almost inaudibly.

Covenant dismissed the question. "I don't know."

She scrutinized him. "Do you trust him?"

"Who has a choice?" Before she could respond, he pushed
away from the stone, used all his energy to force himself into
motion after the old man.

His mouth was full of rain and the sour taste of weakness.
The strain of the past weeks affected him like caducity. But
the torch helped him find handholds on the walls and boulders. With Linden's support, he was able to heave forward
against the heavy stream. Slowly, they made progress.

Some distance up the ravine, the old man entered a cut
branching off to the right. A rough stair in the side of the cut
led to its bottom. Freed of the torrents, Covenant found the
strength to ask himself, *Do you trust him*? But the torch
reassured him. He knew of nobody who could keep a brand
burning in rain except the masters of wood-lore. Or the Lords.
He was ready to trust anybody who served wood or stone with
such potent diligence.

Carefully, he followed the old man along the bottom of the
cut until it narrowed, became a high sheer cleft in the mountain rock. Then, abruptly, the cleft changed directions and
opened into a small dell.

Towering peaks sheltered the vale from the wind. But there
was no escape from the rain. It thrashed Covenant's head and

shoulders like a club. He could barely see the torch as the old man crossed the valley.

With Linden, Covenant waded a swollen stream; and moments later they arrived at a squat stone dwelling which sat against the mountainside. The entry had no door; firelight scattered out at them as they approached. Hurrying now, they burst bedraggled and dripping into the single room of the house.

The old man stood in the center of the room, still clutching his torch though a bright fire blazed in the hearth beyond him. He peered at Covenant with trepidation, ready to cringe, like a child expecting punishment.

Covenant stopped. His bruises ached to be near the fire; but he remained still to look around the room.

At once, a pang of anxiety smote him. Already, he could see that something had changed in the Land. Something fundamental.

The dwelling was furnished with an unexpected mixture of wood and stone. Stoneware bowls and urns sat on wooden shelves affixed to the sidewalls; wooden stools stood around a wooden table in one stone corner. And iron—there were iron utensils on the shelves, iron nails in the stools. Formerly, the people of stone and wood, Stonedownor and Woodhelvennin, had each kept to his own lore—not because they wished to be exclusive, but rather because their special skills and knowledge required all their devotion.

For a moment, he faced the man, bore the old, half-wild gaze. Linden, too, studied the old man, measuring him uncertainly. But Covenant knew she was asking herself questions unlike the ones which mobbed into his mind. Had the Stonedownors and Woodhelvennin grown together, blended their lore? Or had—?

The world is not what it was.

A raw sickness twisted his heart. Without warning, he became conscious of smoke in the room.

Smoke!

He thrust past the old man, hastened to the hearth.

The wood lay on a pile of ash, burning warmly. Coals cracked and fell off the logs, red worms gnawing the flesh of trees. At intervals, wisps of smoke curled up into the room. The rain in the chimney made a low hissing noise.

Hellfire!

The people he had known here would never have voluntarily consumed wood for any purpose. They had always striven to use the life of wood, the Earthpower in it, without destroying the thing they used. Wood, soil, stone, water—the people of the Land had cherished every manifestation of life.

"Ur-Lord," the old man groaned.

Covenant whirled. Grief burned like rage in him. He wanted to howl at the Despiser, What have you *done*? But both Linden and the old man were staring at him. Linden's eyes showed concern, as if she feared he had slipped over the edge into confusion. And the old man was in the grip of a private anguish. Fiercely, Covenant contained the yelling of his passion. But the strain of suppression bristled in his tone. "What keeps that torch burning?"

"I am ashamed!" The man's voice broke as if he were on the verge of weeping. He did not hear Covenant's question; his personal distress devoured him. "This temple," he panted, "built by the most ancient fathers of my father's father—in preparation. We have done nothing! Other rooms fallen to ruin, sanctuaries—" He waved his brand fervidly. "We did nothing. In a score of generations, nothing. It is a hovel—unworthy of you. We did not believe the promise given into our trust—generation after generation of Unfettered too craven to put faith in the proudest prophecies. It would be right for you to strike me."

"Strike you?" Covenant was taken aback. "No." There were too many things here he did not understand. "What's the matter? Why are you afraid of me?"

"Covenant," Linden breathed suddenly. "His hand. Look."

Water dripped from the old man; water ran from them all. But the drops falling from the butt of the torch were red.

"Ur-Lord!" The man plunged to his knees. "I am unworthy." He quivered with dismay. "I have trafficked in the knowledge of the wicked, gaining power against the Sunbane from those who scorn the promises I have sworn to preserve. Ah, spare me! I am shamed." He dropped his brand, opened his left hand to Covenant.

The torch went out the instant he released it. As it struck the floor, it fell into ash.

Across his palm lay two long cuts. Blood ran from them as if it could not stop.

Covenant flinched. Thunder muttered angrily to itself in the distance. Nothing was left of the torch except ash. It had been held together, kept whole and burning, only by the power the old man had put into it. The power of his blood?

Covenant's brain reeled. A sudden memory of Joan stung him—Joan clawing the back of his hand, licking his fingers. Vertigo reft him of balance. He sat down heavily, slumped against the nearest wall. The rain echoed in his ears. Blood? *Blood*?

Linden was examining the old man's hand. She turned it to the firelight, spread the fingers; her grip on his wrist slowed the flow of blood. "It's clean." Her voice was flat, impersonal. "Needs a bandage to stop the bleeding. But there's no infection."

No infection, Covenant breathed. His thoughts limped like cripples. "How can you tell?"

She was concentrating on the wound. "What?"

He labored to say what he meant. "How can you tell there's no infection?"

"I don't know." His question seemed to trigger surprise in her. "I can see it. I can see"— her astonishment mounted —"the pain. But it's clean. How—? Can't you?"

He shook his head. She confirmed his earlier impression; her senses were already becoming attuned to the Land.

His were not. He was blind to everything not written on the surface. Why? He closed his eyes. Old rue throbbed in him. He had forgotten that numbness could hurt so much.

After a moment, she moved; he could hear her searching around the room. When she returned to the old man's side, she was tearing a piece of cloth to form bandages.

You will not fail— Covenant felt that he had already been given up for lost. The thought was salt to his sore heart.

Smoke? Blood? *There's only one way to hurt a man. Give him back something broken.* Damnation.

But the old man demanded his attention. The man had bowed his wet gray head to the stone. His hands groped to touch Covenant's boots. "Ur-Lord," he moaned. "Ur-Lord. At last you have come. The Land is saved."

That obeisance pulled Covenant out of his inner gyre. He could not afford to be overwhelmed by ignorance or loss. And he could not bear to be treated as if he were some kind of saviour; he could not live with such an image of himself. He climbed erect, then took hold of the old man's arms and drew him to his feet.

The man's eyes rolled fearfully, gleaming in the firelight. To reassure him, Covenant spoke evenly, quietly.

"Tell me your name."

"I am Nassic son of Jous son of Prassan," the old man replied in a fumbling voice. "Descended in direct lineage son by son from the Unfettered One."

Covenant winced. The Unfettered Ones he had known were hermits freed from all normal responsibilities so that they could pursue their private visions. An Unfettered One had once saved his life—and died. Another had read his dreams—and told him that he dreamed the truth. He took a stringent grip on himself. "What was his calling?"

"Ur-Lord, he saw your return. Therefore he came to this place—to the vale below Kevin's Watch, which was given its name in an age so long past that none remember its meaning."

Briefly, Nassic's tone stabilized, as if he were reciting something he had memorized long ago. "He built the temple as a place of welcome for you, and a place of healing, for it was not forgotten among the people of those years that your own world is one of great hazard and strife, inflicting harm even upon its heroes. In his vision, he beheld the severe doom of the Sunbane, though to him it was nameless as nightmare, and he foresaw that the Unbeliever, ur-Lord Illender, Prover of Life, would return to combat it. From son to son he handed down his vision, faith un—"

Then he faltered. "Ah, shame," he muttered. "Temple—faith—healing—Land. All ruins." But indignation stiffened him. "Fools will cry for mercy. They deserve only retribution. For lo! the Unbeliever has come. Let the Clave and all its works wail to be spared. Let the very sun tremble in its course! It will avail them nothing! Woe unto you, wicked and abominable! The—"

"Nassic." Covenant forced the old man to stop. Linden was watching them keenly. Questions crowded her face; but Covenant ignored them. "Nassic," he asked of the man's white stare, "what is this Sunbane?"

"Sunbane?" Nassic lost his fear in amazement. "Do you ask—? How can you not—?" His hands tugged at his beard. "Why else have you come?"

Covenant tightened his grip. "Just tell me what it is."

"It is—why, it is—yes, it—" Nassic stumbled to a halt, then cried in a sudden appeal, "Ur-Lord, what is it not? It is sun and rain and blood and desert and fear and the screaming of trees." He squirmed with renewed abasement. "It was—it was the fire of my torch. Ur-Lord!" Misery clenched his face like a fist. He tried to drop to his knees again.

"Nassic." Covenant held him erect, hunted for some way to reassure him. "We're not going to harm you. Can't you see that?" Then another thought occurred to him. Remembering Linden's injury, his own bruises, he said, "Your hand's still bleeding. We've both been hurt. And I—" He almost said, I can't see what she sees. But the words stuck in his throat. "I've been away for a long time. Do you have any hurtloam?"

Hurtloam? Linden's expression asked.

"Hurtloam?" queried Nassic. "What is hurtloam?"

What is—? Distress lurched across Covenant's features. What—? Shouts flared in him like screams. Hurtloam! Earthpower! *Life*! "Hurtloam," he rasped savagely. *"The mud that heals."* His grasp shook Nassic's frail bones.

"Forgive me, Ur-Lord. Be not angry. I   "

"It was here! In this valley!" Lena had healed him with it.

Nassic found a moment of dignity. "I know nothing of hurtloam. I am an old man, and have never heard the name spoken."

"Damnation!" Covenant spat. "Next you're going to tell me you've never heard of Earthpower!"

The old man sagged. "Earthpower?" he breathed. "Earthpower?"

Covenant's hands ground his giddy dismay into Nassic's thin arms. But Linden was at his side, trying to loosen his grip. "Covenant! He's telling the truth!"

Covenant jerked his gaze like a whip to her face.

Her lips were tight with strain, but she did not let herself flinch. "He doesn't know what you're talking about."

She silenced him. He believed her; she could hear the truth in Nassic's voice, just as she could see the lack of infection in his cuts. No hurtloam? He bled inwardly. Forgotten? *Lost*? Images of desecration poured through him. Have mercy. The Land without hurtloam. Without Earthpower? The weight of Nassic's revelation was too much for him. He sank to the floor like an invalid.

Linden stood over him. She was groping for decision, insight; but he could not help her. After a moment, she said, "Nassic." Her tone was severe. "Do you have any food?"

"Food?" he replied as if she had reminded him of his inadequacy. "Yes. No. It is unworthy."

"We need food."

Her statement brooked no argument. Nassic bowed, went at once to the opposite wall, where he began lifting down crude bowls and pots from the shelves.

Linden came to Covenant, knelt in front of him. "What is it?" she asked tightly. He could not keep the despair out of his face. "What's wrong?"

He did not want to answer. He had spent too many years in the isolation of his leprosy; her desire to understand him only aggravated his pain. He could not bear to be so exposed. Yet he could not refuse the demand of her hard mouth, her soft eyes. Her life was at issue as much as his. He made an effort of will. "Later." His voice ached through his teeth. "I need time to think about it."

Her jaws locked; darkness wounded her eyes. He looked away, so that he would not be led to speak before he had regained his self-mastery.

Shortly, Nassic brought bowls of dried meat, fruit, and unleavened bread, which he offered tentatively, as if he knew they deserved to be rejected. Linden accepted hers with a difficult smile; but Nassic did not move until Covenant had mustered the strength to nod his approval. Then the old man took pots and collected rainwater for them to drink.

Covenant stared blindly at his food without tasting it. He seemed to have no reason to bother feeding himself. Yet he knew that was not true; in fact, he was foundering in reasons. But the impossibility of doing justice to them all made his resolution falter. Had he really sold his soul to the Despiser—?

But he was a leper; he had spent long years learning the answer to his helplessness. Leprosy was incurable. Therefore lepers disciplined themselves to pay meticulous attention to their immediate needs. They ignored the abstract immensity of their burdens, concentrated instead on the present, moment by moment. He clung to that pragmatic wisdom. He had no other answer.

Numbly, he put a piece of fruit in his mouth, began to chew.

After that, habit and hunger came to his aid. Perhaps his answer was not a good one; but it defined him, and he stood by it.

Stood or fell, he did not know which.

Nassic waited humbly, solicitously, while Covenant and Linden ate; but as soon as they finished, he said, "Ur-Lord." He sounded eager. "I am your servant. It is the purpose of my life to serve you, as it was the purpose of Jous my father and Prassan his father throughout the long line of the Unfettered." He seemed unmindful of the quaver in his words. "You are not come too soon. The Sunbane multiplies in the Land. What will you do?"

Covenant sighed. He felt unready to deal with such questions. But the ritual of eating had steadied him. And both Nassic and Linden deserved some kind of reply. Slowly, he said, "We'll have to go to Revelstone—" He spoke the name hesitantly. Would Nassic recognize it? If there were no more Lords— Perhaps Revelstone no longer existed. Or perhaps all the names had changed. Enough time had passed for anything to happen.

But Nassic crowed immediately, "Yes! Vengeance upon the Clave! It is good!"

The Clave? Covenant wondered. But he did not ask. Instead, he tested another familiar name. "But first we'll have to go to Mithil Stonedown—"

"No!" the man interrupted. His vehemence turned at once into protest and trepidation. "You must not. They are wicked —wicked! Worshippers of the Sunbane. They say that they abhor the Clave, but they do not. Their fields are sown with blood!"

Blood again; Sunbane; the Clave. Too many things he did not know. He concentrated on what he was trying to ascertain. Apparently, the names he remembered were known to Nassic in spite of their age. That ended his one dim hope concerning the fate of the Earthpower. A new surge of futility beat at him. How could he possibly fight Lord Foul if there were no Earthpower? No, worse—if there were no Earthpower, what was left to fight for?

But Nassic's distraught stare and Linden's clenched, arduous silence demanded responses. Grimacing, he thrust down his sense of futility. He was intimately acquainted with hopelessness, impossibility, gall; he knew how to limit their power over him.

He took a deep breath and said, "There's no other way. We can't get out of here without going through Mithil Stonedown."

"Ah, true," the old man groaned. "That is true." He seemed

almost desperate. "Yet you must not— They are wicked! They harken to the words of the Clave—words of abomination. They mock all old promises, saying that the Unbeliever is a madness in the minds of the Unfettered. You must not go there."

"Then how—?" Covenant frowned grimly. What's happened to them? I used to have friends there.

Abruptly, Nassic reached a decision. "I will go. To my son. His name is Sunder. He is wicked, like the rest. But he is my son. He comes to me when the mood is upon him, and I speak to him, telling him what is proper to his calling. He is not altogether corrupted. He will aid us to pass by the Stonedown. Yes." At once, he threw himself toward the entryway.

"Wait!" Covenant jumped to his feet. Linden joined him.

"I must go!" cried Nassic urgently.

"Wait until the rain stops." Covenant pleaded against the frenzy in Nassic's eyes. The man looked too decrepit to endure any more exposure. "We're not in that much of a hurry."

"It will not halt until nightfall. I must make haste!"

"Then at least take a torch!"

Nassic flinched as if he had been scourged. "Ah, you shame me! I know the path. I must redeem my doubt." Before Covenant or Linden could stop him, he ran out into the rain.

Linden started after him; but Covenant stayed her. Lightning blazed overhead. In the glare, they saw Nassic stumbling frenetically toward the end of the dell. Then thunder and blackness hit, and he disappeared as if he had been snuffed out. "Let him go," sighed Covenant. "If we chase him, we'll probably fall off a cliff somewhere." He held her until she nodded. Then he returned wearily to the fire.

She followed him. When he placed his back to the hearth, she confronted him. The dampness of her hair darkened her face, intensifying the lines between her brows, on either side of her mouth. He expected anger, protest, some outburst against the insanity of her situation. But when she spoke, her voice was flat, controlled.

"This isn't what you expected."

"No." He cursed himself because he could not rise above his dismay. "No. Something terrible has happened."

She did not waver. "How can that be? You said the last time you were here was ten years ago. What can happen in ten years?"

Her query reminded him that he had not yet told her about Lord Foul's prophecy. But now was not the time: she was suffering from too many other incomprehensions. "Ten years in our world." For her sake, he did not say, *the real world.* "Time is different here. It's faster—the way dreams are almost instantaneous sometimes. I've—" He had difficulty meeting her stare; even his knowledge felt like shame. "I've actually been here three times before. Each time, I was unconscious for a few hours, and months went by here. So ten years for me— Oh, bloody hell!" The Despiser had said, *For a score of centuries. For nearly as many centuries more.* "If the ratio stays the same, we're talking about three or four thousand years."

She accepted this as if it were just one more detail that defied rationality. "Well, what could have happened? What's so important about hurtloam?"

He wanted to hide his head, conceal his pain; he felt too much exposed to the new penetration of her senses. "Hurtloam was a special mud that could heal—almost anything." Twice, while in the Land, it had cured his leprosy. But he shied away from the whole subject of healing. If he told her what hurtloam had done for him in the past, he would also have to explain why it had not done him any lasting good. He would have to tell her that the Land was physically self-contained—that it had no tangible connection to their world. The healing of his chest meant nothing. When they regained consciousness, she would find that their bodily continuity in their world was complete. Everything would be the same.

If they did not awaken soon, she would not have time to treat his wound.

Because she was already under so much stress, he spared her that knowledge. Yet he could not contain his bitterness. "But that's not the point. Look." He pointed at the hearth. "Smoke. Ashes. The people I knew never built fires that destroyed wood. They didn't have to. For them, everything around them— wood, water, stone, flesh—every part of the physical world—was full of what they called Earthpower. The power of life. They could raise fire—or make boats flow upstream—or send messages—by using the Earthpower in wood instead of the wood itself.

"That was what made them who they were. The Earthpower was the essence of the Land." Memories thronged in him, visions of the Lords, of the masters of stone- and wood-lore. "It was so vital to them, so sustaining, that they gave their lives to it. Did everything they could to serve it, rather than exploit it. It was strength, sentience, passion. *Life*. A fire like this would have horrified them."

But words were inadequate. He could not convey his long-ing for a world where aspen and granite, water and soil, nature itself, were understood, revered for their potency and loveliness. A world with a soul, deserving to be treasured. Linden gazed at him as if he were babbling. With a silent snarl, he gave up trying to explain. "Apparently," he said, "they've lost it. It's forgotten. Or dead. Now they have this Sunbane. If I understand what I've been hearing—which I doubt—the Sunbane was what kept Nassic's torch burning in the rain. And he had to cut his hand to do it. And the wood was still consumed."

"He says the Sunbane is causing this rain." Covenant shuddered involuntarily; firelight reflecting off the downpour beyond the entryway made the storm look vicious and in-tolerable.

Her eyes searched him. The bones of her face seemed to press against the skin, as if her skull itself protested against so many alien circumstances. "I don't know anything about it. None of this makes sense." She faltered. He could see fears crowding the edges of her vision. "It's all impossible. I can't . . ." She shot a harried glance around the room, thrust her hands into her hair as though she sought to pull imminent hysteria off her features. "I'm going crazy."

"I know." He recognized her desperation. His own wildness when he was first taken to the Land had led him to commit the worst crimes of his life. He wanted to reach out to her, protect her; but the numbness of his hands prevented him. Instead, he said intensely, "Don't give up. Ask questions. Keep trying. I'll tell you everything I can."

For a moment, her gaze ached toward him like the arms of an abandoned child. But then her hands bunched into fists. A grimace like a clench of intransigence knotted her mien. "Questions," she breathed through her teeth. With a severe effort, she took hold of herself. "Yes."

Her tone accused him as if he were to blame for her dis-tress. But he accepted the responsibility. He could have prevented her from following him into the woods. If he had had the courage.

"All right," she gritted. "You've been here before. What makes you so important? What did you do? Why does Foul want you? What's an ur-Lord?"

Covenant sighed inwardly—an exhalation of relief at her determination to survive. That was what he wanted from her. A sudden weariness dimmed his sight; but he took no account of it.

"I was Berek reborn."

The memory was not pleasant; it contained too much guilt, too much sorrow and harm. But he accepted it. "Berek was one of the ancient heroes—thousands of years before I came along. According to the legends, he discovered the Earthpower, and made the Staff of Law to wield it. All the lore of the Earthpower came down from him. He was the Lord-Fatherer, the founder of the Council of Lords. They led the defense of the Land against Foul."

The Council, he groaned to himself, remembering Mhoram, Prothall, Elena. Hell and blood! His voice shook as he continued. "When I showed up, they welcomed me as a sort of avatar of Berek. He was known to have lost the last two fingers of his right hand in a war." Linden's gaze sharpened momentarily; but she did not interrupt. "So I was made an ur-Lord of the Council. Most of those other titles came later. After I defeated Foul.

"But Unbeliever was one I took for myself. For a long time here, I was sure I was dreaming, but I didn't know what to do about it." Sourly, he muttered, "I was afraid to get involved. It had something to do with being a leper." He hoped she would accept this non-explanation; he did not want to have to tell her about his crimes. "But I was wrong. As long as you have some idea of what's happening to you, 'real' or 'unreal' doesn't matter. You have to stand up for what you care about; if you don't, you lose control of who you are." He paused, met her scrutiny so that she could see the clarity of his conviction. "I ended up caring about the Land a lot."

"Because of the Earthpower?"

"Yes." Pangs of loss stung his heart. Fatigue and strain had shorn him of his defenses. "The Land was incredibly beautiful. And the way the people loved it, served it—that was beautiful, too. Lepers," he concluded mordantly, "are susceptible to beauty." In her own way, Linden seemed beautiful to him.

She listened to him like a physician trying to diagnose a rare disease. When he stopped, she said, "You called yourself, 'Unbeliever and white gold wielder.' What does white gold have to do with it?"

He scowled involuntarily. To cover his pain, he lowered himself to the floor, sat against the wall of the hearth. That question touched him deeply, and he was too tired to give it the courage it deserved. But her need for knowledge was peremptory. "My wedding ring," he murmured. "When Joan divorced me, I was never able to stop wearing it. I was a leper—I felt that I'd lost everything. I thought my only link with the human race was the fact that I used to be married.

"But here it's some kind of talisman. A tool for what they call wild magic—'the wild magic that destroys peace.' I can't explain it." To himself, he cursed the paucity of his valor.

Linden sat down near him, kept watching his face. "You think I can't handle the truth."

He winced at her percipience. "I don't know. But I know how hard it is. It sure as hell isn't easy for me."

Outside, the rain beat with steady ire into the valley; thunder and lightning pummeled each other among the mountains. But inside the hut the air was warm, tinged with smoke like a faint soporific. And he had gone for many days without rest. He closed his eyes, partly to acknowledge his exhaustion, partly to gain a respite from Linden's probing.

But she was not finished. "Nassic—" Her voice was as direct as if she had reached out and touched him. "He's crazy."

With an effort of will, Covenant forced himself to ask, "What makes you say that?"

She was silent until he opened his eyes, looked at her. Then, defensively, she said, "I can feel it—the imbalance in him. Can't you? It's in his face, his voice, everything. I saw it right away. When he was coming down the ravine."

Grimly, he put off his fatigue. "What are you trying to tell me? That we can't trust him? Can't believe him?"

"Maybe." Now she could not meet his gaze. She studied the clasp of her hands on her knees. "I'm not sure. All I know is, he's demented. He's been lonely too long. And he believes what he says."

"He's not the only one," Covenant muttered. Deliberately,

he stretched out to make himself more comfortable. He was too tired to worry about Nassic's sanity. But he owed Linden one other answer. Before he let go of himself, he replied, "No, I can't."

As weariness washed over him, he was dimly aware that she stood up and began to pace beside his recumbent form.

He was awakened by silence. The rain had stopped. For a moment, he remained still, enjoying the end of the storm. The rest had done him good; he felt stronger, more capable.

When he raised his head, he saw Linden in the entryway, facing the vale and the clear cool night. Her shoulders were tense; strain marked the way she leaned against the stone. As he got to his feet, she turned toward him. She must have replenished the fire while he slept. The room was bright; he could see her face clearly. The corners of her eyes were lined as if she had been squinting for a long time at something which discomfited her.

"It stopped at nightfall." She indicated the absence of rain with a jerk of her head. "He was right about that."

The trouble in her worried him. He tried to sound casual as he asked, "What have you been thinking?"

She shrugged. "Nothing new. 'Face it. Go forward. Find out what happens.' " Her gaze was bent inward on memories. "I've been living that way for years. It's the only way to find out how much what you're trying to get away from costs."

He searched her for some glimpse of what she meant. "You know," he said slowly, "you haven't told me much about yourself."

She stiffened, drew severity across her countenance like a shield. Her tone denied his question. "Nassic isn't back yet."

For a moment, he considered her refusal. Did she have that much past hurt to hide? Were her defenses aimed at him, or at herself? But then the import of her words penetrated him. "He isn't?" Even an old man should have been able to make the trip twice in this amount of time.

"I haven't seen him."

"Damnation!" Covenant's throat was suddenly dry. "What the hell happened to him?"

"How should I know?" Her ire betrayed the fraying of her nerves. "Remember me? I'm the one who hasn't been here before."

He wanted to snap at her; but he held himself back grimly. "I didn't mean it that way. Maybe he fell off the cliff. Maybe Mithil Stonedown is even more dangerous than he thought. Maybe he doesn't even have a son."

He could see her swallowing her vexation, wishing herself immune to pressure. "What are we going to do?"

"What choice have we got? We'll have to go down there ourselves." Sternly, he compelled himself to face her doubt of Nassic. "It's hard for me to believe we can't trust those people. They were my friends when I didn't deserve to have any friends."

She considered him. "That was three thousand years ago."

Yes, he muttered bleakly. And he had given them little in return except harm. If they remembered him at all, they would be justified in remembering only the harm.

With a sudden nausea, he realized that he was going to have to tell Linden what he had done to Mithil Stonedown, to Lena Atiaran-daughter. The doctor was the first woman he had met in ten years who was not afraid of him. And she had tried to save his life. What other protection could he give her against himself?

He lacked the courage. The words were in his mind, but he could not utter them. To escape her eyes, he moved abruptly past her out of Nassic's stone dwelling.

The night was a vault of crystal. All the clouds were gone. The air was cold and sharp; stars glittered like flecks of broken joy across the immaculate deeps. They gave some visibility. Below the dark crouch of the peaks, he could see the stream flowing turgidly down the length of the dell. He followed it; he remembered this part of the way well enough. But then he slowed his pace as he realized that Linden was not behind him.

"Covenant!"

Her cry scaled the night. Echoes repeated against the mountainsides.

He went back to her at a wild run.

She knelt on a pile of rubble like a cairn beside the hut— the broken remains of Nassic's temple, fallen into desuetude. She was examining a dark form which lay strangely atop the debris.

Covenant sprang forward, peered at the body.

Bloody hell, he moaned. Nassic.

The old man lay embracing the ruins. From the center of his back protruded the handle of a knife.

"Don't touch that," Linden panted. "It's still hot." Her mouth was full of crushed horror.

Still—? Covenant kicked aside his dismay. "Take his legs. We'll carry him into the house."

She did not move. She looked small and abject in the night.

To make her move, he lashed at her, "I told you it was dangerous. Did you think I was kidding? Take his legs!"

Her voice was a still cold articulation of darkness. "He's dead. There's nothing we can do."

The sound of her desolation choked his protests. For one keening moment, he feared that he had lost her—that her mind had gone over the edge. But then she shifted. Her hair fell forward, hid her face, as she bent to slip her arms under Nassic's legs.

Covenant lifted him by the shoulders. Together, they bore him into his house.

He was already stiff.

They set him down gently in the center of the floor. Covenant inspected him. His skin was cold. There was no blood in his robe around the knife; it must have been washed away by the rain. He must have lain dead in the rain for a long time.

Linden did not watch. Her eyes clinched the black iron knife. "It didn't kill him right away," she said hoarsely, "It didn't hit him right. He bled to death." The bones of her face seemed to throb with vehemence. "This is evil."

The way she uttered that word *evil* sent cold fear scrabbling down Covenant's spine. He knew what she meant; he had formerly been able to perceive such things himself. She was looking at the cruelty of the hand which had held that knife, seeing the eager malice which had inspired the blow. And if the iron were still hot— He swallowed harshly. Nassic's killer must have been someone of great and brutal power.

He scrambled for explanations. "Whoever did it knew we were here. Or else why leave him out there? He wanted us to find the body—after he got away." He closed his eyes, forced some clarity onto his spinning thoughts. "Nassic was killed because of us. To keep him from talking to the Stonedown. Or from talking to us. By hell, this stinks of Foul."

Linden was not listening; her own reaction dominated her. "Nobody does this." She sounded lorn, fear-ravaged.

He heard the strangeness of her protest; but he could not stop himself. His old anger for the victims of Despite drove him. "It takes a special kind of killer," he growled, "to leave a hot knife behind. Foul has plenty of that kind of help. He's perfectly capable of having Nassic killed just to keep us from getting too much information. Or to manipulate us somehow."

"Nobody kills like this. For pleasure." Dull anguish blunted her tone, blinded her face. "People don't do that."

"Of course they don't." Her dismay reached him; but the frailty of Nassic's dead limbs affronted him to the marrow of his bones, made his reply savage. "He probably decided to take a nap in the rain, and this knife just fell on him out of nowhere."

She was deaf to his sarcasm—too intimately shocked to recognize him at all. "People kill because they're hungry. Afraid." She struggled for certitude against the indefeasible iron. "Driven. Because someone, something, forces them." Her tone sharpened as if she were gathering screams. "Nobody likes it."

"No." The sight of her distress pulled Covenant to her. He tried to confront her mounting repudiation. "Everybody likes it. Everybody likes power. But most people control it. Because they hate it, too. This is no different than any other murder. It's just more obvious."

A flinch of revulsion twisted her face; his assertion seemed to hurt her. For an instant, he feared that her mind was going to fail. But then her eyes climbed to his face. The effort of self-mastery darkened them like blood. "I want—" Her voice quavered; she crushed it flat. "I want to meet the sonofabitch who did this. So I can see for myself."

Covenant nodded, gritted his own black ire. "I think you're going to get the chance." He, too, wanted to meet Nassic's slayer. "We can't try to second-guess Foul. He knows more than we do. And we can't stay here. But we've lost our guide —our only chance to learn what's happening. We have to go to Mithil Stonedown." Grimly, he concluded, "Since the killer didn't attack us here, he's probably waiting for us in the village."

For a long moment, she remained motionless, mustering her resources. Then she said tightly, "Let's go."

He did not hesitate. Nassic had not even been given the dignity of a clean death. With Linden at his side, he marched out into the night.

But in spite of the violence in him, he did not allow himself to rush. The stars did not shed an abundance of light; and the rain had left the floor of the dell slick with mud. The path to Mithil Stonedown was hazardous. He did not intend to come to harm through recklessness.

He made his way strictly down the valley; and at its end, he followed the stream into a crooked file between sheer walls, then turned away along a crevice that ascended at right angles to the file. The crevice was narrow and crude, difficult going in the star-blocked dark; but it levelled after a while, began to tend downward. Before long, he gained a steep open slope—the eastern face of the Mithil valley.

Dimly in the distance below him, the valley widened like a wedge northward toward an expanse of plains. A deeper blackness along the valley bottom looked like a river.

Beside the river, somewhat to his right, lay a cluster of tiny lights.

"Mithil Stonedown," he murmured. But then vertigo forced him to turn away leftward along a faint path. He could not repress his memory of the time he had walked this path with Lena. Until he told Linden what he remembered, what he had done, she would not know who he was, would not be able to choose how she wished to respond to him. Or to the Land.

He needed her to understand his relationship to the Land. He needed her support, her skills, her strength. Why else had she been chosen?

A cold, penetrating dampness thickened the air; but the exertion of walking kept him warm. And the path became steadily less difficult as it descended toward the valley bottom. As the moon began to crest the peaks, he gave up all pretense of caution. He was hunting for the courage to say what had to be said.

Shortly, the path curved off the slopes, doubled back to follow the river outward. He glanced at Linden from time to time, wondering where she had learned the toughness, unwisdom, or desperation which enabled or drove her to accompany him. He ached for the capacity to descry the truth of her, determine whether her severity came from conviction or dread.

She did not believe in evil.

He had no choice; he had to tell her.

Compelling himself with excoriations, he touched her arm, stopped her. She looked at him. "Linden." She was alabaster in the moonlight—pale and not to be touched. His mouth winced. "There's something I've got to say." His visage felt like old granite. "Before we go any farther." Pain made him whisper.

"The first time I was here, I met a girl. Lena. She was just a kid—but she was my friend. She kept me alive on Kevin's Watch, when I was so afraid it could have killed me." His long loneliness cried out against this self-betrayal.

"I raped her."

She stared at him. Her lips formed soundless words: Raped—? In her gaze, he could see himself becoming heinous.

He did not see the shadow pass over their heads, had no warning of their danger until the net landed on them, tangling them instantly together. Figures surged out of the darkness around them. One of the attackers hit them in the faces with something which broke open and stank like a rotten melon.

Then he could no longer breathe. He fell with Linden in his arms as if they were lovers.

SIX: The Graveler

HE awoke urgently, with a suffocating muck on his face that made him strain to move his arms to clear the stuff away. But his hands were tied behind his back. He gagged helplessly for a moment, until he found that he could breathe.

The dry, chill air was harsh in his lungs. But he relished it. Slowly, it drove back the nausea.

From somewhere near him, he heard Linden say flatly, "You'll be all right. They must have hit us with some kind of anesthetic. It's like ether—makes you feel sick. But the nausea goes away. I don't think we've been hurt."

He rested briefly on the cold stone, then rolled off his chest and struggled into a sitting position. The bonds made the movement difficult; a wave of dizziness went through him. "Friends," he muttered. But the air steadied him. "Nassic was right."

"Nassic was right," she echoed as if the words did not interest her.

They were in a single room, as constricted as a cell. A heavy curtain covered the doorway; but opposite the entrance a barred window let the pale gray of dawn into the room—the late dawn of a sunrise delayed by mountains. The bars were iron.

Linden sat across from him. Her arms angled behind her; her wrists, too, were bound. Yet she had managed to clean the pulp from her cheeks. Shreds of it clung to the shoulders of her shirt.

His own face wore the dried muck like a leper's numbness.

He shifted so that he could lean against the wall. The bonds cut into his wrists. He closed his eyes. A trap, he murmured. Nassic's death was a trap. He had been killed so that Covenant and Linden would blunder into Mithil Stonedown's defenses and be captured. What's Foul trying to do? he asked the darkness behind his eyelids. Make us fight these people?

"Why did you do it?" Linden said. Her tone was level, as if she had already hammered all the emotion out of it. "Why did you tell me about that girl?"

His eyes jumped open to look at her. But in the dim light he was unable to discern her expression. He wanted to say, Leave it alone, we've got other things to worry about. But she had an absolute right to know the truth about him.

"I wanted to be honest with you." His guts ached at the memory. "The things I did when I was here before are going to affect what happens to us now. Foul doesn't forget. And I was afraid"— he faltered at the cost of his desire for rectitude —"you might trust me without knowing what you were trusting. I don't want to betray you—by not being what you think I am."

She did not reply. Her eyes were shadows which told him nothing. Abruptly, the pressure of his unassuaged bitterness began to force words out of him like barbs.

"After my leprosy was diagnosed, and Joan divorced me, I was impotent for a year. Then I came here. Something I couldn't understand was happening. The Land was healing parts of me that had been dead so long I'd forgotten I had them. And Lena—" The pang of her stung him like an acid. "She was so beautiful I still have nightmares about it. The first night— It was too much for me. Lepers aren't supposed to be potent."

He did not give Linden a chance to respond; he went on, reliving his old self-judgment. "Everybody paid for it. I couldn't get away from the consequences. Her mother ended up committing a kind of suicide. Her father's life was warped. The man who wanted to marry her lost everything. Her own mind came apart.

"But I didn't stop there. I caused her death, and the death of her daughter, Elena—*my* daughter. Because I kept trying to escape the consequences. Everybody refused to punish me. I was Berek reborn. They wanted me to save the Land. Lena"— oh, Lena! —"got butchered trying to save my life."

Linden listened without moving. She looked like a figure of stone against the wall, blank and unforgiving, as if no mere recitation of guilt could touch her. But her knees were pressed tightly, defensively, to her chest. When he ceased, she said thickly, "You shouldn't have told me."

"I had to." What else could he say? "It's who I am."

"No." She protested as if an accusation of evil had been raised between them. "It isn't who you are. You didn't do it intentionally, did you? You saved the Land, didn't you?"

He faced her squarely. "Yes. Eventually."

"Then it's over. Done with." Her head dropped to her knees. She squeezed her forehead against them as if to restrain the pounding of her thoughts. "Leave me alone."

Covenant studied the top of her head, the way her hair fell about her thighs, and sought to comprehend. He had expected her to denounce him for what he had done, not for having confessed it. Why was she so vulnerable to it? He knew too little about her. But how could he ask her to tell him things which she believed people should not know about each other?

"I don't understand." His voice was gruff with uncertainty. "If that's the way you feel—why did you keep coming back? You went to a lot of trouble to find out what I was hiding."

She kept her face concealed. "I said, leave me alone."

"I can't." A vibration of anger ran through him. "You wouldn't be here if you hadn't followed me. I need to know why you did it. So I can decide whether to trust you."

Her head snapped up. "I'm a doctor."

"That's not enough," he said rigidly.

The light from the window was growing slowly. Now he could read parts of her countenance—her mouth clenched and severe, her eyes like dark gouges below her forehead.

She regarded him as if he were trespassing on her essential privacy.

After a long moment, she said softly, "I followed you because I thought you were strong. Everytime I saw you, you were practically prostrate on your feet. You were desperate for help. But you stood there acting as if even exhaustion couldn't touch you." Her words were fraught with gall. "I thought you were *strong*. But now it turns out you were just running away from your guilt, like anybody else. Trying to make yourself innocent again by selling yourself for Joan. What was I supposed to do?" Quiet fury whetted her tone. "Let you commit suicide?"

Before he could respond, she went on, "You use guilt the same way you use leprosy. You want people to reject you, stay away from you—make a victim out of you. So you can recapture your innocence." Gradually, her intensity subsided into a dull rasp. "I've already seen more of it than I can stand. If you think I'm such a threat to you, at least leave me alone."

Again she hid her face in her knees.

Covenant stared at her in silence. Her judgment hurt him like a demonstration of mendacity. Was *that* what he was doing—giving her a moral reason to repudiate him because she was unmoved by the physical reason of his leprosy? Was he so much afraid of being helped or trusted? Cared about? Gaping at this vision of himself, he heaved to his feet, lurched to the window as if he needed to defend his eyes by looking at something else.

But the view only gave credence to his memories. It verified that he and Linden were in Mithil Stonedown. The wall and roof of another stone dwelling stood directly in front of him; and on either side of it he could see the corners of other buildings. Their walls were ancient, weathered and battered by centuries of use. They were made without mortar, formed of large slabs and chunks of rock held together by their own weight, topped by flat roofs. And beyond the roofs were the mountains.

Above them, the sky had a brown tinge, as if it were full of dust.

He had been here before, and could not deny the truth; he was indeed afraid. Too many people who cared about him had already paid horrendously to give him help.

Linden's silence throbbed at his back like a bruise; but he remained still, and watched the sunrise flow down into the valley. When the tension in him became insistent, he said without turning, "I wonder what they're going to do with us."

As if in answer, the room brightened suddenly as the curtain was thrust aside. He swung around and found a man in the doorway.

The Stonedownor was about Linden's height, but broader and more muscular than Covenant. His black hair and dark skin were emphasized by the color of his stiff leather jerkin and leggings. He wore nothing on his feet. In his right hand he held a long, wooden staff as if it articulated his authority.

He appeared to be about thirty. His features had a youthful cast; but they were contradicted by two deep frown lines above the bridge of his nose, and by the dullness of his eyes, which seemed to have been worn dim by too much accumulated and useless regret. The muscles at the corners of his jaw bulged as if he had been grinding his teeth for years.

His left arm hung at his side. From elbow to knuckle, it was intaglioed with fine white scars.

He did not speak; he stood facing Covenant and Linden as if he expected them to know why he had come.

Linden lurched to her feet. Covenant took two steps forward, so that they stood shoulder-to-shoulder before the Stonedownor.

The man hesitated, searched Covenant's face. Then he moved into the room. With his left hand, he reached out to Covenant's battered cheek.

Covenant winced slightly, then held himself still while the Stonedownor carefully brushed the dried pulp from his face.

He felt a pang of gratitude at the touch; it seemed to accord him more dignity than he deserved. He studied the man's brown, strong mien closely, trying to decipher what lay behind it.

When he was done, the Stonedownor turned and left the room, holding the curtain open for Covenant and Linden.

Covenant looked toward her to see if she needed encouragement. But she did not meet his gaze. She was already moving. He took a deep breath, and followed her out of the hut.

He found himself on the edge of the broad, round, open

center of Mithil Stonedown. It matched his memory of it closely. All the houses faced inward; and the ones beyond the inner ring were positioned to give as many as possible direct access to the center. But now he could see that several of them had fallen into serious disrepair, as if their occupants did not know how to mend them. If that were true— He snarled to himself. How could these people have forgotten their stone-lore?

The sun shone over the eastern ridge into his face. Squinting at it indirectly, he saw that the orb had lost its blue aurora. Now it wore pale brown like a translucent cymar.

The Stonedown appeared deserted. All the door-curtains were closed. Nothing moved—not in the village, not on the mountainsides or in the air. He could not even hear the river. The valley lay under the dry dawn as if it had been stricken dumb.

A slow scraping of fear began to abrade his nerves.

The man with the staff strode out into the circle, beckoning for Covenant and Linden to follow him across the bare stone. As they did so, he gazed morosely around the village. He leaned on his staff as if the thews which held his life together were tired.

But after a moment he shook himself into action. Slowly, he raised the staff over his head. In a determined tone, he said, "This is the center."

At once, the curtains opened. Men and women stepped purposefully out of their homes.

They were all solid dark people, apparelled in leather garments. They formed a ring like a noose around the rim of the circle, and stared at Covenant and Linden. Their faces were wary, hostile, shrouded. Some of them bore blunt javelins like jerrids; but no other weapons were visible.

The man with the staff joined them. Together, the ring of Stonedownors sat down cross-legged on the ground.

Only one man remained standing. He stayed behind the others, leaning against the wall of a house with his arms folded negligently across his chest. His lips wore a rapacious smile like an anticipation of bloodshed.

Covenant guessed instinctively that this man was Mithil Stonedown's executioner.

The villagers made no sound. They watched Covenant and Linden without moving, almost without blinking. Their silence was loud in the air, like the cry of a throat that had no voice.

The sun began to draw sweat from Covenant's scalp.

"Somebody say something," he muttered through his teeth.

Abruptly, Linden nudged his arm. "That's what they're waiting for. We're on trial. They want to hear what we've got to say for ourselves."

"Terrific." He accepted her intuitive explanation at once; she had eyes which he lacked. "What're we on trial for?"

Grimly, she replied, "Maybe they found Nassic."

He groaned. That made sense. Perhaps Nassic had been killed precisely so that he and Linden would be blamed for the crime. And yet— He tugged at his bonds, wishing his hands were free so that he could wipe the sweat from his face. And yet it did not explain why they had been captured in the first place.

The silence was intolerable. The mountains and the houses cupped the center of the village like an arena. The Stone-downors sat impassively, like icons of judgment. Covenant scanned them, mustered what little dignity he possessed. Then he began to speak.

"My name is ur-Lord Thomas Covenant, Unbeliever and white gold wielder. My companion is Linden Avery." Deliberately, he gave her a title. "The Chosen. She's a stranger to the Land." The dark people returned his gaze blankly. The man leaning against the wall bared his teeth. "But I'm no stranger," Covenant went on in sudden anger. "You threaten me at your peril."

"Covenant," Linden breathed, reproving him.

"I know," he muttered. "I shouldn't say things like that." Then he addressed the people again. "We were welcomed by Nassic son of Jous. He wasn't a friend of yours—or you weren't friends of his, because God knows he was harmless." Nassic had looked so lorn in death— "But he said he had a son here. A man named Sunder. Is Sunder here? Sunder?" He searched the ring. No one responded. "Sunder," he rasped, "whoever you are—do you know your father was murdered? We found him outside his house with an iron knife in his back. The knife was still hot."

Someone in the circle gave a low moan; but Covenant did not see who it was. Linden shook her head; she also had not seen.

The sky had become pale brown from edge to edge. The heat of the sun was as arid as dust.

"I think the killer lives here. I think he's one of you. Or don't you even care about that?"

Nobody reacted. Every face regarded him as if he were some kind of ghoul. The silence was absolute.

"Hellfire." He turned back to Linden. "I'm just making a fool out of myself. You got any ideas?"

Her gaze wore an aspect of supplication. "I don't know— I've never been here before."

"Neither have I." He could not suppress his ire. "Not to a place like this. Courtesy and hospitality used to be so important here that people who couldn't provide them were ashamed." Remembering the way Trell and Atiaran, Lena's parents, had welcomed him to their home, he ground his teeth. With a silent curse, he confronted the Stonedownors. "Are the other villages like this?" he demanded. "Is the whole Land sick with suspicion? Or is this the only place where simple decency has been forgotten?"

The man with the staff lowered his eyes. No one else moved.

"By God, if you can't at least tolerate us, let us go! We'll walk out of here, and never look back. Some other village will give us what we need."

The man behind the circle gave a grin of malice and triumph.

"Damnation," Covenant muttered to himself. The silence was maddening. His head was beginning to throb. The valley felt like a desert. "I wish Mhoram was here."

Dully, Linden asked, "Who is Mhoram?" Her eyes were fixed on the standing man. He commanded her attention like an open wound.

"One of the Lords of Revelstone." Covenant wondered what she was seeing. "Also a friend. He had a talent for dealing with impossible situations."

She wrenched her gaze from the gloating man, glared at Covenant. Frustration and anxiety made her tone sabulous. "He's dead. All your friends are dead." Her shoulders strained involuntarily at her bonds. "They've been dead for three thousand years. You're living in the past. How bad do things have to get before you give up thinking about the way they used to be?"

"I'm trying to understand what's happened!" Her attack

shamed him. It was unjust—and yet he deserved it. Everything he said demonstrated his inadequacy. He swung away from her.

"Listen to me!" he beseeched the Stonedownors. "I've been here before—long ago, during the great war against the Gray Slayer. I fought him. So the Land could be healed. And men and women from Mithil Stonedown helped me. Your ancestors. The Land was saved by the courage of Stonedownors and Woodhelvennin and Lords and Giants and Bloodguard and Ranyhyn.

"But something's happened. There's something wrong in the Land. That's why we're here." Remembering the old song of Kevin Landwaster, he said formally, "So that beauty and truth should not pass utterly from the Earth."

With tone, face, posture, he begged for some kind of response, acknowledgment, from the circle. But the Stonedownors refused every appeal. His exertions had tightened the bonds on his wrists, aggravating the numbness of his hands. The sun began to raise heat-waves in the distance. He felt giddy, futile.

"I don't know what you want," he breathed thickly. "I don't know what you think we're guilty of. But you're wrong about her." He indicated Linden with his head. "She's never been here before. She's innocent."

A snort of derision stopped him.

He found himself staring at the man who stood behind the circle. Their eyes came together like a clash of weapons. The man had lost his grin; he glared scorn and denunciation at Covenant. He held violence folded in the crooks of his elbows. But Covenant did not falter. He straightened his back, squared his shoulders, met the naked threat of the man's gaze.

After one taut moment, the man looked away.

Softly, Covenant said, "We're not on trial here. You are. The doom of the Land is in your hands, and you're blind to it."

An instant of silence covered the village; the whole valley seemed to hold its breath. Then the lone man cried suddenly, "Must we hear more?" Contempt and fear collided in his tone. "He has uttered foulness enough to damn a score of strangers. Let us pass judgment now!"

At once, the man with the staff sprang to his feet. "Be still,

Marid," he said sternly. "I am the Graveler of Mithil Stonedown. The test of silence is mine to begin—and to end."

"It is enough!" retorted Marid. "Can there be greater ill than that which he has already spoken?"

A dour crepitation of assent ran through the circle.

Linden moved closer to Covenant. Her eyes were locked to Marid as if he appalled her. Nausea twisted her mouth. Covenant looked at her, at Marid, trying to guess what lay between them.

"Very well." The Graveler took a step forward. "It is enough." He planted his staff on the stone. "Stonedownors, speak what you have heard."

For a moment, the people were still. Then an old man rose slowly to his feet. He adjusted his jerkin, pulled his gravity about him. "I have heard the Rede of the na-Mhoram, as it is spoken by the Riders of the Clave. They have said that the coming of the man with the halfhand and the white ring bodes unending ruin for us all. They have said that it is better to slay such a man in his slumber, allowing the blood to fall wasted to the earth, than to permit him one free breath with which to utter evil. Only the ring must be preserved, and given to the Riders, so that all blasphemy may be averted from the Land."

Blasphemy? Clave? Covenant grappled uselessly with his incomprehension. Who besides Nassic's Unfettered ancestor had foretold the return of the Unbeliever?

The old man concluded with a nod to the Graveler. Opposite him, a middle-aged woman stood. Jabbing her hand toward Covenant, she said, "He spoke the name of the na-Mhoram as a friend. Are not the na-Mhoram and all his Clave bitter to Mithil Stonedown? Do not his Riders reave us of blood—and not of the old whose deaths are nigh, but of the young whose lives are precious? Let these two die! Our herd has already suffered long days without forage."

"Folly!" the old man replied. "You will not speak so when next the Rider comes. It will be soon—our time nears again. In all the Land only the Clave has power over the Sunbane. The burden of their sacrificing is heavy to us—but we would lack life altogether if they failed to spend the blood of the villages."

"Yet is there not a contradiction here?" the Graveler interposed. "He names the na-Mhoram as friend—and yet the most dire Rede of the Clave speaks against him."

"For both they must die!" Marid spat immediately. "The na-Mhoram is not our friend, but his power is sure."

"True!" voices said around the ring.

"Yes."

"True."

Linden brushed Covenant with her shoulder. "That man," she whispered. "Marid. There's something— Do you see it?"

"No," responded Covenant through his teeth. "I told you I can't. What is it?"

"I don't know." She sounded frightened. "Something—"

Then another woman stood. "He seeks to be released so that he may go to another Stonedown. Are not all other villages our foes? Twice has Windshorn Stonedown raided our fields during the fertile sun, so that our bellies shrank and our children cried in the night. Let the friends of our foes die."

Again the Stonedownors growled, "Yes."

"True."

Without warning, Marid shouted over the grumble of voices, "They slew Nassic father of Sunder! Are we a people to permit murder unavenged? They must die!"

"No!" Linden's instantaneous denial cracked across the circle like a scourge. "We did not kill that harmless old man!"

Covenant whirled to her. But she did not notice him; her attention was consumed by Marid.

In a tone of acid mockery, the man asked, "Do you fear to die, Linden Avery the Chosen?"

"What is it?" she gritted back at him. "What are you?"

"What do you see?" Covenant urged. *"Tell me."*

"Something—" Her voice groped; but her stare did not waver. Perspiration had darkened her hair along the line of her forehead. "It's like that storm. Something evil."

Intuitions flared like spots of sun-blindness across Covenant's mind. "Something hot."

"Yes!" Her gaze accused Marid fiercely. "Like the knife."

Covenant spun, confronted Marid. He was suddenly calm. "You," he said. "Marid. Come here."

"No, Marid," commanded the Graveler.

"Hell and blood!" Covenant rasped like deliberate ice. "My hands are tied. Are you afraid to find out the truth?" He did not glance at the Graveler; he held Marid with his will. "Come here. I'll show you who killed Nassic."

"Watch out," Linden whispered. "He wants to hurt you."

Scorn twisted Marid's face. For a moment, he did not move. But now all the eyes of the Stonedown were on him, watching his reaction. And Covenant gave him no release. A spasm of fear or glee tightened Marid's expression. Abruptly, he strode forward, halted in front of Covenant and the Graveler. "Speak your lies," he sneered. "You will choke upon them before you die."

Covenant did not hesitate. "Nassic was stabbed in the back," he said softly, "with an iron knife. It was a lousy job—he bled to death. When we left him, the knife was still hot."

Marid swallowed convulsively. "You are a fool. What man or woman of Mithil Stonedown could wield a knife with the fire yet within it? Out of your own mouth you are condemned."

"Graveler," Covenant said, "touch him with your staff."

Around him, the Stonedownors rose to their feet.

"For what purpose?" the Graveler asked uncertainly. "It is mere wood. It has no virtue to determine guilt or innocence."

Covenant clinched Marid in his gaze. *"Do it."*

Hesitantly, the Graveler obeyed.

As the tip of the staff neared him, Marid shied. But then a savage exaltation lit his face, and he remained still.

The staff touched his shoulder.

Instantly, the wood burst into red fire.

The Graveler recoiled in astonishment. Stonedownors gasped, gripped each other for reassurance.

With an explosive movement, Marid backhanded Covenant across the side of his head.

The unnatural power of the blow catapulted Covenant backward. He tumbled heavily to the ground. Pain like acid burned through his sore skull.

"Covenant!" Linden cried fearfully.

He heard the Graveler protest, "Marid!"—heard the fright of the Stonedownors turn to anger. Then the pain became a roaring that deafened him. For a moment, he was too dizzy to move. But he fought the fire, heaved himself to his knees so that everyone could see the mark of Marid's blow among his bruises. "Nice work, you bastard," he rasped. His voice seemed to make no sound. "What were you afraid of? Did you think he was going to help us that much? Or were you just having fun?"

He was aware of a low buzzing around him, but could not make out words. Marid stood with arms across his chest, grinning.

Covenant thrust his voice through the roar. "Why don't you tell us your real name? Is it Herem? Jehannum? Maybe Sheol?"

Linden was beside him. She strove fervidly to free her hands; but the bonds held. Her mouth chewed dumb curses.

"Come on," he continued, though he could barely see Marid beyond the pain. "Attack me. Take your chances. Maybe I've forgotten how to use it."

Abruptly, Marid began to laugh: laughter as gelid as hate. It penetrated Covenant's hearing, resounded in his head like a concussion. "It will avail you nothing!" he shouted. "Your death is certain! You cannot harm me!"

The Graveler brandished his flaming staff at Marid. Dimly, Covenant heard the man rage, "Have you slain Nassic my father?"

"With joy!" laughed the Raver. "Ah, how it fed me to plant my blade in his back!"

A woman shrieked. Before anyone could stop her, she sped in a blur of gray hair across the open space, hurled herself at Marid.

He collapsed as if the impact had killed him.

Covenant's strength gave out. He fell to his back, lay panting heavily on the stone.

Then a stench of burned flesh sickened the air. One of the Stonedownors cried out, "Sunder! Her hands!"

Another demanded, "Is he slain?"

"No!" came the reply.

Linden was yelling. "Let me go! I'm a doctor! I can help her!" She sounded frantic. "Don't you know what a doctor is?"

A moment later, hands gripped Covenant's arms, lifted him to his feet. A Stonedownor swam toward him through the hurt; slowly, the face resolved, became the Graveler. His brow was a knot of anger and grief. Stiffly, he said, "Marid sleeps. My mother is deeply burned. Tell me the meaning of this."

"A Raver." Covenant's breathing shuddered in his lungs. "Bloody hell." He could not think or find the words he needed.

The Graveler bunched his fists in Covenant's shirt. "Speak!"

From somewhere nearby, Linden shouted, "Goddamn it, leave him alone! Can't you see he's hurt?"

Covenant fought for clarity. "Let her go," he said to the Graveler. "She's a healer."

The muscles along the Graveler's jaw knotted, released. "I have not been given reason to trust her. Speak to me of Marid."

Marid, Covenant panted. "Listen." Sweating and dizzy, he squeezed the pain out of his mind. "It was a Raver."

The Graveler's glare revealed no comprehension.

"When he wakes up, he'll probably be normal again. May not even remember what happened. He was taken over. That Raver could be anywhere. It isn't hurt. You need a lot of power to knock one of them out, even temporarily. You've got to watch for it. It could take over anybody. Watch for somebody who starts acting strange. Violent. Stay away from them. I mean it."

The Graveler listened first with urgency, then with disgust. Exasperation pulsed in the veins of his temples. Before Covenant finished, the Stonedownor turned on his heel, strode away.

Immediately, the hands holding Covenant's arms dragged him out of the center of the village.

Linden was ahead of him. She struggled uselessly between two burly men. They impelled her back into their jail.

"Damnation," Covenant said. His voice had no force. "I'm trying to warn you."

His captors did not respond. They thrust him into the hut after Linden, and let him fall.

He sank to the floor. The cool dimness of the room washed over him. The suddenness of his release from the sun's brown pressure made the floor wheel. But he rested his pain on the soothing stone; and gradually that quiet touch steadied him.

Linden was cursing bitterly in the stillness. He tried to raise his head. "Linden."

At once, she moved to his side. "Don't try to get up. Just let me see it."

He turned his head to show her his hurt.

She bent over him. He could feel her breath on his cheek. "You're burned, but it doesn't look serious. First-degree." Her tone twitched with nausea and helplessness. "None of the bones are cracked. How do you feel?"

"Dizzy," he murmured. "Deaf. I'll be all right."

"Sure you will," she grated. "You probably have a concussion. I'll bet you want to go to sleep."

He mumbled assent. The darkness in his head offered him cool peace, and he longed to let himself drown in it.

She took a breath through her teeth. "Sit up."

He did not move; he lacked the strength to obey her.

She nudged him with her knee. "I'm serious. If you go to sleep, you might drift into a coma, and I won't be able to do anything about it. You've got to stay awake. Sit up."

The ragged edge in her voice sounded like a threat of hysteria. Gritting his teeth, he tried to rise. Hot pain flayed the bones of his head; but he pried himself erect, then slumped to the side so that his shoulder was braced against the wall.

"Good," Linden sighed. The pounding in his skull formed a gulf between them. She seemed small and lonely, aggrieved by the loss of the world she understood. "Now try to stay alert. Talk to me." After a moment, she said, "Tell me what happened."

He recognized her need. Marid incarnated the fears which Nassic's death had raised for her. A being who lived on hate, relished violence and anguish. She knew nothing about such things.

"A Raver." Covenant tried to slip his voice quietly past the pain. "I should have known. Marid is just a Stonedownor. He was possessed by a Raver."

Linden backed away from him, composed herself against the opposite wall. Her gaze held his face. "What's a Raver?"

"Servant of Foul." He closed his eyes, leaned his head to the stone, so that he could concentrate on what he was saying. "There are three of them. Herem, Sheol, Jehannum—they have a lot of different names. They don't have bodies of their own, so they take over other people—even animals, I guess. Whatever they can find. So they're always in disguise." He sighed—gently, to minimize the effect on his head. "I just hope these people understand what that means."

"So," she asked carefully, "what I saw was the Raver inside Marid? That's why he looked so—so wrong?"

"Yes." When he focused on her voice, his hurt became less demanding; it grew hotter, but also more specific and limited. As a fire in his skin rather than a cudgel in his brain, it crippled his thinking less. "Marid was just a victim. The Raver used him to kill Nassic—set us up for this. What I don't know is why. Does Foul want us killed here? Or is there something else going on? If Foul wants us dead, that Raver made a big mistake when it let itself get caught. Now the Stonedown has something besides us to think about."

"What I don't know," Linden said in a lorn voice like an appeal, "is how I was able to see it. None of this is possible."

Her tone sparked unexpected memories. Suddenly, he realized that the way she had stared at Marid was the same way she had regarded Joan. That encounter with Joan had shaken her visibly.

He opened his eyes, watched her as he said, "That's one of the few things that seems natural to me. I used to be able to see what you're seeing now—the other times I was here." Her face was turned toward him, but she was not looking at him. Her attention was bent inward as she struggled with the lunacy of her predicament. "Your senses," he went on, trying to help her, "are becoming attuned to the Land. You're becoming sensitive to the physical spirit around you. More and more, you're going to look at something, or hear it, or touch it, and be able to tell whether it's sick or healthy—natural or unnatural." She did not appear to hear him. Defying his pain, he rasped, "Which isn't happening to me." He wanted to pull her out of herself before she lost her way. "For all I can see, I might as well be blind."

Her head flinched from side to side. "What if I'm wrong?" she breathed miserably. "What if I'm losing my mind?"

"No! That part of you is never going to be wrong. And you can't lose your mind unless you let it happen." Wildness knuckled her features. *"Don't give up."*

She heard him. With an effort that wrung his heart, she compelled her body to relax, muscle by muscle. She drew a breath that trembled; but when she exhaled, she was calmer. "I just feel so helpless."

He said nothing, waited for her.

After a moment, she sniffed sharply, shook her hair away from her face, met his gaze. "If these Ravers can possess anybody," she said, "why not us? If we're so important—if this Lord Foul is what you say he is—why doesn't he just make us into Ravers, and get it over with?"

With a silent groan of relief, Covenant allowed himself to sag. "That's the one thing he can't do. He can't afford it. He'll manipulate us every way he can, but he has to accept the risk that we won't do what he wants. He needs our freedom. What he wants from us won't have any value if we don't do it by

choice." Also, he went on to himself, Foul doesn't dare let a
Raver get my ring. How could he trust one of them with that
much power?

Linden frowned. "That might make sense—if I understood
what makes us so important. What we've got that he could
possibly want. But never mind that now." She took a deep
breath. "If I could see the Raver—why couldn't anybody
else?"

Her question panged Covenant. "That's what really scares
me," he said tautly. "These people used to be like you. Now
they aren't." And I'm not. "I'm afraid even to think about
what that means. They've lost—" Lost the insight which
taught them to love and serve the Land—to care about it
above everything else. Oh, Foul, you bastard, what have you
done? "If they can't see the difference between a Raver and
a normal man, then they won't be able to see that they should
trust us."

Her mouth tightened. "You mean they're still planning to
kill us."

Before Covenant could reply, the curtain was thrust aside,
and the Graveler entered the room.

His eyes were glazed with trouble, and his brow wore a
scowl of involition and mourning, as if his essential gentleness
had been harmed. He had left his staff behind; his hands hung
at his sides. But he could not keep them still. They moved in
slight jerks, half gestures, as if they sought unconsciously for
something he could hold onto.

After a moment of awkwardness, he sat down on his heels
near the entryway. He did not look at his prisoners; his gaze
lay on the floor between them.

"Sunder," Covenant said softly, "son of Nassic."

The Graveler nodded without raising his eyes.

Covenant waited for him to speak. But the Graveler remained silent, as if he were abashed. After a moment, Covenant said, "That woman who attacked Marid. She was your
mother."

"Kalina Nassic-mate, daughter of Alloma." He held himself
harshly quiet. "My mother."

Linden peered intently at Sunder. "How is she?"

"She rests. But her injury is deep. We have little healing for
such hurts. It may be that she will be sacrificed."

Covenant saw Linden poised to demand to be allowed to
help the woman. But he forestalled her. "Sacrificed?"

"Her blood belongs to the Stonedown." Sunder's voice limped under a weight of pain. "It must not be wasted. Only Nassic my father would not have accepted this. Therefore"— his throat knotted —"it is well he knew not that I am the Graveler of Mithil Stonedown. For it is I who will shed the sacrifice."

Linden recoiled. Aghast, Covenant exclaimed, "You're going to sacrifice your own mother?"

"For the survival of the Stonedown!" croaked Sunder. "We must have blood." Then he clamped down his emotion. "You also will be sacrificed. The Stonedown has made its judgment. You will be shed at the rising of the morrow's sun."

Covenant glared at the Graveler. Ignoring the throb in his head, he rasped, "Why?"

"I have come to make answer." Sunder's tone and his downcast eyes reproved Covenant. The Graveler plainly loathed his responsibility; yet he did not shirk it. "The reasons are many. You have asked to be released so that you may approach another village."

"I'm looking for friends," Covenant countered stiffly. "If I can't find them here, I'll try somewhere else."

"No." The Graveler was certain. "Another Stonedown would do as we do. Because you came to them from Mithil Stonedown, they would sacrifice you. In addition," he continued, "you have spoken friendship for the na-Mhoram, who reaves us of blood."

Covenant blinked at Sunder. These accusations formed a pattern he could not decipher. "I don't know any na-Mhoram. The Mhoram I knew has been dead for at least three thousand years."

"That is not possible." Sunder spoke without raising his head. "You have no more than twoscore years." His hands twisted. "But that signifies little beside the Rede of the Clave. Though the Riders are loathly to us, their power and knowledge is beyond doubt. They have foretold your coming for a generation. And they are nigh. A Rider will arrive soon to enforce the will of the Clave. Retribution for any disregard would be sore upon us. Their word is one we dare not defy. Our sole concern is that the shedding of your blood may aid the survival of the Stonedown."

"Wait," Covenant objected. "One thing at a time." Pain and exasperation vied in his head. "Three thousand years ago, a man with a halfhand and a white gold ring saved the Land from being completely destroyed by the Gray Slayer. Do you mean to tell me that's been forgotten? Nobody remembers the story?"

The Graveler shifted his weight uncomfortably. "I have heard such a tale—perhaps I alone in Mithil Stonedown. Nassic my father spoke of such things. But he was mad—lost in his wits like Jous and Prassan before him. He would have been sacrificed to the need of the Stonedown, had Kalina his wife and I permitted it."

Sunder's tone was a revelation to Covenant. It provided him a glimpse of the Graveler's self-conflict. Sunder was torn between what his father had taught him and what the Stonedown accepted as truth. Consciously, he believed what his people believed; but the convictions of his half-mad father worked on him below the surface, eroding his confidence. He was a man unreconciled to himself.

This insight softened Covenant's vexation. He sensed a range of possibilities in Sunder, intuitions of hope; but he handled them gingerly. "All right," he said. "Let that pass. How is killing us going to help you?"

"I am the Graveler. With blood I am able to shape the Sunbane." The muscles along his jaw clenched and relaxed without rhythm or purpose. "Today we lie under the desert sun—today, and for perhaps as many as three days more. Before this day, the sun of rain was upon us, and it followed the sun of pestilence. Our herd needs forage, as we need crops. With your blood, I will be able to draw water from the hard earth. I will be able to raise an acre, perhaps two acres, of grass and grain. Life for the Stonedown, until the fertile sun comes again."

This made no sense to Covenant. Fumbling for comprehension, he asked, "Can't you get water out of the river?"

"There is no water in the river."

Abruptly, Linden spoke. "No water?" The words conveyed the depth of her incredulity. "That's not possible. It *rained* yesterday."

"I have said," Sunder snapped like a man in pain, "that we lie under the desert sun. Have you not beheld it?"

In his astonishment, Covenant turned to Linden. "Is he telling the truth?"

Sunder's head jerked up. His eyes flicked back and forth between Covenant and Linden.

Through her teeth, she said, "Yes. It's true."

Covenant trusted her hearing. He swung back to the Graveler. "So there's no water." Steadiness rose in him—a mustering of his resources. "Let that pass, too." The throb in his head insisted on his helplessness; but he closed his ears to it. "Tell me how you do it. How you shape the Sunbane."

Sunder's eyes expressed his reluctance. But Covenant held the Graveler with his demand. Whatever strength of will Sunder possessed, he was too unsure of himself now to refuse. How many times had his father told him about the Unbeliever? After a moment, he acceded. "I am the Graveler." He reached a hand into his jerkin. "I bear the Sunstone."

Almost reverently, he drew out a piece of rock half the size of his fist. The stone was smooth, irregularly shaped. By some trick of its surface, it appeared transparent, but nothing showed through it. It was like a hole in his hand.

"Hellfire," Covenant breathed. Keen relief ran through him. Here was one hard solid piece of hope. "*Orcrest.*"

The Graveler peered at him in surprise. "Do you have knowledge of the Sunstone?"

"Sunder." Covenant spoke stiffly to control his excitement and anxiety. "If you try to kill us with that thing, people are going to get hurt."

The Stonedownor shook his head. "You will not resist. *Mirkfruit* will be broken in your faces—the same melon which made you captive. There will be no pain."

"Oh, there will be pain," growled Covenant. "You'll be in pain." Deliberately, he put pressure on the Graveler. "You'll be the only one in this whole Stonedown who knows you're destroying the last hope of the Land. It's too bad your father died. He would have found some way to convince you."

"Enough!" Sunder almost shouted at the laceration of his spirit. "I have uttered the words I came to speak. In this at least I have shown you what courtesy I may. If there is aught else that you would say, then say it and have done. I must be about my work."

Covenant did not relent. "What about Marid?"

Sunder jerked to his feet, stood glowering down at Covenant. "He is a slayer, unshriven by any benefit to the Stonedown—a violator of the Rede which all accept. He will be punished."

"You're going to punish him?" Covenant's control faltered

in agitation. "What for?" He struggled erect, thrust his face at the Graveler. "Didn't you hear what I told you? He's innocent. He was taken over by a Raver. It wasn't his fault."

"Yes," Sunder retorted. "And he is my friend. But you say he is innocent, and your words have no meaning. We know nothing of any Raver. The Rede is the Rede. He will be punished."

"Goddamn it!" snapped Covenant, "did you touch him?"

"Am I a fool? Yes, I put my hand upon him. The fire of his guilt is gone. He has awakened and is tormented with the memory of a noisome thing which came upon him out of the rain. Yet his act remains. He will be punished."

Covenant wanted to take hold of the Graveler, shake him. But his efforts only made the bonds cut deeper into his wrists. Darkly, he asked, "How?"

"He will be bound." The soft violence of Sunder's tone sounded like self-flagellation. "Borne out into the Plains during the night. The Sunbane will have no mercy for him." In ire or regret, he evaded Covenant's glare.

With an effort, Covenant put aside the question of Marid's fate, postponed everything he did not understand about the Sunbane. Instead, he asked, "Are you really going to kill Kalina?"

Sunder's hands twitched as if they wanted Covenant's throat. "Should it ever come to pass that I am free to leave this room," he rasped acidly, "I will do my utmost to heal her. Her blood will not be shed until her death is written on her forehead for all to see. Do you seek to prevent me from her side?"

The Graveler's distress touched Covenant. His indignation fell away. He shook his head, then urged quietly, "Untie Linden. Take her with you. She's a healer. Maybe she—"

Linden interrupted him. "No." Despite its flatness, her voice carried a timbre of despair. "I don't even have my bag. She needs a hospital, not wishful thinking. Let him make his own decisions."

Covenant wheeled toward her. Was this the same woman who had insisted with such passion, *I can help her*! Her face was half hidden by her hair. "Isn't there anything you can do?"

"Third-degree burns"— she articulated each word as if it were a mask for the contradictions of her heart —"are hard enough to treat under the best circumstances. If he wants to commit euthanasia, that's his business. Don't be so goddamn judgmental."

Without transition, she addressed Sunder. "We need food."

He regarded her suspiciously. "Linden Avery, there are things that I would give you for your ease, but food is not among them. We do not waste food on any man, woman, or child who is under judgment. Kalina my mother will not be given food unless I am able to show that she can be healed."

She did not deign to look at him. "We also need water."

Cursing sourly, Sunder turned on his heel, slapped the curtain out of his way. As he left, he snapped, "You will have water." Outside, he yelled at someone, "The prisoners require water!" Then he passed beyond earshot.

Covenant watched the swaying of the curtain, and strove to still his confusion. He could feel his pulse beating like the rhythm of slow flame in the bones of his skull. What was wrong with Linden? Moving carefully, he went to her. She sat with her gaze lowered, her features shrouded by the dimness of the room. He sank to his knees to ask her what was the matter.

She faced him harshly, shook her hair. "I must be hysterical. These people are planning to kill us. For some silly reason, that bothers me."

He studied her for a moment, measuring her belligerence, then retreated to sit against the opposite wall. What else could he do? She was already foundering; he could not insist that she surrender her secrets to him. In her straits, during his first experience with the Land, he had lost himself so badly— He closed his eyes, groped for courage. Then he sighed, "Don't worry about it. They're not going to kill us."

"Naturally not." Her tone was vicious. "You're Thomas Covenant, Unbeliever and white gold wielder. They won't dare."

Her scorn hurt him; but he made an effort to suppress his anger. "We'll get out of here tonight."

"How?" she demanded bluntly.

"Tonight"— he could not silence his weariness —"I'll try to show Sunder why he ought to let us go."

A moment later, someone pushed two large stoneware bowls of water past the curtain. Linden reacted to them as if they were the only explicable things in the room. She shuttled toward them on her knees, lowered her head to drink deeply. When Covenant joined her, she ordered him to use the bowl she had used. He obeyed to avoid an argument; but her reasons became clear when she told him to put his hands in the still-full bowl. The water might reduce their swelling, allow more blood past the bonds—perhaps even loosen the bonds themselves.

Apparently, his wrists were tied with leather; as he followed her instructions, the cool fluid palliated his discomfort; and a short while later he felt a tingle of recovery in his palms. He tried to thank her with a smile; but she did not respond. When he left the water, she took his place, soaked her own hands for a long time.

Gradually, Covenant's attention drifted away from her. The sun was beginning to slant toward afternoon; a bright hot sliver of light dissected by iron bars lay on the floor. He rested his head, and thought about the Sunstone.

Orcrest—a stone of power. The former masters of stone-lore had used *orcrest* to wield the Earthpower in a variety of ways—to shed light, break droughts, test truth. If Sunder's Sunstone were indeed *orcrest*—

But what if it were not? Covenant returned to the dread which had struck him in Nassic's hut. *The world is not what it was.* If there were no Earthpower—

Something broken. He could not deny his anguish. He needed *orcrest*, needed its power; he had to have a trigger. He had never been able to call up wild magic of his own volition. Even in the crisis of his final confrontation with the Despiser, he would have been lost utterly without the catalyst of the Illearth Stone. If the Sunstone were not truly *orcrest*—

He wished that he could feel his ring; but even if his hands had not been bound, his fingers would have been too numb. Leper, he muttered. Make it work. Make it. The sunlight became a white cynosure, growing until it throbbed like the pain in his head. Slowly, his mind filled with a brightness more fearsome and punishing than any night. He opposed it as if he were a fragment of the last kind dark which healed and renewed.

Then Linden was saying, "Covenant. You've slept enough. It's dangerous if you have a concussion. Covenant."

The dazzle in his brain blinded him momentarily; he had to squint to see that the room was dim. Sunset faintly colored the air. The sky beyond the window lay in twilight.

He felt stiff and groggy, as if his life had congealed within him while he slept. His pain had burrowed into the bone; but it, too, seemed imprecise—stupefied by fatigue. At Linden's urging, he drank the remaining water. It cleared his throat, but could not unclog his mind.

For a long time, they sat without speaking. Night filled the valley like an exudation from the mountains; the air turned cool as the earth lost its warmth to the clear heavens. At first, the stars were as vivid as language—an articulation of themselves across the distance and the unfathomable night. But then the sky lost its depth as the moon rose.

"Covenant," Linden breathed, "talk to me." Her voice was as fragile as ice. She was near the limit of her endurance.

He searched for something that would help them both, fortify her and focus him.

"I don't want to die like this," she grated. "Without even knowing why."

He ached because he could not explain why, could not give her his sense of purpose. But he knew a story which might help her to understand what was at stake. Perhaps it was a story they both needed to hear. "All right," he said quietly. "I'll tell you how this world came to be created."

She did not answer. After a moment, he began.

Even to himself, his voice sounded bodiless, as if the dark were speaking for him. He was trying to reach out to her with words, though he could not see her, and had no very clear idea of who she was. His tale was a simple one; but for him its simplicity grew out of long distillation. It made even his dead nerves yearn as if he were moved by an eloquence he did not possess.

In the measureless heavens of the universe, he told her, where life and space were one, and the immortals strode through an ether without limitation, the Creator looked about him, and his heart swelled with the desire to make a new thing to gladden his bright children. Summoning his strength and subtlety, he set about the work which was his exaltation.

First he forged the Arch of Time, so that the world he wished to make would have a place to be. And then within the Arch he formed the Earth. Wielding the greatness of his love and vision as tools, he made the world in all its beauty, so that no eye could behold it without joy. And then upon the Earth he placed all the myriads of its inhabitants—beings to perceive and cherish the beauty which he made. Striving for perfection because it was the nature of creation to desire all things flawless, he made the inhabitants of the Earth capable of creation, and striving, and love for the world. Then he withdrew his hand, and beheld what he had done.

There to his great ire he saw that evil lay in the Earth: malice buried and abroad, banes and powers which had no part in his intent. For while he had labored over his creation, he had closed his eyes, and had not seen the Despiser, the bitter son or brother of his heart, laboring beside him—casting dross into the forge, adding malignancy to his intent.

Then the Creator's wrath shook the heavens, and he grappled with the son or brother of his heart. He overthrew the Despiser and hurled him to the Earth, sealing him within the Arch of Time for his punishment. Thus it became for the inhabitants of the Earth as it was with the Creator; for in that act he harmed the thing he loved, and so all living hearts were taught the power of self-despite. The Despiser was abroad in the Earth, awakening ills, seeking to escape his prison. And the Creator could not hinder him, for the reach of any immortal hand through the Arch would topple Time, destroying the Earth and freeing the Despiser. This was the great grief of the Creator, and the unending flaw and sorrow of those who lived and strove upon the Earth.

Covenant fell silent. Telling this story, essentially as he had heard it ten years ago, brought back many things to him. He no longer felt blurred and ossified. Now he felt like the night, and his memories were stars: Mhoram, Foamfollower, Bannor, the Ranyhyn. While he still had blood in his veins, air in his lungs, he would not turn his back on the world which had given birth to such people.

Linden started to ask a question; but the rustling of the curtain interrupted her. Sunder entered the room carrying an oil lamp. He set it on the floor and seated himself cross-legged in front of it. Its dim, yellow light cast haggard shadows across his visage. When he spoke, his voice wore ashes, as if he had been bereaved.

"I, too, have heard that tale," he said thickly. "It was told to me by Nassic my father. But the tale told in the Rede of the na-Mhoram is another altogether."

Covenant and Linden waited. After a moment, the Graveler went on. "In the Rede it is told that the Earth was formed

as a jail and tormenting-place for the Lord of wickedness—
him whom we name a-Jeroth of the Seven Hells. And life was
placed upon the Earth—men and women, and all other races
—to wreak upon a-Jeroth his proper doom. But time and
again, throughout the ages, the races of the Land failed their
purpose. Rather than exacting pain from a-Jeroth, meting out
upon him the Master's just retribution, they formed alliances
with the Lord, spared him in his weakness and bowed to him
in his strength. And always"— Sunder shot a glance at Covenant, faltered momentarily —"the most heinous of these betrayals have been wrought by men born in the image of the
First Betrayer, Berek, father of cowardice. Halfhanded men.

"Therefore in his wrath the Master turned his face from the
Land. He sent the Sunbane upon us, as chastisement for
treachery, so that we would remember our mortality, and
become worthy again to serve his purpose. Only the interces-
sion of the Clave enables us to endure."

Protests thronged in Covenant. He knew from experience
that this conception of the Land was false and cruel. But
before he could try to reply, Linden climbed suddenly to her
feet. Her eyes were feverish in the lamplight, afflicted by fear
and outrage and waiting. Her lips trembled. "A Master like
that isn't worth believing in. But you probably have to do it
anyway. How else can you justify killing people you don't
even know?"

The Graveler surged erect, faced her extremely. The conflict in him made him grind his teeth. "All the Land knows
the truth which the Clave teaches. It is manifest at every
rising of the sun. None deny it but Nassic my father, who
died in mind before his body was slain, and you, who are
ignorant!"

Covenant remained on the floor. While Linden and Sunder
confronted each other, he drew all the strands of himself
together, braided anger, empathy, determination, memory to
make the cord on which all their lives depended. Part of him
bled to think of the hurt he meant to inflict on Sunder, the
choice he meant to extort; part raged at the brutality which
had taught people like Sunder to think of their own lives as
punishment for a crime they could not have committed; part
quavered in fear at the idea of failure, at the poverty of his
grasp on power. When Linden began to retort to the Graveler,

he stopped her with a wrench of his head. I'll do it, he thought silently to her. If it has to be done. Shifting his gaze to Sunder, he asked, "How's your mother?"

A spasm contorted the Graveler's face; his hands bunched into knots of pain and uselessness. "Her death is plain." His eyes were dull, wounded, articulating the frank torment of his heart. "I must shed her blood with yours at the sun's rising."

Covenant bowed his head for a moment in tacit acknowledgment. Then, deliberately, he created a space of clarity within himself, set his questions and fears aside. All right, he murmured. Leper. It has to be done.

Taking a deep breath, he rose to his feet, faced the Stonedownor.

"Sunder," he said softly, "do you have a knife?"

The Graveler nodded as if the question had no meaning.

"Take it out."

Slowly, Sunder obeyed. He reached to his back, slipped a long iron poniard out of his belt. His fingers held it as if they had no idea how to use it.

"I want you to see that you're safe," Covenant said. "You have a knife. My hands are tied. I can't hurt you."

Sunder stared back at Covenant, transfixed by incomprehension.

All right, Covenant breathed. Leper. Do it now. His heartbeat seemed to fill his chest, leaving no room for air. But he did not waver.

"Get out that piece of *orcrest*. The Sunstone."

Again, Sunder obeyed. Covenant's will held him.

Covenant did not permit himself to glance down at the stone. He was marginally aware that Linden regarded him as if he were no longer sane. A shudder of apprehension threatened his clarity. He had to grit his teeth to keep his voice steady. "Touch me with it."

"Touch—?" Sunder murmured blankly.

"Touch my forehead."

Doubt pinched the corners of Sunder's eyes. His shoulders hunched as he tightened his grip on the knife, the Sunstone.

Do it.

The Graveler's hand seemed to move without volition. The *orcrest* passed Covenant's face, came to rest cool and possible against his tense brow.

His attention dropped through him to his ring, seeking for the link between *orcrest* and white gold. He remembered standing in sunlight and desperation on the slopes of Mount Thunder; he saw Bannor take his hand, place his ring in contact with the Staff of Law. A trigger. He felt the detonation of power.

You are the white gold.

The silence in the room vibrated. His lips stretched back from his teeth. He squeezed his eyes shut against the strain.

A trigger.

He did not want to die, did not want the Land to die. Lord Foul abhorred all life.

Fiercely, he brought the *orcrest* and the white gold together in his mind, chose power.

A burst of argent sprang off his forehead.

Linden let out a stricken gasp. Sunder snatched back the *orcrest*. A gust of force blew out the lamp.

Then Covenant's hands were free. Ignoring the sudden magma of renewed circulation, he raised his arms in front of him, opened his eyes.

His hands blazed the color of the full moon. He could feel the passion of the fire, but it did him no harm.

The flames on his left swiftly faded, died. But his right hand grew brighter as the blaze focused on his ring, burning without a sound.

Linden stared at him whitely, wildly. Sunder's eyes echoed the argent fire like a revelation too acute to bear.

You are stubborn yet. Yes! Covenant panted. You don't begin to know how stubborn.

With a thought, he struck the bonds from Linden's wrists. Then he reached for the Sunstone.

As he took it from Sunder's stunned fingers, a piercing white light exploded from the stone. It shone like a sun in the small room. Linden ducked her head. Sunder covered his eyes with his free arm, waved his poniard uncertainly.

"Wild magic," Covenant said. His voice felt like flame in his mouth. The return of blood to his arms raked his nerves like claws. "Your knife means nothing. I have the wild magic. I'm not threatening you. I don't want to hurt anybody." The night had become cold, yet sweat streamed down his face. "That's not why I'm here. But I won't let you kill us."

"Father!" Sunder cried in dismay. "Was it true? Was every word that you spoke a word of truth?"

Covenant sagged. He felt that he had accomplished his purpose; and at once a wave of fatigue broke through him. "Here." His voice was hoarse with strain. "Take it."

"Take—?"

"The Sunstone. It's yours."

Torn by this vision of power as if it turned the world he had always known to chaos, Sunder stretched out his hand, touched the bright *orcrest*. When its light did not burn him, he closed his fingers on it as if it were an anchor.

With a groan, Covenant released the wild magic. Instantly, the fire went out as if he had severed it from his hand. The Sunstone was extinguished; the room plunged into midnight.

He leaned back against the wall, hugged his pounding arms across his chest. Flares danced along his sight, turning slowly from white to orange and red. He felt exhausted; but he could not rest. He had silenced his power so that the Graveler would have a chance to refuse him. Now he had to meet the cost of his risk. Roughly, he forced out words. "I want to get away from here. Before anything else happens. Before that Raver tries something worse. But we need help. A guide. Somebody who knows the Sunbane. We can't survive alone. I want you."

From out of the darkness, Sunder answered as if he were foundering, "I am the Graveler of Mithil Stonedown. My people hold me in their faith. How shall I betray my home to aid you?"

"Sunder," Covenant replied, striving to convey the extremity of his conviction, "I want to help the Land. I want to save it all. Including Mithil Stonedown."

For a long moment, the Graveler was silent. Covenant clinched his chest, did not allow himself to beg for Sunder's aid; but his heart beat over and over again, *Please; I need you.*

Abruptly, Linden spoke in a tone of startling passion. "You shouldn't have to kill your own mother."

Sunder took a deep quivering breath. "I do not wish to shed her blood. Or yours. May my people forgive me."

Covenant's head swam with relief. He hardly heard himself say, "Then let's get started."

SEVEN: Marid

FOR a moment, there was silence in the small room. Sunder remained still, as if he could not force his reluctant bones to act on his decision. Out of the darkness, he breathed thickly, "Thomas Covenant, do not betray me."

Before Covenant could try to reply, the Graveler turned, eased the curtain aside.

Through the entryway, Covenant saw moonlight in the open center of the Stonedown. Quietly, he asked, "What about guards?"

"There are none here." Sunder's voice was a rigid whisper. "Lives to be shed are left in the charge of the Graveler. It is fitting that one who will commit sacrifice should keep vigil with those whose blood will be shed. The Stonedown sleeps."

Covenant clenched himself against his fatigue and the Graveler's tone. "What about outside the village?"

"Those guards we must evade."

Grimly, Sunder slipped out of the room.

Linden began to follow the Stonedownor. But at Covenant's side she stopped, said softly, "Do you trust him? He already regrets this."

"I know," Covenant responded. In the back of his mind, he cursed the acuity of her hearing. "I wouldn't trust anybody who didn't regret a decision like this."

She hesitated for a moment. She said bitterly, "I don't think regret is such a virtue." Then she let herself out into the night.

He stood still, blinking wearily at the dark. He felt wan with hunger; and the thought of what lay ahead sapped the little strength remaining to him. Linden's severity hurt him. Where had she learned to deny herself the simple humanity of regret?

But he had no time for such things. His need to escape was absolute. Woodenly, he followed his companions out of the room.

119

After the blackness behind him, the moon seemed bright. Sunder and Linden were distinct and vulnerable against the pale walls of the houses, waiting for him. When he joined them, the Graveler turned northward immediately, began moving with barefoot silence between the dwellings. Linden shadowed him; and Covenant stayed within arm's reach of her back.

As they neared the outer houses, Sunder stopped. He signed for Covenant and Linden to remain where they were. When Covenant nodded, Sunder crept away back into the Stonedown.

Covenant tried to muffle his respiration. At his side, Linden stood with her fists clenched. Her lips moved soundlessly as if she were arguing with her fear. The night was chilly; Covenant's anxiety left a cold trail down the small of his back.

Shortly, Sunder returned, bearing a dark oblong the size of a papaya. *"Mirkfruit,"* he whispered. At once, he moved off again.

Like spectres, the three of them left Mithil Stonedown.

From the last houses, Sunder picked his way toward the valley bottom. He traveled in a half crouch, reducing his silhouette as much as possible. Linden followed his example; she seemed to flit through the moonlight as if she had been born sure-footed. But Covenant's toes were numb, and his legs were tired. He stumbled over the uneven ground.

Abruptly, Sunder braced his hands on a rock, vaulted down into the long hollow of the riverbed.

Linden jumped after him. Sand absorbed her landing. Swiftly, she joined Sunder in the shadow under the bank.

Covenant hesitated on the edge. Looking downward, he became suddenly queasy with vertigo. He turned his head away. The barren length of the watercourse stretched serpentine out of the mountains on his left toward the South Plains on his right.

Last night, the Mithil River had been full to overflowing.

"Come!" whispered Sunder. "You will be seen."

Covenant jumped. He landed crookedly, sprawled in the sand. In an instant, Sunder reached his side, urged him to his feet. He ignored the Graveler. He dug his hands into the sand, groping for moisture. But even below the surface, the sand was completely dry. His hands raised dust that made him gag to stifle a cough.

Impossible!

The riverbed was as desiccated as a desert. Had the Law itself become meaningless?

"Covenant!" Linden hissed.

Sunder tugged at his shoulders. Fighting down a rush of blind rage, Covenant pulled his legs under him, stumbled into the shadow of the bank. A moment passed before he regained himself enough to look outward, away from his dismay.

Sunder pointed downriver, toward the black arc of a bridge a few hundred feet away. "One guard," he breathed. "The others can no longer descry us. But him we cannot pass unseen."

"What are we going to do?" whispered Linden.

The Graveler motioned for silence. Hefting his *mirkfruit*, he crept away along the course, staying carefully under the shelter of the bank.

Linden and Covenant followed.

Their progress was slow. The river bottom was littered with rocks and unexpected holes, especially near the banks; Covenant had to watch his footing. Yet his gaze was drawn toward the bridge—the ominous black span blocking their way like a gate. He had crossed that bridge with Lena. And with Atiaran. The memory made his heart squirm.

He caught no glimpse of the guard. The man must have been hiding behind the parapets of the span.

Then they drew near the bridge, made their way under it. Covenant held his breath as Sunder moved to the riverbank. The Graveler climbed with acute caution; he eased his way upward as if every pebble and handful of dirt were treacherous. Slowly, he disappeared around the base of the bridge.

Suspense shivered in the air as if the night were about to shatter. Covenant's lungs knotted, demanding relief. Linden huddled into herself.

They heard a soft thud—the impact of Sunder's *mirkfruit* —followed by a groan, and the sound of a body falling on the stone over their heads.

The Graveler dropped with alacrity back into the riverbed. "Now we must make haste," he warned, "before another comes to ward in his place." He sounded angry. Turning on his heel, he strode away as if what he had just done to someone he had known all his life were unsupportable.

He set a stiff pace. Covenant and Linden had to hurry to keep up with him.

Moonlight gave the night a crisp patina of old silver, as if the darkness itself were a work of fine-spun craft. Stars winked like instances of perfection above the rims of the mountains, which rose rugged into the unattainable heavens on either side. While his strength held, Covenant took pleasure in this opportunity to recover the tangible loveliness of the Land.

But as the moon declined toward setting, and the spur of mountains on his left began to shrink, his momentum faltered. He was too weak. His heart limped as if it could not keep up with him; his muscles felt like sand. And escape was not enough; there was something else he had to do as well. With a dry croak, he called Sunder to a halt. Then he dropped to the ground, stretched out on his back, and sucked air.

Linden stopped nearby, winded but still capable. And Sunder stood erect and impatient; he was tough as well as strong, inured to fatigue by a lifetime of difficult survival. The little he had seen and heard had taught Covenant that life in Mithil Stonedown was arduous and costly. Why else were these villagers willing to sacrifice their own parents—willing to condemn strangers and innocents to death? It was intolerable, that the bountiful Land he loved had come to this.

He was still hunting fortitude when Sunder said stiffly, "Here we are safe enough until the sun's rising—at least while our absence remains undiscovered in the Stonedown. But it avails nothing merely to abide here, awaiting chance or doom. The Rider who approaches Mithil Stonedown may come upon us. He will surely pursue when he is told of our flight. You have asked me to guide you. Thomas Covenant, where will you go?"

Groaning, Covenant pried himself into a sitting position. "First things first." He had learned enough to be sure Sunder would not like the larger answer to that question. So he concentrated on his immediate purpose. "First I want to find Marid."

"Marid?" The Graveler gaped. "Did I not tell you the judgment of the Stonedown? He is condemned by ancient Rede and custom to the mercy of the Sunbane. It has already been done."

"I know," Covenant muttered. "You told me. And I told you. He's innocent."

"Guilt or innocence," retorted Sunder, "it avails nothing. It has already been done! The men and women entrusted with his doom returned before I came to speak with you."

Weariness eroded Covenant's self-mastery. He could hardly restrain his old rage. "What exactly did they do to him?"

Sunder cast a look of exasperation at the stars. "They bore him into the Plains, and left him bound to await his judgment."

"Do you know where they left him?"

"Somewhat. They spoke of their intent before departing. I was not among them to behold the very spot."

"That's good enough." Covenant felt as weak as water; but he climbed to his feet and faced the Graveler. "Take us there."

"There is not time!" Sunder's visage was a tangle of darkness. "The distance is too great. We must find protection, lest we also fall prey to the sun's rising."

"But Marid is *innocent*." Covenant sounded wild to himself, but did not care. "The only reason that Raver used him was because of us. I'm not going to let him be punished. Goddamn it." He grabbed roughly at Sunder's jerkin. "Guide us! I've got too much blood on my hands already."

In a low strained tone, as if he had just glimpsed some crucial and frightening truth, the Graveler said, "You do not understand the Sunbane."

"Then explain it. What are you so afraid of?"

"We will suffer Marid's doom!"

From behind Sunder, Linden said, "He means it. He thinks something awful is going to happen when the sun comes up."

With an effort, Covenant forced himself to release Sunder. He faced Linden, bit down on his voice to keep it quiet. "What do you think?"

She was silent for a moment. Then she said harshly, "I didn't believe you when you said Joan was possessed. But I saw that Raver myself. I saw Marid afterward. The Raver was gone." She carved each word distinctly in the night air. "If you want to stay with Sunder, I'll go looking for Marid myself."

"Heaven and Earth!" protested Sunder. "Did I betray my home merely so that you may meet ruin for a man you cannot save? If you place one foot amiss, you will end in beseeching the stones themselves for death!"

Covenant gazed into the darkness where Linden stood,

gathering strength from her. Softly, he replied to Sunder, "He was your friend."

"You are mad!" Sunder raged. "Nassic my father was mad!" He snatched up a stone, hurled it against the river-bank. "I am mad." Then he whirled on Covenant. Anger hammered in his voice. "Very well. I will guide you. But I will *not*"— his fist hit at the night —"suffer the destruction of the Sunbane for any man or woman, mad or sane."

Wrenching himself into motion, he turned and scrambled up out of the riverbed.

Covenant remained looking toward Linden. He wanted to thank her for her support, her willingness to risk herself in the name of Marid's innocence. But she brushed past him after Sunder. "Come on," she said over her shoulder. "We've got to hurry. Whatever it is he's afraid of, I don't think I'm going to like it."

He watched her while she climbed the bank. *End in beseeching*— He rubbed his right hand across his chin, verified his ring against the stiff stubble of his beard. Then he marshalled his waning resources and struggled to follow his companions.

On level ground, he found himself in an entirely different landscape. Except for the ragged weal of the Mithil, the Plains were nearly featureless. They spread north and west as far as he could see, marked only by the faint undulations of the terrain—bare even of shrubs or piles of rock. The low moonlight gave them an appearance of ghostly sterility, as if they had been weathered barren by ages of implacable thirst.

Sunder headed slightly east of north at a canter, roughly paralleling the mountains which still lay to the east. But Covenant could not endure such a pace. And he did not understand his guide's compelling dread. He called for Sunder to slow down.

The Graveler spun on his heel. *"There is not time."*

"Then there's no reason for us to wear ourselves out."

Sunder spat a curse, started moving again. But in spite of his almost frantic anxiety, he went no faster than a brisk walk.

Some time later, the moon fell below the horizon. But the scant light of the stars sufficed. The terrain was not difficult, and Sunder knew his way. Soon a vague wash of gray from the east began to macerate the night.

The paling of the horizon agitated Sunder. He searched the earth near him while he walked, made digressions from his path like spurts of fright to study irregularities in the ground. But he could not find what he wanted. Within half a league, dawn had become imminent. Urgently, he faced Covenant and Linden. "We must find stone. Any hard rock free of soil. Before the sun's rising. Search, if you value a hale life and a clean death."

Covenant halted woodenly. His surroundings seemed to sway as if they were about to fall apart. He felt stunned by weariness.

"There," Linden said. She was pointing off to her right.

He peered in that direction. He could discern nothing. But he did not have her eyes.

Sunder gaped at her for a moment, then hastened to investigate. With his hands, he explored the surface.

"Stone!" he hissed. "It may suffice." At once, he jumped erect. "We must stand here. The stone will ward us."

Fatigue blurred Covenant's sight. He could not see the Graveler clearly. Sunder's apprehension made no sense to him. Sunrise was only moments away; luminescence cast the horizon into stark relief. Was he supposed to be afraid of the *sun*?

Linden asked Sunder the same question. "Do you think the sun's going to hurt us? That's nonsense. We spent half the morning yesterday in that test of silence of yours, and the only thing we suffered from was prejudice."

"With stone underfoot!" fumed the Graveler. "It is the first touch which destroys! You did not meet the first touch of the Sunbane unwarded by stone!"

I don't have time for this, Covenant muttered to himself. The eyes of his mind saw Marid clearly enough. Left to die in the sun. Unsteadily, he lurched into motion again.

"Fool!" Sunder shouted. "For you I betrayed my born people!"

A moment later, Linden joined Covenant.

"Find stone!" The Graveler's passion sounded like raw despair. "You destroy me! Must I slay you also?"

Linden was silent for a few steps. Then she murmured, "He believes it."

An innominate pang ran through Covenant. Involuntarily, he stopped. He and Linden turned to face the east.

They squinted at the first fiery rim of the rising sun.

It flared red along the skyline; but the sun itself wore an aura of brown, as if it shone through cerements of dust. It touched his face with dry heat.

"Nothing," Linden said tightly. "I don't feel anything."

He glanced back at Sunder. The Graveler stood on his stone. His hands had covered his face, and his shoulders shook.

Because he did not know what else to do, Covenant turned away, went rigidly in search of Marid.

Linden stayed with him. Hunger had abused her face, giving her a sunken aspect; and she carried her head as if the injury behind her ear still hurt. But her jaw was set, emphasizing the firm lines of her chin, and her lips were pale with severity. She looked like a woman who did not know how to fail. He braced himself on her determination, and kept moving.

The rising of the sun had altered the ambience of the Plains. They had been silver and bearable; now they became a hot and lifeless ruin. Nothing grew or moved in the wide waste. The ground was packed and baked until it was as intractable as iron. Loose dirt turned to dust. The entire landscape shimmered with heat like the aftermath of destruction.

Striving against the stupefaction of his fatigue, Covenant asked Linden to tell him about the condition of the terrain.

"It's wrong." She bit out words as if the sight were an obloquy directed at her personally. "It shouldn't be like this. It's like a running sore. I keep expecting to see it bleed. It isn't supposed to be like this."

Isn't supposed to be like this! he echoed. The Land had become like Joan. Something broken.

The heat haze stung his eyes. He could not see the ground except as a swath of pale ichor; he felt that he was treading pain. His numb feet stumbled helplessly.

She caught his arm, steadied him. Clenching his old sorrow, he drew himself upright. His voice shook. "What's causing it?"

"I can't tell," she said grimly. "But it has something to do with that ring around the sun. The sun itself"— her hands released him slowly —"seems natural."

"Bloody hell," he breathed. "What has that bastard done?"

But he did not expect an answer. In spite of her penetrating vision, Linden knew less than he did. Deliberately, he gave himself a VSE. Then he went on looking for Marid. In his rue and pain, the thought of a man lying bound at the mercy of the sun loomed as the one idea which made everything else abominable.

Wearily, doggedly, he and Linden trudged through the heat-leeched landscape. The dust coated his mouth with the taste of failure; the glare lanced through his eyeballs. As his weakness deepened, he drifted into a vague dizziness. Only the landmark of the mountains, now east and somewhat south of him, enabled him to keep his direction. The sun beat down as if onto an anvil, hammering moisture and strength out of him like a smith shaping futility. He did not know how he stayed on his feet. At times, he felt himself wandering over the colorless earth, through the haze, as if he were a fragment of the desolation.

He might have wandered past his goal; but Linden somehow retained more alertness. She tugged him to a stop, dragged his attention out of the slow eddying sopor of the heat. "Look."

His lips framed empty questions. For a moment, he could not understand why he was no longer moving.

"Look," she repeated. Her voice was an arid croak.

They stood in a wide bowl of dust. Clouds billowed from every shuffle of their feet. Before them, two wooden stakes had been driven into the ground. The stakes were some distance apart, as if they had been set to secure the arms of a man lying outstretched. Tied to the stakes were loops of rope.

The loops were intact.

A body's length from the stakes were two holes in the ground—the kind of holes made by stakes pounded in and then pulled out.

Covenant swallowed drily. "Marid." The word abraded his throat.

"He got away," Linden said hoarsely.

Covenant's legs folded. He sat down, coughing weakly at the dust he raised. Got away.

Linden squatted in front of him. The nearness of her face forced him to look at her. Her voice scraped as if it were full of sand. "I don't know how he did it, but he's better off than we are. This heat's going to kill us."

His tongue fumbled. "I had to try. He was innocent."

Awkwardly, she reached out, wiped beads of useless sweat from his forehead. "You look awful."

He peered at her through his exhaustion. Dirt caked her lips and cheeks, collected in the lines on either side of her mouth. Sweat-trails streaked her face. Her eyes were glazed.

"So do you."

"Then we'd better do something about it." A tremor eroded her effort to sound resolute. But she stood up, helped him to his feet. "Let's go back. Maybe Sunder's looking for us."

He nodded. He had forgotten the Graveler.

But when he and Linden turned to retrace their way, they saw a figure coming darkly through the shimmer.

He stopped, squinted. Mirage? Linden stood near him as if to prevent him from losing his balance. They waited.

The figure approached until they recognized Sunder.

He halted twenty paces from them.

In his right hand, he gripped his poniard. This time, he seemed perfectly familiar with its use.

Covenant watched the Graveler dumbly, as if the knife had made them strangers to each other. Linden's hand touched a warning to his arm.

"Thomas Covenant." Sunder's face looked like hot stone. "What is my name?"

What—? Covenant frowned at the intervening heat.

"Speak my name!" the Graveler spat fiercely. "Do not compel me to slay you."

Slay? Covenant made an effort to reach through the confusion. "Sunder," he croaked. "Graveler of Mithil Stonedown. Holder of the Sunstone."

Incomprehension stretched Sunder's countenance. "Linden Avery?" he asked falteringly. "What is the name of my father?"

"Was," she said in a flat tone. "His name was Nassic son of Jous. He's dead."

Sunder gaped as if Covenant and Linden were miraculous. Then he dropped his hands to his sides. "Heaven and Earth! It is not possible. The Sunbane— Never have I beheld—" He shook his head in astonishment. "Ah, you are a mystery! How can such things be? Does one white ring alter the order of life?"

"Sometimes," Covenant muttered. He was trying to follow a fractured sequence of memories. Everything he did was an unintentional assault on the Graveler's preconceptions. He wanted to ease Sunder with some kind of explanation. The heat haze seemed to blur the distinction between past and present. Something about his boots—? He forced words past his parched lips. "The first time I was here—" Boots—yes, that was it. Drool Rockworm had been able to locate him through the alien touch of his boots on the ground. "My boots. Her shoes. They don't come from the Land. Maybe that's what protected us."

Sunder grabbed at the suggestion as if it were a benison. "Yes. It must be so. Flesh is flesh, susceptible to the Sunbane. But your footwear it is unlike any I have seen. Surely you were shielded at the sun's first touch, else you would have been altered beyond any power to know me." Then his face darkened. "But could you not have told me? I feared—" The clenching of his jaws described eloquently the extremity of his fear.

"We didn't know." Covenant wanted to lie down, close his eyes, forget. "We were lucky." A moment passed before he found the will to ask, "Marid—?"

At once, Sunder put everything else aside. He went to look at the stakes, the holes. A frown knotted his forehead. "Fools," he grated. "I warned them to ware such things. None can foretell the Sunbane. Now there is evil upon the Plains."

"You mean," asked Linden, "he didn't escape? He isn't safe?"

In response, the Graveler rasped, "Did I not say there was not time? You have achieved nothing but your own prostration. It is enough," he went on stiffly. "I have followed you to this useless end. Now you will accompany me."

Linden stared at Sunder. "Where are we going?"

"To find shelter," he said in a calmer tone. "We cannot endure this sun."

Covenant gestured eastward, toward a region with which he was familiar. "The hills—"

Sunder shook his head. "There is shelter in the hills. But to gain it we must pass within scope of Windshorn Stonedown. That is certain sacrifice—for any stranger, as for the Graveler of Mithil Stonedown. We go west, to the Mithil River."

Covenant could not argue. Ignorance crippled his ability to make decisions. When Sunder took his arm and turned him away from the sun, he began to scuffle stiffly out of the bowl of dust.

Linden moved at his side. Her stride was unsteady; she

seemed dangerously weak. Sunder was stronger; but his eyes
were bleak, as if he could see disaster ahead. And Covenant
could barely lift his feet. The sun, still climbing toward midmorning, clung to his shoulders, hagriding him. Heat flushed
back and forth across his skin—a vitiating fever which echoed
the haze of the scorched earth. His eyes felt raw from the
scraping of his eyelids. After a time, he began to stumble as if
the ligatures of his knees were parting.

Then he was in the dirt, with no idea of how he had fallen.
Sunder supported him so that he could sit up. The Graveler's
face was gray with dust; he, too, had begun to suffer.
"Thomas Covenant," he panted, "this is fatal to you. You
must have water. Will you not make use of your white ring?"

Covenant's respiration was shallow and ragged. He stared
into the haze as if he had gone blind.

"The white ring," Sunder pleaded. "You must raise water,
lest you die."

Water. He pulled the shards of himself together around that
thought. Impossible. He could not concentrate. Had never
used wild magic for anything except contention. It was not a
panacea.

Both Sunder and Linden were studying him as if he were
responsible for their hopes. They were failing along with him.
For their sakes, he would have been willing to make the
attempt. But it was impossible for other reasons as well. Tor-
tuously, as if he had been disjointed, he shifted forward, got
his knees under him, then his feet.

"Ur-Lord!" protested the Graveler.

"I don't," Covenant muttered, half coughing, "don't know
how." He wanted to shout. "I'm a leper. I can't see—can't
feel—" The Earth was closed to him; it lay blank and meaningless under his feet—a concatenation of haze, nothing
more. "I don't know how to reach it." *We need Earthpower.
And a Lord to wield it.*

There's no Earthpower. The Lords are gone. He had no
words potent enough to convey his helplessness. "I just can't."

Sunder groaned. But he hesitated only momentarily. Then
he sighed in resignation, "Very well. Yet we must have water."
He took out his knife. "My strength is greater than yours.
Perhaps I am able to spare a little blood." Grimly, he directed
the blade toward the mapwork of scars on his left forearm.

Covenant lurched to try to stop him.

Linden was quicker. She seized Sunder's wrist. "No!"

The Graveler twisted free of her, gritted acutely, *"We must have water."*

"Not like that." The cuts on Nassic's hand burned in Covenant's memory; he rejected such power instinctively.

"Do you wish to die?"

"No." Covenant upheld himself by force of will. "But I'm not that desperate. Not yet, anyway."

"Your knife isn't even clean," added Linden. "If septicemia set in, I'd have to burn it out."

Sunder closed his eyes as if to shut out what they were saying. "I will outlive you both under this sun." His jaws chewed his voice into a barren whisper. "Ah, my father, what have you done to me? Is this the outcome of all your mad devoir?"

"Suit yourself," Covenant said brutally, trying to keep Sunder from despair or rebellion. "But at least have the decency to wait until we're too weak to stop you."

The Graveler's eyes burst open. He spat a curse. "Decency, is it?" he grated. "You are swift to cast shame upon people whose lives you do not comprehend. Well, let us hasten the moment when I may decently save you." With a thrust of his arm, he pushed Covenant into motion, then caught him around the waist to keep him from falling, and began half dragging him westward.

In a moment, Linden came to Covenant's other side, shrugged his arm over her shoulders so that she could help support him. Braced in that fashion, he was able to travel.

But the sun was remorseless. Slowly, ineluctably, it beat him toward abjection. By midmorning, he was hardly carrying a fraction of his own weight. To his burned eyes, the haze sang threnodies of prostration; motes of darkness began to flit across his vision. From time to time, he saw small clumps of night crouching on the pale ground just beyond clarity, as if they were waiting for him.

Then the earth seemed to rise up in front of him. Sunder came to a halt. Linden almost fell; but Covenant clung to her somehow. He fought to focus his eyes. After a moment, he saw that the rise was a shelf of rock jutting westward.

Sunder tugged him and Linden forward. They limped past another clump like a low bush, into the shadow of the rock.

The jut of the shelf formed an eroded lee large enough to shelter several people. In the shadow, the rock and dirt felt cool. Linden helped Sunder place Covenant sitting against the balm of the stone. Covenant tried to lie down; but the Graveler stopped him, and Linden panted, "Don't. You might go to sleep. You've lost too much fluid."

He nodded vaguely. The coolness was only relative, and he was febrile with thirst. No amount of shade could answer the unpity of the sun. But the shadow itself was bliss to him, and he was content. Linden sat down on one side of him; Sunder, on the other. He closed his eyes, let himself drift.

Some time later, he became conscious of voices. Linden and Sunder were talking. The hebetude of her tone betrayed the difficulty of staying alert. Sunder's responses were distant, as if he found her inquiries painful but could not think of any way to refuse them.

"Sunder," she asked dimly, "what is Mithil Stonedown going to do without you?"

"Linden Avery?" He seemed not to understand her question.

"Call me Linden. After today——" Her voice trailed away.

He hesitated, then said, "Linden."

"You're the Graveler. What will they do without a Graveler?"

"Ah." Now he caught her meaning. "I signify little. The loss of the Sunstone is of more import, yet even that loss can be overcome. The Stonedown is chary of its lore. My prentice is adept in all the rites which must be performed in the absence of the Sunstone. Without doubt, he shed Kalina my mother at the sun's rising. The Stonedown will endure. How otherwise could I have done what I have done?"

After a pause, she asked, "You're not married?"

"No." His reply was like a wince.

Linden seemed to hear a wide range of implications in that one word. Quietly, she said, "But you were."

"Yes."

"What happened?"

Sunder was silent at first. But then he replied, "Among my people, only the Graveler is given the choice of his own mate. The survival of the Stonedown depends upon its children. Mating for children is not left to the hazard of affection or preference. But by long custom, the Graveler is given freedom. As recompense for the burden of his work.

"The choice of my heart fell upon Aimil daughter of Anest.

Anest was sister to Kalina my mother. From childhood, Aimil and I were dear to each other. We were gladly wed, and gladly sought to vindicate our choosing with children.

"A son came to us, and was given the name Nelbrin, which is 'heart's child.' " His tone was as astringent as the terrain. "He was a pale child, not greatly well. But he grew as a child should grow and was a treasure to us.

"For a score of turnings of the moon he grew. He was slow in learning to walk, and not steady upon his legs, but he came at last to walk with glee. Until—" He swallowed convulsively. "Until by mischance Aimil my wife injured him in our home. She turned from the hearth bearing a heavy pot, and Nelbrin our son had walked to stand behind her. The pot struck him upon the chest.

"From that day, he sickened toward death. A dark swelling grew in him, and his life faltered."

"Hemophilia," Linden breathed almost inaudibly. "Poor kid."

Sunder did not stop. "When his death was written upon his face for all to see, the Stonedown invoked judgment. I was commanded to sacrifice him for the good of the people."

A rot gnawed at Covenant's guts. He looked up at the Graveler. The dryness in his throat felt like slow strangulation. He seemed to hear the ground sizzling.

In protest, Linden asked, "Your own son? What did you do?"

Sunder stared out into the Sunbane as if it were the story of his life. "I could not halt his death. The desert sun and the sun of pestilence had left us sorely in need. I shed his life to raise water and food for the Stonedown."

Oh, Sunder! Covenant groaned.

Tightly, Linden demanded, "How did Aimil feel about that?"

"It maddened her. She fought to prevent me—and when she could not, she became wild in her mind. Despair afflicted her, and she—" For a moment, Sunder could not summon the words he needed. Then he went on harshly, "She committed a mortal harm against herself. So that her death would not be altogether meaningless, I shed her also."

So that her— Hellfire! Covenant understood now why the thought of killing his mother had driven Sunder to abandon his home. How many loved ones could a man bear to kill?

Grimly, Linden said, "It wasn't your fault. You did what

you had to do." Passion gathered in her tone. "It's this Sunbane."

The Graveler did not look at her. "All men and women die. It signifies nothing to complain." He sounded as sun-tormented as the Plains. "What else do you desire to know of me? You need only ask. I have no secrets from you."

Covenant ached to comfort Sunder; but he knew nothing about comfort. Anger and defiance were the only answers he understood. Because he could not ease the Stonedownor, he tried to distract him. "Tell me about Nassic." The words were rough in his mouth. "How did he come to have a son?"

Linden glared at Covenant as if she were vexed by his insensitivity; but Sunder relaxed visibly. He seemed relieved by the question—glad to escape the futility of his mourning. "Nassic my father," he said, with a weariness which served as calm, "was like Jous his father, and like Prassan his father's father. He was a man of Mithil Stonedown.

"Jous his father lived in the place he named his temple, and from time to time Nassic visited Jous, out of respect for his father, and also to ascertain that no harm had befallen him. The Stonedown wed Nassic to Kalina, and they were together as any young man and woman. But then Jous fell toward his death. Nassic went to the temple to bear his father to Mithil Stonedown for sacrifice. He did not return. Dying, Jous placed his hands upon Nassic, and the madness or prophecy of the father passed into the son. Thus Nassic was lost to the Stonedown.

"This loss was sore to Kalina my mother. She was ill content with just one son. Many a time, she went to the temple, to give her love to my father and to plead for his. Always she returned weeping and barren. I fear—" He paused sadly. "I fear she hurled herself at Marid hoping to die."

Gradually, Covenant's attention drifted. He was too weak to concentrate. Dimly, he noted the shifting angle of the sun. Noon had come, laying sunlight within inches of his feet. By midafternoon, the shade would be gone. By midafternoon—

He could not survive much more of the sun's direct weight.

The dark clump which he had passed near the shelf was still there. Apparently, it was not a mirage. He blinked at it, trying to make out details. If not a mirage, then what? A bush? What kind of bush could endure this sun, when every other form of life had been burned away?

The question raised echoes in his memory, but he could not hear them clearly. Exhaustion and thirst deafened his mind.

"Die?"

He was hardly aware that he had spoken aloud. His voice felt like sand rubbing against stone. What kind—? He strove to focus his eyes. "That bush." He nodded weakly toward the patch of darkness. "What is it?"

Sunder squinted. "It is *aliantha*. Such bushes may be found in any place, but they are most common near the River. In some way, they defy the Sunbane." He dismissed the subject. "They are a most deadly poison."

"*Poison*?" Pain sliced Covenant's lips; the vehemence of his outcry split them. Blood began to run through the dust like a trail of fury cleaving his chin. Not *aliantha*!

The Graveler reached toward Covenant's face as if those dirty red drops were precious. Empowered by memories, Covenant struck Sunder's hand aside. "Poison?" he croaked. In times past, the rare aliment of *aliantha* had sustained him more often than he could recollect. If they had become poison—! He was abruptly giddy with violence. If they had become poison, then the Land had not simply lost its Earthpower. The Earthpower had been corrupted! He wanted to batter Sunder with his fists. "*How do you know*?"

Linden caught at his shoulder. "Covenant!"

"It is contained in the Rede of the na-Mhoram," rasped Sunder. "I am a Graveler—it is my work to make use of that knowledge. I know it to be true."

No! Covenant grated. "Have you tried it?"

Sunder gaped at him. "No."

"Do you know anybody who ever tried it?"

"It is poison! No man or woman willingly consumes poison."

"Hell and blood." Bracing himself on the stone, Covenant heaved to his feet. "I don't believe it. He can't destroy the entire Law. If he did, the Land wouldn't exist anymore."

The Graveler sprang erect, gripped Covenant's arms, shook him fiercely. "It is *poison*."

Mustering all his passion, Covenant responded, "*No!*"

Sunder's visage knurled as if only the clench of his muscles kept him from exploding. With one wrench of his hands, he thrust Covenant to the ground. "You are mad." His voice was iron and bitterness. "You seduced me from my home, asking

my aid—but at every turn you defy me. You must seek for
Marid. Madness! You must refuse all safety against the Sunbane. Madness! You must decline to raise water, nor permit
me to raise it. Madness! Now nothing will content you but
poison." When Covenant tried to rise, Sunder shoved him
back. "It is enough. Make any further attempt toward the
aliantha, and I will strike you senseless."

Covenant's gaze raged up at the Graveler; but Sunder did
not flinch. Desperation inured him to contradiction; he was
trying to reclaim some control over his doom.

Holding Sunder's rigid stare, Covenant climbed to his feet,
stood swaying before the Graveler. Linden was erect behind
Sunder; but Covenant did not look at her. Softly, he said, "I
do not believe that *aliantha* is poisonous." Then he turned,
and began to shamble toward the bush.

A howl burst from Sunder. Covenant tried to dodge; but
Sunder crashed into him headlong, carried him sprawling to
the dirt. A blow on the back of his head sent lights across his
vision like fragments of vertigo.

Then Sunder fell away. Covenant levered his legs under
him, to see Linden standing over the Graveler. She held him
in a thumblock which pressed him to the ground.

Covenant stumbled to the bush.

His head reeled. He fell to his knees. The bush was pale
with dust and bore little resemblance to the dark green-and-
viridian plant he remembered. But the leaves were holly-like
and firm, though few. Three small fruit the size of blueberries
clung to the branches in defiance of the Sunbane.

Trembling, he plucked one, wiped the dust away to see the
berry's true color.

At the edge of his sight, he saw Sunder knock Linden's feet
away, break free of her.

Gritting his courage, Covenant put the berry in his mouth.

"Covenant!" Sunder cried.

The world spun wildly, then sprang straight. Cool juice
filled Covenant's mouth with a savor of peach made tangy
by salt and lime. At once, new energy burst through him.
Deliciousness cleansed his throat of dirt and thirst and blood.
All his nerves thrilled to a savor he had not tasted for ten long
years: the quintessential nectar of the Land.

Sunder and Linden were on their feet, staring at him.

A sound like dry sobbing came from him. His sight was a

blur of relief and gratitude. The seed dropped from his lips. "Oh, dear God," he murmured brokenly. "There's Earthpower yet."

A moment later, Linden reached him. She helped him to his feet, peered into his face. "Are you—?" she began, then stopped herself. "No, you're all right. Better. I can already see the difference. How—?"

He could not stop shaking. He wanted to hug her; but he only allowed himself to touch her cheek, lift a strand of hair away from her mouth. Then, to answer her, thank her, he plucked another berry, and gave it to her.

"Eat—"

She held it gently, looked at it. Sudden tears overflowed her eyes. Her lower lip trembled as she whispered, "It's the first healthy—" Her voice caught.

"Eat it," he urged thickly.

She raised it to her mouth. Her teeth closed on it.

Slowly, a look of wonder spread over her countenance. Her posture straightened; she began to smile like a cool dawn.

Covenant nodded to tell her that he understood. "Spit out the seed. Maybe another one will grow."

She took the seed in her hand, gazed at it for a moment as if it had been sanctified before she tossed it to the ground.

Sunder had not moved. He stood with his arms clamped across his chest. His eyes were dull with the horror of watching his life become false.

Carefully, Covenant picked the last berry. His stride was almost steady as he went to Sunder. His heart sang: Earthpower!

"Sunder," he said, half insisting, half pleading, "this is *aliantha*. They used to be called treasure-berries—the gift of the Earth to anybody who suffered from hunger or need. This is what the Land was like."

Sunder did not respond. The glazing of his gaze was complete.

"It's not poison," Linden said clearly. "It's immune to the Sunbane."

"Eat it," Covenant urged. "This is why we're here. What we want to accomplish. Health. Earthpower. Eat it."

With a painful effort, Sunder dredged up his answer. "I do not wish to trust you." His voice was a wilderland. "You violate all my life. When I have learned that *aliantha* are not poison, you will seek to teach me that the Sunbane does not exist—that all the life of the Land through all the generations has had no meaning. That the shedding I have done is no less than murder." He swallowed harshly. "But I must. I must find some truth to take the place of the truth you destroy."

Abruptly, he took the berry, put it in his mouth.

For a moment, his soul was naked in his face. His initial anticipation of harm became involuntary delight; his inner world struggled to alter itself. His hands quavered when he took the seed from his mouth. "Heaven and Earth!" he breathed. His awe was as exquisite as anguish. "Covenant—" His jaw worked to form words. "Is this truly the Land—the Land of which my father dreamed?"

"Yes."

"Then he was mad." One deep spasm of grief shook Sunder before he tugged back about him the tattered garment of his self-command. "I must learn to be likewise mad."

Turning away, he went back to the shelf of rock, seated himself in the shade, and covered his face with his hands.

To give Sunder's disorientation at least a degree of privacy, Covenant shifted his attention to Linden. The new lightness of her expression ameliorated her habitual severity, lifted some of her beauty out from under the streaked dust on her face. "Thank you." He began to say, For trying to save my life. Back there in the woods. But he did not want to remember that blow. Instead, he said, "For getting Sunder off me." I didn't know you trusted me that much. "Where did you learn that thumb-hold?"

"Oh, that." Her grin was half grimness, half amusement. "The med school I went to was in a pretty rough neighborhood. The security guards gave self-defense lessons."

Covenant found himself wondering how long it had been since a woman had last smiled at him. Before he could reply, she glanced upward. "We ought to get out of the sun. One treasure-berry apiece isn't going to keep us going very long."

"True." The *aliantha* had blunted his hunger, eased his body's yearning for water, restored a measure of life to his muscles. But it could not make him impervious to the sun. Around him, the Plains swam with heat as if the fabric of the ground were being bleached away fiber by fiber. He rubbed absent-mindedly at the blood on his chin, started toward Sunder.

Linden halted him. "Covenant."

He turned. She stood facing eastward, back over the shelf of rock. Both hands shaded her eyes.

"Something's coming."

Sunder joined them; together, they squinted into the haze. "What the hell—?" Covenant muttered.

At first he saw nothing but heat and pale dirt. But then he glimpsed an erect figure, shimmering darkly in and out of sight.

The figure grew steadier as it approached. Slowly, it became solid, transubstantiating itself like an avatar of the Sunbane. It was a man. He wore the apparel of a Stonedownor.

"Who—?"

"Oh, my God!" Linden gasped.

The man came closer.

Sunder spat, "Marid!"

Marid? An abrupt weakness struck Covenant's knees.

The Sunbane will have no mercy—

The man had Marid's eyes, chancreous with self-loathing, mute supplication, lust. He still wore stakes tied to each of his ankles. His gait was a shambling of eagerness and dread.

He was a monster. Scales covered the lower half of his face; both mouth and nose were gone. And his arms were snakes. Thick scale-clad bodies writhed from his shoulders; serpent-heads gaped where his hands had been, brandishing fangs as white as bone. His chest heaved for air, and the snakes hissed.

Hellfire.

Linden stared at Marid. Nausea distorted her mouth. She was paralyzed, hardly breathing. The sight of Marid's inflicted ill reft her of thought, courage, motion.

"Ah, Marid, my friend," Sunder whispered miserably. "This is the retribution of the Sunbane, which none can foretell. If you were innocent, as the ur-Lord insists—" He groaned in grief. "Forgive me."

But an instant later his voice hardened. "Avaunt, Marid!" he barked. "Ware us! Your life is forfeit here!"

Marid's gaze flinched as if he understood; but he continued to advance, moving purposefully toward the shelf of rock.

"Marid!" Sunder snatched out his poniard. "I have guilt enough in your doom. Do not thrust this upon me."

Marid's eyes shouted a voiceless warning at the Graveler.

Covenant's throat felt like sand; his lungs labored. In the back of his mind, a pulse of outrage beat like lifeblood.

Three steps to his side, Linden stood frozen and appalled.

Hissing voraciously, Marid flung himself into a run. He sprinted to the rock, up the shelf.

For one splinter of time, Covenant could not move. He saw Marid launch himself at Linden, saw fangs reaching toward her face, saw her standing as if her heart had stopped.

Her need snatched Covenant into motion. He took two desperate strides, crashed head and shoulders against her. They tumbled together across the hard dirt.

He disentangled himself, flipped to his feet.

Marid landed heavily, rolling to get his legs under him.

Wielding his knife, Sunder attempted to close with Marid. But a flurry of fangs drove him back.

At once, Marid rushed toward Linden again.

Covenant met the charge. He stopped one serpent head with his right forearm, caught the other scaly body in his left fist.

The free snake reared back to strike.

In that instant, Sunder reached into the struggle. Too swiftly for the snakes to react, he cut Marid's throat. Viscid fluid splashed the front of Covenant's clothes.

Sunder dropped his dead friend. Blood poured into the dirt. Covenant recoiled several steps. As she rose to her knees, Linden gagged as if she were being asphyxiated by the Sunbane.

The Graveler paid no heed to his companions. A frenetic haste possessed him. "Blood," he panted. "Life." He slapped his hands into the spreading pool, rubbed them together, smeared red onto his forehead and cheeks. "At least your death will be of some avail. It is my guilt-gift."

Covenant stared in dismay. He had not known that a human body could be so lavish of blood.

Snatching out the Sunstone, Sunder bent his head to Marid's neck, sucked blood directly from the cut. With the stone held in both palms, he spewed fluid onto it so that it lay cupped in Marid's life. Then he looked upward and began to chant in a language Covenant could not understand.

Around him, the air concentrated as if the heat took personal notice of his invocation. Energy blossomed from the *orcrest*.

A shaft of vermeil as strait as the line between life and death shot toward the sun. It crackled like a discharge of lightning; but it was steady and palpable, sustained by blood.

It consumed the blood in Sunder's hands, drank the blood from Marid's veins, leeched the blood from the earth. Soon every trace of red was gone. Marid's throat gaped like a dry grin.

Still chanting, Sunder set down the Sunstone near Marid's head. The shaft binding the *orcrest* to the sun did not falter.

Almost at once, water bubbled up around the stone. It gathered force until it was a small spring, as fresh and clear as if it arose from mountain rock rather than from barren dust.

As he watched, Covenant's head began to throb. He was flushed and sweating under the weight of the sun.

Still Sunder chanted; and beside the spring, a green shoot raised its head. It grew with staggering celerity; it became a vine, spread itself along the ground, put out leaves. In a moment, it produced several buds which swelled like melons.

The Graveler gestured Linden toward the spring. Her expression had changed from suffocation to astonishment. Moving as if she were entranced, she knelt beside the spring, put her lips into the water. She jerked back at once, surprised by the water's coldness. Then she was drinking deeply, greedily.

A maleficent fire bloomed in Covenant's right forearm. His breathing was ragged. Dust filled his mouth. He could feel his pulse beating in the base of his throat.

After a time, Linden pulled away from the spring, turned to him. "It's good," she said in dim wonder. "It's good."

He did not move, did not look at her. Dread spurted up in him like water from dry ground.

"Come on," she urged. "Drink."

He could not stop staring at Marid. Without shifting his gaze, he extended his right arm toward her.

She glanced at it, then gave a sharp cry and leaped to him, took hold of his arm to look at it closely.

He was loath to see what she saw; but he forced himself to gaze downward.

His forearm was livid. A short way up from his wrist, two puncture marks glared bright red against the darkness of the swelling. "Bastard bit me," he coughed as if he were already dying.

EIGHT: The Corruption of the Sun

"SUNDER!" Linden barked. "Give me your knife."

The Graveler had faltered when he saw the fang marks; and the spring had also faltered. But he recovered quickly, restored the cadence of his chant. The shaft of Sunbane-fire wavered, then grew stable once more. The melons continued to ripen.

Still chanting, he extended his poniard toward Linden. She strode over to him, took the blade. She did not hesitate; all her actions were certain. Stooping to one of Marid's ankles, she cut a section of the rope which bound the stake.

The pain became a hammer in Covenant's forearm, beating as if it meant to crush the bones. Mutely, he gripped the elbow with his left hand, squeezed hard in an effort to restrict the spread of the venom. He did not want to die like this, with all his questions unanswered, and nothing accomplished.

A moment later, Linden returned. Her lips were set in lines of command. When she said, "Sit down," his knees folded as if she held the strings of his will.

She sat in front of him, straightened his arm between them. Deftly, she looped the rope just above his elbow, pulled it tight until he winced; then she knotted it.

"Now," she said evenly, "I'm going to have to cut you. Get out as much of the venom as I can."

He nodded. He tried to swallow, but could not.

She set the point of the blade against the swelling, abruptly snatched it back. Her tone betrayed a glimpse of strain. "Goddamn knife's too dirty."

Frowning, she snapped, "Don't move," and jumped to her feet. Purposefully, she went to the hot red shaft of Sunder's power. He hissed a warning, but she ignored him. With a physician's care, she touched the poniard to the beam.

142

Sparks sprayed from the contact; fire licked along the knife. When she withdrew it, she nodded grimly to herself.

She rejoined Covenant, braced his arm. For a moment, she met his gaze. "This is going to hurt," she said straight into his eyes. "But it'll be worse if I don't do it."

He fought to clear his throat. "Go ahead."

Slowly, deliberately, she cut a deep cross between the fang marks. A scream tore his flesh. He went rigid, but did not permit himself to flinch. This was necessary; he had done such things himself. Pain was life; only the dead felt no pain. He remained still as she bent her head to suck at the incisions. With his free hand, he gripped his forehead, clutching the bones of his skull for courage.

Her hands squeezed the swelling, multiplying fire. Her lips hurt him like teeth as she drew blood and venom into her mouth.

The taste shattered her composure; she spat his blood fiercely at the ground. "God!" she gasped. "What kind—?" At once, she attacked the wound again, sucked and spat with violent revulsion. Her hands shuddered as she gripped his arm.

What kind—? Her words throbbed along the pressure in his head. What was she talking about?

A third time she sucked, spat. Her features strained whitely, like clenched knuckles. With unintended brutality, she dropped his arm; a blaze shot up through his shoulder. Springing to her feet, she stamped on the spat blood, ground it into the dirt as if it were an outrage she wanted to eradicate from the world.

"Linden," he panted wanly through his pain, "what is it?"

"Venom!" She fulminated with repugnance. "What kind of place is this?" Abruptly, she hastened to Sunder's spring, began rinsing her mouth. Her shoulders were knots of abhorrence.

When she returned to Covenant, her whole body was trembling, and her eyes were hollow. "Poison." She hugged herself as if she were suddenly cold. "I don't have words for it. That wasn't just venom. It was something more—something worse. Like the Sunbane. Some kind of moral poison." She pulled her hands through her hair, fighting for control. "God, you're going to be so sick—! You need a hospital. Except there's no antivenin in the world for poison like that."

Covenant whirled in pain, could not distinguish between it and fear. Moral poison? He did not understand her description, but it clarified other questions. It explained why the Raver in Marid had allowed itself to be exposed. So that Marid would be condemned to the Sunbane, would become a monster capable of inflicting such poison. But why? What would Lord Foul gain if Covenant died like this? And why had Marid aimed his attack at Linden? Because she was sensitive to the Land, could see things the Despiser did not want seen?

Covenant could not think. The reek of blood on his shirt filled his senses. Everything became dread; he wanted to wail. But Linden came to his aid. Somehow, she suppressed her own distress. Urging him upright, she supported him to the water so that he could drink. He was already palsied. But his body recognized its need for water; he swallowed thirstily at the spring.

When he was done, she helped him into the shade of the shelf. Then she sat beside him and held his livid arm with her hands, trying in that way to make him comfortable.

Blood dripped unremarked from his cuts. The swelling spread darkness up toward his elbow.

Sunder had been chanting continuously; but now he stopped. He had at last been able to make his invocation briefly self-sustaining. When he fell silent, the *orcrest*'s vermeil shaft flickered and went out, leaving the stone empty, like a hole in the ground; but the spring continued to flow for a few moments. He had time to drink deeply before the water sank back into the barren earth.

With his poniard, he cut the melons from their vine, then bore them into the shade, and sat down on Covenant's left. Unsteadily, he began slicing the melons into sections, scooping out the seeds. The seeds he put away in a pocket of his jerkin. Then he handed sections of melon across to Linden.

"This is *ussusimiel*," he said in a fragile tone, as if he were exhausted and feared contradiction. "At need it will sustain life with no other food." Wearily, he began to eat.

Linden tasted the fruit. She nodded her approval, then started to devour the sections Sunder had given her. Dully, Covenant accepted a piece for himself. But he felt unable to eat. Pain excruciated the bones of his right arm; and that fire seemed to draw all other strength out of him, leaving him to drown in a wide slow whirl of lassitude. He was going to pass out— And there were so many things his companions did not understand.

One was more important than the others. He tried to focus his sight on the Graveler. But he could not keep his vision clear. He closed his eyes so that he would not have to watch the way the Stonedownor blurred and ran.

"Sunder."

"Ur-Lord?"

Covenant sighed, dreading Sunder's reaction. "Listen." He concentrated the vestiges of his determination in his voice. "We can't stay here. I haven't told you where we're going."

"Let it pass," said his guide quietly. "You are harmed and hungry. You must eat. We will consider such questions later."

"Listen." Covenant could feel midnight creeping toward him. He strove to articulate his urgency. "Take me to Revelstone."

"Revelstone?" Sunder exploded in protest. "You wander in your wits. Do you not know that Revelstone is the Keep of the na-Mhoram? Have I not spoken of the Rede concerning you? The Riders journey throughout the Land, commanding your destruction. Do you believe that they will welcome you courteously?"

"I don't care about that." Covenant shook his head, then found that he could not stop. The muscles of his neck jerked back and forth like the onset of hysteria. "That's where the answers are. I've got to find out how this happened." He tried to gesture toward the barrenness; but all his horizons were dark, blinded by dust and dead air. "What the Sunbane is. I can't fight it if I don't know what it is."

"Ur-Lord, it is three hundred leagues."

"I know. But I've got to go. I have to know what happened." He insisted weakly, like a sick child. "So I can fight it."

"Heaven and Earth!" Sunder groaned. "This is the greatest madness of all." For a long moment, he remained still, scouring himself for endurance or wisdom. *Please*, Covenant breathed into the silence. *Sunder. Please.*

Abruptly, the Graveler muttered, "Ah, well. I have no longer any other demand upon me. And you are not to be denied. In the name of Nassic my father—and of Marid my friend, whose life you strove to redeem at your cost—I will guide you where you wish to go. Now eat. Even prophets and madmen require sustenance."

Covenant nodded dimly. Shutting his mind to the smell of blood, he took a bite of the *ussusimiel*.

It could not compare with *aliantha* for taste and potency; but it felt clean in his mouth, and seemed to relieve some of the congestion of his pain. As he ate, the darkness receded somewhat.

After he had consumed his share of the fruit, he settled himself to rest for a while. But Sunder stood up suddenly. "Come," he said to Linden. "Let us be on our way."

"He shouldn't be moved," she replied flatly.

"There will be *aliantha* nigh the River. Perhaps they will have power to aid him."

"Maybe. But he shouldn't be moved. It'll make the venom spread."

"Linden Avery," Sunder breathed. "Marid was my friend. I cannot remain in this place."

Covenant became conscious of a dim fetor in the air. It came from his arm. Or from Marid's corpse.

For a moment, Linden did not respond. Then she sighed, "Give me the knife. He can't travel with his arm like that."

Sunder handed her his poniard. She looked closely at Covenant's swelling. It had grown upward past his elbow. Its black pressure made the rope bite deeply into his arm.

He watched tabidly as she cut away the tourniquet.

Blood rushed at his wound. He cried out.

Then the darkness came over him for a time. He was on his feet, and his arms were hooked over the shoulders of his companions, and they were moving westward. The sun beat at them as if they were an affront to its suzerainty. The air was turgid with heat; it seemed to resist respiration. In all directions, the stone and soil of the Plains shimmered as if they were evaporating. Pain laughed garishly in his head at every step. If Linden or Sunder did not find some kind of febrifuge for him soon—

Linden was on his left now, so that her stumbling would not directly jar his sick arm. Oblivion came and went. When Covenant became aware of the voice, he could not be sure of it. It might have been the voice of a dream.

"And he who wields white wild magic gold
is a paradox—
for he is everything and nothing,
hero and fool,
potent, helpless—
and with the one word of truth or treachery
he will save or damn the Earth
because he is mad and sane,
cold and passionate,
lost and found."

Sunder fell silent. After a moment, Linden asked, "What is that?" She panted the words raggedly.

"A song," said the Graveler. "Nassic my father sang it whenever I became angry at his folly. But I have no understanding of it, though I have seen the white ring, and the wild magic shining with a terrible loveliness."

Terrible, Covenant breathed as if he were dreaming.

Later, Linden said, "Keep talking. It helps— Do you know any other songs?"

"What is life without singing?" Sunder responded. "We have songs for sowing and for reaping—songs to console children during the sun of pestilence—songs to honor those whose blood is shed for the Stonedown. But I have set aside my right to sing them." He made no effort to conceal his bitterness. "I will sing for you one of the songs of a-Jeroth, as it is taught by the Riders of the Clave."

He straightened his shoulders, harrowing Covenant's arm. When he began, his voice was hoarse with dust, short-winded with exertion; but it suited his song.

" 'Oh, come, my love, and bed with me;
Your mate knows neither lust nor heart—
Forget him in this ecstasy.
I joy to play the treacher's part.'
Acute with blandishments and spells
Spoke a-Jeroth of the Seven Hells.

"Diassomer Mininderain,
The mate of might, and Master's wife,
All stars' and heavens' chatelaine,

With power over realm and strife,
Attended well, the story tells,
To a-Jeroth of the Seven Hells.

"With a-Jeroth the lady ran;
Diassomer with fear and dread
Fled from the Master's ruling span.
On Earth she hides her trembling head,
While all about her laughter wells
From a-Jeroth of the Seven Hells.

" 'Forgive!' she cries with woe and pain;
Her treacher's laughter hurts her sore.
'His blandishments have been my bane.
I yearn my Master to adore.'
For in her ears the spurning knells
Of a-Jeroth of the Seven Hells.

"Wrath is the Master—fire and rage.
Retribution fills his hands.
Attacking comes he, sword and gage,
'Gainst treachery in all the lands.
Then crippled are the cunning spells
Of a-Jeroth of the Seven Hells.

"Mininderain he treats with rue;
No heaven-home for broken trust,
But children given to pursue
All treachery to death and dust.
Thus Earth became a gallow-fells
For a-Jeroth of the Seven Hells."

The Graveler sighed. "Her children are the inhabitants of
the Earth. It is said that elsewhere in the Earth—across the
seas, beyond the mountains—live beings who have kept faith.
But the Land is the home of the faithless, and on the descendants of betrayal the Sunbane wreaks the Master's wrath."

Covenant expostulated mutely. He knew as vividly as leprosy that the Clave's view of history was a lie, that the people
of the Land had been faithful against Lord Foul for millennia.
But he could not understand how such a lie had come to be
believed. Time alone did not account for this corruption.

He wanted to deny Sunder's tale. But his swelling had risen

black and febrile halfway to his shoulder. When he tried to find words, the darkness returned.

After a time, he heard Linden say, "You keep mentioning the Riders of the Clave." Her voice was constricted, as if she suffered from several broken ribs. "What do they ride?"

"Great beasts," Sunder answered, "which they name Coursers."

"Horses?" she panted.

"Horses? I do not know this word."

Do not—? Covenant groaned as if the pain in his arm were speaking. Not know the Ranyhyn? He saw a sudden memory in the heat-haze: the great horses of Ra rearing. They had taught him a lesson he could hardly bear about the meaning of fidelity. Now they were gone? Dead? The desecration which Lord Foul had wrought upon the Land seemed to have no end.

"Beasts are few in the Land," Sunder went on, "for how can they endure the Sunbane? My people have herds—some goats, a few cattle—only because large effort is made to preserve their lives. The animals are penned in a cave near the mountains, brought out only when the Sunbane permits.

"But it is otherwise with the Coursers of the Clave. They are bred in Revelstone for the uses of the Riders—beasts of great swiftness and size. It is said that those on their backs are warded from the Sunbane." Grimly, he concluded, "We must evade all such aid if we wish to live."

No Ranyhyn? For a time, Covenant's grief became greater than his pain. But the sun was coquelicot malice in his face, blanching what was left of him. The sleeve of his T-shirt formed a noose around his black arm; and his arm itself on Sunder's shoulder seemed to be raised above him like a mad, involuntary salute to the Sunbane. Even sorrow was leprosy, numb corruption: meaningless and irrefragable. Venom slowly closed around his heart.

Sometime later, the darkness bifurcated, so that it filled his head, and yet he could gaze out at it. He lay on his back, looking at the moon; the shadows of the riverbanks rose on either side. A breeze drifted over him, but it seemed only to fan his fever. The molten lead in his arm contradicted the taste of *aliantha* in his mouth.

His head rested in Linden's lap. Her head leaned against the slope of the watercourse; her eyes were closed; perhaps she slept. But he had lain with his head in a woman's lap once before, and knew the danger. *Of your own volition—* He bared his teeth at the moon. "It's going to kill me." The words threatened to strangle him. His body went rigid, straining against invisible poison. "I'll never give you the ring. Never."

Then he understood that he was delirious. He watched himself, helpless, while he faded in and out of nightmare, and the moon crested overhead.

Eventually, he heard Sunder rouse Linden. "We must journey now for a time," the Graveler said softly, "if we wish to find new *aliantha*. We have consumed all that is here."

She sighed as if the vigil she kept galled her soul.

"Does he hold?" asked Sunder.

She shifted so that she could get to her feet. "It's the *aliantha*," she murmured. "If we keep feeding him—"

Ah, you are stubborn yet. Are stubborn yet stubborn yet.

Then Covenant was erect, crucified across the shoulders of his companions. At first, he suffered under unquiet dreams of Lord Foul, of Marid lying throat-cut beneath an angry sun. But later he grew still, drifted into visionary fields—dew-bedizened leas decked with eglantine and meadow rue. Linden walked among them. She was Lena and Atiaran: strong, and strongly hurt; capable of love; thwarted. And she was Elena, corrupted by a misbegotten hate—child of rape, who destroyed herself to break the Law of Death because she believed that the dead could bear the burdens of the living.

Yet she was none of these. She was herself, Linden Avery, and her touch cooled his forehead. His arm was full of ashes, and his sleeve no longer cut into the swelling. Noon held the watercourse in a vise of heat; but he could breathe, and see. His heart beat unself-consciously. When he looked up at her, the sun made her hair radiant about her head.

"Sunder." Her tone sounded like tears. "He's going to be all right."

"A rare poison, this *aliantha*," the Graveler replied grimly. "For that lie, at least, the Clave must give an accounting."

Covenant wanted to speak; but he was torpid in the heat, infant-weak. He shifted his hips in the sand, went back to sleep.

* * *

When he awakened again, there was sunset above him. He lay with his head on Linden's lap under the west bank of the river, and the sky was streaked with orange and pink, sunlight striking through dust-laden air. He felt brittle as an old bone; but he was lucid and alive. His beard itched. The swelling had receded past his elbow; his forearm had faded from blackness to the lavender of shadows. Even the bruises on his face seemed to have healed. His shirt was long dry now, sparing him the smell of blood.

Dimness obscured Linden's mien; but she was gazing down at him, and he gave her a wan smile. "I dreamed about you."

"Something good, I hope." She sounded like the shadows.

"You were knocking at my door," he said because his heart was full of relief. "I opened it, and shouted, 'Goddamn it, if I wanted visitors I'd post a sign!' You gave me a right cross that almost broke my jaw. It was love at first sight."

At that, she turned her head away as if he had hurt her. His smile fell apart. Immediately, his relief became the old familiar ache of loneliness, isolation made more poignant by the fact that she was not afraid of him. "Anyway," he muttered with a crooked grimace like an apology, "it made sense at the time."

She did not respond. Her visage looked like a helm in the crepuscular air, fortified against any affection or kinship.

A faint distant pounding accentuated the twilight; but Covenant hardly heard it until Sunder leaped suddenly down the east bank into the watercourse. "Rider!" he cried, rushing across the sand to crouch at Linden's side. "Almost I was seen."

Linden coiled under Covenant, poised herself to move. He clambered into a sitting position, fought his heart and head for balance. He was in no condition to flee.

Fright sharpened Linden's whisper. "Is he coming this way?"

"No," replied Sunder quickly. "He goes to Mithil Stonedown."

"Then we're safe?" Already the noise was almost gone.

"No. The Stonedown will tell him of our flight. He will not ignore the escape of the halfhand and the white ring."

Her agitation increased. "He'll come after us?"

"Beyond doubt. The Stonedown will not give pursuit.

Though they have lost the Sunstone, they will fear to encounter Marid. But no such fear will restrain the Rider. At the sun's rising—if not before—he will be ahunt for us." In a tone like a hard knot, he concluded, "We must go."

"Go?" Linden murmured in distraction. "He's still too weak." But an instant later she pulled herself erect. "We'll have to."

Covenant did not hesitate. He extended a hand to Sunder. When the Graveler raised him to his feet, he rested on Sunder's shoulder while frailty whirled in his head, and forced his mouth to shape words. "How far have we come?"

"We are no more than six leagues by the River from Mithil Stonedown," Sunder answered. "See," he said, pointing southward. "It is not far."

Rising there roseate in the sunset were mountain-heads—the west wall of the Mithil valley. They seemed dangerously near. Six! Covenant groaned to himself. In two days. Surely a Rider could cover that distance in one morning.

He turned back to his companions. Standing upright in the waterway, he had better light; he could see them clearly. Loss and self-doubt, knowledge of lies and fear of truth, had burrowed into Sunder's countenance. He had been bereft of everything which had enabled him to accept what he had done to his son, to his wife. In exchange, he had been given a weak driven man who defied him, and a hope no larger than a wedding band.

And Linden, too, was suffering. Her skin had been painfully sunburned. She was caught in a world she did not know and had not chosen, trapped in a struggle between forces she could not comprehend. Covenant was her only link to her own life; and she had almost lost him. Ordinary mortality was not made to meet such demands. And yet she met them and refused even to accept his gratitude. She stored up pain for herself as if no other being had the right to touch her, care about her.

Regret raked at Covenant's heart. He had too much experience with the way other people bore the cost of his actions.

But he accepted it. There was a promise in such pain. It gave him power. With power, he had once wrested meaning for all the blood lost in his name from Lord Foul's worst Despite.

For a moment while his companions waited, trying to contain their haste, he gave himself a VSE. Then he said tightly, "Come on. I can walk," and began to shamble northward along the watercourse.

With the thought of a Rider pressing against his back, he kept his legs in motion for half a league. But the aftermath of the venom had left him tabid. Soon he was forced to ask for help. He turned to Sunder; but the Graveler told him to rest, then scrambled out of the riverbed.

Covenant folded unwillingly to the ground, sat trying to find an answer to the incapacity which clung to his bones. As the moon rose, Sunder returned with a double handful of *aliantha.*

Eating his share of the treasure-berries, Covenant felt new strength flow into him, new healing. He needed water, but his thirst was not acute. When he was done, he was able to regain his feet, walk again.

With the help of frequent rests, more *aliantha*, and support from his companions, he kept moving throughout the night. Darkness lay cool and soothing on the South Plains, as if all the fiery malison of the Sunbane had been swept away, absorbed by the gaps of midnight between the stars. And the sandy bottom of the Mithil made easy going. He drove himself. The Clave had commanded his death. Under the moon, he held his weakness upright; but after moonset, his movements became a long stagger of mortality, dependent and visionless.

They rested before dawn; but Sunder roused them as sunrise drew near. "The doom of the Sunbane approaches," he murmured. "I have seen that your footwear spares you. Yet you will ease my heart if you join me." He nodded toward a broad plane of rock nearby—clean stone large enough to protect a score of people.

Trembling with exhaustion, Covenant tottered to his feet. Together, the companions stood on the rock to meet the day.

When the sun broke the horizon, Sunder let out a cry of exultation. The brown was gone. In its place, the sun wore a coronal of chrysoprase. The light green touch on Covenant's face was balmy and pleasant, like a caress after the cruel pressure of the desert sun.

"A fertile sun!" Sunder crowed. "This will hamper pursuit, even for a Rider." Leaping off the rock as if he had been made young again, he hurried to find a clear patch of sand.

With the haft of his poniard, he plowed two swift furrows across the sand; and in them he planted a handful of his *ussusimiel* seeds. "First we will have food!" he called. "Can water be far behind?"

Covenant turned toward Linden to ask her what she saw in the sun's green. Her face was slack and puffy, untouched by Sunder's excitement; she was pushing herself too hard, demanding too much of her worn spirit. And her eyes were dull, as if she were being blinded by the things she saw—essential things neither Covenant nor Sunder could discern.

He started to frame a question; but then the sunshine snatched his attention away. He gaped at the west bank.

The light had moved partway down the side of the watercourse. And wherever it touched soil, new-green sprouts and shoots thrust into view.

They grew with visible rapidity. Above the rim of the river, a few bushes raised their heads high enough to be seen. Green spread downward like a mantle, following the sun-line cast by the east wall; plants seemed to scurry out of the dirt. More bush tops appeared beyond the bank. Here and there, young saplings reached toward the sky. Wherever the anademed sunlight fell, the wasteland of the past three days became smothered by verdure.

"The fertile sun," Sunder breathed gladly. "None can say when it will rise. But when it rises, it brings life to the Land."

"Impossible," Covenant whispered. He kept blinking his eyes, unconsciously trying to clear his sight, kept staring at the way grass and vines came teeming down the riverbank, at the straight new trees which were already showing themselves beyond the shrubs along the river's edge. The effect was eldritch, and frightening. It violated his instinctive sense of Law. "Impossible."

"Forsooth," chuckled the Graveler. He seemed new-made by the sun. "Do your eyes lack credence? Surely you must now acknowledge that there is truth in the Sunbane."

"Truth—?" Covenant hardly heard Sunder. He was absorbed in his own amazement. "There's still Earthpower— that's obvious. But it was never like this." He felt an intuitive chill of danger. "What's wrong with the Law?" Was that it? Had Foul found some way to destroy the Law itself? The *Law*?

"Often," Sunder said, "Nassic my father sang of Law. But he did not know its import. What is Law?"

Covenant stared sightlessly at the Graveler. "The Law of Earthpower." Fearsome speculations clogged his throat; dread rotted his guts. "The natural order. Seasons. Weather. Growth and decay. What happened to it? What has he done?"

Sunder frowned as if Covenant's attitude were a denial of his gladness. "I know nothing of such matters. The Sunbane I know—and the Rede which the na-Mhoram has given us for our survival. But seasons—Law. These words have no meaning."

No meaning, Covenant groaned. No, of course not. If there were no Law, if there had been no Law for centuries, the Stonedownor could not possibly understand. Impulsively, he turned to Linden. "Tell him what you see."

She appeared not to hear him. She stood at the side of the rock, wearing an aspect of defenseless hebetude.

"Linden!" he cried, driven by his mortal apprehension. "Tell him what you *see*."

Her mouth twisted as if his demand were an act of brutality. She pushed her hands through her hair, glanced up at the green-wreathed sun, then at the green-thick bank.

Shuddering, she permitted herself to see.

Her revulsion was all the answer Covenant needed. It struck him like an instant of shared vision, momentarily gifting or blighting his senses with the acuity they lacked. Suddenly, the long grass and curling vines, the thick bushes, the saplings no longer seemed lush to him. Instead, they looked frenetic, hysterical. They did not spring with spontaneous luxuriance out of the soil; they were forced to grow by the unnatural scourge of the sun. The trees clawed toward the sky like drowners; the creepers writhed along the ground as if they lay on coals; the grass grew as raw and immediate as a shriek.

The moment passed, leaving him shaken.

"It's wrong." Linden rubbed her arms as if what she saw made her skin itch like an infestation of lice. The redness of her sunburn aggravated all her features. "Sick. Evil. It's not supposed to be like this. It's killing me." Abruptly, she sat down, hid her face in her hands. Her shoulders clenched as if she did not dare to weep.

Covenant started to ask, Killing you? But Sunder was already shouting.

"Your words signify nothing! This is the fertile sun! It is

not *wrong*. It simply *is*. Thus the Sunbane has been since the punishment began. Behold!"

He stabbed a gesture toward the sandy patch in which he had planted his seeds. The sun-line lay across one of his furrows. In the light, *ussusimiel* were sprouting.

"Because of this, we will have food! The fertile sun gives life to all the Land. In Mithil Stonedown—now, while you stand thus decrying wrong and ill—every man, woman, and child sings. All who have strength are at labor. While the fertile sun holds, they will labor until they fall from weariness. Searching first to discover places where the soil is of a kind to support crops, then striving to clear that ground so seeds may be planted. Thrice in this one day, crops will be planted and harvested, thrice each day of the fertile sun.

"And if people from another Stonedown come upon this place, seeking proper soil for themselves, then there will be killing until one Stonedown is left to tend the crops. And the people will *sing*! The fertile sun is life! It is fiber for rope and thread and cloth, wood for tools and vessels and fire, grain for food, and for the *metheglin* which heals weariness. Speak not to me of wrong!" he cried thickly. But then his passion sagged, leaving him stooped and sorrowful. His arms hung at his sides as if in betraying his home he had given up all solace. "I cannot bear it."

"Sunder." Covenant's voice shook. How much longer could he endure being the cause of so much pain? "That isn't what I meant."

"Then enlighten me," the Graveler muttered. "Comfort the poverty of my comprehension."

"I'm trying to understand your life. You endure so much— just being able to sing is a victory. But that isn't what I meant." He gripped himself so that his anger would not misdirect itself at Sunder. "This isn't a punishment. The people of the Land aren't criminals—betrayers. No!" *I have been preparing retribution*. "Your lives aren't wrong. The Sunbane is wrong. It's an evil that's being done to the Land. I don't know how. But I know who's responsible. Lord Foul—you call him a-Jeroth. It's his doing.

"Sunder, he can be fought. Listen to me." He appealed to the scowling Graveler. "He can be fought."

Sunder glared at Covenant, clinging to ideas, perceptions, he could understand. But after a moment he dropped his gaze.

When he spoke, his words were a recognition. "The fertile sun is also perilous, in its way. Remain upon the safety of the rock while you may." With his knife, he went to clean away grass and weeds from around his vines.

Ah, Sunder, Covenant sighed. You're braver than I deserve.

He wanted to rest. Fatigue made the bones of his skull hurt. The swelling of his forearm was gone now; but the flesh was still deeply bruised, and the joints of his elbow and wrist ached. But he held himself upright, turned to face Linden's mute distress.

She sat staring emptily at nothing. Pain dragged her mouth into lines of failure, acutely personal and forlorn. Her hands gripped her elbows, hugging her knees, as if she strove to anchor herself on the stiff mortality of her bones.

Looking at her, he thought he recognized his own first ordeals in the Land. He made an effort to speak gently. "It's all right. I understand."

He meant to add, Don't let it overwhelm you. You're not alone. There are reasons for all this. But her reply stopped him. "No, you don't." She did not have even enough conviction for bitterness. "You can't see."

He had no answer. The flat truth of her words denied his empathy, left him groping within himself as if he had lost all his fingers. Defenseless against his incapacity, his responsibility for burdens he was unable to carry, he sank to the stone, stretched out his tiredness. She was here because she had tried to save his life. He yearned to give her something in return, some help, protection, ease. Some answer to her own severity. But there was nothing he could do. He could not even keep his eyes open.

When he looked up again, the growth on both sides of the watercourse, and down the west bank to the edge of the rock, had become alarmingly dense. Some of the grass was already knee-deep. He wondered how it would be possible to travel under such a sun. But he left that question to Sunder.

While melon buds ripened on his vines, the Graveler occupied himself by foraging for wild creepers. These he cut into strands. When he was satisfied with what he had gathered, he returned to the rock, and began knotting and weaving the vines to form a mesh sack.

By the time he had finished this chore, the first of the *ussusimiel* were ripe. He sectioned them, stored the seeds in his pocket, then meted out rations to his companions. Covenant accepted his share deliberately, knowing his body's need for aliment. But Sunder had to nudge Linden's shoulder to gain her attention. She frowned at the *ussusimiel* as if it were unconscionable, received it with a look of gall.

When they had eaten, Sunder picked the rest of the melons and put them in his sack. He appeared to be in a lighter mood; perhaps his ability to provide food had strengthened his sense of how much he was needed; or perhaps he was now less afraid of pursuit. Firmly, he announced, "We must leave the riverbed. We will find no water here." He nodded toward the east bank. "At first it will be arduous. But as the trees mount, they will shade the ground, slowing the undergrowth. But mark me—I have said that the fertile sun is perilous. We must travel warily, lest we fall among plants which will not release us. While this sun holds, we will sojourn in daylight, sleeping only at night."

Covenant rubbed lightly at the scabs on his forearm, eyed the rim of the bank. "Did you say water?"

"As swiftly as strength and chance permit."

Strength, Covenant muttered. Chance. He lacked one, and did not trust the other. But he did not hesitate. "Let's go."

Both men looked at Linden.

She rose slowly to her feet. She did not raise her eyes; but she nodded mutely.

Sunder glanced a question at Covenant; but Covenant had no answer. With a shrug, the Graveler lifted his sack to his shoulder and started down the river bottom. Covenant followed, with Linden behind him.

Sunder avoided the grass and weeds as much as possible until he reached a place where the sides were less steep. There he dug his feet into the dirt, and scrambled upward.

He had to burrow through the underbrush which lipped the slope to gain level ground. Covenant watched until the Graveler disappeared, then attempted the climb himself. Handholds on long dangling clumps of grass aided his ascent. After a moment of slippage, he crawled into Sunder's burrow.

Carefully, he moved along the tunnel of bracken and brush which Sunder had brunted clear. The teeming vegetation made progress difficult; he could not rise above his hands and knees. He felt enclosed by incondign verdancy, a savage ecstasy of growth more insidious than walls, and more stifling. He could not control the shudders of his muscles.

Crawling threatened to exhaust him; but after some distance, the tunnel ended. Sunder had found an area where the bracken was only waist-high, shaded by a crowded young copse of wattle. He was stamping down the brush to make a clearing when Covenant and then Linden caught up with him.

"We are fortunate," Sunder murmured, nodding toward one of the nearest trees. It was a new mimosa nearly fifteen feet tall; but it would not grow any more; it was being strangled by a heavy creeper as thick as Covenant's thigh. This plant had a glossy green skin, and it bore a cluster of yellow-green fruit which vaguely resembled papaya. "It is *mirkfruit*."

Mirkfruit? Covenant wondered, remembering the narcoleptic pulp with which he and Linden had been captured by Mithil Stonedown. "How is that fortunate?"

Sunder took out his knife. "The fruit is one matter, the vine another." Drawing Covenant with him, he stepped toward the creeper, gripped his poniard in both hands. "Stand ready," he warned. Then he leaped upward and spiked his blade into the plant above the level of his head.

The knife cut the vine like flesh. When Sunder snatched back his blade, clear water gushed from the wound.

In his surprise, Covenant hesitated.

"Drink!" snapped Sunder. Brusquely, he thrust Covenant under the spout.

Then Covenant was gulping at water that splashed into his face and mouth. It was as fresh as night air.

When he had satisfied his body's taut thirst, Linden took his place, drank as if she were frantic for something, anything, which did not exacerbate the soreness of her nerves. Covenant feared the vine would run dry. But after she stepped aside, Sunder was able to drink his fill before the stream began to slacken.

While the water lasted, the companions used it to wash their hands and faces, sluice some of the dust from their clothes. Then the Graveler shouldered his sack. "We must continue. Nothing motionless is free of hazard under this sun." To demonstrate his point, he kicked his feet, showed how the grass tried to wind around his ankles. "And the Rider will be abroad. We will journey as near the Mithil as soil and sun allow."

He gestured northward. In that direction, beyond the shade of the copse, lay a broad swath of raw gray grass, chest-high and growing. But then the grass faded into a stand of trees, an incongruous aggregation of oak and sycamore, eucalyptus and jacaranda. "There is great diversity in the soil," Sunder explained, "and the soil grows what is proper to it. I cannot foresee what we will encounter. But we will strive to stay among trees and shade." Scanning the area as if he expected to see signs of the Rider, he began to breast his way through the thick grass.

Covenant followed unsteadily, with Linden at his back.

By the time they neared the trees, his arms were latticed with fine scratches from the rough blades; and the grass itself waved above his head.

But later, as Sunder had predicted, the shade of the trees held the undergrowth to more natural proportions. And these trees led to a woodland even more heavily shadowed by cypress, flowering mulberry, and a maple-like tree with yellow leaves which Covenant recognized poignantly as Gilden. The sight of these stately trees, which the people of the Land had once treasured so highly, now being grown like puppets by the Sunbane, made ire pound like vertigo in the bones of his forehead.

He turned to share his outrage with Linden. But she was consumed by her own needs, and did not notice him. Her gaze was haunted by misery; her eyes seemed to wince away from everything around her, as if she could not blind herself to the screaming of the trees. Neither she nor Covenant had any choice but to keep moving.

Shortly after noon, Sunder halted in a bower under a dense willow. There the companions ate a meal of *ussusimiel*. Then, half a league farther on, they came across another *mirkfruit* creeper. These things sustained Covenant against his convalescent weakness. Nevertheless, he reached the end of his stamina by midafternoon. Finally, he dropped to the ground, allowed himself to lie still. All his muscles felt like mud; his head wore a vise of fatigue that constricted his sight and balance. "That's enough," he mumbled. "I've got to rest."

"You cannot," the Graveler said. He sounded distant. "Not until the sun's setting—or until we have found barren ground."

"He has to," panted Linden. "He hasn't got his strength back. He still has that poison in him. He could relapse."

After a moment, Sunder muttered, "Very well. Remain with him—ward him. I will search for a place of safety." Covenant heard the Graveler stalking away through the brush.

Impelled by Sunder's warning, Covenant crawled to the shade of a broad Gilden trunk, seated himself against the bark. For a short time, he closed his eyes, floated away along the wide rolling of his weariness.

Linden brought him back to himself. She must have been tired, but she could not rest. She paced back and forth in front of him, gripping her elbows with her hands, shaking her head as if she were arguing bitterly with herself. He watched for a moment, tried to squeeze the fatigue from his sight. Then he said carefully, "Tell me what's the matter."

"That's the worst." His request triggered words out of her; but she replied to herself rather than to him. "It's all terrible, but that's the worst. What kind of tree is that?" She indicated the trunk against which he sat.

"It's called a Gilden." Spurred by memories, he added, "The wood used to be considered very special."

"It's the worst." Her pacing tightened. "Everything's hurt. In such pain—" Tremors began to scale upward in her voice. "But that's the worst. All the Gilden. They're on fire inside. Like an auto-da-fé." Her hands sprang to cover the distress on her face. "They ought to be put out of their misery."

Put out of—? The thought frightened him. Like Sunder's mother? "Linden," he said warily, "tell me what's the matter."

She spun on him in sudden rage. "Are you deaf as well as blind? Can't you feel anything? I said they're in pain! They ought to be put out of their misery!"

"No." He faced her fury without blinking. That's what Kevin did. The Land's need broke his heart. So he invoked the Ritual of Desecration, trying to extirpate evil by destroying what he loved. Covenant winced to remember how close he had come to walking that path himself. "You can't fight Lord Foul that way. That's just what he wants."

"Don't tell me that!" she spat at him. "I don't want to hear it. You're a leper. Why should you care about pain? Let the whole world scream! It won't make any difference to you." Abruptly, she flung herself to the ground, sat against a tree with her knees raised to her chest. "I can't take any more." Suppressed weeping knurled her face. She bowed her head, sat with her arms outstretched and rigid across her knees. Her hands curled into fists, clinging futilely to thin air. "I can't."

The sight of her wrung his heart. "Please," he breathed. "Tell me why this hurts you so much."

"I can't shut it out." Hands, arms, shoulders—every part

of her was clenched into a rictus of damned and demanding passion. "It's all happening to me. I can see—feel—the trees. In me. It's too personal. I can't take it. It's killing me."

Covenant wanted to touch her, but did not dare. She was too vulnerable. Perhaps she would be able to feel leprosy in the contact of his fingers. For a moment, he grappled with a desire to tell her about Kevin. But she might hear that story as a denial of her pain. Yet he had to offer her something.

"Linden," he said, groaning inwardly at the arduousness of what he meant to say, "when he summoned us here, Foul spoke to me. You didn't hear him. I'm going to tell you what he said."

Her hands writhed; but she made no other reply. After a difficult moment, he began to repeat the Despiser's cold scorn.

Ah, you are stubborn yet.

He remembered every word of it, every drop of venom, every inflection of contempt. The memory came upon him like a *geas*, overwhelming his revulsion, numbing his heart. Yet he did not try to stop. He wanted her to hear it all. Since he could not ease her, he tried to share his sense of purpose.

You will be the instrument of my victory.

As the words fell on her, she coiled into herself—curled her arms around her knees, buried her face against them—shrank from what he was saying like a child in terror.

There is despair laid up for you here beyond anything your petty mortal heart can bear.

Yet throughout his recitation he felt that she hardly heard him, that her reaction was private, an implication of things he did not know about her. He half expected her to break out in keening. She seemed so bereft of the simple instinct for solace. She could have sustained herself with anger at the Despiser, as he did; but such an outlet seemed to have no bearing on her complex anguish. She sat folded trembling into herself, and made no sound.

Finally, he could no longer endure watching her. He crawled forward as if he were damning himself, and sat beside her. Firmly, he pried her right hand loose from its clinch, placed his halfhand in her grip so that she could not let go of his maimed humanity unless she released her hold on herself. "Lepers aren't numb," he said softly. "Only the body gets numb. The rest compensates. I want to help you, and I don't know how." Through the words, he breathed, Don't hurt yourself like this.

Somehow, the touch of his hand, or the empathy in his voice, reached her. As if by a supreme act of will, she began to relax her muscles, undo the knots of her distress. She drew a shuddering breath, let her shoulders sag. But still she clung to his hand, held the place of his lost fingers as if that amputation were the only part of him she could understand.

"I don't believe in evil." Her voice seemed to scrape through her throat, come out smeared with blood. "People aren't like that. This place is *sick*. Lord Foul is just something you made up. If you can blame sickness on somebody, instead of accepting it for what it is, then you can avoid being responsible for it. You don't have to try to end the pain." Her words were an accusation; but her grip on his hand contradicted it. "Even if this is a dream."

Covenant could not answer. If she refused to admit the existence of her own inner Despiser, how could he persuade her? And how could he try to defend her against Lord Foul's manipulations? When she abruptly disengaged her hand, rose to her feet as if to escape the implications of his grasp, he gazed after her with an ache of loneliness indistinguishable from fear in his heart.

NINE: River-Ride

A SHORT time later, Sunder returned. If he noticed Linden's tension as she stood there pale and absolute with her back to Covenant, he did not ask for any explanation. Quietly, he announced that he had found a place where they could rest safely until the next morning. Then he offered Covenant his hand.

Covenant accepted the help, let himself be pulled to his feet. His muscles felt like ashes in his limbs; but by leaning on Sunder's shoulder he was able to travel another half a league to reach a stretch of rock. It was hidden among high brush, which provided at least some protection against discovery. Reclining on the rough stone, Covenant went to sleep for the remainder of the afternoon. After a supper of *ussusimiel*, he surprised himself by sleeping throughout the night.

In spite of the hardness of his bed, he did not awaken until shortly after sunrise. By that time, Sunder had already cleared a patch of ground and planted a new crop of melons.

When Covenant arose, Linden joined him. Avoiding his gaze as if she could not tolerate the sight of his thoughts, his concern for her, his countervailing beliefs, she examined him mutely, then pronounced him free of fever, fit to travel. Something she saw disturbed her, but she did not say what it was, and he did not ask.

As soon as Sunder's new crop was ripe, he replenished his stock of seeds and refilled his sack of melons. Then he led Covenant and Linden away into the brush.

The Mithil River had turned toward the northwest, and they continued to follow its course as closely as the terrain permitted. Initially, their progress was slow; their way traversed a tangle of ground-ivy which threatened to baffle even the Graveler's strength. But beyond the ivy they entered a deep forest of banyan trees, and walking became easier.

The second day of the fertile sun raised the banyans to heights far beyond anything Covenant would have believed possible. Huge avenues and galleries lay between the trunks; the prodigious intergrown branches arched and stretched like the high groined ceiling and towering pillars of a place of reverence in Revelstone—or like the grand cavern of Earthroot under *Melenkurion* Skyweir. But the effect was ominous rather than grand. Every bough and trunk seemed to be suffering under its own weight.

Several times, Covenant thought he heard a rumble of hooves in the distance, though he saw nothing.

The next day, the companions met some of the consequences of the sun's necrotic fecundity. By midmorning, they found themselves struggling through an area which, just the day before, had been a stand of cedars many hundreds of feet tall. But now it looked like the scene of a holocaust.

Sometime during the night, the trees had started to topple; and each falling colossus had chopped down others. Now the entire region was a chaos of broken timber—trunks and branches titanically rent, splintered, crushed. The three companions spent the whole day wrestling with the ruins.

Near sunset, they won through to a low hillside of heather,

seething in the breeze and twice their height. Sunder attacked the wrist-thick stems with his poniard, and eventually succeeded in clearing an area large enough for them to lie down. But even then he could not rest; he was taut with anxiety. While they ate, Covenant made no comment; and Linden, wrapped in her privacy, seemed unaware of the Graveler. But later Covenant asked him what troubled him.

Grimly, Sunder replied, "I have found no stone. The moon wanes, and will not penetrate this heather sufficiently to aid my search. I know not how to avoid Marid's fate."

Covenant considered for a moment, then said, "I'll carry you. If I'm protected, you ought to be safe, too."

The Graveler acceded with a stiff shrug. But still he did not relax. Covenant's suggestion violated a lifetime of ingrained caution. Quietly, Covenant said, "I think you'll be all right. I was right about the *aliantha*, wasn't I?"

Sunder responded by settling himself for sleep. But when Covenant awakened briefly during the night and looked about him, he saw the Graveler staring up into the darkness of the heather like a man bidding farewell to the use of his eyes.

The companions rose in the early gray of dawn. Together, they moved through the heather until they found a thinning through which they could glimpse the eastern horizon. The breeze had become stronger and cooler since the previous evening. Covenant felt a low chill of apprehension. Perhaps he and Linden had not been protected by their footwear; perhaps they were naturally immune to the Sunbane. In that case—

They had no time to search for alternatives. Sunrise was imminent. Linden took the sack of melons. Covenant stooped to let Sunder mount his back. Then they faced the east. Covenant had to compel himself not to hold his breath.

The sun came up flaring azure, blue-clad in an aura of sapphire. It shone for only a moment. Then black clouds began to roll westward like the vanguard of an attack.

"The sun of rain." With an effort, Sunder ungnarled his fingers from Covenant's shoulders and dropped to the ground. "Now," he rasped against the constriction of his chest, "we will at last begin to travel with some swiftness. If we do not foil pursuit altogether, we will at least prolong our lives."

At once, he turned toward the River, started plunging hurriedly through the heather as if he were racing the clouds.

Covenant faced Linden across the rising wind. "Is he all right?"

"Yes," she replied impatiently. "Our shoes block the Sunbane." When he nodded his relief, she hastened after Sunder.

The heather spread westward for some distance, then changed abruptly into a thicket of knaggy bushes as tall as trees along the riverbank. The clouds were overhead, and a few raindrops had begun to spatter out of the sky, as Sunder forged into the high brush. While he moved, he hacked or broke off stout branches nearly eight feet along, cut loose long sections of creeper. These he dragged with him through the thicket. When he had collected all he could manage, he gave the branches and vines to his companions, then gathered more wood of the same length.

By the time they came in sight of the riverbed, only a small strip of sky remained clear in the west.

Sunder pressed forward to the edge of the bank. There he prepared a space in which he could work. Obeying his terse orders, though they did not know what he had in mind, Covenant and Linden helped him strip his vines and branches of twigs and leaves. Then they put all the wood together lengthwise, and Sunder lashed it into a secure bundle with the vines. When he was done, he had a tight stack thicker than the reach of his arms.

Wind began to rip the top of the thicket. Heavy drops slapped against the leaves, producing a steady drizzle within the brush. But Sunder appeared to have forgotten his haste. He sat down and did what he could to make himself comfortable.

After a moment, Covenant asked, "Now what?"

Sunder looked at him, at Linden. "Are you able to swim?"

They both nodded.

"Then we will await the rising of the River."

Covenant blinked the water out of his eyes. Damnation, he muttered. A raft.

The idea was a good one. The current of the Mithil would provide a faster pace than anything they could hope to match by traveling overland. And Sunder's raft would give them something to hold onto so that they did not exhaust themselves. The Graveler had been in such a hurry because the chore of making even this small raft would have been far more difficult under the full weight of the rain. Covenant nodded to himself. Sunder was a more resourceful guide than he deserved.

Linden seated herself near the raft and folded her arms over her knees. In a flat voice, she said, "It's going to be cold."

That was true; the rain was already chilly. But Covenant ignored it, moved to look down into the river bottom.

The sight made him dubious. The bed was choked with growth almost to the level of the rim. He did not know how long the water would take to rise; but when it did, the trees and brush would make it extremely hazardous.

As Sunder handed out rations of *ussusimiel*, Covenant continued studying the watercourse. The downpour was hard and flat now, beating into the brush as steadily as a waterfall, and the air darkened gradually; but he could see well enough to make out the first muddy stirrings of the River. Initially, he feared that the water would rise too slowly. But the thicket had caused him to underestimate the force of the storm. The torrents fell heavily—and more heavily moment by moment. The rain sounded like a great beast thrashing in the brush.

The water began to run more rapidly. Moiling like a current of snakes, the stream slipped between the trees, rushed slapping and gurgling through the shrubs. All this region of the South Plains drained into the watercourse. Covenant had barely finished his meal when a sudden change came over the flow. Without warning, the current seemed to leap upward, forward, like a pouncing predator; and some of the bushes shifted.

They were shallow-rooted. The stream tugged them free. They caught promptly in the limbs of the trees, hung there like desperation in the coils of the current. But the water built up against them. The trees themselves started to topple.

Soon uprooted trunks and branches thronged the River, beating irresistibly downstream. The water seethed with the force of an avalanche. Rain crashed into the Mithil, and it rose and ran avidly. Foot by foot, it swept itself clean.

The current was more than halfway up the banks when Sunder got to his feet. He spent a moment ensuring that his few possessions were secure, then stooped to the raft, lashed the sack of melons tightly to the wood.

A spasm of fear twisted Covenant's chest. "It's too dangerous!" he shouted through the noise of the rain. "We'll be battered to pieces!" I'm a leper!

"No!" Sunder returned. "We will ride with the current—with the trees! If the hazard surpasses you, we must wait! The River will not run clear until the morrow!"

Covenant thought about the Rider, about beings he had encountered who could sense the presence of white gold. Before he could respond, Linden barked, "I'll go crazy if I have to spend my time sitting here!"

Sunder picked up one end of the raft. "Cling to the wood, lest we become lost to each other!"

At once, she bent to the other end of the bundle, locked her hands among the branches, lifted them.

Cursing silently, Covenant placed himself beside her and tried to grip the wet branches. The numbness of his fingers threatened to betray him; he could not be sure of his hold.

"We must move as one!" Sunder warned. "Out into the center!"

Covenant growled his understanding. He wanted to pause for a VSE. The watercourse looked like an abyss to his ready vertigo.

The next moment, Sunder yelled, "Now!" and hurled himself toward the edge.

Hellfire! The raft yanked at Covenant as Sunder and Linden heaved it forward. He lurched into motion.

Sunder sprang for the water. The raft dove over the bank. Covenant's grip tore him headlong past the edge. With a shattering jolt, he smashed into the water.

The impact snatched his inadequate fingers from the raft. The Mithil swept him away and down. He whirled tumbling along the current, lost himself in turbulence and suffocation. An instant of panic made his brain as dark as the water. He flailed about him without knowing how to find the surface.

Then a bush still clinched to its roots struck his leg a stinging blow. It righted him. He clawed upward.

With a gasp that made no sound, he broke water.

Amid the tumult of the rain, he was deaf to everything except air and fear, the current shoving at his face, and the gelid fire of the water. The cold stunned his mind.

But a frantic voice was howling, "Covenant!"

The urgency of Linden's cry reached him. Fighting the drag of his boots, he surged head and shoulders out of the racing boil, scanned the darkness.

Before he plunged underwater again, he caught a glimpse of the raft.

It was nearby, ten feet farther downriver. As he regained the surface, he struck out along the current.

An arm groped for him. He kicked forward, grabbed at Linden's wrist with his half-hand. His numb fingers could not hold. Water closed over his head.

Her hand clamped onto his forearm, heaved him toward the raft. He grappled for one of the branches and managed to fasten himself to the rough bark.

His weight upset Sunder's control of the raft. The bundle began to spin. Covenant had an impression of perilous speed. The riverbanks were only a vague looming; they seethed past him as he hurtled along the watercourse.

"Are you all right?" Linden shouted.

"Yes!"

Together, they battled the cold water, helped Sunder right the raft's plunging.

The rain deluged them, rendered them blind and mute. The current wrestled constantly for mastery of the raft. Repeatedly, they had to thrash their way out of vicious backwaters and fend off trees which came beating down the River like triremes. Only the width of the Mithil prevented logjams from developing at every bend.

And the water was cold. It seemed to suck at their muscles, draining their strength and warmth. Covenant felt as if his bones were being filled with ice. Soon he could hardly keep his head above water, hardly hold onto the wood.

But as the River rose, its surface gradually grew less turbulent. The current did not slow; but the increase of water blunted the moiling effect of the uneven bottom and banks. The raft became easier to manage. Then, at Sunder's instructions, the companions began to take turns riding prone on the raft while the other two steered, striving to delay the crisis of their exhaustion.

Later, the water became drinkable. It still left a layer of grit on Covenant's teeth; but rain and runoff slowly macerated the mud, clarifying the Mithil.

He began to hear an occasional dull booming like the sounds of battle. It was not thunder; no lightning accompanied it. Yet it broke through the loud water-sizzle of the rain.

Without warning, a sharp splintering rent the air. A monstrous shadow hove above him. At the last instant, the current rushed the raft out from under the fall of an immense tree.

Too tall for its roots, overburdened by the weight of the storm, the tree had riven its moorings and toppled across the River.

Now Covenant heard the same rending everywhere, near and far. The Mithil traversed a region of megalithic trees; the clamor of their destruction broke and boomed incessantly.

He feared that one of them would strike the raft or dam the River. But that did not happen. The trees which landed in the Mithil occluded the current without blocking it. And then the noise of their ruin receded as the River left that region behind.

Rain continued to fall like the collapse of the sky. Covenant placed himself at one end of the raft and used the weight of his boots to steady its course. Half paralyzed with cold, he and his companions rode through a day that seemed to have no measure and no end. When the rain began to dwindle, that fact could not penetrate his dogged stupor. As the clouds rolled back from the east, uncovering the clear heavens of evening, he gaped at the open air as if it spoke a language which had become alien to him.

Together, the companions flopped like dying fish to the riverbank, crawled out of the water. Somehow, Sunder mustered the strength to secure the raft against the rising of the River. Then he joined Covenant and Linden in the wind-shelter of a copse of preternatural gorse, and slumped to the ground. The teeming black clouds slid away to the west; and the sun set, glorious with orange and red. The gloaming thickened toward night.

"Fire." Linden's voice quivered; she was trembling from head to foot. "We've got to have a fire."

Covenant groaned his mind out of the mud on which he lay, raised his head. Long vibrations of cold ran through him; shivers knotted his muscles. The sun had not shone on the Plains all day, and the night was as clear as perfect ice.

"Yes," Sunder said through locked teeth. "We must have fire."

Fire. Covenant winced to himself. He was too cold to feel anything except dread. But the need was absolute. And he could not bear to think of blood. To forestall the Graveler, he struggled to his hands and knees, though his bones seemed to clatter together. "I'll do it."

They faced each other. The silence between them was

marked only by the chill breeze rubbing its way through the
copse, and by the clenched shudder of breathing. Sunder's
expression showed that he did not trust Covenant's strength,
did not want to set aside his responsibility for his companions.
But Covenant kept repeating inwardly, You're not going to
cut yourself for me, and did not relent. After a moment,
Sunder handed him the *orcrest*.

Covenant accepted it with his trembling half-hand, placed it
in contact with his ring, glared at it weakly. But then he
faltered. Even in ten years, he had not been able to unlearn
his instinctive fear of power.

"Hurry," Linden whispered.

Hurry? He covered his face with his left hand, striving to
hide his ague. Bloody hell. He lacked the strength. The *orcrest*
lay inert in his fist; he could not even concentrate on it. You
don't know what you're asking.

But the need was indefeasible. His anger slowly tightened.
He became rigid, clenched against the chills. He indistinguishable from pain or exhaustion shaped itself to the circle of his
ring. The Sunstone had no life; the white gold had no life. He
gave them his life. There was no other answer.

Cursing silently, he hammered his fist at the mud.

White light burst in the *orcrest*: flame sprang from his ring
as if the metal were a band of silver magma. In an instant, his
whole hand was ablaze.

He raised his fist, brandished fire like a promise of retribution against the Sunbane. Then he dropped the Sunstone. It
went out; but his ring continued to spout flame. In a choking
voice, he gasped, "Sunder!"

At once, the Graveler gave him a dead gorse-branch. He
grasped the wet bark in his half-hand: his arm shook as he
squeezed white flame into the wood. When he set it down, it
was afire.

Sunder supplied more wood, then knelt to tend the weak
fire. Covenant set flame to the second branch, to a third and
fourth. Sunder fed the burning with leaves and twigs, blew
carefully on the flames. After a moment, he announced, "It is
enough."

With a groan, Covenant let his mind fall blank, and the
blaze of his ring plunged into darkness. Night closed over the
copse, huddled around the faint yellow light and smoke of
the fire.

Soon he began to feel heat on his face.

Sagging within himself, he tried to estimate the consequences of what he had done, measure the emotional umbrage
of power.

Shortly, the Graveler recovered his sack of melons from the
raft, and dealt out rations of *ussusimiel*. Covenant felt too
empty to eat; but his body responded without his volition. He
sat like an effigy, with wraiths of moisture curling upward
from his clothes, and looked dumbly at the inanition of his
soul.

When she finished her meal, Linden threw the rinds away.
Staring into the flames, she said remotely, "I don't think I can
take another day of this."

"Is there choice?" Fatigue dulled Sunder's eyes. He sat
close to the heat, as if his bones were thirsty for warmth.
"The ur-Lord aims toward Revelstone. Very well. But the
distance is great. Refusing the aid of the River, we must
journey afoot. To gain the Keep of the na-Mhoram would
require many turnings of the moon. But I fear we would not
gain it. The Sunbane is too perilous. And there is the matter
of pursuit."

The set of Linden's shoulders showed her apprehension.
After a moment, she asked tightly, "How much longer?"

The Graveler sighed. "None can foretell the Sunbane," he
said in a dim voice. "It is said that in generations past each
new sun shone for five and six, even as many as seven days.
But a sun of four days is now uncommon. And with my own
eyes I have beheld only one sun of less than three."

"Two more days," Linden muttered. "Dear God."

For a while, they were silent. Then, by tacit agreement,
they both arose to gather wood for the fire. Scouring the
copse, they collected a substantial pile of brush and branches.
After that, Sunder stretched out on the ground. But Linden
remained sitting beside the fire. Slowly, Covenant noticed
through his numbness that she was studying him.

In a tone that seemed deliberately inflectionless, she asked,
"Why does it bother you to use your ring?"

His ague had abated, leaving only a vestigial chill along his
bones. But his thoughts were echoes of anger. "It's hard."

"In what way?" In spite of its severity, her expression said
that she wanted to understand. Perhaps she needed to understand. He read in her a long history of self-punishment. She

was a physician who tormented herself in order to heal others, as if the connection between the two were essential and compulsory.

To the complexity of her question, he gave the simplest answer he knew. "Morally."

For a moment, they regarded each other, tried to define each other. Then, unexpectedly, the Graveler spoke. "There at last, ur-Lord," he murmured, "you have uttered a word which lies within my comprehension." His voice seemed to arise from the wet wood and the flames. "You fear both strength and weakness, both power and lack of power. You fear to be in need—and to have your need answered. As do I.

"I am a Graveler—well acquainted with such fear. A Stonedown trusts the Graveler for its life. But in the name of that life, that trust, he must shed the blood of his people. Those who trust must be sacrificed to meet the trust. Thus trust becomes a matter of blood and death. Therefore I have fled my home"—the simple timbre of lament in his tone relieved what he said of any accusation—"to serve a man and a woman whom I cannot trust. I know not how to trust you, and so I am freed of the burden of trust. There is naught between us which would require me to shed your lives. Or to sacrifice my own."

Listening to Sunder's voice and the fire, Covenant lost some of his fear. A sense of kinship came over him. This dour self-doubting Stonedownor had suffered so much, and yet had preserved so much of himself. After a long moment, Covenant chose to accept what Sunder was saying. He could not pay every price alone. "All right," he breathed like the night breeze in the copse. "Tomorrow night you can start the fire."

Quietly, Sunder replied, "That is well."

Covenant nodded. Soon he closed his eyes. His weariness lowered him to the ground beside the fire. He wanted to sleep.

But Linden held his attention. "It isn't enough," she said stiffly. "You keep saying you want to fight the Sunbane, but you can hardly light a fire. You might as well be afraid of rubbing sticks together. I need a better answer than that."

He understood her point. Surely the Sunbane—capable of torturing nature itself at its whim—could not be abrogated by anything as paltry as a white gold ring. He distrusted power because no power was ever enough to accomplish his heart's desires. To heal the world. Cure leprosy. Bridge the loneliness which thwarted his capacity for love. He made an effort not to sound harsh. "Then find one. Nobody else can do it for you."

She did not respond. His words seemed to drive her back into her isolation. But he was too tired to contend with her. Already he had begun to fade. As she settled herself for the night, he rode the susurration of the River into sleep.

He awoke cramped and chilled beside a pile of dead embers. The stars had been effaced; and in the dawn, the rapid Mithil looked dark and cold, as fatal as sleet. He did not believe he could survive another day in the water.

But, as Sunder had said, they had no choice. Shivering in dire anticipation, he awakened his companions. Linden looked pale and haggard, and her eyes avoided the River as if she could not bear to think about it. Together, they ate a scant breakfast, then stood on a boulder to face the dawn. As they had expected, the sun rose in a glow of blue, and menacing clouds began to pile out of the east. Sunder shrugged in resignation and went to retie his shrinking sack of melons to the raft.

The companions launched the bundle of wood. The sting of the water burned Covenant's breath out of his lungs; but he fought the cold and the current and the weight of his boots with his old leper's intransigence, and survived the first shock.

Then the rain commenced. During the night, the River had become less violent; it had washed itself free of floating brush and trees and had risen above the worst of its turbulence. But the rain was more severe, had more wind behind it. Gusts drove the raindrops until they hit like flurries of hail. Torrents lashed into the water with a hot, scorching sound.

The downpour rapidly became torment for the companions. They could not escape from the sodden and insidious cold. From time to time, Covenant glimpsed a burst of lightning in the distance, rupturing the dark; but the unremitting slash of rain into the Mithil drowned out any thunder. Soon his muscles grew so leaden, his nerves so numb, that he could no longer grip the raft. He jammed his hand in among the branches, hooked his elbow over one of the bindings, and survived.

Somehow, the day passed. At last, a line of clear sky broke open along the east. Gradually, the rain and wind eased. More by chance than intent, the companions gained a small cove of gravel and sand in the west bank. As they drew their raft out of the water, Covenant's legs failed, and he collapsed face-down on the pebbles as if he would never be able to move again.

Linden panted, "Firewood." He could hear the stumbling scrunch of her shoes. Sunder also seemed to be moving.

Her groan jerked up his head, heaved him to his hands and knees. Following her wounded stare, he saw what had dismayed her.

There was no firewood. The rain had washed the gravel clean. And the small patch of shore was impenetrably surrounded by a tangle of briar with long barbed thorns. Exhaustion and tears thickened her voice as she moaned, "What are we going to do?"

Covenant tried to speak, but was too weak to make any sound.

The Graveler locked his weary knees, mustered a scant smile. "The ur-Lord has granted permission. Be of good heart. Some little warmth will ease us greatly."

Lurching to his feet, Covenant watched blankly as Sunder approached the thickest part of the briar.

The muscles of his jaw knotted and released irrhythmically, like a faltering heartbeat. But he did not hesitate. Reaching his left hand in among the thorns, he pressed his forearm against one of the barbs and tore a cut across his skin.

Covenant was too stunned by fatigue and cold and responsibility to react. Linden flinched, but did not move.

With a shudder, Sunder smeared the welling blood onto his hands and face, then took out his *orcrest*. Holding the Sunstone so that his cut dripped over it, he began to chant.

For a long moment, nothing happened. Covenant trembled in his bones, thinking that without sunlight Sunder would not be able to succeed. But suddenly a red glow awakened in the translucent stone. Power the color of Sunder's blood shafted in the direction of the sun.

The sun had already set behind a line of hills, but the Sunstone was unaffected by the intervening terrain; Sunder's vermeil shaft struck toward the sun's hidden position. Some distance from the cove, the shaft disappeared into the dark base of the hills; but its straight, bright power was not hindered.

Still chanting, Sunder moved his hands so that the shaft encountered a thick briar stem. Almost at once, flame burst from the wood.

When the stem was well afire, he shifted his power to the nearest branches.

The briar was wet and alive; but his shaft lit new stems and twigs easily, and the tangle was so dense that the flames fed each other. Soon he had created a self-sustaining bonfire.

He fell silent; and the blood-beam vanished. Tottering weakly, he went to the River to wash himself and the Sunstone.

Covenant and Linden hunched close to the blaze. Twilight was deepening around them. At their backs, the Mithil sounded like the respiration of the sea. In the firelight, Covenant could see that her lips were blue with cold, her face drained of blood. Her eyes reflected the flames as if they were devoid of any other vision. Grimly, he hoped that she would find somewhere the desire or the resolution to endure.

Shortly, Sunder returned, carrying his sack of *ussusimiel*. Linden bestirred herself to tend his arm; but he declined quietly. "I am a Graveler," he murmured. "Such work would not have fallen to me, were I slow of healing." He raised his forearm, showed her that the bleeding had already stopped. Then he sat down near the flames, and began to prepare a ration of melons for supper.

The three of them ate in silence, settled themselves for the night in silence. Covenant was seeking within himself for the courage to face another day under the sun of rain. He guessed that his companions were doing the same. They wore their private needs like cerements, and slept in isolation.

The next day surpassed Covenant's worst expectations. As clouds sealed the Plains, the wind mounted to rabid proportions, whipping the River into froth and flailing rain like the barbs of a scourge. Lightning and thunder bludgeoned each other across the heavens. In flashes, the sky became as lurid as the crumbling of a firmament, as loud as an avalanche. The raft rode the current like dead wood, entirely at the mercy of the Mithil.

Covenant thrashed and clung in constant fear of the lightning, expecting it to strike the raft, to fry him and his companions. But that killing blow never fell. Late in the day, the lightning itself granted them an unexpected reprieve. Downriver from them, a blue-white bolt sizzled into a stand of prodigious eucalyptus. One of the trees burned like a torch.

Sunder yelled at his companions. Together, they heaved the raft toward the bank, then left the River and hastened to the trees. They could not approach the burning eucalyptus; but when a blazing branch fell nearby, they used other dead wood to drag the branch out from under the danger of the tree. Then they fed brush, broken tree limbs, eucalyptus leaves as big as scythes to the flames until the blaze was hot enough to resist the rain.

The burning tree and the campfire shed heat like a benediction. The ground was thick with leaves which formed the softest bed Covenant and his companions had had for days. Sometime after sunset, the tree collapsed, but it fell away from them; after that they were able to rest without concern.

Early in the dawn, Sunder roused Covenant and Linden so that they would have time to break their fast before the sun rose. The Graveler was tense and distracted, anticipating a change in the Sunbane. When they had eaten, they went down to the riverbank and found a stretch of flat rock where they could stand to await the morning. Through the gaunt and blackened trees, they saw the sun cast its first glance over the horizon.

It appeared baleful, fiery and red; it wore coquelicot like a crown of thorns, and cast a humid heat entirely unlike the fierce intensity of the desert sun. Its corona seemed insidious and detrimental. Linden's eyes flinched at the sight. And Sunder's face was strangely blanched. He made an instinctive warding gesture with both hands. "Sun of pestilence," he breathed; and his tone winced. "Ah, we have been fortunate. Had this sun come upon us after the desert sun, or the fertile—" The thought died in his throat. "But now, after a sun of rain—" He sighed. "Fortunate, indeed."

"How so?" asked Covenant. He did not understand the attitude of his companions. His bones yearned for the relief of one clear clean day. "What does this sun do?"

"Do?" Sunder gritted. "What harm does it not? It is the dread and torment of the Land. Still water becomes stagnant. Growing things rot and crumble. All who eat or drink of that which has not been shaded are afflicted with a disease which few survive and none cure. And the insects—!"

"He's right," Linden whispered with her mouth full of dismay. "Oh, my God."

"It is the Mithil River which makes us fortunate, for it will not stagnate. Until another desert sun, it will continue to flow from its springs, and from the rain. And it will ward us in other ways also." The reflected red in Sunder's eyes made him look like a cornered animal. "Yet I cannot behold such a sun without faintheartedness. My people hide in their homes at such a time and pray for a sun of two days. I ache to be hidden also. I am homeless and small against the wideness of the world, and in all the Land I fear a sun of pestilence more than any other thing."

Sunder's frank apprehension affected Covenant like guilt. To answer it, he said, "You're also the only reason we're still alive."

"Yes," the Graveler responded as if he were listening to his own thoughts rather than to Covenant.

"Yes!" Covenant snapped. "And someday every Stonedown is going to know that this Sunbane is not the only way to live. When that day comes, you're going to be just about the only person in the Land who can teach them anything."

Sunder was silent for a time. Then he asked distantly, "What will I teach them?"

"To remake the Land." Deliberately, Covenant included Linden in his passion. "It used to be a place of such health and loveliness—if you saw it, it would break your heart." His voice gave off gleams of rage and love. "That can be true again." He glared at his companions, daring them to doubt him.

Linden covered her gaze; but Sunder turned and met Covenant's ire. "Your words have no meaning. No man or woman can remake the Land. It is in the hands of the Sunbane, for good or ill. Yet this I say to you," he grated when Covenant began to protest. "Make the attempt." Abruptly, he lowered his eyes. "I can no longer bear to believe that Nassic my father was a mere witless fool." Retrieving his sack of melons, he went brusquely and tied it to the center of the raft.

"I hear you," Covenant muttered. He felt an unexpected desire for violence. "I hear you."

Linden touched his arm. "Come on." She did not meet his glance. "It's going to be dangerous here."

He followed mutely as she and Sunder launched the raft.

Soon they were out in the center of the Mithil, riding the current under a red-wreathed sun and a cerulean sky. The

warmer air made the water almost pleasant; and the pace of
the River had slowed during the night, easing the management
of the raft. Yet the sun's aurora nagged at Covenant. Even to
his superficial sight, it looked like a secret threat, mendacious
and bloodthirsty. Because of it, the warm sunlight and clear
sky seemed like concealment for an ambush.

His companions shared his trepidation. Sunder swam with a
dogged wariness, as if he expected an attack at any moment.
And Linden's manner betrayed an innominate anxiety more
acute than anything she had shown since the first day of the
fertile sun.

But nothing occurred to justify this vague dread. The morning passed easily as the water lost its chill. The air filled with
flies, gnats, midges, like motes of vehemence in the red-tinged
light; but such things did not prevent the companions from
stopping whenever they saw *aliantha*. Slowly, Covenant began
to relax. Noon had passed before he noticed that the River
was becoming rougher.

During the days of rain, the Mithil had turned directly
northward; and now it grew unexpectedly broader, more
troubled. Soon, he descried what was happening. The raft was
moving rapidly toward the confluence of the Mithil and another river.

Their speed left the companions no time for choice. Sunder
shouted, "Hold!" Linden thrust her hair away from her face,
tightened her grip. Covenant jammed his numb fingers in
among the branches of the raft. Then the Mithil swept them
spinning and tumbling into the turbulent center of the confluence.

The raft plunged end over end. Covenant felt himself
yanked through the turmoil, and fought to hold his breath.
But almost at once the current rushed the raft in another
direction. Gasping for air, he shook water from his eyes and
saw that now they were traveling northeastward.

For more than a league, the raft seemed to hurtle down the
watercourse. But finally the new stream eased somewhat between its banks. Covenant started to catch his breath.

"What was that?" Linden panted.

Covenant searched his memory. "Must have been the Black
River." From Garroting Deep. And from *Melenkurion* Sky-
weir, where Elena had broken the Law of Death to summon
Kevin Landwaster from his grave, and had died herself as a

result. Covenant flinched at the recollection, and at the thought that perhaps none of the Land's ancient forests had survived the Sunbane. Gritting himself, he added, "It separates the South and Center Plains."

"Yes," said the Graveler. "And now we must choose. Revelstone lies north of northwest from us. The Mithil no longer shortens our way."

Covenant nodded. But the seine of his remembering brought up other things as well. "That's all right. It won't increase the distance." He knew vividly where the Mithil River would take him. "Anyway, I don't want to walk under this sun."

Andelain.

He shivered at the suddenness of his hope and anxiety. If *aliantha* could endure the Sunbane, could not Andelain also preserve itself? Or had the chief gem and glory of the Land already been brought to ruin?

That thought outweighed his urgency to reach Revelstone. He estimated that they were about eighty leagues from Mithil Stonedown. Surely they had outdistanced any immediate pursuit. They could afford this digression.

He noticed that Sunder regarded him strangely. But the Graveler's face showed no desire at all to brave the sun of pestilence afoot. And Linden seemed to have lost the will to care where the River carried them.

By turns, they began trying to get some rest after the strain of the confluence.

For a time, Covenant's awareness of his surroundings was etiolated by memories of Andelain. But then a flutter of color almost struck his face, snatching his attention to the air over his head. The atmosphere thronged with bugs of all kinds. Butterflies the size of his open hand, with wings like flakes of chiaroscuro, winked and skimmed erratically over the water; huge horseflies whined past him; clusters of gnats swirled like mirages. They marked the air with constant hums and buzzings, like a rumor of distant violence. The sound made him uneasy. Itching skirled down his spine.

Sunder showed no specific anxiety. But Linden's agitation mounted. She seemed inexplicably cold; her teeth chattered until she locked her jaws to stop them. She searched the sky and the riverbanks apprehensively, looking—

The air became harder to breathe, humid and dangerous.

Covenant was momentarily deaf to the swelling hum. But then he heard it—a raw thick growling like the anger of bees.

Bees!

The noise augered through him. He gaped in dumb horror as a swarm dense enough to obscure the sun rose abruptly out of the brush along the River and came snarling toward the raft.

"Heaven and Earth!" Sunder gasped.

Linden thrashed the water, clutched at Covenant. "Raver!" Her voice scaled into a shriek. "Oh, my God!"

TEN: Vale of Crystal

THE presence of the Raver, lurid and tangible, burned through Linden Avery's nerves like a discharge of lightning, stunning her. She could not move. Covenant thrust her behind him, turned to face the onslaught. Her cry drowned as water splashed over her.

Then the swarm hit. Black-yellow bodies as long as her thumb clawed the air, smacked into the River as if they had been driven mad. She felt the Raver all around her—a spirit of ravage and lust threshing viciously among the bees.

Impelled by fear, she dove.

The water under the raft was clear; she saw Sunder diving near her. He gripped his knife and the Sunstone as if he intended to fight the swarm by hand.

Covenant remained on the surface. His legs and body writhed; he must have been swatting wildly at the bees.

At once, her fear changed directions, became fear for him. She lunged toward him, grabbed one ankle, heaved him downward as hard as she could. He sank suddenly in her grasp. Two bees still clung to his face. In a fury of revulsion, she slapped them away. Then she had to go up for air.

Sunder rose nearby. As he moved, he wielded his knife. Blood streamed from his left forearm.

She split the surface, gulped air, and dove again.

The Graveler did not. Through the distortion of the water, she watched red sunfire raging from the *orcrest*. The swarm concentrated darkly around Sunder. His legs scissored, lifting his shoulders. Power burst from him, igniting the swarm; bees flamed like hot spangles.

An instant later, the attack ended.

Linden broke water again, looked around rapidly. But the Raver was gone. Burnt bodies littered the face of the Mithil.

Sunder hugged the raft, gasping as if the exertion of so much force had ruptured something in his chest.

She ignored him. Her swift scan showed her that Covenant had not regained the surface.

Snatching air into her lungs, she went down for him.

She wrenched herself in circles, searching the water. At first, she could find nothing. Then she spotted him. He was some distance away across the current, struggling upward. His movements were desperate. In spite of the interference of the River, she could see that he was not simply desperate for air.

With all the strength of her limbs, she swam after him.

He reached the surface; but his body went on thrashing as if he were still assailed by bees.

She raised her head into the air near him, surged to his aid.

"Hellfire!" he spat like an ague of fear or agony. Water streamed through his hair and his ragged beard, as if he had been immersed in madness. His hands slapped at his face.

"Covenant!" Linden shouted.

He did not hear her. Wildly, he fought invisible bees, pounded his face. An inchoate cry tore through his throat.

"Sunder!" she panted. "Help me!" Ducking around Covenant, she caught him across the chest, began to drag him toward the bank. The sensation of his convulsions sickened her; but she bit down her nausea, wrestled him through the River.

The Graveler came limping after her, dragging the raft. His mien was tight with pain. A thin smear of blood stained his lips.

Reaching the bank, she dredged Covenant out of the water. Spasms ran through all his muscles, resisting her involuntarily. But his need gave her strength; she stretched him out on the ground, knelt at his side to examine him.

For one horrific moment, her fear returned, threatening to swamp her. She did not want to see what was wrong with him. She had already seen too much; the wrong of the Sunbane had excruciated her nerves so long, so intimately, that she half believed she had lost her mind. But she was a doctor; she had chosen this work for reasons which brooked no excuse of fear or repugnance or incapacity. Setting her self aside, she bent the new dimension of her senses toward Covenant.

Clenchings shook him like bursts of brain-fire. His face contorted around the two bee stings. The marks were bright red and swelling rapidly; but they were not serious. Or they were serious in an entirely different way.

Linden swallowed bile, and probed him more deeply.

His leprosy became obvious to her. It lay in his flesh like a malignant infestation, exigent and dire. But it was quiescent.

Something else raged in him. Baring her senses to it, she suddenly remembered what Sunder had said about the sun of pestilence—and what he had implied about insects. He stood over her. In spite of his pain, he swatted grimly at mosquitoes the size of dragonflies, keeping them off Covenant. She bit her lips in apprehension, looked down at Covenant's right forearm.

His skin around the pale scars left by Marid's fangs and Sunder's poniard was already bloated and dark, as if his arm had suffered a new infusion of venom. The swelling worsened as she gazed at it. It was tight and hot, as dangerous as a fresh snake-bite. Again, it gave her a vivid impression of moral wrong, as if the poison were as much spiritual as physical.

Marid's venom had never left Covenant's flesh. She had been disturbed by hints of this in days past, but had failed to grasp its significance. Repulsed by *aliantha*, the venom had remained latent in him, waiting— Both Marid and the bees had been formed by the Sunbane: both had been driven by Ravers. The bee-stings had triggered this reaction.

That must have been the reason for the swarm's attack, the reason why the Raver had chosen bees to work its will. To produce this relapse.

Covenant gaped back at her sightlessly. His convulsions began to fade as his muscles weakened. He was slipping into shock. For a moment, she glimpsed a structure of truth behind his apparent paranoia, his belief in an Enemy who sought to destroy him. All her instincts rebelled against such a conception. But now for an instant she seemed to see something deliberate in the Sunbane, something intentional and cunning in these attacks on Covenant.

The glimpse reft her of self-trust. She knelt beside him, unable to move or choose. The same dismay which had incapacitated her when she had first seen Joan came upon her.

But then the sounds of pain reached her—the moan of Sunder's wracked breathing. She looked up at him, asking mutely for answers. He must have guessed intuitively the connection between venom and bees. That was why he defied his own hurt to prevent further insect bites. Meeting her sore gaze, he said, "Something in me has torn." He winced at every word. "It is keen—but I think not perilous. Never have I drawn such power from the Sunstone." She could feel his pain as a palpable emission; but he had clearly rent some of the ligatures between his ribs, not broken any of the ribs themselves, or damaged anything vital.

Yet his hurt, and his resolute self-expenditure on Covenant's behalf, restored her to herself. A measure of her familiar severity returned, steadying the labor of her heart. She climbed to her feet. "Come on. Let's get him back in the water."

Sunder nodded. Gently, they lifted Covenant down the bank. Propping his left arm over the raft so that his right arm could hang free in the cool water, they shoved out into the center of the current. Then they let the River carry them downstream under the bale of a red-ringed sun.

During the remainder of the afternoon, Linden struggled against her memory of Joan, her sense of failure. She could almost hear her mother whining for death. Covenant regained consciousness several times, lifted his head; but the poison always dragged him back before he could speak. Through the water, she watched the black tumescence creep avidly up his arm. It seemed much swifter than the previous time; Marid's poison had increased in virulence during its dormancy. The sight blurred her eyes. She could not silence the fears gnawing at her heart.

Then, before sunset, the River unbent among a clump of hills into a long straight line leading toward a wide ravine which opened on the Mithil. The sides of the ravine were as sheer as a barranca, and they reflected the low sunshine with a strange brilliance. The ravine was like a vale of diamonds; its walls were formed of faceted crystal which caught the light and returned it in delicate shades of white and pink. When the sun of pestilence dipped toward the horizon, washing the terrain in a bath of vermilion, the barranca became a place of rare glory.

People moved on the rivershore; but they gave no indication that they saw the raft. The River was already in shadow, and the brightness of the crystal was dazzling. Soon they left the bank and went up into the ravine.

Linden and Sunder shared a look, and began to steer toward the mouth of the barranca. In dusk macerated only by the last gleamings along the vale rim, they pulled their raft partway up the shore and carefully eased Covenant to dry ground. His arm was black and thick to the shoulder, cruelly pinched by both his ring and his shirt, and he moaned when they moved him.

She sat beside him, stroked his forehead; but her gaze was fixed on Sunder. "I don't know what to do," she said flatly. "We're going to have to ask these people for help."

The Graveler stood with his arms around his chest, cradling his pain. "We cannot. Have you forgotten Mithil Stonedown? We are blood that these people may shed without cost to themselves. And the Rede denounces him. I redeemed you from Mithil Stonedown. Who will redeem us here?"

She gripped herself. "Then why did we stop?"

He shrugged, winced. "We must have food. Little *ussusimiel* remains to us."

"How do you propose to get it?" She disliked the sarcasm in her tone, but could not stifle it.

"When they sleep"— Sunder's eyes revealed his reluctance as clearly as words —"I will attempt to steal what we must have."

Linden frowned involuntarily. "What about guards?"

"They will ward the hills, and the River from the hills. There is no other approach to this place. If they have not yet observed us, perhaps we are safe."

She agreed. The thought of stealing was awkward to her; but she recognized that they had no alternative. "I'll come with you." Sunder began to protest; she stopped him with a brusque shake of her head. "You're not exactly healthy. If nothing else, you'll need me to watch your back. And," she sighed, "I want to get some *mirkfruit*. He needs it."

The Graveler's face was unreadable in the twilight. But he

acquiesced mutely. Retrieving the last of his melons from the raft, he began to cut them open.

She ate her ration, then did what she could to feed Covenant. The task was difficult; she had trouble making him swallow the thin morsels she put in his mouth. Again, dread constricted her heart. But she suppressed it. Patiently, she fed slivers of melon to him, then stroked his throat to trigger his swallowing reflex, until he had consumed a scant meal.

When she finished, the night was deep around her, and a waning moon had just begun to crest the hills. She rested beside Covenant for a while, trying to gather up the unraveled ends of her competence. But she found herself listening to his respiration as if she expected every hoarse intake to be his last. She loathed her helplessness so keenly— A distinct fetor rode the breeze from across the River, the effect of the sun of pestilence on the vegetation. She could not rest.

Abruptly, Covenant began to flinch. A faint white light winked along his right side—burned and vanished in an instant.

She sat up, hissed, "Sunder."

The light came again—an evanescent stutter of power from the ring embedded deep in Covenant's swollen finger.

"Heaven and Earth!" whispered Sunder. "It will be seen."

"I thought—" She watched stupidly as the Graveler slid Covenant's hand into the pocket of his pants. The movement made him bare his teeth in a grin of pain. His dry stare was fixed on the moon. "I thought he needed the Sunstone. To trigger it." His pocket muffled the intermittent gleaming, but did not conceal it entirely. "Sunder." Her clothing was still damp; she could not stop shivering. "What's happening to him?"

"Ask me not," Sunder breathed roughly. "I lack your sight." But a moment later he inquired, "Can it be that this Raver of which he speaks—that this Raver is within him?"

"No!" she snapped, repudiating the idea so swiftly that she had no chance to control her vehemence. "He isn't Marid." Her senses were certain of this; Covenant was ill, not possessed. Nevertheless, Sunder's suggestion struck chords of anger which took her by surprise. She had not realized that she was investing so much of herself in Thomas Covenant. Back on Haven Farm, in the world she understood, she had chosen to support his embattled integrity, hoping to learn a lesson of strength. But she had had no conception of where that decision would carry her. She had already witnessed too much when she had watched him smile for Joan—smile, and forfeit his life. An inchoate part of her clung to this image of him; his self-sacrifice seemed so much cleaner than her own. Now, with a pang, she wondered how much more she had yet to comprehend about him. And about herself. Her voice shook. "Whatever else he is, he isn't a Raver."

Sunder shifted in the darkness as if he were trying to frame a question. But before he could articulate it, the dim flicker of Covenant's ring was effaced by a bright spangling from the walls of the barranca. Suddenly, the whole ravine seemed to be on fire.

Linden sprang erect, expecting to find scores of angry Stonedownors rushing toward her. But as her eyes adjusted, she saw that the source of the reflection was some distance away. The village must have lit an immense bonfire. Flames showed the profile of stone houses between her and the light; fire echoed off the crystal facets in all directions. She could hear nothing to indicate that she and her companions were in danger.

Sunder touched her shoulder. "Come," he whispered. "Some high purpose gathers the Stonedown. All its people will attend. Perhaps we have been granted an opportunity to find food."

She hesitated, bent to examine Covenant. A complex fear made her reluctant. "Should we leave him?" His skin felt crisp with fever.

"Where will he go?" the Graveler responded simply.

She bowed her head. Sunder would probably need her. And Covenant seemed far too ill to move, to harm himself. Yet he looked so frail— But she had no choice. Pulling herself upright, she motioned for the Graveler to lead the way.

Without delay, Sunder crept up the ravine. Linden followed as stealthily as she could.

She felt exposed in the brightness of the vale; but no alarm was raised. And the light allowed them to approach the Stonedown easily. Soon they were among the houses.

Sunder stopped at every corner to be sure that the path was clear. But they saw no one. All the dwellings seemed to be empty. The Graveler chose a house. Motioning for Linden to guard the doorway, he eased himself past the curtain.

The sound of voices reached her. For an instant, she froze

with a warning in her throat. But then her hearing clarified located the sound. It came from the center of the Stonedown She gripped her relief and waited.

Moments later, Sunder returned. He had a bulging leathe knapsack under his arm. In her ear, he breathed that he ha found *mirkfruit* as well as food.

He started to leave. But she stopped him, gestured inward For a moment, he considered the advantages of knowing wha transpired in the village. Then he agreed.

Together, they sneaked forward until only one house stoo between them and the center. The voices became distinct; sh could hear anger and uncertainty in them. When Sunde pointed at the roof, she nodded at once. He set his knapsac down, lifted her to the flat eaves. Carefully, she climbed ont the roof.

Sunder handed her the sack. She took it, then reache down to help him join her. The exertion tore a groan from hi sore chest; but the sound was too soft to disturb the voices Side by side, they slid forward until they were able to see an hear what was happening in the center of the Stonedown.

The people were gathered in a tight ring around the ope space. They were a substantially larger number than the popu lation of Mithil Stonedown. In an elusive way, they seeme more prosperous, better-fed, than the folk of Sunder's home But their faces were grim, anxious, fearful. They watched th center of the circle with tense attention.

Beside the bonfire stood three figures—two men and woman. The woman was poised between the men in an atti tude of prayer, as if she were pleading with both of them. Sh wore a sturdy leather shift like the other Stonedowno women. Her pale delicate features were urgent, and the dis array of her raven hair gave her an appearance of fatality.

The man nearest to Linden and Sunder was also a Stone downor, a tall square individual with a bristling black beard and eyes darkened by conflict. But the person opposite him was unlike anyone Linden had seen before. His raiment was a vivid red robe draped with a black chasuble. A hood shad owed his features. His hands held a short iron rod like a scepter with an open triangle affixed to its end. Emanations of heiratic pride and vitriol flowed from him as if he were defy ing the entire Stonedown.

"A Rider!" Sunder whispered. "A Rider of the Clave."

The woman—she was hardly more than a girl—faced the tall Stonedownor. "Croft!" she begged. Tears suffused her mien. "You are the Graveler. You must forbid!"

"Aye, Hollian," he replied with great bitterness. While he spoke, his hands toyed with a slim wooden wand. "By right of blood and power, I am the Graveler. And you are an eh-Brand—a benison beyond price to the life of Crystal Stonedown. But he is Sivit na-Mhoram-wist. He claims you in the name of the Clave. How may I refuse?"

"You may refuse—" began the Rider in a sepulchral tone.

"You must refuse!" the woman cried.

"But should you refuse," Sivit continued remorselessly, "should you think to deny me, I swear by the Sunbane that I will levy the na-Mhoram's *Grim* upon you, and you will be ground under its might like chaff!"

At the word *Grim*, a moan ran through the Stonedown; and Sunder shivered.

But Hollian defied their fear. "Croft!" she insisted, "forbid! I care nothing for the na-Mhoram or his *Grim*. I am an eh-Brand. I foretell the Sunbane! No harm, no *Grim* or any curse, will find you unwary while I abide here. Croft! My people!" She appealed to the ring of Stonedownors. "Am I nothing, that you cast me aside at the whim of Sivit na-Mhoram-wist?"

"Whim?" barked the Rider. "I speak for the Clave. I do not utter whims. Harken to me, girl. I claim you by right of service. Without the mediation of the Clave—without the wisdom of the Rede and the sacrifice of the na-Mhoram—there would be no life left in any Stonedown or Woodhelven, despite your arrogance. And we must have life for our work. Do you think to deny *me*? Contemnable folly!"

"She is precious to us," said the tall Graveler softly. "Do not enforce your will upon us."

"Is she?" Sivit raged, brandishing his scepter. "You are sick with her folly. She is not precious. She is an abomination! You think her an eh-Brand, a boon rare in the Land. I say to you, she is a Sun-Sage! Damned as a servant of a-Jeroth! She does not foretell the Sunbane. She causes it to be as she chooses. Against her and her foul kind the Clave strives, seeking to undo the harm such beings wreak."

The Rider continued to rant; but Linden turned away. To Sunder, she whispered, "Why does he want her?"

"Have you learned nothing?" he replied tightly. "The Clave has power over the Sunbane. For power, they must have blood."

"Blood?"

He nodded. "At all times, Riders journey the Land, visiting again and again every village. At each visit, they take one or two or three lives—ever young and strong lives—and bear them to Revelstone, where the na-Mhoram works his work."

Linden clenched her outrage, kept her voice at a whisper. "You mean they're going to kill her?"

"Yes!" he hissed.

At once, all her instincts rebelled. A shock of purpose ran through her, clarifying for the first time her maddening relationship to the Land. Some of Covenant's ready passion became suddenly explicable. "Sunder," she breathed, "we've got to save her."

"Save—?" He almost lost control of his voice. "We are two against a Stonedown. And the Rider is mighty."

"We've got to!" She groped for a way to convince him. The murder of this woman could not be allowed. Why else had Covenant tried to save Joan? Why else had Linden herself risked her life to prevent his death? Urgently, she said, "Covenant tried to save Marid."

"Yes!" rasped Sunder. "And behold the cost!"

"No." For a moment, she could not find the answer she needed. Then it came to her. "What's a Sun-Sage?"

He stared at her. "Such a being cannot exist."

"What," she enunciated, "is it?"

"The Rider has said," he murmured. "It is one who can cause the Sunbane."

She fixed him with all her determination. "Then we need her."

His eyes seemed to bulge in their sockets. His hands grasped for something to hold onto. But he could not deny the force of her argument. "Mad," he exhaled through his teeth. "All of us—mad." Briefly, he searched the Stonedown as if he were looking for valor. Then he reached a decision. "Remain here," he whispered. "I go to find the Rider's Courser. Perhaps it may be harmed, or driven off. Then he will be unable to bear her away. We will gain time to consider other action."

"Good!" she responded eagerly. "If they leave here, I'll try to see where they take her."

He gave a curt nod. Muttering softly to himself, "Mad. Mad," he crept to the rear of the roof and dropped to the ground, taking his knapsack with him.

Linden returned her attention to Hollian's people. The young woman was on her knees, hiding her face in her hands. The Rider stood over her, denouncing her with his scepter; but he shouted at the Stonedownors.

"Do you believe that you can endure the na-Mhoram's *Grim*? You are fey and anile. By the Three Corners of Truth! At one word from me, the Clave will unleash such devastation upon you that you will grovel to be permitted to deliver up this foul eh-Brand, and it will avail you nothing!"

Abruptly, the woman jerked upright, threw herself to confront the Graveler. "Croft!" she panted in desperation, "slay this Rider! Let him not carry word to the Clave. Then I will remain in Crystal Stonedown, and the Clave will know nothing of what we have done." Her hands gripped his jerkin, urging him. "Croft, hear me. Slay him!"

Sivit barked a contemptuous laugh. Then his voice dropped, became low and deadly. "You have not the power."

"He speaks truly," Croft murmured to Hollian. Misery knurled his countenance. "He requires no *Grim* to work our ruin. I must meet his claim, else we will not endure to rue our defiance."

An inarticulate cry broke from her. For a moment, Linden feared that the young woman would collapse into hysteria. But out of Hollian's distress came an angry dignity. She raised her head, drew herself erect. "You surrender me," she said bitterly. "I am without help or hope. Yet you must at least accord to me the courtesy of my worth. Restore to me the *lianar*."

Croft looked down at the wand in his hands. The rictus of his shoulders revealed his shame and decision. "No," he said softly. "With this wood you perform your foretelling. Sivit na-Mhoram-wist has no claim upon it—and for you it has no future. Crystal Stonedown will retain it. As a prayer for the birth of a new eh-Brand."

Triumph shone from the Rider as if he were a torch of malice.

At the far side of the village, Linden glimpsed a sudden hot flaring of red. Sunder's power. He must have made use of his Sunstone. The beam cast vermeil through the crystal, then vanished. She held her breath, fearing that Sunder had given himself away. But the Stonedownors were intent on the conflict in their midst: the instant of force passed unnoticed.

Mute with despair, Hollian turned away from the Graveler, then stopped as if she had been slapped, staring past the corner of the house on which Linden lay. Muffled gasps spattered around the ring; everyone followed the eh-Brand's stare.

What—?

Linden peered over the eaves in time to see Covenant come shambling into the center of the village. He moved like a derelict. His right arm was hideously swollen. Poison blazed in his eyes. His ring spat erratic bursts of white fire.

No! she cried silently. Covenant!

He was so weak that any of the Stonedownors could have toppled him with one hand. But the rage of his fever commanded their restraint; the circle parted for him involuntarily, admitting him to the open space.

He lurched to a stop, stood glaring flames around him. "Linden," he croaked in a parched voice. "Linden."

Covenant!

Without hesitation, she dropped from the roof. Before they could realize what was happening, she thrust her way between the Stonedownors, hastened to Covenant.

"Linden?" He recognized her with difficulty; confusion and venom wrestled across his visage. "You left me."

"The Halfhand!" Sivit yelled. "The white ring!"

The air was bright with peril; it sprang from the bonfire, leaped off the walls of the barranca. Scores of people trembled on the verge of violence. But Linden held everything else in abeyance, concentrated on Covenant. "No. We didn't leave you. We came to find food. And to save her." She pointed at Hollian.

The stare of his delirium did not shift. "You left me."

"I say it is the Halfhand!" shouted the Rider. "He has come as the Clave foretold! Take him! Slay him!"

The Stonedownors flinched under Sivit's demand; but they made no move. Covenant's intensity held them back.

"No!" Linden averred to him urgently. "Listen to me! That man is a Rider of the Clave. The *Clave*. He's going to kill her so that he can use her blood. We've got to save her!"

His gaze twisted toward Hollian, then returned to Linden. He blinked at her incomprehendingly. "You left me." The pain of finding himself alone had closed his mind to every other appeal.

"Fools!" Sivit raged. Suddenly, he flourished his scepter. Blood covered his lean hands. Gouts of red fire spewed from the iron triangle. Swift as vengeance, he moved forward.

"She's going to be sacrificed!" Linden cried at Covenant's confusion. "Like Joan! *Like Joan!*"

"Joan?" In an instant, all his uncertainty became anger and poison. He swung to face the Rider. "Joan!"

Before Sivit could strike, white flame exploded around Covenant, enveloping him in conflagration. He burned with silver fury, coruscated the air. Linden recoiled, flung up her hands to ward her face. Wild magic began to erupt in all directions.

A rampage of force tore Sivit's scepter from his hands. The iron fired black, red, white, then melted into slag on the ground. Argent lashed the bonfire; flaming brands scattered across the circle. Wild lightning sizzled into the heavens until the sky screamed and the crystal walls rang out celestial peals of power.

The very fabric of the dirt stretched under Linden's feet, as if it were about to tear. She staggered to her knees.

The Stonedownors fled. Shrieks of fear escaped among the houses. A moment later, only Croft, Hollian, and Sivit remained. Croft and Hollian were too stunned to move. Sivit huddled on the ground like a craven, with his arms over his head.

Abruptly, as if Covenant had closed a door in his mind, the wild magic subsided. He emerged from the flame; his ring flickered and went out. His legs started to fold.

Linden surged to her feet, caught him before he fell. Wrapping her arms around him, she held him upright.

Then Sunder appeared, carrying the knapsack. He ran forward, shouting, "Flee! Swiftly, lest they regain their wits and pursue us!" Blood still marked a new cut on his left forearm. As he passed her, he snatched at Hollian's arm. She resisted; she was too numb with shock to understand what was happening. He spun on her, fumed into her face, *"Do you covet death?"*

His urgency pierced her stupor. She regained her alertness with a moan. "No. I will come. But—but I must have my *lianar*." She pointed at the wand in Croft's hands.

Sunder marched over to the tall Stonedownor. Croft's grasp tightened reflexively on the wood.

Wincing with pain, Sunder struck Croft a sharp blow in the stomach. As the taller man doubled over, Sunder neatly plucked the *lia·ar* from him.

"Come!" Sunder shouted at Linden and Hollian. "Now!"

A strange grim relief came over Linden. Her first assessments of Covenant had been vindicated; at last, he had shown himself capable of significant power. Bracing his left arm over her shoulders, she helped him out of the center of the Stonedown.

Sunder took Hollian's wrist. He led the way among the houses as fast as Covenant could move.

The vale was dark now; only the crescent moon, and the reflection of dying embers along the walls, lit the ravine. The breeze carried a sickly odor of rot from across the Mithil, and the water looked b!ack and viscid, like an evil chrism. But no one hesitated. Hollian seemed to accept her rescue with mute incomprehension. She helped Linden ease Covenant into the water, secure him across the raft. Sunder urged them out into the River, and they went downstream clinging to the wood.

ELEVEN: The Corruption of Beauty

THERE was no pursuit. Covenant's power had stunned the people of Crystal Stonedown; the Rider had lost both scepter and Courser; and the River was swift. Soon Linden stopped looking behind her, stopped listening for the sounds of chase. She gave her concern to Covenant.

He had no strength left, made no effort to grip the raft, did not even try to hold up his head. She could not hear his respiration over the lapping of the water, and his pulse seemed to have withdrawn to a place beyond her reach. His face looked ghastly in the pale moonlight. All her senses groaned to her that he suffered from a venom of the soul.

His condition galled her. She clung to him, searching among her ignorances and incapacities for some way to succor him. A voice in her insisted that if she could feel his distress so acutely she ought to be able to affect it somehow, that surely the current of perception which linked her to him could run both ways. But she shied away from the implications. She had no power, had nothing with which to oppose his illness except the private blood of her own life. Her fear of so much vulnerability foiled her, left her cursing because she lacked even the limited resources of her medical bag—lacked anything which could have spared her this intimate responsibility for his survival.

For a time, her companions rode the River in silence. But at last Hollian spoke. Linden was dimly cognizant of the young woman's plight. The eh-Brand had been surrendered to death by her own village, and had been impossibly rescued— Eventually, all the things she did not understand overcame her reluctance. She breathed clenched apprehension into the darkness. "Speak to me. I do not know you."

"Your pardon." Sunder's tone expressed weariness and useless regret. "We have neglected courtesy. I am Sunder son of Nassic, at one time"— he became momentarily bitter —"Graveler of Mithil Stonedown, fourscore leagues to the south. With me are Linden Avery the Chosen and ur-Lord Thomas Covenant, Unbeliever and white gold wielder. They are strangers to the Land."

Strangers, Linden murmured. She saw herself as an unnatural visitant. The thought had sharp edges on all sides.

The eh-Brand answered like a girl remembering her manners with difficulty. "I am Hollian Amith-daughter, eh-Brand of Crystal Stonedown. I am—" She faltered, then said in a sore voice, "I know not whether to give you thanks for redeeming my life—or curses for damning my home. The na-Mhoram's *Grim* will blacken Crystal Stonedown forever."

Sunder spoke roughly. "Perhaps not."

"How not?" she demanded in her grief. "Surely Sivit na-Mhoram-wist will not forbear. He will ride forthwith to Revelstone, and the *Grim* will be spoken. Nothing can prevent it."

"He will not ride to Revelstone. I have slain his Courser." Half to himself, Sunder muttered, "The Rede did not reveal to me that a Sunstone may wield such might."

Hollian gave a low cry of relief. "And the *rukh* with which he molds the Sunbane is destroyed. Thus he cannot call down ill upon my people." A recovery of hope silenced her. She relaxed in the water as if it were a balm for her fears.

Covenant's need was loud in Linden's ears. She tried to deafen herself to it. "The Rider's scepter—his *rukh*? Where did he get the blood to use it? I didn't see him cut himself."

"The Riders of the Clave," Sunder responded dourly, "are not required to shed themselves. They are fortified by the young men and women of the Land. Each *rukh* is hollow, and contains the blood with which the Sunbane is wielded."

Echoes of the outrage which had determined her to rescue Hollian awoke in Linden. She welcomed them, explored them, hunting for courage. The rites of the Sunbane were barbaric enough as Sunder practiced them. To be able to achieve such power without personal cost seemed to her execrable. She did not know how to reconcile her ire with what she had heard of the Clave's purpose, its reputation for resistance to the Sunbane. But she was deeply suspicious of that reputation. She had begun to share Covenant's desire to reach Revelstone.

But Covenant was dying.

Everything returned to Covenant and death.

After a while, Hollian spoke again. A different fear prompted her to ask, "Is it wild magic? Wild magic in sooth?"

"Yes," the Graveler said.

"Then why—?" Linden could feel Hollian's disconcertion. "How did it transpire that Mithil Stonedown did not slay him, as the Rede commands?"

"I did not permit it," replied Sunder flatly. "In his name, I turned from my people, so that he would not be shed."

"You are a Graveler," Hollian whispered in her surprise. "A Stonedownor like myself. Such a deed—surely it was difficult for you. How were you brought to commit such transgression?"

"Daughter of Amith," Sunder answered like a formal confession, "I was brought to it by the truth of the Rede. The words of the ur-Lord were words of beauty rather than evil. He spoke as one who owns both will and power to give his words substance. And in my heart the truth of the Rede was unbearable.

"Also," he went on grimly, "I have been made to learn that the Rede itself contains falsehood."

"Falsehood?" protested Hollian. "No. The Rede is the life of the Land. Were it false, all who rely upon it would die."

Sunder considered for a moment, then said, "Eh-Brand, do you know the *aliantha*?"

She nodded. "It is most deadly poison."

"No." His certitude touched Linden. In spite of all that had happened, he possessed an inner resilience she could not match. "It is good beyond any other fruit. I speak from knowledge. For three suns, we have eaten *aliantha* at every chance."

"Surely"— Hollian groped for arguments —"it is the cause of the ur-Lord's sickness?"

"No. This sickness has come upon him previously, and the *aliantha* gave him healing."

At this, she paused, trying to absorb what she had heard. Her head turned from side to side, searching the night for guidance. When she spoke again, her voice came faintly over the wet sounds of the River. "You have redeemed my life. I will not doubt you. I am homeless and without purpose, for I cannot return to Crystal Stonedown, and the world is perilous, and I do not comprehend my fate. I must not doubt you.

"Yet I would ask you of your goal. All is dark to me. You have incurred the wrath of the Clave for me. You journey great distances under the Sunbane. Will you give me reason?"

Sunder said deliberately, "Linden Avery?" passing the question to her. She understood; he was discomfited by the answer, and Hollian was not likely to take it calmly. Linden wanted to reject the difficulty, force Sunder and Hollian to fend for themselves. But, because her own weakness was intolerable to her, she responded squarely, "We're going to Revelstone."

Hollian reacted in horror. "Revelstone? You betray me!" At once, she thrust away from the raft, flailing for an escape.

Sunder lunged after her. He tried to shout something, but his damaged chest changed it to a gasp of pain.

Linden ignored him. His lunge had rolled the raft, dropping Covenant into the water.

She grappled for Covenant, brought him back to the surface. His respiration was so shallow that he did not even cough at the water which streamed from his mouth. In spite of his weight, he conveyed a conviction of utter frailty.

Sunder fought to prevent Hollian's flight; but he was hampered by his hurt ribs. "Are you mad?" he panted at her. "If we sought your harm, Sivit's intent would have sufficed!"

Struggling to support Covenant, Linden snapped, "Let her go!"

"Let—?" the Graveler protested.

"Yes!" Ferocity burned through her. "I need help. By God, if she wants to leave, that's her right!"

"Heaven and Earth!" retorted Sunder. "Then why have we imperiled our lives for her?"

"Because she was going to be killed! I don't care if we need her or not. We don't have the right to hold her against her will. *I need help*."

Sunder spat a curse. Abruptly, he abandoned Hollian, came limping through the water to take some of Covenant's weight. But he was livid with pain and indignation. Over his shoulder, he rasped at Hollian, "Your suspicion is unjust!"

"Perhaps." The eh-Brand trod water twenty feet away; her head was a piece of darkness among the shadows of the River. "Assuredly, I have been unjust to Linden Avery." After a moment, she demanded, "What purpose drives you to Revelstone?"

"That's where the answers are." As quickly as it had come, Linden's anger vanished, and a bone-deep dread took its place. She had been through too much. Without Sunder's aid, she could not have borne Covenant back to the raft. "Covenant thinks he can fight the Sunbane. But he has to understand it first. That's why he wants to talk to the Clave."

"Fight?" asked Hollian in disbelief. "Do you speak of altering the Sunbane?"

"Why not?" Linden clung to the raft. Dismay clogged her limbs. "Isn't that what you do?"

"I?"

"Aren't you a Sun-Sage?"

"No!" Hollian declared sharply. "That is a lie, uttered by Sivit na-Mhoram-wist to strengthen his claim upon me. I am an eh-Brand. I see the sun. I do not shape it."

To Linden, Sunder growled, "Then we have no need of her."

Dimly, Linden wondered why he felt threatened by Hollian. But she lacked the courage to ask him. "We need all the help we can get," she murmured. "I want her with us. If she's willing."

"Why?"

At the same time, Hollian asked, "Of what use am I to you?"

Without warning, Linden's throat filled with weeping. She felt like a lorn child, confronted by extremities she could not meet. She had to muster all her severity in order to articulate, "He's dying. I can feel it." In a shudder of memory, she saw Marid's fangs. "It's worse than it was before. I need help." The help she needed was vivid and appalling to her; but she could not stop. "One of you isn't enough. You'll just bleed to death. Or I will." Impelled by her fear of losing Covenant, she wrenched her voice at Hollian. "I need power. To heal him."

She had not seen the eh-Brand approach; but now Hollian was swimming at her side. Softly, the young woman said, "Perhaps such shedding is unnecessary. It may be that I can succor him. An eh-Brand has some knowledge of healing. But I do not wish to fall prey to the Clave a second time."

Linden gritted her teeth until her jaw ached, containing her desperation. "You've seen what he can do. Do you think he's going to walk into Revelstone and just let them sacrifice him?"

Hollian thought for a moment, touched Covenant's swelling gently. Then she said, "I will attempt it. But I must await the sun's rising. And I must know how this harm came upon him."

Linden's self-command did not reach so far. Sunrise would be too late. Covenant could not last until dawn. *The Chosen!* she rasped at herself. Dear God. She left the eh-Brand's questions for Sunder to answer. As he began a taut account of what had happened to Covenant, Linden's attention slipped away to the Unbeliever's wracked and failing body.

She could feel the poison seeping past the useless constriction of his shirt sleeve. Death gnawed like leprosy at the sinews of his life. He absolutely could not last until dawn.

Her mother had begged to die; but he wanted to live. He had exchanged himself for Joan, had smiled as if the prospect were a benison; yet his every act showed that he wanted to live. Perhaps he *was* mad; perhaps his talk about a Despiser *was* paranoia rather than truth. But the conclusions he drew from it were ones she could not refute. She had learned in Crystal Stonedown that she shared them.

Now he was dying.

She had to help him. She was a doctor. Surely she could do

something about his illness. Impossible that her strange acuity could not cut both ways. With an inward whimper, she abandoned resistance, bared her heart.

Slowly, she reached her awareness into him, inhabited his flesh with her private self. She felt his eviscerated respiration as her own, suffered the heat of his fever, clung to him more intimately than she had ever held to any man.

Then she was foundering in venom. She was powerless to repel it. Nausea filled her like the sick breath of the old man who had told her to *Be true.* No part of her knew how to give life in this way. But what she could do, she did. She fought for him with the same grim and secretly hopeless determination which had compelled her to study medicine as if it were an act of rage against the ineffectuality of her parents—a man and woman who had understood nothing about life except death, and had coveted the thing they understood with the lust of lovers. They had taught her the importance of efficacy. She had pursued it without rest for fifteen years.

That pursuit had taken her to Haven Farm. And there her failure in the face of Joan's affliction had cast her whole life into doubt. Now that doubt wore the taste and corruption of Covenant's venom. She could not quench the poison. But she tried by force of will to shore up the last preterite barriers of his life. This sickness was a moral evil; it offended her just as Marid had offended her, as Nassic's murder and the hot knife had offended her; and she denied it with every beat of her heart. She squeezed air into his lungs, pressured his pulse to continue, opposed the gnawing and spread of the ill.

Alone, she kept him alive through the remainder of the night.

The bones of her forehead ached with shared fever when Sunder brought her back to herself. Dawn was in the air. He and Hollian had drawn the raft toward the riverbank. Linden looked about her tabidly. Her soul was full of ashes. A part of her panted over and over, No. Never again. The River ran through a lowland which should have been composed of broad leas; but instead, the area was a gray waste where mountains of preternatural grass had been beaten down by three days of torrential rain, then rotted by the sun of pestilence. As the approach of day stirred the air, currents of putrefaction shifted back and forth across the Mithil.

But she saw why Sunder and Hollian had chosen this place.

Near the bank, a sandbar angled partway across the watercourse, forming a swath where Covenant could lie, away from the fetid grass.

The Stonedownors secured the raft, lifted Covenant to the sand, then raised him into Linden's arms. Hugging him erect, though she herself swayed with exhaustion, she watched as Sunder and Hollian hastened to the riverbank and began hunting for stone. Soon they were out of sight.

With the thin remnant of her strength, Linden confronted the sun.

It hove over the horizon wearing incarnadine like the sails of a plague-ship. She welcomed its warmth—needed to be warm, yearned to be dry—but its corona made her moan with empty repugnance. She lowered Covenant to the sand, then sat beside him, studied him as if she were afraid to close her eyes. She did not know how soon the insects would begin to swarm.

But when Sunder and Hollian returned, they were excited. The tension between them had not relaxed; but they had found something important to them both. Together, they carried a large bush which they had uprooted as if it were a treasure.

"*Voure!*" Hollian called as she and Sunder brought the bush to the sandbar. Her pale skin was luminous in the sunlight. "This is good fortune. *Voure* is greatly rare." They set the bush down nearby, and at once began to strip its leaves.

"Rare, indeed," muttered Sunder. "Such names are spoken in the Rede, but I have never beheld *voure*."

"Does it heal?" Linden asked faintly.

In response, the eh-Brand gave her a handful of leaves. They were as pulpy as sponges; clear sap dripped from their broken stems. Their pungent odor made her wince.

"Rub the sap upon your face and arms," said Hollian. "*Voure* is a potent ward against insects."

Linden stared until her senses finally registered the truth of the eh-Brand's words. Then she obeyed. When she had smeared sap over herself, she did the same to Covenant.

Sunder and Hollian were similarly busy. After they had finished, he stored the remaining leaves in his knapsack.

"Now," the eh-Brand said promptly, "I must do what lies within my capacity to restore the Halfhand."

"His name is Covenant," Linden protested dimly. To her, *Halfhand* was a Clave word: she did not like it.

Hollian blinked as if this were irrelevant, made no reply.

"Do you require my aid?" asked Sunder. His stiffness had returned. In some way that Linden could not fathom, Hollian annoyed or threatened him.

The eh-Brand's response was equally curt. "I think not."

"Then I will put this *voure* to the test." He stood up. "I will go in search of *aliantha*." Moving brusquely, he went back to the riverbank, stalked away through the rotting grass.

Hollian wasted no time. From within her shift, she drew out a small iron dirk and her *lianar* wand. Kneeling at Covenant's right shoulder, she placed the *lianar* on his chest, took the dirk in her left hand.

The sun was above the horizon now, exerting its corruption. But the pungence of the *voure* seemed to form a buckler against putrefaction. And though large insects had begun to buzz and gust in all directions, they did not come near the sandbar. Linden ached to concentrate on such things. She did not want to watch the eh-Brand's bloody rites. Did not want to see them fail. Yet she attached her eyes to the knife, forced herself to follow it.

Like Sunder's left forearm, Hollian's right palm was laced with old scars. She drew the iron across her flesh. A runnel of dark rich blood started down her bare wrist.

Setting down her dirk, she took up the *lianar* in her bleeding hand. Her lips moved, but she made no sound.

The atmosphere focused around her wand. Abruptly, flames licked the wood. Fire the color of the sun's aura skirled around her fingers. Her voice became an audible chant, but the words were alien to Linden. The fire grew stronger; it covered Hollian's hand, began to tongue the blood on her wrist.

As she chanted, her fire sent out long delicate shoots like tendrils of wisteria. They grew to the sand, stretched along the water like veins of blood in the current, went searching up the riverbank as if they sought a place to root.

Supported by a shimmering network of power tendrils, she tightened her chant, and lowered the *lianar* to Covenant's envenomed forearm. Linden flinched instinctively. She could taste the ill in the fire, feel the preternatural force of the Sunbane. Hollian drew on the same sources of power which Sunder tapped with his Sunstone. But after a moment Linden discerned that the fire's effect was not ill. Hollian fought poison with poison. When she lifted her wand from Covenant's arm, the tension of his swelling had already begun to recede.

Carefully, she shifted her power to his forehead, set flame to the fever in his skull.

At once, his body sprang rigid, head jerked back; a scream ripped his throat. From his ring, an instant white detonation blasted sand over the two women and the River.

Before Linden could react, he went completely limp.

The eh-Brand sagged at his side. The flame vanished from her *lianar*, leaving the wood pale, clean, and whole. In the space of a heartbeat, the fire-tendrils extinguished themselves; but they continued to echo across Linden's sight.

She rushed to examine Covenant. Apprehension choked her. But as she touched him, he inhaled deeply, began to breathe as if he were only asleep. She felt for his pulse; it was distinct and secure.

Relief flooded through her. The Mithil and the sun grew oddly dim. She was prone on the sand without realizing that she had reclined. Her left hand lay in the water. That cool touch seemed to be all that kept her from weeping.

In a weak voice, Hollian asked, "Is he well?"

Linden did not answer because she had no words.

Shortly, Sunder returned, his hands laden with treasureberries. He seemed to understand the exhaustion of his companions. Without speaking, he bent over Linden, slipped a berry between her lips.

Its deliciousness restored her. She sat up, estimated the amount of *aliantha* Sunder held, took her share. The berries fed a part of her which had been stretched past its limits by her efforts to keep Covenant alive.

Hollian watched in weariness and dismay as Sunder consumed his portion of the *aliantha*. But she could not bring herself to touch the berries he offered her.

As her strength returned, Linden propped Covenant into a half-sitting position, then pitted berries and fed them to him. Their effect was almost immediate; they steadied his respiration, firmed his muscle tone, cleansed the color of his skin.

Deliberately, she looked at Hollian. The exertion of aiding Covenant had left the eh-Brand in need of aliment. And her searching gaze could find no other answer. With a shudder of resolution, she accepted a berry, put it in her mouth. After a moment, she bit down on it.

Her own pleasure startled her. Revelation glowed in her eyes, and her fear seemed to fall away like a discarded mantle.

With a private sigh, Linden lowered Covenant's head to the sand, and let herself rest.

The companions remained on the sandbar for a good part of the morning, recuperating. Then, when Covenant's swelling had turned from black to a mottled yellow-purple, and had declined from his shoulder, Linden judged that he was able to travel. They set off down the Mithil once more.

The *voure* continued to protect them from insects. Hollian said the sap would retain its potency for several days; and Linden began to believe this when she discovered that the odor still clung to her after more than half a day immersed in the water.

In the lurid red of sunset, they stopped on a broad slope of rock spreading northward out of the River. After the strain of the past days, Linden hardly noticed the discomfort of sleeping on stone. Yet part of her stayed in touch with Covenant, like a string tuned to resonate sympathetically at a certain pitch. In the middle of the night, she found herself staring at the acute sickle of the moon. Covenant was sitting beside her. He seemed unaware of her. Quietly, he moved to the water's edge for a drink.

She followed, anxious that he might be suffering from a relapse of delirium. But when he saw her, he recognized her with a nod, and drew her away to a place where they could at least whisper without disturbing their companions. The way he carried his arm showed that it was tender but utile. His expression was obscure in the vague light; but his voice sounded lucid.

"Who's the woman?"

She stood close to him, peered into the shadow of his countenance. "You don't remember?"

"I remember bees." He gave a quick shudder. "That Raver. Nothing else."

Her efforts to preserve his life had left her vulnerable to him. She had shared his extremity; and now he seemed to have a claim on her which she would never be able to refuse. Even her heartbeat belonged to him. "You had a relapse."

"A relapse—?" He tried to flex his sore arm.

"You were stung, and went into shock. It was like another

snakebite in the same place, only worse. I thought—" She touched his shoulder involuntarily. "I thought you weren't going to make it."

"When was that?"

"A day and a half ago."

"How did—?" he began, then changed his mind. "Then what?"

"Sunder and I couldn't do anything for you. We just went on." She started to speak rapidly. "That night, we came to another Stonedown." She told him the story as if she were in a hurry to reach the end of it. But when she tried to describe the power of his ring, he stopped her. "That's impossible," he whispered.

"You don't remember at all?"

"No. But I tell you it's impossible. I've always—always had to have some kind of trigger. The proximity of some other power. Like the *orcrest*. It never happens by itself. Never."

"Maybe it was the Rider."

"Yes." He grasped the suggestion gratefully. "That must be it. That scepter—his *rukh*." He repeated the name she had told him as if he needed reassurance.

She nodded, then resumed her narration.

When she was done, he spoke his thoughts hesitantly. "You say I was delirious. I must have been—I don't remember any of it. Then this Rider tried to attack. All of a sudden, I had power." His tone conveyed the importance of the question. "What set me off? I shouldn't have been able to defend myself, if I was that sick. Did you get hurt? Did Sunder—?"

"No." Suddenly, the darkness between them was full of significance. She had risked herself extravagantly to keep him alive—and for what? In his power and delirium he had believed nothing about her except that she had abandoned him. And even now he did not know what he had cost her. No. She could hardly muffle her bitterness as she replied, "We're all right. It wasn't that."

Softly, he asked, "Then what was it?"

"I made you think Joan was in danger." He flinched; but she went on, struck at him with words. "It was the only thing I could find. You weren't going to save yourself—weren't going to save me. You kept accusing me of deserting you. By God," she grated, "I've stood by you since the first time I saw Joan. No matter how crazy you are, I've stood by you. You'd be dead now if it weren't for me. But you kept accusing me, and I couldn't reach you. The only name that meant anything to you was *Joan*."

She hurt him. His right hand made a gesture toward her, winced away. In the darkness, he seemed to have no eyes; his sockets gaped at her as if he had been blinded. She expected him to protest that he had often tried to help her, often striven to give her what support he could. But he stood there as he had stood when she had first confronted him on Haven Farm, upright under the weight of impossible burdens. When he spoke, his voice was edged with rage and exquisite grief.

"She was my wife. She divorced me because I had leprosy. Of all the things that happened to me, that was the worst. God knows I've committed crimes. I've raped—killed—betrayed— But those were things I *did*, and I did everything I could to make restitution. She treated me as if I were a crime. Just being who I was, just suffering from a physical affliction I couldn't have prevented or cured anymore than I could have prevented or cured my own mortality, I terrified her. That was the *worst*. Because I believed it. I felt that way about leprosy myself.

"It gave her a claim on me. I spent eleven years living with it—I couldn't bear being the cause. I sold my soul to pay that debt, and it doesn't make any difference." The muscles of his face contorted at the memory. "I'm a leper. I'm never going to stop being a leper. I'm never going to be able to quit her claim on me. It goes deeper than any choice." His words were the color of blood.

"But, Linden," he went on; and his direct appeal stung her heart. "She's my *ex*-wife." In spite of his efforts to control it, his voice carried fatality like a lament. "If the past is any indication, I'm never going to see her again."

She clung to him with her eyes. Uncertainties thronged in her. Why would he not see Joan again? How had he sold himself? How much had he withheld? But in her vulnerability one question mattered more than all the others. As steadily, noncommittally, as she could, she asked, "Do you want to see her again?"

To her tense ears, the simplicity of his reply bore the weight of a declaration. "No. I don't particularly like being a leper."

She turned away so that he would not see the tears in her eyes. She did not want to be so exposed to him. She was in danger of losing herself. And yet her relief was as poignant as love. Over her shoulder, she said flatly, "Get some rest. You need it." Then she went back to where Sunder and Hollian lay, stretched out on the rock, and spent a long time shivering as if she were caught in a winter of unshielded loneliness.

The sun had already risen, red and glowering, when she awoke. A pile of *aliantha* near Sunder's knapsack showed that the Stonedownors had foraged successfully for food. Covenant and the eh-Brand stood together, making each other's acquaintance. Sunder sat nearby as if he were grinding his teeth.

Linden climbed to her feet. Her body felt abused by the hardness of her bed, but she ignored it. Averting her eyes from Covenant as if in shame, she went to the river to wash her face.

When she returned, Sunder divided the treasure-berries. The travelers ate in silence; *aliantha* was a food which imposed stillness. Yet Linden could not deafen herself to the ambience of her companions. Covenant was as rigid as he had ever been on Haven Farm. Hollian's delicate features wore perplexity as if it were a kind of fear. And the darkness of the Graveler's mood had not lifted—resentment directed at the eh-Brand, or at himself.

They made Linden feel lost. She was responsible for their various discomforts and inadequate to do anything about it. In sustaining Covenant, she had opened doors which she now could not close, though she swore she would close them. Muttering sourly to herself, she finished her *aliantha*, scattered the seeds beyond the rock, then went severely through the motions of preparing to enter the River.

But Hollian could not bear her own trouble in silence. After a moment, she addressed the Unbeliever. "You say that I am to name you Covenant—though it is a name of ill omen, and sits unquietly in my mouth. Very well. Covenant. Have you considered where you go? The Graveler and Linden Avery say that you are destined for Revelstone. My heart shrinks from the thought—but if such is your goal, I will not gainsay it. Yet Revelstone lies there." She pointed northwestward. "Elevenscore leagues distant. The Mithil no longer shares your way."

"That is known to us, eh-Brand," Sunder muttered.

She ignored him. "It may be that we can journey afoot, with the aid of *voure*." She hesitated, recognizing the difficulty of what she proposed. "And great good fortune." Her eyes did not leave Covenant's face.

"Maybe." His tone betrayed that he had already made his decision. "But I don't want to take the chance of getting stung again. We'll stay on the River for another day or two, anyway."

"Covenant." Hollian's gaze was poignant. "Do you know what lies that way?"

"Yes." He met her squarely. "Andelain."

Andelain? The concealed intensity with which he said that name brought Linden to alertness.

"Do you—" Hollian wrestled against her apprehension. "Do you *choose* to approach Andelain?"

"Yes." Covenant's resolution was complete. But he studied the eh-Brand closely, as if her concern disturbed him. "I want to see it. Before I go to Revelstone."

His assertion appalled her. She recoiled. Gasping, she strove to shout, but could not find enough air in all the wide morning. "You are mad. Or a servant of a-Jeroth, as the Rede proclaims." She turned toward Linden, then Sunder, beseeching them to hear her. "You must not permit it." She snatched a raw breath, cried out, "You must not!"

Covenant sprang at her, dug his fingers into her shoulders, shook her. "*What's wrong with Andelain?*"

Hollian's mouth worked; but she could find no words.

"Sunder!" Covenant barked.

Stiffly, the Graveler replied, "I am fourscore leagues from my home. I know nothing of this Andelain."

Hollian fought to master herself. "Covenant," she said in a livid tone, "you may eat *aliantha*. You may defy the Clave. You may trample upon the Rede, and cast your challenge to the Sunbane itself. But you must not enter Andelain."

Covenant lowered his voice, demanded dangerously, "Why not?"

"It is a snare and a delusion!" she moaned. "An abomination in the Land. It lies lovely and cruel before the eyes, and seduces all who look upon it to their destruction. It is impervious to the Sunbane!"

"Impossible!" snapped Sunder.

"No!" Hollian panted. "I speak truly. Sun after sun, it remains unaltered, imitating paradise." She thrust all her dismay at Covenant. "Many people have been betrayed— The tale of them is often told in all this region. But I speak not only of tales. I have known four—four brave Stonedownors who succumbed to that lure. Distraught by their lives, they left Crystal Stonedown to test the tale of Andelain. Two entered, and did not return. Two made their way to Crystal Stonedown once more—and the madness in them raved like the na-Mhoram's *Grim*. No succor could anele their violence. Croft was driven to sacrifice them.

"Covenant," she begged, "do not journey there. You will meet a doom more terrible than any unshielded Sunbane." Her every word vibrated with conviction, with honest fear. "Andelain is a desecration of the soul."

Roughly, Covenant thrust the eh-Brand away from him. He whirled, strode down the slope to stand at the water's edge. His fists clenched and unclenched, trembling, at his sides.

Linden went to him at once, seeking a way to dissuade him. She believed Hollian. But when she touched his arm, the savagery in him struck her mute. "Andelain." His voice was taut with fatality and rage. Without warning, he turned on her. His eyes blazed through her. "You say you've stood by me." His whisper expressed more bloodshed than any shout. "Do it now. Nothing else matters. Stand by me."

Before she could try to respond, he spun toward Sunder and Hollian. They stared at him, dumbfounded by his passion. The sun limned his profile like a cynosure. "Andelain used to be the heart of the Land." He sounded as if he were strangling. "I have to find out what happened to it." The next moment, he was in the water, swimming downriver with all his strength.

Linden checked herself, did not follow him. He could not keep up that pace; she would be able to rejoin him. *Stand by me.* Her senses told her that Hollian spoke the truth. There was something heinous concealed in Andelain. But Covenant's appeal outweighed any conviction of peril. She had striven with the intimacy of a lover to save his life. The cost of that intimacy she could not endure; but she could do other things for him. She faced the Stonedownors. "Sunder?"

The Graveler glanced away along the River, then over at Hollian, before he met Linden's demand. "The eh-Brand is a Stonedownor," he replied, "like myself. I trust her fear. But my lot now lies with the ur-Lord. I will accompany him."

With a simple nod, Linden accepted his decision. "Hollian?"

The eh-Brand seemed unable to confront the choice she had to make. Her eyes wandered the stone, searching it for answers it did not contain. "Does it come to this?" she murmured bitterly, "that I have been rescued from peril into peril?" But slowly she summoned up the strength which had enabled her to face Croft and Sivit with dignity. "It is stated in the Rede beyond any doubt that the Halfhand is a servant of a-Jeroth."

Flatly, Linden said, "The Rede is wrong."

"That cannot be!" Hollian's fear was palpable in the air. "If the Rede is false, how can it sustain life?"

Unexpectedly, Sunder interposed himself. "Eh-Brand." His voice knotted as if he had arrived without warning or preparation at a crisis. "Linden Avery speaks of another wrong altogether. To her, all things are wrong which arise from the Sunbane."

Hollian stared at him. And Linden, too, watched him narrowly. She chaffed to be on her way; but the Graveler's efforts to resolve his own feelings kept her still.

"Eh-Brand," he went on, gritting his teeth, "I have held you in resentment. Your presence is a reproach to me. You are a Stonedownor. You comprehend what has come to pass when a Graveler betrays his home. Whether you choose or no, you accuse me. And your plight is enviable to me. You are innocent of where you stand. Whatever path you follow from this place, none can lay blame upon you. All my paths are paths of blame.

"My vindication has been that I am necessary to the ur-Lord, and to Linden Avery, and to their purpose. His vision touched my heart, and the survival of that vision has been in my hands. Lacking my aid, they would be long dead, and with them the one clear word of beauty I have been given to hear.

"Whether you choose or no, you deprive me of my necessity. Your knowledge of the Sunbane and of the perils before us surely excels mine. You give healing where I cannot. You have not shed life. In your presence, I have no answer to my guilt."

"Sunder," Hollian breathed. "Graveler. This castigation avails nothing. The past is beyond change. Your vindication cannot be taken from you."

"All things change," he replied tightly. "Ur-Lord Covenant

alters the past at every turning. Therefore"— he cut off her protest—"I am without choice. I cannot bear that this alteration should be undone. But there is choice for you. And because you own choice, eh-Brand, I implore you. Give your service to the ur-Lord. He offers much—and is in such need. Your aid is greater than mine."

Hollian's gaze scoured him as he spoke. But she did not find any answer to her fear. "Ah," she sighed bitterly, "I do not see this choice. Death lies behind me and horror before. This is not choice. It is torment."

"It is *choice*!" Sunder shouted, unable to restrain his vehemence. "Neither death nor horror is compulsory for you. You may depart from us. Find a new people to be your home. They will distrust you for a time—but that will pass. No Stonedown would willingly sacrifice an eh-Brand."

His words took both Hollian and Linden by surprise. Hollian had plainly given no thought to the idea he raised. And Linden could not guess why he used such an argument. "Sunder," she said carefully, "what do you think you're doing?"

"I seek to persuade her." He did not take his eyes from Hollian. "A choice made freely is stronger than one compelled. We must have her strength—else I fear we will not gain Revelstone."

Linden strove to understand him. "Do you mean to tell me that now you *want* to go to Revelstone?"

"I must," he responded; but his words were directed toward the eh-Brand. "No other purpose remains to me. I must see the lies of the Rede answered. Throughout all the generations of the Sunbane, the Riders have taken blood in the name of the Rede. Now they must be required to speak the truth."

Linden nodded, bent her attention on Hollian as the eh-Brand absorbed his argument, hunted for a reply. After a moment, she said slowly, holding his gaze, "In the *aliantha*— if in no other way—I have been given cause to misdoubt the Rede. And Sivit na-Mhoram-wist sought my death, though it was plain for all to see that I was of great benefit to Crystal Stonedown. If you follow ur-Lord Covenant in the name of truth, I will accompany you." At once, she turned to Linden. "But I will not enter Andelain. That I will not do."

Linden acknowledged this proviso. "All right. Let's go." She had been too long away from Covenant; her anxiety for him tightened all her muscles. But one last requirement held her back. "Sunder," she said deliberately. "Thanks."

Her gratitude seemed to startle him. But then he replied with a mute bow. In that gesture, they understood each other.

Leaving the knapsack and the raft to the Stonedownors, Linden dove into the water and went after Covenant.

She found him resting on a sand-spit beyond a bend in the River. He looked weary and abandoned, as if he had not expected her to come. But when she pulled herself out of the water near him, shook her eyes clear, she could see the relief which lay half-hidden behind his convalescence and his unkempt beard.

"Are you alone?"

"No. They're coming. Sunder talked her into it."

He did not respond. Lowering his head to his knees, he hid his face as if he did not want to admit how intensely he felt that he had been reprieved.

Shortly, Sunder and Hollian swam into view; and soon the companions were on their way downriver again. Covenant rode the current in silence, with his gaze always fixed ahead. And Linden, too, remained still, trying to gather up the scattered pieces of her privacy. She felt acutely vulnerable, as if any casual word, any light touch, could drive her to the edges of her own secrets. She did not know how to recollect her old autonomy. Through the day, she could feel the sun of pestilence impending over her as she swam; and her life seemed to be composed of threats against which she had no protection.

Then, late in the afternoon, the River began to run straight into the east, and the terrain through which it flowed underwent a dramatic change. Steep hills lay ahead on both sides like poised antitheses. Those on the right were rocky and barren—a desolation unlike the wilderland of the desert sun. Linden saw at once that they were always dead, that no sun of fertility ever alleviated their detrition. Some ancient and concentrated ruin had blasted their capacity for life long ago, before the Sunbane ever came upon them.

But the hills on the left were a direct contradiction. The power with which they reached her senses sent a shock through all her nerves.

North of the Mithil lay a lush region untouched by stress or wrong. The stands of elm and Gilden which crowned the boundary were naturally tall and vividly healthy; no fertile sun had aggravated their growth, no sun of pestilence had corroded their strong wood and clean sap. The grass sweeping away in long greenswards from the riverbank was pristine with *aliantha* and amaryllis and buttercups. An analystic air blew from these hills, forever sapid and virginal.

The demarcation between this region and the surrounding terrain was as clear as a line drawn in the dirt; at that border, the Sunbane ended and loveliness began. On the riverbank, like a marker and ward to the hills, stood an old oak, gnarled and somber, wearing long shrouds of bryony like a cloak of power—a hoary majesty untrammeled by desert or rot. It forbade and welcomed, according to the spirit of those who approached.

"Andelain," Covenant whispered thickly, as if he wanted to sing, and could not unclose his throat. "Oh, Andelain."

But Hollian gazed on the Hills with unmitigated abhorrence. Sunder glowered at them as if they posed a danger he could not identify.

And Linden, too, could not share Covenant's gladness. Andelain touched her like the taste of *aliantha* embodied in the Land. It unveiled itself to her particular percipience with a visionary intensity. It was as hazardous as a drug which could kill or cure, according to the skill of the physician who used it.

Fear and desire tore at her. She had felt the Sunbane too personally, had exposed herself too much in Covenant. She wanted loveliness as if her soul were starving for it. But Hollian's dread was entirely convincing. Andelain's emanations felt as fatal as prophecy against Linden's face. She saw intuitively that the Hills could bereave her of herself as absolutely as any wrong. She had no ability to gauge or control the potency of this drug. Impossible that ordinary trees and grass could articulate so much might! She was already engaged in a running battle against madness. Hollian had said that Andelain drove people mad.

No, she repeated to herself. Not again. Please.

By mute consent, she and her companions stopped for the night among the ruins opposite the oak. A peculiar spell was on them, wrapping them within themselves. Covenant gazed, entranced, at the shimmer of health. But Hollian's revulsion did not waver. Sunder carried distrust in the set of his shoulders. And Linden could not shake her senses free of the deadness of the southern hills. The waste of this region was like a shadow cast by Andelain, a consequence of power. It affected her as if it demonstrated the legitimacy of fear.

Early in the evening, Hollian pricked her palm with the point of her dirk, and used the blood to call up a slight green flame from her *lianar*. When she was done, she announced that the morrow would bring a fertile sun. But Linden was locked within her own apprehensions, and hardly heard the eh-Brand.

When she arose in the first gray of dawn with her companions, she said to Covenant, "I'm not going with you."

The crepuscular air could not conceal his surprise. "Not? Why?" When she did not answer immediately, he urged her. "Linden, this is your chance to taste something besides sickness. You've been so hurt by the Sunbane. Andelain can heal you."

"No." She tried to sound certain, but memories of her mother, of the old man's breath, frayed her self-command. She had shared Covenant's illness, but he had never shared his strength. "It only looks healthy. You heard Hollian. Somewhere in there, it's cancerous." I've already lost too much.

"Cancerous?" he demanded. "Are you losing your eyes? That is *Andelain*."

She could not meet his dark stare. "I don't know anything about Andelain. I can't tell. It's too powerful. I can't stand anymore. I could lose my mind in there."

"You could find it in there," he returned intensely. "I keep talking about fighting the Sunbane, and you don't know whether to believe me or not. The answer's in there. Andelain denies the Sunbane. Even I can see that. The Sunbane isn't omnipotent.

"Of course Andelain's powerful," he went on in a rush of ire and persuasion. "It has to be. But we need power. We've got to know how Andelain stays clear.

"I can understand Hollian. Even Sunder. The Sunbane made them what they are. It's cruel and terrible, but it makes sense. A world full of lepers can't automatically trust someone with good nerves. But *you*. You're a doctor. Fighting sickness is your business.

"Linden." His hands gripped her shoulders, forced her to look at him. His eyes were gaunt and grim, placing demands upon her as if he believed that anybody could do the things he did. As if he did not know that he owed her his life, that all his show of determination or bravery would already have come to nothing without her. "Come with me."

In spite of his presumption, she wanted to be equal to him. But her recollections of venom were too acute to be endured. She needed to recover herself. "I can't. I'm afraid."

The fury in his gaze looked like grief. She dropped her eyes. After a moment, he said distantly, "I'll be back in two or three days. It's probably better this way. Numbness has its advantages. I probably won't be so vulnerable to whatever's in there. When I get back, we'll decide what to do."

She nodded dumbly. He released her.

The sun was rising, clothed in a cymar of emerald. When she raised her head again, he was in the River, swimming toward Andelain as if he were capable of anything. Green-tinged light danced on the ripples of his passing. The venom was still in him.

PART II

Vision

TWELVE: The Andelainian Hills

As Thomas Covenant passed the venerable oak and began angling his way up into Andelain, he left a grieved and limping part of himself with Linden. He was still weak from the attack of the bees, and did not want to be alone. Unwillingly, almost unconsciously, he had come to depend on Linden's presence. He felt bound to her by many cords. Some of them he knew: her courage and support; her willingness to risk herself on his behalf. But others seemed to have no name. He felt almost physically linked to her without knowing why. Her refusal to accompany him made him afraid.

Part of his fear arose from the fear of his companions; he dreaded to learn that behind its beauty Andelain was secretly chancrous. But he had been a leper for too long, was too well acquainted with cunning disease, that kind of dread could only increase his determination. Most of his trepidation sprang from Linden's rejection, from what that decision might mean.

For most of his hopes revolved around her. Doubt eroded his previous victory in the Land. He could not shake the gnawing conviction that in choosing to buy Joan's safety he had sold himself to the Despiser, had given up the freedom on which efficacy against Despite depended; he had felt that knife strike his chest, and knew he might fail. *The wild magic is no longer potent against me. Of your own volition you will give the white gold into my hand.* But Linden was another question. She had been chosen by the old man who had once told him to *Be true.* In their summoning, Lord Foul had betrayed no knowledge of or desire for her presence. And since then she had showed herself capable of many things.

Behind her self-severity, she was beautiful. How could he not place hope in such a woman?

But now her refusal of Andelain seemed to imply that his hope was based on quicksand, that her clenched will was an articulation of cowardice rather than courage.

He understood such things. He was a leper, and lepers were taught cowardice by every hurt in all the world. If anything, her decision increased his empathy for her. But he was alone; and he knew from long and brutal experience how little he could accomplish alone. Even the apotheosis of his former power against Lord Foul would have gone for nothing without the support and laughter of Saltheart Foamfollower.

So as he climbed into Andelain, he felt that he was walking into a bereavement, a loss of comradeship, of hope, perhaps of courage, from which he might never recover.

At the hillcrest, he paused to wave at his companions. But they did not reply; they were not looking at him. Their lack of response hurt him as if they had deliberately turned their backs.

But he was a man who had always been faithful to his griefs; and the Land had become a rending and immedicable sorrow to him. He went on into Andelain because he needed health, power, knowledge. So that he could try to restore what had been lost.

Soon, however, his mood changed. For this was Andelain, as precious to his memory as his dearest friendships in the Land. In this air—ether as crisp as sempiternal spring—he could not even see the sun's chrysoprastic aura; the sunshine contained nothing except an abundance of beauty. The grass unrolling under his feet was lush and beryl-green, freshly jeweled with dew. Woodlands extended north and east of him. Broad Gilden fondled the breeze with their wide gold leaves; stately elms fronted the azure of the sky like princes; willows as delicate as filigree beckoned to him, inviting him into their heart-healing shade. All about the hale trunks, flowers enriched the greensward: daisies and columbine and elegant forsythia in profusion. And over everything lay an atmosphere of pristine and vibrant loveliness, as if here and in no other place lived quintessential health, nature's pure gift to assuage the soul.

Munching *aliantha* as he passed, loping down long hillsides, bursting occasionally into wild leaps of pleasure, Thomas Covenant traveled swiftly into Andelain.

Gradually, he grew calmer, became more attuned to the taintless tranquility of the Hills. Birds sang among the branches; small woodland animals darted through the trees. He did nothing to disturb them. And after he had walked for some distance, drinking in thirstily the roborant of Andelain, he returned his thoughts to his companions, to Hollian and Sunder. He felt sure now that the Hills were not cancerous, that they contained no secret and deadly ill. Such an idea had become inconceivable. But at the same time the intensity of what he saw and felt and loved increased his comprehension of the Stonedownors.

They were like lepers; all the people of the Land were like lepers. They were the victims of the Sunbane, victims of an ill for which there was no cure and no escape. Outcast from the beauty of the world. And under such conditions, the need to survive exacted harsh penalties. No thing under the sun was as perilous to a leper as his own yearning for the kind of life, companionship, hope, denied him by his disease. That susceptibility led to despair and self-contempt, to the conviction that the outcasting of the leper was just—condign punishment for an affliction which must have been deserved.

Seen in that way, Andelain was a living vindication of the Sunbane. The Land was not like Andelain because the people of the Land merited retribution rather than loveliness. What else could they believe, and still endure the penury of their lives? Like so many lepers, they were driven to approve their own destitution. Therefore Sunder could not trust anything which was not ruled by the Sunbane. And Hollian believed that Andelain would destroy her. They had no choice.

No choice at all. Until they learned to believe that the Sunbane was not the whole truth of their lives. Until Covenant found an answer which could set them free.

He was prepared to spend everything he possessed, everything he was, to open the way for Sunder, and Hollian, and Linden to walk Andelain unafraid.

Through the day, he journeyed without rest. He did not need rest. The *aliantha* healed the effects of the venom, and the water in the cleanly streams made him feel as fresh as a newborn; and each new vista was itself a form of sustenance, vivid and delicious. The sun set in splendor long before he was ready to stop. He could not stop. He went on, always northeastward, until the gloaming became night, and the stars came smiling out of their celestial deeps to keep him company.

But the darkness was still young when he was halted by the sight of a faint yellow-orange light, flickering through the trees like a blade of fire. He did not seek to approach it; memories held him still. He stood hushed and reverent while the flame wandered toward him. And as it came, it made a fine clear tinkling sound, like the chime of delicate crystal.

Then it bobbed in the air before him, and he bowed low to it, for it was one of the Wraiths of Andelain—a flame no larger than his hand dancing upright as if the darkness were an invisible wick. Its movement matched his obeisance; and when it floated slowly away from him, he followed after it. Its lustre made his heart swell. Toward the Wraiths of Andelain he felt a keen grief which he would have given anything to relieve. At one time, scores of them had died because he had lacked the power to save them.

Soon this Wraith was joined by another—and then by still others—and then he was surrounded by dancing as he walked. The bright circle and high, light ringing of the flames guided him, so that he went on and on as if he knew his way until a slim sliver-moon rose above the eastern Hills.

Thus the Wraiths brought him to a tall knoll, bare of trees but opulently grassed. There the chiming faded into a stronger music. The very air became the song to which the stars measured out their gavotte, and every blade of grass was a note in the harmony. It was a stern song behind its quietude, and it held a long sorrow which he understood. The Wraiths remained at the base of the knoll, forming a long ring around it; but the music carried him upward, toward the crest.

And then the song took on words, so distinct that they could never be forgotten. They were sad and resolute, and he might have wept at them if he had been less entranced.

"Andelain I hold and mold within my fragile spell,
    While world's ruin ruins wood and wold.
Sap and bough are grief and grim to me, engrievement fell,
    And petals fall without relief.
    Astricken by my power's dearth,
I hold the glaive of Law against the Earth.

"Andelain I cherish dear within my mortal breast;
    And faithful I withhold Despiser's wish.

But faithless is my ache for dreams and slumbering and rest,
    And burdens make my courage break.
    The Sunbane mocks my best reply,
And all about and in me beauties die.

"Andelain! I strive with need and loss, and ascertain
    That the Despiser's might can rend and rive.
Each falter of my ancient heart is all the evil's gain;
    And it appalls without relent.
    I cannot spread my power more,
Though teary visions come of wail and gore.

"Oh, Andelain! forgive! for I am doomed to fail this war.
    I cannot bear to see you die—and live,
Foredoomed to bitterness and all the gray Despiser's lore.
    But while I can I heed the call
    Of green and tree; and for their worth,
I hold the glaive of Law against the Earth."

Slowly through the music, Covenant beheld the singer.

The man was tall and strong, and robed all in whitest
sendaline. In his hand, he held a gnarled tree limb as a staff.
Melody crowned his head. Music flowed from the lines of his
form in streams of phosphorescence. His song was the very
stuff of power, and with it he cupped the night in the palm
of his hand.

His face had neither eyes nor eye sockets. Though he had
changed mightily in the ten years or thirty-five centuries since
Covenant had last seen him, he did not appear to have aged at
all.

An impulse to kneel swept through Covenant, but he refused it. He sensed that if he knelt now there would be no end
to his need to prostrate himself. Instead, he stood quiet before
the man's immense white music, and waited.

After a moment, the man hummed sternly, "Thomas Covenant, do you know me?"

Covenant met his eyeless gaze. "You're Hile Troy."

"No." The song was absolute. "I am Caer-Caveral, the
Forestal of Andelain. In all the Land I am the last of my
kind."

"Yes," Covenant said. "I remember. You saved my life at
the Colossus of the Fall—after I came out of Morinmoss. I
think you must have saved me in Morinmoss, too."

"There is no Morinmoss." Caer-Caveral's melody became bleakness and pain. "The Colossus has fallen."

No Morinmoss? No forests? Covenant clenched himself, held the tears down. "What do you want from me? I'll do anything."

The Forestal hummed for a moment without answering. Then he sang, "Thomas Covenant, have you beheld Andelain?"

"Yes." Clenching himself. "I've seen it."

"In all the Land, it is the last keep of the Law. With my strength, I hold its fabric unrent here. When I fail in the end—as fail I must, for I am yet Hile Troy withal, and the day comes when I must not refuse to sacrifice my power—there will be no restitution for the abysm of that loss. The Earth will pass into its last age, and nothing will redeem it."

"I know." With his jaws locked. "I know."

"Thomas Covenant," the tall man sang, "I require from you everything and nothing. I have not brought you here this night to ask, but to give. Behold!" A sweeping gesture of his staff scattered the grass with music; and there, through the melody like incarnations of song, Covenant saw them. Pale silver as if they were made of moonshine, though the moon had no such light, they stood before him. Caer-Caveral's streaming argence illumined them as if they had been created out of Forestal-fire.

Covenant's friends.

High Lord Mhoram, with the wise serenity of his eyes, and the crookedness of his smile.

Elena daughter of Lena and rape, herself a former High Lord, beautiful and passionate. Covenant's child; almost his lover.

Bannor of the Bloodguard, wearing poise and capability and the power of judgment which could never be wrested from him.

Saltheart Foamfollower, who towered over the others as he towered over all mortals in size, and humor, and purity of spirit.

Covenant stared at them through the music as if the sinews of his soul were fraying. A moan broke from his chest, and he went forward with his arms outstretched to embrace his friends.

"Hold!"

The Forestal's command froze Covenant before he could close the separation. Immobility filled all his muscles.

"You do not comprehend," Caer-Caveral sang more kindly. "You cannot touch them, for they have no flesh. They are the Dead. The Law of Death has been broken, and cannot be made whole again. Your presence here has called them from their sleep, for all who enter Andelain encounter their Dead here."

Cannot—? After all this time? Tears streamed down Covenant's cheeks; but when Caer-Caveral released him, he made no move toward the specters. Almost choking on his loss, he said, "You're killing me. What do you want?"

"Ah, beloved," Elena replied quickly, in the clear irrefusable voice which he remembered with such anguish, "this is not a time for grief. Our hearts are glad to behold you here. We have not come to cause you pain, but to bless you with our love. And to give you gifts, as the Law permits."

"It is a word of truth," added Mhoram. "Feel joy for us, for none could deny the joy we feel in you."

"Mhoram," Covenant wept. "Elena. Bannor. Oh, Foamfollower!"

The Forestal's voice took on a rumble like the threat of thunder. "Thus it is that men and women find madness in Andelain. This must not be prolonged. Thomas Covenant, it is well that your companions did not accompany you. The man and woman of the Land would break at the sight of their Dead. And the woman of your world would raise grim shades here. We must give our gifts while mind and courage hold."

"Gifts?" Covenant's voice shook with yearning. "Why—? How—?" He was so full of needs that he could not name them all.

"Ah, my friend, forgive us," Mhoram said. "We may answer no questions. That is the Law."

"As in the summoning of dead Kevin which broke the Law of Death," interposed Elena, "the answers of the Dead rebound upon the questioner. We will not harm you with our answers, beloved."

"And you require no answers." Foamfollower was laughing in his gladness. "You are sufficient to every question."

Foamfollower! Tears burned Covenant's face like blood. He was on his knees, though he could not remember kneeling.

"Enough," the Forestal hummed. "Even now he falters."

Graceful and stately, he moved to Covenant's side. "Thomas Covenant, I will not name the thing you seek. But I will enable you to find it." He touched Covenant's forehead with his staff. A white blaze of music ran through Covenant's mind. "The knowledge is within you, though you cannot see it. But when the time has come, you will find the means to unlock my gift." As the song receded, it left nothing in its wake but a vague sense of potential.

Caer-Caveral stepped aside; and High Lord Mhoram came soundlessly forward. "Ur-Lord and Unbeliever," he said gently, "my gift to you is counsel. When you have understood the Land's need, you must depart the Land, for the thing you seek is not within it. The one word of truth cannot be found otherwise. But I give you this caution: do not be deceived by the Land's need. The thing you seek is not what it appears to be. In the end, you must return to the Land."

He withdrew before Covenant could ask him to say more.

Elena took the High Lord's place. "Beloved," she said with a smile of deep affection, "it has befallen me to speak a hard thing to you. The truth is as you have feared it to be; the Land has lost its power to remedy your illness, for much great good has been undone by the Despiser. Therefore I rue that the woman your companion lacked heart to accompany you, for you have much to bear. But she must come to meet herself in her own time. Care for her, beloved, so that in the end she may heal us all."

Then her voice grew sharper, carrying an echo of the feral hate which had led her to break the Law of Death. "This one other thing I say to you also. When the time is upon you, and you must confront the Despiser, he is to be found in Mount Thunder—in Kiril Threndor, where he has taken up his abode."

Elena, Covenant moaned. You still haven't forgiven me, and you don't even know it.

A moment later, Bannor stood before him. The Bloodguard's *Haruchai* face was impassive, implacable. "Unbeliever, I have no gift for you," he said without inflection. "But I say to you, Redeem my people. Their plight is an abomination. And they will serve you well."

Then Foamfollower came forward; and Covenant saw that the Giant was not alone. "My dear friend," said Foamfollower gaily, "to me has fallen the giving of a gift beyond price. Behold!"

He indicated his companion; and Covenant could tell at once that this figure was not one of the Dead. He wore a short gray tunic, and under it all his skin from head to foot was as black as the gaps between the stars. His form was perfectly shaped and strong; but his hair was black, his teeth and gums were black, his pupilless eyes were pure midnight. He held himself as if he were oblivious to the Dead and the Forestal and Covenant. His eyes gazed emptily, regarding nothing.

"He is Vain," said Foamfollower, "the final spawn of the ur-viles." Covenant flinched, remembering ur-viles. But the Giant went on, "He crowns all their generations of breeding. As your friend, I implore you: take him to be your companion. He will not please you, for he does not speak, and serves no purpose but his own. But that purpose is mighty, and greatly to be desired. His makers have ever been lore-wise, though tormented, and when it comes upon him he, at least, will not fail.

"I say that he serves no purpose but his own. Yet in order that you may accept him, the ur-viles have formed him in such a way that he may be commanded once. Once only, but I pray it may suffice. When your need is upon you, and there is no other help, say to him, '*Nekhrimah*, Vain,' and he will obey.

"Thomas Covenant. My dear friend." Foamfollower bent close to him, pleading with him. "In the name of Hotash Slay, where I was consumed and reborn, I beg you to accept this gift."

Covenant could hardly refrain from throwing his arms around the Giant's neck. He had learned a deep dread of the ur-viles and all their works. But Foamfollower had been his friend, and had died for it. Thickly, he said, "Yes. All right."

"I thank you," the Giant breathed, and withdrew.

For a moment, there was silence. Wraith-light rose dimly, and the Dead stood like icons of past might and pain. Caer-Caveral's song took on the cadence of a threnody. Crimson tinged the flow of his phosphorescence. Covenant felt suddenly that his friends were about to depart. At once, his heart began to labor, aching for the words to tell them that he loved them.

The Forestal approached again; but High Lord Mhoram stayed him. "One word more," Mhoram said to Covenant. "This must be spoken, though I risk much in saying it. My friend, the peril upon the Land is not what it was. Lord Foul works in new ways, seeking ruin, and his evil cannot be answered by any combat. He has said to you that you are his Enemy. Remember that he seeks always to mislead you. It boots nothing to avoid his snares, for they are ever beset with other snares, and life and death are too intimately intergrown to be severed from each other. But it is necessary to comprehend them, so that they may be mastered. When—" He hesitated momentarily. "When you have come to the crux, and have no other recourse, remember the paradox of white gold. There is hope in contradiction."

Hope? Covenant cried. Mhoram! Don't you know I'm going to fail?

The next moment, Caer-Caveral's song came down firmly on the back of his neck, and he was asleep in the thick grass.

THIRTEEN: Demondim-Spawn

WHEN he awoke, his face itched as if the grass had grown into his beard, and his back was warm with midmorning sun.

He raised his head. He was still atop the knoll where he had met Caer-Caveral and the Dead. Andelain lay around him, unfolded like a flower to the sun. But he observed the trees and sky abstractly; the Hills had temporarily lost their power over him. He was too full of ashes to be moved.

He remembered the previous night clearly. He remembered everything about it except the conviction of its reality.

But that lasted for only a moment. When he sat up, changed his range of sight, he saw Vain.

The Demondim-spawn made everything else certain.

He stood just as he had the night before, lightly poised and oblivious. Covenant was struck once again by Vain's physical perfection. His limbs were smooth and strong; his flesh bore no blemish; he might have been an idealized piece of statuary.

He gave no sign that he was aware of Covenant's awakening, that he was cognizant of Covenant at all. His arms hung relaxed, with the elbows slightly crooked, as if he had been made for readiness but had not yet been brought to life. No respiration stirred his chest; his eyes neither blinked nor shifted.

Slowly, Covenant reviewed the other gifts he had been given. They were all obscure to him. But Vain's solidity conveyed a kind of reassurance. Covenant took his companion as a promise that the other gifts would prove to be equally substantial.

Seeking relief from his sense of loss, he rose to his feet, faced Vain. He considered the dark form briefly, then said, "Foamfollower says you don't talk. Is that true?"

Vain did not react. An ambiguous smile hung on his lips, but no expression altered the fathomless ebony of his orbs. He might as well have been blind.

"All right," Covenant muttered. "You don't speak. I hope the other things he said are true, too. I don't want to test it. I'm going to put off commanding you as long as I can. If those ur-viles lied—" He frowned, trying to penetrate the mystery of his companion; but no intuition came to his aid. "Maybe Linden can tell me something about you." Vain's black gaze did not shift. After a moment, Covenant growled, "I also hope I don't get in the habit of talking to you. This is ridiculous."

Feeling vaguely foolish, he glanced at the sun to ascertain his directions, then started down the knoll to begin the journey back to his friends.

The Demondim-spawn followed a few paces behind him. Vain moved as if he had memorized his surroundings long ago, and no longer needed to take notice of them. In spite of his physical solidity, his steps made no sound, left no impression in the grass.

Covenant shrugged, and set off southwestward through the Hills of Andelain.

By noon, he had eaten enough *aliantha* to comprise a feast, and had begun to recover his joy. Andelain did far more for him than give comfort to his eyes and ears or provide solace for his loss. Lord Foul had deprived him of the most exquisite pleasure of his previous visit here—the ability to *feel* health like a palpable cynosure in every green and living thing about him. But the Hills seemed to understand his plight, and adjust their appeal to offer him what he could enjoy. The air was refulgent with gay birds. The grass cushioned his feet, so that his knees and thighs felt exuberant at every stride. *Aliantha* nourished him until all his muscles were suffused with vitality.

Thus Andelain transformed his grief, melded it into a granitic sense of purpose. He considered the hazards ahead of him without dread, and swore an implacable oath without fear or fury, an oath that Andelain would not fall while he still had breath or pulse to defend it.

In the middle of the afternoon, he came upon a stream running placidly over a bed of fine sand, and stopped to give himself a bath. He knew that he would not be able to rejoin his companions by nightfall, so he did not begrudge the time. Stripping off his clothes, he scrubbed himself from head to foot with sand until he began to feel clean for the first time in many days.

Vain stood beside the stream as if he had been rooted to that spot all his life. A mischievous impulse came over Covenant; without warning, he slapped a spray of water at the Demondim-spawn. Droplets gleamed on Vain's obsidian flesh and dripped away, but he betrayed no flicker of consciousness.

Hellfire, Covenant muttered. A touch of prescience darkened his mood. He began almost grimly to wash his clothes.

Soon he was on his way again, with Vain trailing behind him.

He had planned to continue walking until he reached the Mithil valley and his companions. But this night was the dark of the moon, and the stars did not give much light. As the last illumination of evening faded from the air, he decided to stop.

For a time, he had trouble sleeping. An innominate anxiety disturbed his rest. Vain held himself like an effigy of darkness, hinting at dangers. An ur-vile, Covenant growled. He could not trust an ur-vile. They, the Demondim-spawn, were one of the ancient races of the Land; and they had served Lord Foul for millennia. Covenant had been attacked time and again by the roynish creatures. Eyeless and bloodthirsty, they had devoured scores of Wraiths at a time when he had been empty of power. Now he could not believe that the ur-viles which had given Vain to Foamfollower had told the truth.

But the air and grass of Andelain were an elixir that answered his vague distress; and eventually he slept.

He was awake and traveling in the exultation of sunrise. Regret clouded his mood now; he did not want to leave Andelain. But he did not let that slow him. He was concerned for his companions. Well before noon, he crested the last line of hills above the Mithil River.

He had reached the valley too far east; the old oak at the corner of Andelain was half a league or more away to his right. He moved briskly toward it along the crests, watching intently for a glimpse of his friends.

But when he neared the majestic tree, he could see no sign of Linden, Sunder, or Hollian.

He stopped, scanned the barren region across the Mithil for some sign of his companions. It was larger than he had realized. In his eagerness to enter Andelain, he had paid little attention to the area. Now he saw that the wrecked rock and dead shale spread some distance south through the hills, and perhaps a league west into the Plains. Nothing grew anywhere in that blasted region; it lay opposite him like a corpse of stone. But its edges were choked by the teeming verdure of the fertile sun. Two periods of fertility without a desert interval between them to clear the ground made the area look like a dead island under green siege.

But of Linden and the two Stonedownors there was no trace.

Covenant pelted down the hillside. He hit the water in a shallow dive, clawed the surface of the Mithil to the south bank. In moments, he stood on the spot where he had said farewell to Linden.

He remembered the place exactly, all the details matched his recollection, it was here, here—! "Linden!" His shout sounded small against the desolation of the rocks, disappeared without echo into the surrounding jungle. *"Linden!"*

He could find no evidence that she had been here, that he had ever had any companions at all.

The sun wore its green carcanet like a smirk of disdain. His mind went blank with dread for a moment. Curses he could not utter beat against his stupefaction. His companions were gone. He had left them, and in his absence something had happened to them. Another Rider? Without him to defend them—! What have I done? Pounding his fists dumbly at each other, he found himself staring into Vain's unreachable eyes.

The sight jarred him. "They were *here!*" he spat as if the Demondim-spawn had contradicted him. A shudder ran through him, became cold fury. He began to search the region. "They didn't abandon me. Something chased them off. Or they were captured. They weren't killed—or badly hurt. There's no blood."

He picked a tall pile of boulders and scrambled up it, regardless of his vertigo. Standing precariously atop the rocks, he looked across the River toward the Plains bordering Andelain. But the tangle of the monstrous vegetation was impenetrable; his companions could have been within hailing distance, and he would not have been able to see them. He turned, studied the wreckage south and west of him. That wilderland was rock-littered and chaotic enough to conceal a myriad perils.

"Linden!" he yelled. "Sunder! Hollian!"

His voice fell stricken to the ground. There was no answer.

He did not hesitate. A *geas* was upon him. He descended from the boulders, returned to the place where he had last seen Linden. As he moved, he gathered small stones. With them, he made an arrow on the rock, pointing toward the interior of the wilderland, so that, if his companions returned for him, they would know where he had gone. Then he set off along the line of his arrow.

Vain followed him like an embodied shadow.

Covenant moved rapidly, urgently. His gaze hunted the terrain like a VSE. He wanted to locate or fall prey to whatever was responsible for the disappearance of his friends. When he knew the nature of the peril, he would know how to respond. So he made no attempt at stealth. He only kept his eyes alert, and went scuttling across the rocks and shale like a man bent on his own destruction.

He drove himself for a league through the ruins before he paused to reconsider his choice of directions. He was badly winded by his exertions; yet Vain stood nearby as if he had never stood anywhere else—indefatigable as stone. Cursing Vain's blankness or his own mortality, Covenant chose a leaning stone spire, and climbed it to gain a vantage on his surroundings.

From the spire, he saw the rims of a long canyon perhaps

half a league due west of him. At once, he decided to turn
toward it; it was the only prominent feature in the area.

He slid back down the spire too quickly. As he landed, he
missed his balance and sprawled in front of Vain.

When he regained his feet, he and the Demondim-spawn
were surrounded by four men.

They were taller than Stonedownors, slimmer. They wore
rock-hued robes of a kind which Covenant had learned to
associate with Woodhelvennin. But their raiment was ill-
kempt. A fever of violence glazed their eyes. Three of them
wielded long stone clubs; the fourth had a knife. They held
their weapons menacingly, advanced together.

"Hellfire," Covenant muttered. His hands made unconscious warding gestures. "Hell and blood."

Vain gazed past the men as if they were trivial.

Malice knotted their faces. Covenant groaned. Did every
human being in the Land want to kill him? But he was too
angry to retreat. Hoping to take the Woodhelvennin by surprise, he snapped abruptly, "Where's Linden?"

The man nearest him gave a glint of recognition.

The next instant, one of them charged. Covenant flinched;
but the others did not attack. The man sprang toward Vain.
With his club, he levelled a smashing blow at Vain's skull.

The stone burst into slivers. The man cried out, backed
away clutching his elbows.

Vain's head shifted as if he were nodding. He did not
acknowledge the strike with so much as a blink of his black
eyes. He was uninjured and oblivious.

Amazed uncertainty frightened the other men. A moment
later, they started forward with the vehemence of fear.

Covenant had no time for astonishment. He had a purpose
of his own, and did not intend to see it fail like this. Before
the men had advanced two steps, he spread his arms and
shouted, "Stop!" with all the ferocity of his passion.

His cry made the air ring. The men halted.

"Listen!" he rasped. "I'm not your enemy, and I don't
intend to get beaten to death for my innocence!" The man
with the knife waved it tentatively. Covenant jabbed a finger
in his direction. "I mean it! If you want us, here we are. But
you don't have to kill us." He was trembling; but the sharp
authority in his voice leashed his attackers.

The man who had recognized Linden's name hesitated, then

revealed himself as the leader. "If you resist," he said tautly, "all Stonemight Woodhelven will arise to slay you."

Covenant let bitterness into his tone. "I wouldn't dream of resisting. You've got Linden. I want to go wherever she is."

Angry and suspicious, the man tried to meet Covenant's glare, but could not. With his club, he pointed toward the canyon. "There."

"There," Covenant muttered. "Right." Turning his back on the Woodhelvennin, he marched off in that direction.

The leader barked an order; and the man with the stunned arms hurried past Covenant. The man knew the rocks and ruins intimately; the path he chose was direct and well-worn. Sooner than he had expected, Covenant was led into a crevice which split the canyon-rim. The floor of the crevice descended steeply before it opened into its destination.

Covenant was surprised by the depth of the canyon. The place resembled a gullet; the rock of the upper edges looked like dark teeth silhouetted against the sky. Unforeseen dangers seemed to crouch, waiting, in the shadows of the walls. For a moment, he faltered. But his need to find his companions impelled him. As he was steered toward the dwellings of the Woodhelven, he studied everything he could see, searching for information, hope.

He was struck initially by the resemblance between the village and the men who had captured him. Stonemight Woodhelven was slovenly; its inhabitants were the first careless people he had met in the Land. The canyon floor around the houses was strewn with refuse; and the people wore their robes as if they had no interest in the appearance or even the wholeness of their apparel. Many of them looked dirty and ill-used, despite the fact that they were obviously well-fed. And the houses were in a similar condition. The wooden structures were fundamentally sound. Each stood on massive stilts for protection against the force of water which ran through the canyon during a sun of rain; and all had frames of logs as heavy as vigas. But the construction of the walls was sloppy, leaving gaps on all sides; and many of the door-ladders had broken rungs and twisted runners.

Covenant stared with surprise and growing trepidation as he moved through the disorganized cluster of huts. How——? he wondered. How can people this careless survive the Sun-bane?

Yet in other ways they did not appear careless. Their eyes smoldered with an odd combination of belligerence and fright as they regarded him. They reminded him strangely of Drool Rockworm, the Cavewight who had been ravaged almost to death by his lust for the Illearth Stone.

Covenant's captors took him to the largest and best-made of the houses. There, the leader called out, "Graveler!" After a few moments, a woman emerged and came down the ladder to face Covenant and Vain. She was tall, and moved with a blend of authority and desperation. Her robe was a vivid emerald color—the first bright raiment Covenant had seen— and it was whole; but she wore it untidily. Her hair lay in a frenzy of snarls. She had been weeping; her visage was dark and swollen, battered by tears.

He was vaguely confused to meet a Graveler in a Woodhelven. Formerly, the people of wood and stone had kept their lores separate. But he had already seen evidence that such distinctions of devotion no longer obtained. After Lord Foul's defeat, the villages must have had a long period of interaction and sharing. Therefore Crystal Stonedown had raised an eh-Brand who used wood, and Stonemight Woodhelven was led by a Graveler.

She addressed the leader of the captors. "Brannil?"

The man poked Covenant's shoulder. "Graveler," he said in a tone of accusation, "this one spoke the name of the stranger, companion to the Stonedownors." Grimly, he continued, "He is the Halfhand. He bears the white ring."

She looked down at Covenant's hand. When her eyes returned to his face, they were savage. "By the Stonemight!" she snarled, "we will yet attain recompense." Her head jerked a command. Turning away, she went toward her house.

Covenant was slow to respond. The woman's appearance— and the mention of his friends—had stunned him momentarily. But he shook himself alert, shouted after the Graveler, "Wait!"

She paused. Over her shoulder, she barked, "Brannil, has he shown power against you?"

"No, Graveler," the man replied.

"Then he has none. If he resists you, strike him senseless." Stiffly, she reentered her dwelling and closed the door.

At once, hands grabbed Covenant's arms, dragged him toward another house, thrust him at the ladder. Unable to regain his balance, he fell against the rungs. Immediately, several men forced him up the ladder and through the doorway with such roughness that he had to catch himself on the far wall.

Vain followed him. No one had touched the Demondim-spawn. He climbed into the hut of his own accord, as if he were unwilling to be separated from Covenant.

The door slammed shut. It was tied with a length of vine.

Muttering, "Damnation," Covenant sank down the wall to sit on the woven-wood floor and tried to think.

The single room was no better than a hovel. He could see through chinks in the walls and the floor. Some of the wood looked rotten with age. Anybody with strength or a knife could have broken out. But freedom was not precisely what he wanted. He wanted Linden, wanted to find Sunder and Hollian. And he had no knife. His resources of strength did not impress him.

For a moment, he considered invoking his one command from Vain, then rejected the idea. He was not that desperate yet. For some time, he studied the village through the gaps in the walls, watched the afternoon shadows lengthen toward evening in the canyon. But he saw nothing that answered any of his questions. The hovel oppressed him. He felt more like a prisoner—more ineffectual and doomed—than he had in Mithil Stonedown. A sense of impending panic constricted his heart. He found himself clenching his fists, glaring at Vain as if the Demondim-spawn's passivity were an offense to him.

His anger determined him. He checked through the front wall to be sure the two guards were still there. Then he carefully selected a place in the center of the door where the wood looked weak, measured his distance from it, and kicked.

The house trembled. The wood let out a dull splitting noise.

The guards sprang around, faced the door.

Covenant kicked the spot again. Three old branches snapped, leaving a hole the size of his hand.

"Ware, prisoner!" shouted a guard. "You will be clubbed!"

Covenant answered with another kick. Splinters showed along one of the inner supports.

The guards hesitated, clearly reluctant to attempt opening the door while it was under assault.

Throwing his weight into the blow, Covenant hit again.

One guard poised himself at the foot of the ladder. The other sprinted toward the Graveler's dwelling.

Covenant grinned fiercely. He went on kicking at the door, but did not tire himself by expending much effort. When the Graveler arrived, he gave the wood one last blow and stopped.

At a command from the Graveler, a guard ascended the ladder. Watching Covenant warily through the hole, he untied the lashings, then sprang away to evade the door if Covenant kicked it again.

Covenant did not. He pushed the door aside with his hand and stood framed in the entryway to confront the Graveler. Before she could address him, he snapped, "I want to talk to you."

She drew herself up haughtily. "Prisoner, I do not wish to speak with you."

He overrode her. "I don't give a good goddamn what you wish. If you think I don't have power, you're sadly mistaken. Why else does the Clave want me dead?" Bluffing grimly, he rasped, "Ask your men what happened when they attacked my companion."

The narrowing of her eyes revealed that she had already been apprised of Vain's apparent invulnerability.

"I'll make a deal with you," he went on, denying her time to think. "I'm not afraid of you. But I don't want to hurt you. I can wait until you decide to release me yourself. If you'll answer some questions, I'll stop breaking this house down."

Her eyes wandered momentarily, returned to his face. "You have no power."

"Then what are you afraid of?"

She hesitated. He could see that she wanted to turn away; but his anger undermined her confidence. Apparently, her confidence had already taken heavy punishment from some other source. After a moment, she murmured thickly, "Ask."

At once, he said, "You took three prisoners—a woman named Linden Avery and two Stonedownors. Where are they?"

The Graveler did not meet his gaze. Somehow, his question touched the cause of her distress. "They are gone."

"Gone?" A lurch of dread staggered his heart. "What do you mean?" She did not reply. "*Did you kill them?*"

"No!" Her look was one of outraged hunger, the look of a predator robbed of its prey. "It was our *right*! The Stonedownors were enemies! Their blood was forfeit by right of capture. They possessed Sunstone and *lianar*, also forfeit. And

the blood of their companion was forfeit as well. The friend
of enemies is also an enemy. It was our right."

"But we were reft of our right." A corrupt whine wounded
her voice. "The three fell to us in the first day of the fertile
sun. And that same night came Santonin na-Mhoram-in on
his Courser." Her malignant grief was louder than shouting.
"In the name of the Clave, we were riven of that which was
ours. Your companions are nothing, Halfhand. I acceded
them to the Rider without compunction. They are gone to
Revelstone, and I pray that their blood may rot within them."

Revelstone? Covenant groaned. Hellfire! The strength
drained from his knees; he had to hold himself up on the
doorframe.

But the Graveler was entranced by her own suffering, and
did not notice him. "Yes, and rot the Clave as well," she
screamed. "The Clave and all who serve the na-Mhoram. For
by Santonin we were riven also of the power to live. The
Stonemight—!" Her teeth gnashed. "When I discover who
betrayed our possession of the Stonemight to Santonin na-
Mhoram-in, I will rend the beating heart from that body and
crush it in my hands!"

Abruptly, she thrust her gaze, as violent as a lance, at
Covenant. "I pray your white ring is such a periapt as the
Riders say. That will be our recompense. With your ring, I
will bargain for the return of the Stonemight. Yes, and more
as well. Therefore make ready to die, Halfhand. In the dawn I
will spill your life. It will give me joy."

Fear and loss whirled through Covenant, deafening him to
the Graveler's threat, choking his protests in his throat. He
could grasp nothing clearly except the peril of his friends.
Because he had insisted on going into Andelain—

The Graveler turned on her heel, strode away: he had to
struggle to gasp after her, "When did they go?"

She did not reply. But one of the guards said warily, "At
the rising of the second fertile sun."

Damnation! Almost two days—! On a Courser! As the
guards shoved him back into the hovel and retied the door,
Covenant was thinking stupidly, I'll never catch up with them.

A sea of helplessness broke over him. He was emprisoned
here while every degree of the sun, every heartbeat of time,
carried his companions closer to death. Sunder had said that
the Earth was a prison for a-Jeroth of the Seven Hells, but
that was not true: it was a jail for him alone, Thomas Cove-

nant the Incapable. If Stonemight Woodhelven had released him at this moment, he would not have been able to save his friends.

And the Woodhelven would not release him; that thought penetrated his dismay slowly. They intended to kill him. At dawn. To make use of his blood. He unclenched his fists, raised his head. Looking through the walls, he saw that the canyon had already fallen into shadow. Sunset was near; evening approached like a leper's fate. Mad anguish urged him to hurl himself against the weakened door; but the futility of that action restrained him. In his fever for escape, for the power to redeem what he had done to his companions, he turned to his wedding band.

Huddling there against the wall in the gathering dusk, he considered everything he knew about wild magic, remembered everything that had ever given rise to white fire. But he found no hope. He had told Linden the truth: in all his past experiences, every exertion of wild magic had been triggered by the proximity of some other power. His final confrontation with Lord Foul would have ended in failure and Desecration if the Despiser's own weapon, the Illearth Stone, had not been so mighty, had not raised such a potent response from the white gold.

Yet Linden had told him that in his delirium at Crystal Stonedown his ring had emitted light even before the Rider had put forth power. He clung to that idea. High Lord Mhoram had once said to him, *You are the white gold.* Perhaps the need for a trigger arose in him, in his own unresolved reluctance, rather than in the wild magic itself. If that were true—

Covenant settled into a more comfortable position and composed his turmoil with an effort of will. Deliberately, he began to search his memory, his passions, his need, for the key which had unlocked wild magic in his battle with Lord Foul.

He remembered the completeness of his abjection, the extremity of his peril. He remembered vividly the cruelty with which the Despiser had wracked him, striving to compel the surrender of his ring. He remembered the glee with which Lord Foul had envisioned the Land as a cesspit of leprosy.

And he remembered the awakening of his rage for lepers, for victims and destitution. That passion—clear and pure beyond any fury he had ever felt—had carried him into the eye of the paradox, the place of power between conflicting impossibilities: impossible to believe the Land real; impossible to refuse the Land's need. Anchored by the contradiction itself, made strong by rage, he had faced Lord Foul, and had prevailed.

He remembered it all, re-experienced it with an intensity that wrung his heart. And from his intensity he fashioned a command for the wild magic—a command of fire.

The ring remained inert on the second finger of his half-hand. It was barely visible in the dimness.

Despair twisted his guts; but he repressed it, clenched his purpose in both hands like a strangler. Trigger, he panted. Proximity. Bearing memory like an intaglio of flame in his mind, he rose to his feet and confronted the only external source of power available to him. Swinging his half-fist through a tight arc, he struck Vain in the stomach.

Pain shot through his hand; red bursts like exploding carbuncles staggered across his mind. But nothing happened. Vain did not even look at him. If the Demondim-spawn contained power, he held it at a depth Covenant could not reach.

"God damn it!" Covenant spat, clutching his damaged hand and shaking with useless ire. "Don't you understand? They're going to kill me!"

Vain did not move. His black features had already disappeared in the darkness.

"Damnation." With an effort that made him want to weep, Covenant fought down his pointless urge to smash his hands against Vain. "Those ur-viles probably lied to Foamfollower. You're probably just going to stand there and watch them cut my throat."

But sarcasm could not save him. His companions were in such peril because he had left them defenseless. And Foamfollower had been killed in the cataclysm of Covenant's struggle with the Illearth Stone. Foamfollower, who had done more to heal the Despiser's ill than any wild magic—killed because Covenant was too frail and extreme to find any other answer. He sank to the floor like a ruin overgrown with old guilt, and sat there dumbly repeating his last hope until exhaustion dragged him into slumber.

Twice he awakened, pulse hammering, heart aflame, from dreams of Linden wailing for him. After the second, he gave up sleep; he did not believe he could bear that nightmare a third time. Pacing around Vain, he kept vigil among his inadequacies until dawn.

Gradually, the eastern sky began to etiolate. The canyon walls detached themselves from the night, and were left behind like deposits of darkness. Covenant heard people moving outside the hut, and braced himself.

Feet came up the ladder; hands fumbled at the lashings.

When the vine dropped free, he slammed his shoulder against the door, knocking the guard off the ladder. At once, he sprang to the ground, tried to flee.

But he had misjudged the height of the stilts. He landed awkwardly, plunged headlong into a knot of men beyond the foot of the ladder. Something struck the back of his head, triggering vertigo. He lost control of his limbs.

The men yanked him to his feet by the arms and hair. "You are fortunate the Graveler desires you wakeful," one of them said. "Else I would teach your skull the hardness of my club." Dizziness numbed Covenant's legs; the canyon seemed to suffer from nystagmus. The Woodhelvennin hauled him away like a collection of disarticulated bones.

They took him toward the north end of the canyon. Perhaps fifty or sixty paces beyond the last house, they stopped.

A vertical crack split the stone under his feet. Wedged into it was a heavy wooden post, nearly twice his height.

He groaned sickly and tried to resist. But he was helpless.

The men turned him so that he faced the village, then bound his arms behind the post. He made a feeble effort to kick at them; they promptly lashed his ankles as well.

When they were done, they left without a word.

As the vertigo faded, and his muscles began to recover, he gagged on nausea; but his guts were too empty to release anything.

The houses were virtually invisible, lost in the gloaming of the canyon. But after a moment he realized that the post had been placed with great care. A deep gap marked the eastern wall above him; and through it came a slash of dawn. He would be the first thing in Stonemight Woodhelven to receive the sun.

Moments passed. Sunlight descended like the blade of an axe toward his head.

Though he was protected by his boots, dread ached in his bones. His pulse seemed to beat behind his eyeballs.

The light touched his hair, his forehead, his face. While the Woodhelven lay in twilight, he experienced the sunrise like an annunciation. The sun wore a corona of light brown haze. A breath of arid heat blew across him.

Damnation, he muttered. Bloody damnation.

As the glare covered his mien, blinding him to the Woodhelven, a rain of sharp pebbles began to fall on him. Scores of people threw small stones at him.

He squeezed his eyes shut, bore the pain as best he could.

When the pebbles stopped, he looked up again and saw the Graveler approaching out of the darkness.

She held a long, iron knife, single-edged and hiltless. The black metal appeared baleful in her grasp. Her visage had not lost its misery; but it also wore a corrupt exaltation which he could not distinguish from madness.

Twenty paces or more behind the Graveler stood Vain. The Woodhelvennin had wrapped him in heavy vines, trying to restrain him; but he seemed unaware of his bonds. He held himself beyond reach as if he had come simply to watch Covenant die.

But Covenant had no time to think about Vain. The Graveler demanded his attention. "Now," she rasped. "Recompense. I will shed your life, and your blood will raise water for the Woodhelven." She glanced down at the narrow crevice. "And with your white ring we will buy back our Stonemight from the Clave."

Clutching his dismally-rehearsed hope, Covenant asked, "Where's your *orcrest*?"

"*Orcrest*?" she returned suspiciously.

"Your Sunstone."

"Ah," she breathed, "Sunstone. The Rede speaks of such matters." Bitterness twisted her face. "Sunstone is permitted— yet we were reft of our Stonemight. It is not just!" She eyed Covenant as if she were anticipating the taste of his blood. "I have no Sunstone, Halfhand."

No Sunstone? Covenant gasped inwardly. He had hoped with that to ignite his ring. But the Graveler had no Sunstone. No Sunstone. The desert sun shone on him like the bright, hot flood which had borne him into the Land. Invisible vulture-wings beat about his head—heart strokes of insanity. He could barely thrust his voice through the noise. "How can—? I thought every Graveler needed a Sunstone." He knew this was not true, but he wanted to make her talk, delay her. He had already been stabbed once: any similar blow would surely end him. "How else can you work the Sunbane?"

"It is arduous," she admitted, though the hunger in her gaze did not blink. "I must make use of the Rede. The Rede!" Abruptly, she spat into the crack at her feet. "For generations Stonemight Woodhelven has had no need of such knowledge. From Graveler to Graveler the Stonemight has been handed down, and with it we made *life*! Without it, we must grope for survival as we may."

The sun sent sweat trickling through Covenant's beard, down the middle of his back. His bonds cut off the circulation in his arms, tugged pain into his shoulders. He had to swallow several times to clear his throat. "What is it? The Stonemight?"

His question reached her. He saw at once that she could not refuse to talk about the Stonemight. A nausea of love or lust came into her face. She lowered her knife; her eyes lost their focus on him. "Stonemight," she breathed ardently. "Ah, the Stonemight." Her breasts tightened under her green robe as if she were remembering rapture. "It is power and glory, wealth and comfort. A stone of dearest emerald, alight with possibility and cold beyond the touch of any stone. That such might is contained in so small and lovely a periapt! For the Stonemight is no larger than my palm. It is flat, and sharp of edge, like a flake stricken from a larger stone. And it is admirable beyond price."

She went on, unable to rein the rush of her entrancement. But Covenant lost her words in a flash of intuitive horror. Suddenly he was certain that the talisman she described was a fragment of the Illearth Stone.

That conviction blazed through him like appalled lightning. It explained so many things: the ruined condition of this region; the easiness of the Woodhelven's life; the gratuitous violence of the people; the Graveler's obsession. For the Illearth Stone was the very essence of corruption, a bane so malignant that he had been willing to sacrifice Foamfollower's life as well as his own in order to extirpate that evil from the Land. For a moment of dismay, he believed he had failed to destroy the Stone, that the Illearth Stone itself was the source of the Sunbane.

But then another explanation occurred to him. At one time, the Despiser had given each of his Ravers a piece of the Stone. One of these Ravers had marched to do battle against the Lords, and had been met here, at the southwest corner of

Andelain—met and held for several days. Perhaps in that conflict a flake of the Raver's Stone had fallen undetected among the hills, and had remained there, exerting its spontaneous desecration, until some unhappy Woodhelvennin had stumbled across it.

But that did not matter now. A Rider had taken the Stonemight. To Revelstone. Suddenly, Covenant knew that he had to live, had to reach Revelstone. To complete the destruction of the Illearth Stone. So that his past pain and Foamfollower's death would not have been for nothing.

The Graveler was sobbing avidly, "May they rot!" She clenched the haft of her knife like a spike. "Be damned to interminable torment for bereaving me! I curse them from the depths of my heart and the abyss of my anguish!" She jerked the knife above her head. The blade glinted keen and evil in the desert sun. She had lost all awareness of Covenant; her gaze was bent inward on a savage vision of the Clave. "I will slay you all!"

Covenant's shout tore his throat. In horror and desperation, he yelled, "*Nekhrimah*, Vain! Save me."

The Graveler paid no heed. With the whole force of her body, she drove her knife at his chest.

But Vain moved. While the blade arced through its swing, he shrugged his arms free of the bindings.

He was too far away, too late—

From a distance of twenty paces, he closed his fist.

Her arms froze in mid-plunge. The knife tip strained at the center of Covenant's shirt; but she could not complete the blow.

He watched wildly as Vain approached the Graveler. With the back of his hand, Vain struck her. She crumpled. Blood burst from her mouth. As it ran, she twitched once, then lay still.

Vain ignored her. He gestured at the post, and the wood sprang into splinters. Covenant fell; but Vain caught him, set him on his feet.

Covenant allowed himself no time to think. Shedding splinters and vines, he picked up the knife, thrust it into his belt. His arms felt ferocious with the return of circulation. His heart labored acutely. But he forced himself forward. He knew that if he did not keep moving he would collapse in an outrage of reaction. He strode among the paralyzed Woodhelvennin back into the village, and entered the first large house he reached.

His eyes took a moment to pierce the dimness. Then he made out the interior of the room. The things he sought hung on the walls: a woven-vine sack of bread, a leather pouch containing some kind of liquid. He had taken them before he noticed a woman sitting in one of the corners. She held herself small and still in an effort to protect the baby sucking at her breast.

He unstopped the pouch and swallowed deeply. The liquid had a cloying taste, but it washed some of the gall from his throat. Roughly, he addressed the woman. "What is it?"

In a tiny voice, she answered, *"Metheglin."*

"Good." He went to the door, then halted to rasp at her, "Listen to me. This world's going to change. Not just here— not just because you lost your bloody Stonemight. The whole Land is going to be different. You've got to learn to live like human beings. Without all this sick killing."

As he left the house, the baby started crying.

FOURTEEN: Pursuit

He moved brusquely among the stupefied Woodhelvennin. The baby's crying was like a spur in the air; the men and women began to shift, blink their eyes, glance around. In moments, they would recover enough to act. As he reached Vain, he muttered, "Come on. Let's get out of here," and strode away toward the north end of the canyon.

Vain followed.

The sunrise lit Covenant's path. The canyon lay crookedly beyond him, and its rims began to draw together, narrowing until it was little more than a deep sheer ravine. He marched there without a backward look, clinched by the old intransigent stricture of his illness. His friends were already two days ahead of him, and traveling swiftly.

Shouts started to echo along the walls: anger, fear, loss. But he did not falter. Borne on the back of a Courser, Linden and the two Stonedownors might easily reach Revelstone ten days before him. He could conceive of no way to catch up with them in time to do them any good. But leprosy was also a form of despair for which there was no earthly cure; and he had learned to endure it, to make a life for himself in spite of it, by stationing himself in the eye of the paradox, affirming the acceptable humanity of all the contradictions—and by locking his soul in the most rigid possible discipline. The same resources enabled him to face the futile pursuit of his friends.

And he had one scant reason for hope. The Clave had decreed *his* death, not Linden's, Sunder's, Hollian's. Perhaps his companions would be spared, held hostage, so that they could be used against him. Like Joan. He clung to that thought, and strode down the narrowing canyon to the tight beat of his will.

The shouts rose to a crescendo, then stopped abruptly. In the frenzy of their loss, some of the Woodhelvennin set out after him. But he did not look back, did not alter his pace. The canyon was constricted enough now to prevent his pursuers from reaching him without first passing Vain. He trusted that the Demondim-spawn would prove too intimidating for the Woodhelvennin.

Moments later, he heard bare feet slapping stone, echoing. Apprehension knotted his shoulders. To ease himself, he attempted a bluff. "Vain!" he shouted without turning his head. "Kill the first one who tries to get past you!" His words danced between the walls like a threat of murder.

But the runners did not hesitate. They were like their Graveler, addicts of the Illearth Stone; violence was their only answer to loss. Their savage cries told Covenant that they were berserk.

The next instant, one of them screamed hideously. The others scrambled to a halt.

Covenant whirled.

Vain stood facing the Woodhelvennin—five of them, the nearest still ten paces away. That man knelt with his back arched and straining, black agony in his face. Vain clenched his fist toward the man. With a wrench, he burst the man's heart.

"Vain!" Covenant yelled. "Don't—! I didn't mean it!"

The next Woodhelvennin was fifteen paces away. Vain made a clawing gesture. The man's face, the whole front of his skull, tore open, spilling brains and gore across the stone.

"*Vain!*"

But Vain had not yet satisfied Covenant's command. Knees slightly bent, he confronted the three remaining men. Covenant howled at them to flee; but the berserkergang was on them, and they could not flee. Together, they hurled themselves at Vain.

He swept them into his embrace, and began to crush them with his arms.

Covenant leaped at Vain's back. "Stop!" He strove to pry Vain's head back, force him to ease his grip. "You don't have to do this!" But Vain was granite and unreachable. He squeezed until the men lost the power to scream, to breathe. Their ribs broke like wet twigs. Covenant pounded his fury at the Demondim-spawn; but Vain did not release the men until they were dead.

Then in panic Covenant saw a crowd of Woodhelvennin surging toward him. "No!" he cried, "get back!" and the echoes ran like terror down the canyon. But the people did not stop.

He could not think of anything else to do. He left Vain and fled. The only way he could prevent Vain from butchering more people was by saving himself, completing the command. Desperately, he dashed away, running like the virulence of his curses.

Soon the rims of the canyon closed above him, forming a tunnel. But the light behind him and the glow at the far end of the passage enabled him to keep up his pace. The loud reiteration of his boots deafened him to the sounds of pursuit.

When he cast a glance backward, he saw Vain there, matching his speed without effort.

After some distance, he reached sunlight in the dry riverbed of the Mithil. Panting raggedly, he halted, rested against the bank. As soon as he could muffle his respiration, he listened at the tunnel; but he heard nothing. Perhaps five corpses were enough to check the extremity of the Woodhelvennin. With rage fulminating in his heart, he swung on Vain.

"Listen to me," he spat. "I don't care how bad it gets. If you *ever* do something like that again, I swear to God I'll take you back where I found you, and you and your whole bloody purpose can just *rot!*"

But the Demondim-spawn looked as blank as stone. He stood with his elbows slightly bent, his eyes unfocused, and betrayed no awareness of Covenant's existence.

"Sonofabitch," Covenant muttered. Deliberately, he turned away from Vain. Gritting his will, he forced his anger into another channel, translated it into strength for what he had to do. Then he went to climb the north bank of the Mithil.

The sack of bread and the pouch of *metheglin* hampered him, making the ascent difficult; but when he gained the edge and stopped, he did not stop because he was tired. He was halted by the effect of the desert sun on the monstrous vegetation.

The River was dry. He had noticed that fact without pausing to consider it. But he considered it now. As far as he could see, grass as high as houses, shrubs the size of hillocks, forests of bracken, trees that pierced the sky—all had already been reduced to a necrotic gray sludge lying thigh-deep over every contour of the terrain.

The brown-clad sun melted every form of plant fiber, desiccated every drop of sap or juice, sublimated everything that grew. Every wood and green and fertile thing simply ran down itself like spilth, making one turgid puddle which the Sunbane sucked away as if the air were inhaling sludge. When he stepped into the muck in order to find out whether or not he could travel under these conditions, he was able to see the level of the viscid slop declining. It left a dead gray stain on his pants.

The muck sickened him. Involuntarily, he delayed. To clear his throat, he drank some of the *metheglin*, then chewed slowly at half a loaf of unleavened bread as he watched the sludge evaporate. But the pressure in him would not let him wait long. As the slop sank to the middle of his shins, he took a final swig of *metheglin*, stopped the pouch, and began slogging northwestward toward Revelstone, elevenscore leagues distant.

The heat was tremendous. By midmorning, the ground was bare and turning arid; the horizons had begun to shimmer, collapsing in on Covenant as if the desert sun shrank the world. Now there was nothing to hinder his progress across the waste of the Center Plains—nothing except light as eviscerating as fire, and air which seemed to wrench the moisture from his flesh, and giddy heatwaves, and Sunbane.

He locked his face toward Revelstone, marched as if neither sun nor wilderland had the power to daunt him. But dust and dryness clogged his throat. By noon, he had emptied half his leather pouch. His shirt was dark with sweat. His forehead felt blistered, flushed by chills. The haze affected his balance, so that he stumbled even while his legs were still strong enough to be steady. And his strength did not last; the sun leeched it from him, despite his improvident consumption of bread and *metheglin*.

For a time, indecision clouded his mind. His only hope of gaining on Linden lay in traveling day and night without letup. If he acted rationally, journeyed only at night while the desert sun lasted, then the Rider's Courser would increase the distance between them every day. But he could not endure this pace. The hammer of the Sunbane was beating his endurance thinner and thinner; at confused moments, he felt translucent already.

When his brain became so giddy that he found himself wondering if he could ask Vain to carry him, he acknowledged his limitations. In a flinch of lucidity, he saw himself clinging to Vain's shoulders while the Demondim-spawn stood motionless under the sun because Covenant was not moving. Bitterly, he turned northeast toward Andelain.

He knew that the marge of Andelain ran roughly parallel to his direct path toward Revelstone; so in the Hills he would be able to stay near the route the Rider must have taken. Yet Andelain was enough out of his way to gall him. From the Hills he might not be able to catch sight of Linden and her companions, even if by some piece of good fortune the Rider was delayed; and the rumpled terrain of Andelain might slow him. But the choice was not one of speed: not under this sun. In Andelain he might at least reach the Soulsease River alive.

And perhaps, he thought, trying to encourage himself, perhaps even a Rider of the Clave could not travel swiftly through the various avatars of the Sunbane. Clenching that idea in his sore throat, he angled in the direction of the Hills.

With Vain striding impassively behind him, he crossed into lushness shortly before dusk. In his bitterness, he did not rejoice to be back within the Land's last bastion of health and Law; but the spring of the turf and the vitality of the *aliantha* affected him like rejoicing. Strength flowed back into his veins; his sight cleared; his raw mouth and throat began to heal. Through the gold-orange emblazonry of the sunset, he stiffened his pace and headed grimly along the skirts of the Hills.

All that night, he did not stop for more than scant moments at a time. Sustained by Andelain, his body bore the merciless demand of his will. The moon was too new to give him aid; but few trees grew along the edges of the Hills and, under an open sky, star-glister sufficed to light his way. Drinking *metheglin* and chewing bread for energy, he stalked the hillsides and the vales. When his pouch was empty, he discarded it. And at all times his gaze was turned westward, searching the Plains for any sign of a fire which might indicate, beyond hope or chance, that the Rider and his prisoners were still within reach. By dawn, he was twenty leagues from Stonemight Woodhelven, and still marching, as if by sheer stubbornness he had abrogated his mortality.

But he could not make himself immune to exhaustion. In spite of *alantha* and clear spring water, bounteous grass and air as vital as an elixir, his exertions eroded him like leprosy. He had passed his limits, and traveled now on borrowed endurance—stamina wrested by plain intransigence from the ruinous usury of time. Eventually, he came to believe that the end was near, waiting to ambush him at the crest of every rise, at the bottom of every slope. Then his heart rose up in him and, because he was Thomas Covenant the Unbeliever, responsible beyond any exculpation for the outcome of his life, he began to run.

Staggering, stumbling at every third stride, he lumbered northwest, always northwest, within the marge of Andelain, and did not count the cost. Only one concession did he make to his wracked breathing and torn muscles: he ate treasureberries from every *alantha* he passed, and threw the seeds out into the wasteland. Throughout the day he ran, though by midafternoon his pace was no better than a walk; and throughout the day Vain followed, matching stride for stride with his own invulnerability the exhaustion which crumbled Covenant.

Shortly after dark, Covenant broke. He missed his footing, fell, and could not rise. His lungs shuddered for air, but he was not aware of them. Everything in his chest seemed numb, beyond help. He lay stunned until his pulse slowed to a limp and his lungs stopped shivering. Then he slept.

He was awakened near midnight by the touch of a cold hand on his soul. A chill that resembled regret more than fear ran through him. He jerked up his head.

Three silver forms like distilled moonlight stood before him. When he had squeezed the blur of prostration from his sight, he recognized them.

Lena, the woman he had raped.

Atiaran and Trell, her parents.

Trell—tall, bluff, mighty Trell—had been deeply hurt by the harm Covenant had done to Lena and by the damage Atiaran had inflicted on herself in her efforts to serve the Land by saving her daughter's rapist. But the crowning anguish of his life, the pain which had finally unbalanced his mind, had been dealt him by the love Elena Lena-daughter bore for Covenant.

Atiaran had sacrificed all her instincts, all her hard-won sense of rectitude, for Covenant's sake; she had believed him necessary to the Land's survival. But the implications of that self-injury had cost her her life in the end.

And Lena—ah, Lena! She had lived on for almost fifty years, serene in the mad belief that Covenant would return and marry her. And when he had returned—when she had learned that he was responsible for the death of Elena, that he was the cause of the immense torment of the Ranyhyn she adored—she had yet chosen to sacrifice herself in an attempt to save his life.

She did not appear before him in the loveliness of youth, but rather in the brittle caducity of age; and his worn heart cried out to her. He had paid every price he could find in an extravagant effort to rectify his wrongs; but he had never learned to shed the burden of remorse.

Trell, Atiaran, Lena. In each of their faces, he read a reproach as profound as human pain could make it. But when Lena spoke, she did not derogate him. "Thomas Covenant, you have stressed yourself beyond the ability of your body. If you sleep further, it may be that Andelain will spare you from death, but you will not awaken until a day has been lost. Perhaps your spirit has no bounds. Still you are not wise to punish yourself so. Arise! You must eat and move about, lest your flesh fail you."

"It is truth," Atiaran added severely. "You punish yourself for the plight of your companions. But such castigation is a doom which achieves itself. Appalling yourself thus, you ensure that you will fail to redeem your companions. And failure demonstrates your unworth. In punishing yourself, you come to merit punishment. This is Despite, Unbeliever. Arise and eat."

Trell did not speak. But his mute stare was unarguable. Humbly, because of who they were, and because he recognized what they said, Covenant obeyed. His body wept in every joint and thew; but he could not refuse his Dead. Tears ran down his face as he understood that these three—people who in life had had more cause to hate him than anyone else—had come to him here in order to help him.

Lena's arm pointed silver toward a nearby *aliantha.* "Eat every berry. If you falter, we will compel you."

He obeyed, ate all the ripe fruit he could find in the darkness with his numb fingers. Then, tears cold on his cheeks, he set off once again in the direction of Revelstone with his Dead about him like a cortege.

At first, every step was a torment. But slowly he came to feel the wisdom of what his Dead required him to do. His heart grew gradually steadier; the ache of his breathing receded as his muscles loosened. None of the three spectres spoke again, and he had neither the temerity nor the stamina to address them. In silence, the meager procession wound its argent, ghostly way along the border of Andelain. For a long time after his weeping stopped, Covenant went on shedding grief inwardly because his ills were irrevocable, and he could never redeem the misery he had given Trell, Atiaran, and Lena. Never.

Before dawn, they left him—turned abruptly away toward the center of Andelain without allowing him an opportunity to thank them. This he understood; perhaps no gall would have been as bitter to them as the thanks of the Unbeliever. So he said nothing of his gratitude. He stood facing their departure like a salute, murmuring promises in his heart. When their silver had faded, he continued along the path of his purpose.

Dawn and a fresh, gay brook, which lay like music across his track, gave him new strength; he was able to amend his pace until it bore some resemblance to his earlier progress. With Vain always behind him like a detached shadow, he spent the third day of the desert sun traveling Andelain as swiftly as he could without risking another collapse.

That evening, he stopped soon after sunset, under the shelter of a hoary willow. He ate a few *aliantha*, finished the last of his bread, then spent some time seated with his back to the trunk. The tree stood high above the Plains, and he sat facing westward, studying the open expanse of the night without hope, almost without volition, because the plight of his companions did not allow him to relax.

The first blink of fire snatched him instantly to his feet.

The flame vanished as suddenly as it had appeared. But a moment later it recurred. This time, it caught. After several tentative flickers, it became steady.

It was due west of him.

In the darkness, he could not estimate the distance. And he knew logically that it could not be a sign of Linden and the Stonedownors; surely a Rider could travel farther than this on a Courser in five days. But he did not hesitate. Gesturing to Vain, he started down the hill.

The pressure within him mounted at every stride. As he crossed out of Andelain, he was moving at a lope. The fire promptly disappeared beyond a rise in the ground. But he had the direction firmly fixed in his mind. Across the Sunbane-ruined earth he went with alacrity and clenched breath, like a man eager to confront his doom.

He had covered half a league before he glimpsed the fire again. It lay beyond still another rise. But he was close enough now to see that it was large. As he ascended the second rise, he remembered caution and slowed his pace. Climbing the last way in a stealthy crouch, he carefully peered over the ridge.

There: the fire.

Holding his breath, he scanned the area around the blaze.

From the ridge, the ground sloped sharply, then swept away in a long shallow curve for several hundred feet before curling steeply upward to form a wide escarpment. In a place roughly opposite his position, the contour of the ground and the overhang of the escarpment combined to make a depression like a bowl half-buried on edge against the wall of the higher terrain.

The fire burned in this vertical concavity. The half bowl reflected much of the light, but the distance still obscured some details. He could barely see that the fire blazed in a long, narrow mound of wood. The mound lay aimed toward the heart of the bowl; and the fire had obviously been started at the end away from the escarpment, so that, as new wood caught flame, the blaze moved into the bowl. Half the length of the woodpile had already been consumed.

The surrounding area was deserted. Covenant descried no sign of whoever had contrived such a fire. Yet the arrangement was manifestly premeditated. Except for the hunger of the flames, an eerie silence lay over the Plains.

A figure snagged the corner of Covenant's vision. He turned, and saw Vain standing beside him. The Demondim-spawn made no attempt to conceal himself below the ridge.

"Idiot!" whispered Covenant fiercely. "Get down!"

Vain paid no attention. He regarded the fire with the same blind, ambiguous smile that he had worn while traveling through Andelain. Or while killing the people of Stonemight Woodhelven. Covenant grabbed at his arm; but Vain was immovable.

Through his teeth, Covenant muttered, "Damn you, anyway. Someday you're going to be the death of me."

When he looked back toward the fire, it had moved noticeably toward the escarpment, and the bowl was brighter. With a sudden rush of dismay, he saw that the mound of wood ended in a pile around an upright stake as tall and heavy as a man.

Someone or something was tied to the stake. Tied alive. The indistinct figure was struggling.

Hell and blood! Covenant instinctively recognized a trap. For a moment, he was paralyzed. He could not depart, leave that bound figure to burn. And he could not approach closer. An abominable purpose was at work here, malice designed to snare him—or someone else equally vulnerable. Someone else? That question had no answer. But as he gritted himself, trying to squeeze a decision out of his paralysis, he remembered Mhoram's words: *It boots nothing to avoid his snares*—

Abruptly, he rose to his feet. "Stay here," he breathed at Vain. "No sense both of us getting into trouble." Then he went down the slope and strode grimly toward the fire.

Vain followed as usual. Covenant could hardly keep from raging at the Demondim-spawn. But he did not stop.

As he neared the escarpment, the fire began to lick at the woodpile around the stake. He broke into a run. In moments, he was within the bowl and staring at the bait of the trap.

The creature bound to the stake was one of the Waynhim.
Like the ur-viles, the Waynhim were Demondim-spawn.
Except for their gray skin and smaller stature, they resembled
the ur-viles closely. Their hairless bodies had long trunks and
short limbs, with the arms and legs matched in length so that
the creatures could run on all fours as well as walk erect.
Their pointed ears sat high on their bald skulls; their mouths
were like slits. And they had no eyes; they used scent instead
of vision. Wide nostrils gaped in the centers of their faces.

As products of the Demondim, the Waynhim were lore-
wise and cunning. But, unlike their black kindred, they had
broken with Lord Foul after the Ritual of Desecration. Covenant had heard that the Waynhim as a race served the Land
according to their private standards; but he had seen nothing
more of them since his last stay at Revelstone, when a Waynhim had escaped from Foul's Creche to bring the Council
word of Lord Foul's power.

The creature before Covenant now was in tremendous pain.
Its skin was raw. Dark blood oozed from scores of lash-marks.
One of its arms bent at an angle of agony, and its left ear
had been ripped away. But it was conscious. Its head followed
his approach, nostrils quivering. When he stopped to consider
its situation, it strained toward him, begging for rescue.

"Hang on," he rasped, though he did not know if the creature could understand him. "I'll get you out." Fuming in
outrage, he began to scatter the wood, kicking dead boughs
and brush out of his way as he reached toward the stake.

But then the creature seemed to become aware of a new
scent. Perhaps it caught the smell of his wedding ring. He
knew that Demondim-spawn were capable of such perceptions.
It burst into a fit of agitation, began barking in its harsh,
guttural tongue. Urgency filled its voice. Covenant grasped
none of its language; but he heard one word which sent a chill
of apprehension down his spine. Again and again, the Waynhim barked, "*Nekhrimah!*"

Bloody hell! The creature was trying to give Vain some
kind of command.

Covenant did not stop. The creature's desperation became
his. Heaving wood aside, he cleared a path to the stake. At
once, he snatched the Graveler's knife from his belt and began
to slash the vines binding the Waynhim.

In a moment, the creature was free. Covenant helped it

limp out of the woodpile. Immediately, the creature turned on Vain, emitted a stream of language like a curse. Then it grabbed Covenant's arm and tugged him away from the fire. Southward.

"No." He detached his arm with difficulty. Though the Waynhim probably could not comprehend him, he tried to explain. "I'm going north. I've got to get to Revelstone."

The creature let out a muffled cry as if it knew the significance of that word *Revelstone*. With a swiftness which belied its injuries, it scuttled out of the bowl along the line of the escarpment. A moment later, it had vanished in the darkness.

Covenant's dread mounted. What had the Waynhim tried to tell him? It had infected him with a vivid sense of peril. But he did not intend to take even one step that increased the distance between him and Linden. His only alternative was to flee as quickly as possible. He turned back toward Vain.

The suddenness of the surprise froze him.

A man stood on the other side of the fire.

He had a ragged beard and frenzied eyes. In contrast, his lips wore a shy smile. "Let it be," he said, nodding after the Waynhim. "We have no more need of it." He moved slowly around the fire, drawing closer to Covenant and Vain. For all its surface nonchalance, his voice was edged with hysteria.

He reached Covenant's side of the blaze. A sharp intake of air hissed through Covenant's teeth.

The man was naked to the waist, and his torso was behung with salamanders. They grew out of him like excrescences. Their bodies twitched as he moved. Their eyes glinted redly in the firelight, and their jaws snapped.

A victim of the Sunbane!

Remembering Marid, Covenant brandished his knife. "That's close enough," he warned; but his voice shook, exposing his fear. "I don't want to hurt you."

"No," the man replied, "you do not wish to hurt me." He grinned like a friendly gargoyle. "And I have no wish to hurt you." His hands were clasped together in front of him as if they contained something precious. "I wish to give you a gift."

Covenant groped for anger to master his fear. "You hurt that Waynhim. You were going to kill it. What's the matter with you? There isn't enough murder in the world—you have to add more?"

The man was not listening. He gazed at his hands with an expression of mad delight. "It is a wondrous gift." He shuffled forward as if he did not know that he was moving. "No man but you can know the wonder of it."

Covenant willed himself to retreat; but his feet remained rooted to the ground. The man exerted a horrific fascination. Covenant found himself staring involuntarily at those hands as if they truly held something wonderful.

"Behold," the man whispered with gentle hysteria. Slowly, carefully, like a man unveiling treasure, he opened his hands.

A small furry spider sat on his palm.

Before Covenant could flinch, recoil, do anything to defend himself, the spider jumped.

It landed on his neck.

As he slapped it away, he felt the tiny prick of its sting.

For an instant, a marvelous calm came over him. He watched unperturbed as the man moved forward as if he were swimming through the sudden thickness of the firelight. The sound of the blaze became woolly. Covenant hardly noticed when the man took away his knife. Vain gazed at him for no reason at all. With imponderable delicacy, the floor of the bowl began to tilt.

Then his heart gave a beat like the blow of a sledgehammer, and everything shattered. Flying shards of pain shredded his thoughts. His brain had time to form only two words: *venom relapse.* After that, his heart beat again; and he was conscious of nothing except one long raw howl.

For some time, he wandered lorn in a maze of anguish, gibbering for release. Pain was everywhere. He had no mind, only pain—no respiration that was not pain—no pulse which did not multiply pain. Agony swelled inside his right forearm. It hurt as if his limb were nothing but a bloody stump; but that harm was all of him, everything, his chest and bowels and head and on and on in an unbearable litany of pain. If he screamed, he did not hear it; he could not hear anything except pain and death.

Death was a dervish, vertigo, avalanche, sweeping him over the precipice of his futility. It was everything he had ever striven to redeem, every pointless anguish to which he had ever struggled to give meaning. It was unconsolable grief and ineradicable guilt and savage wrath; and it made a small clear space of lucidity in his head.

Clinging shipwrecked there, he opened his eyes.

Delirium befogged his sight; gray shapes gamboled incomprehensibly across his fever, threatening the last lucid piece of himself. But he repulsed the threat. Blinking as if the movement of his eyelids were an act of violence, he cleared his vision.

He was in the bowl, bound at the stake. Heaps of firewood lay around him. Flames danced at the edges of the pyre.

The bowl was full of figures dancing like flames. They capered around the space like ghouls. Cries of blood-lust sprang off the walls of the escarpment; voices shrill with cannibalism battered his ears. Men with chatoyant eyes and prehensile noses leered at him. Women with adder-breasts, fingers lined by fangs, flared past him like fragments of insanity, cackling for his life. Children with hideous facial deformities and tiger maws in their bellies puked frogs and obscenities.

Horror made him spin, tearing clarity from his grasp. His right arm blasted pain into his chest. Every nerve of that limb was etched in agony. For an instant, he almost drowned.

But then he caught sight of Vain.

The Demondim-spawn stood with his back to the Plains, regarding the fervid dancers as if they had been created for no other purpose than to amuse him. Slowly, his eyes shifted across the frenzy until they met Covenant's.

"Vain!" Covenant gasped as if he were choking on blood. "Help me!"

In response, Vain bared his teeth in a black grin.

At the sight, Covenant snapped. A white shriek of fury exploded from his chest. And with his shriek came a deflagration that destroyed the night.

FIFTEEN: "Because you can *see*"

No. Never again.

After Covenant had passed beyond the hillcrest in Andelain, Linden Avery sat down among the dead stones, and tried to recover her sense of who she was. A black mood was on her. She felt futile and bereft of life, as she had so often felt in recent years; all her efforts to rise above her parents had accomplished nothing. If Sunder or Hollian had spoken to her, she might have screamed, if she were able to summon the energy.

Now that she had made her decision, had struck a blow in defense of her difficult autonomy against Covenant's strange power to persuade her from herself, she was left with the consequences. She could not ignore them; the old and forever unassuaged barrenness around her did not permit them to be ignored. These dead hills climbed south and west of her, contradicting Andelain as if she had chosen death when she had been offered life.

And she was isolated by her blackness. Sunder and Hollian had found companionship in their mutual rejection of the Hills. Their lives had been so fundamentally shaped by the Sunbane that they could not question the discomfiture Andelain gave them. Perhaps they could not perceive that those lush trees and greenswards were healthy. Or that health was beautiful.

But Linden accepted the attitude of the Stonedownors. It was explicable in the context of the Sunbane. Her separateness from them did not dismay her.

The loss of Covenant dismayed her. She had made her decision, and he had walked out of her life as if he were taking all her strength and conviction with him. The light of the fertile sun had danced on the Mithil as he passed, burning about him like a recognition of his efficacy against the Land's doom. She had shared the utmost privacy of his life, and yet he had left her for Andelain. And the venom was still in him.

She would not have been more alone if he had riven her of all her reasons for living.

But she had made her decision. She had experienced Covenant's illness as if it were her own, and knew she could not have chosen otherwise. She preferred this lifeless waste of stone over the loveliness of Andelain because she understood it better, could more effectively seal herself against it. After her efforts to save Covenant, she had vowed that she would never again expose herself so intimately to anything, never again permit the Land-born sensitivity of her senses to threaten her independent identity. That vow was easier to keep when the perceptions against which she closed her heart were perceptions of ruin, of dead rock like the detritus of a cataclysm, rather than of clean wood, aromatic grasses, bountiful *alianctha*. In her private way, she shared Hollian's distrust. Andelain was far more seductive than the stone around her. She knew absolutely that she could not afford to be seduced.

Lost in her old darkness, with her eyes and ears closed as if she had nailed up shutters, barred doors, she did not understand Sunder's warning shout until too late. Suddenly, men with clubs and knives boiled out of hiding. They grappled with Sunder as he fought to raise his poniard, his Sunstone. Linden heard a flat thud as they stunned him. Hollian's arms were pinioned before her dirk could make itself felt. Linden leaped into motion; but she had no chance. A heavy blow staggered her. While she retched for breath, her arms were lashed behind her.

A moment later, brutal hands dragged her and her companions away from the River.

For a time while she gasped and stumbled, she could not hold up her defenses. Her senses tasted the violence of the men, experiencing their roughness as if it were a form of ingrained lust. She felt the contorted desecration of the terrain. Involuntarily, she knew that she was being taken toward the source of the deadness, that these people were creatures of the same force which had killed this region. She had to shut her eyes, tie her mind in dire knots, to stifle her unwilling awareness of her straits.

Then the companions were manhandled down a narrow crevice into the canyon of Stonemight Woodhelven.

Linden had never seen a Woodhelven before, and the sight of it revolted her. The carelessly made homes, the slovenly people, the blood-eagerness of the Graveler—these things debased the arduous rectitude she had learned to see in people like Sunder and Hollian. But everything else paled when she caught her first glimpse of the Graveler's steaming, baleful green stone. It flooded her eyes with ill, stung her nostrils like virulent acid; it dwarfed every other power she had encountered, outshone everything except the Sunbane itself. That emerald chip was the source of the surrounding ruin, the cause of the imminent and uncaring wildness of the Woodhelvennin. Tears blinded her. Spasms clenched her mind like a desire to vomit. Yet she could not deafen herself to the Graveler's glee when that woman announced her intention to slay her captives the next morning.

Then Linden and the Stonedownors were impelled into a rude hut on stilts, and left to face death as best they could. She could not resist. She had reached a crisis of self protection. This close to the Stonemight, she was always aware of it. Its emanations leeched at her heart, sucked her toward dissolution. Rocking against the wall to remind herself that she still existed, still possessed a separate physical identity, she repeated, No, never again. She iterated the words as if they were a litany against evil, and fought for preservation.

She needed an answer to Joan, to venom and Ravers, to the innominate power of the Stonemight. But the only answer she found was to huddle within herself and close her mind as if she were one of her parents, helpless to meet life, avid for death.

Yet when dawn came, the door of the hut was flung open, not by the Graveler or any of the Woodhelvennin, but by a Rider of the Clave. The fertile sun vivified his stark red robe, etched the outlines of his black *rukh*, made the stiff thrust of his beard look like a grave digger's spade. He was tall with authority and unshakably confident. "Come," he said as if disobedience were impossible. "I am Santonin na-Mhoram-in. You are mine." To Sunder's glower and Hollian's groan, he replied with a smile like the blade of a scimitar.

Outside, the Woodhelvennin stood moaning and pleading. The Graveler protested abjectly. But Santonin compelled her. Weeping, she surrendered her Stonemight. Another man delivered to him the Stonedownors' Sunstone, *lianar*, knives.

Watching the transaction, Linden was unable to think anything except that Covenant would return from Andelain soon, and his companions would be gone. For one mad instant, Santonin's smile almost drew her to confess Covenant's existence; she wanted to keep him from falling into the hands of Stonemight Woodhelven. But Sunder and Hollian were silent; and their silence reminded her that the Clave desired Covenant's death. With the remnants of her will, she swallowed everything which might betray him.

After that, her will was taken from her altogether. Under the green doom of the sun, Santonin na-Mhoram-in ignited his *rukh*. Coercion sprang from the blaze, seized possession of her soul. All choice left her. At his word, she mounted Santonin's Courser. The shred of her which remained watched Sunder and Hollian as they also obeyed. Then Santonin took them away from Stonemight Woodhelven. Away toward Revelstone.

His control could not be broken. She contained nothing with which she might have resisted it. For days, she knew that she should attempt to escape, to fight. But she lacked the simple volition to lift her hands to her face or push her hair out of her eyes without Santonin's explicit instructions. Whenever he looked into her dumb gaze, he smiled as if her imposed docility pleased him. At times, he murmured names that meant nothing to her, as if he were mocking her: Windscour, Victuallin Tayne, Andelainscion. And yet he did not appear to be corrupt. Or she was not capable of perceiving his corruption.

Only once did his mastery fail. Shortly after sunrise on the first day of a desert sun, eight days after their departure from Stonemight Woodhelven, a silent shout unexpectedly thrilled the air, thrilled Linden's heart. Santonin's hold snapped like an overtight harpstring.

As if they had been straining at the leash for this moment, Sunder and Hollian grappled for the *rukh*. Linden clamped an arm-lock on Santonin, flung him to the ground, then broke away southeastward in the direction of the shout.

But a moment later, she found herself wandering almost aimlessly back to Santonin's camp. Sunder and Hollian were packing the Rider's supplies. Santonin wore a fierce grin. The triangle of his *rukh* shone like blood and emerald. Soon he took his captives on toward Revelstone, as if nothing had happened.

Nothing had happened. Linden knew nothing, understood nothing, chose nothing. The Rider could have abused her in any way he desired. She might have felt nothing if he had elected to exercise a desire. But he did not. He seemed to have a clear sense of his own purpose. Only the anticipation in his eyes showed that his purpose was not kind.

After days of emptiness, Linden would have been glad for any purpose which could restore her to herself. Any purpose at all. Thomas Covenant had ceased to exist in her thoughts. Perhaps he had ceased to exist entirely. Perhaps he had never existed. Nothing was certain except that she needed Santonin's instructions in order to put food in her mouth.

Even the sight of Revelstone itself, the Keep of the na-Mhoram rising from the high jungle of a second fertile sun like a great stone ship, could not rouse her spirit. She was only distantly aware of what she was seeing. The gates opened to admit the Rider, closed behind his Courser, and meant nothing.

Santonin na-Mhoram-in was met by three or four other figures like himself; but they greeted him with respect, as if he had stature among them. They spoke to him, words which Linden could not understand. Then he commanded his prisoners to dismount.

Linden, Sunder, and Hollian obeyed in an immense, ill-lit hall. With Santonin striding before them, they walked the ways of the great Keep. Passages and chambers, stairs and junctions, passed unmarked, unremembered. Linden moved like a hollow vessel, unable to hold any impression of the ancient gut-rock. Santonin's path had no duration and no significance.

Yet his purpose remained. He brought his captives to a huge chamber like a pit in the floor of Revelstone. Its sloping sides were blurred and blunt, as if a former gallery or arena had been washed with lava. At its bottom stood a man in a deep ebony robe and a chasuble of crimson. He gripped a tall iron crozier topped with an open triangle. His hood was thrown back, exposing features which were also blurred and blunt in the torchlight.

His presence pierced Linden's remaining scrap of identity like a hot blade. Behind her passivity, she began to wail.

He was a Raver.

"Three fools," he said in a voice like cold scoria. "I had hoped for four."

Santonin and the Raver spoke together in alien, empty words. Santonin produced the Stonemight and handed it to the Raver. Emerald reflected in the Raver's eyes; an eloquent smile shaped the flesh of his lips. He closed his fist on the green chip, so that it plumed lush ferns of force. Linden's wail died of starvation in the poverty of her being.

Then the Rider stepped to one side, and the Raver faced the captives. His visage was a smear of ill across Linden's sight. He gazed at her directly, searched out the vestiges of her self, measured them, scorned them. "You I must not harm," he said dully, almost regretfully. "Unharmed, you will commit all harm I could desire." His eyes left her as if she were too paltry to merit further notice. "But these treachers are another matter." He confronted Sunder and Hollian. "It signifies nothing if they are broken before they are shed."

He held the Stonemight against his chest. Its steam curled up his face. Nostrils dilating, he breathed the steam as if it were a rare narcotic. "Where is Thomas Covenant?"

The Stonedownors did not react, could not react. Linden stood where she had been left, like a disregarded puppet. But her heart contracted in sudden terror.

The Raver made a slight gesture. Santonin muttered softly over his *rukh*. Abruptly, the control holding Sunder and Hollian ended. They stumbled as if they had forgotten how to manage their limbs and jerked trembling erect. Fear glazed Sunder's eyes, as if he were beholding the dreadful font and master of his existence. Hollian covered her face like a frightened child.

"Where is Thomas Covenant?"

Animated by an impulse more deeply inbred than choice or reason, the Stonedownors struggled into motion and tried to flee.

The Raver let Hollian go. But with the Stonemight he put out a hand of force which caught Sunder by the neck. Hot emerald gripped him like a garrote, snatched him to his knees.

Reft of her companion, Hollian stopped and swung around to face the Raver. Her raven hair spread about her head like wings.

The Raver knotted green ill at Sunder's throat. "Where is Thomas Covenant?"

Sunder's eyes were blind with fear and compulsion. They bulged in their sockets. But he did not answer. Locking his jaws, he held himself still.

The Raver's fingers tightened. "Speak."

The muscles of Sunder's jaw pulled together, clenched as if he were trying to break his teeth, grind his voice into silence forever. As the force at his throat grew stronger, those muscles became distinct, rigid, etched against the darkness of his fear and strangulation. It seemed impossible that he could so grit his teeth without tearing the ligatures of his jaw. But he did not answer. Sweat seemed to burst from his pores like bone marrow squeezed through his skin. Yet his rictus held.

A frown of displeasure incused the Raver's forehead. "You will speak to me," he soughed. "I will tear words from your soul, if need be." His hand clinched the Stonemight as if he were covetous to use all its power. "Where is Thomas Covenant?"

"Dead." Whimpers contorted Hollian's voice. Linden felt the lie in the core of her helplessness. "Lost."

The Raver did not glance away from Sunder, did not release his garrote. "How so?"

"In Andelain," the eh-Brand panted. "He entered. We awaited him. He did not return." To complete her lie, she moaned, "Forgive me, Sunder."

"And the white ring?"

"I know not. Lost. He did not return."

Still the Raver gave no look or answer to Hollian. But he eased slightly his grasp on the Graveler. "Your refusal," he breathed, "says to me that Thomas Covenant lives. If he is lost, why do you wish me to believe that he lives?"

Within the scraps of herself, Linden begged Sunder to support Hollian's lie, for his own sake as well as for Covenant's.

Slowly, the Graveler unlocked his jaw. Clarity moved behind the dullness of his eyes. Terribly through his knotted throat, he grated, "I wish you to fear."

A faint smile like a promise of murder touched the Raver's lips. But, as with Santonin, the certainty of his purpose restrained him. To the Rider, he said, "Convey them to the hold." Linden could not see whether he believed Hollian's lie. She could descry nothing but the loud wrong of the Raver's purpose.

With a few words, Santonin returned the Stonedownors to Linden's condition. Walking like wooden articulations of his will, his captives followed him dumbly out of the stone pit.

Again, they traversed halls which had no meaning, crossed thresholds that seemed to appear only to be forgotten. Soon they entered a cavern lined into the distance on both sides with iron doors. Small barred windows in the doors exposed each cell, but Linden was incapable of looking for any glimpse of other prisoners. Santonin locked away first Sunder, then Hollian. Farther down the row of doors, he sent Linden herself into a cell.

She stood, helpless and soul-naked, beside a rank straw pallet while he studied her as if he were considering the cost of his desires. Without warning, he quenched his *rukh*. His will vanished from her mind, leaving her too empty to hold herself upright. As she crumpled to the pallet, she heard him chuckling softly. Then the door clanged shut and bolts rasped into place. She was left alone in her cell as if it contained nothing except the louse-ridden pallet and the blank stone of the walls.

She huddled foetally on the straw, while time passed over her like the indifference of Revelstone's granite. She was a cracked gourd and could not refill herself. She was afraid to make the attempt, afraid even to think of making any attempt. Horror had burrowed into her soul. She desired nothing but silence and darkness, the peace of oblivion. But she could not achieve it. Caught in the limbo between revulsion and death, she crouched among her emptinesses, and waited for the contradictions of her dilemma to tear her apart.

Guards came and went, bringing her unsavory food and stale water; but she could not muster enough of herself to notice them. She was deaf to the clashing of iron which marked the movements of the guards, the arrival or departure of prisoners. Iron meant nothing. There were no voices. She would have listened to voices. Her mind groped numbly for some image to preserve her sanity, some name or answer to reinvoke the identity she had lost. But she lost all names, all images. The cell held no answers.

Then there was a voice, a shout as if a prisoner had broken free. She heard it through her stupor, clung to it. Fighting the cramps of motionlessness, the rigidity of hunger and thirst, she crawled like a cripple toward the door.

Someone spoke in a flat tone. A voice unlike any she had heard before. She was so grateful for it that at first she hardly caught the words. She was clawing herself up toward the bars of her window when the words themselves penetrated her.

"Ur-Lord Thomas Covenant," the voice was saying. "Unbeliever and white gold wielder, I salute you. You are remembered among the *Haruchai*." The speaker was inflexible, denying his own need. "I am Brinn. Will you set us free?"

Covenant! She would have screamed the name, but her throat was too dry even to whisper.

The next instant, she heard the impact of iron on flesh. Covenant! A body slumped to the stone. Guards moved around it. Hauling herself to the window, she crushed her face against the bars and tried to see; but no one entered her range of vision. A moment later, feet made heavy by a burden moved out of the hold, leaving her lorn under a cairn of silence.

She wanted to sob; but even that was an improvement for her. She had been given a name to fill her emptiness. Covenant. Helplessness and hope. Covenant was still alive. He was here. He could save her. He did not know that she needed saving.

For a time which seemed long and full of anguish, she slumped against the door while her chest shook with dry sobs and her heart clung to the image of Thomas Covenant. He had smiled for Joan. He was vulnerable to everything, and yet he appeared indomitable. Surely the guards had not killed him?

Perhaps they had. Perhaps they had not. His name itself was hope to her. It gave her something to be, restored pieces of who she was. When exhaustion etiolated her sobbing, she crept to her water-bowl, drank it dry, then ate as much of the rancid food as she could stomach. Afterward, she slept for a while.

But the next iron clanging yanked her awake. The bolts of her door were thrown back. Her heart yammered as she rolled from the pallet and lurched desperately to her feet. Covenant—?

Her door opened. The Raver entered her cell.

He seemed to have no features, no hands; wherever his robe bared his flesh, such potent emanations of ill lanced from him that she could not register his physical being. Wrong scorched the air between them, thrusting her back against the wall. He reeked of Marid, of the malice of bees. Of Joan. His breath filled the cell with gangrene and nausea. When he spoke, his voice seemed to rot in her ears.

"So it appears that your companions lied. I am astonished. I had thought all the people of the Land to be cravens and children. But no matter. The destruction of cravens and children is small pleasure. I prefer the folly of courage in my victims. Fortunately, the Unbeliever"— he sneered the name —"will not attempt your redemption. He is unwitting of your plight."

She tried to squeeze herself into the stone, strove to escape through bluff granite. But her body, mortal and useless, trapped her in the Raver's stare. She could not shut her eyes to him. He burned along her nerves, etching himself into her, demeaning her soul with the intaglio of his ill.

"But he also," continued the Raver in a tone like stagnant water, "is no great matter. Only his ring signifies. He will have no choice but to surrender it. Already he has sold himself, and no power under the Arch of Time can prevent his despair.

"No, Linden Avery," the Raver said without a pause. "Abandon all hope of Thomas Covenant. The principal doom of the Land is upon your shoulders."

No! She had no defense against so much corruption. Night crowded around her, more cruel than any darkness—night as old as the pain of children, parents who sought to die. Never!

"You have been especially chosen for this desecration. You are being forged as iron is forged to achieve the ruin of the Earth." His voice violated all her flesh. "You have been chosen, Linden Avery, because you can *see*. Because you are open to that which no other in the Land can discern, you are open to be forged. Through eyes and ears and touch, you are made to be what the Despiser requires. Descrying destruction, you will be driven to commit all destruction. I will relish that ruin.

"Therefore I have forewarned you. So that you will know your peril, and be unable to evade it. So that as you strive to evade it, the Despiser may laugh in scorn and triumph."

No. It was not possible. She was a doctor; she could not be forced to destroy. No power, no cunning, no malevolence, could unmake who she chose to be. Never! A rush of words surged up in her, burst from her as if she were babbling.

"You're sick. This is all sickness. It's just disease. You have some disease that rots your mind. Physiological insanity. A chemical imbalance of the brain. You don't know what you're saying. I don't believe in *evil*!"

"No?" The Raver was mildly amused. "Forsooth. That lie, at least, I must rectify." He advanced on her like a tide of slaughter. "You have committed murder. Are you not evil?"

He spread his arms as if he meant to embrace her. He had no face, no hands. A bright hallucination at the sleeve of his robe stretched toward her, caressed her cheek.

Terror bloomed from the touch like a nightshade of the soul. Gelid ill froze her face, spread ice across her senses like the concatenation and fulfillment of all her instinctive revulsion. It flamed through her and became truth. The truth of Despite. Wrong suppurated over her features, festering her severity and beauty, corrupting who she was. The Sunbane shone in her flesh: desert, pestilence, the screaming of trees. She would have howled, but she had no voice.

She fled. There was no other defense. Within herself, she ran away. She closed her eyes, her ears, her mouth, closed the nerves of her skin, sealed every entrance to her mind. *No.* Horror gave her the power of paralysis. *Never.* Striking herself blind and deaf and numb, she sank into the darkness as if it were death, the ineluctable legacy of her birth.

Never again.

SIXTEEN: The Weird of the Waynhim

I won't!

Covenant fought to sit up, struggled against blankets that clogged his movements, hands that restrained him.

I'll never give it up!

Blindly, he wrestled for freedom. But a massive weakness fettered him where he lay. His right arm was pinned by a preterite memory of pain.

I don't care what you do to me!

And the grass under him was fragrant and soporific. The hands could not be refused. An uncertain blur of vision eased the darkness. The face bending over him was gentle and human.

"Rest, ring-wielder," the man said kindly. "No harm will come upon you in this sanctuary. There will be time enough for urgency when you are somewhat better healed."

The voice blunted his desperation. The analystic scent of the grass reassured and comforted him. His need to go after Linden mumbled past his lips, but he could no longer hear it.

The next time he awakened, he arrived at consciousness slowly, and all his senses came with him. When he opened his eyes, he was able to see. After blinking for a moment at the smooth dome of stone above him, he understood that he was underground. Though he lay on deep fresh grass, he could not mistake the fact that this spacious chamber had been carved out of the earth. The light came from braziers in the corners of the room.

The face he had seen earlier returned. The man smiled at him, helped him into a sitting position. "Have care, ring-wielder. You have been mortally ill. This weakness will be slow to depart." The man placed a bowl of dark fluid in Covenant's hands and gently pressed him to drink. The liquid had a musty, alien flavor; but it steadied him as it went down into his emptiness.

He began to look around more closely. His bed was in the center of the chamber, raised above the floor like a catafalque of grass. The native stone of the walls and dome had been meticulously smoothed and shaped. The ceiling was not high, but he would be able to stand erect. Low entryways marked opposite walls of the room. The braziers were made of un-adorned gray stone and supported by iron tripods. The thick, black fluid in them burned without smoke.

When he turned his head far enough, he found Vain near him.

The Demondim-spawn stood with his arms hanging slightly bent. His lips wore a faint, ambiguous smile, and his eyes, black without pupil or iris, looked like the orbs of a blind man.

A quiver of revulsion shook Covenant. "Get—" His voice scraped his throat like a rusty knife. "Get him out of here."

The man supported him with an arm around his back. "Perhaps it could be done," he said, smiling wryly. "But great force would be required. Do you have cause to fear him?"

"He—" Covenant winced at chancrous memories: Sunbane victims dancing; Vain's grin. He had difficulty forcing words past the blade in his throat. "Refused to help me." The thought of his own need made him tremble. "Get rid of him."

"Ah, ring-wielder," the man said with a frown, "such questions are not so blithely answered. There is much that I must tell you—and much I wish to be told."

He faced Covenant; and Covenant observed him clearly for the first time. He had the dark hair and stocky frame of a Stonedownor, though he wore nothing but a wide piece of leather belted around his waist. The softness of his brown eyes suggested sympathy; but his cheeks had been deeply cut by old grief, and the twitching of his mouth gave the impression that he was too well acquainted with fear and incomprehension. His skin had the distinctive pallor of a man who had once been richly tanned. Covenant felt an immediate surge of empathy for him.

"I am Hamako," the man said. "My former name was one which the Waynhim could not utter, and I have foresworn it. The Waynhim name you ring-wielder in their tongue—and as ring-wielder you are well known to them. But I will gladly make use of any other name you desire."

Covenant swallowed, took another drink from the bowl. "Covenant," he said hoarsely. "I'm Thomas Covenant."

The man accepted this with a nod. "Covenant." Then he returned to the question of Vain. "For two days," he said, "while you have lain in fever, the Waynhim have striven with the riddle of this Demondim-spawn. They have found purpose in him, but not harm. This is an astonishment to them, for they perceive clearly the hands of the ur-viles which made him, and they have no trust for ur-viles. Yet he is an embodiment of lore which the Waynhim comprehend. Only one question disturbs them." Hamako paused as if reluctant to remind Covenant of past horrors. "When you freed *dhraga* Waynhim from fire, thus imperiling your own life, *dhraga* spoke the word of command to this Demondim-spawn, ordering him to preserve you. Why did he not obey?"

The dark fluid salved Covenant's throat, but he still sounded harsh. "I already used the command. He killed six people."

"Ah," said Hamako. He turned from Covenant, and called down one of the entryways in a barking tongue. Almost immediately, a Waynhim entered the chamber. The creature sniffed inquiringly in Covenant's direction, then began a rapid conversation with Hamako. Their voices had a roynish sound that grated on Covenant's nerves—he had too many horrid memories of ur-viles—but he suppressed his discomfort, tried not to think balefully of Vain. Shortly, the Waynhim trotted away as if it carried important information. Hamako returned his attention to Covenant.

The man's gaze was full of questions as he said, "Then you came not upon this Demondim-spawn by chance. He did not seek you out without your knowledge."

Covenant shook his head.

"He was given to you," Hamako continued, "by those who know his purpose. You comprehend him."

"No. I mean, yes, he was given to me. I was told how to command him. I was told to trust him." He scowled at the idea of Vain's trustworthiness. "But nothing else."

Hamako searched for the right way to phrase his question. "May I ask—who was the giver?"

Covenant felt reluctant to answer directly. He did not distrust Hamako; he simply did not want to discuss his experience with his Dead. So he replied gruffly, "I was in Andelain."

"Ah, Andelain," Hamako breathed. "The Dead." He nodded in comprehension, but it did not relieve his awkwardness.

Abruptly, Covenant's intuition leaped. "You know what his purpose is." He had often heard that the lore of the Waynhim was wide and subtle. "But you're not going to tell me."

Hamako's mouth twitched painfully. "Covenant," he said, pleading to be understood, "the Dead were your friends, were they not? Their concern for you is ancient and far-seeing. It is sooth—the Waynhim ken much, and guess more. Doubtless there are many questions to which they hold answers. But—"

Covenant interrupted him. "You know how to fight the Sunbane, and you're not going to tell me that either."

His tone made Hamako wince. "Surely your Dead have given to you all which may be wisely told. Ah, Thomas Covenant! My heart yearns to share with you the lore of the Waynhim. But they have instructed me strictly to forbear. For many reasons.

"They are ever loath to impart knowledge where they cannot control the use to which their knowledge is placed. For the ring-wielder, perhaps they would waive such considerations. But they have not the vision of the Dead, and fear to transgress the strictures which have guided the gifts of the Dead. This is the paradox of lore, that it must be achieved rather than granted, else it misleads. This only I am permitted to say: were I to reveal the purpose of this Demondim-spawn, that revelation could well prevent the accomplishment of his purpose." Hamako's face held a look of supplication. "That purpose is greatly desirable."

"At any rate, the ur-viles desire it greatly." Frustration and weakness made Covenant sarcastic. "Maybe these Waynhim aren't as different as you think."

He emptied the bowl, then tried to get to his feet. But Hamako held him back. Covenant had touched anger in the man. Stiffly, Hamako said, "I owe life and health and use to the succor of the Waynhim. Aye, and many things more. I will not betray their wishes to ease your mind, ring-wielder though you are."

Covenant thrust against Hamako's grasp, but could not break free. After an effort like palsy, he collapsed back on the grass. "You said two days," he panted. Futility enfeebled him. Two more days! "I've got to go. I'm already too far behind."

"You have been deeply harmed," Hamako replied. "Your flesh will not yet bear you. What urgency drives you?"

Covenant repressed a querulous retort. He could not denigrate Hamako's refusal to answer crucial questions; he had done such things himself. When he had mastered his gall, he said, "Three friends of mine were kidnapped by a Rider. They're on their way to Revelstone. If I don't catch up with them in time, they'll be killed."

Hamako absorbed this information, then called again for one of the Waynhim. Another rapid conversation took place. Hamako seemed to be stressing something, urging something; the responses of the Waynhim sounded thoughtful, unpersuaded. But the creature ended on a note which satisfied Hamako. As the Waynhim departed, he turned back to Covenant.

"*Durhisitar* will consult the Weird of the Waynhim," the man said, "but I doubt not that aid will be granted. No Waynhim will forget the redemption of *dhraga*—or the peril of the trap which ensnared you. Rest now, and fear not. This *rhysh* will accord you power to pursue your companions."

"How? What can they do?"

"The Waynhim are capable of much," returned Hamako, urging Covenant to lie back. "Rest, I say. Hold only this much trust, and put care aside. It will be bitter to you if you are offered aid, and are too weak to avail yourself of it."

Covenant could not resist. The grass exuded a somnolent

air. His body was leaden with weariness; and the roborant he had drunk seemed to undermine his anxiety. He allowed Hamako to settle him upon the bed. But as the man prepared to leave, Covenant said distantly, "At least tell me how I ended up here. The last thing I remember"— he did not look at Vain —"I was as good as dead. How did you save me?"

Hamako sat on the edge of the bed. Once again, his countenance wore an awkward sympathy. "That I will relate," he said. "But I must tell you openly that we did not save you."

Covenant jerked up his head. "No?"

"Softly." Hamako pushed him flat again. "There is no need for this concern."

Grabbing the man's arms with both hands, Covenant pulled their faces together. "What the hell am I doing alive?"

"Covenant," said Hamako with a dry smile, "how may I tell the tale if you are so upwrought?"

Slowly, Covenant released him. "All right." Specters crowded his head; but he forced himself to relax. "Tell it."

"It came to pass thus," the man said. "When *dhraga* Waynhim was set free by your hand, and learned that this Demondim-spawn would not obey the word of command, it desired you to share its flight. But it could not gain your comprehension. Therefore *dhraga* summoned all the haste which the harm to its body permitted, and sped to inform the *rhysh* of your plight. *Dhraga* had been made the bait of a snare. This snare—"

Covenant interrupted him. "What's a *rhysh*?"

"Ah, pardon me. For a score of turnings of the moon, I have heard no human voice but those warped by the Sunbane. I forget that you do not speak the Waynhim tongue.

"In our speech, the word *rhysh* means stead. It gives reference to a community of Waynhim. In all the Land, there are many hundredscore Waynhim, but all live in *rhysh* of one or two score. Each *rhysh* is private unto itself—though I am told that communication exists between them. In the great war of Revelstone, nigh two score centuries past, five *rhysh* fought together against the ur-viles of the Despiser. But such sharing is rare. Each *rhysh* holds to itself and interprets the Weird in its own way. Long has this *rhysh* lived here, serving its own vision."

Covenant wanted to ask the meaning of the term *Weird*; but he already regretted having halted Hamako's tale.

"The *rhysh*," Hamako resumed, "was informed of your plight by *dhraga*. At once we set out to attempt your aid. But the distance was too great. When first *dhraga* was captured the decision was taken to make no rescue. It was bitter to all the *rhysh* to abandon one of its own. But we had cause to fear this snare. Long have we labored all too near a strong number of those warped by the Sunbane." Unexplained tears blurred his eyes. "Long have the ill souls that captured you striven to undo us. Therefore we believed the snare to be for us. Having no wish to slay or be slain, we abandoned *dhraga* to its doom."

Covenant was struck by the closeness with which Hamako identified himself with the *rhysh*, and by the man's evident grief over the Sunbane victims. But he did not interrupt again.

"Also," Hamako went on, suppressing his emotion, "for three days of desert sun prior to the setting of this snare, the Waynhim tasted Raver spoor."

A Raver! Covenant groaned. Hellfire! That explained the trap. And the spider.

"Therefore we feared the snare deeply. But when we learned that the ring-wielder had fallen prey, we comprehended our error, and ran to succor you. But the distance," he repeated, "was too great. We arrived only in time to behold the manner in which you redeemed yourself with wild magic."

Redeemed——! An ache wrung Covenant's heart. No!

"Though your arm was terrible and black, your white ring spun a great fire. The bonds dropped from you. The wood was scattered. The Sunbane-warped were cast aside like chaff, and fled in terror. Rocks were riven from the escarpment. Only this Demondim-spawn stood scatheless amid the fire.

"The power ended as you fell. Perceiving your venom-ill, we bore you here, and the Waynhim tended you with all their cunning until your death receded from you. Here you are safe until your strength returns."

Hamako fell silent. After studying Covenant for a moment, he rose to his feet and began to depart.

"The Raver?" Covenant gritted.

"All spoor of him is gone," Hamako replied quietly. "I fear his purpose was accomplished."

Or else he's afraid of me, Covenant rasped inwardly. He did not see Hamako leave the chamber. He was consumed by his thoughts. Damnation! First Marid, then the bees, now this.

Each attack worse than the one before. And a Raver involved each time. Hell and blood! Why? Bile rose in him. Why else? Lord Foul did not want him dead, not if his ring might fall to a Raver. The Despiser wanted something entirely different. He wanted surrender, voluntary abdication. Therefore the purpose of these attacks lay in their effect on him, in the way they drew power from his delirium, violence over which he had no control.

No control!

Was Foul trying to scare him into giving up his ring?

God bloody damn it to hell! He had always felt an almost overwhelming distrust of power. In the past, he had reconciled himself to the might with which he had defeated Lord Foul only because he had refrained from making full use of it; rather than attempting to crush the Despiser utterly, he had withheld the final blow, though in so doing he had ensured that Lord Foul would rise to threaten the Land again. Deliberately, he had made himself culpable for Lord Foul's future ill. And he had chosen that course because the alternative was so much worse.

For he believed that Lord Foul was part of himself, an embodiment of the moral peril lurking for the outcast in the complex rage against being outcast, a leper's doom of Despite for everything including himself. Restraint was the only possible escape from such a doom. If he had allowed his power to rise unchecked, committed himself completely to wild magic in his battle against Lord Foul, he would have accomplished nothing but the feeding of his own inner Despiser. The part of him which judged, believed, affirmed, was the part which refrained. Utter power, boundless and unscrupulous rage, would have corrupted him, and he would have changed in one stroke from victim to victimizer. He knew how easy it was for a man to become the thing he hated.

Therefore he profoundly feared his wild magic, his capacity for power and violence. And that was precisely the point of Foul's attack. The venom called up his might when he was beyond all restraint—called it up and increased it. In Mithil Stonedown, he had almost failed to light Sunder's *orcrest*; but two days ago he had apparently broken boulders. Without volition.

And still he did not know why. Perhaps in saving Joan, he *had* sold himself; perhaps he was no longer free. But no lack of freedom could force him to surrender. And every increase in his power improved his chances of besting the Despiser again.

His danger lay in the venom, the loss of restraint. But if he could avoid further relapses, learn control—

He was a leper. Control and discipline were the tools of his life. Let Lord Foul consider that before he counted his victory.

With such thoughts, Covenant grew grim and calm. Slowly, the effects of his illness came over him. The scent of the grass soothed him like an anodyne. After a time, he slept.

When Hamako nudged him awake again, he had the impression that he had slept for a long time. Nothing in the chamber had changed; yet his instincts were sure. Groaning at the way everything conspired to increase the peril of his friends, he groped into a sitting position. "How many days have I lost now?"

Hamako placed a large bowl of the dark, musty liquid in Covenant's hands. "You have been among us for three days of the sun of pestilence," he answered. "Dawn is not yet nigh, but I have awakened you because there is much I wish to show and say before you depart. Drink."

Three days. Terrific! Dismally, Covenant took a deep swallow from the bowl.

But as the liquid passed into him, he recognized the improvement in his condition. He held the bowl steadily: his whole body felt stable. He looked up at Hamako. To satisfy his curiosity, he asked, "What is this stuff?"

"It is *vitrim*." Hamako was smiling: he seemed pleased by what he saw in Covenant. "It resembles an essence of *aliantha*, but has been created by the lore of the Waynhim rather than drawn from the *aliantha* itself."

In a long draught, Covenant drained the bowl, and felt immediately more substantial. He returned the bowl, and rose to his feet. "When can I get started? I'm running out of excuses."

"Soon after the sun's rising, you will renew your sojourn," answered Hamako. "I assure you that you will hold your days among us in scant regret." He handed the bowl to a Waynhim standing nearby and accepted a leather pouch like a wineskin. This he gave to Covenant. "*Vitrim*," he said. "If you consume it prudently, you will require no other aliment for three days."

Covenant acknowledged the gift with a nod and tied the pouch to his belt by its drawstring. As he did so, Hamako said, "Thomas Covenant, it pains me that we have refused to answer your most urgent questions. Therefore I desire you to comprehend the Weird of the Waynhim ere you depart. Then perhaps you will grasp my conviction that their wisdom must be trusted. Are you willing?"

Covenant faced Hamako with a rueful grimace. "Hamako, you saved my life. I may be a natural-born ingrate, but I can still appreciate the significance of not being dead. I'll try to understand anything you want to tell me." Half involuntarily, he added, "Just don't take too long. If I don't *do* something soon, I won't be able to live with myself."

"Then come," Hamako said, and strode out of the chamber.

Covenant paused to tuck in his shirt, then followed.

As he stooped to pass through the entryway, he noted sourly that Vain was right behind him.

He found himself in a corridor, scrupulously delved out of native rock, where he could barely walk erect. The passage was long, and lit at intervals by small censers set into the walls. In them, a dark fluid burned warmly, without smoke.

After some distance, the passage branched, became a network of tunnels. As Covenant and Hamako passed, they began to meet Waynhim. Some went by in silence; others exchanged a few comments with Hamako in their roynish tongue; but all of them bowed to the ring-wielder.

Abruptly, the tunnel opened into an immense cavern. It was brightly-lit by vats of burning liquid. It appeared to be more than a hundred feet high and three times that across. At least a score of Waynhim were busily at work around the area.

With a thrill of astonishment, Covenant saw that the whole cavern was a garden.

Thick grass covered the floor. Flowerbeds lay everywhere, hedged by many different varieties of bushes. Trees—pairs of Gilden, oak, peach, sycamore, elm, apple, jacaranda, spruce, and others—stretched their limbs toward the vaulted ceiling. Vines and creepers grew up the walls.

The Waynhim were tending the plants. From plot to tree they moved, barking chants and wielding short iron staves; and dark droplets of power sprang from the metal, nourishing flowers and shrubs and vines like a distilled admixture of loam and sunshine.

The effect was incomparably strange. On the surface of the Land, the Sunbane made everything unnatural; nothing grew without violating the Law of its own being, nothing died without ruin. Yet here, where there was no sunlight, no free air, no pollinating insects, no age-nurtured soil, the garden of the Waynhim blossomed lush and lovely, as natural as if these plants had been born to fructify under a stone sky.

Covenant gazed about with undisguised wonder; but when he started to ask a question, Hamako gestured him silent, and led him into the garden.

Slowly, they walked among the flowers and trees. The murmurous chanting of the Waynhim filled the air; but none of the creatures spoke to each other or to Hamako; they were rapt in the concentration of their work. And in their concentration, Covenant caught a glimpse of the prodigious difficulty of the task they had set for themselves. To keep such a garden healthy underground must have required miracles of devotion and lore.

But Hamako had more to show. He guided Covenant and Vain to the far end of the cavern, into a new series of corridors. These angled steadily upward; and as he ascended, Covenant became aware of a growing animal smell. He had already guessed what he was about to see when Hamako entered another large cave, not as high as the garden, but equally broad.

It was a zoo. The Waynhim here were feeding hundreds of different animals. In small pens cunningly devised to resemble their natural dens and habitats lived pairs of badgers, foxes, hounds, marmosets, moles, raccoons, otters, rabbits, lynx, muskrats. And many of them had young.

The zoo was less successful than the garden. Animals without space to roam could not be healthy. But that problem paled beside the amazing fact that these creatures were alive at all. The Sunbane was fatal to animal life. The Waynhim preserved these species from complete extinction.

Once again, Hamako silenced Covenant's questions. They left the cave, and continued to work upward. They met no Waynhim in these tunnels. Soon their ascent became so pronounced that Covenant wondered just how deep in the Earth he had slept for three days. He felt a pang over the insensitivity of his senses; he missed the ability to gauge the rock weight above him, assess the nature of the *vitrim*, probe the spirits of his companions. That regret made him ache for

Linden. She might have known whether or not he could trust Vain.

Then the passageway became a spiral stair which rose to a small round chamber. No egress was visible; but Hamako placed his hands against a section of the wall, barked several Waynhim words, and thrust outward. The stone divided along an unseen crack and opened.

Leaving the chamber, Covenant found himself under the stars. Along the eastern horizon, the heavens had begun to pale. Dawn was approaching. At the sight, he felt an unexpected reluctance to leave the safety and wonder of the Waynhim desmesne. Grimly, he tightened his resolve. He did not look back when Hamako sealed the entrance behind him.

Vague in the darkness, Hamako led him through an impression of large, crouching shapes to a relatively open area. There he sat down, facing the east. As he joined Hamako, Covenant discovered that they were on a flat expanse of rock —protection against the first touch of the Sunbane.

Vain stood off to one side as if he neither knew nor cared about the need for such protection.

"Now I will speak," Hamako said. His words went softly into the night. "Have no fear of the Sunbane-warped who sought your life. Never again will they enter this place. That much at least of mind and fear they retain." His tone suggested that he held the area sacred to some private and inextinguishable sorrow.

Covenant settled himself to listen; and after a deep pause Hamako began.

"A vast gulf," he breathed, a darker shape amid the dark crouchings of the night, "lies between creatures that are born and those that are made. Born creatures, such as we are, do not suffer torment at the simple fact of physical form. Perhaps you desire keener sight, greater might of arm, but the embodiment of eyes and limbs is not anguish to you. You are born by Law to be as you are. Only a madman loathes the nature of his birth.

"It is far otherwise with the Waynhim. They were made— as the ur-viles were made—by deliberate act in the breeding dens of the Demondim. And the Demondim were themselves formed by lore rather than blood from the Viles who went before them. Thus the Waynhim are not creatures of law. They are entirely alien in the world. And they are unnaturally long of life. Some among this *rhysh* remember the Lords and the ancient glory of Revelstone. Some tell the tale of the five *rhysh* which fought before the gates of Revelstone in the great siege—and of the blue Lord who rode to their aid in folly and valor. But let that pass.

"The numbers of the Waynhim are only replenished because the ur-viles continue the work of their Demondim makers. Much breeding is yet done in the deeps of the Earth, and some are ur-viles, some Waynhim—and some are altogether new, enfleshed visions of lore and power. Such a one is your companion. A conscious making to accomplish a chosen aim."

In the east, the sky slowly blanched. The last stars were fading. The shapes around Covenant and Hamako grew more distinct, modulating toward revelation.

"That is the Weird of all Demondim-spawn. Each Waynhim and ur-vile beholds itself and sees that it need not have been what it is. It is the fruit of choices it did not make. From this fact both Waynhim and ur-viles draw their divergent spirits. It has inspired in the ur-viles a quenchless loathing for their own forms and an overweening lust for perfection, for the power to create what they are not. Their passion is extreme, careless of costs. Therefore they have given millennia of service to the Despiser, for Lord Foul repays them with both knowledge and material for their breedings. Thus comes your companion.

"And therefore the Waynhim have been greatly astonished to find no ill in him. He is an—an apotheosis. In him, it appears that the ur-viles have at last transcended their unscrupuling violence and achieved perfection. He is the Weird of the ur-viles incarnate. More of him I may not say.

"But the spirit of the Waynhim is different entirely. They are not reckless of costs; from the great Desecration which Kevin Landwaster and Lord Foul conceived upon the Land, they learned a horror of such passions. They foresaw clearly the price the ur-viles paid, and will ever pay, for self-loathing, and they turned in another way. Sharing the Weird, they chose to meet it differently. To seek self-justification."

Hamako shifted his position, turned more squarely toward the east.

"In the Waynhim tongue, Weird has several meanings. It is fate or destiny—but it is also choice, and is used to signify council or decision-making. It is a contradiction—fate and choice. A man may be fated to die, but no fate can determine whether he will die in courage or cowardice. The Waynhim choose the manner in which they meet their doom.

"In their loneness, they have chosen to serve the Law of which they do not partake. Each *rhysh* performs its own devoir. Thus the garden and the animals. In defiance of the Sunbane and all Lord Foul's ill, this *rhysh* seeks to preserve things which grow by Law from natural seed, in the form which they were born to hold. Should the end of Sunbane ever come, the Land's future will be assured of its natural life."

Covenant listened with a tightness in his throat. He was moved by both the scantness and the nobility of what the Waynhim were doing. In the myriad square leagues which comprised the vast ruin of the Sunbane, one cavern of healthy plants was a paltry thing. And yet that cavern represented such commitment, such faith in the Land, that it became grandeur. He wanted to express his appreciation, but could find no adequate words. Nothing could ever be adequate except the repeal of the Sunbane, allowing the Waynhim to have the future they served. The fear that their self-consecration might prove futile in the end blurred his vision, made him cover his eyes with his hands.

When he looked up again, the sun was rising.

It came in pale brown across the Plains, a desert sun. Land features were lifted out of darkness as the night bled away. When he glanced about him, he saw that he was sitting in the center of a wrecked Stonedown.

Houses lay in rubble; lone walls stood without ceilings to support; architraves sprawled like corpses; slabs of stone containing windows canted against each other. At first, he guessed that the village had been hit by an earthquake. But as the light grew stronger, he saw more clearly.

Ragged holes the size of his palm riddled all the stone as if a hail of vitriol had fallen on the village, chewing through the ceilings until they collapsed, tearing the walls into broken chunks, burning divots out of the hard ground. The place where he sat was pocked with acid marks. Every piece of rock in the area which had ever stood upright had been sieved into ruin.

"Hellfire!" he murmured weakly. "What happened here?"

Hamako had not moved; but his head was bowed. When he

spoke, his tone said plainly that he was acutely familiar with the scene. "This also I desire to tell," he sighed. "For this purpose I brought you here."

Behind him, a hillock cracked and opened, revealing within it the chamber from which he and Covenant had left the underground corridors. Eight Waynhim filed into the sunrise, closing the entrance after them. But Hamako seemed unaware of them.

"This is During Stonedown, home of the Sunbane-warped who sought your life. They are my people."

The Waynhim ranged themselves in a circle around Hamako and Covenant. After an initial glance, Covenant concentrated on Hamako. He wanted to hear what the man was saying.

"My people," the former Stonedownor repeated. "A proud people—all of us. A score of turnings of the moon ago, we were hale and bold. Proud. It was a matter of great pride to us that we had chosen to defy the Clave.

"Mayhap you have heard of the way in which the Clave acquires blood. All submit to this annexation, as did we for many generations. But it was gall and abhorrence to us, and at last we arose in refusal. Ah, pride. The Rider departed from us, and During Stonedown fell under the na-Mhoram's *Grim.*"

His voice shuddered. "It may be that you have no knowledge of such abominations. A fertile sun was upon us, and we were abroad from our homes, planting and reaping our sustenance—recking little of our peril. Then of a sudden the green of the sun became black—blackest ill—and a fell cloud ran from Revelstone toward During Stonedown, crossing against the wind."

He clenched his hand over his face, gripping his forehead in an effort to control the pain of memory.

"Those who remained in their homes—infants, mothers, the injured and the infirm—perished as During Stonedown perished, in agony. All the rest were rendered homeless."

The events he described were vivid to him, but he did not permit himself to dwell on them. With an effort of will, he continued, "Then despair came upon us. For a day and a night, we wandered the brokenness of our minds, heeding nothing. We had not the heart to heed. Thus the Sunbane took my people unprotected. They became as you have seen them.

"Yet I was spared. Stumbling alone in my loss—bemoaning the death of wife and daughter—I came by chance upon three of the Waynhim ere the sun rose. Seeing my plight, they compelled me to shelter."

He raised his head, made an attempt to clear his throat of grief. "From that time, I have lived and worked among the *rhysh*, learning the tongue and lore and Weird of the Waynhim. In heart and will, I have become one of them as much as a man may. But if that were the extent of my tale"— he glanced painfully at Covenant —"I would not have told it. I have another purpose."

Abruptly, he stood and gazed around the gathered Waynhim. When Covenant joined him, he said, "Thomas Covenant, I say to you that I have become of the Waynhim. And they have welcomed me as kindred. More. They have made my loss a part of their Weird. The Sunbane-warped live dire lives, committing all possible harm ere they die. In my name, this *rhysh* has taken upon itself the burden of my people. They are watched and warded—preserved from hurt, sustained in life— prevented from wreaking the damage of their wildness. For my sake, they are kept much as the animals are kept, both aided and controlled. Therefore they remain alive in such numbers. Therefore the *rhysh* was unwilling to redeem *dhraga*. And therefore"— he looked squarely at Covenant —"both *rhysh* and I are to blame for the harm you suffered."

"No," Covenant protested. "It wasn't your fault. You can't blame yourself for things you can't foresee."

Hamako brushed this objection aside. "The Waynhim did not foresee their own creation. Yet the Weird remains." But then, somehow, he managed a smile. "Ah, Covenant," he said, "I do not speak for any love of blame. I desire only your comprehension." He gestured around him. "The Waynhim have come to offer their aid in pursuit of your companions. I wish you to know what lies behind this offer, so that you may accept it in the spirit of its giving, and forgive us for what we have withheld from you."

A surge of respect and empathy blurred Covenant's responses again. Because he had no other way to express what he felt, he said formally, as Atiaran had taught him, "I thank you. The giving of this gift honors me. Accepting it, I return honor to the givers." Then he added, "You've earned the right."

Slowly, the strain faded from Hamako's smile. Without releasing Covenant's gaze, he spoke to the Waynhim; and they answered in a tone of readiness. One of them stepped forward, placed something in his hand. When Hamako raised his hand, Covenant saw that the object was a stone dirk.

He winced inwardly. But Hamako's smile was the smile of a friend. Seeing Covenant's uncertainty, the man said, "There is no harm for you in this. May I have your hand?"

Consciously repressing a tremor, Covenant extended his right hand, palm downward.

Hamako grasped his wrist, looked for a moment at the scars left by Joan's nails, then abruptly drew a cut across the veins.

Covenant flinched; but Hamako held him, did not permit him to withdraw.

His anxiety turned to amazement as he saw that the cut did not bleed. Its edges opened, but no blood came from the wound.

Dhraga approached. Its broken arm hung in a splint, but its other wounds were healing.

It raised its uninjured hand. Carefully, Hamako made an incision in the exposed palm. At once, dark blood swarmed down *dhraga*'s forearm.

Without hesitation, the Waynhim reached out, placed its cut directly on Covenant's. Hot blood smeared the back of his hand.

At that instant, he became aware of the other Waynhim. They were chanting softly in the clear desert dawn.

Simultaneously, strength rushed up his arm, kicked his heart like a burst of elation. He felt suddenly taller, more muscular. His vision seemed to expand, encompassing more of the terrain. He could easily have wrested free of Hamako's grasp. But he had no need to do so.

Dhraga lifted its hand away.

The bleeding had stopped. Its blood was being sucked into his cut.

Dhraga withdrew. Hamako gave the dirk to *durhisitar*. While *durhisitar* cut its palm just as *dhraga*'s had been cut, Hamako said, "Soon the power will come to appear unbearable, but I ask you to bear it. Remain quiet until all the Waynhim have shared this giving. If the ritual is completed, you will have the strength you require for a day—perhaps two."

Durhisitar put its cut upon Covenant's. More might surged into him. He felt abruptly giddy with energy, capable of anything, everything. His incision absorbed *durhisitar's* blood. When the creature stepped back, he could hardly hold himself still for the next Waynhim.

Only after the third infusion did he realize that he was receiving something more than power. *Dhraga* he had recognized by its injuries—but how had he known *durhisitar*? He had never looked closely at that particular Waynhim. Yet he had known it by name, just as he knew the third Waynhim, *dhubha*, and the fourth, *vraith*. He felt ecstatic with knowledge.

Drhami was fifth; *ghohritsar*, sixth. He was dancing with uncontainable might. Hamako's knuckles whitened; but his grip had the weight of a feather. Covenant had to leash himself firmly to keep from exploding free and cavorting around the ruins like a wild man. The range of his hearing had become so wide that he could hardly distinguish words spoken nearby.

Hamako was saying, "—remember your companions. Waste not this power. While it remains, stop for neither night nor doom."

Ghramin.

Covenant felt as colossal as Gravin Threndor, as mighty as Fire-Lions. He felt that he could crush boulders in his arms, destroy Ravers with his hands.

Dhurng: eighth and last.

Hamako snatched back his hand as if the power in Covenant burned him. "Go now!" he cried. "Go for Land and Law, and may no malison prevail against you!"

Covenant threw back his head, gave a shout that seemed to echo for leagues:

"*Linden!*"

Swinging around to the northwest, he released the flood-fire of his given strength and erupted, running toward Revelstone like a coruscation in the air.

SEVENTEEN: Blood-Speed

THE sun ascended, brown-mantled and potent, sucking the moisture of life from the Land. Heat pressed down like the weight of all the sky. Bare ground was baked as hard as travertine. Loose dirt became dust and dust became powder until brown clogged the air and every surface gave off clouds like dead steam. Chimeras roamed the horizons, avatars of the Sunbane. The Center Plains lay featureless and unaneled under the bale of that sun.

But Waynhim strength was glee in Covenant's veins. Running easily, swiftly, he could not have stopped, even by choice; his muscles thronged with power; gaiety exalted his heart; his speed was delicious to him. Without exertion, he ran like the Ranyhyn.

His progress he measured on a map in his mind—names of regions so dimly remembered that he could no longer identify when he had first heard them.

Across the wide wilderland of Windscour: eleven leagues. Through the ragged hills of Kurash Festillin: three leagues.

By noon he had settled into a long, fast stride, devouring distance as if his appetite for it were insatiable. Fortified by *vitrim* and power, he was immune to heat, dust, hallucination.

Yet Vain followed as if the Demondim-spawn had been made for such swiftness. He ran the leagues lightly, and the ground seemed to leap from under his feet.

Along the breadth of Victuallin Tayne, where in ancient centuries great crops had flourished: ten leagues. Up the long stone rise of Greshas Slant to higher ground: two leagues. Around the dry hollow of Lake Pelluce in the center of Andelainscion, olden fruiterer to the Land: five leagues.

Covenant moved like a dream of strength. He had no sense of time, of strides measured by sweat and effort. The Waynhim had borne the cost of this power for him, and he was free to run and run. When evening came upon him, he feared he would have to slacken his pace; but he did not. Stars burnished the crisp desert night, and the moon rose half full, shedding silver over the waste. Without hesitation or hinderance, he told out the dark in names.

Across the Centerpith Barrens: fourteen leagues. Down the Fields of Richloam, Sunbane-ruined treasure of the Plains: six leagues. Up through the jagged ridges of Emacrimma's Maw: three leagues. Along Boulder Fash, strewn with confusion like the wreckage of a mountain: ten leagues.

The night unfurled like an oriflamme: it snapped open over the Plains, and snapped away; and he went on running through the dawn. Outdistancing moon and stars, he caught the sunrise in the dry watercourse of the Soulsease River, fivescore leagues and more from Stonemight Woodhelven. Speed was as precious to him as a heart-gift. With Vain always at his back, he sipped *vitrim* and left the Soulsease behind, left the Center Plains behind to run and run, northwest toward Revelstone.

Over the open flat of Riversward: five leagues. Through the fens of Graywightswath, which the desert sun made traversable: nine leagues. Up the rocks of the Bandsoil Bounds: three leagues.

Now the sun was overhead, and at last he came to the end of his exaltation. His eldritch strength did not fail—not yet—but he began to see that it would fail. The knowledge gave him a pang of loss. Consciously, he increased his pace, trying to squeeze as many leagues as possible from the gift of Hamako's *rhysh*.

Across the rolling width of Riddenstretch: twelve leagues.

Gradually his mortality returned. He had to exert effort now to maintain his speed. His throat ached on the dust.

Among the gentle hills, smooth as a soft-rumpled mantle, of Consecear Redoin: seven leagues.

As the last rays of sunset spread from the Westron Mountains, he went running out of the hills, stumbled and gasped—and the power was gone. He was mortal again. The air rasped his lungs as he heaved for breath.

For a while, he rested on the ground, lay panting until his respiration eased. Mutely, he searched Vain for some sign of fatigue; but the Demondim-spawn's black flesh was vague in the gloaming, and nothing could touch him. After a time, Covenant took two swallows from his dwindling *vitrim*, and started walking.

He did not know how much time he had gained; but it was

enough to renew his hope. Were his companions two days ahead of him? Three? He could believe that the Clave might not harm them for two or three days. If he met no more delays—

He went briskly on his way, intending to walk through the night. He needed sleep; but his body felt less tired than it usually did after a hike of five leagues. Even his feet did not hurt. The power and the *vitrim* of the Waynhim had sustained him wondrously. With the sharpness of the air to keep him alert, he expected to cover some distance before he had to rest.

But within a league he caught sight of a fire burning off to the left ahead of him.

He could have bypassed it; he was far enough from it for that. But after a moment he shrugged grimly and started toward the fire. His involuntary hope that he had caught up with his friends demanded an answer. And if this light represented a menace, he did not want to put it behind him until he knew what it was.

Creeping over the hard uneven ground, he crouched forward until he could make out details.

The light came from a simple campfire. A few pieces of wood burned brightly. A bundle of faggots lay near three large sacks.

Across the fire sat a lone figure in a vivid red robe. The hood of the robe had been pushed back, revealing the lined face and gray-raddled hair of a middle-aged woman. Something black was draped around her neck.

She triggered an obscure memory in Covenant. He felt he had seen someone like her before, but could not recollect where or when. Then she moved her hands, and he saw that she held a short iron scepter with an open triangle affixed to its end. Curses crowded against his teeth. He identified her from Linden's description of the Rider at Crystal Stonedown.

Gritting to himself, he began to withdraw. This Rider was not the one he wanted. The Graveler of Stonemight Woodhelven had indicated that Linden's abductor, Santonin na-Mhoram-in, was a man. And Covenant had no intention of risking himself against any Rider until no other choice remained. With all the stealth he could muster, he edged away from the light.

Suddenly, he heard a low snarl. A huge shape loomed out

of the darkness, catching him between it and the fire. Growling threats, the shape advanced like the wall of a house.

Then a voice cut the night.

"Din!"

The Rider. She stood facing Covenant and Vain and the snarl. "Din!" she commanded. "Bring them to me!"

The shape continued to approach, forcing Covenant toward the campfire. As he entered the range of the light, he became gradually able to see the immense beast.

It had the face and fangs of a saber-tooth, but its long body resembled that of a horse—a horse with shoulders as high as the top of his head, a back big enough to carry five or six people, and hair so shaggy that it hung to the creature's thighs. Its feet were hooved. From the back of each ankle grew a barbed spur as long as a swordthorn.

Its eyes were red with malice, and its snarl vibrated angrily. Covenant hastened to retreat as much as he could without moving too close to the Rider.

Vain followed calmly with his back to the beast.

"Halfhand!" the Rider barked in surprise. "I was sent to await you, but had no thought to meet with you so soon." A moment later, she added, "Have no fear of Din. It is true— the Coursers are creatures of the Sunbane. But therefore they have no need of meat. And they are whelped in obedience. Din will lift neither fang nor spur against you without my command."

Covenant put the fire between him and the woman. She was a short, square individual, with a blunt nose and a determined chin. Her hair was bound carelessly at the back of her neck as if she had no interest in the details of her appearance. But her gaze had the directness of long commitment. The black cloth hanging around her neck ritualized the front of her robe like a chasuble.

He distrusted her completely. But he preferred to take his chances with her rather than with her Courser. "Show me." He cast a silent curse at the unsteadiness of his voice. "Send it away."

She regarded him over the flames. "As you wish." Without shifting her gaze, she said, "Begone, Din! Watch and ward."

The beast gave a growl of disappointment. But it turned away and trotted out into the night.

In an even tone, the Rider asked, "Does this content you?"

Covenant answered with a jerk of his knotted shoulders. "It takes orders from you." He did not relax a jot of his wariness. "How content do you expect me to get?"

She considered him as if she had reason to fear him, and did not intend to show it. "You misdoubt me, Halfhand. Yet it appears to me that the right of misdoubt is mine."

Harshly, he rasped, "How do you figure that?"

"In Crystal Stonedown you reft Sivit na-Mhoram-wist of his rightful claim, and nigh slew him. But I give you warning." Her tone involuntarily betrayed her apprehension. "I am Memla na-Mhoram-in. If you seek my harm, I will not be so blithely dispatched." Her hands gripped her *rukh*, though she did not raise it.

He suppressed an angry denial. "Crystal Stonedown is just about a hundred and fifty leagues from here. How do you know what happened there?"

She hesitated momentarily, then decided to speak. "With the destruction of his *rukh*, Sivit was made helpless. But the fate of every *rukh* is known in Revelstone. Another Rider who chanced to be in that region was sent at once to his aid. Then that Rider spoke with his *rukh* to Revelstone, and the story was told. I knew of it before I was sent to await you."

"Sent?" Covenant demanded, thinking, Be careful. One thing at a time. "Why? How did you know I was coming?"

"Where else but Revelstone would the Halfhand go with his white ring?" she replied steadily. "You fled Mithil Stonedown in the south, and appeared again at Crystal Stonedown. Your aim was clear. As for why I was sent—I am not alone. Seven of the Clave are scattered throughout this region, so that you would not find the Keep unforewarned. We were sent to escort you if you come as friend. And to give warning if you come as foe."

Deliberately, Covenant let his anger show. "Don't lie to me. You were sent to kill me. Every village in the Land was told to kill me on sight. You people think I'm some kind of threat."

She studied him over the jumping flames. "Are you not?"

"That depends. Whose side are you on? The Land's—or Lord Foul's?"

"Lord Foul? That name is unknown to me."

"Then call him a Jeroth. A-Jeroth of the Seven Hells."

She stiffened. "Do you ask if I serve a-Jeroth? Have you come such a distance in the Land, and not learned that the

Clave is dedicated entirely to the amelioration of the Sunbane? To accuse—"

He interrupted her like a blade. "Prove it." He made a stabbing gesture at her *rukh*. "Put that thing down. Don't tell them I'm coming."

She stood still, trapped by indecision.

"If you really serve the Land," he went on, "you don't need to be afraid of me. But I've got no reason to trust you. Goddamn it, you've been trying to kill me! I don't care how much tougher you are than Sivit." He brandished his ring, hoping she had no way of recognizing his incapacity. "I'll take you apart. Unless you give me some reason not to."

Slowly, the Rider's shoulders sagged. In a tight voice, she said, "Very well." Taking her scepter by the triangle, she handed it past the fire to him.

He accepted it with his left hand to keep it away from his ring. A touch of relief eased some of his tension. He slipped the iron into his belt, then tugged at his beard to keep himself from becoming careless, and began to marshall his questions.

Before he could speak, Memla said, "Now I am helpless before you. I have placed myself in your hands. But I desire you to understand the Clave before you choose my doom. For generations, the soothreaders have foretold the coming of the Halfhand and the white ring. They saw it as an omen of destruction for the Clave—a destruction which only your death could prevent.

"Halfhand, we are the last bastion of power in the Land. All else has been undone by the Sunbane. Only our might, constant and vigilant, preserves any life from Landsdrop to the Westron Mountains. How can our destruction be anything other than heinous to the Land? Therefore we sought your death.

"But Sivit's tale held great meaning for Gibbon na-Mhoram. Your power was revealed to the Clave for the first time. The na-Mhoram took counsel for several days, and at last elected to dare his doom. Power such as yours, he declared, is rare and precious, and must be used rather than resisted. Better, he said, to strive for your aid, risking fulfillment of the soothreaders' word, than to lose the hope of your puissance. Therefore I do not seek your hurt, though Sivit did, to his cost."

Covenant listened intently, yearning for the ability to hear whether or not she spoke the truth. Sunder and Hollian had taught him to fear the Clave. But he needed to reach Revelstone—and reach it in a way which would not increase the danger to his friends. He decided to attempt a truce with Memla.

"All right," he said, moderating the harshness of his tone. "I'll accept that—for now. But there's something I want *you* to understand. I didn't lift a finger against Sivit until he attacked me." He had no memory of the situation; but he felt no need to be scrupulously candid. Bluffing for his safety, he added, "He forced me. All I wanted was the eh-Brand."

He expected her to ask why he wanted an eh-Brand. Her next sentence took him by surprise.

"Sivit reported that you appeared to be ill."

A chill spattered down his spine. Careful, he warned himself. Be careful. "Sunbane-fever," he replied with complex dishonesty. "I was just recovering."

"Sivit reported," she went on, "that you were accompanied by a man and a woman. The man was a Stonedownor, but the woman appeared to be a stranger to the Land."

Covenant clenched himself, decided to chance the truth. "They were captured by a Rider. Santonin na-Mhoram-in. I've been chasing them for days."

He hoped to surprise a revelation from her; but she responded with a frown, "Santonin? He has been absent from Revelstone for many days—but I think he has taken no captives."

"He's got three," rasped Covenant. "He can't be more than two days ahead of me."

She considered for a moment, then shook her head. "No. Had he taken your companions, he would have spoken of it through his *rukh* to the Readers. I am na-Mhoram-in. Such knowledge would not be withheld from me."

Her words gave him a sick sense of being out of his depth—caught in a web of falsehood with no possibility of extrication. Who was lying? The Graveler of Stonemight Woodhelven? Memla? Or Santonin, so that he could keep a fragment of the Illearth Stone for himself? His inability to discern the truth hurt Covenant like vertigo. But he fought to keep his visage flat, free of nausea. "Do you think I'm making this up?"

Memla was either a consummate prevaricator or a brave woman. She met his glare and said evenly, "I think you have told me nothing concerning your true companion." With a nod, she indicated Vain.

The Demondim-spawn had not moved a muscle since he had first come to a halt near the fire.

"He and I made a deal," Covenant retorted. "I don't talk about him, and he doesn't talk about me."

Her eyes narrowed. Slowly, she said, "You are a mystery, Halfhand. You enter Crystal Stonedown with two companions. You reave Sivit of an eh-Brand. You show power. You escape. When you appear once more, swift beyond belief, your three companions are gone, replaced by this black enigma. And you demand to be trusted. Is it power which gives you such arrogance?"

Arrogance, is it? Covenant grated. I'll show you arrogance. Defiantly, he pulled the *rukh* from his belt, tossed it to her. "All right," he snapped. "Talk to Revelstone. Tell them I'm coming. Tell them anybody who hurts my friends is going to answer for it!"

Startlement made her hesitate. She looked at the iron and back at him, debating rapidly with herself. Then she reached her decision. Reluctantly, she put the *rukh* away within her robe. Straightening her black chasuble, she sighed, "As you wish." Her gaze hardened. "If your companions have indeed been taken to Revelstone, I will answer for their safety."

Her decision softened his distrust. But he was still not satisfied. "Just one more thing," he said in a quieter tone. "If Santonin was on his way to Revelstone while you were coming here, could he get past you without your knowing it?"

"Clearly," she responded with a tired lift of her shoulders. "The Land is wide, and I am but one woman. Only the Readers know the place and state of every *rukh*. Though seven of us were sent to await you, a Rider could pass by unseen if he so chose. I rely on Din to watch and ward, but any Rider could command Din's silence, and I would be none the wiser. Thus if you desire to believe ill of Santonin, I cannot gainsay you.

"Please yourself," she continued in a tone of fatigue. "I am no longer young, and mistrust wearies me. I must rest." Bending like an old woman, she seated herself near the fire. "If you are wise, you will rest also. We are threescore leagues from Revelstone—and a Courser is no palanquin."

Covenant gazed about him, considering his situation. He felt too tight—and too trapped—to rest. But he intended to remain with Memla. He wanted the speed of her mount. She was either honest or she was not; but he would probably not learn the truth until he reached Revelstone. After a moment, he, too, sat down. Absent-mindedly, he unbound the pouch of *vitrim* from his belt, and took a small swallow.

"Do you require food or water?" she asked. "I have both." She gestured toward the sacks near her bundle of firewood.

He shook his head. "I've got enough for one more day."

"Mistrust." Reaching into a sack, she took out a blanket and spread it on the ground. With her back to Covenant, she lay down, pulled the blanket over her shoulders like a protection against his suspicions, and settled herself for sleep.

Covenant watched her through the declining flames. He was cold with a chill which had nothing to do with the night air. Memla na-Mhoram-in challenged too many of his assumptions. He hardly cared that she cast doubt on his distrust of the Clave; he would know how to regard the Clave when he learned more about the Sunbane. But her attack on his preconceptions about Linden and Santonin left him sweating. Was Santonin some kind of rogue Rider? Was this a direct attempt by Lord Foul to lay hands on the ring? An attack similar to the possession of Joan? The lack of any answers made him groan.

If Linden were not at Revelstone, then he would need the Clave's help to locate Santonin. And he would have to pay for that help with cooperation and vulnerability.

Yanking at his beard as if he could pull wisdom from the skin of his face, he glared at Memla's back and groped for prescience. But he could not see past his fear that he might indeed be forced to surrender his ring.

No. Not that. Please. He gritted his teeth against his chill dread. The future was a leper's question, and he had been taught again and again that the answer lay in single-minded dedication to the exigencies of the present. But he had never been taught how to achieve single-mindedness, how to suppress his own complex self-contradictions.

Finally, he dozed. His slumber was fitful. The night was protracted by fragmentary nightmares of suicide—glimpses of a leper's self-abandonment that terrified him because they came so close to the facts of his fate, to the manner in which he had given himself up for Joan. Waking repeatedly, he strove to elude his dreams; but whenever he faded back toward unconsciousness, they renewed their ubiquitous grasp.

Some time before dawn, Memla roused herself. Muttering at the stiffness in her bones, she used a few faggots to restore the fire, then set a stoneware bowl full of water in the flames to heat. While the water warmed, she put her forehead in the dirt toward Revelstone and mumbled orisons in a language Covenant could not understand.

Vain ignored her as if he had been turned to stone.

When the water was hot enough, she used some of it to lave her hands, face, and neck. The rest she offered to Covenant. He accepted. After the night he had just spent, he needed to comfort himself somehow. While he performed what ablutions he could, she took food for breakfast from one of her sacks.

He declined her viands. True, she had done nothing to threaten him. But she was a Rider of the Clave. While he still had *vitrim* left, he was unwilling to risk her food. And also, he admitted to himself, he wanted to remind her of his distrust. He owed her at least that much candor.

She took his refusal sourly. "The night has not taught you grace," she said. "We are four days from Revelstone, Halfhand. Perhaps you mean to live on air and dust when the liquid in your pouch fails."

"I mean," he articulated, "to trust you exactly as much as I have to, and no more."

She scowled at his reply, but made no retort.

Soon dawn approached. Moving briskly now, Memla packed away her supplies. As soon as she had tied up her sacks, bound her bundles together by lengths of rope, she raised her head, and barked, "Din!"

Covenant heard the sound of hooves. A moment later, Memla's Courser came trotting out of the dusk.

She treated it with the confidence of long familiarity. Obeying her brusque gesture, Din lowered itself to its belly. At once, she began to load the beast, heaving her burdens across the middle of its back so that they hung balanced in pairs. Then, knotting her fingers in its long hair, she pulled herself up to perch near its shoulders.

Covenant hesitated to follow. He had always been uncomfortable around horses, in part because of their strength, in part because of their distance from the ground; and the Courser was larger and more dangerous than any horse. But he had no choice. When Memla snapped at him irritably, he took his courage in both hands, and heaved himself up behind her.

Din pitched to its feet. Covenant grabbed at the hair urgently to keep himself from falling. A spasm of vertigo made everything reel as Memla turned Din to face the sunrise.

The sun broke the horizon in brown heat. Almost at once, haze began to ripple the distance, distorting all the terrain. His memories of the aid the Waynhim had given him conflicted with his vertigo and with his surprise at Memla's immunity.

Answering his unspoken question, she said, "Din is a creature of the Sunbane. His body wards us as stone does." Then she swung her beast in the direction of Revelstone.

Din's canter was unexpectedly smooth; and its hair gave Covenant a secure hold. He began to recover his poise. The ground still seemed fatally far away; but it no longer appeared to bristle with falling. Ahead of him, Memla sat cross-legged near the Courser's shoulders, trusting her hands to catch her whenever she was jostled off balance. After a while, he followed her example. Keeping both fists constantly clutched in Din's coat, he made himself as secure as he could.

Memla had not offered Vain a seat. She had apparently decided to treat him exactly as he treated her. But Vain did not need to be carried by any beast. He loped behind Din effortlessly and gave no sign that he was in any way aware of what he was doing.

Covenant rode through the morning in silence, clinging to the Courser's back and sipping *vitrim* whenever the heat made him dizzy. But when Memla resumed their journey after a brief rest at noon, he felt a desire to make her talk. He wanted information; the wilderness of his ignorance threatened him. Stiffly, he asked her to explain the Rede of the Clave.

"The Rede!" she ejaculated over her shoulder. "Halfhand, the time before us is reckoned in days, not turnings of the moon."

"Summarize," he retorted. "If you don't want me dead, then you want my help. I need to know what I'm dealing with."

She was silent.

Deliberately, he rasped, "In other words, you *have* been lying to me."

Memla leaned abruptly forward, hawked and spat past Din's shoulder. But when she spoke, her tone was subdued, almost chastened. "The Rede is of great length and complexity, comprising all the accumulated knowledge of the Clave in reference to life in the Land, and to survival under the Sunbane. It is the task of the Riders to share this knowledge throughout the Land, so that Stonedown and Woodhelven may endure."

Right, Covenant muttered. And to kidnap people for their blood.

"But little of this knowledge would have worth to you," she went on. "You have sojourned scatheless under the Sunbane. What skills it to tell you of the Rede?

"Yet you desire comprehension. Halfhand, there is only one matter which the bearer of the white ring need understand. It is the triangle." She took the *rukh* from her robe, showed it to him over her shoulder. "The Three Corners of Truth. The foundation of all our service."

To the rhythm of Din's strides, she began to sing:

> "Three the days of Sunbane's bale:
> Three the Rede and sooth:
> Three the words na-Mhoram spake:
> Three the Corners of Truth."

When she paused, he said, "What do you mean—'three the days'? Isn't the Sunbane accelerating? Didn't each sun formerly last for four or five days, or even more?"

"Yes," she replied impatiently, "beyond doubt. But the soothreaders have ever foretold that the Clave would hold at three—that the generations-long increase of our power and the constant mounting of the Sunbane would meet and match at three days, producing balance. Thus we hope now that in some way we may contrive to tilt the balance to our side, sending the Sunbane toward decline. Therefore the na-Mhoram desires your aid.

"But I was speaking of the Three Corners of Truth," she continued with asperity before Covenant could interrupt again. "This knowledge at least you do require. On these three facts the Clave stands, and every village lives.

"First, there is no power in Land or life comparable to the Sunbane. In might and efficacy, the Sunbane surpasses all other puissance utterly.

"Second, there is no mortal who can endure the Sunbane. Without great knowledge and cunning, none can hope to en-

dure from one sun to the next. And without opposition to the
Sunbane, all life is doomed. Swift or slow, the Sunbane will
wreak entire ruin.

"Third, there is no power sufficient to oppose the Land's
doom, except power which is drawn from the Sunbane itself.
Its might must be reflected against it. No other hope exists.
Therefore does the Clave shed the blood of the Land, for
blood is the key to the Sunbane. If we do not unlock that
power, there will be no end to our perishing.

"Hear you, Halfhand?" Memla demanded. "I doubt not
that in your sojourn you have met much reviling of the Clave.
Despite all our labor, Stonedown and Woodhelven must believe
that we exact their blood for pleasure or self." To Covenant's
ears, her acidity was the gall of a woman who instinctively
abhorred her conscious convictions. "Be not misled! The cost
is sore to us. But we do not flinch from it because it is our
sole means to preserve the Land. If you must cast blame, cast
it upon a-Jeroth, who incurred the just wrath of the Master
—and upon the ancient betrayers, Berek and his ilk, who
leagued with a-Jeroth."

Covenant wanted to protest. As soon as she mentioned
Berek as a betrayer, her speech lost its persuasiveness. He had
never known Berek Halfhand; the Lord-Fatherer was already
a legend when Covenant had entered the Land. But his knowledge of the effects of Berek's life was nearly two score centuries more recent than Memla's. Any set of beliefs which
counted Berek a betrayer was founded on a lie; and so any
conclusions drawn from that foundation were false. But he
kept his protest silent because he could conceive of no way to
demonstrate its accuracy. No way short of victory over the
Sunbane.

To spare himself a pointless argument, he said, "I'll reserve
judgment on that for a while. In the meantime, satisfy my
curiosity. I've got at least a dim notion of who a-Jeroth is. But
what are the seven Hells?"

Memla was muttering sourly to herself. He suspected that
she resented his distrust precisely because it was echoed by a
distrust within herself. But she answered brusquely, "They are
rain, desert, pestilence, fertility, war, savagery, and darkness.
But I believe that there is also an eighth. Blind hostility."

After that, she rebuffed his efforts to engage her in any
more talk.

When they halted for the night, he discarded his empty

pouch and accepted food from her. And the next morning, he did what he could to help her prepare for the day's journey.

Sitting on Din, she faced the sunrise. It crested the horizon like a cynosure in green; and she shook her head. "A fertile sun," she murmured. "A desert sun wreaks much ruin, and a sun of rain may be a thing of great difficulty. A sun of pestilence carries peril and abhorrence. But for those who must journey, no other sun is as arduous as the sun of fertility. Speak not to me under this sun, I adjure you. If my thoughts wander, our path will also wander."

By the time they had covered half a league, new grass blanketed the ground. Young vines crawled visibly from place to place: bushes unfolded buds the color of mint.

Memla raised her *rukh*. Uncapping the hollow scepter, she decanted enough blood to smear her hands. Then she started chanting under her breath. A vermilion flame, pale and small in the sunlight, burned within the open triangle.

Under Din's hooves, the grass parted along a straight line stretching like a plumb toward Revelstone. Covenant watched the parting disappear into the distance. The line bared no ground; but everything nearby—grass, shrubs, incipient saplings—bent away from it as if an invisible serpent were sliding northwestward through the burgeoning vegetation.

Along the parting, Din cantered as if it were incapable of surprise.

Memla's chant became a low mumble. She rested the end of her *rukh* on Din's shoulders; but the triangle and the flame remained erect before her. At every change in the terrain, the verdure thickened, compressing whole seasons into fractions of the day. Yet her line remained open. Trees shunned it; copses parted as if they had been riven by an axe; bushes edging the line had no branches or leaves on that side.

When Covenant looked behind him, he saw no trace of the path; it closed the moment Memla's power passed. As a result, Vain had to fend for himself. But he did so with characteristic disinterest, slashing through grass and brush at a run, crashing thickets, tearing across briar patches which left no mark on his black skin. He could not have seemed less conscious of difficulty. Watching the Demondim-spawn, Covenant did not know which amazed him more: Memla's ability to create this path; or Vain's ability to travel at such speed without any path.

That night, Memla explained her line somewhat. Her *rukh*, she said, drew on the great Banefire in Revelstone, where the Clave did its work against the Sunbane, and the Readers tended the *master-rukh*. Only the power for the link to the *master-rukh* came from her; the rest she siphoned from the Banefire. So the making of her path demanded stern concentration, but did not exhaust her. And the nearer she drew to Revelstone, the easier her access to the Banefire became. Thus she was able to form her line again the next day, defying the resistance of huge trees, heather and bracken as high as Din's shoulders, grass like thickets and thickets like forests.

Yet Vain was able to match the Courser's pace. He met the sharper test of each new league as if no size or density of vegetation could ever estimate his limits. And the third day made no change. It intensified still more the extravagance of the verdure, but did not hamper the nonchalant ease with which he followed Din. Time and again, Covenant found himself craning his neck, watching Vain's progress and wondering at the sheer unconscious force it represented.

But as the afternoon passed, his thoughts turned from Vain, and he began to look ahead. The mammoth jungle concealed any landmarks the terrain might have offered, but he knew that Revelstone was near. All his anxiety, dread, and anticipation returned to him; and he fought to see through the thronging foliage as if only an early glimpse of the ancient Keep would forewarn him of the needs and hazards hidden there.

But he received no forewarning. Late in the afternoon, Memla's path started up a steep hillside. The vegetation suddenly ended on the rock of the foothills. Revelstone appeared before Covenant as if in that instant it had been unfurled from the storehouse of his most vivid memories.

The Courser had arrived athwart the great stone city, Giant-wrought millennia ago from the gutrock of the plateau. Out of the farthest west, mountains came striding eastward, then, two leagues away on Covenant's left, dropped sheer to the upland plateau, still a thousand feet and more above the foothills. The plateau narrowed to form a wedged promontory half a league in length; and into this promontory the ancient Giants had delved the immense and intricate habitation of Revelstone.

The whole cliff-face before Covenant was coigned and fortified, lined with abutments and balconies, punctuated by oriels, architraves, embrasures, from a level fifty or a hundred feet above the foothills to the rim of the plateau. On his left, Revelstone gradually faded into native rock; but on his right, it filled the promontory to the wedge-tip, where the watchtower guarded the massive gates of the Keep.

The tremendous and familiar size of the city made his heart ache with pride for the Giants he had loved—and with sharp grief, for those Giants had died in a body, slain by a Raver during the war against Lord Foul's Illearth Stone. He had once heard that there was a pattern graven into the walls of Revelstone, an organization of meaning too huge for un-Giantish minds to grasp; and now he would never have it explained to him.

But that was not all his grief. The sight of Revelstone recalled other people, friends and antagonists, whom he had hurt and lost: Trell Atiaran-mate; Hile Troy, who had sold his soul to a Forestal so that his army might survive; Saltheart Foamfollower; Elena. High Lord Mhoram. Then Covenant's sorrow turned to anger as he considered that Mhoram's name was being used by a Clave which willingly shed innocent blood.

His wrath tightened as he studied Revelstone itself. Memla's line ran to a point in the middle of the city; and from the plateau above that point sprang a prodigious vermeil beam, aimed toward the heart of the declining sun. It was like the Sunbane shaft of Sunder's *orcrest*; but its sheer size was staggering. Covenant gaped at it, unable to conceive the number of lives necessary to summon so much power. Revelstone had become a citadel of blood. He felt poignantly that it would never be clean again.

But then his gaze caught something in the west, a glitter of hope. There, halfway between Revelstone and the Westron Mountains, lay Furl Falls, where the overflow of Glimmermere came down the cliff to form the White River. And the Falls held water; tumbling spray caught the approaching sunset, and shone. The Land had been eighteen days without a sun of rain, and six of them had been desert; yet the springs of Glimmermere had not failed.

Gripping anger and hope between his teeth, Covenant set himself to face whatever lay ahead.

Memla gave a sigh of accomplishment, and lowered her *rukh*. Turning Din's head with a muttered command, she sent the beast trotting toward the gates under the southeast face of the tower.

The watchtower was barely half the height of the plateau, and its upper reaches stood independent of the main Keep, joined only by wooden crosswalks. Covenant remembered that a courtyard lay open to the sky within the granite walls which sealed the base of the tower to the Keep; and the megalithic stone gates under the watchtower were repeated beyond the courtyard, so that Revelstone possessed a double defense for its only entrance. But as he approached the tower, he was shocked to see that the outer gates lay in rubble. Sometime in the distant past, Revelstone had needed its inner defense.

The abutments over the ruined gates were deserted, as were the fortifications and embrasures above it; the whole tower seemed empty. Perhaps it was no longer defensible. Perhaps the Clave saw no need to fear the entry of strangers. Or perhaps this air of desertion was a trap to catch the unwary.

Memla headed directly into the tunnel, which led to the courtyard; but Covenant slipped off Din's back, lowering himself by handholds of hair. She stopped, looked back at him in surprise. "Here is Revelstone," she said. "Do you not wish to enter?"

"First things first." His shoulders were tight with apprehension. "Send the na-Mhoram out here. I want him to tell me in person that I'll be safe."

"He is the na-Mhoram!" she snapped indignantly. "He does not come or go according to the whims of others."

"Good for him." He controlled his tension with sarcasm. "The next time I have a whim, I'll keep that in mind." She opened her mouth to retort. He cut her off. "I've already been taken prisoner twice. It's not going to happen to me again. I'm not going in there until I talk to the na-Mhoram." On the spur of a sudden intuition, he added, "Tell him I understand the necessity of freedom as well as he does. He can't get what he wants by coercion. He's just going to have to cooperate."

Memla glared at him for a moment, then muttered, "As you wish." With a gruff command, she sent Din into the tunnel, leaving Covenant alone with Vain.

Covenant took hold of his anxiety, and waited. Across the peaks, the sun was setting in green and lavender; the shadow of Revelstone spread out over the monstrous verdure like an aegis of darkness. Watching the tower for signs of hostile intent, he observed that no pennons flew from its crown. None were needed: the hot red shaft of Sunbane-force marked Revelstone as the home of the Clave more surely than any oriflamme.

Unable to possess himself in patience, he growled to Vain, "I'm damned if I know what you want here. But I've got too many other problems. You'll have to take care of yourself."

Vain did not respond. He seemed incapable of hearing.

Then Covenant saw movement in the tunnel. A short man wearing a stark black robe and a red chasuble came out past the ruined gates. He carried an iron crozier as tall as himself, with an open triangle at one end. He did not use the hood of his robe; his round face, bald head, and beardless cheeks were exposed. His visage was irenic, formed in a mold of habitual beatitude or boredom, as if he knew from experience that nothing in life could ruffle his composure. Only his eyes contradicted the hebetude of his mien. They were a piercing red.

"Halfhand," he said dully. "Be welcome in Revelstone. I am Gibbon na-Mhoram."

The simple blandness of the man's manner made Covenant uncomfortable. "Memla tells me I'm safe here," he said. "How am I supposed to believe that, when you've been trying to kill me ever since I first set foot in the Land?"

"You represent great peril to us, Halfhand." Gibbon spoke as if he were half asleep. "But I have come to believe that you also represent great promise. In the name of that promise, I accept the risk of the peril. The Land has need of every power. I have come to you alone so that you may see the truth of what I say. You are as safe among us as your own purposes permit."

Covenant wanted to challenge that assertion; but he was not ready to hazard a test. He changed his tack. "Where's Santonin?"

Gibbon did not blink. "Memla na-Mhoram-in spoke to me of your belief that your companions have fallen into the hands of a Rider. I know nothing of this. Santonin has been long from Revelstone. We feel concern for him. His *rukh* is silent. Perhaps—if what you say of him is true—your companions have mastered him, and taken his *rukh*. I have already commanded the Riders who were sent to meet you to begin a search. If your companions are found, I assure you that we shall value their safety."

Covenant had no answer. He scowled at the na-Mhoram, and remained silent.

The man showed no uncertainty or confusion. He nodded toward Vain, and said, "Now I must ask you concerning your companion. His power is evident, but we do not comprehend him."

"You see him," Covenant muttered. "You know as much about him as I do."

Gibbon permitted his gaze to widen. But he did not mention his incredulity. Instead, he said, "My knowledge of him is nothing. Therefore I will not permit him to enter Revelstone."

Covenant shrugged. "Suit yourself. If you can keep him out, you're welcome."

"That will be seen." The na-Mhoram gestured toward the tunnel. "Will you accompany me?"

For one more moment, Covenant hesitated. Then he said, "I don't think I have much choice."

Gibbon nodded ambiguously, acknowledging either Covenant's decision or his lack of options, and turned toward the tower.

Walking behind the na-Mhoram, Covenant entered the tunnel as if it were a gullet into peril. His shoulders hunched involuntarily against his fear that people might leap on him from the openings in the ceiling. But nothing attacked him. Amid the echoing of his footsteps, he passed through to the courtyard.

There he saw that the inner gates were intact. They were open only wide enough to admit the na-Mhoram. Members of the Clave stood guard on the fortifications over the entrance.

Motioning for Covenant to follow him, Gibbon slipped between the huge stone doors.

Hellfire, Covenant rasped, denying his trepidation. With Vain at his back, he moved forward.

The gates were poised like jaws. The instant he passed them, they closed with a hollow granite thud, sealing Vain outside.

There was no light. Revelstone crouched around Covenant, as dark as a prison.

EIGHTEEN: Revelstone in Rain

"GIBBON!" Fear and ire lashed Covenant's voice.

"Ah, your pardon," the na-Mhoram replied out of the darkness. "You desire light. A moment."

Robes rustled around Covenant. He flung his arms wide to ward them off; but they did not assail him. Then he heard a word of command. Red flame burst from the triangle of a *rukh*. Other lights followed. In moments, the high, wide entry hall of Revelstone was garishly incarnadine.

"Your pardon," Gibbon repeated. "Revelstone is a place of caution. The Clave is unjustly despised by many, as your own mistrust demonstrates. Therefore we admit strangers warily."

Groping to recover his inner balance, Covenant grated, "Have you ever stopped to consider that maybe there's a reason why people don't like you?"

"Their mislike is natural," said the na-Mhoram, unperturbed. "Their lives are fear from dawn to dusk, and they do not behold the fruit of our labor. How should they believe us when we say that without us they would perish? We do not resent this. But we take caution against it."

Gibbon's explanation sounded dangerously plausible. Yet Covenant distrusted the na-Mhoram's lack of passion. Because he could think of no apt retort, he simply nodded when Gibbon asked, "Will you come?" At the na-Mhoram's side, he walked down the hall, flanked by members of the Clave carrying fires.

The hall was as large as a cavern; it had been formed by Giants to accommodate Giants. But Gibbon soon turned from it into a side passage, and began to ascend broad stairways toward the upper levels of the city. Revelstone was as complex as a maze because it had been laid out according to criteria known only to the long-dead Giants. However, it was familiar to Covenant; though he had not been here for ten of his years, he found that he knew his way. He took a grim satisfaction from the fact.

Loyal to the Keep he remembered, he followed Gibbon upward and away from the spine of Revelstone. Once the entry hall was well behind them, their way was lit by torches smoking in sconces along the walls. Before long, they entered a corridor marked at long intervals by granite doors with wooden handles. Opposite one of them stood a hooded figure wearing a red robe but no chasuble. When the na-Mhoram approached, the figure opened the door for him. Covenant took a moment to be sure the entrance had no hidden locks or bolts, then went in after Gibbon.

Beyond the door lay a suite of rooms: a central area containing stone chairs and a table; a bedroom to one side and a bathroom to the other; an outer balcony. On the table was a tray of food. Brands lit the suite, covering the air with a patina of smoke. Remembering the untrammeled fires of the Lords, Covenant began to marshal bitter questions for the na-Mhoram.

"You will have comfort here," Gibbon said. "But if you are displeased, we will provide any quarters you require. Revelstone is larger than the Clave, and much unused." Beckoning for the hooded figure beyond the doorway, he continued, "This is Akkasri na-Mhoram-cro. She will answer your wants. Speak to her of any lack or desire." The hooded woman bowed without revealing her face or hands, and withdrew. "Halfhand, are you content?"

Content? Covenant wanted to snarl. Oh, sure! Where the goddamn bloody hell is Linden? But he repressed that impulse. He did not wish to betray how much his companions mattered to him. Instead, he said, "I'll be fine. As long as nobody tries to stick a knife into me—or lock my door—or poison my food."

Gibbon's beatitude smothered every emotion. His eyes were as bland as their color permitted. He regarded Covenant for a moment, then moved to the table. Slowly, he ate a bite from every dish on the tray—dried fruit, bread, stew—and washed them down with a swallow from the flask. Holding Covenant's gaze, he said, "Halfhand, this mistrust does not become you. I am moved to ask why you are here, when you expect such ill at our hands."

That question Covenant was prepared to answer honestly. "Not counting what happened to my friends, I need information. I need to understand this Sunbane. So I need the Clave. The villagers I've met—" They had been too busy trying to kill him to answer questions. "They just survive. They don't understand. I want to know what causes the Sunbane. So I can fight it."

Gibbon's red eyes glinted ambiguously. "Very well," he replied in a tone that expressed no interest in what he heard or said. "As to fighting the Sunbane, I must ask you to wait until the morrow. The Clave rests at night. But the causes of the Sunbane are plain enough. It is the Master's wrath against the Land for the evil of past service to a-Jeroth."

Covenant growled inwardly. That idea was either a lie or a cruel perversion. But he did not intend to argue metaphysics with Gibbon. "That isn't what I mean. I need something more practical. How is it done? How did it happen? How does it work?"

Gibbon's gaze did not waver. "Halfhand, if I possessed such knowledge, I would make use of it myself."

Terrific. Covenant did not know whether to believe the na-Mhoram. A wave of emotional fatigue rolled over him. He began to see how hard it would be to glean the information he needed; and his courage quailed. He did not know the right questions. He simply nodded when Gibbon said, "You are weary. Eat, now. Sleep. Perhaps the morrow will bring new insight."

But as Gibbon moved to the door, Covenant felt compelled to try once more. "Tell me. How come Glimmermere still has water?"

"We moderate the Sunbane," the na-Mhoram answered with easy patience. "Therefore the Earth retains some vitality." A blink of hesitation touched his eyes, vanished. "An old legend avers that a nameless periapt lies in the deeps of the lake, sustaining it against the Sunbane."

Covenant nodded again. He knew of at least one thing, powerful or not, which lay at the bottom of Glimmermere.

Then Gibbon left the room, closing the door behind him, and Covenant was alone.

He remained still for a while, allowing his weakness to flow over him. Then he took a chair out onto the balcony, so that he could sit and think in the privacy of the night.

His balcony stood halfway up the south face of the Keep. A gibbous moon was rising, and he was able to descry the vast dark jumble of trees left by the fertile sun. Sitting with his feet braced against the rail of the balcony to appease his fear of heights, he ran his fingers through his tangled beard, and tried to come to grips with his dilemma.

He did not in fact anticipate a physical attempt upon his life. He had insisted on the necessity of freedom in order to remind the Clave that they would gain nothing by killing him; but the truth was that he accused the Clave of meditating murder primarily as a release for an entirely different dread.

He was afraid for Linden, poignantly afraid that his friends were in far more danger than he was. And this fear was aggravated by his helplessness. Where were they? Were Gibbon and Memla lying about Santonin? If so, how could he learn the truth? If not, what could he do? He felt crippled without Linden; he needed her perceptions. She would have been able to tell him whether or not Gibbon was honest.

Cursing the numbness of his leprosy, he asked the night why *he* of all people in the Land—Thomas Covenant, Unbeliever and white gold wielder, who had once mastered the Despiser in mortal combat—why he should feel so helpless. And the answer was that his self-knowledge, his fundamental confidence in what he was, was torn by doubt. His resources had become a contradiction. All the conscious extremity of his will was unable to call up one jot or tittle of power from his ring; yet when he was delirious, he exerted a feral might utterly beyond conscious control. Therefore he distrusted himself, and did not know what to do.

But to that question the night turned a deaf ear. Finally he abandoned the interrogation, and set about preparing for sleep.

In the bathroom, he stripped off his clothes, scrubbed both them and himself thoroughly, then draped them over chairbacks to dry. He felt vulnerable in his nakedness; but he accepted that risk by eating the food he had been given, drinking to the bottom the flask of *metheglin*. The mead added a physical drowsiness to his moral fatigue. When he investigated the bed, he found it comfortable and clean-smelling. Expecting nightmares, surprises, anguish, he crouched under the blankets, and slept.

He awoke to the sound of rain—torrents beating like the rush of a river against Revelstone's granite. The air of the bedroom felt moist; he had not closed off the balcony before going to bed. But for a time he did not move; he lay in the streaming susurration and let the sound carry him toward alertness.

When at last he rolled over onto his back and opened his eyes, he found Vain standing near the bed.

The Demondim-spawn bore himself as always—arms hanging slightly bent, stance relaxed, eyes focused on nothing.

"What the hell—?" Covenant jerked out of bed and hurried into the next room. Rain came slashing in from the balcony, drenching the floor. He braved the deluge, went outside to look for some indication of how Vain had reached him.

Through the downpour, he saw a huge tree bough leaning against the end of the balcony. The butt of the limb rested on another balcony thirty or forty feet below; apparently, Vain had climbed several hundred feet up the wall of Revelstone by scaling his bough to the lower abutments, then pulling it up behind him and using it to reach the next parapets, ascending by stages until he gained Covenant's room. How Vain had known the right room Covenant had no idea.

Scattering water, he rushed back into his suite and swung shut the balcony-door. Naked and dripping, he gaped at the Demondim-spawn, amazed by Vain's inexplicable capabilities. Then a grim grin twisted his mouth. "Good for you," he rasped. "This will make them nervous." Nervous people made mistakes.

Vain gazed vacuously past him like a deaf-mute. Covenant nodded sharply at his thoughts and started toward the bathroom to get a towel. But he was pulled to a halt by the sight of the livid raw patch running from the left side of Vain's head down his shoulder. He had been injured; his damaged skin oozed a black fluid as if he had been severely burned.

How—? Over the past days, Covenant had become so convinced of Vain's invulnerability that now he could not think. The Demondim-spawn could be hurt? Surely— But the next instant his astonishment disappeared in a flaring of comprehension. Vain had been attacked by the Clave-Riders testing the mysterious figure outside their gates. They had burned him. Perhaps he had not even deigned to defend himself.

But his mien betrayed no knowledge of pain. After a moment, Covenant went cursing into the bathroom and began to towel himself dry. Bastards! I'll bet he didn't lift a finger. Swiftly, he donned his clothes, though they were still somewhat damp. Striding to the door of his suite, he pushed it open.

Akkasri na-Mhoram-cro stood in the passage with a fresh

tray of food at her feet. Covenant beckoned roughly to her. She picked up the tray and carried it into his suite.

He stopped her inside the doorway, took the new tray and handed her the old one, then dismissed her. He wanted her to have a chance to report Vain's presence to the na-Mhoram. It was a small revenge, but he took it. Her hood concealed her face, so that he could not see her reaction. But she left with alacrity.

Muttering darkly, he sat down to breakfast.

Shortly after he finished, there was a knock at his door. He thrust the slab of stone open, and was disappointed to find Akkasri alone outside.

"Halfhand," she said in a muffled tone, "you have asked for knowledge concerning the Clave's resistance of the Sunbane. The na-Mhoram commands me to serve you. I will guide you to the place where our work is wrought and explain it as best I may."

This was not what Covenant had expected. "Where's Gibbon?"

"The na-Mhoram," replied Akkasri, stressing Gibbon's title, "has many duties. Though I am only na-Mhoram-cro, I can answer certain inquiries. Gibbon na-Mhoram will attend you, if I do not suffice to your need."

Oh, hell, he growled. But he concealed his disconcertion. "We'll see. I've got a lot of questions." He stepped out into the hallway, held the door open for Vain. "Let's go."

At once, Akkasri moved off down the passage, ignoring Vain completely. This struck Covenant as unnatural; the Demondim-spawn was not easily discounted. Perhaps she had been told what to do? Then his revenge had not been wasted.

His nerves tightened. Striding at Akkasri's side, he began his search for comprehension by asking bluntly, "What's a na-Mhoram-cro?"

"Halfhand," the woman said without giving him a glimpse of her face, "the na-Mhoram-cro are the novices of the Clave. We have been taught much, but have not yet mastered the *rukh* sufficiently to become Riders. When we have gained that skill, we will be na-Mhoram-wist. And with much experience and wisdom, some of us will advance to become the hands of the na-Mhoram himself, the na-Mhoram-in. Such is Memla, who bore you to Revelstone. She is greatly honored for her courage and sagacity."

"If you're a novice," he demanded, "how much can you explain?"

"Only Gibbon na-Mhoram holds all the knowledge of the Clave." Akkasri's tone was tinged with indignation. "But I am unskilled, not ignorant."

"All right." With Vain behind them, she led Covenant downward, tending generally toward the central depths of the Keep. "Tell me this. Where did the Clave come from?"

"Halfhand?"

"It hasn't been here forever. Other people used to live in Revelstone. What happened to them? How did the Clave get started? Who started it?"

"Ah." She nodded. "That is a matter of legend. It is said that many and many generations ago, when the Sunbane first appeared in the sky, the Land was governed by a Council. This Council was decadent, and made no effort to meet the peril. Therefore precious time was lost before the coming of the Mhoram."

Covenant began to recognize where she was taking him; this was the way to the sacred enclosure. He was faintly surprised by the general emptiness of the halls and passages. But he reflected that Revelstone was huge. Several thousand people could live in it without crowding each other.

"It is his vision which guides us now," the na-Mhoram-cro was saying. "Seeing that the Council had fallen to the guile of a-Jeroth, he arose with those few who retained leal and fore-sight, and drove out the treachers. Then began the long strug-gle of our lives to preserve the Land. From the Mhoram and his few has the Clave descended, generation after generation, na-Mhoram to na-Mhoram, seeking ever to consummate his opposition to the Sunbane.

"It is a slow work. We have been slow to master the skill and gain the numbers which we need—and slow as well to muster blood." She said the word *blood* with perfect imper-sonality, as if it cost nothing. "But now we approach the fruition of our long dream. The Sunbane has reached a rhythm of three days—and we hold. We hold, Halfhand!" She claimed pride; but she spoke blandly, as if pride, too, were impersonal. As if she had been carefully groomed to answer Covenant's questions.

But he held his suspicion in abeyance. They walked one of the main hallways along the spine of the Keep; and ahead he could see the passage branching to circle left and right around the outer wall of the sacred enclosure, where the long-dead Lords had held their Vespers of self-consecration to the Land and to Peace.

As he drew closer, he observed that all the many doors, which were regularly spaced around the wall and large enough for Giants, were kept shut. The brief opening as a Rider came out of the enclosure revealed a glimpse of lurid red heat and muffled roaring inside.

The na-Mhoram-cro stopped before one of the doors, addressing Covenant. "Speech is difficult within this place." He wanted to behold her face; she sounded as if she had evasive eyes. But her hood concealed her visage. If he had not seen Memla and Gibbon, he might have suspected that all the Clave were hiding some kind of deformity. "It is the hall of the Bancfire and the *master-rukh*. When you have seen it, we will withdraw, and I will tell you concerning it."

He nodded in spite of a sudden reluctance to see what the Clave had done to the sacred enclosure. When Akkasri opened the nearest door, he followed her into a flood of heat and noise.

The place blazed with garish fire. The enclosure was an immense cavity in the gut-rock of Revelstone, a cylinder on end, rising from below the level of the foothills more than halfway up the height of the Keep. From a dais on the floor, the Lords had spoken to the city. And in the walls were seven balconies circling the space, one directly above the next. There the people of Revelstone had stood to hear the Lords.

No more. Akkasri had brought Covenant to the fourth balcony; but even here, at least two hundred feet above the floor, he was painfully close to the fire.

It roared upward from a hollow where the dais had been, sprang yowling and raging almost as high as the place where he stood. Red flame clawed the air as if the very roots of the Keep were afire. The blast of heat half-blinded him; the fire seemed to scorch his cheeks, crisp his hair. He had to blink away a blur of tears before he could make out any details.

The first thing he saw was the *master-rukh*. It rested at three points on the rail of this balcony, a prodigious iron triangle. The center of each arm glowed dull vermeil.

Two members of the Clave stood at each corner of the *master-rukh*. They seemed impervious to the heat. Their hands gripped the iron, concentrated on it as if the Banefire were a script which they could read by touch. Their faces shone ruddy and fanatical above the flames.

Clearly, this was the place from which the red shaft of Sunbane power leaped to the sun.

The doors at the base of the cavity and around the highest balcony were open, providing ventilation. In the lurid brilliance, Covenant saw the domed ceiling for the first time. Somehow, the Giants had contrived to carve it ornately. Bold figures strode the stone, depicting scenes from the early history of the Giants in the Land: welcome, gratitude, trust. But the fire made the images appear strangely distorted and malefic.

Grinding his teeth, he cast his gaze downward. A movement at the base of the fire caught his attention. He saw now that several troughs had been cut into the floor, feeding the hollow. A figure apparelled like the na-Mhoram-cro approached one of the troughs, carrying two heavy pails which were emptied into the trough. Dark fluid ran like the ichor of Revelstone into the hollow. Almost at once, the Banefire took on a richer texture, deepened toward the ruby hue of blood.

Covenant was suffocating on heat and inchoate passion. His heart struggled in his chest. Brushing past Akkasri and Vain, he hastened toward the nearest corner of the *master-rukh*.

The people there did not notice him; the deep roar of the flame covered the sound of his boots, and their concentration was intent. He jerked one of them by the shoulder, pulled the individual away from the iron. The person was taller than he—a figure of power and indignation.

Covenant yelled up at the hooded face, "Where's Santonin?"

A man's voice answered, barely audible through the howl of the Banefire. "I am a Reader, not a soothreader!"

Covenant gripped the man's robe. "What happened to him?"

"He has lost his *rukh*!" the Reader shouted back. "At the command of the na-Mhoram, we have searched for him diligently! If his *rukh* were destroyed—if he were slain with his *rukh* still in his hands—we would know of it. Every *rukh* answers to the *master-rukh*, unless it falls into ignorant hands. He would not choose to release his *rukh*. Therefore he has been overcome and bereft. Perhaps then he was slain. We cannot know!"

"Halfhand!" Akkasri clutched at Covenant's arm, urging him toward the door.

He let her draw him out of the sacred enclosure. He was dizzy with heat and blind wild hope. Maybe the Reader spoke the truth; maybe his friends had overpowered their captor; maybe they were safe! While the na-Mhoram-cro closed the door, he leaned against the outer wall and panted at the blessedly cool air.

Vain stood near him, as blank and attentive as ever.

Studying Covenant, Akkasri asked, "Shall we return to your chamber? Do you wish to rest?"

He shook his head. He did not want to expose that much of his hope. With an effort, he righted his reeling thoughts. "I'm fine." His pulse contradicted him; but he trusted she could not perceive such things. "Just explain it. I've seen the *master-rukh*. Now tell me how it works. How you fight the Sunbane."

"By drawing its power from it," she answered simply. "If more water is taken from a lake than its springs provide, the lake will be emptied. Thus we resist the Sunbane.

"When the Mhoram first created the Banefire, it was a small thing, and accomplished little. But the Clave has increased it generation after generation, striving for the day when sufficient power would be consumed to halt the advance of the Sunbane."

Covenant fumbled mentally, then asked, "What do you do with all this power? It's got to go somewhere."

"Indeed. We have much use for power, to strengthen the Clave and continue our work. As you have learned, much is drawn by the Riders, so that they may ride and labor in ways no lone man or woman could achieve without a ruinous expenditure of blood. With other power are the Coursers wrought, so that the Sunbane will have no mastery over them. And more is consumed by the living of Revelstone. Crops are grown on the upland plateau—kine and goats nourished—looms and forges driven. In earlier generations, the Clave was hampered by need and paucity. But now we flourish, Half-hand. Unless some grave disaster falls upon us," Akkasri said in a pointed tone, "we will not fail."

"And you do it all by killing people," he rasped. "Where do you get that much blood?"

She turned her head away in distaste for his question. "Doubtless you possess that knowledge," she said stiffly. "If you desire further enlightenment, consult the na-Mhoram."

"I will," he promised. The state of the sacred enclosure reminded him that the Clave saw as evil a whole host of things which he knew to be good; and actions which they called good made his guts heave. "In the meantime, tell me what the na-Mhoram"— to irritate her, he used the title sardonically —"has in mind for me. He wants my help. What does he want me to do?"

This was obviously a question for which she had come prepared. Without hesitation, she said, "He desires to make of you a Reader."

A Reader, he muttered to himself. Terrific.

"For several reasons," she went on evenly. "The distinction between Reading and soothreading is narrow, but severe. Perhaps with your white ring the gap may be bridged, giving the Clave knowledge to guide its future. Also with your power, perhaps still more of the Sunbane may be consumed. Perhaps you may exert a mastery over the region around Revelstone, freeing it from the Sunbane. This is our hope. As you wielded more power, the Sunbane would grow weaker, permitting the expansion of your mastery, spreading safety farther out into the Land. Thus the work of generations might be compressed into one lifetime.

"It is a brave vision, Halfhand, worthy of any man or woman. A great saving of life and Land. For that reason Gibbon na-Mhoram rescinded the command of your death."

But he was not persuaded. He only listened to her with half his mind. While she spoke, he became aware of an alteration in Vain. The Demondim-spawn no longer stood completely still. His head shifted from side to side, as if he heard a distant sound and sought to locate its source. His black orbs were focused. When Akkasri said, "Will you answer, Halfhand?" Covenant ignored her. He felt suddenly sure that Vain was about to do something. An obscure excitement pulled him away from the wall, poised him for whatever might happen.

Abruptly, Vain started away along the curving hall.

"Your companion!" the na-Mhoram-cro barked in surprise and agitation. "Where does he go?"

"Let's find out." At once, Covenant strode after Vain.

The Demondim-spawn moved like a man with an impeccable knowledge of Revelstone. Paying no heed to Covenant and Akkasri, or to the people he passed, he traversed corridors and stairways, disused meeting halls and refectories; and at every opportunity he descended, working his way toward the roots of the Keep.

Akkasri's agitation increased at every descent. But, like Vain, Covenant had no attention to spare for her. Searching his memory, he tried to guess Vain's goal. He could not. Before long, Vain led him into passages he had never seen before. Torches became infrequent. At times, he could barely distinguish the black Demondim-spawn from the dimness.

Then, without warning, Vain arrived in a cul-de-sac lit only by light reflecting from some distance behind him. As Covenant and Akkasri caught up with him, he was staring at the end of the corridor as if the thing he desired were hidden beyond it.

"What is it?" Covenant did not expect Vain to reply; he spoke only to relieve his own tension. "What are you after?"

"Halfhand," snapped the na-Mhoram cro, "he is your companion." She seemed afraid, unprepared for Vain's action. "You must control him. He must stop here."

"Why?" Covenant drawled, trying to vex her into a lapse of caution, a revelation. "What's so special about this place?"

Her voice jumped. "It is forbidden!"

Vain faced the blind stone as if he were thinking. Then he stepped forward and touched the wall. For a long moment, his hands probed the surface.

His movements struck a chord in Covenant's memory. There was something familiar about what Vain was doing.

Familiar?

The next instant, Vain reached up to a spot on the wall above his head. Immediately, lines of red tracery appeared in the stone. They spread as if he had ignited an intaglio: in moments, red limned a wide doorway.

The door swung open, revealing a torch-lit passage.

Yes! Covenant shouted to himself. When he and Foamfollower had tried to enter Foul's Creche, the Giant had found and opened a similar door just as Vain had found and opened this one.

But what was that kind of door doing in Revelstone? Neither the Giants nor the Lords had ever used such entrances.

In a sudden rush of trepidation, he saw Akkasri's movement a moment too late to stop her. Swift with urgency, she snatched a *rukh* from under her robe and decanted blood onto her hands. Now fire sprang from the triangle; she began shouting words he could not understand.

Vain had already disappeared into the passage. Before the

door could close itself again, Covenant sprinted after the Demondim-spawn.

This hall doubled back parallel to the one he had just left. It was well-lit. He could see that this place had not been part of the original Giant-work. Walls, floor, ceiling, all were too roughly formed. The Giants had never delved stone so carelessly. Leaping intuitively ahead of himself, he guessed that this tunnel had not been cut until after the passing of the Council. It had been made by the Clave for their own secret purposes.

Beyond him, a side corridor branched off to the left. Vain took this turning. Covenant followed rapidly.

In ten strides, the Demondim-spawn reached a massive iron door. It had been sealed with heavy bolts sunk deep into the stone, as if the Clave intended it to remain shut forever.

A faint pearly light marked the cracks around the metal.

Vain did not hesitate. He went to the door, found a place to wedge his fingers into the cracks. His back and shoulders tensed. Pressure squeezed new fluid from his burns.

Covenant heard running behind him, but did not turn away. His amazement tied him to Vain.

With a prodigious burst of strength, Vain tore the door from its moorings. Ringing like an anvil, it fell to the floor. In a wash of nacreous illumination, he stepped past the threshold.

Covenant followed like a man in a trance.

They entered a large chamber crammed with tables, walled to the ceiling with shelves. Hundreds of scrolls, caskets, pouches, periapts filled the shelves. The tables were piled high with staffs, swords, scores of talismans. The light came from three of the richest caskets, set high on the back wall, and from several objects on the tables. Dumb with astonishment, Covenant recognized the small chest which had once held the *krill* of Loric Vilesilencer. The chest was open and empty.

He gaped about him, unable to think, realize, understand.

A moment later, Akkasri and two people dressed like Riders raced into the chamber and leaped to a halt. They brandished flaming *rukhs.* "Touch nothing!" one of them barked.

Vain ignored them as if he had already forgotten they had the power to harm him. He moved to one of the far tables. There he found what he sought: two wide bands of dull gray iron.

Covenant identified them more by instinct than any distinctive feature.

The heels of the Staff of Law.

The Staff of Law, greatest tool of the Council of Lords, formed by Berek Halfhand from a branch of the One Tree. It was destroyed by wild magic when Lord Foul had forced dead Elena to wield it against the Land. Bannor had borne the heels back to Revelstone after the Despiser's defeat.

Before anyone could react, Vain donned the bands.

One he slipped over his right hand. It should have been too small; but it went past his knuckles without effort, and fitted snugly to his wrist.

The other he pulled onto his left foot. The iron seemed elastic. He drew it over his arch and heel easily, settled it tight about his ankle.

A Rider gasped. Akkasri and another woman faced Covenant. "Halfhand," Akkasri's companion snapped, "this is upon your head. The Aumbrie of the Clave is forbidden to all. We will not tolerate such violation."

Her tone brought Covenant back to himself. Dangers bristled in the air. Thinking rapidly, he said, "All the lore of the Lords—everything that used to belong to the Council. It's all here. It's all intact."

"Much is intact," Akkasri said rigidly. "The Council was decadent. Some was lost."

Covenant hardly heard her. "The First and Second Wards." He gestured toward the shining caskets. "The Third Ward? Did they find the Third Ward?" Foreseeing the Ritual of Desecration, Kevin Landwaster had hidden all his knowledge in Seven Wards to preserve it for future Councils; but during High Lord Mhoram's time, only the first two and the last had been found.

"Evidently," a Rider retorted. "Little good it did them."

"Then why"— Covenant put all his appalled amazement into his voice —"don't you *use* it?"

"It is lore for that which no longer exists." The reply had the force of an indictment. "It has no value under the Sunbane."

Oh, hell. Covenant could find no other words for his dismay. Hell and blood.

"Come!" The Rider's command cut like a lash. But it was not directed at Covenant. She and her companions had turned toward Vain. Their *rukhs* burned redly, summoning power.

Vain obeyed, moving as if he had remembered the source

of his injury. Akkasri grabbed his arm, tried to pull the band from his wrist; but the metal was iron and inflexible.

Gesturing with their *rukhs*, she and the Riders escorted Vain from the Aumbrie as if Covenant were not present.

He followed them. To his surprise, they herded Vain away from the hidden doorway.

They went some distance down the rough corridor. Then the passage turned sharply, and debouched into a huge hall lit by many torches. The air was gray with smoke.

With a stab of shock, Covenant realized that the hall was a dungeon.

Scores of bolted iron doors seriated both walls. In each, heavy bars guarded a small window. Half a thousand people could have been emprisoned here, and no one who lacked Vain's instincts or knowledge could ever have found them.

As Covenant stared about him, the implications of the Riders' anger burned into clarity in his mind. Gibbon had not intended him to know of this place.

How many other secrets were there in Revelstone?

One of the Riders hurried to a door and shot back the bolts. Within lay a cell barely wide enough to contain a straw pallet.

With their *rukhs*, Akkasri and the other Rider forced Vain toward the door.

He turned under the architrave. His captors flourished threats of fire; but he made no move against them. He aimed one look at Covenant. His black face wore an expression of appeal.

Covenant glared back, uncomprehending. Vain?

A gift beyond price, Foamfollower had said. *No purpose but his own.*

Then it was too late. The door clanged shut on Vain. The Rider thrust home the bolts.

Uselessly Covenant protested, What do you want from me?

The next instant, a brown arm reached between the window bars of a nearby cell. Fingers clawed the air, desperate for freedom.

The gesture galvanized Covenant. It was something he understood. He dashed toward that door.

A Rider shouted at him, forbidding him. He paid no heed.

As he gained the door, the arm withdrew. A flat face pressed against the bars. Impassive eyes gazed out at him.

He almost lost his balance in horror. The prisoner was one

of the *Haruchai*—one of Bannor's people, who made their home high in the fastnesses of the Westron Mountains. He could not mistake the stern characteristic mien of the race that had formed the Bloodguard, could not mistake the resemblance to Bannor, who had so often saved his life.

In Andelain, Bannor's shade had said, *Redeem my people. Their plight is an abomination.*

Suppressing the tonal lilt of his native tongue, the *Haruchai* said, "Ur-Lord Thomas Covenant, Unbeliever and white gold wielder, I salute you. You are remembered among the *Haruchai*." The implacable rigor of his personality seemed incapable of supplication. "I am Brinn. Will you set us free?"

Then hot iron struck the back of Covenant's neck, and he stumbled like a cripple into darkness.

His unconsciousness was agony, and he could do nothing to assuage it. For a time as painful as frenzy, he lay deaf and blind. But gradually the darkness turned to rain. Torrents, muffled by granite, poured down walls, cascaded off eaves and parapets, rattled against oriels. The sound carried him back to himself. He became aware of the texture of blankets against his skin, aware of the deadness in his fingers and feet, the numbness of loss.

Remembering leprosy, he remembered everything, with an acuteness that made him press his face to the bed, knot his hands in the blanket under him. Vain. The *Haruchai*. The attack of the Riders.

That hidden door, which led to the Aumbrie, and the dungeon.

It was the same kind of door which the Despiser had formerly used in Foul's Creche. What was such a door doing in Revelstone?

A shudder ran through him. He rolled over, wincing at the movement. The back of his neck was stiff and sore. But the bones were intact, and the damage to his muscles did not seem permanent.

When he opened his eyes, he found Gibbon sitting beside his bed. The na-Mhoram's beatific face was tightened to express concern; but his red eyes held only peril.

A quick glance showed Covenant that he lay in the bedroom of his suite. He struggled to sit up. Sharp pains lanced through his back and shoulders; but the change of position enabled him to cast a glance at his right hand.

His ring was still there. Whatever else the Clave intended, they apparently did not intend to steal the white gold.

That steadied him. He looked at the na-Mhoram again, and made an intuitive decision not to raise the issue of the door. He had too many other dangers to consider.

"Doubtless," Gibbon said with perfect blandness, "your neck gives you pain. It will pass. Swarte employed excessive force. I have reprimanded her."

"How—?" The hurt seemed to cramp his voice. He could barely squeeze out a hoarse whisper. "How long have I been out?"

"It is now midday of the second day of rain."

Damnation, Covenant groaned. At least one whole day. He tried to estimate how many people the Clave had killed in that period of time, but could not. Perhaps they had killed Brinn— He thrust the idea away.

"Akkasri," he breathed, filling the name with accusation.

Gibbon nodded calmly. "Akkasri na-Mhoram-in."

"You lied to me."

The na-Mhoram's hebetude seemed impervious to offense. "Perhaps. My intent was not false. You came to Revelstone rife with hostility and suspicion. I sought means to allay your mistrust—and at the same time to ward against you if your purpose was evil. Therefore I informed you that Akkasri was of the na-Mhoram-cro. I desired to win your faith. In that I was not false. Guised as a na-Mhoram-cro, Akkasri could answer many questions without presenting to you the apparent threat of power. This I believed because of your treatment of Memla na-Mhoram-in. I regret that the outcome went amiss."

This sounded plausible; but Covenant rejected it with a shake of his head. Immediately, a stab of soreness made him grimace. Muttering darkly to himself, he massaged his neck. Then he changed the subject, hoping to unsettle Gibbon. "What the hell are you doing with one of the *Haruchai* in your goddamn prison?"

But the na-Mhoram appeared immune to discomfiture. Folding his arms, he said, "I sought to withhold that knowledge from you. Already you believe that you have sufficient cause for mistrust. I desired that you should have no more such reasons until you learned to see the sovereign importance of our work."

Abruptly, Gibbon went in another direction. "Halfhand, did the *Haruchai* name you truly? Are you indeed ur-Lord Thomas Covenant, Unbeliever and white gold wielder?"

"What difference does that make?" growled Covenant.

"That name is mentioned often in the ancient legends. After the First Betrayer, Thomas Covenant was the greatest of all a-Jeroth's servants."

"That's ridiculous." This new distortion of the Land's history dismayed him. But he was determined to evade Gibbon's snare. "How could I possibly be that Thomas Covenant? Where I come from, the name's common. So are white gold rings."

Gibbon gazed redly at him; but Covenant did not blink. A lie for a lie, he rasped. Finally, the na-Mhoram admitted, "You have not the look of such age." Then he went on, "But I was speaking of the *Haruchai*.

"Halfhand, we have not one *Haruchai* in our hold. We have threescore and seven."

Three—! Covenant could not keep the horror off his face.

"There." Gibbon gestured at him. "I had cause to fear your response."

"By God!" Covenant spat fiercely. "You ought to fear the *Haruchai*! Don't you know what you're dealing with?"

"I respect them entirely." The na-Mhoram's dull calm was complete. "Their blood is potent and precious."

They were my friends! Covenant could hardly refrain from shouting aloud. What in the name of all bloody hellfire and damnation do you think you're doing?

"Halfhand, you know that our work requires blood," Gibbon continued reasonably. "As the Sunbane grows, the Banefire must grow to resist it. We are long beyond the time when the people of the Land could meet all our need.

"Five generations past, when Offin na-Mhoram led the Clave, he was faced with the defeat of our dream. He had neared the limit of what the Land could supply, and it did not suffice. I will not dwell on his despair. It is enough to say that at that time—by chance or mercy—the *Haruchai* came to our aid."

He shrugged. "It is true that they did not intend the aid we found in them. Five came from the Westron Mountains in the name of their legends, seeking the Council. But Offin did not flinch his opportunity. He took the five captive.

"With the passage of time, five more came in search of their lost kindred. These also were captured. They were hardy and feral, but the power of the Banefire mastered them. And later more *Haruchai* came seeking the lost. First by five, then by ten, then by the score they came, with long lapses between. They are a stubborn people, and generation after generation they did not relent. Generation after generation, they were captured." Covenant thought he saw a glint of amusement in Gibbon's red eyes. "As their numbers increased, so grew the Banefire. Thus not a one of them prevailed or escaped.

"Their most recent foray comprised fivescore—a veritable army in their sight." Gibbon's blandness sounded like the serenity of a pure heart. "Three score and seven remain."

An abomination. The na-Mhoram's tale made Covenant ache for violence. He could hardly muffle his vehemence as he asked, "Is this supposed to convince me that you're my friend?"

"I do not seek your conviction here," replied Gibbon. "I seek only to explain, so that you will comprehend why I sought to withhold this knowledge—and why Swarte struck you when you beheld the *Haruchai*. You must perceive the extent of our consecration to our task. We count any one life—or any score of lives—or any myriad—as nothing against the life of the Land. The Sunbane is an immense ill, and we must spend immensely to combat it.

"Also I desire you to understand that *your* aid—the service of your white ring—promises the redemption of the Land, the saving of many times many lives. Does our shedding distress you? Then aid us, so that the need for blood may be brought to an end. You cannot serve the Land in any other way."

Covenant held Gibbon with a glare. Through his teeth, he breathed, "I knew the original Mhoram. The last time I was here, I made him choose between the hope of the Land and the life of one little girl. He chose the girl." No words could articulate all the bile in his mouth. "You're worse than the Sunbane."

He expected the na-Mhoram to retort; but Gibbon only blinked, and said, "Then it is sooth that you are the Unbeliever?"

"Yes!" Covenant snapped, casting subterfuge and safety aside. "And I'm not going to let you commit genocide on the *Haruchai.*"

"Ah," Gibbon sighed, rising to his feet, "I feared that we would come to this." He made a placating gesture. "I do not seek your harm. But I see only one means by which we may win your aid. I will ready the Clave for a soothtell. It will reveal the truth you covet. Lies will be exposed, hearts laid bare."

He moved to the doorway. "Rest now, Halfhand. Eat— regain your strength. Walk where you wish. I ask only that you eschew the Aumbrie and the hold until that which stands between us has been resolved. I will send for you when the soothtell has been prepared." Without waiting for an answer, he left the suite.

Soothtell, Covenant snarled. His inner voice sounded like a croak. By God, yes!

Ignoring the pain in his neck, he threw off the blankets and went to the next room in search of food.

There was a fresh tray on the table. The room had been closed against the rain, and the air reeked of smoke. Strangely certain now that the Clave would not try to poison or drug him, he attacked the food, wolfing it down to appease his empty rage. But he did not touch the flask of *metheglin*; he did not want anything to dull his alertness, hamper his reflexes. He sensed that Gibbon's soothtell would be a crisis, and he meant to survive it.

He felt a compelling need to leave his suite and roam Revelstone, measuring his tension and resolve against the huge Keep. But he did not. Exerting a leper's discipline, he sat down in one of the chairs, stretched his legs to another, rested his sore neck on the chairback, and forced himself to be still. Muscle by muscle, he loosened his body, relaxed his forehead, softened his pulse, in an effort to achieve the concentration and poise he required in order to be ready.

Faces intruded on him: Linden, Sunder, Brinn. Brinn's visage was as absolute as Bannor's. Linden's features were strained, not by severity or choice, but by fear. He closed his mind to them, so that his own passion would not blind him. Instead, he thought about the hidden door Vain had discovered.

He could sense the answer in him, mumbling toward clarity. But it was still blocked by his preconceptions. Yet its very nearness drew beads of trepidation-sweat from his face. He was not prepared for the mendacity it represented.

Mendacity. He reached out for that idea, tried to take hold of its implications. But the hands of his mind were half-hands, inadequate.

The knock at his door jerked him erect. A pang stung his neck; droplets of sweat spattered the floor.

Before he could leave his chair, the door sprang open. Memla burst into the room.

A tangle of gray-streaked hair framed her pale visage. She clutched her *rukh* as if she meant to strike him with it. But it held no flame. Her eyes were full of broken honesty.

"False!" she gasped. "They have been false to me!"

He lurched to confront her across the table.

She gaped momentarily for words, unable to compress the enormity of her indignation into mere speech. Then she broke out, "They are here! Santonin—your companions! All here!"

Covenant gripped the table to keep himself from falling.

"Two Stonedownors and a stranger. In the hold." Passion obstructed her breathing. "Santonin I saw, where he did not expect to be seen. The na-Mhoram uttered direct falsehood to me!

"I challenged Santonin. He revealed the truth—why I and others were sent to meet you. Smirking! Not to escort you, no. To ensure that you did not catch him. He gained Revelstone on the second day of the fertile sun. One day before us!"

One day? Something in Covenant began to howl. *One day*?

"Had I not halted you—had you walked through the night —you might have come upon him before dawn. He passed near me."

With an inchoate snarl, Covenant swung his arm, swept the tray from the table. Stoneware broke; *metheglin* splashed the floor. But the act steadied him. "Memla." He had been unjust to her. He regained control of his limbs, his purpose; but he could not control his voice. "Take me to Gibbon."

She stared at him. His demand took her aback. "You must flee. You are in peril."

"Now." He needed to move, begin, so that the trembling in his chest would not spread to his legs. "Take me to him now."

She hesitated, then gave a fierce nod. "Yes. It is right." Turning on her heel, she strode out of the room.

He surged after her in anguish and fury. Down toward the roots of Revelstone she guided him, along ways which he remembered. It was a long descent, but it seemed to pass swiftly. When she entered a familiar hall lit from its end by torches, he recognized the place where the Lords of the Council had had their private quarters.

The wide, round court beyond the hall both was and was not as he remembered it. The floor was burnished granite, as smooth as if it had been polished by ages of use and care. The ceiling rose far above the floor; and the walls were marked at intervals with coigns by which other levels of the Keep communicated with the dwellings spaced around the base of the cavity. These things accorded with his memory. But the light was altogether different. The Lords had not needed torches; the floor itself had shone with Earthpower. According to the old tales, the stone had been set aglow by Kevin Landwaster and the Staff of Law. But that illumination—so expressive of the warmth and fidelity of the Council—was gone now. The torches which replaced it seemed garish and unreliable by comparison.

But Covenant had neither time nor attention to spare for lost wonder. A score of the Clave stood around the center of the floor. All held their *rukhs* ready; and the na-Mhoram's crozier dominated them. They had turned to the sound of Covenant's entrance. Their hoods concealed their faces.

Within their circle lay a stone slab like a catafalque. Heavy iron fetters chained a man to it.

One of the *Haruchai*.

When Covenant stalked ahead of Memla to approach the circle, he recognized Brinn.

"Halfhand," the na-Mhoram said. For the first time, Covenant heard excitement in Gibbon's tone. "The soothtell is prepared. All your questions will be answered now."

NINETEEN: Soothtell

THE vibration of augury in the na-Mhoram's voice stopped Covenant. The high dome of the space was dark, untouched by the light of the torches; the Riders stood on the dead floor as if it were the bottom of an abyss. Behind the concealment of their hoods, they might have been ur-viles; only the pale flesh of their hands revealed that they were human as they poised their *rukhs* for fire. Santonin was probably among them. Stonemight Woodhelven's fragment of the Illearth Stone was probably hidden somewhere in this circle. Gibbon's tone told Covenant that the Clave had not gathered here to do him any benefit.

He came to a halt. Echoes of his rage repeated within him like another voice iterating ridicule. Instinctively, he clenched his half-fist around his wedding band. But he did not retreat. In a raw snarl, he demanded, "What the bloody hell have you done with my friends?"

"The soothtell will answer." Gibbon was eager, hungry. "Do you choose to risk the truth?"

Brinn gazed at Covenant. His mien was impassive; but sweat sheened his forehead. Abruptly, he tensed against his fetters, straining with stubborn futility to break the chains.

Memla had not left the mouth of the hall. "Ware, Half-hand!" she warned in a whisper. "There is malice here."

He felt the force of her warning. Brinn also was striving to warn him. For an instant, he hesitated. But the *Haruchai* had recognized him. Somehow, Brinn's people had preserved among them the tale of the Council and of the old wars against Corruption—the true tale, not a distorted version. And Covenant had met Bannor among his Dead in Andelain.

Gripping his self-control, he stepped into the circle, went to the catafalque. He rested a hand momentarily on Brinn's arm. Then he faced the na-Mhoram.

"Let him go."

The na-Mhoram did not reply directly. Instead, he turned toward Memla. "Memla na-Mhoram-in," he said, "you have no part in this soothtell. I desire you to depart."

"No." Her tone brandished outrage. "You have been false to him. He knows not what he chooses."

"Nevertheless," Gibbon began quietly, then lost his hebetude in a strident yell, "you will *depart*!"

For a moment, she refused. The air of the court was humid with conflicting intentions. Gibbon raised his crozier as if to strike at her. Finally, the combined repudiation of the circle was too strong for her. In deep bitterness, she said, "I gave promise to the Halfhand for the safety of his companions. It is greatly wrong that the na-Mhoram holds the word of a na-

Mhoram-in in such slight trust." Turning on her heel, she strode away down the hall.

Gibbon dismissed her as if she had ceased to exist. Facing Covenant once again, he said, "There is no power without blood." He seemed unable to suppress the acuity of his excitement. "And the soothtell requires power. Therefore this *Haruchai.* We will shed him to answer your questions."

"No!" Covenant snapped. "You've killed enough of them already."

"We must have blood," the na-Mhoram said.

"Then kill one of your bloody Riders!" Covenant was white with fury. "I don't give a good goddamn what you do! Just leave the *Haruchai* alone!"

"As you wish." Gibbon sounded triumphant.

"Ur-Lord!" Brinn shouted.

Covenant misread Brinn's warning. He sprang backward, away from the catafalque—into the hands of the Riders behind him. They grappled with him, caught his arms. Faster than he could defend himself, two knives flashed.

Blades slit both his wrists.

Two red lines slashed across his sight, across his soul. Blood spattered to the floor. The cuts were deep, deep enough to kill him slowly. Staring in horror, he sank to his knees. Pulsing rivulets marked his arms to the elbows. Blood dripped from his elbows, spreading his passion on the stone.

Around him, the Riders began to chant. Scarlet rose from their *rukhs*; the air became vermeil power.

He knelt helpless within the circle. The pain in his neck paralysed him. A spike of utter trepidation had been driven through his spine, nailing him where he crouched. The outcry of his blood fell silently.

Gibbon advanced, black and exalted. With the tip of his crozier, he touched the growing pool, began to draw meticulous red lines around Covenant.

Covenant watched like an icon of desolation as the na-Mhoram enclosed him in a triangle of his blood.

The chanting became words he could not prevent himself from understanding.

> "Power and blood, and blood and flame:
> Soothtell visions without name:
> Truth as deep as Revelstone,
> Making time and passion known.

"Time begone, and space avaunt—
Nothing may the seeing daunt.
Blood uncovers every lie:
We will know the truth, or die."

When Gibbon had completed the triangle, he stepped back
and raised his iron. Flame blossomed thetic and incarnadine
from its end.

And Covenant exploded into vision.

He lost none of his self-awareness. The fires around him
became more lurid and compelling; his arms felt as heavy as
millstones; the chant labored like the thudding of his heart.
But behind the walls he saw and the stone he knew, other
sights reeled, other knowledge gyred, tearing at his mind.

At first, the vision was chaos, impenetrable. Images ruptured past the catafalque, the Riders, burst in and out of view
so feverishly that he comprehended none of them. But when
in anguish he surrendered to them, let them sweep him into
the eye of their vertigo, some of them sprang toward clarity.

Like three blows of a fist, he saw Linden, Sunder, Hollian.
They were in the hold, in cells. Linden lay on her pallet in a
stupor as pale as death.

The next instant, those images were erased. With a wrench
that shook him to the marrow of his bones, the chaos gathered toward focus. The Staff of Law appeared before him. He
saw places: Revelstone besieged by the armies of the Despiser;
Foul's Creche crumbling into the Sea; Glimmermere opening
its waters to accept the *krill* of Loric. He saw faces: dead
Elena in ecstasy and horror; High Lord Mhoram wielding the
krill to slay a Raver's body; Foamfollower laughing happily in
the face of his own death. And behind it all he saw the Staff
of Law. Through everything, implied by everything, the Staff.
Destroyed by an involuntary deflagration of wild magic when
dead Elena was forced to use it against the Land.

Kneeling there like a suicide in a triangle of blood, pinned
to the stone by an iron pain, with his life oozing from his
wrists, Covenant saw.

The Staff of Law. Destroyed.

The root of everything he needed to know.

For the Staff of Law had been formed by Berek Halfhand
as a tool to serve and uphold the Law. He had fashioned the
Staff from a limb of the One Tree as a way to wield Earthpower in defense of the health of the Land, in support of the

natural order of life. And because Earthpower was the strength of mystery and spirit, the Staff became the thing it served. It was the Law; the Law was incarnate in the Staff. The tool and its purpose were one.

And the Staff had been destroyed.

That loss had weakened the very fiber of the Law. A crucial support was withdrawn, and the Law faltered.

From that seed grew both the Sunbane and the Clave.

They came into being together, gained mastery over the Land together, flourished together.

After the destruction of Foul's Creche, the Council of Lords had prospered in Revelstone for centuries. Led first by High Lord Mhoram, then by successors equally dedicated and idealistic, the Council had changed the thrust and tenor of its past service. Mhoram had learned that the Lore of the Seven Wards, the knowledge left behind by Kevin Landwaster, contained within it the capacity to be corrupted. Fearing a renewal of Desecration, he had turned his back on that Lore, thrown the *krill* into Glimmermere, and commenced a search for new ways to use and serve the Earthpower.

Guided by his decision, Councils for generations after him had used and served, performing wonders. Trothgard had been brought back to health. All the old forests—Grimmerdhore, Morinmoss, Garroting Deep, Giant Woods—had thrived to such an extent that Caerroil Wildwood, the Forestal of Garroting Deep, had believed his labor ended at last, and had passed away; and even the darkest trees had lost much of their enmity for the people of the Land. All the war-torn wastes along Landsdrop between Mount Thunder and the Colossus of the Fall had been restored to life. The perversity of Sarangrave Flat had been reduced; and much had been done to ease the ruin of the Spoiled Plains.

For a score of centuries, the Council served the Land's health in peace and fruitfulness. And at last the Lords began to believe that Lord Foul would never return, that Covenant had driven Despite utterly from the Earth. Paradise seemed to be within their grasp. Then in the confidence of peace, they looked back to High Lord Mhoram, and chose to change their names to mark the dawning of a new age. Their High Lord they christened the na-Mhoram; their Council they called the Clave. They saw no limit to the beauty they could achieve. They had no one to say to them that their accomplishments came far too easily.

For the Staff of Law had been destroyed. The Clave flourished in part because the old severity of the Law, the stringency which matched the price paid to the beauty of the thing purchased, had been weakened; and they did not know their peril.

Finding the Third Ward, they had looked no further for knowledge. Through the centuries, they had grown blind, and had lost the means to know that the man who had been named the na-Mhoram, who had transformed the Council in the Clave, was a Raver.

For when Covenant had defeated the Despiser, reduced him by wild magic and laughter to a poverty of spirit so complete that he could no longer remain corporeal, the Despiser had not died. Despite did not die. Fleeing the destruction of his Creche, he had hidden at the fringes of the one power potent enough to heal even him: the Earthpower itself.

And this was possible because the Staff had been destroyed. The Law which had limited him and resisted him since the creation of the Earth had been weakened; and he was able to endure it while he conceived new strength, new being. And while he endured, he also corrupted. As he gained stature, the Law sickened.

The first result of this decay was to make the work of the Council more easy; but every increment strengthened Lord Foul, and all his might went to increase the infection. Slowly, he warped the Law to his will.

His Ravers shared his recovery; and he did not act overtly against the Land until *samadhi* Sheol had contrived his way into the Council, had begun its perversion, until several generations of na-Mhorams, each cunningly mastered by *samadhi*, had brought the Clave under Lord Foul's sway.

Slowly, the Oath of Peace was abandoned; slowly, the ideals of the Clave were altered. Therefore when the Clave made a secret door to its new hold and Aumbrie, it made one such as the Ravers had known in Foul's Creche. Slowly, the legends of Lord Foul were transmogrified into the tales of a-Jeroth, both to explain the Sunbane and to conceal Lord Foul's hand in it.

Laboring always in secret, so that the Clave at all times had many uncorrupted members—people like Memla, who believed the Raver's lies, and were therefore sincere in their service—*samadhi* Sheol fashioned a tool for the Despiser, ill enough to preach the shedding of blood, pure enough to be persuasive. Only then did Lord Foul let his work be seen.

For the Staff of Law had been destroyed, and his hands were on the reins of nature. By degrees, mounting gradually over centuries, he inflicted his abhorrence upon the Land, corrupting the Earthpower with Sunbane. This he was able to do because the Clave had been made incapable of conceiving any true defense. The Banefire was not a defense, had never been a defense. Rather, it was *samadhi*'s means to commit further afflictions. The shedding of blood to invoke the Sunbane only made the Sunbane stronger. Thus Lord Foul caused the increase of the Sunbane without cost to himself.

And all this, Covenant saw as his blood-deepened around his knees, had been done in preparation for one thing, the capstone and masterstroke of Lord Foul's mendacity: the summoning of white gold to the Land. Lord Foul desired possession of the wild magic; and he did to the Land what he had done to Joan, so that Covenant would have no final choice except surrender.

The loss of the Staff explained why Covenant's summoning had been so elaborate. In the past, such summons had always been an act of Law, performed by the holder of the Staff. Only when he had been close to death from starvation and rattlesnake venom, and the Law of Death had been broken, had summoning been possible without the Staff. Therefore this time the Despiser had been forced to go to great lengths to take hold of Covenant. A specific location had been required, specific pain, a triangle of blood, freedom of choice and death. Had any of these conditions failed, the summoning would have failed, and Lord Foul would have been left to harm the Land, the Earth, without hope of achieving his final goal—the destruction of the Arch of Time. Only by destroying the Arch could he escape the prison of Time. Only with wild magic could he gain freedom and power to wage his hatred of the Creator across the absolute heavens of the cosmos.

But the summoning had not failed, and Covenant was dying. He understood now why Gibbon had driven Memla from the court. If she had shared this vision of the truth, her outrage might have led her to instigate a revolt among the uncorrupted Riders; for Gibbon, too, was a Raver.

He understood what had happened to the Colossus of the Fall. It had been an avatar of the ancient forests, erected on

Landsdrop to defend against Ravers; and the Sunbane had destroyed the forests, unbinding the will of wood which had upheld for millennia that stone monolith.

He understood how Caer-Caveral had been driven to Andelain by the erosion of Morinmoss—and why the last of the Forestals was doomed to fail. At its root, the power of the Forestal was an expression of Law, just as Andelain was the quintessence of Law; and the Sunbane was a corruption Caer-Caveral could resist but not defeat.

He understood what had become of the Ranyhyn, the great horses, and of the Ramen who served them. Perceiving the ill of the Sunbane in its earliest appearances, both Ranyhyn and Ramen had simply fled the Land, sojourning south along the marge of the Sunbirth Sea in search of safer grasslands.

These things came to him in glimpses, flares of vision across the central fact of his situation. But there were also things he could not see: a dark space where Caer-Caveral had touched his mind; a blur that might have explained Vain's purpose; a blankness which concealed the reason why Linden was chosen. Loss gripped him: the ruin of the Land he loved; all the fathomless ill of the Sunbane and the Clave was his fault, his doing.

He had no answer for the logic of his guilt. The Staff of Law had been destroyed—and he had destroyed it. Wild magic had burst from his ring to save his life; power beyond all choice or mastery had riven the Staff, so that nothing remained but its heels. For such an act, he deserved to die. The lassitude of blood-loss seemed condign and admirable. His pulse shrank toward failure. He was culpable beyond any redemption and had no heart to go on living.

But a voice spoke in his mind:

Ur-Lord.

It was a voice without sound, a reaching of thought to thought. It came from Brinn. He had never before heard the mind-speech of the *Haruchai*; but he recognized the speaker in the intensity of Brinn's gaze. The power of the soothtell made possible things which could not otherwise have occurred.

Unbeliever. Thomas Covenant.

Unbeliever, he answered to himself. Yes. It's my fault. My responsibility.

You must fight.

The images before him whirled toward chaos again.

Responsible. Yes. On my head. He could not fight. How could any man hope to resist the Desecration of a world?

But guilt was the voice of the Clave, the Riders and the Raver who had committed such atrocities. Brinn strained against his bonds as if he would rupture his thews rather than accept failure. Linden still lay in the hold, unconscious or dead. And the Land— Oh, the Land! That it should die undefended!

Fight!

Somewhere deep within him, he found the strength for curses. Are you nothing but a leper? Even lepers don't have to surrender.

Visions reeled through the air. The scarlet light faded as Gibbon brought the soothtell to an end.

Stop! He still needed answers: how to fight the Sunbane; how to restore the Law; to understand the venom in him; to cure it. He groped frantically among the images, fought to bring what he needed into clarity.

But he could not. He could see nothing now but the gaping cuts in his wrists, the ooze of his blood growing dangerously slower. The Riders took the soothtell away from him before he gained the most crucial knowledge. They were reducing their power— No, they were not reducing it, they were changing it, translating it into something else.

Into coercion.

He could feel them now, a score of wills impending on the back of his neck, commanding him to abandon resistance, take off his ring and surrender it before he died. Telic red burned at him from all sides; every *rukh* was aflame with compulsion. Release the ring. Set it aside. Before you die. This, he knew, was not part of Lord Foul's intent. It was Gibbon's greed; *samadhi* Sheol wanted the white gold for himself.

The ring!

Brinn's mind-voice was barely audible:

Unbeliever! They will slay us all!

All, he thought desperately. Threescore and seven of the *Haruchai*. Vain, if they could. Sunder. Hollian. Linden.

The Land.

Release the *ring!*

No.

His denial was quiet and small, like the first ripple presaging a tsunami.

I will not permit this.

Extravagant fury and need gathered somewhere beyond the shores of his consciousness, piled upward like a mighty sea.

His mind was free now of everything except helplessness and determination. He knew he could not call up wild magic to save him. He required a trigger; but the Riders kept their power at his back, out of reach. At the same time, his need was absolute. Slashing his wrists was a slow way to kill him, but it would succeed unless he could stop the bleeding, defend himself.

He did not intend to die. Brinn had brought him back to himself. He was more than a leper. No abjections could force him to abide his doom. No. There were other answers to guilt. If he could not find them, he would create them out of the raw stuff of his being.

He was going to fight.

Now.

The tsunami broke. Wrath erupted in him like the madness of venom.

Fire and rage consumed all his pain. The triangle and the will of the Clave splintered and fell away.

A wind of passion blew through him. Wild argent exploded from his ring.

White blazed over his right fist. Acute incandescence covered his hand as if his flesh were power. Conflagration tore the red air.

Fear assailed the Clave. Riders cried out in confusion. Gibbon shouted commands.

For a moment, Covenant remained where he was. His ring flamed like one white torch among the vermeil *rukhs*. Deliberately, he drew power to his right wrist; shaping the fire with his will, he stopped the flow of blood, closed the knife wound. A flash of ire seared and sealed the cut. Then he turned the magic to his left wrist.

His concentration allowed Gibbon time to marshal a defense. Covenant could feel the Riders surging around him, mustering the Banefire to their *rukhs*. But he did not care. The venom in him counted no opposition, no cost. When his wrists were healed, he rose direly to his feet and stood erect like a man who had lost no blood and could not be touched.

His force staggered the atmosphere of the court. It blasted from his entire body as if his very bones were avid for fire.

Gibbon stood before him. The Raver wielded a crozier so fraught with heat and might that the iron screamed. A shaft of red malice howled at Covenant's heart.

Covenant quenched it with a shrug.

One of the Riders hurled a coruscating *rukh* at his back.

Wild magic evaporated the metal in mid-flight.

Then Covenant's wrath became ecstasy, savage beyond all restraint. In an instant of fury which shocked the very gut-rock of Revelstone, his wild magic detonated.

Riders screamed, fell. Doors in the coigns above the floor burst from their hinges. The air sizzled like frying flesh.

Gibbon shouted orders Covenant could not hear, threw an arc of emerald across the court, then disappeared.

Under a moil of force, the floor began to shine like silver magma.

Somewhere amid the wreckage of the soothtell, he heard Lord Foul laughing.

The sound only strung his passion tighter.

When he looked about him, bodies lay everywhere. Only one Rider was left standing. The man's hood had been blown back, revealing contorted features and frantic eyes.

Intuitively, Covenant guessed that this was Santonin.

In his hands, he grasped a flake of stone which steamed like green ice, held it so that it pressed against his *rukh*. Pure emerald virulence raged outward.

The Illearth Stone.

Covenant had no limits, no control. A rave of force hurled Santonin against the far wall, scorched his raiment to ashes, blackened his bones.

The Stone rolled free, lay pulsing like a diseased heart on the bright floor.

Reaching out with flames, Covenant drew the Stone to himself. He clenched it in his half-hand. Foamfollower had died so that the Illearth Stone could be destroyed.

Destroyed!

A silent blast stunned the cavity—a green shriek devoured by argent. The Stone-flake vanished in steam and fury.

With a tremendous splitting noise, the floor cracked from wall to wall.

"Unbeliever!"

He could barely hear Brinn.

"Ur-Lord!"

He turned and peered through fire at the *Haruchai*.

"The prisoners!" Brinn barked. "The Clave holds your friends! Lives will be shed to strengthen the Banefire!"

The shout penetrated Covenant's mad rapture. He nodded. With a flick of his mind, he shattered Brinn's chains.

At once, Brinn sprang from the catafalque and dashed out of the cavity.

Covenant followed in flame.

At the end of the hall, the *Haruchai* launched himself against three Riders. Their *rukhs* burned. Covenant lashed argent at them, sent them sprawling, reduced their *rukhs* to scoria.

He and Brinn hastened away through the passages of Revelstone.

Brinn led; he knew how to find the hidden door to the hold. Shortly, he and Covenant reached the Raver-made entrance. Covenant summoned fire to break down the door; but before he could strike, Brinn slapped the proper spot in the invisible architrave. Limned in red tracery, the portal opened.

Five Riders waited within the tunnel. They were prepared to fight; but Brinn charged them with such abandon that their first blasts missed. In an instant, he had felled two of them. Covenant swept the other three aside, and followed Brinn, running toward the hold.

The dungeon had no other defenders; the Clave had not had time to organize more Riders. And if Gibbon were still alive, he might conceivably withdraw his forces rather than risk losses which would cripple the Clave. When Brinn and Covenant rushed into the hold and found it empty, Brinn immediately leaped to the nearest door and began to throw back the bolts.

But Covenant was rife with might, wild magic which demanded utterance. Thrusting Brinn aside, he unleashed an explosion that made the very granite of Revelstone stagger. With a shrill scream of metal, all the cell doors sprang from their moorings and clanged to the floor, ringing insanely.

At once, scores of *Haruchai* emerged, ready to fight. Ten of them raced to defend the entrance to the tunnel; the rest scattered toward other cells, searching for more prisoners.

Eight or nine people of the Land—Stonedownors and Woodhelvennin—appeared as if they were dazzled by the miracle of their reprieve.

Vain left his cell slowly. When he saw Covenant, saw Covenant's passionate fire, his face stretched into a black grin, the grin of a man who recognized what Covenant was doing. The grin of a fiend.

Two *Haruchai* supported Sunder. The Graveler had a raw weal around his neck, as if he had been rescued from a gibbet, and he looked weak. He gaped at Covenant.

Hollian came, wan and frightened, from her cell. Her eyes flinched from Covenant as if she feared to know him. When she saw Sunder, she hastened to him and wrapped herself in his arms.

Covenant remained still, aching for Linden. Vain grinned like the sound of Lord Foul's laughter.

Then Brinn and another *Haruchai* bore Linden out into the hall. She lay limp in their arms, dead or unconscious, in sopor more compulsory than any sleep.

When Covenant saw her, he let out a howl which tore chunks from the ceiling and pulverized them until the air was full of fine powder.

He could not stop himself until Brinn yelled to him that she was alive.

PART III

Purpose

TWENTY: The Quest

HE left the hold, left his companions, because he could not bear to watch the impenetrable nightmares writhe across Linden's mien. She was not afraid of his leprosy. She had supported him at every crisis. This was the result. No one could rouse her. She lay in a stupor like catatonia, and dreamed anguish.

He went toward the upland plateau because he needed to recover some kind of hope.

Already, the frenzy of his power had begun to recoil against him. Vain's smile haunted him like an echo of horror and scorn. His rescue from Stonemight Woodhelven was no different than this. How many people had he killed? He had no control over his power. Power and venom controlled him.

Yet he did not release the wild magic. Revelstone was still full of Riders. He glimpsed them running past the ends of long halls, preparing themselves for defense or counterattack. He did not have enough blood in his veins to sustain himself without the fire of his ring: once he dropped his power, he would be beyond any self-protection. He would have to trust the *Haruchai* to save him, save his friends. And that thought also was bitter to him. Bannor's people had paid such severe prices in his name. How could he permit them to serve him again?

How many people had he killed?

Shedding flames like tears, he climbed up through the levels of Revelstone toward the plateau.

And Brinn strode at his side as if the *Haruchai* had already committed himself to this service. Somewhere he had found a

343

cloak which he now draped across Covenant's shoulders. The Unbeliever shrugged it into place, hardly noticing. It helped to protect him against the shock of blood-loss.

Covenant needed hope. He had gained much from the soothtell; but those insights paled beside the shock of Linden's straits, paled beside the mounting self-abomination of what he had done with his power. He had not known he was so capable of slaughter. He could not face the demands of his new knowledge without some kind of hope.

He did not know where else to turn except to Glimmermere. To the Earthpower which remained still vital enough to provide Glimmermere with water, even when all the Land lay under a desert sun. To the blade which lay in the deeps of the lake.

Loric's *krill*.

He did not want it because it was a weapon. He wanted it because it was an alternative, a tool of power which might prove manageable enough to spare him any further reliance upon his ring.

And he wanted it because Vain's grin continued to knell through his head. In that grin, he had seen Vain's makers, the roynish and cruel beings he remembered. They had lied to Foamfollower. Vain's purpose was not greatly to be desired. It was the purpose of a fiend. Covenant had seen Vain kill, seen himself kill, and knew the truth.

And Loric, who was Kevin's father, had been called Vilesilencer. He had formed the *krill* to stem the harm of Vain's ancestors. Perhaps the *krill* would provide an answer to Vain.

That, too, was a form of hope. Covenant needed hope. When he reached the open plateau, the brightness of his power made the night seem as black and dire as Vain's obsidian flesh.

No one had been able to rouse Linden. She was caught in the toils of a heinous nightmare, and could not fight free. What evil had been practiced upon her?

And how many people had he killed? He, who had sworn never to kill again, and had not kept that oath. How many?

His own fire blinded him; he could not see any stars. The heavens gaped over him like a leper's doom. How could any man who lacked simple human sensitivity hope to control wild magic? *The wild magic which destroys peace*. He felt numb, and full of venom, and could not help himself.

Wrapped in argent like a new incarnation of the Sunbane, he traversed the hills toward Glimmermere. The tarn was hidden by the terrain; but he knew his way.

Brinn walked beside him, and did not speak. The *Haruchai* seemed content to support whatever Covenant intended. In this same way, the Bloodguard had been content to serve the Lords. Their acceptance had cost them two thousand years without love or sleep or death. And it had cost them corruption; like Foamfollower, Bannor had been forced to watch his people become the thing they hated. Covenant did not know how to accept Brinn's tacit offer. How could he risk repeating the fate of the Bloodguard? But he was in need, and did not know how to refuse.

Then he saw it: Glimmermere lying nestled among the hills. Its immaculate surface reflected his silver against the black night, so that the water looked like a swath of wild magic surrounded, about to be smothered, by the dark vitriol of ur-viles. Avid white which only made Vain grin. But Covenant's power was failing; he had lost too much blood; the reaction to what he had done was too strong. He lumbered stiff-kneed down to the water's edge, stood trembling at the rim of Glimmermere, and fought himself to remain alight just a little longer.

Fire and darkness sprang back at him from the water. He had bathed once in Glimmermere; but now he felt too tainted to touch this vestige of Earthpower. And he did not know the depth of the pool. High Lord Mhoram had thrown the *krill* here as an act of faith in the Land's future. Surely he had believed the blade to be beyond reach. Covenant would never be able to swim that far down. And he could not ask Brinn to do it. He felt dismayed by the implications of Brinn's companionship; he could not force himself to utter an active acceptance of Brinn's service. The *krill* seemed as distant as if it had never existed.

Perhaps none of this had ever existed. Perhaps he was merely demented, and Vain's grin was the leer of his insanity. Perhaps he was already dead with a knife in his chest, experiencing the hell his leprosy had created for him.

But when he peered past the flaming silver and midnight, he saw a faint echo from the depths. The *krill*. It replied to his power as it had replied when he had first awakened it. Its former arousal had led ineluctably to Elena's end and the breaking of the Law of Death. For a moment, he feared it, feared the keenness of its edges and the weight of culpability it implied. He had loved Elena— But the wild magic was worse. The venom was worse. He could not control them.

"How many—?" His voice tore the silence clenched in his throat. "How many of them did I kill?"

Brinn responded dispassionately out of the night, "One score and one, ur-Lord."

Twenty-one? Oh, God!

For an instant, he thought that the sinews of his soul would rend, must rend, that his joints would be ripped asunder. But then a great shout of power blasted through his chest, and white flame erupted toward the heavens.

Glimmermere repeated the concussion. Suddenly, the whole surface of the lake burst into fire. Flame mounted in a gyre; the water of the lake whirled. And from the center of the whirl came a clear white beam in answer to his call.

The *krill* rose into view. It shone, bright and inviolate, in the heart of the lake—a long double-edged dagger with a translucent gem forged into the cross of its guards and haft. The light came from its gem, reiterating Covenant's fire, as if the jewel and his ring were brothers. The night was cast back by its radiance, and by his power, and by the high flames of Glimmermere.

Still the *krill* was beyond reach. But he did not hesitate now. The whirl of the water and the gyring flames spoke to him of things which he understood: vertigo and paradox; the eye of stability in the core of the contradiction. Opening his arms to the fire, he stepped out into the lake.

Earthpower unheld him. Conflagration which replied to his conflagration spun around him and through him, and bore his weight. Floating like a flicker of shadow through the argence, he walked toward the center of Glimmermere.

In his weakness, he felt that the fire would rush him out of himself, reduce him to motes of mortality and hurl him at the empty sky. The *krill* seemed more substantial than his flesh; the iron more full of meaning than his wan bones. But when he stooped to it and took hold of it, it lifted in his hands and arced upward, leaving a slash of brilliance across the night.

He clutched it to his chest and turned back toward Brinn.

Now his fatigue closed over him. No longer could he keep his power alight. The fingers of his will unclawed their grip and failed. At once, the flames of Glimmermere began to subside.

But still the lake upheld him. The Earthpower gave him this gift as it had once gifted Berek Halfhand's despair on the slopes of Mount Thunder. It sustained him, and did not let him go until he stumbled to the shore in darkness.

Night lay about him and in him. His eyes descried nothing but the dark as if they had been burned out of his head. Even the shining of the gem seemed to shed no illumination. Shorn now of power, he could no longer grasp the *krill*. It became hot in his hands, hot enough to touch the nerves which still lived. He dropped it to the ground, where it shone like the last piece of light in the world. Mutely, he knelt beside it, with his back to Glimmermere as if he had been humbled. He felt alone in the Land, and incapable of himself.

But he was not alone. Brinn tore a strip from his tunic—a garment made from an ochre material which resembled vellum—and wrapped the *krill* so that it could be handled. For a moment, he placed a gentle touch on Covenant's shoulder. Then he said quietly, "Ur-Lord, come. The Clave will attempt to strike against us. We must go."

As the gleam of the *krill* was silenced, the darkness became complete. It was a balm to Covenant, solace for the aggrievement of power. He ached for it to go on assuaging him forever. But he knew Brinn spoke the truth. Yes, he breathed. We must go. Help me.

When he raised his head, he could see the stars. They glittered as if only their own beauty could console them for their loneliness. The moon was rising. It was nearly full.

In silence and moonlight, Covenant climbed to his feet and began to carry his exhaustion back toward Revelstone.

After a few steps, he accepted the burden of the *krill* from Brinn and tucked it under his belt. Its warmth rested there like a comfort against the knotted self-loathing in his stomach.

Stumbling and weary, he moved without knowing how he could ever walk as far as Revelstone. But Brinn aided him, supported him when he needed help, let him carry himself when he could. After a time that passed, like the sequences of delirium, they gained the promontory and the mouth of the na-Mhoram's Keep.

One of the *Haruchai* awaited them outside the tunnel which led down into Revelstone. As Covenant lurched to a halt, the *Haruchai* bowed; and Brinn said, "Ur-Lord, this is Ceer."

"Ur-Lord," Ceer said.

Covenant blinked at him, but could not respond. He seemed to have no words left.

Expressionlessly, Ceer extended a leather pouch toward him.

He accepted it. When he unstopped the pouch, he recognized the smell of *metheglin*. At once, he began to drink. His drained body was desperate for fluid. Desperate. He did not lower the pouch until it was empty.

"Ur-Lord," Ceer said then, "the Clave gathers about the Banefire. We harry them, and they make no forays—but there is great power in their hands. And four more of the *Haruchai* have been slain. We have guided all prisoners from Revelstone. We watch over them as we can. Yet they are not safe. The Clave holds coercion to sway our minds, if they but choose to exert it. We know this to our cost. We must flee."

Yes, Covenant mumbled inwardly. Flee. I know. But when he spoke, the only word he could find was, "Linden—?"

Without inflection, Ceer replied, "She has awakened."

Covenant did not realize that he had fallen until he found himself suspended in Brinn's arms. For a long moment, he could not force his legs to straighten. But the *metheglin* helped him. Slowly, he took his own weight, stood upright again.

"How—?"

"Ur-Lord, we strove to wake her." Suppressing the lilt of his native tongue to speak Covenant's language made Ceer sound completely detached. "But she lay as the dead, and would not be succored. We bore her from the Keep, knowing not what else to do. Yet your black companion—" He paused, asking for a name.

"Vain," Covenant said, almost choking on the memory of that grin. "He's an ur-vile."

A slight contraction of his eyebrows expressed Ceer's surprise; but he did not utter his thoughts aloud. "Vain," he resumed, "stood by unheeding for a time. But then of a sudden he approached Linden Avery the Chosen." Dimly, Covenant reflected that the *Haruchai* must already have spoken to Sunder or Hollian. "Knowing nothing of him, we strove to prevent him. But he cast us aside as if we were not who we are. He knelt to the Chosen, placed his hand upon her. She awakened."

A groan of incomprehension and dread twisted Covenant's throat; but Ceer went on. "Awakening, she cried out and sought to flee. She did not know us. But the Stonedownors your companions comforted her. And still"— a slight pause betrayed Ceer's uncertainty —"Vain had not done. Ur-Lord, he bowed before her—he, who is heedless of the *Haruchai*, and deaf to all speech. He placed his forehead upon her feet.

"This was fear to her," Ceer continued. "She recoiled to the arms of the Stonedownors. They also do not know this Vain. But they stood to defend her if need be. He rose to his feet, and there he stands yet, still unheeding, as a man caught in the coercion of the Clave. He appears no longer conscious of the Chosen, or of any man or woman."

Ceer did not need to speak his thought; Covenant could read it in his flat eyes.

We do not trust this Vain.

But Covenant set aside the question of Vain. The *krill* was warm against his belly; and he had no strength for distractions. His path was clear before him, had been clear ever since he had absorbed the meaning of the soothtell. And Linden was awake. She had been restored to him. Surely now he could hold himself together long enough to set his purpose in motion.

Yet he took the time for one more inquiry. "How is she?"

Ceer shrugged fractionally. "She has gazed upon the face of Corruption. Yet she speaks clearly to the Stonedownors." He paused, then said, "She is your companion. You have redeemed us from abomination. While we live, she and all your companions will suffer no further hurt." He looked toward Brinn. "But she has warned us of a Raver. Ur-Lord, surely we must flee."

A Raver, thought Covenant. Gibbon. Yes.

What did he do to her? The nightmare on her face was still vivid to him. What did that bastard do to her?

Without a word, he locked himself erect, and started stiffly down the tunnel into Revelstone.

The way was long; but *metheglin* and darkness sustained him. Vain's grin sustained him. The Demondim-spawn had awakened her? Had knelt to her? The ur-viles must have lied to Foamfollower. Hamako's *rhysh* must have been mistaken or misled. Did Vain bow in acknowledgment of Gibbon's effect on her?

What did that bastard do to her?

If Covenant had doubted his purpose before, or had doubted himself, he was sure now. No Clave or distance or impossibility was going to stand in his way.

Down through the city he went, like a tight curse. Down past *Haruchai* who scouted the city and watched the Riders. Down to the gates, and the passage under the watchtower. He had already killed twenty-one people; he felt that for himself he had nothing left to fear. His fear was for his companions; and his curse was for the Despiser. His purpose was clear.

As he moved through the tunnel, a score of *Haruchai* gathered around him like an honor-guard. They bore supplies which they had scoured from Revelstone for the flight of the prisoners.

With them, he passed the broken outer gates into the night.

Below him on the rocky slope of the foothill burned a large bonfire. Stark against the massed jungle beyond it, it flamed with a loud crepitation, fighting the rain-drenched green wood which the *Haruchai* fed to it. Its yellow light enclosed all the prisoners, defending them from darkness.

He could see a group of Stonedownors and Woodhelvennin huddling uncertainly near the fire. *Haruchai* moved around the area, preparing supplies, wresting more firewood from the jungle, standing watch. Vain stood motionless among them. Sunder, Hollian, and Linden sat close together as if to comfort each other.

He had eyes only for Linden. Her back was to him. He hardly noticed that all Brinn's people had turned toward him and dropped to one knee, as if he had been announced by silent trumpets. With the dark citadel rising behind him, he went woodenly toward Linden's back as if he meant to fall at her feet.

Sunder saw him, spoke quickly to Linden and Hollian. The Stonedownors jumped upright and faced Covenant as if he came bearing life and death. More slowly, Linden, too, climbed erect. He could read nothing but pain in the smudged outlines of her mien. But her eyes recognized him. A quiver like urgency ran through her. He could not stop himself. He surged to her, wrapped his arms around her, hid his face in her hair.

Around him, the *Haruchai* went back to their tasks.

For a moment, she returned his embrace as if she were grateful for it. Then, suddenly, she stiffened. Her slim, abused body became nausea in his arms. He tried to speak, but could not, could not sever the knots in his chest. When she tried to pull away from him, he let her go; and still he could not speak.

She did not meet his stare. Her gaze wandered his frame to the old cut in the center of his shirt. "You're sick."

Sick? Momentarily, he failed to understand her. "Linden—?"

"Sick." Her voice trailed like blood between her lips. "Sick." Moving as if she were stunned by abhorrence or grief, she turned her back on him. She sank to the ground, covered her face with her hands, began to rock back and forth. Faintly, he heard her murmuring, "Sick. Sick."

His leprosy.

The sight almost tore away his last strength. If he could have found his voice, he would have wailed, What did that bastard do to you? But he had come too far and had too many responsibilities. The pressure of the *krill* upheld him. Clenching himself as if he, too, could not be touched, he looked at Sunder and Hollian.

They seemed abashed by Linden's reaction. "Ur-Lord," Sunder began tentatively, then faltered into silence. The weal around his neck appeared painful; but he ignored it. Old frown-marks bifurcated his forehead as if he were caught between rage and fear, comradeship and awe, and wanted Covenant to clarify them for him. His jaws chewed words he did not know how to utter.

"Ur-Lord," Hollian said for him, "she has been sorely hurt in some way. I know not how, for Gibbon na-Mhoram said to her, 'You I must not harm.' Yet an anguish torments her." Her pale features asked Covenant to forgive Linden.

Dumbly, he wondered where the eh-Brand found her courage. She was hardly more than a girl, and her perils often seemed to terrify her. Yet she had resources— She was a paradox of fright and valor; and she spoke when Sunder could not.

"You have bought back our lives from the na-Mhoram," she went on, "at what cost to yourself I cannot know. I know not how to behold such power as you wield. But I have tasted the coercion of the Riders, and the emprisonment of the Clave. I thank you from my heart. I pray I may be given opportunity to serve you."

Serve—? Covenant groaned. How can I let you serve me?

You don't know what I'm going to do. Yet he could not refuse her. Somewhere in his own inchoate struggle of need and conviction, he had already accepted the service of the *Haruchai*, though their claim on his forbearance was almost forty centuries older than hers. Gripping himself rigid because he knew that if he bent he would break, he asked the only question he could articulate in the poverty of his courage. "Are you all right?"

She glanced at Sunder, at his neck. When he nodded, she replied, "It is nothing. A little hunger and fear. We are acquainted with such things. And," she continued more strongly, "we have been blessed with more than our lives. The *Haruchai* are capable of wonders." With a gesture, she indicated three of Brinn's people who stood nearby. "Ur-Lord, here are Cail, Stell, and Harn." The three sketched bows toward Covenant.

"When we were guided from the hold, I was content with my life. But the *Haruchai* were not content." Reaching into her robe, she brought out her dirk and *lianar*. "They sought throughout Revelstone and recovered these for me. Likewise they recovered Sunder's Sunstone and blade." Sunder agreed. Covenant wondered vaguely at the new intimacy which allowed Hollian to speak for Sunder. How much had they been through together? "How does it come to pass," Hollian concluded, "that the Land has so forgotten the *Haruchai*?"

"You know nothing of us," the one named Harn responded. "We know nothing of you. We would not have known to seek your belongings, had not Memla na-Mhoram-in revealed that they had been taken from you."

Memla, Covenant thought. Yes. Another piece of his purpose became momentarily lucid. "Brinn." The night seemed to be gathering around him. Sunder and Hollian had drifted out of focus. "Find her. Tell her what we need."

"Her?" Brinn asked distantly. "What is it that we need?"

Until he understood the question, Covenant did not perceive that he was losing consciousness. He had lost too much blood. The darkness on all sides was creeping toward vertigo. Though he yearned to let himself collapse, he lashed out with curses until he had brought his head up again, reopened his eyes.

"Memla," he said thickly. "Tell her we need Coursers."

"Yes, ur-Lord." Brinn did not move. But two or three

Haruchai left the fire and loped easily up toward the watch-tower.

Someone placed a bowl of *metheglin* in Covenant's hands. He drank it, tried to squeeze a semblance of clarity into his vision, and found himself staring at Vain.

The Demondim-spawn stood with his arms slightly bent, as if he were ready to commit acts which could not be foreseen. His black eyes stared at nothing; the ghoul grin was gone from his black lips. But he still wore the heels of the Staff of Law, one on his right wrist, the other on his left ankle. The burns he had received two nights ago were almost healed.

As a man caught in the coercion— Was that it? Was the Clave responsible for Vain? Ur-viles serving the Clave? How far did the na-Mhoram's mendacity extend? Vain's blackness echoed the night. How had he roused Linden? And *why?* Covenant wanted to rage at the Demondim-spawn. But he himself had killed—without control or even reluctance. He lacked the rectitude to unravel Vain's intent. There was too much blood on his head.

And not enough in his veins. He was failing. The illumination cast by the bonfire seemed to shrink around him. He had so little time left—

Listen, he started to say. This is what we're going to do. But his voice made no sound.

His hand groped for Brinn's shoulder. Help me. I've got to hold on. A little longer.

"Covenant."

Linden's voice tugged him back into focus. She stood before him. Somehow, she had pulled herself out of her inner rout. Her eyes searched him. "I thought I saw—" She regarded the wild tangle of his beard as if it had prevented her from identifying him earlier. Then her gaze found the thick red scars on his wrists. A sharp gasp winced through her teeth.

At once, she grabbed his forearms, drew his wrists into the light. "I was right. You've lost blood. A lot of it." Her physician's training rose up in her. She studied him, gauging his condition with her eyes and hands. "You need a transfusion."

The next moment, she perceived the newness of the scars. Her gaze jumped to his face. "What did they do to you?"

At first, he could not respond. The soothtell was too exigent; he felt unable to bear the answer she needed.

But she misunderstood his silence. Abomination stretched her visage. "Did you——?"

Her apprehension broke him out of his paralysis. "No. Not that. They did it to me. I'll be all right."

A sag of relief softened her expression. But her eyes did not leave his face. She struggled for words as if the conflict of her emotions blocked her throat. Finally, she said hoarsely, "I heard you shout. We almost got free." Her stare drifted out of focus, turned inward. "For a while, I would have given my soul to hear you shout again." But memories made her flee outward again. "Tell me——" she began, fighting for severity as if it were essential to her. "Tell me what happened to you."

He shook his head. "I'm all right." What else could he say? "Gibbon wanted blood. I didn't have a chance to refuse." He knew that he should explain, that all his companions needed to know what he had learned in the soothtell. But he had no strength.

As if to spare Covenant the necessity of speech, Brinn said flatly, "The ur-Lord's life was forfeit in the soothtell. Yet with wild magic he healed himself."

At that, Linden's orbs darkened. Her lips echoed soundlessly, Healed? Her gaze dropped to the old scar behind the cut in his shirt. The recovery of determination which had drawn her out of herself seemed to crumple. Losses which he could not begin to understand overflowed from her eyes. She turned away from him, turned her face toward the night. "Then you don't need me."

Hollian reached out to her. Like a child, Linden put her arms around Hollian's neck and buried her face in the eh-Brand's shoulder.

Covenant did not react. The pressure of his rage and grief was all that stood between him and darkness. He could not move without falling. *What did that bastard do to you?*

"Ur-Lord," Brinn said, "we must not delay. The na-Mhoram was not slain. Surely the Clave will soon strike against us."

"I know." Covenant's heart was crying uselessly, Linden! and hot streaks of self-reproach ran from his eyes; but his voice was adamantine. "We'll go. As soon as Memla gets here." He did not doubt that Memla would come. She had no choice; she had already betrayed the Clave for him. Too many people had already done too much for him.

"That is well," Brinn replied. "Where will we go?"

Covenant did not falter. He was sure of what he had to do. His Dead had prepared him for this. "To find the One Tree. I'm going to make a new Staff of Law."

His auditors fell abruptly silent. Incomprehension clouded Hollian's face. Sunder frowned as if he wanted to speak but could not find the right words. The knot of Stonedownors and Woodhelvennin held themselves still. Vain betrayed no flicker of interest. But the eyes of the *Haruchai* shone.

"The old tellers," Brinn said slowly, "relate that the Lords, even at the time of Kevin, had a legend of the One Tree, from which the Staff of Law was made. Ur-Lord Covenant, you conceive a bold undertaking. You will be accompanied. But how will you seek the One Tree? We have no knowledge of it."

No knowledge, Covenant breathed wanly. He had guessed as much. South of the Land lay the lifeless Gray Desert. In the north, the long winter of the Northron Climbs was said to be impassable. And to the west, where the *Haruchai* lived, there was no knowledge of the One Tree. He accepted that. If Berek had gone west to find the One Tree, he would surely have encountered Brinn's people. With an effort, Covenant answered, "Neither do I. But we'll go east. To the Sea." Where the Giants had come from. "To get away from the Clave. After that— I don't know."

Brinn nodded. "It is good. This the *Haruchai* will do. Cail, Stell, Ceer, Harn, Hergrom, and myself will share your quest, to ward you and your companions. Two score will return to our people, to give them the knowledge we have gained." His voice sharpened slightly. "And to consider our reply to the depredations of this Clave. Those who remain will see these Stonedownors and Woodhelvennin to their homes—if such aid is desired."

The faces of the nine freed people of the Land expressed immediately their eagerness to accept Brinn's offer.

"The old tellers speak much of the Giants—of their fidelity and laughter, and of their dying," Brinn concluded. "Gladly will we look upon their home and upon the Sea which they loved."

Now, Covenant said to himself. If ever he intended to refuse the *Haruchai*, escape his being dependent on and responsible for them again after four thousand years, now was the time. But he could not. He was no longer able to stand without Brinn's support. Isn't it bad enough, he groaned, that I'm the one who destroyed the Staff? Opened the door for the Sunbane? Do I have to carry this, too? But he needed the *Haruchai* and could not refuse.

For a moment, the night reeled; but then he felt hands touch his chest, and saw Sunder standing before him. The Graveler held his chin up, exposing his damaged neck as if with that injury he had earned answers. His eyes reflected the firelight like the echoing of his torn mind.

"Covenant," he said in a clenched tone, using that name instead of the title ur-Lord, as if he sought to cut through awe and power and command to the man behind them. "I have journeyed far in your name, and will journey farther. But there is fear in me. The eh-Brand foretells a sun of pestilence —after but two days of rain. In freeing us, you have damaged the Clave. And now the Sunbane quickens. Perhaps you have done such harm that the Clave can no longer moderate the Sunbane. Perhaps you have wrought a great peril for the Land."

Covenant heard the personal urgency of Sunder's question; but for a time he lacked the fortitude to reply. Sunder's doubt pained him, weakened him. His veins were empty of life, and his muscles could no longer support him. Even the warmth of the *krill* under his belt had faded into his general inurement. But Sunder was his friend. The Graveler had already sacrificed too much for him. Fumbling among his frailties, he gave the first answer he found.

"The na-Mhoram is a Raver. Like Marid."

But that did not satisfy Sunder. "So Linden Avery has said. Yet the Clave moderated the Sunbane for the sake of the Land, and now that moderation has been weakened."

"No." Somewhere within him, Covenant discovered a moment of strength. "The Clave doesn't moderate the Sunbane. They've been using it to hurt the Land. Feeding it with blood. They've been serving Lord Foul for centuries."

Sunder stared; incredulity seemed to hurt his face. Covenant's asseveration violated everything he had ever believed. "Covenant." Dismay scarred his voice. His hands made imploring gestures. "How can it be true? It is too much. How can I know that it is true?"

"Because I say it's true." The moment passed, leaving

Covenant as weary as death. "I paid for that soothtell with my blood. And I was here. Four thousand years ago. When the Land was healthy. What the Clave taught you is something they made up to justify all that bloodshed." A distant part of him saw what he was doing, and protested. He was identifying himself with the truth, making himself responsible for it. Surely no man could keep such a promise. Hile Troy had tried—and had lost his soul to the Forestal of Garroting Deep as a consequence.

"Then—" Sunder wrestled for comprehension. His features showed horror at the implications of what Covenant said— horror turning to rage. "Then why do you not fight? Destroy the Clave—end this ill? If they are such an abomination?"

Covenant drooped against Brinn. "I'm too weak." He hardly heard himself. "And I've already killed—" A spasm of grief twisted his face. Twenty-one people! "I swore I would never kill again." But for Sunder's sake, he made one more effort to articulate what he believed. "I don't want to fight them until I stop hating them."

Slowly, the Graveler nodded. The bonfire became a roaring in Covenant's ears. For an instant of giddiness, he thought that Sunder was Nassic. Nassic with young, sane eyes. The Graveler, too, was capable of things which humbled Covenant.

There was movement around him. People were readying themselves for departure. They saluted him; but his numbness prevented him from responding. Escorted by nearly a score of *Haruchai*, they left the foothills. He did not watch them go. He hung on the verges of unconsciousness and fought to remain alive.

For a time, he drifted along the current of the bonfire. But then he felt himself turned in Brinn's arms, gently shaken erect. He pried his eyes wide, scraped his eyelids across the sabulous exhaustion in his gaze, and saw Memla.

She stood grimly before him. Her chasuble was gone, and her robe had been singed in places. Her age-stained hair straggled about her shoulders. Fire blisters marred her right cheek; her blunt features were battered. But her eyes were angry, and she faced Covenant with her *rukh* held ready.

At her back champed five of the Clave's huge Coursers.

Brinn nodded to her. "Memla na-Mhoram-in," he said flatly. "The ur-Lord has awaited you."

She gave Brinn a gesture of recognition without taking her

eyes from Covenant. Her gruff voice both revealed and controlled her wrath. "I cannot live with lies. I will accompany you."

Covenant had no words for her. Mutely, he touched his right hand to his heart, then raised the palm toward her.

"I have brought Coursers," she said. "They were not well defended—but well enough to hamper me. Only five could I wrest from so many of the na-Mhoram-cro." The beasts were laden with supplies. "They are Din, Clang, Clangor, Annoy, and Clash."

Covenant nodded. His head went on bobbing feebly, as if the muscles of his neck had fallen into caducity.

She gripped his gaze. "But one matter must be open between us. With my *rukh*, I can wield the Banefire to aid our journey. This the Clave cannot prevent. But I in turn cannot prevent them from knowing where I am and what I do, through my *rukh*. Halfhand." Her tone took on an inflection of appeal. "I do not wish to set aside the sole power I possess."

Her honesty and courage demanded an answer. With an effort that disfocused his eyes and made his head spin, he said, "Keep it. I'll take the chance."

His reply softened her features momentarily. "When first we met," she said, "your misdoubt was just, though I knew it not. Yet trust is preferrable." Then, abruptly, she stiffened again. "But we must depart. Gibbon has gathered the Clave at the Banefire. While we delay, they raise the *Grim* against us."

The *Grim*! Covenant could not block the surge of his dismay. It carried him over the edge, and he plunged like dead stone into darkness.

As he fell, he heard a cold wail from Revelstone—a cry like the keening of the great Keep, promising loss and blood. Or perhaps the wail was within himself.

TWENTY-ONE: Sending

SOMETIME during the night, he wandered close to consciousness. He was being rocked on the back of a Courser. Arms reached around him from behind and knotted together over his heart. They supported him like bands of stone. *Haruchai* arms.

Someone said tensely, "Are you not a healer? You must succor him."

"No." Linden's reply sounded small and wan, and complete. It made him moan deep in his throat.

Glints of *rukh*-fire hurt his eyes. When he shut out the sight, he faded away once more.

The next time he looked up, he saw the gray of dawn in fragments through the monstrous jungle. The lightening of the sky lay directly ahead of him. He was mounted on Din, with Memla before him and Brinn behind. Another Courser, carrying Ceer and Hergrom, led the way along the line Memla created with her *rukh*. The rest of the company followed Din.

As Covenant fumbled toward wakefulness, Memla's path ran into an area of relatively clear ground under the shade of a towering stand of rhododendron. There she halted. Over her shoulder, she called to the company, "Remain mounted. The Coursers will spare us from the Sunbane."

Behind him, Covenant heard Sunder mutter, "Then it is true—"

But Hergrom dropped to the ground, began to accept supplies handed down by Ceer; and Brinn said, "The *Haruchai* do not share this need to be warded."

Immune? Covenant wondered dimly. Yes. How else had so many of them been able to reach Revelstone unwarped?

Then the sun began to rise, sending spangles of crimson and misery through the vegetation. Once again, the eh-Brand had foretold the Sunbane accurately.

When the first touch of the sun was past, Memla ordered the Coursers to their knees, controlling them all with her command. The company began to dismount.

Covenant shrugged off Brinn's help and tried to stand alone. He found that he could. He felt as pale and weak as an invalid; but his muscles were at least able to hold his weight.

Unsteadily, he turned to look back westward through the retreating night for some sign of the na-Mhoram's *Grim*.

The horizon seemed clear.

Near him, Sunder and Stell had descended from one Courser, Hollian and Harn from another. Cail helped Linden down from the fifth beast. Covenant faced her with his frailty and concern; but she kept her gaze to herself, locked herself in her loneliness as if the very nerves of her eyes, the essential marrow of her bones, had been humiliated past bearing.

He left her alone. He did not know what to do, and felt too tenuous to do it.

While the *Haruchai* prepared food for the company—dried meat, bread, fruit, and *metheglin*—Memla produced from one of her sacks a large leather pouch of distilled *voure*, the pungent sap Covenant's friends had once used to ward off insects under the sun of pestilence. Carefully, she dabbed the concentrate on each of her companions, excluding only Vain. Covenant nodded at her omission. Perhaps *rukh*-fire could harm the Demondim-spawn. The Sunbane could not.

Covenant ate slowly and thoroughly, feeding his body's poverty. But all the time, a weight of apprehension impended toward him from the west. He had seen During Stonedown, had seen what the *Grim* could do. With an effort, he found his voice to ask Memla how long the raising of a *Grim* took.

She was clearly nervous. "That is uncertain," she muttered. "The size of the *Grim*, and its range, must be considered." Her gaze flicked to his face, leaving an almost palpable mark of anxiety across his cheek. "I read them. Here." Her hands tightened on her *rukh*. "It will be very great."

Very great, Covenant murmured. And he was so weak. He pressed his hands to the *krill*, and tried to remain calm.

A short time later, the company remounted. Memla drew on the Banefire to open a way for the huge Coursers. Again, Hergrom and Ceer—on Annoy, Memla said: the names of the beasts seemed important to her, as if she loved them in her blunt fashion—went first, followed by Covenant, Brinn, and the Rider on Din, then by Cail and Linden on Clash, Sunder and Stell on Clang, Harn and Hollian on Clangor. Vain brought up the rear as if he were being sucked along without volition in the wake of the Coursers.

Covenant dozed repeatedly throughout the day. He had been too severely drained; he could not keep himself awake. Whenever the company paused for food, water, and rest, he consumed all the aliment he was given, striving to recover some semblance of strength. But between stops the rocking of Din's stride unmoored his awareness, so that he rode tides of dream and dread and insects, and could not anchor himself.

In periods of wakefulness, he knew from the rigidity of Memla's back that she wanted to flee and flee, and never stop. She, too, knew vividly what the *Grim* could do. But, toward evening, her endurance gave out. Under the shelter of a prodigious Gilden, she halted the quest for the night.

At first, while she started a fire, the air thronged with flying bugs of every description; and the boughs and leaves of the tree seethed with things which crawled and bored. But *voure* protected the company. And gradually, as dusk seeped into the jungle, macerating the effect of the Sunbane, the insects began to disappear. Their viscid stridulation faded as they retreated into gestation or sleep. Memla seated her weary bones beside the fire, dismissed the Coursers, and let the *Haruchai* care for her companions.

Sunder and Hollian seemed tired, as if they had not slept for days; but they were sturdy, with funds of stamina still untapped. Though they knew of the *Grim*, at least by rumor, their relief at escaping Revelstone outweighed their apprehension. They stood and moved together as if their emprisonment had made them intimate. Sunder seemed to draw ease from the eh-Brand, an anodyne for his old self-conflicts; her youth and her untormented sense of herself were a balm to the Graveler, who had shed his own wife and son and had chosen to betray his people for Covenant's sake. And she, in turn, found support and encouragement in his knotted resourcefulness, his determined struggle for conviction. They both had lost so much; Covenant was relieved to think that they could comfort each other. He could not have given them comfort.

But their companionship only emphasized Linden's isolation in his eyes. The Raver had done something to her. And Covenant, who had experience with such things, dreaded knowing what it was—and dreaded the consequences of not knowing.

As he finished his meal, he arrived at the end of his ability to support his ignorance. He was sitting near the fire. Memla rested, half-asleep, on one side of him. On the other sat Sunder and Hollian. Four of the *Haruchai* stood guard beyond the tree. Brinn and Cail moved silently around the fringes of the Gilden, alert for peril. Vain stood at the edge of the light like the essence of all black secrets. And among them, across the fire from Covenant, Linden huddled within herself, with her arms clasped around her knees and her eyes fixed on the blaze, as if she were a complete stranger.

He could not bear it. He had invested so much hope in her and knew so little about her; he had to know why she was so afraid. But he had no idea how to confront her. Her hidden wound made her untouchable. So for his own sake, as well as for the sake of his companions, he cleared his throat and began to tell his tale.

He left nothing out. From Andelain and the Dead to Stone-might Woodhelven, from Vain's violence to Hamako's *rhysh*, from his run across the Center Plains to Memla's revelation of the Clave's mendacity, he told it all. And then he described the soothtell as fully as he could. His hands would not remain still as he spoke; so much of the memory made him writhe. He tugged at his beard, knitted his fingers together, clutched his left fist over his wedding band, and told his friends what he had witnessed.

He understood now why the Raver had been willing to let him see the truth of the Land's history. Lord Foul wanted him to perceive the fetters of action and consequence which bound him to his guilt, wanted him to blame himself for the destruction of the Staff, and for the Sunbane, and for every life the Clave sacrificed. So that he would founder in culpability, surrender his ring in despair and self-abhorrence. Lord Foul, who laughed at lepers. *At the last there will be but one choice for you.* In that context, the venom in him made sense. It gave him power he could not control. Power to kill people. Guilt. It was a prophecy of his doom—a self-fulfilling prophecy.

That, too, he explained, hoping Linden would raise her eyes, look at him, try to understand. But she did not. Her mouth stretched into severity; but she held to her isolation. Even when he detailed how the seeds planted by his Dead had led him to conceive a quest for the One Tree, intending to make a new Staff of Law so that thereby he could oppose Lord Foul and contest the Sunbane without self-abandonment, even then she did not respond. Finally, he fell silent, bereft of words.

For a time, the company remained still with him. No one asked any questions; they seemed unwilling to probe the pain he had undergone. But then Sunder spoke. To answer Covenant, he told what had happened to Linden, Hollian, and him after Covenant had entered Andelain.

He described Santonin and the Stonemight, described the Rider's coercion, described the way in which he and Hollian had striven to convince Gibbon that Covenant was lost or dead. But after that, he had not much to tell. He had been cast into a cell with little food and water, and less hope. Hollian's plight had been the same. Both had heard the clamor of Covenant's first entrance into the hold, and nothing more.

Then Covenant thought that surely Linden would speak. Surely she would complete her part of the tale. But she did not. She hid her face against her knees and sat huddled there as if she were bracing herself against a memory full of whips.

"Linden." How could he leave her alone? He needed the truth from her. "Now you know how Kevin must have felt."

Kevin Landwaster, last of Berek's line. Linden had said, *I don't believe in evil.* Kevin also had tried not to believe in evil. He had unwittingly betrayed the Land by failing to perceive Lord Foul's true nature in time, and had thereby set the Despiser on the path to victory. Thus he had fallen into despair. Because of what he had done, he had challenged the Despiser to the Ritual of Desecration, hoping to destroy Lord Foul by reaving the Land. But in that, too, he had failed. He had succeeded at laying waste the Land he loved, and at losing the Staff of Law; but Lord Foul had endured.

All this Covenant told her. "Don't you see?" he said, imploring her to hear him. "Despair is no answer. It's what Foul lives on. Whatever happened to you, it doesn't have to be like this." Linden, listen to me!

But she did not listen, gave no sign that she was able to hear him. If he had not seen the shadows of distress shifting behind her eyes, he might have believed that she had fallen back into the coma which Gibbon had levied upon her.

Sunder sat glowering as if he could not choose between his empathy for Linden and his understanding of Covenant. Hollian's dark eyes were blurred with tears. Brinn and Cail watched as if they were the models for Vain's impassivity. None of them offered Covenant any help.

He tried a different tack. "Look at Vain." *Linden*! "Tell me what you see."

She did not respond.

"I don't know whether or not I can trust him. I don't have your eyes. I need you to tell me what he is."

She did not move. But her shoulders tautened as if she were screaming within herself.

"That old man." His voice was choked by need and fear. "On Haven Farm. You saved his life. He told you to *Be true*."

She flinched. Jerking up her head, she gaped at him with eyes as injured as if they had been gouged into the clenched misery of her soul. Then she was on her feet, fuming like a magma of bitterness. "*You*!" she cried. "You keep talking about desecration. This is your doing. Why did you have to sell yourself for Joan? Why did you have to get us into this? Don't you call *that* desecration?"

"Linden." Her passion swept him upright; but he could not reach out to her. The fire lay between them as if she had lit it there in her fury.

"Of course you don't. You can't *see*. You don't *know*." Her hands clawed the air over her breasts as if she wanted to tear her flesh. "You think it will help if you go charging off on some crazy quest. Make a new Staff of Law." She was savage with gall. "You don't count, and you don't even *know it*!"

He repeated her name. Sunder and Hollian had risen to their feet. Memla held her *rukh* ready, and Cail stood poised nearby, as if both Rider and *Haruchai* felt violence in the air.

"What did he do to you?" *What did that bastard do to you?*

"He said you don't count!" Abruptly, she was spouting words, hurling them at him as if he were the cause of her distress. "All they care about is your ring. The rest is me. He said, 'You have been especially chosen for this desecration. You are being forged as iron is forged to achieve the ruin of the Earth.' " Her voice thickened like blood around the memory. "Because I can *see*. That's how they're going to make me do what they want. By torturing me with what I see, and feel, and hear. You're making me do exactly what they want!"

The next instant, her outburst sprang to a halt. Her hands leaped to her face, trying to block out visions. Her body went rigid, as if she were on the verge of convulsions; a moan tore its way between her teeth. Then she sagged.

In desolation, she whispered, "He touched me."

Touched—?

"Covenant." She dropped her hands, let him see the full anguish in her visage. "You've got to get me out of here. Back to where I belong. Where my life means something. Before they make me kill you."

"I know," he said, because she had to have an answer. "That's another reason why I want to find the One Tree." But within himself he felt suddenly crippled. *You don't count.* He had placed so much hope in her, in the possibility that she was free of Lord Foul's manipulations; and now that hope lay in wreckage. "The Lords used the Staff to call me here." In one stroke, he had been reft of everything. "A Staff is the only thing I know of that can send us back."

Everything except the *krill*, and his old intransigence.

Especially chosen— Hell and blood! He wanted to cover his face; he could have wept like a child. But Linden's eyes clung to him desperately, trying to believe in him. Sunder and Hollian held each other against a fear they could not name. And Memla's countenance was blunt-molded into a shape of sympathy, as if she knew what it meant to be discounted. Only the *Haruchai* appeared unmoved—the *Haruchai*, and Vain.

When Linden asked, "Your ring?" he met her squarely.

"I can't control it."

Abruptly, Memla's expression became a flinch of surprise, as if he had uttered something appalling.

He ignored her. While his heart raged for grief, as if tears were a debt which he owed to his mortality and could not pay, he stretched out his arms. There in front of all his companions he gave himself a VSE.

Ah, you are stubborn yet.

Yes. By God. Stubborn.

Acting with characteristic detached consideration, Brinn handed Covenant a pouch of *metheglin*. Covenant lifted it between himself and his friends, so that they could not see his face, and drank it dry. Then he walked away into the darkness around the Gilden, used the night to hide him. After a time, he lay down among the things he had lost, and closed his eyes.

Brinn roused him with the dawn, got him to his feet in time to meet the second rising of the sun of pestilence, protected by his boots. The rest of the quest was already awake. Sunder and Hollian had joined Memla on pieces of stone; the *Haruchai* were busy preparing food; Linden stood gazing at the approaching incarnadine. Her face was sealed against its own vulnerability; but when she noticed Covenant, her eyes acknowledged him somberly. After the conflicts of the previous evening, her recognition touched him like a smile.

He found that he felt stronger. But with recovery came a renewal of fear. The na-Mhoram's *Grim*—

Memla bore herself as if throughout the night she had not forgotten that peril. Her aging features were lined with apprehension, and her hands trembled on her *rukh*. To answer Covenant's look, she murmured, "Still he raises it, and is not content. It will be a *Grim* to rend our souls." For a moment, her eyes winced to his face as if she needed reassurance. But then she jerked away, began snapping at her companions to make them hurry.

Soon the company was on its way, moving at a hard canter down the path which Memla invoked from the Banefire. Her urgency and Covenant's tight dread infected the Stonedownors, marked even Linden. The quest rode in silence, as if they could feel the *Grim* poised like a blade at the backs of their necks.

The jungle under the sun of pestilence aggravated Covenant's sense of impending disaster. The insects thronged around him like incarnations of disease. Every malformed bough and bush was a-crawl with malformed bugs. Some of the trees were so heavily veined with termites that the wood looked leprous. And the smell of rot had become severe. Under the aegis of the Sunbane, his guts ached, half expecting the vegetation to break open and begin suppurating.

Time dragged. Weakness crept through his muscles again. When the company finally rode into the relief of sunset, his neck and shoulders throbbed from the strain of looking backward for some sign of the *Grim*. Shivers ran through the marrow of his bones. As soon as Memla picked a camping place under the shelter of a megalithic stand of eucalyptus, he dropped to the ground, hoping to steady himself on the Earth's underlying granite. But his hands and feet were too numb to feel anything.

Around him, his companions dismounted. Almost at once, Linden went over to Hollian. The flesh of Linden's face was pale and taut, stretched tight over her skull. She accosted the eh-Brand purposefully, but then had to fumble for words. "The insects," she murmured. "The smell. It's worse. Worse than any other sun. I can't shut it all out." Her eyes watched the way her hands clung together, as if only that knot held her in one piece. "I can't— What's it going to be tomorrow?"

Sunder had moved to stand near Hollian. As Linden fell silent, he nodded grimly. "Never in all my life have I faced a sun of pestilence and encountered so little harm." His tone was hard. "I had not known the Clave could journey so untouched by that which is fear and abhorrence to the people of the Land. And now ur-Lord Covenant teaches us that the Clave's immunity has been purchased by the increase rather than the decline of the Sunbane." His voice darkened as if he were remembering all the people he had shed. "I do not misdoubt him. But I, too, desire tidings of the morrow's sun."

Memla indicated with a shrug that such tidings could not alter her anxiety. But Covenant joined Linden and Sunder. He felt suddenly sickened by the idea that perhaps the soothtell had been a lie designed by Gibbon-Raver to mislead him. If two days of rain were followed by only two days of pestilence— Gripping himself, he waited for Hollian's response.

She acceded easily. Her light smile reminded him that she was not like Sunder. With her *lianar* and her skill, she had always been able to touch the Sunbane for the benefit of others; she had never had to kill people to obtain blood. Therefore she did not loathe her own capabilities as Sunder did his.

She stepped a short distance away to give herself space, then took out her dirk and wand. Seating herself on the leaves which littered the ground, she summoned her concentration. Covenant, Linden, and Sunder watched intently as she placed the *lianar* on her lap, gripped her dirk in her left hand and directed the point against her right palm. The words of invocation soughed past her lips. They clasped the company like a liturgy of worship for something fatal. Even the *Haruchai* left their tasks to stand ready. The thought that she was about to cut herself made Covenant scowl; but he had long ago left behind the days when he could have protested what she was doing.

Slowly, she drew a small cut on her palm. As blood welled from the incision, she closed her fingers on the *lianar*. Dusk had deepened into night around the quest, concealing her from the watchers. Yet even Covenant's impercipient senses could feel her power thickening like motes of fire concatenating toward flame. For a bated moment, the air was still. Then she sharpened her chant, and the wand took light.

Red flames bloomed like Sunbane orchids. They spread up into the air and down her forearm to the ground. Crimson tendrils curled about her as if she were being overgrown. They seemed bright; but they cast no illumination; the night remained dark.

Intuitively, Covenant understood her fire. With chanting and blood and *lianar*, she reached out toward the morrow's sun; and the flames took their color from what that sun would be. Her fire was the precise hue of the sun's pestilential aura.

A third sun of pestilence. He sighed his relief softly. Here, at least, he had no reason to believe that the soothtell had been false.

But before the eh-Brand could relax her concentration, release her foretelling, the fire abruptly changed.

A streak of blackness as absolute as Vain's skin shot from the wood, scarred the flames with ebony. At first, it was only a lash across the crimson. But it grew, expanded among the flames until it dominated them, obscured them.

Quenched them.

Instantly, night covered the companions, isolating them from each other. Covenant could perceive nothing except a faint tang of smoke in the air, as if Hollian's wand had been in danger of being consumed.

He swore hoarsely under his breath and swung out his arms until he touched Brinn on one side, Linden on the other. Then he heard feet spring through the leaves and heard Sunder cry, "Hollian!"

The next moment, Memla also cried out in horror. "Sending!" Fire raged from her *rukh*, cracked like a flail among the trees, making the night lurid. "It comes!" Covenant saw Ceer standing behind the Rider as if to protect her from attack. The other *Haruchai* formed a defensive ring around the company.

"*Gibbon!*" Memla howled. "Abomination!" Her fire savaged the air as if she were trying to strike at Revelstone from a distance of nearly two score leagues. "By all the Seven Hells—!"

Covenant reacted instinctively. He surged into the range of Memla's fire and gripped her forearms to prevent her from striking at him. "Memla!" he yelled into her face. "*Memla!* How much time have we got?"

His grip or his demand reached her. Her gaze came into focus on him. With a convulsive shudder, she dropped her fire, let darkness close over the quest. When she spoke, her voice came out of the night like the whispering of condor wings.

"There is time. The *Grim* cannot instantly cross so many leagues. Perhaps as much as a day remains to us.

"But it is the na-Mhoram's *Grim*, and has been two days in the raising. Such a sending might break Revelstone itself."

She took a breath which trembled. "Ur-Lord, we cannot evade this *Grim*. It will follow my *rukh* and rend us utterly." Her voice winced in her throat. "I had believed that the wild magic would give us hope. But if it is beyond your control—"

At Covenant's back, a small flame jumped into life and caught wood. Sunder had lit a faggot. He held it up like a torch, lifting the company out of the dark.

Hollian was gasping through her teeth, fighting not to cry out. The violation of her foretelling had hurt her intimately.

"That's right," Covenant gritted. "I can't control it." His hands manacled Memla's wrists, striving to keep her from hysteria. "Hang on. Think. We've got to do something about this." His eyes locked hers. "Can you leave your *rukh* behind?"

"Covenant!" she wailed in immediate anguish. "It is who I am! I am nothing to you without it." He tightened his grasp. She flinched away from his gaze. Her voice became a dry moan. "Without my *rukh*, I cannot part the trees. And I cannot command the Coursers. It is the power to which they have been bred. Losing it, my hold upon them will be lost. They will scatter from us. Perhaps they will turn against us." Her mien appeared to be crumbling in the unsteady torchlight. "This doom is upon my head," she breathed. "In ignorance and folly, I lured you to Revelstone."

"Damnation!" Covenant rasped, cursing half to himself. He felt trapped; and yet he did not want Memla to blame herself. He had asked for her help. He wrestled down his dismay. "All right," he panted. "Call the Coursers. Let's try to outrun it."

She gaped at him. "It is the *Grim*! It cannot be outrun."

"Goddamn it, he's only one Raver!" His fear made him livid. "The farther he has to send it, the weaker it's going to be. Let's try!"

For one more moment, Memla could not recover her courage. But then the muscles of her face tightened, and a look of resolution or fatality came into her eyes. "Yes, ur-Lord," she gritted. "It will be weakened somewhat. Let us make the attempt."

As he released her, she began shouting for the Coursers.

They came out of the night like huge chunks of darkness. The *Haruchai* threw sacks of supplies and bundles of firewood onto the broad backs. Covenant wheeled to face his companions.

Sunder and Hollian stood behind Linden. She crouched among the leaves, with her hands clamped over her face. The Stonedownors made truncated gestures toward her but did not know how to reach her. Her voice came out as if it were being throttled.

"I can't—"

Covenant exploded. "*Move!*"

She flinched, recoiled to her feet. Sunder and Hollian jerked into motion as if they were breaking free of a trance. Cail abruptly swept Linden from the ground and boosted her lightly onto Clash. Scrambling forward, Covenant climbed up behind Memla. In a whirl, he saw Sunder and Hollian on their mounts, saw the *Haruchai* spring into position, saw Memla's *rukh* gutter, then burst alive like a scar across the dark.

At once, the Coursers launched themselves down the line of Memla's path.

The night on either side of her fire seemed to roil like thunderheads. Covenant could not see past her back; he feared that Din would career at any moment into a failure of the path, crash against boulders, plunge into lurking ravines or gullies. But more than that, he feared his ring, feared the demand of power which the *Grim* would put upon him.

Memla permitted no disaster. At unexpected moments, her line veered past sudden obstacles; yet with her fire and her will she kept the company safe and swift. She was running for her life, for Covenant's life, for the hope of the Land; and she took her Coursers through the ruinous jungle like bolts from a crossbow.

They ran while the moon rose—ran as it arced overhead —ran and still ran after it had set. The Coursers were creatures of the Sunbane, and did not tire. Just after dawn, Memla slapped them to a halt. When Covenant dismounted, his legs trembled. Linden moved as if her entire body had been beaten with clubs. Even Sunder and Hollian seemed to have lost their hardiness. But Memla's visage was set in lines of extremity; and she held her *rukh* as if she strove to tune her soul to the pitch of iron.

She allowed the company only a brief rest for a meal. But even that time was too long. Without warning, Stell pointed toward the sun. The mute intensity of his gesture snatched every eye eastward.

The sun stood above the horizon, its sick red aura burning like a promise of infirmity. But the corona was no longer perfect. Its leading edge wore a stark black flaw.

The mark was wedge-shaped, like an attack of ur-viles, and aligned as if it were being hammered into the sun from Revelstone.

Linden's groan was more eloquent than any outcry.

Shouting a curse, Memla drove her companions back to the Coursers. In moments, the quest had remounted, and the beasts raced against black malice.

They could not win. Though Memla's path was strong and true—though the Coursers ran at the full stretch of their great legs—the blackness grew swiftly. By midmorning, it had devoured half the sun's anadem.

Pressure mounted against Covenant's back. His thoughts took on the rhythm of Din's strides: I must not— Must not— Visions of killing came: ten years or four millennia ago, at the battle of Soaring Woodhelven, he had slain Cavewights. And later, he had driven a knife into the heart of the man who had murdered Lena. He could not think of power except in terms of killing.

He had no control over his ring.

Then the company burst out of thick jungle toward a savannah. There, nothing obstructed the terrain except the coarse grass, growing twice as tall as the Coursers, north, south, and east, and the isolated mounds of rock standing like prodigious cairns at great distances from each other. Covenant had an instant of overview before the company plunged down the last hillside into the savannah. The sky opened; and he could not understand how the heavens remained so un-trammeled around such a sun. Then Memla's path sank into the depths of the grass.

The quest ran for another league before Hollian cried over the rumble of hooves, "It comes!"

Covenant flung a look behind him.

A thunderhead as stark as the sun's wound boiled out of the west. Its seething was poised like a fist; and it moved with such swiftness that the Coursers seemed not to be racing at all.

"Run!" he gasped at Memla's back.

As if in contradiction, she wrenched Din to a halt. The Courser skidded, almost fell. Covenant nearly lost his seat. The other beasts veered away, crashing frenetically through the grass. "Heaven and Earth!" Sunder barked. Controlling all the Coursers, Memla sent them wheeling and stamping around her, battering down the grass to clear a large circle.

As the vegetation east of him was crushed, Covenant saw why she had stopped.

Directly across her path marched a furious column of creatures.

For a moment, he thought that they were Cavewights—Cavewights running on all fours in a tight swath sixty feet wide, crowding shoulder to shoulder out of the south in a stream without beginning or end. They had the stocky frames, gangrel limbs, blunt heads of Cavewights. But if these were Cavewights they had been hideously altered by the Sunbane. Chitinous plating armored their backs and appendages; their fingers and toes had become claws; their chins were split into horned jaws like mandibles. And they had no eyes, no features; their faces had been erased. Nothing marked their fore-skulls except long antennae which hunted ahead of them, searching out their way.

They rushed as if they were running headlong toward prey. The line of their march had already been torn down to bare dirt by the leaders. In their haste, they sounded like the swarming of gargantuan ants—formication punctuated by the sharp clack of jaws.

"Hellfire!" Covenant panted. The blackness around the sun was nearly complete; the *Grim* was scant leagues away, and closing rapidly. And he could see no way past this river of pestilential creatures. If they were of Cavewightish stock— He shuddered at the thought. The Cavewights had been mighty earth delvers, tremendously strong. And these creatures were almost as large as horses. If anything interrupted their single-minded march, they would tear even Memla's beasts limb from limb.

Linden began to whimper, then bit herself into silence. Sunder stared at the creatures with dread-glazed eyes. Hollian's hair lay on her shoulders like raven wings, emphasizing her pale features as if she were marked for death. Memla sagged in front of Covenant like a woman with a broken spine.

Turning to Brinn, Covenant asked urgently, "Will it pass?"

In answer, Brinn nodded toward Hergrom and Ceer. Ceer had risen to stand erect on Annoy's back. Hergrom promptly climbed onto Ceer's shoulders, balanced there to gain a view over the grass. A moment later, Brinn reported, "We are farsighted, but the end of this cannot be seen."

Bloody hell! He was afraid of wild magic, power beyond control or choice. I must not I But he knew that he would use it if he had to. He could not simply let his companions die.

The thunderhead approached like the blow of an axe. Blackness garroted the sun. The light began to dim.

A rush of protest went through him. Fear or no fear, this doom was intolerable. "All right." Ignoring the distance to the ground, he dropped from Din's back. "We'll have to fight here."

Brinn joined him. Sunder and Stell dismounted from Clang, Hollian and Harn from Clangor. Cail pulled Linden down from Clash and set her on her feet. Her hands twitched as if they were searching for courage; but she found none. Covenant tore his gaze away, so that her distress would not make him more dangerous. "Sunder," he rapped out, "you've got your *orcrest*. Memla has her *rukh*. Is there some way you can work together? Can you hit that thing"— he grimaced at the *Grim* —"before it hits us?"

The cloud was almost overhead. It shed a preternatural twilight across the savannah, quenching the day.

"No." Memla had not dismounted. She spoke as if her mouth were full of ashes. "There is not time. It is too great."

Her dismay hurt Covenant like a demand for wild magic. He wanted to shout, I can't control it! Don't you understand? I might kill you all! But she went on speaking as if his power or incapacity had become irrelevant. "You must not die. That is certain." Her quietness seemed suddenly terrible. "When the way is clear, cross instantly. This march will seal the gap swiftly." She straightened her shoulders and lifted her face to the sky. "The *Grim* has found you because of me. Let it be upon my head."

Before anyone could react, she turned Din and guided it toward the blind rushing creatures. As she moved, she brought up the fire of her *rukh*, holding it before her like a saber.

Covenant and Sunder sprang after her. But Brinn and Stell interposed themselves. Cursing, the Graveler fought to break free; but Stell mastered him without effort. Furiously, Sunder shouted, "Release me! Do you not see that she means to die?"

Covenant ignored Sunder: he locked himself to Brinn's flat eyes. Softly, dangerously, he breathed, "Don't do this."

Brinn shrugged. "I have sworn to preserve your life."

"Bannor took the same Vow." Covenant did not struggle. But he glared straight at the *Haruchai*. People have died because of me. How much more do you think I can stand? "That's how Elena got killed. I might have been able to save her."

The *Grim* began to boil almost directly above the quest. But the Cavewightlike creatures were unaware of it. They marched on like blind doom, shredding the dirt of the plains.

"Bannor maintained his Vow," Brinn said, as if it cost him no effort to refute Covenant. "So the old tellers say, and their tale has descended from Bannor himself. It was First Mark Morin, sworn to the High Lord, who failed." He nodded toward Ceer. In response, Ceer sprinted after Memla and vaulted lightly onto Din's back. "We also," Brinn concluded, "will maintain the promise we have made, to the limit of our strength."

But Memla reacted in rage too thick for shouting. "By the Seven Hells!" she panted, "I will not have this. You have sworn nothing to me." Brandishing her *rukh*, she faced Ceer. "If you do not dismount, I will burn you with my last breath, and all this company shall die for naught!"

Memla! Covenant tried to yell. But he could not. He had nothing to offer her; his fear of wild magic choked him. Helplessly, he watched as Ceer hesitated, glanced toward Brinn. The *Haruchai* consulted together in silence, weighing their commitments. Then Ceer sprang to the ground and stepped out of Din's way.

No! Covenant protested. She's going to get herself killed!

He had no time to think. Gloaming occluded the atmosphere. The ravening *Grim* poised itself above Memla, focused on her fire. The heavens around the cloud remained impossibly cerulean; but the cloud itself was pitch and midnight. It descended as it seethed, dropping toward its victims.

Under it, the air crackled as if it were being scorched.

The Coursers skittered. Sunder took out his *orcrest*, then seized Hollian's hand and pulled her to the far side of the circle, away from Memla. The *Haruchai* flowed into defensive positions among the companions and the milling beasts.

Amid the swirl of movement, Vain stood, black under black, as if he were inured to darkness.

Hergrom placed himself near Vain. But Memla was planning to die; Linden was foundering in ill; and Covenant felt outraged by the unanswerable *must/must not* of his ring. He yelled at Hergrom, "Let him take care of himself!"

The next instant, he staggered to his knees. The air shattered with a heart-stopping concussion. The *Grim* broke into bits, became intense black flakes floating downward like a fall of snow.

With fearsome slowness, they fell—crystals of sun-darkness, tangible night, force which not even stone could withstand.

Howling defiance, Memla launched fire at the sky.

Din bunched under her and charged out into the march of the creatures. A series of tremendous heaves carried beast and Rider toward the center of the stream.

The flakes of the *Grim* drifted in her direction, following the lodestone of her *rukh*. Its dense center, the nexus of its might, passed beyond the quest.

The creatures immediately mobbed her mount. Din let out a piercing scream at the tearing of claws and mandibles. Only the plunging of its hooves, the slash of its spurs, the thickness of its coat, protected it.

Then the *Grim* fell skirling around her head. Her fire blazed: she lashed out, trying to keep herself and Din from being touched. Every flake her flame struck burst in a glare of darkness, and was gone. But for every flake she destroyed, she was assailed by a hundred more.

Covenant watched her in an agony of helplessness, knowing

that if he turned to his ring now he could not strike for her without striking her. The *Grim* was thickest around her; but its edges covered the march as well as the quest. The creatures were swept into confusion as killing bits as big as fists fell among them.

Vermeil shot from Sunder's *orcrest* toward the darkened sun. Covenant yelled in encouragement. By waving the Sunstone back and forth, the Graveler picked flakes out of the air with his shaft, consuming them before they could reach him or Hollian.

Around the company, the *Haruchai* dodged like dervishes. They used flails of pampas grass to strike down the flakes. Each flake destroyed the whip which touched it; but the *Haruchai* snatched up more blades and went on fighting.

Abruptly, Covenant was thrust from his feet. A piece of blackness missed his face. Brinn pitched him past it, then jerked him up again. Heaving Covenant from side to side, Brinn danced among the falling *Grim*. Several flakes hit where they had been standing. Obsidian flares set fire to the grass.

The grass began to burn in scores of places.

Yet Vain stood motionless, with a look of concentration on his face. Flakes struck his skin, his tunic. Instead of detonating, they melted on him and ran hissing down his raiment, his legs, like water on hot metal.

Covenant gaped at the Demondim-spawn, then lost sight of him as Brinn went dodging through the smoke.

He caught a glimpse of Memla. She fought extravagantly for her life, hurled fire with all the outrage of her betrayal by the na-Mhoram. But the focus of the *Grim* formed a mad swarm around her. And the moiling creatures had already torn Din to its knees. In patches, its hide had been bared to the bone.

Without warning, a flake struck the Courser's head. Din collapsed, tumbling the Rider headlong among the creatures.

Memla! Covenant struggled to take hold of his power. But Brinn's thrusting and dodging reft him of concentration. And already he was too late.

Yet Ceer leaped forward with the calm abandon of the *Haruchai*. Charging into the savagery, he fought toward Memla.

She regained her feet in a splash of fire. For an instant, she stood, gallant and tattered, hacking fury at the creatures. Ceer almost reached her.

Then Covenant lost her as Brinn tore him out from under a black flurry. Flames and *Haruchai* reeled about him; the flakes were everywhere. But he fought upright in time to see Memla fall with a scream of darkness in her chest.

As she died and dropped her *rukh*, the four remaining Coursers went berserk.

They erupted as if only her will had contained the madness of their fear. Yowling among the grassfires, two of them dashed out of the circle and fled across the savannah. Another plowed into the breach the *Grim* had made in the march. As it passed, Ceer suddenly appeared at its side. Fighting free of the creatures, he grabbed at the Courser's hair and used the beast to pull him away.

The fourth beast attacked the company. Its vehemence caught the *Haruchai* unprepared. Its eyes burned scarlet as it plunged against Hergrom, struck him down with its chest.

Hergrom had been helping Cail to protect Linden.

Instantly, the beast reared at her.

Cail tried to shove her aside. She stumbled, fell the wrong way.

Covenant saw her sprawl under the Courser's hooves. One of them clipped her head as the beast stamped, trying to crush her.

Again, the Courser reared.

Cail stood over her. Covenant could not strike without hitting the *Haruchai*. He fought to run forward.

As the Courser hammered down, Cail caught its legs. For one impossible moment, he held the huge animal off her. Then it began to bend him.

Linden!

With a prodigious effort, Cail heaved the Courser to the side. Its hooves missed Linden as they landed.

Blood appeared. From shoulder to elbow, Cail's left arm had been ripped open by one of the beast's spurs.

It reared again.

Covenant's mind went instantly white with power. But before he could grasp it, use it, Brinn knocked him away from another cluster of flakes. The grass was giddy fire and death, whirling. He flipped to his feet and swung back toward Linden; but his heart had already frozen within him.

As his vision cleared, he saw Sunder hurl a blast of Sunbane-fire which struck the Courser's chest, knocking it to its knees. Lurching upright again, it pounded its pain away from the quest.

But Linden lay under the *Grim*, surrounded by growing fires, and did not move.

TWENTY-TWO: Plain of Fire

FIRES leaped in front of him, obscuring her from his sight. The *Grim*-fall darkened the air. The thrashing and clatter of the creatures filled his ears. He could not see if Linden were still alive. Brinn kept heaving him from side to side, kept lashing handsful of grass around his head.

Sunder's fire scored the atmosphere like straight red lightning. Now the corrosive flakes began to concentrate around him.

Covenant broke free of Brinn, went surging toward Linden. Hergrom had lifted her from the ground. The *Haruchai* carried her in an elaborate dance of evasion. She hung limp in his arms. Blood seeping from the back of her head matted her hair.

An argent shout gathered in Covenant's chest.

But as he raised his head to howl power, he saw the blackness around the sun fraying. Pestilential red glistered through the ebony. The last *Grim*-flakes were drifting toward Sunder's head. The Graveler was able to consume them all.

At once, Covenant locked his throat, left the wild magic unspoken. In a rush, he reached Hergrom and Linden.

Cail stood nearby. He had torn a strip from his tunic; with Harn's help, he bound the cloth as a tourniquet about his arm. His ripped flesh bled heavily.

The other *Haruchai* were marked with smoke and fire, but had not been injured. And Sunder and Hollian were unharmed, though his exertions left the Graveler tottering. Hollian supported him.

Vain stood a short distance away as if nothing had happened. Flames licked about his feet like crushed serpents.

Covenant ignored them all. Linden's visage was lorn alabaster. Blood stained her wheaten tresses. Her lips wore an unconscious grimace of pain. He tried to take her from Hergrom's arms; but Hergrom would not release her.

"Ur-Lord." Brinn's alien voice seemed incapable of urgency. "We must go. Already the gap closes."

Covenant pulled uselessly at Hergrom's grasp. It was intolerable that she might die! She was not meant to end like this. Or why had she been Chosen? He called out to her, but did not know how to reach her.

"Covenant!" Sunder's ragged breathing made his tone hoarse. "It is as Brinn says. The na-Mhoram-in spent her life to provide this passage. We must go."

Memla. That name pierced Covenant. She had given him life. Like Lena. And so many others. With a shudder, he turned from Hergrom. His hands groped for support. "Yes." He could hardly hear himself through the flames. "Let's go."

At once, the *Haruchai* sprang into motion. Harn and Stell led the way; Hergrom and Brinn followed with Covenant; Cail guarded Sunder and Hollian. They paid no attention to Vain. In a body, they dodged the grassfires toward the breach in the march.

The creatures milled insanely around the scorched and pitted ground where Memla had fallen. Their leaders had already marched out of sight, uncognizant of what had happened behind them. But more warped beings poured constantly from the south. They would have overrun the company immediately; but their own dead delayed them. The arriving creatures fell on the many slain and injured, tearing flesh apart with claws and mandibles, feeding ravenously. And the fires added fear to their hunger.

Into the confusion, the *Haruchai* guided Covenant and the Stonedownors.

The quest appeared small and fragile beside those large, blind creatures, vulnerable against those ferocious jaws, those plated limbs. But Brinn's people threaded the roil with uncanny stealth. And whenever a creature blundered toward them, Stell and Harn struck cunningly, breaking the antennae so that the creature could not locate its prey. Thus maimed, the beasts were swept into mortal combat with other creatures. Covenant, Sunder, and Hollian were impelled past gaping jaws, under rearing bellies, across moments of clear ground, as if their lives were preserved by the charm of *Haruchai* competence.

A few shreds of red cloth marked the place of Memla's death, unambergrised by any grave or chance for mourning.

Running as well as they could, the companions broke into the thick grass beyond the march. Creatures veered to follow. With all their strength, Stell and Harn attacked the grass, forcing a way through it. Only Vain did not make haste. He had no need for haste: every creature which touched him fell dead, and was devoured by the oncoming surge.

A short distance into the grass, Ceer joined the company. He did not speak; but the object he held explained what he had done.

Memla's *rukh*.

The sight of it halted Covenant. Possibilities reeled through his head. He grappled to take hold of them.

But he had no time. A sharp crepitation cut the grass like a scythe; thousands of creatures were chewing their way in pursuit.

Brinn thrust Covenant forward. The company ran.

Ceer, Stell, Brinn, and Harn dropped back to defend the rear. Now Cail led. In spite of his wounded arm and the abrasion of the raw, stiff grass, he forced a path with his body. Hergrom followed, carrying Linden; and Covenant crowded on Hergrom's heels, with Hollian and Sunder behind him.

The creatures gave chase as if they were prepared to reap the savannah in order to feast on human flesh. The noise of their charge hunted the company like fire.

Cail attacked the thick blades with all the ancient valor of the *Haruchai*; but he could not open a path swiftly enough to outdistance the pursuit. Covenant soon began to waver in exhaustion. He was still convalescing from the soothtell. Sunder and Hollian were in little better condition. Linden lay like defeat in Hergrom's arms. And Cail left smears of blood across the grass.

In the back of Covenant's desperation, a demand panted. Use your ring! But he could not, could not. He was so weak. He began to lose ground. Cail and Hergrom seemed to fade through the whipping backlash of the grass. If he let the venom rise in him, he did not know what he would kill. He heard himself yelling as if his exertions were a knife in his chest; but he could not silence the pain.

Suddenly, Brinn was at his side. Speaking only loud enough to be heard, the *Haruchai* reported, "Cail has found a place which may be defended."

Covenant staggered, fell thrashing among serrated grass-spears. A miasma of rot clogged his breathing. But Brinn heaved him back to his feet. Vertigo whirled through him. Clinging to Brinn's shoulder as if it were the only solid thing left in the world, he let the *Haruchai* half carry him forward.

Cail's path led to a pile of boulders rising incongruously out of the savannah, like a cairn left by Giants. It stood half again as high as the surrounding grass. Hergrom had already climbed to the crown, set Linden down in relative safety, and returned to help Sunder and Hollian ascend. Ignoring his pain, Cail joined Hergrom. Stell and Harn followed. They caught Covenant when Brinn and Ceer boosted him upward.

He scrambled to Linden's side, fought down his weakness, tried to examine her. Lifting her head, parting her hair as gently as he could with his numb fingers, he found that the wound in her scalp did not appear serious. The bleeding had almost ceased. Yet she remained unconscious. All her muscles were limp. Her face looked like the aftermath of a battle. His truncated senses could not measure her condition. He was useless to her.

Sunder and Hollian climbed up to him. Kneeling beside Linden, Sunder scrutinized her. Fatigue and trepidation dragged at his features. "Ah, Linden Avery," he breathed. "This is a sore mischance."

Covenant stifled a groan and sought to contradict the dismay in Sunder's tone. "It doesn't look that serious."

The Graveler avoided Covenant's stare. "The injury itself— Perhaps even Cail's hurt does not threaten his life. But this is a sun of pestilence." He faltered into silence.

"Ur-Lord," Hollian said tightly, "any wound is fatal under a sun of pestilence. There is no healing for the Sunbane sickness."

"*None?*" The word was torn from Covenant.

"None," Sunder rasped through his teeth. And Hollian said with pain in her gaze, "None that is known to the people of the Land. If the Clave has knowledge of a cure—"

She did not need to complete her thought. Covenant understood her; Memla was dead. Because she was honest, she had turned against the na-Mhoram; because she was brave, she had drawn the *Grim* onto herself; and because Covenant had not used his wild magic, she was dead. His fear had cost her her life.

He had cost the company even the bare possibility that she might have known how to treat Linden. And Cail.

Any wound is fatal.

And that was not all. The Coursers were gone. The quest had no supplies.

It was his fault, because he had been afraid. With power, he killed. Without power, he caused people to die.

Memla had given her life for him.

Eyes burning, he rose dangerously to his feet. The height of his perch threatened him; but he ignored it as if he were impervious to vertigo, or lost.

"Brinn!"

The *Haruchai* had ranged themselves defensively around the rocks at the level of the grass tops. Over his shoulder, Brinn said, "Ur-Lord?"

"Why did you let Memla die?"

Brinn replied with a shrug. "The choice was hers." His confidence in his own rectitude seemed immaculate. "Ceer made offer of his life. She refused."

Covenant nodded. Memla had refused. Because he had told her he could not control his ring.

He was not satisfied with Brinn's answer. The Bloodguard had once made a similar decision about Kevin—and had never forgiven themselves for the outcome. But such questions did not matter now. Memla was dead. Linden and Cail were going to die. Blinking at the heat in his eyes, he looked around him.

The quest was poised on the mound of boulders—all except Vain, who remained below, as if he were comfortable among the grass and the stench. The jungle lay out of sight to the west. In all directions, the savannah stretched to the horizons, an inland sea of gray-green, waving lightly in the breeze.

But it wore a scar of bare dirt running imponderably northward. And from this scar, a similar swath had veered toward the company's knoll. Already, the fires of the *Grim* had faded to smoke and smoldering. Freed from that peril, the creatures rushed in a straight line toward the boulders. The grass boiled as it was thrust aside, tramped down, eaten. Soon the knoll stood alone among a seethe of beasts.

Covenant could barely discern Vain. The Demondim-spawn held his ground with perfect nonchalance, and every creature which touched him died.

The *Haruchai* were ready when the attack began. As the

creatures scrambled up the rocks, Brinn and his people used
the advantage of elevation to break each assailant's antennae,
then strove to dislodge the creature so that it fell back into the
boil and was consumed.

They were surprisingly successful. Their strength, accuracy,
and balance made them effective; and the fallen beasts slowed
the rest of the attack.

But the knoll was too large; five *Haruchai* could not defend
it completely. Gradually, they were driven backward.

Covenant did not hesitate. Cold fury filled his bones like
power. Snarling at himself, he pulled the bundle from under
his belt and unwrapped the *krill* of Loric Vilesilencer.

The brightness of its gem stopped him momentarily; he had
forgotten the intensity of that white, pure light, the keenness
of the edges, the heat of the metal. A leper's fear made him
reluctant to touch the *krill* without the protection of cloth.

But then the company's need came over him like a *geas*.
His fingers were already numb, irrelevant. No burn could alter
the doom which defined him. He dropped the cloth, took the
krill in his half-hand, and went to join the *Haruchai*.

Beings like misborn Cavewights came jerking upward on
their long limbs. Their claws scored the stone; their jaws
gaped and clacked. One gouge could disembowel him; one
bite could sever an arm. Their feelers reached toward him.

Moving as if he were accursed, he began to slash at them.

The *krill* sliced their plating like bare flesh, cut through
antennae, even mandibles, as if the blade were a broadsword
with the weight and puissance of a Giant behind it. The *krill*
was a tool of Law, and the creatures were the Lawless spawn
of the Sunbane. A dull ache of fire spread up through Covenant's palm to his wrist, his arm; but he hacked and flailed
urgently, and his every stroke sent a beast to the ungentle
death of the mass below it.

Soon Sunder joined the defense. His poniard was not a
good weapon for such work; but he was sturdy, and his blade
could cripple feelers. He was unable to dislodge the beasts as
the *Haruchai* did. But often that was unnecessary. With damaged antennae, the creatures became disoriented, turned aside,
grappled with each other, toppled to the ground. And Stell or
Ceer warded him.

The attack did not falter; hundreds of creatures replaced
the scores which fell. But the company held. In time, all the
ground around the knoll was denuded of grass; and a storm of

mute rage covered the bare dirt, seeking to strike upward. But only a certain number of beasts could assail the boulders at any one moment. Against these limited numbers, the company held. Their ordeal dragged out like slow torture. Covenant's arms became leaden; he had to grip the *krill* in both hands. Sunder kept up a mutter of curses, lashing himself to continue the struggle long after he had exhausted his strength. But Hollian gave him periods of rest by taking his place, using his poniard because her dirk was too small for the task. And Vain's power helped, though he seemed unaware of what he did. The company held.

The afternoon wore on. Covenant became little more than a blank reflex. He grew numb to the passage of time, the progress of the assault. His joints were cramped with fire. Time and again, Brinn saved him from attacks he was too slow to meet.

He hardly noticed when the sun started to set, and the frenzy of the creatures began to abate. At the onset of twilight, the beasts seemed to lose purpose or direction. By ones and twos, then by scores, they scuttled away, wandering hurriedly into the grass. As dusk thickened over the savannah, the goad of the Sunbane faded. Soon all the creatures were fleeing.

Covenant stopped. His heart trembled like prostration in his chest. He was gasping for breath. He dropped the *krill* among the rocks. The knoll tilted under him. On his hands and knees, he tried to crawl up to Linden. But he could not reach her. His dizziness became suddenly violent. It whirled him out into the blind night.

Sometime after the moon had passed its apex, he was awakened by Linden's knotted retching as she went into convulsions.

He lurched upright and groped through a blur of fatigue, hunger, thirst, to try to see what was happening.

The crown of the boulders was lit by the *krill*; it had been wedged among the stones so that it shed illumination over the company. Sunder and Hollian crouched beside Linden, watching her anxiously. Ceer and Hergrom restrained her so that she would not hurt herself, as long, mad clenchings shook her muscles.

On the lower boulders, the other *Haruchai* clustered as if they were fighting each other. With a quick glance, Covenant saw Brinn, Stell, and Harn struggling to quell Cail. Like Linden, the injured *Haruchai* lay in the grip of frenetic seizures.

Seeing Covenant, Sunder rasped grimly, "The sun of pestilence has infected her wound. From this sickness none recover."

Oh, God.

A rush of panic started up in him, then shattered as he realized that Linden was gagging, choking on her tongue.

He grabbed for her face and tried to pry her jaws open. But he could not break the locking of her teeth. Her whole body sprang rigid.

"She's swallowed her tongue! Get her mouth open!"

Instantly, Ceer clinched both her wrists in his left hand. With his right, he tried to wedge open her jaws. For one heartbeat, even his strength was not enough. Then he succeeded in forcing her teeth apart. She quivered under a lash of pain. Holding her mouth open with the width of his hand, he reached deftly down her throat, cleared her tongue.

She drew breath as if she wanted to scream; but convulsions blocked the wail in her chest.

With a feral spasm, Cail hurled Brinn from him. Twisting in the air, Brinn landed lightly on the ground, came bounding upward again as Stell and Harn grappled with their kinsman.

Linden's face was ghastly in the *krill*-light. Her breathing wept in and out of her excruciated lungs.

Cail sounded as if he were asphyxiating. An obscure part of Covenant thought, He's immune to the Sunbane. There must have been poison in the spur.

He concentrated on Linden as if he could keep her alive by sheer force of will. His hand shook as he stroked her forehead, wiped the sweat away; but he could feel nothing.

"Ur-Lord," Hollian said in a stretched whisper, "I must speak of this. It must be uttered." He could not read her countenance; her face was averted from the *krill*. Out of the shadow, she breathed, "I have consulted the *lianar*. The morrow will bring a desert sun."

Covenant clung to Linden's torment, willing it to ease. "I don't give a damn."

"There is more." Hollian's tone sharpened. She was an eh-Brand, accustomed to respect. "There will be fire, as if the sun were a sun of flame. This will become a place of ill. We must flee."

"Now?"

"At once. We must return to the west—to the soil where trees grow. The earth of this grassland will be death to us."

"She's in no condition!" His sudden fury shocked the night, struck the company into a silence punctuated only by the hoarse breathing of the injured. With a wrench of his shoulders, he dismissed Hollian's warning. "I'm not going to move her."

She started to protest. Sunder interrupted her gruffly. "He is the ur-Lord."

"He is *wrong*. The truth must be met. These deaths cannot be prevented. To remain here will be death for us all."

"He is the ur-Lord." Sunder's roughness grew gentle. "Every task to which he sets his hand is impossible—yet it is accomplished. Have courage, eh-Brand."

Linden broke into another series of spasms. Watching the way her illness brutalized her, Covenant feared that every breath would be her last. But then, abruptly, her convulsions ended; she fell limp as if the puppet strings of her plight had been cut. Slowly, her respiration deepened as she sank into the sleep of exhaustion.

Cail's affliction was more advanced. The fits which wracked him went on until moonset. Brinn's people had to fight incessantly to prevent him from battering himself to death on the rocks.

"Dawn is near," Sunder murmured softly, as if he feared to disturb the stillness, feared that the sound of his voice might trigger Linden or Cail into frenzy again.

"We are too late." Hollian could not suppress her bitterness. "We must remain here. We cannot gain safety in time."

Covenant ignored both of them. He sat with Linden in his embrace and sought to believe that she would live.

No one moved. They sat in the *krill*-light while the east paled toward sunrise. A dusty glow began to silhouette the earth. All the stars were washed away. The sky modulated as brown gathered around the imminence of the dawn. The atmosphere grew palpably drier, foretelling heat.

When the sun rose, it wore a cloak of desiccation. Its touch reminded Covenant that he had not had food or fluid since the previous morning. A giddy dispassion began to revolve in him, distancing him from his fate. Linden's flagrant slumber felt like an accomplished fact in his arms.

As the Sunbane colored the savannah, the pampas grass began to melt. Its fiber turned to a dead gray sludge, and slumped to the ground like spilth. This, Covenant mused in a mood of canted detachment, was what had happened to Morinmoss. To Grimmerdhore and Garroting Deep. A desert sun had risen over them, and tens of thousands of years of sentient forest had simply dissolved into muck. *And the glory of the world becomes less than it was.* For a moment, he recovered enough passion to ache out, Damn you, Foul! It would be better if you just killed me.

In a voice like Covenant's inanition, but infinitely steadier, Brinn addressed Hollian. "Eh-Brand, you spoke of fire."

"The *lianar* spoke of fire." Both affronted dignity and nagging self-doubt marked her words. "Never have I seen such a flame in my foretelling. Do not question me. I cannot answer."

Covenant thought dimly that there was no reason for fire. The quest was without water under a desert sun. Nothing else was necessary.

The truth of Hollian's augury became clear when the sun rose high enough, and the grass sank low enough, for light to contact the bare ground around the knoll. And with the light came a faint shimmer which seemed to transmogrify the texture of the soil. The dirt began to glow.

Covenant believed that he was hallucinating.

Without warning, Vain ascended the boulders. Everyone stared at him; but his black eyes remained unfocused, private, as if he were unaware of his own intentions.

Brinn and Hergrom placed themselves to guard Covenant and Linden. But Vain stopped without acknowledging the *Haruchai* and stood gazing like a void into the blank air.

Slowly, the soil took on a reddish tinge enriched with yellow. The color deepened, hardened.

Heat radiated from the ground.

Around the edges of the clearing, the sludge started to smolder. Viscid smoke went up in wisps, then in billows which thickened steadily, clogging the atmosphere.

In moments, the muck was afire.

As it burned, smoke began to mount in other places across the savannah. Soon there were blazes everywhere.

And the bare dirt continued to darken.

The company watched tensely; even the *Haruchai* seemed to be holding their breath. Only Linden and Cail were oblivious. Vain was not. He studied Linden between the shoulders of Brinn and Hergrom, and his visage sharpened, as if vague purposes were being whetted toward clarity within him.

Numbly, Covenant studied the ground. That rich, half-orange light and heat brought up recollections. Gradually, the face of Lena's father, Trell, became vivid to him; he did not know why. He could see Trell standing like granite in Lena's home. The big Stonedownor's face was ruddy with light. Reflections gleamed in his beard—the precise color of these emanations.

Then Covenant remembered.

Graveling. Fire-stones.

Under the touch of the desert sun, this entire savannah was being transformed into a sea of graveling.

Fire consumed the sludge; and under it lay clear graveling which sent one long, silent shout of heat into the heavens.

Covenant and his companions might as well have been perched above a flow of lava.

He sat and stared as if his eyeballs had been scorched blind. He could feel death lying like a familiar in his arms.

Memla had sacrificed herself. Linden and Cail were going to die. Everyone was going to die.

Vain gave no hint of his intent. The suddenness of his movement took even the wary *Haruchai* by surprise. With a frightening swiftness, he thrust Brinn and Hergrom aside and stepped between them toward Covenant and Linden.

Hergrom caught himself on an outcropping of rock. Brinn was saved from a fall into the graveling only by the celerity with which Ceer grabbed for him.

Effortlessly, Vain took Linden from Covenant's arms.

Stell surged forward, pounded Vain between the eyes. The Demondim-spawn did not react; he went about his purpose as if he had not been touched. Stell was knocked back against Harn.

Cradling Linden gently, Vain stepped to the eastern edge of the mound and leaped down into the fire-stones.

"*Vain!*"

Covenant was on his feet. His hearing roared as if the heat had become a gale. Venom pulsed in his veins. He wanted wild magic, wanted to strike—!

But if he hit Vain, hurt him, the Demondim-spawn might drop Linden into the graveling.

Linden!

Vain paid no heed to the danger behind him. Firmly, surely, he strode away.

At that instant, Hergrom sprang pantherish from the boulders. At the farthest stretch of his leap, he impacted against Vain's shoulders.

The Demondim-spawn did not even stumble. He walked on across the graveling with Linden held before him and Hergrom clinging to his back as if he were unconscious of them both.

Covenant's shouting died in his chest. He was hardly aware that Brinn and Sunder were holding his arms as if to prevent him from pursuing Vain.

"He does not feel the fire," Brinn remarked distantly. "Perhaps he will save her. Perhaps he intends to save her."

To save—? Covenant sagged. Was it possible? The muscles of his face hurt, but he could not unclench his grimace. To save her so that she could serve Lord Foul? "Then why"—his voice knotted —"didn't he help her before? During the *Grim*?"

Brinn shrugged. "Perhaps he saw then that his aid was not needed. He acts now to save her because we are helpless."

Vain? Covenant panted. No. He could not suppress the tremors in him. "We're not helpless." It was unbearable. Not even a leper could bear it. *We are not helpless.*

He cast one abrupt glance toward Vain. The Demondim-spawn was running, fading into the shimmer of the graveling.

Covenant wrenched free of Brinn and Sunder. He confronted his companions. The effort to control his trembling made him savage. "Ceer. Give me the *rukh*."

Sunder scowled. Hollian's eyes widened as if she felt an intuitive hope or fear. But the *Haruchai* showed no surprise. Ceer took Memla's *rukh* from his tunic and handed it to Covenant.

With a jerk, Covenant thrust the iron toward Sunder. "All right. You're the Graveler. Use it."

Sunder's lips formed words without sound: Use it?

"Call the Coursers back. They're bred to the Sunbane. They can carry us out of here."

The Graveler breathed a strangled protest. "Covenant!"

Covenant jabbed the *rukh* against Sunder's chest. "Do it. I can't. I don't know the Sunbane the way you do. I can't touch it. I'm a leper."

"And I am not a Rider!"

"I don't care." Covenant clinched ire around his dread.

"We're all going to die. Maybe I don't count. But you do. Hollian does. You know the truth about the Clave." Again, he punched Sunder with the *rukh*. "*Use* it."

The heat spread sweat across Sunder's face, made his features look like they were about to melt like the grass. Desperately, he turned an imploring gaze toward Hollian.

She touched his scarred forearm. The stature of her calling was upon her. "Sunder," she said quietly. "Graveler. Perhaps it may be done. Surely the Sunstone empowers you to the attempt. And I will aid you as I can. Through the *lianar*, I am able to perceive the state of the Sunbane. It may be that I can guide you to mastery."

For a moment, they held each other's eyes, measuring what they saw. Then Sunder swung back to Covenant. The Graveler's expression was rent by fear of failure, by instinctive loathing for anything which belonged to the Clave. But he accepted the *rukh*.

Grimly, he climbed to sit atop the highest boulder, near the white radiance of the *krill*.

Hollian stood on a lower rock so that her head was level with his. She watched gravely as he set his *orcrest* in his lap, then fumbled to uncap the hollow handle of the *rukh*.

Covenant's legs quavered as if they could no longer bear the weight of who he was. But he braced himself on the rocks, remained erect like a witness and a demand.

Sunder poured the last fluid from the *rukh* into his hand. Hollian placed her palm in his, let it rest there for a moment, sharing the blood like a gesture of comradeship. Then she wrapped her stained fingers around the *lianar*, and began to chant softly to herself. Sunder rubbed his hands together, dabbed red onto his forehead and cheeks, then picked up the Sunstone.

The rigid accents of his invocation formed a counterpoint to her lilting murmur. Together, they wove the silence into a skein of Sunbane-power: bloodshed and fire.

Soon, his familiar vermeil shaft shot like a quarrel toward the sun. A crepitation like the discharge of slow lightning made the air squirm.

He lifted the *rukh* and held it so that the Sunstone's beam ran along the iron. His knuckles whitened, cording the backs of his hands.

Delicate flames opened like buds along the *lianar*. Hollian closed her eyes. Her fire turned slowly to the color of the sun's brown aura, began to put out tendrils. One of them reached Sunder's hands. It wound around his grasp, then started to climb the *rukh* and the Sunstone shaft.

He blinked fiercely at the sweat in his eyes, glared as if the *rukh* were an adder he could neither hold nor release.

The poignance in Covenant's chest told him that he had forgotten to breathe. When he forced himself to inhale, he seemed to suck in vertigo from the air. Only his braced arms kept him from losing his balance.

None of the *Haruchai* were watching Sunder and Hollian. Cail had gone into convulsions. The others fought to keep him still.

Memories of Linden wrung Covenant's guts. He shut his eyes against the nausea.

He looked up again when the chanting ended. Sunder's shaft and Hollian's flame vanished. The Stonedownors clung to each other. The Graveler's shoulders shook.

Covenant knelt without knowing how he had lost his feet.

When Sunder spoke, his voice was muffled against Hollian's neck. "After all, it is not greatly difficult to be a Rider. I am attuned to the *rukh*. The Coursers are distant. But they have heard. They will come."

Eventually, Cail's seizure receded. For a while, he regained consciousness; but he spoke in the alien tongue of the *Haruchai*, and Covenant did not understand what he said.

The first of the great beasts returned shortly before noon. By then, thirst and hunger had reduced Covenant to stupefaction; he could not focus his eyes to see which of the Coursers it was, or whether the animal still bore any supplies. But Brinn reported, "It is Clangor, the Courser which assailed Linden Avery. It limps. Its chest is burned. But it suffers no harm from the graveling." A moment later, he added, "Its burdens are intact."

Intact, Covenant thought dizzily. He peered through the haze as Ceer and Stell leaped down to the Courser, then returned carrying sacks of water and food. Oh dear God.

By the time he and the Stonedownors had satisfied the first desperation of their thirst and had begun to eat a meal, Annoy came galloping from the south. Like Clangor, it was unscathed by the graveling; but it skittered uncomfortably around the knoll, champing to escape the fire-stones.

Clash and Clang also returned. Sunder frowned at them as

if he did not like the pride he felt in what he had achieved; but Hollian's smile shone.

At once, the *Haruchai* began to prepare for departure.

Using the piece of cloth he had discarded, Covenant re-wrapped the *krill* and tucked it under his belt. Then he descended the boulders to the level of the Coursers' backs.

At close range, the heat of the graveling felt severe enough to char his flesh. It triggered involuntary memories of Hotash Slay and Saltheart Foamfollower. The Giant had spent himself in lava and agony to help Covenant.

Distrusting the Coursers and himself, Covenant could not leap the small distance to a mount. No more, he yearned. Don't let any more friends die for me. He had to cling where he was, squinting against the radiance, until the *Haruchai* could help him.

In a moment, Ceer and Brinn joined him, carrying Cail. Sunder raised the *rukh*, uncertain of his mastery; but the Coursers obeyed, crowding close to the knoll. Leaving Cail, Ceer stepped to Annoy's back. Harn tossed the sacks to him. He placed them across Annoy's huge withers, then accepted Cail from Brinn.

Cail's arm was livid and suppurating badly. It made Covenant groan. Cail needed Linden. She was a doctor.

She was as sick as the *Haruchai*.

Practicing his control, Sunder sent Annoy out of the way of the other Coursers. Then Harn and Hollian mounted Clangor. The Graveler joined Stell on Clang. Before Covenant could suppress his dread, Brinn lifted him onto Clash.

He dropped to the broad back, knotted his fists in Clash's hair. Heat blasted at him like slow roasting and suffocation. But he fought to raise his voice. "Find Vain. Fast."

With a gesture, Sunder launched the beasts eastward. They galloped away through air burnished orange by graveling.

Clang bore Sunder and the *rukh* at a staggering pace; but the other mounts matched it. Even Clangor, oozing pain from its wound, did not fall behind; it ran like a storm-wind with frenzy in its red eyes. It had been formed by the power of the Banefire to obey any *rukh*. It could not refuse Sunder's authority.

Covenant could not gauge their speed; he could hardly keep his eyes open against the sharp heat, hardly breathe. He only knew that he was traveling swiftly. But he did not know how fast Vain could run. The Demondim-spawn's lead was as long as the morning.

Wind scorched his face. His clothes felt hot on his skin, as if the fabric had begun to smolder. He wore warm sweat down the length of his body. His eyes bled tears against the shine and heat of the graveling. But the Coursers ran as if they were being borne by the passion of the fire-stones. Hollian clung to Harn's back. Sunder hunched over Clang's neck. The *Haruchai* rode with magisterial detachment. And the Coursers ran.

The graveling unfurled as if it would never end. Fire deepened the sky, colored the heavens with molten grandeur. Through the haze, the sun's coronal looked like an outer ring of incandescence. The entire savannah was a bed of coals; the Coursers were traversing an accentuated hell. But Sunder had mastered the *rukh*. While he lived, the beasts could not falter.

They did not. They ran as if they had been born in flames. Smoothly, indefatigably, they swept the leagues behind them like dead leaves into a furnace.

Covenant's breathing sobbed, not because he lacked air, but rather because his lungs were being seared. He began to have visions of Glimmermere, the cool tarn tinged with Earthpower. His bones throbbed to inhale water. And the Coursers ran.

When they broke out of the graveling onto hard dirt, the suddenness of the change made the desert air feel like bliss. It snatched his head up. Relief slammed into his chest like a polar wind. In an instant, the Coursers were clattering across dead, sun-baked soil, raising pennons of dust. The haze retreated; abruptly, the terrain had features, texture, meaning.

As his sight cleared, he saw Vain ahead of him.

The Demondim-spawn stood, black and fatal, on the bank of a gully which twisted emptily across the company's way. The dull iron bands of the Staff of Law emphasized his midnight form. He watched the Coursers thunder toward him as if he had been waiting for them.

He was alone.

Alone?

Covenant tumbled from Clash's back as the beast pounded to a halt. He landed hard, sprawled across the dirt. Rolling his feet under him, he hurled himself at Vain.

"What have you done with her?"

Vain did not move: Covenant crashed into the Demondim-spawn, recoiled as if he had hit a wall of obsidian.

The next moment, Hergrom appeared out of the gully. He seemed uninjured, though his raiment had been singed by the graveling. Without expression, as if he did not deign to judge Covenant's precipitation, he said, "She is here. In the shade."

Covenant surged past him, jumped down into the gully.

The dry watercourse was not deep. He landed in sand and whirled, searching for Linden.

She lay on her back under the shadow of the gully wall. Her skin seemed faintly red in the dimmer light; she had been so close to the graveling. He could see her as clearly as if she were engraved on his mind: her raw color, the streaks of sweat in her wheaten hair, the frown scar between her brows like an expostulation against the life she had lived.

She was in convulsions. Her heels drummed the sand; her fingers attacked the ground on either side; spasms racked her body, arched her back. A skull-grin clinched her face. Small gasps whimpered through her teeth like shreds of pain.

Covenant dove to her side, gripped her shoulders to restrain her arms. He could not make a sound, could not thrust words past his panic.

Sunder and Hollian joined him, followed by Harn and Hergrom. Brinn, Ceer, and Stell came a moment later, bearing Cail. He, too, was in the throes of another seizure.

Sunder rested a hand on Covenant's shoulder. "It is the Sunbane sickness," he said softly. "I am sorry. She cannot endure."

Her whimpering turned to a rasp in her throat like a death-rattle. She seemed to be groaning, "Covenant."

Linden! he moaned. I can't help you!

Abruptly, her eyes snapped open, staring wildly. They gaped over the rictus which bared her teeth.

"Cove—" Her throat worked as the muscles knotted, released. Her jaws were locked together like the grip of a vise. Her eyes glared white delirium at him. "Help—"

Her efforts to speak burned his heart. "I don't—" He was choking. "Don't know how."

Her lips stretched as if she wanted to sink her teeth into the skin of his cheek. Her neck cords stood out like bone. She had to force the word past her seizure by sheer savagery.

"Voure."

"What?" He clung to her. "*Voure*?"

"Give—" Her extremity cut him like a sword. "*Voure*."

The sap that warded off insects? His orbs were as dry as fever. "You're delirious."

"*No*." The intensity of her groan pierced the air. "Mind—" Her wild, white stare demanded, beseeched. With every scrap of her determination, she fought her throat. "Clear." The strain aggravated her convulsions. Her body kicked against his weight as if she were being buried alive. "I—" For an instant, she dissolved into whimpers. But she rallied, squeezed out, "Feel."

Feel? he panted. Feel what?

"*Voure*."

For one more horrific moment, he hung on the verge of understanding her. Then he had it.

Feel!

"Brinn!" he barked over his shoulder. "Get the *voure*!"

Feel! Linden could feel. She had the Land-born health sense; she could perceive the nature of her illness, understand it precisely. And the *voure* as well. She knew what she needed.

The angle of her stare warned him. With a jolt, he realized that no one had moved, that Brinn was not obeying him.

"Covenant," Sunder murmured painfully. "Ur-Lord. She— I beg you to hear me. She has the Sunbane sickness. She knows not what she says. She—"

"Brinn." Covenant spoke softly, but his lucid passion sliced through Sunder's dissuasion. "Her mind is clear. She knows exactly what she's saying. Get the *voure*."

Still the *Haruchai* did not comply. "Ur-Lord," he said, "the Graveler has knowledge of this sickness."

Covenant had to release Linden's arms, clench his fists against his forehead to keep from screaming. "The only reason"— his voice juddered like a cable in a high wind —"Kevin Landwaster was able to perform the Ritual of Desecration, destroy all the life of the Land for hundreds of years, was because the Bloodguard stood by and let him do it. He ordered them not to do anything, and he had knowledge, so they obeyed. For the rest of their lives, their Vow was corrupt, and they didn't know it. They didn't even know they were tainted until Lord Foul rubbed their noses in it. Until he proved he could make them serve him." Foul had maimed three of them to make them resemble Covenant. "Are you

going to just stand there again and let more people die?"
Abruptly, his control shattered. He hammered the sand with
his fists. *"Get the VOURE!"*

Brinn glanced at Sunder, at Cail. For a moment, he seemed
to hesitate. Then he sprang from the gully toward the Coursers.

He was back almost at once, carrying Memla's leather flask
of *voure*. With an air of disinterest, as if he eschewed responsibility, he handed it to Covenant.

Trembling, Covenant unstopped the flask. He had to apply
a crushing force of will to steady his hands so that he could
pour just a few drops through Linden's teeth. Then he
watched in a trance of dread and hope as she fought to
swallow.

Her back arched, went slack as if she had broken her
spine.

His gaze darkened. The world spun in his head. His mind
became the swooping and plunge of condors. He could not
see, could not think, until he heard her whisper, "Now Cail."

The *Haruchai* responded immediately. Her understanding
of Cail's plight demonstrated her clarity of mind. Brinn took
the flask, hurried to Cail's side. With Stell's help, he forced
some of the *voure* between Cail's locked jaws.

Relaxation spread through Linden, muscle by muscle. Her
breathing eased; the cords of her neck loosened. One by one,
her fingers uncurled. Covenant lifted her hand, folded her
broken nails in his clasp, as he watched the rigor slipping out
of her. Her legs became limp along the sand. He held to her
hand because he could not tell whether she were recovering or
dying.

Then he knew. When Brinn came over to him and announced without inflection, "The *voure* is efficacious. He will
mend," she gave a low sigh of relief.

TWENTY-THREE: Sarangrave Flat

COVENANT watched her while she slept, human and frail, until some time after sunset. Then, in the light of a campfire built by the *Haruchai*, he roused her. She was too weak for solid food, so he fed her *metheglin* diluted with water.

She was recovering. Even his blunt sight could not be mistaken about it. When she went back to sleep, he stretched out on the sand near her, and fell almost instantly into dreams.

They were dreams in which wild magic raged, savage and irremediably destructive. Nothing could be stopped, and every flare of power was the Despiser's glee. Covenant himself became a waster of the world, became Kevin on a scale surpassing all conceivable Desecrations. The white fire came from the passions which made him who he was, and he could not—!

But the stirring of the company awakened him well before dawn. Sweating in the desert chill, he climbed to his feet and looked around. The embers of the fire revealed that Linden was sitting up, with her back against the gully wall. Hergrom attended her soundlessly, giving her food.

She met Covenant's gaze. He could not read her expression in the dim light, did not know where he stood with her. His sight seemed occluded by the afterimages of nightmare. But the obscurity and importance of her face drew him to her. He squatted before her, studied her mien. After a moment, he murmured to explain himself, "I thought you were finished."

"I thought," she replied in a restrained voice, "I was never going to make you understand."

"I know." What else could he say? But the inadequacy of his responses shamed him. He felt so unable to reach her.

But while he fretted against his limitations, her hand came to him, touched the tangle of his beard. Her tone thickened. "It makes you look older."

One of the *Haruchai* began to rebuild the fire. A red gleam reflected from her wet eyes as if they were aggravated by coals, were bits of fire in her mind. She went on speaking, fighting the emotion in her throat.

"You wanted me to look at Vain." She nodded toward the Demondim-spawn; he stood across the gully from her. "I've tried. But I don't understand. He isn't alive. He's got so much power, and it's imperative. But it's—it's inanimate. Like your ring. He could be anything."

Her hand covered her eyes. For a moment, she could not steady herself. "Covenant, it hurts. It hurts to see him. It hurts to see anything." Reflections formed orange-red beads below the shadow of her hand.

He wanted to put his arms around her; but he knew that was not the comfort she needed. A Raver had touched her, had impaled her soul. Gibbon had told her that her health sense would destroy her. Gruffly, he answered, "It saved your life."

Her shoulders clenched.

"It saved Cail's life."

She shuddered, dropped her hand, let him see her eyes streaming in the new light of the fire. "It saved *your* life."

He gazed at her as squarely as he could, but said nothing, gave her all the time she required.

"After Crystal Stonedown." The words came huskily past her lips. "You were dying. I didn't know what to do." A grimace embittered her mouth. "Even if I'd had my bag— Take away hospitals, labs, equipment, and doctors aren't much good." But a moment later she swallowed her insufficiency. "I didn't know what else to do. So I went inside you. I felt your heart and your blood and your lungs and your nerves— Your sickness. I kept you alive. Until Hollian was able to help you."

Her eyes left his, wandered the gully like guilt. "It was horrible. To feel all that ill. *Taste* it. As if I were the one who was sick. It was like breathing gangrene." Her forehead knotted in revulsion or grief; but she forced her gaze back to his visage. "I swore I would never do anything like that again as long as I lived."

Pain made him bow his head. He glared into the shadows between them. A long moment passed before he could say without anger, "My leprosy is that disgusting to you."

"No." Her denial jerked his eyes up again. "It wasn't leprosy. It was venom."

Before he could absorb her asseveration, she continued, "It's still in you. It's growing. That's why it's so hard to look at you." Fighting not to weep, she said hoarsely, "I can't keep it out. Any of it. The Sunbane gets inside me. I can't keep it out. You talk about desecration. Everything desecrates *me*."

What can I do? he groaned. Why did you follow me? Why did you try to save my life? Why doesn't my leprosy disgust you? But aloud he tried to give her answers, rather than questions. "That's how Foul works. He tries to turn hope into despair. Strength into weakness. He attacks things that are precious, and tries to make them evil." The Despiser had used Kevin's love of the Land, used the Bloodguard's service, the Giants' fidelity, used Elena's passion, to corrupt them all. And Linden had looked at Vain because he, Covenant, had asked it of her. "But that knife cuts both ways. Every time he tries to hurt us is an opportunity to fight him. We have to find the strength of our weakness. Make hope out of despair.

"Linden." He reached out with his half-hand, took one of her hands, gripped it. "It doesn't do any good to try to hide from him." *It boots nothing to avoid his snares.* "If you close your eyes, you'll just get weaker. We have to accept who we are. And deny him." But his fingers were numb; he could not tell whether or not she answered his clasp.

Her head had fallen forward. Her hair hid her face.

"Linden, it saved your *life*."

"No." Her voice seemed to be muffled by the predawn dusk and the shadows. "You saved my life. I don't have any power. All I can do is see." She pulled her hand away. "Leave me alone," she breathed. "It's too much. I'll try."

He wanted to protest. But her appeal moved him. Aching stiffly in all his joints, he stood up and went to the fire for warmth.

Looking vaguely around the gully, he noticed the Stonedownors. The sight of them stopped him.

They sat a short distance away. Sunder held the *rukh*. Faint red flames licked the triangle. Hollian supported him as she had when he had first attuned himself to the *rukh*.

Covenant could not guess what they were doing. He had not paid any attention to them for too long, had no idea what they were thinking.

Shortly, they dropped their fires. For a moment, they sat gazing at each other, holding hands as if they needed courage.

"It cannot be regretted." Her whisper wafted up the gully like a voice of starlight. "We must bear what comes as we can."

"Yes," Sunder muttered. "As we can." Then his tone softened. "I can bear much—with you." As they rose to their feet, he drew her to him, kissed her forehead.

Covenant looked away, feeling like an intruder. But the Stonedownors came straight to him; and Sunder addressed him with an air of grim purpose. "Ur-Lord, this must be told. From the moment of your request"— he stressed the word ironically —"that I take up this *rukh*, there has been a fear in me. While Memla held her *rukh*, the Clave knew her. Therefore the *Grim* came upon us. I feared that in gaining mastery of her *rukh* I, too, would become known to the Clave.

"Covenant—" He faltered for only an instant. "My fear is true. We have ascertained it. I lack the skill to read the purpose of the Clave—but I have felt their touch, and know that I am exposed to them."

"Ur-Lord," asked Hollian quietly, "what must we do?"

"Just what we've been doing." Covenant hardly heard her, hardly heard his answer. "Run. Fight, if we have to." He was remembering Linden's face in convulsions, her rigid mouth, the sweat streaks in her hair. And wild magic. "Live."

Fearing that he was about to lose control, he turned away.

Who was he, to talk to others about living and striving, when he could not even handle the frightening growth of his own power? The venom! It was part of him now. As the wild magic became more possible to him, everything else seemed more and more impossible. He was so capable of destruction. And incapable of anything else.

He picked up a jug of *metheglin* and drank deeply to keep himself from groaning aloud.

He was thinking, Power corrupts. Because it is unsure. It is not enough. Or it is too much. It teaches doubt. Doubt makes violence.

The pressure for power was growing in him. Parts of him were hungry for the rage of wild fire.

For a time, he was so afraid of himself, of the consequences of his own passions, that he could not eat. He drank the thick mead and stared into the flames, trying to believe that he would be able to contain himself.

He had killed twenty-one people. They were vivid to him now in the approaching dawn. Twenty-one! Men and women whose only crime had been that their lives had been deformed by a Raver.

When he raised his head, he found Linden standing near him.

She was insecure on her feet, still extremely weak; but she was able to hold herself upright. She gazed at him soberly. As he dropped his eyes, she said with an echo of her old severity, "You should eat something."

He could not refuse her. He picked up a piece of dried meat. She nodded, then moved woodenly away to examine Cail. Covenant chewed abstractly while he watched her.

Cail appeared to be both well and ill. He seemed to have recovered from the Sunbane sickness, regained his native solidity and composure. But his injury was still hotly infected; *voure* had no efficacy against the poison of the Courser's spur.

Linden glared at the wound as if it wrung her nerves, then demanded fire and boiling water. Hergrom and Ceer obeyed without comment. While the water heated, she borrowed Hollian's dirk, burned it clean in the flames, then used it to lance Cail's infection. He bore the pain stoically; only a slight tension between his brows betrayed what he felt. Blood and yellow fluid splashed a stain onto the sand. Her hands were precise in spite of her weakness. She knew exactly where and how deeply to cut.

When the water was ready, she obtained a blanket from Brinn. Slashing the material into strips, she used some of them to wash out the wound; with others, she made a crude bandage. Fine beads of sweat mirrored the firelight from Cail's forehead; but he did not wince. He did not appear to be breathing.

"You'll be all right as soon as we stop the infection." Her voice sounded impersonal, as if she were reading from some medical tome. "You're healthy enough for any five people." Then her severity frayed. "This is going to hurt. If I could think of any way to kill the pain, I'd do it. But I can't. I left everything in my bag."

"Have no concern, Linden Avery," Cail replied evenly. "I am well. I will serve you."

"Serve yourself!" she grated at once. "Take care of that arm." As she spoke, she made sure that his bandage was secure. Then she poured boiling water over the fabric.

Cail made no sound. She stumbled to her feet, moved away

from him and sat down against the gully wall, as if she could not bear the sight of his courage.

A moment later, Vain caught Covenant's attention. The first light of the sun touched Vain's head, etched it out of the gloaming—a cynosure of blackness and secrets. Sunder and Hollian went quickly to find rock. Covenant helped Linden erect. The *Haruchai* stood. All the company faced the dawn.

The sun broached the rim of the gully, wearing brown like the cerements of the world. Thirst and hallucination, bleached bones, fever-blisters. But Linden gasped involuntarily, "It's weaker!"

Then, before Covenant could grasp what she meant, she groaned in disappointment. "No. I must be losing my mind. It hasn't changed."

Changed? Her bitterness left him in a whirl of anxiety as the quest broke camp, mounted the Coursers, and set off eastward. Was she so badly stressed by fear that she could no longer trust her eyes? In her convulsions, sweat had darkened her hair like streaks of damp anguish. But she seemed to be recovering. Her wound had been relatively minor. The company rode the sun-trammeled wasteland of the North Plains as if they were traversing an anvil. Why did he know so little about her?

But the next morning she was steadier, surer. She carried her head as if it had ceased to pain her. When she faced the dawn and saw the third desert sun rise, her whole body tensed. "I was right," she gritted. "It *is* weaker." A moment later, she cried, "There!" Her arm accused the horizon. "Did you see it? Right there, it changed! It was weaker and then it became as strong as ever. As if it crossed a boundary."

No one spoke. Sunder and Hollian watched Linden as if they feared that the Sunbane sickness had affected her mind. The *Haruchai* gazed at her without expression.

"I saw it." Her voice stiffened. "I'm not crazy."

Covenant winced. "We don't have your eyes."

She glared at him for an instant, then turned on her heel and strode away toward the waiting Coursers.

Now she rode as if she were angry. In spite of the dry brutality of the sun and the strain of clinging to Clash's back, her strength was returning. And with it came ire. Her ability to see had already cost her so much; and now her companions appeared to doubt what she saw. Covenant himself half disbelieved her. Any weakening of the Sunbane was a sign of hope. Surely therefore it was false? After what she had been through?

When the company stopped for the night, she ate a meal, tended Cail's arm, and set herself to sleep. But long before dawn, she was pacing the dead shale as if she were telling the moments until a revelation. Her tension articulated clearly how much she needed to be right, how sorely her exacerbated soul needed relief.

That morning, the sun rose in red pestilence. It tinged the stark outlines of the wilderland crimson, making the desert roseate, lovely, and strange, like a gilded burial ground; but though he strained his sight until his brain danced with images of fire, Covenant could not descry any lessening of the Sunbane. Yet Linden gave a fierce nod as if she had been vindicated. And after a moment, Brinn said impassively, "The Chosen is farsighted." He used her title like a recognition of power. "The corruption about the sun has lessened."

"I am surpassed," Sunder muttered in frustration. "I do not see this lessening."

"You will," Linden replied. "We're getting closer."

Covenant was suddenly dizzy with hope. "Closer to what?" Was the Sunbane failing?

"Inquire of the Chosen." Brinn's shrug disavowed all responsibility for what he saw. "We know nothing of this."

Covenant turned to her.

"I'll tell you." She did not meet his gaze. "When I'm sure."

He swallowed a curse, gritted himself still. *It's too much*, she had said. *I'll try.* He understood. She was trying. She wanted to trust what she saw and feared to be misled, to be hurt again. With difficulty, he left her alone.

She continued to stare eastward while the *Haruchai* distributed food, water, and *voure*. She ate heedlessly, ignoring Brinn's people as they readied the Coursers. But then, just as Sunder brought the beasts forward, her arm stabbed out, and she barked, "There!"

Brinn glanced at the sun. "Yes. The corruption regains its strength."

Covenant groaned to himself. No wonder she did not wish to explain what she saw. How could she bear it?

Morosely, he mounted Clash behind Linden and Brinn. The quest moved out across the ragged wasteland.

Under this sun, the desert became a place of silence and

scorpions. Only the rattle of the Coursers' hooves punctuated the windless air; and soon that noise became part of the silence as well. Insects scuttled over the rocks, or waded the sand, and made no sound. The sky was as empty of life as a tomb. Slowly, Covenant's mood became red and fatal. The Plains seemed eerie with all the blood he had shed. Involuntarily, he toyed with his ring, turning it around his finger as if his bones itched for fire. Yet he loathed killing, loathed himself. And he was afraid.

We have to accept who we are. Where had he learned the arrogance or at least the insensitivity to say such things?

That night, his memories and dreams made his skin burn as if he were eager for immolation, for a chance to anneal his old guilt in flame. Lena filled his sight as if she had been chiseled on the backs of his eyes. A child, in spite of her body's new maturity. He had struck her, knotted his hands in her shift and rent— The memory of her scream was distilled nightmare to him. *A moral leper.*

You are mine.

He was a creature of wild magic and doubt; and the long night, like the whole Land stretched helpless under the Sunbane, was also a desert.

But the next morning, when the sun rose in its crimson infestation, he, too, could see that its aurora was weaker. It seemed pale, almost uncertain. Sunder and Hollian could see it as well.

And this time the weakness did not vanish until midmorning. Ascending from the first quarter of the sky, the aura crossed a threshold; and the Sunbane closed over the Plains like a lid. Intuitions tried to clarify themselves in Covenant's head; he felt that he should have been able to name them. But he could not. Lacking Linden's eyes, he seemed also to lack the ability to interpret what he saw. A strange blindness—

That evening, the company reached Landsdrop.

Now Covenant knew where he was. Landsdrop was the precipice which separated the Upper Land in the west from the Lower Land in the east. It stretched roughly north-northwest from deep in the Southron Range far toward the unexplored Northron Climbs. Many leagues south of him, Mount Thunder, ancient Gravin Threndor, crouched against the cliff, kneeling with its knees on the Lower Land and its elbows on the Upper. Deep in its dark roots lay the place where the

Illearth Stone had been found. And deep in its dark heart was the secret chamber of Kiril Threndor, where Lord Foul the Despiser now made his home.

The sun was setting as the quest halted. The shadow of Landsdrop, three or four thousand feet high in this region, obscured all the east. But Covenant knew what lay ahead. The deadly marsh of Sarangrave Flat.

In past ages, the Sarangrave had become what it was—a world of intricate waterways, exotic life, and cunning peril—through the effects of the river called the Defiles Course. This water emerged between the knees of Mount Thunder from the catacombs in the bowels of the mountain, where it had run through Wightwarrens and Demondim breeding dens, through charnals and offal pits, laboratories and forges, until it was polluted by the most irrefragable filth. As sewage spread throughout the Flat from the river, it corrupted a once-fair region, changed a marsh home for egrets and orchids into a wild haven for the misborn. During the last wars, Lord Foul had found much of the raw material for his armies in Sarangrave Flat.

Covenant knew about the Flat because at one time he had seen it for himself, from Landsdrop to the south of Mount Thunder. He had seen with Land-sharpened eyes, vision he no longer possessed. But he had other knowledge of the region as well. He had heard some things during his visits to Revelstone. And he had learned more from Runnik of the Bloodguard. At one time, Runnik had accompanied Korik and two Lords, Hyrim and Shetra, on a mission to Seareach, to ask the aid of the Giants against Lord Foul. Lord Shetra had been slain in the Sarangrave, and Runnik had barely survived to bring back the tale.

Covenant's guts squirmed at the thought of the Sarangrave under a sun of pestilence. Beyond doubt, he was going to have to tell Runnik's tale to his companions.

The *Haruchai* set camp a stone's throw from the great cliff because Covenant refused to go any closer in the dark; he already felt too susceptible to the lure of precipices. After he had eaten, fortified himself with *metheglin*, he huddled near the jumping allusions of the campfire, wrapped his memories around him, and asked the quest to listen.

Linden sat down opposite him. He wanted to feel that she was nearby; but the intervening fire distanced her. Sunder and

Hollian were vague at the edges of his sight. His attention narrowed to the crackling wood and the recollection of Runnik's tale.

Fist and faith, the Bloodguard had said. *We will not fail.* But they had failed. Covenant knew that now. They had failed, and fallen into Corruption, and died. The Vow had been broken. And the Giants had been slain.

But such things were not part of what he had to tell. To control the old ache of remembrance, he envisioned Runnik's face before him. The Bloodguard had stood, with a pang in his eyes, before High Lord Elena, Lord Mhoram, Hile Troy, and the Unbeliever. A bonfire had made the night poignant. Covenant could recall Runnik's exact words. *The attacks of the lurker. The fall of Lord Shetra.* Bloody hell.

In a dull tone, he told the essentials of that tale. When he had first seen the Sarangrave, it had been a place of fervid luxuriance and subtle death: alive with shy water-bred animals and malicious trees; adorned with pools of clear poison; waylaid with quicksand; spangled with flowers of loveliness and insanity. A place where nature had become vastly treacherous, polluted and hungry. But not evil. It was blameless in the same way that storms and predators were blameless. The Giants, who knew how to be wary, had always been able to travel the Flat.

But forty years later, when Korik's mission had looked out from Landsdrop, the Sarangrave had changed. Slumbering ill had been stirred to wakefulness. And this ill, which Runnik had called *the lurker of the Sarangrave*, had snatched Lord Shetra to her death, despite the fact that she had been under the protection of fifteen Bloodguard. Fifteen— The lurker had been alert to strength, attracted to power. First the Ranyhyn, then the Bloodguard themselves, had unwittingly brought peril down on Korik's mission. And of the messengers Korik had sent to carry the tale back to the High Lord, only Runnik had survived.

After Covenant fell silent, his companions remained still for a moment. Then Hollian asked unsurely, "May we not ride around this place of risk?"

Covenant did not raise his head. "That used to be a hundred leagues out of the way. I don't know what it is now." Had Sarangrave Flat grown or dwindled under the Sunbane?

"We have not such time," Sunder said immediately. "Do

you desire to confront a second *Grim*? The Clave reads us as
we speak of such matters. When I place my hand upon the
iron, I feel the eyes of the Banefire fixed in my heart. They
hold no benison."

"The Clave can't—" Linden began, then stopped herself.

"The Clave," Covenant responded, "kills people every day.
To keep that bloody Banefire going. How many lives do you
think a hundred leagues are going to cost?"

Hollian squirmed. "Mayhap this lurker no longer lives? The
Sunbane alters all else. Will not Sarangrave Flat be altered
also?"

"No," Linden said. But when Covenant and the Stonedownors looked at her sharply, she muttered, "I'll tell you
about it in the morning." Wrapping blankets around her as if
they were a buckler against being touched, she turned away.

For a while after Sunder and Hollian had gone to their rest,
Covenant sat and watched the fire die, striving with himself,
trying to resist the way Landsdrop plucked at the bottom of
his mind, to guess what Linden had learned about the Sunbane, to find the courage he needed for the Sarangrave.

You are mine.

He awoke, haggard and power-haunted, shortly before
dawn and found that Linden and the Stonedownors, with
Cail, Harn, and Stell, had already left their beds to stand on
the edge of Landsdrop. The air was cold; and his face felt stiff
and dirty, as if his beard were the grip of his dreams, clutching his visage with unclean fingers. Shivering, he arose,
slapped his arms to warm them, then accepted a drink of
metheglin from Brinn.

As Covenant drank, Brinn said, "Ur-Lord."

His manner caught Covenant's attention like a hand on his
shoulder. Brinn looked as inscrutable as stone in the crepuscular air; yet his very posture gave an impression of importance.

"We do not trust these Coursers."

Covenant frowned. Brinn had taken him by surprise.

"The old tellers," Brinn explained, "know the tale which
Runnik of the Bloodguard told to High Lord Elena. We have
heard that the mission to the Giants of Seareach was betrayed
to the lurker of the Sarangrave by Earthpower. The Earthpower of the Ranyhyn was plain to all who rode them. And
the Vow of the Bloodguard was a thing of Earthpower.

"But we have sworn no life-shaping Vow. The wild magic need not be used. The Graveler and the eh-Brand need not employ their lore. The lurker need not be aware of us."

Covenant nodded as he caught Brinn's meaning. "The Coursers," he muttered. "Creatures of the Sunbane. You're afraid they'll give us away."

"Yes, ur-Lord."

Covenant winced, then shrugged. "We don't have any choice. We'll lose too much time on foot."

Brinn acquiesced with a slight bow. For an instant, the *Haruchai* seemed so much like Bannor that Covenant almost groaned. Bannor, too, would have voiced his doubt—and then would have accepted Covenant's decision without question. Suddenly, Covenant felt that his Dead were coming back to life, that Bannor was present in Brinn, impassive and infrangibly faithful; that Elena was reborn in Linden. The thought wrenched his heart.

But then a shout snatched him toward Landsdrop.

The sun was rising.

Gritting himself against incipient vertigo, he hurried to join his companions on the lip of the cliff.

Across the east, the sun came up in pale red, as if it had just begun to ooze blood. Light washed the top of the precipice, but left all the Lower Land dark, like a vast region where night was slowly sucked into the ground. But though he could see nothing of the Flat, the sun itself was vivid to him.

Its aura was weaker.

Weaker than it had been the previous morning.

Linden stared intently at it for a moment, then whirled and sent her gaze arcing up and down the length of Landsdrop. Covenant could hear insects burring as if they had been resurrected from the dead ground.

"By God." She was exultant. "I was *right*."

He held himself still, hardly daring to exhale.

"This is the line." She spoke in bursts of excitement, comprehension. "Landsdrop. It's like a border." Her hands traced consequences in the air. "You'll see. When the sun passes over the cliff—at noon—the Sunbane will be as strong as ever."

Covenant swallowed thickly. "Why?"

"Because the atmosphere is different. It doesn't have anything to do with the sun. That corona is an illusion. We see it because we're looking at the sun through the atmosphere. The

Sunbane is in the air. The sun doesn't change. But the *air*—"

He did not interrupt. But in the back of his mind he sifted what she said. Some of it made sense: the power required literally to change the sun was inconceivable.

"The Sunbane is like a filter. A way of warping the normal energy of the sun. Corrupting it." She aimed her words at him as if she were trying to drive insight through his blindness. "And it's all west from here. The Upper Land. What you see out there"— she jerked her head eastward —"is just spill-over. That's why it looks weak. The Clave won't be able to reach us anymore. And the Sarangrave might be just as you remember it."

All—? Covenant thought. But how? Winds shift—storms—

Linden seemed to see his question in his face. "It's in the air," she insisted. "But it's like an emanation. From the ground. It must have something to do with the Earthpower you keep talking about. It's a corruption of the Earthpower."

A corruption of the Earthpower! At those words, his head reeled, and his own vague intuitions came into focus. She was right. Absolutely. He should have been able to figure it out for himself. The Staff of Law had been destroyed—

And Lord Foul had made his new home in Mount Thunder, which crouched on the edge of Landsdrop, facing west. Naturally, the Despiser would concentrate his Sunbane on the Upper Land. Most of the east already lay under his power. It was all so clear. Only a blind man could fail to see such things.

For a long moment, other facets of the revelation consumed him. Lord Foul had turned the Earthpower itself against the Land. The Sunbane was limited in its reach. But if it became intense enough, deep enough—

But then he seemed to hear for the first time something else Linden had said. *The Sarangrave might be*—

Bloody hell! He forced himself into motion, drove his reluctant bones toward Landsdrop so that he could look over the edge.

The shadow of the horizon had already descended halfway down the cliff. Faint, pink light began to reflect off the waters of the Sarangrave. Pale jewels, rosy and tenuous, spread across the bottom of the shadow, winking together to form reticular lines, intaglios, like a map of the vanishing night. Or a snare. As the sun rose, the gems yellowed and grew more intricate. In links and interstices, they articulated the venous life of the Flat—explication, trap, and anatomy in one. Then all the waterways burned white, and the sun itself shone into Sarangrave Flat.

After five days in the wasted plains, Covenant felt that the lush green and water below him were exquisite, lovely and fascinating, as only adders and belladonna could be. But Linden stood beside him, staring white-eyed at the marsh. Her lips said over and over again, Oh, my God. But the words made no sound.

Covenant's heart turned over in fear. "What do you see?"

"Do you want to go down there?" Horror strangled her voice. "Are you crazy?"

"Linden!" he snapped, as if her dread were an accusation he could not tolerate. The backs of his hands burned venomously, lusting of their own volition to strike her. Was she blind to the pressures building in him? Deaf to the victims of the Clave? "I can't see what you see."

"I'm a doctor," she panted as if she were bleeding internally. "Or I was. I can't bear all this *evil*."

No! His anger vanished at the sight of her distress. Don't say that. You'll damn us both. "I understand. Better than anybody. Tell me what it is."

She did not raise her eyes, would not look at him. "It's alive." Her voice was a whisper of anguish. "The whole thing's alive." Gibbon had promised her that she would destroy the Land. "It's hungry." Covenant knew nothing about her. "It's like a Raver."

A Raver? He wanted to shout, What kind of person are you? Why did Foul choose you? But he crushed himself to quietness. "*Is* it a Raver?"

She shook her head. She went on shaking her head, as if she could not reach the end of all the things she wanted to deny. "Ravers are more—" She had to search herself for an adequate description. "More specific. Self-conscious. But it's still *possession*." She said that word as if it sickened her. Her hands fumbled toward her mouth. "Help me."

"No." He did not mean to refuse her; his arms ached to hold her. But that was not what she needed. "You can stand it. That old man chose you for a reason." Groping for ways to succor her, he said, "Concentrate on it. Use what you see to help yourself. Know what you're up against. Can that thing see us? Is it that specific? If we try to cross—will it know we're there?"

She closed her eyes, covered them to shut out the sight. But then she forced herself to look again. Struggling against revulsion, she jerked out, "I don't know. It's so big. If it doesn't notice us— If we don't attract its attention—"

If, he finished for her, we don't show the kind of power it feeds on. Yes. But a sudden vision of wild magic stunned him. He did not know how long he could contain the pressure. With a wrench, he made himself move, turned to Brinn, then winced at the way his voice spattered emotion. "Get the Coursers ready. Find a way down there. As soon as we eat, we're going through."

Swinging away from the *Haruchai*, he almost collided with Sunder and Hollian. They were leaning against each other as if for support. The knots at the corners of Sunder's jaw bulged; a frown of apprehension or dismay incused his forehead. The young eh-Brand's features were pale with anxiety.

The sight was momentarily more than Covenant could bear. Why was he forever so doomed to give pain? With unwanted harshness, he rasped, "You don't have to go."

Sunder stiffened. Hollian blinked at Covenant as if he had just slapped her face. But before he could master himself enough to apologize, she reached out and placed her hand on his arm. "Ur-Lord, you miscomprehend us." Her voice was like the simple gesture of her touch. "We have long and long ago given up all thought of refusing you."

With an effort, Sunder loosened the clenching of his teeth. "That is sooth. Do you not understand this of us? The peril is nothing. We have sojourned so far beyond our knowledge that all perils are become equal. And Linden Avery has said that soon we will be free of the threat of the Clave."

Covenant stared at the Graveler, at the eh-Brand.

"No, Covenant," Sunder went on. "Our concern is otherwise. We journey where the Sunbane does not obtain. We do not love the Sunbane. We are not mad. But without it—" He hesitated, then said, "What purpose do we serve? What is our value to you? We have not forgotten Andelain. The Sunbane has made us to be who we are. Perhaps under another sun we will merely burden you."

The frankness of their uncertainty touched Covenant. He was a leper; he understood perfectly what they were saying. But he believed that the Sunbane could be altered, had to believe that it was not the whole truth of their lives. How else

could he go on? Against the sudden thickness in his throat, he
said, "You're my friends. Let's try it and see."

Fumbling for self-control, he went to get something to eat.

His companions joined him. In silence, they ate as if they
were chewing the gristle of their apprehensions.

Shortly, Ceer brought word of a path down the cliff. Hergrom and Cail began to load the Coursers. Long before Covenant had found any courage, the quest was mounted and
moving.

Ceer, Hergrom, and Cail led the way on Annoy. With
Linden's care and the native health of the *Haruchai*, Cail had
essentially recovered from his wound. Brinn, Linden, and
Covenant followed on Clash. Then came Harn and Hollian on
Clangor, Stell and Sunder on Clang. Vain brought up the
rear.

They went northward for half a league to a wide trail cut
into the face of Landsdrop. This was a vestige of one of the
ancient Giantways, by which the Unhomed had traveled between Seareach and Revelstone. Covenant locked his hands in
Clash's hair, and fought his vertigo as the company began to
descend.

The sheer drop to the Lower Land pulled at him constantly.
But the trail had been made by Giants; though it angled and
doubled steeply, it was wide enough for the huge Coursers.
Still, the swing of Clash's back made him feel that he was
about to be pitched over the edge. Even during a brief rest,
when Brinn halted the company to refill the waterskins from a
rill trickling out of the cliff-face, the Flat seemed to reel
upward at him like a green storm. He spun, sweating, down
the last slope and lurched out into the humid air of the foothills with a pain in his chest, as if he had forgotten how to
breathe.

The foothills were clear for some distance before they
rolled down into the peril of the Sarangrave. Brinn took the
Coursers forward at a clattering run, as if he meant to plunge
straight into the verdant sea. But he stopped on the verge of
the thick marshgrass which lapped the hills. For a moment, he
surveyed the quest, studying Vain briefly, as if he wondered
what to expect from the Demondim-spawn. Then he addressed Linden.

"Chosen," he said with flat formality, "the old tellers say
that the Bloodguard had eyes such as yours. That is not true
of us. We understand caution. But we also understand that

your sight surpasses ours. You must watch with me, lest we fall to the snares of the Sarangrave."

Linden swallowed. Her posture was taut, keyed beyond speech by dread. But she answered with a stiff nod.

Now Clash led. Covenant glared out past Linden and Brinn, past Clash's massive head, toward the Sarangrave. The hillside descended into a breeze-ruffled lake of marshgrass, and beyond the grass stood the first gnarled brush of the Flat. Dark shrubs piled toward trees which concealed the horizon. The green of their leaves seemed vaguely poisonous under the pale red sun. In the distance, a bird cried, then fell silent. The Sarangrave was still, as if it waited with bated breath. Covenant could hardly force himself to say, "Let's go."

Brinn nudged Clash forward. Bunched together like a fist, the company entered Sarangrave Flat.

Clash stepped into the marshgrass, and immediately sank to its knees in hidden mire.

"Chosen," Brinn murmured in reproof as the Courser lumbered backward to extricate itself.

Linden winced. "Sorry. I'm not—" She took a deep breath, straightened her back. "Solid ground to the left."

Clash veered in that direction. This time, the footing held. Soon, the beast was breasting its way through chest-high grass.

An animal the size of a crocodile suddenly thrashed out from under Clash's hooves—a predator with no taste for such large prey. Clash shied; but the *rukh* steadied it quickly. Clinging to his seat, Covenant forced his gaze ahead and tried not to believe that he was riding into a morass from which there was no outlet and no escape.

Guided by Linden's senses, Brinn led the company toward the trees. In spite of past suns, the growth here was of normal size; yet even to Covenant's blunt perceptions, the atmosphere felt brooding and chancrous, like an exhalation of disease, the palpable leprosy of pollution.

As they reached the trees, the quest passed under thickening blotches of shade. At first, clear ground lay between the trunks, wind-riffled swaths of bland grass concealed things at which Covenant could not guess. But as the riders moved inward, the trees intensified. The grass gave way to shallow puddles, stretches of mud which sucked like hunger at the hooves of the Coursers. Branches and vines variegated the sky. At the edges of hearing came the sounds of water, almost subliminal, as if wary behemoths were drinking from a nearby pool. The ambience of the Sarangrave settled in Covenant's chest like a miasma.

Abruptly, an iridescent bird blundered, squalling, skyward out of the brush. His guts lurched. Sweating, he gaped about him. The jungle was complete; he could not see more than fifty feet in any direction. The Coursers followed a path which wandered out of sight between squat gray trees with cracked bark and swollen trunks. But when he looked behind him, he could see no sign of the way he had come. The Sarangrave sealed itself after the company. Somewhere not far away, he could hear water dripping, like the last blood from Marid's throat.

His companions' nerves were raw. Sunder's eyes seemed to flinch from place to place. Hollian's mien wore a look of unconscious fright, as if she were a child expecting to be terrified. Linden sat hunched forward, gripping Brinn's shoulders. Whenever she spoke, her voice was thin and tense, etiolated by her vulnerability to the ill on all sides. Yet Vain looked as careless as the accursed, untouched even by the possibility of wrong.

Covenant felt that his lungs were filling up with moisture. The Coursers seemed to share his difficulty. He could hear them snuffling stertorously. They grew restive by degrees, choppy of gait, alternately headstrong and timorous. What do they—? he began. But the question daunted him, and he did not finish it.

At noon, Brinn halted the company on a hillock covered with pimpernels, and defended on two sides by a pool of viscid sludge which smelled like tar. In it, pale flagellant creatures swam. They broke the surface, spread sluggish ripples about them, then disappeared. They looked like corpses, wan and necrotic, against the darkness of the fluid.

Then Linden pointed through the branches toward the sun. When Covenant peered at the faint aura, he saw it change, just as she had predicted. The full power of the Sunbane returned, restoring pestilence to the Sarangrave.

At the sight, a nameless chill clutched his viscera. The Sarangrave under a sun of pestilence—

Hollian's gasp yanked the company toward her. She was gaping at the pool, with her knuckles jammed between her teeth.

At every spot where sunlight touched the dark surface, pale creatures rose. They thrust blind heads into the light, seemed to yearn upward. A slight wind ruffled the trees, shifting pieces of sunshine back and forth. The creatures flailed to follow the spots of light.

When any creature had kept its head in the light for several moments, it began to expand. It swelled like ripening fruit, then split open, scattering green droplets around the pool. The droplets which fell in shadow quickly turned black and faded. But the ones which fell in light became bright—

Covenant closed his eyes; but he could not shut out the sight. Green flecks danced against red behind his eyelids. He looked again. The droplets were luminescent and baleful, like liquid emeralds. They grew as they swam, feeding on sludge and pestilence.

"Good God!" Horror compacted Linden's whisper. "We've got to get out of here!"

Her tone carried complete conviction. The *Haruchai* sprang into motion. Sunder called the Coursers forward. Cail boosted first Linden, then Covenant, upward, so that Clash would not have to kneel. Stell and Harn did the same for the Stonedownors.

Skirting the pool, Brinn guided the beasts eastward as swiftly as he dared, deeper into the toils of Sarangrave Flat.

Fortunately, the Sunbane seemed to steady the Coursers, enforcing the hold of Sunder's *rukh*. Their ponderous skittishness eased. When malformed animals scuttled out from under their hooves, or shrieking birds flapped past their heads, they remained manageable. After half a league, the riders were able to eat a meal without dismounting.

As they ate, Covenant looked for a way to question Linden. But she forestalled him. "Don't ask." Specters haunted the backs of her eyes. "It hurt. I just knew we were in danger. I don't want to know what it was."

He nodded. The plight of the company required her to accept visions which wrung her soul. She was so exposed. And he had no way to help her.

The *Haruchai* passed around a pouch of *voure*. As he dabbed the pungent sap on his face and arms, Covenant became aware that the air was alive with butterflies.

Fluttering red and blue, yellow like clean sunshine, gleams of purple and peacock-green, they clouded the spaces between the trees like particolored snow, alert and lovely. The dance of the Sarangrave— Sarangrave Flat under a sun of pestilence. The insects made him feel strangely bemused and violent. They were beautiful. And they were born of the Sunbane. The venom in him answered their entrancement as if, despite himself, he yearned to fry every lambent wing in sight. He hardly noticed when the company began moving again through the clutches of the marsh. At one time, he had watched helplessly while Wraiths died. Now every memory increased the pressure in him, urged him toward power. But in this place power was suicide.

Piloted by Brinn's caution and Linden's sight, the questors worked eastward. For a time, they traveled the edges of a water channel clogged with lilies. But then the channel cut toward the north, and they were forced to a decision. Linden said that the water was safe. Brinn feared that the lily-stems might fatally tangle the legs of the Coursers.

The choice was taken out of their hands. Hergrom directed their attention northwestward. For a moment, Covenant could see nothing through the obscure jungle. Then he caught a glimpse.

Fragments of livid green. The same green he had watched aborning in the pool of tar.

They were moving. Advancing—

Linden swore urgently. "Come on." She clinched Brinn's shoulders. "Cross. We've got to stay away from those things."

Without hesitation, Brinn sent Clash into the water.

At once, the Courser's legs were toiled in the stems. But the channel was shallow enough to give the beast a purchase on its bottom. Clash fought forward in a series of violent heaves, thrashing spray in all directions.

The other mounts followed to the east bank. Cascading water from their thick coats, they began to move as swiftly as Sarangrave Flat allowed.

Through stretches of jungle so dense that the trees seemed to claw at the quest, and the creepers dangled like garrotes. Across waving greenswards intricately beset with quagmires. Along the edges of black bogs which reeked like carrion eaters, pools which fulminated trenchantly. Into clear streams, slime-covered brooks, avenues of mud. Everywhere the riders went, animals fled from them; birds betrayed them in raucous fear or outrage; insects hove and swarmed, warded away only by the smell of *voure*.

And behind them came glimpses of green, elusive spangles, barely seen, as if the company were being stalked by emeralds.

Throughout the afternoon, they wrestled with the Flat; but, as far as Covenant could see, they gained nothing except a sense of panic. They could not outdistance those iridescent green blinks. He felt threats crawling between his shoulder blades. From time to time, his hands twitched as if they ached to fight, as if he knew no other answer to fear except violence.

In the gloaming of sunset, Brinn halted the company for supper. But no one suggested that they should make camp. The pursuit was more clearly visible now.

Green shapes the size of small children, burning inwardly like swamp lights, crept furtively through the brush—creatures of emerald stealth and purpose. Scores of them. They advanced slowly, like a malison that had no need for haste.

A thin rain began to fall, as if the ambience of the Sarangrave were sweating in eagerness.

One of the Coursers snorted. Annoy stamped its feet, tossed its head. Covenant groaned. Shetra had been one of the most potent Lords of Elena's Council, adept at power. Fifteen Bloodguard and Lord Hyrim had been unable to save her.

He clutched at his mount and yearned forward as Brinn and Linden picked their way through the drizzle.

Water slowly soaked his hair and trickled into his eyes. The susurrus of the rain filled the air like a sigh. Everything else had fallen still. The advance of the lambent green creatures was as silent as gravestones. Sunder began to mutter at the Coursers, warning them to obedience.

"Quicksand," Linden gritted. "To the right."

Through his knees, Covenant could feel Clash trembling.

For a moment, the quicksand made a sucking noise. Then the sound of the rain intensified. It became an exhalation of wet lust. Behind the drizzle, Sarangrave Flat waited.

The creatures were within a stone's throw of the company and drawing closer.

A gasp stiffened Linden. Covenant jerked his gaze ahead, searched the night.

In the distance lay a line of green lights.

It cut the quest off from the east.

The line arced to the north, spreading out to join the pursuit.

Hellfire!

The company had ridden into a snare. Flickering through

the trees and brush and rain, the fires began to contract around the riders like a noose. They were being herded southward.

Clangor stumbled to its knees, then lurched upright again, blowing fearfully.

Linden panted curses under her breath. Covenant heard them as if they were the voice of the rain. She was desperate, dangerously close to hysteria. Opening her senses in this place must have violated her like submitting to a rape.

A stream he could not see gave an undertone to the rain, then faded. For a time, the beasts slapped through shallow water between knurled old cypresses. The drizzle fell like chrism, anointing the company for sacrifice. He did not want to die like this, unshriven and without meaning. His half-hand clenched and loosened around his ring like an unconscious prophecy.

Linden continued instructing Brinn, barking what she saw into his ear as if that were her only defense against the mad night; but Covenant no longer heard her. He twisted in his seat, trying to gauge the pursuit. The rain sounded like the sizzling of water against hot gems. If the fell from Clash's back, the creatures would be on him in moments.

Out of the darkness, Sunder croaked, "Heaven and Earth!" A noise like a whimper broke from Hollian.

Covenant turned and saw that the south, too, was lined with green fires. They pent the company on all sides.

The terrain had opened; nothing obscured the encirclement. To one side, streaks of green reflected off a small pond. The water seemed to be leering. The creatures advanced like leprosy. The night held no sound except the sighing of the rain.

Clang danced like a nervous colt. Annoy snorted heavily, winced from side to side. But Sunder kept the Coursers under control. He urged them forward until they stood in the center of the green circle. There he stopped.

In a flat voice, Brinn said, "Withhold your power. The lurker must not be made to notice us."

Linden panted as if she could hardly breathe.

The creatures came seething noiselessly through the dark. The ones beyond the water stopped at its edge; the others continued to approach. They were featureless and telic, like lambent gangrene. They looked horribly like children.

Hergrom dismounted, became a shadow moving to meet

the line. For a moment, he was limned by slime fire. Rain stippled his silhouette.

Then Linden coughed, "No! Don't touch them!"

"Chosen." Brinn's voice was stone. "We must breach this snare. Hergrom will make trial, that we may learn how to fight."

"*No.*" Her urgency suffocated her. "They're acid. They're made out of acid."

Hergrom stopped.

Pieces of darkness whirled at him from Ceer's direction. He caught them, two brands from the quest's store of firewood.

Hefting them by their ends, he confronted the creatures.

Stark against the green, he swung one of the faggots like a club, striking the nearest child-form.

It burst like a wineskin, spilling emerald vitriol over the ground. His brand broke into flame.

The creatures on either side appeared not to care that one of them had fallen. But they promptly shifted to close the gap.

He struck with the other brand, ruptured another shape. Then he returned, bearing the faggots like torches.

In the firelight, Covenant saw that the company stood in an incongruously open stretch of grass. Beyond the advancing children, black trees crouched like craven ghouls. The pool on his left was larger than he had guessed it to be. Scant inches below its surface lay thick, dark mud. A quagmire.

The green creatures sought to herd the quest into it.

As if he could read Covenant's thoughts, Brinn said warningly, "Ur-Lord. Withhold."

Covenant tried to reply, could not. His lungs were full of moisture. His chest tugged at the air. He seemed to be asphyxiating on rain. Water ran down his face like blood-sweat.

No, it was not the rain. It was the air itself, strangling him.

Gradually, the drizzle changed pitch. It began to sound like a cry. From deep in the night, a wail rose toward the sky.

It was in Covenant's lungs. The very air was howling. He could hear Sunder gasp, feel Linden's muscles jerking to breathe, taste his own acrid fear.

The lurker.

Damnation!

The cry scaled upward in pitch and passion, became a

throtting scream. It clawed the depths of his chest, sucked at his courage like quicksand.

Panic.

The company stood like sacrificial cattle, trembling and dumb, while the acid-creatures advanced.

An instant later, Clash's distress became a convulsion. Bucking savagely, the Courser scattered Linden and Covenant to the grass, then sprang insanely against Clang. With Brinn clinging to its neck, Clash knocked Sunder and Stell from Clang's back. At once, the rampaging Courser tried to leap over Clang.

Covenant regained his feet in time to see Clangor go mad. Ignoring Hollian's cries and Harn's commands, the beast plunged against Clash and Clang and drove them to their knees.

Suddenly, all four mounts were possessed by a mad frenzy to attack Sunder and Stell. Annoy crashed squealing into the roil of Coursers. Ceer and Cail dove free. Stell and Harn snatched Hollian out from under Clangor's hooves.

Vain stood near the edge of the pool, watching the confusion as if it pleased him.

Covenant could not understand why the acid-creatures did not charge. They continued to approach incrementally, but did not take this opportunity to attack.

Brinn still clung to Clash's neck, fending off the teeth of the other Coursers with his free hand. The *Haruchai* appeared insignificant, helpless, amid the madness of the beasts.

Darkness gathered in Covenant like venom. It leaped instinctively toward his ring. White gold. Power.

He wanted to shout, but could not get enough air. The howl of the lurker made the rain ring, choked his chest, covered his skin with formication.

He cocked his arm. But Linden, catching his half-hand in both her fists, gasped at him like hysteria, "No!"

The force of her desperation struck him still and cold. A gelid wind blew in his mind. Use it! Pressure threatened to burst him. His ring. Don't! But the lurker—

The lurker was already aware. It was—

Why was it aware? What had alerted it?

Diving forward, Ceer joined Brinn among the Coursers. Together, the two of them began casting down sacks of supplies and bundles of firewood.

Before they could finish, the tangle abruptly clarified itself. Clangor surged to its feet, followed by Annoy. Clash and Clang heaved upright.

Driven mad by the rain and the piercing shriek of the lurker, they assailed Sunder.

The Graveler ducked under Clangor, dodged Annoy, so that the beasts collided with each other. But the grass was slick under his feet. As he tried to spin out of the way, he went down. A chaos of hooves exploded around him.

Linden clinched Covenant's arm as if he had tried to break free. But he had not, could not have moved to save his life. The acid-children— The howl— Coursers whirling. Rain swarming against his skin.

What had alerted—?

Stell appeared somehow among the beasts, stood over Sunder, and fought to protect him; he heaved legs aside, punched at heads, forced animals against each other.

Brinn and Ceer sought to distract the Coursers. But their insane fury at Sunder consumed them. He rolled from side to side, avoiding blows. But their savagery was too great.

The Coursers! Covenant gagged. His eyes bulged under the pressure of asphyxiation, vertigo. Creatures of the Sunbane. Corrupted Earthpower.

The lurker was alert to such power.

Then this attack was directed against the Coursers. And they knew it. They were mad with fear.

Why didn't they flee?

Because they were held!

Hellfire!

Covenant sprang into motion with a wrench that knocked Linden to the ground. His eyes locked onto Sunder. He could not breathe, had to breathe. The howl filled his lungs, strangling him. But he could not let Sunder die. With a convulsion of will, he ripped words out of himself.

"The *rukh*! Throw it away!"

Sunder could not have heard him. The screaming of the lurker drowned every other sound. The Graveler jerked over onto his chest as if he had been pounded by a hoof, then jerked back again.

With the *rukh* in his hands.

Stell snatched it from him, hurled it. Arcing over the Coursers, it splashed into the center of the quagmire.

Instantly, the beasts wheeled. They charged after the iron as if it were the lure of their doom. In their terror, they strove to destroy the thing which prevented them from flight.

One of them smashed into Vain.

He made no effort to evade the impact. In his habitual pose, he stood as if no power on Earth could touch him. But the beast was a creature of the Sunbane, made feral and tremendous by fear. Its momentum knocked him backward.

He toppled into the pool.

The Coursers crashed after him, drove him down with their hooves. Then they, too, were caught in the quagmire.

At once, the water began to boil. Turbulence writhed across the surface, wringing screams from the Coursers; upheavals squirmed as if the quag were about to erupt. One by one, the beasts were wrenched downward, disappearing in dark froth like blood. Sucking noises came from the pool as if it were a gullet.

Moments later, the turmoil ended. The water relaxed with a sigh of satiation.

When the heaving subsided, Vain stood alone in the center of the pool.

He was sinking steadily. But the unfocus of his eyes was as blind as ever in the light of the torches. The water reached his chest. He did not struggle or cry out.

"Brinn!" Covenant panted. But the *Haruchai* were already moving. Harn pulled a coil of rope from one of the rescued sacks and threw it to Brinn. Promptly, but without haste, Brinn unwound one end of the rope and tossed it toward Vain.

The rope landed across Vain's shoulder.

He did not blink, gave no sign that he had seen it. His arms remained at his sides. The diffusion of his gaze was as complete as the quagmire.

"Vain!" Linden's protest sounded like a sob. The Demon-dim-spawn did not acknowledge it.

Brinn snatched back the rope, swiftly made a loop with a slip-knot. The water lapped at Vain's neck as the *Haruchai* prepared to throw again.

With a flick, Brinn sent the rope snaking outward. The loop settled around Vain's head. Carefully, Brinn tugged it taut, then braced himself to haul on the rope. Ceer and Harn joined him.

Abruptly, Vain sank out of sight.

When the *Haruchai* pulled, the rope came back empty. The loop was intact.

Until he heard himself swearing, Covenant did not realize that he could breathe.

The howling of the lurker was gone. The acid-creatures were gone. They had vanished into the night.

There was nothing left except the rain.

TWENTY-FOUR: The Search

COVENANT hugged his chest in an effort to steady his quivering heart. His lungs seized air as if even the rain of the Sarangrave were sweet.

Through the stillness, he heard Hollian moan Sunder's name. As Sunder groaned, she gasped, "You are hurt."

Covenant squeezed water out of his eyes, peered through the torchlight at the Graveler.

Pain gnarled Sunder's face. Together, Hollian and Linden were removing his jerkin. As they bared his ribs, they exposed a livid bruise where one of the Coursers had kicked him.

"Hold still," Linden ordered. Her voice shook raggedly, as if she wanted to scream. But her hands were steady. Sunder winced instinctively at her touch, then relaxed as her fingers probed his skin without hurting him. "A couple broken," she breathed. "Three cracked." She placed her right palm over his lung. "Inhale. Until it hurts."

He drew breath; a spasm knotted his visage. But she gave a nod of reassurance. "You're lucky. The lung isn't punctured." She demanded a blanket from one of the *Haruchai*, then addressed Sunder again. "I'm going to strap your chest—immobilize those ribs as much as possible. It's going to hurt. But you'll be able to move without damaging yourself." Stell handed her a blanket, which she promptly tore into wide strips. Caring for Sunder seemed to calm her. Her voice lost its raw edge.

Covenant left her to her work and moved toward the fire

Hergrom and Ceer were building. Then a wave of reaction flooded him, and he had to squat on the wet grass, hunch inward with his arms wrapped around his stomach to keep himself from whimpering. He could hear Sunder hissing thickly through his teeth as Linden bound his chest; but the sound was like the sound of the rain, and Covenant was already soaked. He concentrated instead on the way his heart flinched from beat to beat, and fought for control. When the attack passed, he climbed to his feet, and went in search of *metheglin*.

Brinn and Ceer had been able to save only half the supplies; but Covenant drank freely of the mead which remained. The future would have to fend for itself. He was balanced precariously on the outer edge of himself and did not want to fall.

He had come within instants of calling up the wild magic— of declaring to the lurker that the Coursers were not the only available prey. If Linden had not stopped him— The drizzle felt like mortification against his skin. If she had not stopped him, he and his companions might already have met Lord Shetra's doom. His friends—he was a snare for them, a walking deathwatch. How many of them were going to die before Lord Foul's plans fructified?

He drank *metheglin* as if he were trying to drown a fire, the fire in which he was fated to burn, the fire of himself. Leper outcast unclean. Power and doubt. He seemed to feel the venom gnawing hungrily at the verges of his mind.

Vaguely, he watched the *Haruchai* fashion scant shelters out of the remaining blankets, so that the people they guarded would not have to lie in rain. When Linden ordered Sunder and Hollian to rest, he joined them.

He awoke, muzzy-headed, in the dawn. The two women were still asleep—Linden lay like a battered wife with her hair sticking damply to her face—but Sunder was up before him. The rain had stopped. Sunder paced the grass slowly, carrying his damaged ribs with care. Concentration or pain accentuated his forehead.

Covenant lurched out of his sodden bed and shambled to the supplies for a drink of water. Then, because he needed companionship, he went to stand with the Graveler.

Sunder nodded in welcome. The lines above his nose seemed to complicate his vision. Covenant expected him to say something about the *rukh* or the Coursers; but he did not. Instead, he muttered tightly, "Covenant, I do not like this Sarangrave. Is all life thus, in the absence of the Sunbane?"

Covenant winced at the idea. It made him think of Andelain. The Land was like the Dead; it lived only in Andelain, where for a while yet the Sunbane could not stain or ravish. He remembered Caer-Caveral's song:

> But while I can I heed the call
> Of green and tree; and for their worth,
> I hold the glaive of Law against the Earth.

The mourning of that music brought back grief and old rage. Was he not Thomas Covenant, who had beaten the Despiser and cast Foul's Creche into the Sea? "If it is," he answered to the tone of dirges, poisons, "I'm going to tear that bastard's heart out."

Distantly, the Graveler asked, "Is hate such a good thing? Should we not then have remained at Revelstone, and given battle to the Clave?"

Covenant's tongue groped for a reply; but it was blocked by recollections. Unexpectedly, he saw *turiya* Raver in the body of Triock, a Stonedownor who had loved Lena. The Raver was saying, *Only those who hate are immortal.* His ire hesitated. Hate? With an effort, he took hold of himself. "No. Whatever else happens, I've already got too much innocent blood on my hands."

"I hear you," Sunder breathed. His wife and son were in his eyes; he had reason to understand Covenant's denial.

Sunlight had begun to angle into the clearing through the trees, painting streaks across the damp air. A sunrise free of the Sunbane. Covenant stared at it for a moment, but it was indecipherable to him.

The sun roused Linden and Hollian. Soon the company began to prepare for travel. No one spoke Vain's name, but the loss of him cast a pall over the camp. Covenant had been trying not to think about it. The Demondim-spawn was unscrupulous and lethal. He smiled at unreined power. But he was also a gift from Saltheart Foamfollower. And Covenant felt irrationally shamed by the thought that he had let a companion, any companion, sink into that quagmire, even though Linden had said that Vain was not alive.

A short time later, the *Haruchai* shouldered the supplies,

and the quest set off. Now no one spoke at all. They were
afoot in Sarangrave Flat, surrounded by hazards and by the
ears of the lurker. Betrayals seemed to wait for them behind
every tree, in every stream. None of them had the heart to
speak.

Brinn and Cail led the way, with Linden between them.
Turning slightly north of east, they crossed the clearing, and
made their way back into the jungle.

For a while, the morning was white and luminous with sun-
gilt mist. It shrouded the trees in evanescence. The company
seemed to be alone in the Flat, as if every other form of life
had fled. But as the mist frayed into wisps of humidity and
faded, the marsh began to stir. Birds rose in brown flocks or
individual blurs of color; secretive beasts scurried away from
the travelers. At one point, the quest encountered a group of
large gray monkeys, feeding at a thicket of berries as scarlet
as poison. The monkeys had canine faces and snarled menacingly. But Brinn walked straight toward them with no expression in his flat eyes. The monkeys broke for the trees, barking
like hyenas.

For most of the morning, the company edged through a
stretch of jungle with solid ground underfoot. But during the
afternoon, they had to creep across a wide bog, where hillocks
of sodden and mangy grass were interspersed with obscure
pools and splotches of quicksand. Some of the pools were
clear; others, gravid and mephitic. At sudden intervals, one or
another of them was disturbed, as if something vile lay on its
bottom. Linden and the *Haruchai* were hard pressed to find a
safe path through the region.

In the distance behind them, the sun passed over Landsdrop
and took on the blue aura of rain. But the sky over Sarangrave Flat stayed deep cerulean, untainted and unscathed.

By sunset, they had traveled little more than five leagues.

It would have been better, Covenant thought as he chewed
his disconsolate supper, if we'd ridden around. But he knew
that such regrets had no meaning. It would have been better if
he had never harmed Lena or Elena—never lost Joan—never
contracted leprosy. The past was as indefeasible as an amputation. But he could have borne his slow progress more lightly
if so many lives, so much of the Land, had not been at
stake.

That night came rain. It filled the dark, drenched the dawn, and did not lift until the company had been slogging through mud for half the morning.

In the afternoon, they had to wade a wetland of weeds and bulrushes. The water covered Covenant's thighs; the rushes grew higher than his head. A preterite fear of hidden pits and predators scraped at his nerves. But the company had no choice; this swamp blocked their way as far as the *Haruchai* could see.

The density of the rushes forced them to move in single file. Brinn led, followed immediately by Linden and Cail; then went Harn, Hollian, Stell, Sunder, Covenant, Ceer, and Hergrom. The water was dark and oily; Covenant's legs vanished as if they had been cut off at the waterline. The air was clouded with mosquitoes; and the marsh stank faintly, as if its bottom were littered with carcasses. The sack perched high on Stell's shoulders blocked Covenant's view ahead; he did not know how far he would have to go like this. Instinctively, he tried to hurry, but his boots could not keep their footing in the mud, and the water was as heavy as blood.

The mirk dragged at his legs, stained his clothes. His hands clutched the reeds involuntarily, though they could not have saved him if he fell. His mind cursed at thoughts of Vain. The Demondim-spawn had not even looked at the people who were trying to rescue him. Covenant's pulse labored in his temples.

Without warning, the rushes beside him thrashed. The water seethed. A coil as thick as his thigh broke the surface.

Instantly, Sunder was snatched out of sight.

Twenty feet away, he heaved up again, with a massive serpent body locked around his hips and neck. Gleaming scales covered strength enough to snap his back like a dry stick.

All the celerity of the *Haruchai* seemed insignificant to Covenant. He saw Stell release his sack, crouch, start a long dive forward, as if each piece of the action were discrete, time-consuming. Ceer carried no sack; he was one fraction of a heartbeat ahead of Stell. Hollian's mouth stretched toward a scream. Every one of the reeds was distinct and terrible. The water had the texture of filthy wool. Covenant saw it all: wet scales; coils knotted to kill; Ceer and Stell in the first reach of their dives; Hollian's mouth—

Marid! A man with no mouth, agony in his eyes, snakes for

arms. Fangs agape for Linden's face. Sunder. Marid. Fangs fixed like nails of crucifixion in Covenant's right forearm.

Venom.

In that instant, he became a blaze of fury.

Before Ceer and Stell covered half the distance, Covenant fried the coils straining Sunder's back. Wild magic burned the flesh transparent, lit spine, ribs, entrails with incandescence.

Linden let out a cry of dismay.

The serpent's death throes wrenched Sunder underwater.

Ceer and Stell dove into the convulsions. They disappeared, then regained their feet, with the Graveler held, gasping, between them. Dead coils thudded against their backs as they bore Sunder out of danger.

All Covenant's power was gone, snuffed by Linden's outcry. Cold gripped the marrow of his bones. Visions of green children and suffocation. Bloody hell.

His companions gaped at him. Linden's hands squeezed the sides of her head, fighting to contain her fear. Covenant expected her to shout abuse at him. But she did not. "It's my fault." Her voice was a low rasp. "I should have seen that thing."

"No." Stell spoke as if he were immune to contradiction. "It came when you had passed. The fault is mine. The Graveler was in my care."

Hellfire, Covenant groaned uselessly. Hell and damnation.

With an effort, Linden jerked down her hands and forced herself to the Graveler's side. He breathed in short gasps over the pain in his chest. She examined him for a moment, scowling at what she perceived. Then she muttered, "You'll live." Outrage and helplessness made her voice as bitter as bile.

The *Haruchai* began to move. Stell retrieved his sack. Brinn reformed the line of the company. Holding herself rigid, Linden took her place. They went on through the swamp.

They tried to hurry. But the water became deeper, holding them back. Its cold rank touch shamed Covenant's skin. Hollian could not keep her feet; she had to cling to Harn's sack and let him pull her. Sunder's injury made him wheeze as if he were expiring.

But finally the reeds gave way to an open channel; and a short distance beyond it lay a sloping bank of marshgrass. The bottom dropped away. The company had to swim.

When they gained solid ground, they saw that all their apparel was covered with a slick brown slime. It stank in

Covenant's nostrils. Linden could not keep the nausea off her mien.

With characteristic dispassion, the *Haruchai* ignored their uncleanliness. Brinn stood on the bank, studying the west. Hergrom moved away until he reached a tree he could climb. When he returned, he reported flatly that none of the green acid-creatures were in sight.

Still the company hurried. Beyond the slope, they dropped into a chaos of stunted copses and small poisonous creeks which appeared to run everywhere without moving. Twilight came upon them while they were still winding through the area, obeying Linden's strident command to let no drop of the water touch them.

In the dusk, they saw the first sign of pursuit. Far behind them among the copses was a glimpse of emerald. It disappeared at once. But no one doubted its meaning.

"Jesus God," Linden moaned. "I can't stand it."

Covenant cast an intent look at her. But the gloaming obscured her face. The darkness seemed to gnaw at her features. In silence, the quest ate a meal and tried to prepare to flee throughout the night.

Dark tensed about them as the sunset was cut off by Landsdrop. But then, strangely, the streams began to emit light. A nacreous glow, ghostly and febrile, shone out of the waters like diseased phosphorescence. And this light, haunting the copses with lines of pearly filigree, seemed to flow, though the water had appeared stagnant. The glow ran through the region, commingling and then separating again like a web of moonlight, but tending always toward the northeast.

In that direction, some distance away, Sarangrave Flat shone brightly. Eldritch light marked the presence of a wide radiance.

Covenant touched Brinn's arm, nodding toward the fire. Brinn organized the company, then carefully led the way forward.

Darkness made the distance deceptive; the light was farther away than it appeared to be. Before the questers covered half the intervening ground, tiny emerald fires began to gather behind them. Shifting in and out of sight as they passed among the copses, the acid-creatures stole after the company.

Covenant closed his mind to the pursuit, locked his gaze on the silver ahead. He could not endure to think about the coming attack—the attack which he had made inevitable.

Tracking the glow lines of the streams as if they were a map, Brinn guided the quest forward as swiftly as his caution permitted.

Abruptly, he stopped.

Pearl-limned, he pointed ahead. For a moment, Covenant saw nothing. Then he caught his breath between his teeth to keep himself still.

Stealthy, dark shapes were silhouetted between the company and the light. At least two of them, as large as saplings.

Firmly, Hergrom pressed Covenant down into a crouch. His companions hid against the ground. Covenant saw Brinn gliding away, a shadow in the ghost-shine. Then the *Haruchai* was absorbed by the copses and the dark.

Covenant lost sight of the moving shapes. He stared toward where he had last seen them. How long would Brinn take to investigate and return?

He heard a sound like a violent expulsion of breath.

Instinctively, he tried to jump to his feet. Hergrom restrained him.

Something heavy fell through underbrush. Blows were struck. The distance muffled them; but he could hear their strength.

He struggled against Hergrom. An instant later, the *Haruchai* released him. The company rose from hiding. Cail and Ceer moved forward. Stell and Harn followed with the Stonedownors.

Covenant took Linden's hand and pulled her with him after Sunder.

They crossed two streams diagonally, and then all the glowing rills lay on their right. The flow of silver gathered into three channels, which ran crookedly toward the main light. But the quest had come to firm ground. The brush between the trees was heavy. Only the *Haruchai* were able to move silently.

Near the bank of the closest stream, they found Brinn. He stood with his fists on his hips. Nacre reflected out of his flat eyes like joy.

He confronted a figure twice as tall as himself. A figure like a reincarnation in the eldritch glow. A dream come to life. Or one of the Dead.

A Giant!

"The old tellers spoke truly," Brinn said. "I am gladdened." The Giant folded his thick arms over his chest, which was as deep and solid as the trunk of an oak. He wore a sark of mail, formed of interlocking granite discs, and heavy leather leggings. Across his back, he bore a huge bundle of supplies. He had a beard like a fist. His eyes shone warily from under massive brows. The blunt distrust of his stance showed that he and Brinn had exchanged blows—and that he did not share Brinn's gladness.

"Then you have knowledge which I lack." His voice rumbled like stones in a subterranean vault. "You and your companions." He glanced over the company. "And your gladness"— he touched the side of his jaw with one hand —"is a weighty matter."

Suddenly, Covenant's eyes were full of tears. They blinded him; he could not blink away visions of Saltheart Foamfollower—Foamfollower, whose laughter and pure heart had done more to defeat Lord Foul and heal the Land than any other power, despite the fact that his people had been butchered to the last child by a Giant-Raver wielding a fragment of the Illearth Stone, thus fulfilling the unconscious prophecy of their home in Seareach, which they had named *Coercri*, The Grieve.

All killed, all the Unhomed. They sprang from a sea-faring race, and in their wandering they had lost their way back to their people. Therefore they had made a new place for themselves in Seareach where they had lived for centuries, until three of their proud sons had been made into Giant-Ravers, servants of the Despiser. Then they had let themselves be slain, rather than perpetuate a people who could become the thing they hated.

Covenant wept for them, for the loss of so much love and fealty. He wept for Foamfollower, whose death had been gallant beyond any hope of emulation. He wept because the Giant standing before him now could not be one of the Unhomed, not one of the people he had learned to treasure.

And because, in spite of everything, there were still Giants in the world.

He did not know that he had cried aloud until Hollian touched him. "Ur-Lord. What pains you?"

"Giant!" he cried. "Don't you know me?" Stumbling, he went past Linden to the towering figure. "I'm Thomas Covenant."

"Thomas Covenant." The Giant spoke like the murmuring of a mountain. With gentle courtesy, as if he were moved by the sight of Covenant's tears, he bowed. "The giving of your name honors me. I take you as a friend, though it is strange to meet friends in this fell place. I am Grimmand Honninscrave." His eyes searched Covenant. "But I am disturbed at your knowledge. It appears that you have known Giants, Giants who did not return to give their tale to their people."

"No," Covenant groaned, fighting his tears. Did not return? Could not. They lost their way, and were butchered. "I've got so much to tell you."

"At another time," rumbled Honninscrave, "I would welcome a long tale, be it however grievous. The Search has been scarce of story. But peril gathers about us. Surely you have beheld the *skest*? By mischance, we have placed our necks in a garrote. The time is one for battle or cunning rather than tales."

"*Skest*?" Sunder asked stiffly over the pain of his ribs. "Do you speak of the acid-creatures, which are like children of burning emerald?"

"Grimmand Honninscrave." Brinn spoke as if Sunder were not present. "The tale of which the ur-Lord speaks is known among us also. I am Brinn of the *Haruchai*. Of my people, here also are Cail, Stell, Harn, Ceer, and Hergrom. I give you our names in the name of a proud memory." He met Honninscrave's gaze. "Giant," he concluded softly, "you are not alone."

Covenant ignored both Brinn and Sunder. Involuntarily, only half conscious of what he was doing, he reached up to touch the Giant's hand, verify that Honninscrave was not a figment of silvershine and grief. But his hands were numb, dead forever. He had to clench himself to choke down his sorrow.

The Giant gazed at him sympathetically. "Surely," he breathed, "the tale you desire to tell is one of great rue. I will hear it—when the time allows." Abruptly, he turned away. "Brinn of the *Haruchai*, your name and the names of your people honor me. Proper and formal sharing of names and tales is a joy for which we also lack time. In truth, I am not alone.

"Come!" he cried over his shoulder.

At his word, three more Giants detached themselves from the darkness of the trees and came striding forward.

The first to reach his side was a woman. She was starkly beautiful, with hair like fine-spun iron, and stern purpose on her visage. Though she was slimmer than he, and slightly shorter, she was fully caparisoned as a warrior. She wore a corselet and leggings of mail, with greaves on her arms; a helm hung from her belt, a round iron shield from her shoulders. In a scabbard at her side, she bore a broadsword nearly as tall as Covenant.

Honninscrave greeted her deferentially. He told her the names which the company had given him, then said to them, "She is the First of the Search. It is she whom I serve."

The next Giant had no beard. An old scar like a sword cut lay under both his eyes across the bridge of his nose. But in countenance and apparel he resembled Honninscrave closely. His name was Cable Seadreamer. Like Honninscrave, he was unarmed and carried a large load of supplies.

The fourth figure stood no more than an arm's reach taller than Covenant. He looked like a cripple. In the middle of his back, his torso folded forward on itself, as if his spine had crumbled, leaving him incapable of upright posture. His limbs were grotesquely muscled, like tree boughs being choked by heavy vines. And his mien, too, was grotesque—eyes and nose misshapen, mouth crookedly placed. The short hair atop his beardless head stood erect as if in shock. But he was grinning, and his gaze seemed quaintly gay and gentle; his ugliness formed a face of immense good cheer.

Honninscrave spoke the deformed Giant's name: "Pitchwife."

Pitchwife? Covenant's old empathy for the destitute and the crippled made him wonder, Doesn't he even rate two names?

"Pitchwife, in good sooth," the short Giant replied as if he could read Covenant's heart. His chuckle sounded like the running of a clear spring. "Other names have I been offered in plenty, but none pleased me half so well." His eyes sparkled with secret mirth. "Think on it, and you will comprehend."

"We comprehend." The First of the Search spoke like annealed iron. "Our need now is for flight or defense."

Covenant brimmed with questions. He wanted to know where these Giants had come from, why they were here. But the First's tone brought him back to his peril. In the distance, he caught glimpses of green, a line forming like a noose.

"Flight is doubtful," Brinn said dispassionately. "The creatures of this pursuit are a great many."

"The *skest*, yes," rumbled Honninscrave. "They seek to herd us like cattle."

"Then," the First said, "we must prepare to make defense."

"Wait a minute." Covenant grasped at his reeling thoughts. "These *skest*. You know them. What do you know about them?"

Honninscrave glanced at the First, then shrugged. "Knowledge is a tenuous matter. We know nothing of this place or of its life. We have heard the speech of these beings. They name themselves *skest*. It is their purpose to gather sacrifices for another being, which they worship. This being they do not name."

"To us"— Brinn's tone hinted at repugnance —"it is known as the lurker of the Sarangrave."

"It *is* the Sarangrave." Linden sounded raw, over-wrought. Days of intimate vulnerability had left her febrile and defenseless. "This whole place is alive somehow."

"But how do you even know that much?" Covenant demanded of Honninscrave. "How can you understand their language?"

"That also," the Giant responded, "is not knowledge. We possess a gift of tongues, for which we bargained most acutely with the *Elohim*. But what we have heard offers us no present aid."

Elohim. Covenant recognized that name. He had first heard it from Foamfollower. But such memories only exacerbated his sense of danger. He had hoped that Honninscrave's knowledge would provide an escape; but that hope had failed. With a wrench, he pulled himself into focus.

"Defense isn't going to do you any good either." He tried to put force into his gaze. "You've got to escape." Foamfollower died because of me. "If you break through the lines, they'll ignore you. I'm the one they want." His hands made urging gestures he could not restrain. "Take my friends with you."

"Covenant!" Linden protested, as if he had announced an intention to commit suicide.

"It appears," Pitchwife chuckled, "that Thomas Covenant's knowledge of Giants is not so great as he believes."

Brinn did not move; his voice held no inflection. "The ur-Lord knows that his life is in the care of the *Haruchai*. We will not leave him. The Giants of old also would not depart a companion in peril. But there is no bond upon you. It would sadden us to see harm come upon you. You must flee."

"Yes!" Covenant insisted.

Frowning, Honninscrave asked Brinn, "Why does the ur-Lord believe that the *skest* gather against him?"

Briefly, Brinn explained that the company knew about the lurker of the Sarangrave.

At once, the First said, "It is decided." Deftly, she unbound her helm from her belt, settled it on her head. "This the Search must witness. We will find a place to make defense."

Brinn nodded toward the light in the northeast. The First glanced in that direction. "It is good." At once, she turned on her heel and strode away.

The *Haruchai* promptly tugged Covenant, Linden, and the Stonedownors into motion. Flanked by Honninscrave and Seadreamer, with Pitchwife at their backs, the company followed the First.

Covenant could not resist. He was paralyzed with dread. The lurker knew of him, wanted him; he was doomed to fight or die. But his companions—the Giants— Foamfollower had walked into the agony of Hotash Slay for his sake. They must not—!

If he hurt any of his friends, he felt sure he would go quickly insane.

The *skest* came in pursuit. They thronged out of the depths of the Flat, forming an unbroken wall against escape. The lines on either side tightened steadily. Honninscrave had described it accurately: the questors were being herded toward the light.

Oh, hell!

It blazed up in front of them now, chasing the night with nacre, the color of his ring. He guessed that the water glowed as it did precisely because his ring was present. They were nearing the confluence of the streams. On the left, the jungle retreated up a long hillside, leaving the ground tilted and clear as far ahead as he could see; but the footing was complicated by tangled ground creepers and protruding roots. On the right, the waters formed a lake the length of the hillside. Silver hung like a preternatural vapor above the surface. Thus concentrated, the light gave the surrounding darkness a ghoul-begotten timbre, as if such glowing were the peculiar dirge and lamentation of the accursed. It was altogether lovely and heinous.

A short way along the hillside, the company was blocked by a barrier of *skest*. Viscid green fire ran in close-packed child forms from the water's edge up the hillside to curve around behind the quest.

The First stopped and scanned the area. "We must cross this water."

"No!" Linden yelped at once. "We'll be killed."

The First cocked a stern eyebrow. "Then it would appear," she said after a moment of consideration, "that the place of our defense has been chosen for us."

A deformed silence replied. Pitchwife's breathing whistled faintly in and out of his cramped lungs. Sunder hugged Hollian against the pain in his chest. The faces of the *Haruchai* looked like death masks. Linden was unraveling visibly toward panic.

Softly, invidiously, the atmosphere began to sweat under the ululation of the lurker.

It mounted like water in Covenant's throat, scaled slowly upward in volume and pitch. The *skest* poured interminably through the thick scream. Perspiration crawled his skin like formication. Venom beat in him like a fever.

Cable Seadreamer clamped his hands over his ears, then dropped them when he found he could not shut out the howl. A mute snarl bared his teeth.

Calmly, as if they felt no need for haste, the *Haruchai* unpacked their few remaining bundles of firewood. They meted out several brands apiece among themselves, offering the rest to the Giants. Seadreamer glared at the wood incomprehendingly; but Pitchwife took several faggots and handed the rest to Honninscrave. The wood looked like mere twigs in the Giants' hands.

Linden's mouth moved as if she were whimpering; but the yammer and shriek of the lurker smothered every other cry.

The *skest* advanced, as green as corruption.

Defying the sheen of suffocation on his face, Brinn said, "Must we abide this? Let us attempt these *skest*."

The First looked at him, then looked around her. Without warning, her broadsword leaped into her hands, seemed to ring against the howl as she whirled it about her head. "Stone and Sea!" she coughed—a strangled battle cry.

And Covenant, who had known Giants, responded:

"Stone and Sea are deep in life,
two unalterable symbols of the world."

He forced the words through his anoxia and vertigo as he had learned them from Foamfollower.

> "Permanence at rest, and permanence in motion;
> participants in the Power that remains."

Though the effort threatened to burst his eyeballs, he spoke so that the First would hear him and understand.

Her eyes searched him narrowly. "You have known Giants indeed," she rasped. The howling thickened in her throat. "I name you Giantfriend. We are comrades, for good or ill."

Giantfriend. Covenant almost gagged on the name. The Seareach Giants had given that title to Damelon father of Loric. To Damelon, who had foretold their destruction. But he had no time to protest. The *skest* were coming. He broke into a fit of coughing. Emeralds dizzied him as he struggled for breath. The howl tore at the marrow of his bones. His mind spun. Giantfriend, Damelon, Kevin; names in gyres. Linden Marid venom.

Venomvenomvenom.

Holding brands ready, Brinn and Ceer went out along the edge of the lake to meet the *skest*.

The other *Haruchai* moved the company in that direction. Sweat running into Pitchwife's eyes made him wink and squint like a madman. The First gripped her sword in both fists.

Reft by vertigo, Covenant followed only because Hergrom impelled him.

Marid. Fangs.

Leper outcast unclean.

They were near the burning children now. Too near.

Suddenly, Seadreamer leaped past Brinn like a berserker to charge the *skest*.

Brinn croaked, "Giant!" and followed.

With one massive foot, Seadreamer stamped down on a creature. It ruptured, squirting acid and flame.

Seadreamer staggered as agony screamed up his leg. His jaws stretched, but no sound came from his throat. In an inchoate flash of perception, Covenant realized that the Giant was mute. Hideously, Seadreamer toppled toward the *skest*.

The lurker's voice bubbled and frothed like the lust of quicksand.

Brinn dropped his brands, caught Seadreamer's wrist. Planting his strength against the Giant's weight, he pivoted Seadreamer away from the creatures.

The next instant, Pitchwife reached them. With prodigious ease, the cripple swept his injured comrade onto his shoulders. Pain glared across Seadreamer's face; but he clung to Pitchwife's shoulders and let Pitchwife carry him away from the *skest*.

At the same time, Ceer began to strike. He splattered one of the acid-children with a back-handed blow of a brand. Conflagration tore half the wood to splinters. He hurled the remains at the next creature. As this *skest* burst, he was already snatching up another faggot, already striking again.

Stell and Brinn joined him. Roaring, Honninscrave slashed at the line with a double handful of wood, scattering five *skest* before the brands became fire and kindling in his grasp.

Together, they opened a gap in the lurker's noose.

The howl tightened in fury, raked the lungs of the company like claws.

Hergrom picked up Covenant and dashed through the breach. Cail followed, carrying Linden. Brinn and Ceer kept the gap open with the last of the firewood while Honninscrave and the First strode past the flames, relying on their Giantish immunity to fire. Pitchwife waded after them, with Seadreamer on his back.

Then the *Haruchai* had no more wood. *Skest* surged to close the breach, driven by the lurker's unfaltering shriek.

Stell leaped the gap. Harn threw Hollian bodily to Stell, then did the same with Sunder.

As one, Brinn, Ceer, and Harn dove over the creatures.

Already, the *skest* had turned in pursuit. The lurker gibbered with rage.

"Come!" shouted the First, almost retching to drive her voice through the howl. The Giants raced along the lakeshore, Pitchwife bearing Seadreamer with the agility of a *Haruchai*.

The company fled. Sunder and Hollian sprinted together, flanked by Harn and Stell. Covenant stumbled over the roots and vines between Brinn and Hergrom.

Linden did not move. Her face was alabaster with suffocation and horror. Covenant wrenched his gaze toward her to see the same look which had stunned her mien when she had first seen Joan. The look of paralysis.

Cail and Ceer took her arms and started to drag her forward.

She fought; her mouth opened to scream.

Urgently, the First gasped, "Ware!"

A wail ripped Hollian's throat.

Brinn and Hergrom leaped to a stop, whirled toward the lake.

Covenant staggered at the sight and would have fallen if the *Haruchai* had not upheld him.

The surface of the lake was rising. The water became an arm like a concatenation of ghost-shine—a tentacle with scores of fingers. It mounted and grew, reaching into the air like the howling of the lurker incarnate.

Uncoiling like a serpent, it struck at the company, at the people who were nearest.

At Linden.

Her mouth formed helpless mewling shapes. She struggled to escape. Cail and Ceer pulled at her. Unconsciously, she fought them.

As vividly as nightmare, Covenant saw her left foot catch in the fork of a root. The *Haruchai* hauled at her. In a spasm of pain, her ankle shattered. It seemed to make no sound through the rage of the lurker.

The arm lashed phosphorescence at her. Cail met the blow, tried to block it. The arm swatted him out of the way. He tumbled headlong toward the advancing *skest*.

They came slowly, rising forward like a tide.

Linden fought to scream, and could not.

The arm swung back again, slamming Ceer aside.

Then Honninscrave passed Covenant, charging toward Linden.

Covenant strove with all his strength to follow the Giant. But Brinn and Hergrom did not release him.

Instantly, he was livid with fury. A flush of venom pounded through him. Wild magic burned.

His power hurled the *Haruchai* away as if they had been kicked aside by an explosion.

The arm of the lurker struck. Honninscrave dove against it, deflected it. His weight bore it to the ground in a chiaroscuro of white sparks. But he could not master it. It coiled about him, heaved him into the air. The pain of its clutch seemed to shatter his face. Viciously, the arm hammered him down. He hit the hard dirt, bounced, and lay still.

The arm was already reaching toward Linden.

Blazing like a torch, Covenant covered half the distance to her. But his mind was a chaos of visions and vertigo. He saw Brinn and Hergrom blasted, perhaps hurt, perhaps killed. He saw fangs crucifying his forearm, felt venom committing murders he could not control.

The shining arm sprang on its fingers at Linden.

For one lurching beat of his heart, horror overcame him. All his dreads became the dread of venom, of wild magic he could not master, of himself. If he struck at the arm now, he would hit Linden. The power ran out of him like a doused flame.

The lurker's fingers knotted in her hair. They yanked her toward the lake. Her broken ankle remained caught in the root fork. The arm pulled, excruciating her bones. Then her foot twisted free.

Linden!

Covenant surged forward again. The howling had broken his lungs. He could not breathe.

As he ran, he snatched out Loric's *krill*, cast aside the cloth, and locked his fingers around the haft. Bounding to the attack, he drove the blade like a spike of white fire into the arm.

The air became a detonation of pain. The arm released Linden, wrenched itself backward, almost tore the *krill* out of his grasp. Argent poured from the wound like moon flame, casting arcs of anguish across the dark sky.

In hurt and fury, the arm coiled about him, whipping him from the ground. For an instant, he was held aloft in a crushing grip; the lurker clenched him savagely at the heavens. Then it punched him into the water.

It drove him down as if the lake had no bottom and no end. Cold burned his skin, plugged his mouth; pressure erupted in his ears like nails pounding into his skull; darkness drowned his mind. The lurker was tearing him in half.

But the gem of the *krill* shone bright and potent before him. Loric's *krill*, forged as a weapon against ill. A weapon.

With both hands, Covenant slammed the blade into the coil across his chest.

A convulsion loosened the grip. Lurker blood scoured his face.

He was still being dragged downward, forever deeper into the abysm of the lurker's desmesne. The need for air shredded his vitals. Water and cold threatened to burst his bones. Pressure spots marked his eyes like scars of mortality and failure, failure, the Sunbane, Lord Foul laughing in absolute triumph.

No!

Linden in her agony.

No!

He twisted around before the lurker's grasp could tighten again, faced in the direction of the arm. Downward forever. The *krill* blazed indomitably against his sight.

With all the passion of his screaming heart—with everything he knew of the *krill*, wild magic, rage, venom—he slashed at the lurker's arm.

His hot blade severed the flesh, passed through the appendage like water.

Instantly, all the deep burned. Water flashed and flared; white coruscations flamed like screams throughout the lake. The lurker became tinder in the blaze. Suddenly, its arm was gone, its presence was gone.

Though he still held the *krill*, Covenant could see nothing. The lurker's pain had blinded him. He floated alone in depths so dark that they could never have held any light.

He was dying for air.

TWENTY-FIVE: "In the name of the Pure One"

MISERABLY, stubbornly, he locked his teeth against the water and began to struggle upward. He felt power-seared and impotent, could not seem to move through the rank depths. His limbs were dead for lack of air. Nothing remained to him except the last convulsion of his chest which would rip his mouth open—nothing except death, and the memory of Linden with her ankle shattered, fighting to scream.

In mute refusal, he went on jerking his arms, his legs, like a prayer for the surface.

Then out of the darkness, a hand snagged him, turned him. Hard palms took hold of his face. A mouth clamped over his.

The hands forced his jaws open; the mouth expelled breath into him. That scant taste of air kept him alive.

The hands drew him upward.

He broke the surface and exploded into gasping. The arms upheld him while he sobbed for air. Time blurred as he was pounded in and out of consciousness by his intransigent heart.

In the distance, a voice—Hollian's?—called out fearfully, "Brinn? Brinn?"

Brinn answered behind Covenant's head. "The ur-Lord lives."

Another voice said, "Praise to the *Haruchai*." It sounded like the First of the Search. "Surely that name was one of great honor among the Giants your people have known."

Then Covenant heard Linden say as if she were speaking from the bottom of a well of pain, "That's why the water looked so deadly." She spoke in ragged bursts through her teeth, fighting to master her hurt with words. "The lurker was there. Now it's gone." In the silence behind her voice, she was screaming.

Gone. Slowly, the burn of air starvation cleared from Covenant's mind. The lurker was gone, withdrawn though certainly not dead; no, that was impossible; he could not have slain a creature as vast as the Sarangrave. The lake was lightless. The fires started by the spilling of *skest* acid had gone out for lack of fuel. Night covered the Flat. But somehow he had retained his grip on the *krill*. Its shining enabled him to see.

Beyond question, the lurker was still alive. When Brinn swam him to the shore and helped him out onto dry ground, he found that the atmosphere was too thick for comfort. Far away, he heard the creature keening over its pain; faint sobs seemed to bubble in the air like the self-pity of demons.

On either hand, *skest* gleamed dimly. They had retreated; but they had not abandoned the lurker's prey.

He had only injured the creature. Now it would not be satisfied with mere food. Now it would want retribution.

A torch was lit. In the unexpected flame, he saw Hergrom and Ceer standing near Honninscrave with loads of wood which they had apparently foraged from the trees along the hill crest. Honninscrave held a large stone firepot, from which Ceer lit torches, one after another. As Hergrom passed brands to the other *Haruchai*, light slowly spread over the company.

Dazedly, Covenant looked at the *krill*.

Its gem shone purely, as if it were inviolable. But its light brought back to him the burst of fury with which he had first awakened the blade, when Elena was High Lord. Whatever else Loric had made the *krill* to be, Covenant had made it a thing of savagery and fire. Its cleanliness hurt his eyes.

In silent consideration, Brinn reached out with the cloth Covenant had discarded. He took the *krill* and wrapped its heat into a neat bundle, as if thereby he could make the truth bearable for Covenant. But Covenant went on staring at his hands.

They were unharmed; free even of heat-damage. He had been protected by his own power; even his flesh had become so accustomed to wild magic that he guarded himself instinctively, without expense to any part of himself except his soul. And if that were true—

He groaned.

If that were true, then he was already damned.

For what did damnation mean, if it did not mean freedom from the mortal price of power? Was that not what made Lord Foul what he was? The damned purchased might with their souls; the innocent paid for it with their lives. Therein lay Sunder's true innocence, though he had slain his own wife and son—and Covenant's true guilt. Even in Foul's Creche, he had avoided paying the whole price. At that time, only his restraint had saved him, his refusal to attempt Lord Foul's total extirpation. Without restraint, he would have been another Kevin Landwaster.

But where was his restraint now? His hands were undamaged. Numb with leprosy, blunt and awkward, incapable, yes; yet they had held power without scathe.

And Brinn offered the bundle of the *krill* to him as if it were his future and his doom.

He accepted it. What else could he do? He was a leper; he could not deny who he was. Why else had he been chosen to carry the burden of the Land's need? He took the bundle and tucked it back under his belt, as if in that way he could at least spare his friends from sharing his damnation. Then, with an effort like an acknowledgment of fatality, he forced himself to look at the company.

In spite of his bruises, Honninscrave appeared essentially whole. Seadreamer was able to stand on his acid-burned foot; and Pitchwife moved as if his own fire walk were already forgotten. They reminded Covenant of the *caamora*, the ancient Giantish ritual fire of grief. He remembered Foamfol-

lower burying his bloody hands among the coals of a bonfire
to castigate and cleanse them. Foamfollower had been horrified by the lust with which he had slaughtered Cavewights
and he had treated his dismay with fire. The flames had hurt
him, but not damaged him; when he had withdrawn his hands,
they had been hale and clean.

Clean, Covenant murmured. He ached for the purification
of fire. But he compelled his eyes to focus beyond the Giants.

Gazing directly at Brinn, he almost cried out. Both Brinn
and Hergrom had been scorched by the lash of wild magic;
eyebrows and hair were singed, apparel darkened in patches.
He had come so close to doing them real harm—

Like Honninscrave, Cail and Ceer were battered but intact.
They held torches over Linden.

She lay on the ground with her head in Hollian's lap. Sunder knelt beside her, holding her leg still. His knuckles were
white with strain; and he glowered as if he feared that he
would have to sacrifice her for her blood.

The First stood nearby with her arms folded over her mail
like an angry monolith, glaring at the distant *skest*.

Linden had not stopped talking: the pieces of her voice
formed a ragged counterpoint to the moaning of the lurker.
She kept insisting that the water was safe now, the lurker had
withdrawn, it could be anywhere, it was the Sarangrave, but it
was primarily a creature of water, the greatest danger came
from water. She kept talking so that she would not sob.

Her left foot rested at an impossible angle. Bone splinters
pierced the skin of her ankle, and blood oozed from the
wounds in spite of the pressure of Sunder's grip.

Covenant's guts turned at the sight. Without conscious
transition, he was kneeling at her side. His kneecaps hurt as if
he had fallen. Her hands closed and unclosed at her sides,
urgent to find something that would enable her to bear the
pain.

Abruptly, the First left her study of the *skest*. "Giantfriend,"
she said, "her hurt is sore. We have *diamondraught*. For one
who is not of Giantish stature, it will bring swift surcease."
Covenant did not lift his eyes from Linden's embattled visage.
He was familiar with *diamondraught*; it was a liquor fit for
Giants. "Also, it is greatly healing," the First continued, "distilled for our restitution." Covenant heard glints of compassion
along her iron tone. "But no healing known to us will repair
the harm. Her bones will knit as they now lie. She—"

She will be crippled.

No. Anger mounted in him, resentment of his helplessness, rage for her pain. The exhaustion of his spirit became irrelevant. "Linden." He hunched forward to make her meet his gaze. Her eyes were disfocused. "We've got to do something about your ankle." Her fingers dug into the ground. "You're the doctor. Tell me what to do." Her countenance looked like a mask, waxen and aggrieved. *"Linden."*

Her lips were as white as bone. Her muscles strained against Sunder's weight. Surely she could not bear any more.

But she breathed hoarsely, "Immobilize the leg." Wails rose in her throat; she forced them down. "Above the knee."

At once, Sunder shifted to obey. But the First gestured him aside. "The strength of a Giant is needed." She wrapped Linden's leg in her huge hands, holding it like a vise of stone.

"Don't let me move."

The company answered her commands. Her pain was irrefusable. Ceer grasped her shoulders. Harn anchored one of her arms; Sunder pinned the other. Brinn leaned along her uninjured leg.

"Give me something to bite."

Hollian tore a strip from the fringe of her robe, folded it several times, and offered it to Linden's mouth.

"Take hold of the foot." Dry dread filled her eyes. "Pull it straight away from the break. Hard. Keep pulling until all the splinters slip back under the skin. Then turn it into line with the leg. Hold the foot so the bones don't shift. When I feel everything's right"—she panted feverishly, but her doctor's training controlled her—"I'll nod. Let go of the foot. Slowly. Put a splint on it. Up past the knee. Splint the whole leg."

Immediately, she squeezed her eyes shut, opened her mouth to accept Hollian's cloth.

A nausea of fear twisted in Covenant's bowels; but he ignored it. "Right," he grated. "I'll do it." Her courage appalled him. He moved to her foot.

Cail brushed him away.

Curses jumped through Covenant's teeth; but Cail responded without inflection, "This I will do for her."

Covenant's vitals trembled. His hands had held power enough to maim the lurker and had suffered no harm. "I said *I'll do it.*"

"No." Cail's denial was absolute. "You have not the

strength of the *Haruchai*. And the blame for this injury is mine."

"Don't you understand?" Covenant could not find sufficient force for his remonstration. "Everything I touch turns to blood. All I do is kill." His words seemed to drop to the ground, vitiated by the distant self-pity of the lurker. "She's here because she tried to save my life. I need to help her."

Unexpectedly, Cail looked up and met Covenant's wounded gaze. "Ur-Lord," he said as if he had judged the Unbeliever to the marrow of his bones, "you have not the strength."

You don't understand! Covenant tried to shout. But no sound came past the knot of self-loathing in his throat. Cail was right; with his half-hand, he would not be able to grip Linden's foot properly; he could never help her, had not the strength. And yet his hands were unharmed. He could not resist when Pitchwife took hold of him, drawing him away from the group around Linden.

Without speaking, the malformed Giant led him to the campfire Honninscrave was building. Seadreamer sat there, resting his acid-burned foot. He gazed at Covenant with eloquent, voiceless eyes. Honninscrave gave Covenant a sharp glance, then picked up a stone cup from one of his bundles and handed it to Covenant. Covenant knew from the smell that the cup contained *diamondraught*, potent as oblivion. If he drank from that cup, he might not regain consciousness until the next day. Or the day after that.

Unconsciousness bore no burdens, felt no blame.

He did not drink. He stared into the flames without seeing them, without feeling the clench of grief on his features. He did nothing but listen to the sounds of the night: the lurker bubbling pain softly to itself; Pitchwife's faint stertorous breathing; Linden's gagged scream as Cail started to pull at her foot. Her bones made a noise like the breaking of sodden sticks as they shifted against each other.

Then the First said tightly, "It is done."

The fire cast streaks of orange and yellow through Covenant's tears. He did not want ever to be able to see again, wished himself forever deaf and numb. But he turned to Pitchwife and lifted the stone cup toward the Giant. "Here. She needs this."

Pitchwife carried the cup to Linden. Covenant followed like a dry leaf in his wake.

Before Covenant reached her, he was met by Brinn and

Cail. They blocked his way; but they spoke deferentially. "Ur-Lord." Brinn's alien inflection expressed the difficulty of apologizing. "It was necessary to deny you. No disservice was intended."

Covenant fought the tightness of his throat. "I met Bannor in Andelain. He said, 'Redeem my people. Their plight is an abomination. And they will serve you well.' "

But no words were adequate to articulate what he meant. He fumbled past the *Haruchai*, went to kneel at Linden's side.

She was just emptying the cup which the First held for her. The skin of her face looked as bloodless as marble; a patina of pain clouded her gaze. But her respiration was growing steadier, and the clench of her muscles had begun to loosen. With numb fingers, he rubbed the tears from his eyes, trying to see her clearly, trying to believe that she would be all right.

The First looked at him. Quietly, she said, "Trust the *diamondraught*. She will be healed."

He groped for his voice. "She needs bandages. A splint. That wound should be cleaned."

"It will be done." The quaver of stress in Hollian's tone told him that she needed to help. "Sunder and I—"

He nodded mutely, remaining at Linden's side while the Stonedownors went to heat water and prepare bandages and splints. She seemed untouchable in her weakness. He knelt with his arms braced on the ground and watched the *diamondraught* carry her to sleep.

He also watched the care with which Hollian, Sunder, and Stell washed and bandaged Linden's ankle, then splinted her leg securely. But at the same time, a curious bifurcation came over him—a split like the widening gulf between his uselessness and his power. He was sure now—though he feared to admit it to himself—that he had healed himself with wild magic when he had been summoned to Kevin's Watch with the knife-wound still pouring blood from his chest. He remembered his revulsion at Lord Foul's refrain, *You are mine*, remembered heat and white flame—

Then why could he not do the same for Linden, knit her bones just as he had sealed his own flesh? For the same reason that he could not draw water from the Earth or oppose the Sunbane. Because his senses were too numb for the work, unattuned to the spirit within the physical needs around him. Clearly, this was deliberate, a crucial part of the Despiser's intent. Clearly, Lord Foul sought at every turn to increase both Covenant's might and his helplessness, stretch him on the rack of self-contradiction and doubt. But why? What purpose did it serve?

He had no answer. He had invested too much hope in Linden, in her capacity for healing. And Lord Foul had chosen her on precisely the same grounds. It was too much. Covenant could not think. He felt weak and abject of soul. For a moment, he listened to the misery of the lurker. Then, numbly, he left Linden's side and returned to the campfire, seeking warmth for his chilled bones.

Sunder and Hollian joined him. They held each other as if they, too, felt the cold of his plight. After a few moments, Harn and Hergrom brought food and water. Covenant and the Stonedownors ate like the survivors of a shipwreck.

Covenant's dullness grew in spite of the meal. His head felt as heavy as prostration; his heart lay under a great weight. He hardly noticed that the First of the Search had come to speak with Honninscrave. He stood, leaning toward the flames like a man contemplating his own dissolution. When Honninscrave addressed him, veils of fatigue obscured the Giant's words.

"The First has spoken," Honninscrave said. "We must depart. The lurker yet lives. And the *skest* do not retreat. We must depart while they are thus thinly scattered and may be combated. Should the lurker renew its assault now, all your power—and all the Chosen's pain—will have gained us naught."

Depart, Covenant mumbled. Now. The importance of the words was hidden. His brain felt like a tombstone.

"You speak truly," Brinn replied for Covenant. "It would be a gladness to travel with Giants, as the old tellers say *Haruchai* and Giants traveled together in the ancient days. But perhaps our paths do not lie with each other. Where do you go?"

The First and Honninscrave looked at Seadreamer. Seadreamer closed his eyes as if to ignore them; but with one long arm he pointed toward the west.

Brinn spoke as if he were immune to disappointment. "Then we must part. Our way is eastward, and it is urgent."

Part? A pang penetrated Covenant's stupor. He wanted the company of the Giants. He had a world of things to tell them. And they were important to him in another way as well, a way he could not seem to articulate. He shook his head. "No."

Honninscrave cocked an eyebrow. The First frowned at Covenant.

"We just met," Covenant murmured. But that was not what he had to say. He groped for clarity. "Why west?" Those words disentangled some of his illucidity. "Why are you here?"

"Giantfriend," the First responded with a hint of iron, "that tale is long, and the time is perilous. This lurker is a jeopardy too vast to be disdained."

Covenant knotted his fists and tried to insist. "Tell me."

"Thomas Covenant—" Honninscrave began in a tone of gentle dissuasion.

"I beat that thing once," Covenant croaked. "I'll beat it again if I have to." Don't you understand? All your people were killed. "Tell me why you're here."

The First considered her companions. Honninscrave shrugged. Seadreamer kept his eyes closed, communing with a private pain. Pitchwife hid his face behind a cup of *diamondraught.*

Stiffly, she said, "Speak briefly, Grimmand Honninscrave."

Honninscrave bowed, recognizing her right to command him. Then he turned to Covenant. His body took on a formal stance, as if even his muscles and sinews believed that tales were things which should be treated with respect. His resemblance to Foamfollower struck Covenant acutely.

"Hear, then, Thomas Covenant," Honninscrave said with a cadence in his deep voice, "that we are the leaders of the Search—the Search of the Giants, so called for the purpose which has brought us thus far across the world from our Home. To our people, from time to time among the generations, there is born one possessed of a gift which we name the Earth-Sight—a gift of vision such as only the *Elohim* comprehend. This gift is strange surpassingly, and may be neither foretold nor bound, but only obeyed. Many are the stories I would wish to tell, so that you might grasp the import of what I say. But I must content myself with this one word: the Earth-Sight has become a command to all Giants, which none would willingly shirk or defy. Therefore we are here.

"Among our generation, a Giant was born, brother of my bone and blood, and the Earth-Sight was in him. He is Cable Seadreamer, named for the vision which binds him, and he is voiceless, scalded mute by the extravagance and horror of what the Earth-Sight has seen. With the eyes of the gift, he beheld a wound upon the Earth, sore and terrible—a wound like a great nest of maggots, feeding upon the flesh of the world's heart. And he perceived that this wound, if left uncleansed, unhealed, would grow to consume all life and time, devouring the foundation and corner-stone of the Earth, unbinding Stone and Sea from themselves, birthing chaos.

"Therefore a Giantclave was held, and the Search given its duty. We are commanded to seek out this wound and oppose it, in defense of the Earth. For that reason, we set sail from our Home in the proudest *dromond* of all Giantships, Starfare's Gem. For that reason, we have followed Seadreamer's gaze across the wide oceans of the world—we, and twoscore of our people, who tend the Gem. And for that reason, we are here. The wound lies in this land, in the west. We seek to behold it, discover its nature, so that we may summon the Search to resist or cleanse it."

Honninscrave stopped and stood waiting for Covenant's reply. The other Giants studied the Unbeliever as if he held the key to a mystery, the First grimly, Seadreamer as intensely as an oracle, Pitchwife with a gaze like a chuckle of laughter or loss. Possibilities widened the faces of the Stonedownors as they began to understand why Covenant had insisted on hearing the explanation of the Giants. But Covenant was silent. He saw the possibilities, too; Honninscrave's narration had opened a small clear space in his mind, and in that space lay answers. But he was preoccupied with an old grief. Foamfollower's people had died because they were unable to find their way Home.

"Ur-Lord," Brinn said. "Time demands us. We must depart."

Depart. Covenant nodded. Yes. Give me strength. He swallowed, asked thickly, "Where's your ship?"

"The *dromond* Starfare's Gem," Honninscrave replied as if he desired Covenant to use the ship's title, "stands anchored off the delta of a great swamp which lies in the east. A distance of perhaps sevenscore leagues."

Covenant closed his eyes. "Take me there. I need your ship."

The First's breath hissed through her teeth. Pitchwife gaped at the ur-Lord's audacity. After a moment, Honninscrave began hesitantly, "The First has named you Giantfriend. We desire to aid you. But we cannot—"

"Thomas Covenant," the First said in a voice like a broadsword, "what is your purpose?"

"Oh, forsooth!" Pitchwife laughed. "Let this lurker await our good readiness. We will not be hastened." His words could have been sarcastic; but he spoke them in a tone of clean glee. "Are we not Giants? Are not tales more precious to us than life?"

Quietly, almost gently, the First said, "Peace, Pitchwife."

At her command, Pitchwife stopped; but his grin went on contradicting the grief of the lurker.

In the core of his numbness, Covenant held to the few things he understood, kept his eyes shut so that he would not be distracted. Distanced from himself by darkness and concentration, he hardly heard what he was saying.

"I know that wound. I know what it is. I think I know what to do about it. That's why we're here. I need you—your ship, your knowledge—your help."

The thing you seek is not within the Land.

The Staff of Law. The One Tree.

Yet Mhoram had also said, *Do not be deceived by the Land's need. The thing you seek is not what it appears to be.*

Carefully, Honninscrave said, "Cable Seadreamer asks that you speak more plainly."

More plainly? For an instant, Covenant's grasp on clarity faltered. Do I have to tell you that it's my fault? That I'm the one who opened the door? But he steadied himself in the eye of all the things he did not understand and began to speak.

There in the night, with his eyes closed against the firelight and the immaculate stars, he described the Sunbane and the purpose for which Lord Foul had created the Sunbane. He outlined its origin in the destruction of the Staff of Law, then told of his own role in that destruction, so that the Giants would understand why the restitution of the Staff was his responsibility. And he talked about what he had learned in Andelain. All these things ran together in his mind; he did not know whether the words he spoke aloud made any sense.

When he finished, he fell silent and waited.

After a time, the First said thoughtfully, "You ask the use of Starfare's Gem so that you may seek across the world for this One Tree. You ask our aid and our knowledge of the Earth, to aid your seeking."

Covenant opened his eyes then, let his mortal weariness speak for him. Yes. Look at me. How else can any of this be healed?

"Stone and Sea!" she muttered, "this is a hard matter. If you speak truly, then the path of the Search lies with you."

"The ur-Lord," Brinn said without inflection, "speaks truly."

She rejected his assertion with a brusque shrug. "I doubt not that he speaks truly concerning his own belief. But is his belief a sure knowledge? He asks us to place all the Search into his hands—without any secure vision of what we do. Granted, he is mighty, and has known the friendship of Giants. But might and surety are not children of the same parent."

"Do you"— Covenant could feel himself failing into stupidity again, becoming desperate —"know where the One Tree is?"

"No," she replied stiffly. She hesitated for only a moment. "But we know where such knowledge may be gained."

"Then take me there." His voice was husky with supplication. "The Sunbane's getting worse. People are killed every day to feed it. The Land is dying." *I swore I'd never kill again—swore it in the name of Foamfollower's* caamora. *But I can't stop.* "Please."

Indecision held the First. She glared at the dilemma he had given her. Honninscrave knelt by the fire, tending it as if he needed something to do with his hands. Seadreamer's face wore pain as if he were maimed by his muteness. Near him, Sunder and Hollian waited in suspense.

Whistling thinly through his teeth, Pitchwife began to repack the Giants' bundles. His features expressed a complete confidence that the First would make the right choice.

Without warning, a bolt of white shot through the depths of the lake. It flickered, disappeared. Fired again.

Instantly, the whole lake caught silver. Ghost-shine sprang into the night. The water came to life.

In the distance, the lurker's sobbing mounted toward rage. At once, the air seemed to congeal like fear.

Sunder spat a hoarse curse. Harn and Hergrom dove toward the quest's supplies. Pitchwife tossed a bundle to Honninscrave. Honninscrave caught it, slipped his shoulders into the bindings. The First had already kicked the campfire apart. She and Honninscrave picked up brands to use as torches. Pitchwife threw the other bundle to Seadreamer, then snatched up a torch himself.

Ceer and Cail had lifted Linden. But the splint made her

awkward for them. Covenant saw dazedly that they would not be able to carry her, run with her, without hurting her ankle.

He did not know what to do. His lungs ached. The lurker's rising howl tore open the scars of past attacks. Sweat burst from the bones of his skull. The *skest* were moving, tightening their fire around the company. There was nothing he could do.

Then Seadreamer reached Cail and Ceer. The Giant took Linden from them; his huge arms supported her as securely as a litter.

The sight unlocked Covenant's paralysis. He trusted the Giant instinctively. The company began to climb the hillside northward. He left them, turned to confront the water.

Just try it! His fists jerked threats at the fell luster and the howl. Come on! Try to hurt us again!

Brinn yanked him away from the lakeshore and dragged him stumbling up the hill.

Reeling with exertion and anoxia, he fought to keep his feet. Dark trees leaped across his vision like aghast dancers in the nacreous light. He tripped repeatedly. But Brinn upheld him.

The lurker's cry whetted itself on pain and frustration, shrilled into his ears. At the fringes of his sight, he could see the *skest*. They moved in pursuit, as if the lurker's fury were a scourge at their backs.

Then Brinn impelled him over the crest of the hill.

At once, the ghost-light was cut off. Torches bounded into the jungle ahead of him. He struggled after them as if he were chasing swamp-fires. Only Brinn's support saved him from slamming into trunks, thick brush, vines as heavy as hawsers.

The howling scaled toward a shriek, then dropped to a lower, more cunning pitch. But the sound continued to impale Covenant like a swordthorn. He retched for air; the night became vertigo. He did not know where he was going.

A lurid, green blur appeared beyond the torches. The *skest* angled closer on the left, forcing the company to veer to the right.

More *skest*.

The flight of the torches swung farther to the right.

Lacking air, strength, courage, Covenant could hardly bear his own weight. His limbs yearned to fall, his chest ached for oblivion. But Hergrom gripped his other arm. Stumbling between *Haruchai*, he followed his companions.

For long moments, they splashed down the length of a cold

stream which ran like an aisle between advancing hordes of
skest. But then the stream faded into quicksand. The company
lost time hunting for solid ground around the quagmire.

They gained a reach of clear dirt, soil so dead that even
marshgrass could not grow there. They began to sprint. Brinn
and Hergrom drew Covenant along more swiftly than he
could move.

Suddenly, the whole group crashed to a halt, as if they had
blundered against an invisible wall.

The First hissed an oath like a sword-cut. Sunder and Hollian sobbed for air. Pitchwife hugged his crippled chest.
Honninscrave swung in circles, scanning the night. Seadreamer stood like a tree with Linden asleep in his arms and
stared into the darkness as if he had lost his sight.

With his own breath rending like an internal wound, Covenant jerked forward to see why the company had stopped.

Herded! Bloody hell.

The dead ground stretched like a peninsula out into a region of mud: mire blocked the way for more than a stone's
throw on three sides. The muck stank like a charnal, seething
faintly, as if corpses writhed in its depths. It looked thick
enough to swallow even Giants without a trace.

Already, *skest* had begun to mass at the head of the peninsula, sealing the company in the lurker's trap. Hundreds of
skest, scores of hundreds. They made the whole night green,
pulsing like worship. Even armed with a mountain of wood,
no Giant or *Haruchai* could have fought through that throng;
and the company had no wood left except the torches.

Covenant's respiration became febrile with cursing.

He looked at his companions. Emerald etched them out of
the darkness, as distinct as the accursed. Linden lay panting in
Seadreamer's arms as if her sleep were troubled by nightmares.
Hollian's face was bloodless under her black hair, pale as
prophecy. Sunder's whole visage clenched around the grinding
of his teeth. Their vulnerability wrung Covenant's heart. The
Haruchai and the Giants could at least give some account of
themselves before they fell. What could Linden, Sunder, and
Hollian do except die?

"Ur-Lord." Brinn's singed hair and dispassion looked
ghastly in the green light. "The white ring. May these *skest* be
driven back?"

Thousands of them? Covenant wanted to demand. I don't
have the strength. But his chest could not force out words.

One of Honninscrave's torches burned down to his hand. With a grimace, he tossed the sputtering wood into the mire.

Instantly, the surface of the mud lake caught fire.

Flames capered across the mire like souls in torment. Heat like a foretaste of hell blasted against the company, drove them into a tight cluster in the center of the peninsula.

The First discarded her torches, whipped out her sword, and tried to shout something. The lurker drowned her voice. But the Giants understood. They placed themselves around their companions, using their bodies as shields against the heat. The First, Honninscrave, and Pitchwife faced outward; Seadreamer put his back to the fire, protecting Linden.

The next instant, a concussion shook the ground. Pitchwife stumbled. Hollian, Sunder, and Covenant fell.

As Covenant climbed back to his feet, he saw a tremendous spout of flame mounting out of the mud.

It rose like a fire-storm and whirled toward the heavens. Its fury tore a gale through the night. Towering over the peninsula, it leaned to hammer the company. The howl of the lurker became a gyre of conflagration.

No!

Covenant eluded Brinn's grasp, wrenched past Honninscrave. He forged out into the heat to meet the firespout.

Baring the *krill*, he raised it so that its gem shone clear. Purest argent pierced the orange mudfire, defying it as hotly as lightning.

In the silence of his clogged lungs, Covenant raged words he did not understand. Words of power.

Melenkurion abatha! Duroc minas mill khabaal!

Immediately, the firespout ruptured. In broken gouts and fear, it crashed backward as if he had cut off another arm of the lurker. Flames skirled like frustrated ire across the mud. Abruptly, the air was free. Wind empty of howling fed the fire. Covenant's companions coughed and gasped as if they had been rescued from the hands of a strangler.

He knelt on the dead ground. Peals of light rang in his head, tintinnabulating victory or defeat; either one, there was no difference; triumph and desecration were the same thing. He was foundering—

But hands came to succor him. They were steady and gentle. They draped cloth over the *krill*, took it from his power-cramped fingers. Relative darkness poured through his eye-sockets as if they were empty pits, gaping for night. The dark

spoke in Brinn's voice. "The lurker has been pained. It fears
to be pained again."

"Sooth," the First muttered starkly. "Therefore it has given
our deaths into the hands of its acolytes."

Brinn helped Covenant to his feet. Blinking at numberless
krill echoes, he fought to see. But the afterflares were too
bright. He was still watching them turn to emerald when he
heard Hollian's gasp. The Giants and *Haruchai* went rigid.
Brinn's fingers dug reflexively into Covenant's arm.

By degrees, the white spots became orange and green—
mudfire and *skest*. The acid-creatures thronged at the head
of the peninsula, shimmering like religious ecstasy. They
oozed forward slowly, not as if they were frightened, but
rather as if they sought to prolong the anticipation of their
advance.

Covenant's companions stared in the direction of the *skest*.
But not at the *skest*.

Untouched amid the green forms, as if he were impervious
to every conceivable vitriol, stood Vain.

His posture was one of relaxation and poise; his arms hung,
slightly bent, at his sides. But at intervals he took a step, two
steps, drew gradually closer to the leading edge of the *skest*.
They broke against his legs and had no effect.

His gaze was unmistakably fixed on Linden.

In a flash of memory, Covenant saw Vain snatch Linden
into his arms, leap down into a sea of graveling. The Demondim-spawn had returned from quicksand and loss to rescue
her.

"Who—?" the First began.

"He is Vain," Brinn replied, "given to ur-Lord Thomas
Covenant by the Giant Saltheart Foamfollower among the
Dead in Andelain."

She cleared her throat, searching for a question which would
produce a more useful answer. But before she could speak,
Covenant heard a soft popping noise like the bursting of a
bubble of mud.

At once, Vain came to a halt. His gaze flicked past the
company, then faded into disfocus.

Covenant turned in time to see a short figure detach itself
from the burning mud, step queasily onto the hard ground.

The figure was scarcely taller than the *skest*, and shaped
like them, a misborn child without eyes or any other features.

But it was made of mud. Flames flickered over it as it climbed from the fire, then died away, leaving a dull brown creature like a sculpture poorly wrought in clay. Reddish pockets embedded in its form glowed dully.

Paralyzed by recognition, Covenant watched as a second clay form emerged like a damp sponge from the mud. It looked like a crocodile fashioned by a blind man.

The two halted on the bank and faced the company. From somewhere within themselves, they produced modulated squishing noises which sounded eerily like language. Mud talking.

The First and Pitchwife stared, she sternly, he with a light like hilarity in his eyes. But Honninscrave stepped forward and bowed formally. With his lips, he made sounds which approximated those of the clay forms.

In a whisper, Pitchwife informed his companions, "They name themselves the *sur-jheherrin*. They ask if we desire aid against the *skest*. Honninscrave replies that our need is absolute." The clay creatures spoke again. A look of puzzlement crossed Pitchwife's face. "The *sur-jheherrin* say that we will be redeemed. 'In the name of the Pure One,' " he added, then shrugged. "I do not comprehend it."

The *jheherrin*. Covenant staggered inwardly as memories struck him like blows. Oh dear God.

The soft ones. They had lived in the caves and mud pits skirting Foul's Creche. They had been the Despiser's failures, the rejected mischances of his breeding dens. He had let them live because the torment of their craven lives amused him.

But he had misjudged them. In spite of their ingrown terror, they had rescued Covenant and Foamfollower from Lord Foul's minions, had taught Covenant and Foamfollower the secrets of Foul's Creche, enabling them to reach the thronehall and confront the Despiser. In the name of the Pure One—

The *sur-jheherrin* were clearly descendants of the soft ones. They had been freed from thrall, as their old legend had foretold. But not by Covenant, though he had wielded the power. His mind burned with remembrance; he could hear himself saying, because he had had no choice, *Look at me. I'm not pure. I'm corrupt.* The word *jheherrin* meant "the corrupt." His reply had stricken the clay creatures with despair. And still they had aided him.

But Foamfollower— The Pure One. Burned clean by the *caamora* of Hotash Slay, he had cast down the Despiser, broken the doom of the *jheherrin*.

And now their inheritors lived in the mud and mire of Sarangrave Flat. Covenant clung to the *sur-jheherrin* with his eyes as if they were an act of grace, the fruit of Foamfollower's great clean heart, which they still treasured across centuries that had corroded all human memories of the Land.

The acid-creatures continued to advance, oblivious to Vain and the *sur-jheherrin*. The first *skest* were no more than five paces away, radiating dire emerald. Hergrom, Ceer, and Harn stood poised to sacrifice themselves as expensively as possible, though they must have known that even *Haruchai* were futile against so much green vitriol. Their expressionlessness appeared demonic in that light.

The two *sur-jheherrin* speaking with Honninscrave did not move. Yet they fulfilled their offer of aid. Without warning, the muck edging the peninsula began to seethe. Mud rose like a wave leaping shoreward, then resolved into separate forms. *Sur-jheherrin* like stunted apes, misrecollected reptiles, inept dogs. Scores of them came wetly forward, trailing fires which quickly died on their backs. They surged with surprising speed past the *Haruchai*. And more of them followed. Out of mud lit garishly by the lurker's fire, they arose to defend the company.

The forces met, vitriol and clay pouring bluntly into contact. There was no fighting, no impact of strength or skill. *Skest* and *sur-jheherrin* pitted their essential natures against each other. The *skest* were created to spill green flame over whatever opposed them. But the clay forms absorbed acid and fire. Each *sur-jheherrin* embraced one of the *skest*, drew the acid-creature into itself. For an instant, emerald glazed the mud. Then the green was quenched, and the *sur-jheherrin* moved to another *skest*.

Covenant watched the contest distantly. To his conflicted passions, the battle seemed to have no meaning apart from the *sur-jheherrin* themselves. While his eyes followed the struggle, his ears clinched every word of the dialogue between Honninscrave and the first mud-forms. Honninscrave went on questioning them as if he feared that the outcome of the combat was uncertain, and the survival of the Search might come to depend on what he could learn.

"Honninscrave asks"— Pitchwife continued to translate

across the mute conflict —"if so many *skest* may be defeated. The *sur-jheherrin* reply that they are greatly outnumbered. But in the name of the Pure One, they undertake to clear our way from this trap and to aid our flight from the Sarangrave."

More clay forms climbed from the mud to join the struggle. They were needed. The *sur-jheherrin* were not able to absorb *skest* without cost. As each creature took in more acid, the green burning within it became stronger, and its clay began to lose shape. Already, the leaders were melting like heated wax. With the last of their solidity, they oozed out of the combat and ran down the sides of the peninsula back into the mud.

"Honninscrave asks if the *sur-jheherrin* who depart are mortally harmed. They reply that their suffering is not fatal. As the acid dissipates, their people will be restored."

Each of the clay forms consumed several of the *skest* before being forced to retreat. Slowly, the assault was eaten back, clearing the ground. And more *sur-jheherrin* continued to rise from the mud, replacing those which fled.

Another part of Covenant knew that his arms were clamped over his stomach, that he was rocking himself from side to side, like a sore child. Everything was too vivid. Past and present collided in him: Foamfollower's agony in Hotash Slay; the despair of the soft ones; innocent men and women slaughtered; Linden helpless in Seadreamer's arms; fragments of insanity.

Yet he could hear Pitchwife's murmur as distinctly as a bare nerve. "Honninscrave asks how the *sur-jheherrin* are able to survive so intimately with the lurker. They reply that they are creatures of mire, at home in quicksand and bog and claybank, and the lurker cannot see them."

Absorbing their way forward, the *sur-jheherrin* reached Vain, shoved past his thighs. The Demondim-spawn did not glance at them. He remained still, as if time meant nothing to him. The clay forms were halfway to the head of the peninsula.

"Honninscrave asks if the *sur-jheherrin* know this man whom you name Vain. He asks if they were brought to our aid by Vain. They reply that they do not know him. He entered their clay pits to the west, and began journeying at once in this direction, traversing their desmesne as if he knew all its ways. Therefore they followed him, seeking an answer to his mystery." Again, Pitchwife seemed puzzled. "Thus he brought them by apparent chance to an awareness that the people of the Pure One were present in Sarangrave Flat—and imperiled. At once, they discarded the question of this Vain and set themselves to answer their ancient debt."

Back-lit by emeralds, orange mudfire in his face, Vain gazed enigmatically through the company, revealing nothing.

Behind him, the *skest* began to falter. Some sense of peril seemed to penetrate their dim minds; instead of oozing continuously toward absorption, they started to retreat. The *sur-jheherrin* advanced more quickly.

Honninscrave made noises with his lips. Pitchwife murmured, "Honninscrave asks the *sur-jheherrin* to speak to him of this Pure One, whom he does not know."

"No," the First commanded over her shoulder. "Inquire into such matters at another time. Our way clears before us. The *sur-jheherrin* have offered to aid us from this place. We must choose our path." She faced Covenant dourly, as if he had given her a dilemma she did not like. "It is my word that the duty of the Search lies westward. What is your reply?"

Seadreamer stood at her side, bearing Linden lightly. His countenance wore a suspense more personal than any mere question of west or east.

Covenant hugged his chest, unable to stop rocking. "No." His mind was a jumble of shards like a broken stoneware pot, each as sharp-edged and vivid as blame. "You're wrong." The Stonedownors stared at him; but he could not read their faces. He hardly knew who he was. "You need to know about the Pure One."

The First's eyes sharpened. "Thomas Covenant," she rasped, "do not taunt me. The survival and purpose of the Search are in my hands. I must choose swiftly."

"Then choose." Suddenly, Covenant's hands became fists, jerking blows at the invulnerable air. "Choose, and be ignorant." His weakness hurt his throat. "I'm talking about a Giant."

The First winced, as if he had unexpectedly struck her to the heart. She hesitated, glancing past the company to gauge the progress of the *sur-jheherrin*. The head of the peninsula would be clear in moments. To Covenant, she said sternly, "Very well, Giantfriend. Speak to me of this Pure One."

Giantfriend! Covenant ached. He wanted to hide his face in grief; but the passion of his memories could not be silenced.

"Saltheart Foamfollower. A Giant. The last of the Giants who lived in the Land. They'd lost their way Home." Foamfollower's visage shone in front of him. It was Honninscrave's face. All his Dead were coming back to him. "Every other hope was gone. Foul had the Land in his hands, to crush it. There was nothing left. Except me. And Foamfollower.

"He helped me. He took me to Foul's Creche, so that I could at least fight, at least make that much restitution, die if I had to. He was burned—" Shuddering, he fought to keep his tale in order. "Before we got there, Foul trapped us. We would have been killed. But the *jheherrin*—the ancestors— They rescued us. In the name of the Pure One.

"That was their legend—the hope that kept them sane. They believed that someday somebody pure—somebody who didn't have Foul's hands clenched in his soul—would come and free them. If they were worthy. Worthy! They were so tormented. There wasn't enough weeping in all the world to describe their worth. And I couldn't—" He choked on his old rage for victims, the preterite and the dispossessed. "I had power, but I wasn't pure. I was so full of disease and violence—" His hands groped the air, came back empty. "And they still helped us. They thought they had nothing to live for, and they helped—"

His vision of their courage held him silent for a moment. But his friends were waiting; the First was waiting. The *sur-jheherrin* had begun to move off the peninsula, absorbing *skest*. He drove himself to continue.

"But they couldn't tell us how to get across Hotash Slay. It was lava. We didn't have any way to get across. Foamfollower—" The Giant had shouted, *I am the last of the Giants. I will give my life as I choose.* Covenant's memory of that cry would never be healed. "Foamfollower carried me. He just walked the lava until it sucked him down. Then he threw me to the other side." His grief resounded in him like a threat of wild magic, unaneled power. "I thought he was dead."

His eyes burned with recollections of magma. "But he wasn't dead. He came back. I couldn't do it alone, couldn't even get into Foul's Creche, never mind find the thronehall, save the Land. He came back to help me. Purified. All his hurts seared, all his hate and lust for killing and contempt for himself gone. He gave me what I needed when I didn't have anything left, gave me joy and laughter and courage. So that I could finish what I had to do without committing another Desecration. Even though it killed him."

Oh, Foamfollower!

"He was the Pure One. The one who freed the *jheherrin*. Freed the Land. By laughing. A Giant."

He glared at the company. In the isolation of what he remembered, he was prepared to fight them all for the respect Foamfollower deserved. But his unquenched passion had nowhere to go. Tears reflected orange and green from Honninscrave's cheeks. Pitchwife's mien was a clench of sorrow. The First swallowed thickly, fighting for sternness. When she spoke, her words were stiff with the strain of self-mastery.

"I must hear more of the Giants you have known. Thomas Covenant, we will accompany you from this place."

A spasm of personal misery knotted Seadreamer's face. The scar under his eyes ached like a protest; but he had no voice.

In silence, Brinn took Covenant's arm and drew him away toward the end of the peninsula. The company followed. Ahead, the *sur-jheherrin* had consumed a passage through the *skest*. Brinn moved swiftly, pulling Covenant at a half-run toward the free night.

When they had passed the *skest*, the *Haruchai* turned eastward.

As the company fled, a screech of rage shivered the darkness, rang savagely across the Sarangrave. But in front of Covenant and Brinn, *sur-jheherrin* appeared, glowing orange and red.

Guided by clay forms, the company began to run.

TWENTY-SIX: *Coercri*

FIVE days later, they reached the verge of Sarangrave Flat and broke out of jungle and wetland into the late afternoon of a cloudless sky. The *sur-jheherrin* were unexpectedly swift, and their knowledge of the Flat was intimate; they set a pace Covenant could not have matched. And Sunder and Hollian were in little better condition. Left to their own strength, they would have moved more slowly. Perhaps they would have died.

So for a large portion of each day, the Giants carried them. Seadreamer still bore Linden supine in his arms to protect her leg; but Sunder sat against the First's back, using her shield as a sling; Hollian straddled Pitchwife's hunched shoulders; and Covenant rode in the crook of Honninscrave's elbow. No one protested this arrangement. Covenant was too weary to feel any shame at his need for help. And peril prevented every other form of pride.

At intervals throughout those five days, the air became turgid screams, afflicting the company with an atavistic dread for which there was no anodyne except flight. Four times, they were threatened. Twice, hordes of *skest* appeared out of dark streams and tar-pits; twice, the lurker itself attacked. But, aided by the *sur-jheherrin* and by plentiful supplies of green wood, the *Haruchai* and the Giants were able to repulse the *skest*. And Covenant opposed the lurker with the light of the *krill*, lashing white fire from the unveiled gem until the lurker quailed and fled, yowling insanely.

When he had the chance, during times of rest or less frenetic travel, Honninscrave asked the *sur-jheherrin* more questions, gleaning knowledge of them. Their story was a terse one, but it delineated clearly enough the outlines of the past.

For a time which must have been measured in centuries after the fall of Foul's Creche, the *jheherrin* had huddled fearfully in their homes, not daring to trust their redemption, trust that they had been found worthy. But at last they had received proof strong enough for their timorous hearts. Freed from the Despiser's power and from the corruptive might of the Illearth Stone, the *jheherrin* had regained the capacity to bring forth children. That was redemption, indeed. Their children they named the *sur-jheherrin*, to mark their new freedom. In the age which followed, the soft ones began the long migration which took them from the place of their former horror.

From cave to mud pit, quagmire to swamp, underground spring to riverbed, they moved northward across the years, seeking terrain in which they could flourish. And they found what they needed in the Sarangrave. For them, it was a place of safety: their clay flesh and mobility, their ability to live in the bottoms of quicksands and streams, suited them perfectly to the Flat. And in safety they healed their old terror, became creatures who could face pain and risk, if need arose. Thus their gratitude toward the Pure One grew rather than diminished through the generations. When they saw Giants in peril, their decision of aid was made without hesitation for all the *sur-jheherrin* throughout the Sarangrave.

And with that aid, the company finally reached the narrow strip of open heath which lay between the time-swollen Sarangrave and the boundary hills of Seareach. The quest was in grim flight from the most desperate assault of the *skest*. But suddenly the trees parted, unfurling the cerulean sky like a reprieve overhead. The smell of bracken replaced the dank stenches and fears of the Flat. Ahead, the grass-mantled hills rose like the battlements of a protected place.

The Giants ran a short distance across the heath like Ranyhyn tasting freedom, then wheeled to look behind them.

The *skest* had vanished. The air was still, unappalled by lust or rage, empty of any sound except bird calls and breeze. Even the solidity of the ground underfoot was a surcease from trepidation.

The *sur-jheherrin*, too, melted back into the Flat as if to avoid thanks. At once, Covenant shrugged himself from Honninscrave's arm and returned to the edges of the jungle, trying to find the words he wanted. But his heart had become a wilderland where few words grew. He could do nothing except stare dumbly through the trees with the sun in his face, thinking like an ache, Foamfollower would be proud.

The First joined him and gazed into the Sarangrave with an unwonted softness in her eyes. Brinn joined him; all his companions joined him, standing like a salute to the unquestionable worth of the *sur-jheherrin*.

Later, the *Haruchai* unpacked their supplies and prepared a meal. There between the Sarangrave and Seareach, the company fed and tried to measure the implications of their situation.

Linden sat, alert and awkward, with her back braced against Seadreamer's shin; she needed the support because of the rigid splint on her left leg. She had awakened a day and a half after her injury and had taken pains to assure her companions that her ankle was knitting properly. *Diamondraught* was a potent healer. But since then, Covenant had had no chance to talk to her. Though Seadreamer carried a constant unhappiness on his face, he tended Linden as if she were a child.

Covenant sorely wanted to speak with her. But for the present, sitting in the bracken with the afternoon sun slanting toward evening across his shoulders, he was preoccupied by other questions. The Giants had brought him this far; but they had not been persuaded to give him the help he needed. And he had promised them the tale of the Unhomed. He could not imagine ever having enough courage to tell it.

Yet he had to say something. Sunder and Hollian had moved away into the dark, seeking a private relief. Covenant understood. After all their other losses, they now had before them a world for which they were not equipped—a world without the Sunbane that made them valuable to their companions. But the Giants sat expectantly around the flames, waiting to hear him argue for their aid. Something he must say. Yet it was not in him.

At last, the First broke the silence. "Giantfriend." She used the title she had given him gently. "You have known Giants—the people of your friend, Saltheart Foamfollower. We deeply desire to hear their story. We have seen in you that it is not a glad tale. But the Giants say that joy is in the ears that hear, not in the mouth that speaks. We will know how to hear you with joy, though the telling pains you."

"Joy." Covenant swallowed the breaking of his voice. Her words seemed to leech away what little fortitude he had left. He knew what the Giants would do when they heard his story. "No. Not yet. I'm not ready."

From his position behind Covenant, Brinn said, "That tale is known among the old tellers of the *Haruchai*." He moved closer to the fire, met the sudden dismay in Covenant's face. "I will tell it, though I have not been taught the skill of stories." In spite of its dispassion, his gaze showed that he was offering a gift, offering to carry one of Covenant's burdens for him.

But Covenant knew the story too well. The fate of the Bloodguard and their Vow was inextricably bound up with the doom of the Seareach Giants. In his *Haruchai* honesty, Brinn would certainly reveal parts of the story which Covenant would never choose to tell. Brinn would disclose that Korik's mission to the Unhomed had reached *Coercri* with Lord Hyrim during the slaughter of the Giants by a Giant-Raver. Three of the Bloodguard had survived, had succeeded in killing the Giant-Raver, had captured a fragment of the Ill-earth Stone. But the Stone had corrupted them, turning them to the service of Lord Foul. And this corruption had so appalled the Bloodguard that they had broken their Vow, had abandoned the Lords during the Land's gravest peril. Surely Brinn would describe such things as if they were not a great grief to his people, not the reason why group after group of *Haruchai* had returned to the Land, falling prey to the butchery of the Clave. This Covenant could not bear. The Bloodguard had always judged themselves by standards which no mortal could meet.

"No," Covenant almost moaned. He faced Brinn, gave the only answer he had. You don't have to do that. It's past. It wasn't their fault. " 'Corruption wears many faces.' " He was quoting Bannor. " 'Blame is a more enticing face than others, but it is none the less a mask for the Despiser.' " Do you know that Foul maimed those three Bloodguard? Made them into half-hands? "I'll tell it." It's on my head. "When I'm ready." A pang of augury told him that *Haruchai* were going to die because of him.

Brinn studied him for a moment. Then the *Haruchai* shrugged fractionally, withdrew to his place guarding Covenant's back. Covenant was left with nothing between him and the intent eyes of the Giants.

"Giantfriend," the First said slowly, "such tales must be shared to be borne. An untold tale withers the heart. But I do not ask that you ease your heart. I ask for myself. Your tale concerns my kindred. And I am the First of the Search. You have spoken of the Sunbane which so appalls the Earth. My duty lies there. In the west. Seadreamer's Earth-Sight is clear. We must seek out this evil and oppose it. Yet you desire our aid. You ask for our proud *dromond* Starfare's Gem. You assert that your path is the true path of the Search. And you refuse to speak to us concerning our people.

"Thomas Covenant, I ask for your tale because I must choose. Only in stories may the truth to guide me be found. Lacking the knowledge which moves your heart, I lack means to judge your path and your desires. You must speak."

Must? In his emotional poverty, he wanted to cry out, You don't know what you're doing! But the Giants regarded him with eyes which asked and probed. Honninscrave wore his resemblance to Foamfollower as if that oblique ancestry became him. Seadreamer's stare seemed rife with Earth-Sight. Empathy complicated Pitchwife's smile. Covenant groaned inwardly.

"These hills—" He gestured eastward, moving his half-hand like a man plucking the only words he could find. "They're the boundary of Seareach. Where the Giants I knew used to live. They had a city on the Sea. *Coercri*: The Grieve. I want to go there."

The First did not reply, did not blink.

He clenched his fist and strove to keep himself intact. "That's where they were murdered."

Honninscrave's eyes flared. Pitchwife drew a hissing breath through his teeth. "In their homes?"

"Yes."

The First of the Search glared at Covenant. He met her look, saw dismay, doubt, judgment seethe like sea shadows behind her eyes. In spite of his fear, he felt strangely sure that her anger would give him what he wanted.

In a tone of quiet iron, she said, "Honninscrave will return to Starfare's Gem. He will bring the Giantship northward. We will meet at this *Coercri*. Thus I prepare to answer your desires—if I am persuaded by your tale. And the others of the Search will wish to behold a city of Giants in this lost land.

"Thomas Covenant, I will wait. We will accompany you to the coast of Seareach. But"— her voice warned him like a sword in her hands —"I will hear this tale of murder."

Covenant nodded. He folded his arms over his knees, buried his face between his elbows; he needed to be alone with his useless rue. You'll hear it. Have mercy on me.

Without a word, Honninscrave began to pack the supplies he would need. Soon he was gone, striding briskly toward the Sea as if his Giantish bones could do without rest forever.

The sound of Honninscrave's departure seemed to stretch out Covenant's exhaustion until it covered everything. He settled himself for sleep as if he hoped that he would never awaken.

But he came out of dreams under the full light of the moon. In the last flames of the campfire, he could see the Giants and the Stonedownors slumbering. Dimly, he made out the poised, dark shapes of the *Haruchai*. Vain stood at the edge of the light, staring at nothing like an entranced prophet.

A glimpse of orange-red reflecting from Linden's eyes revealed that she also was awake. Covenant left his blankets. His desire for the escape of sleep was strong, but his need to talk to her was stronger. Moving quietly, he went to her side.

She acknowledged him with a nod, but did not speak. As he sat beside her, she went on staring into the embers.

He did not know how to approach her; he was ignorant of any names which might unlock her. Tentatively, he asked, "How's your leg?"

Her whisper came out of the dark, like a voice from another world. "Now I know how Lena must have felt."

Lena? Surprise and shame held him mute. He had told her about that crime when she had not wanted to hear. What did it mean to her now?

"You raped her. But she believed in you and she let you go. It's like that for me."

She fell silent. He waited for a long moment, then said in a stiff murmur, "Tell me."

"Almost everything I see is a rape." She spoke so softly that he had to strain to hear her. "The Sunbane. The Sarangrave. When that Raver touched me, I felt as if I had the Sunbane inside me. I don't know how you live with that venom. Sometimes I can't even stand to look at you. That touch denied everything about me. I've spent half my life fighting to be a doctor. But when I saw Joan, I was so horrified— I couldn't bear it. It made me into a lie. That's why I followed you.

"That Raver— It was like with Joan, but a thousand times worse. Before that, I could at least survive what I was seeing —the Sunbane, what it did to the Land—because I thought it was a disease. But when he touched me, he made everything evil. My whole life. Lena must have felt like that."

Covenant locked his hands together and waited. After a while, she went on. "But my ankle is healing. I can feel it. When it was broken, I could see inside it, see everything that needed to be done, how to get the bones back into place. I knew when they were set right. And now I can feel them healing. They're fusing just the way they should. The tissues, the blood-vessels and nerves—" She paused as if she could not contain all her emotion in a whisper. "And that *diamondraught* speeds up the process. I'll be able to walk in a few days."

She turned to face him squarely. "Lena must have felt like that, too. Or she couldn't have let you get away with it.

"Covenant." Her tone pleaded for his understanding. "I need to heal things. I need it. That's why I became a doctor, and why I can't stand all this evil. It isn't something I can heal. I can't cure souls. I can't cure myself."

He wanted to understand, yearned to comprehend her. Her

eyes reflected the embers of the fire like echoes of supplication. But he had so little knowledge of who she was, how she had come to be such a person. Yet the surface of her need was plain enough. With an effort, he swallowed his uncertainty, his fear. "The One Tree," he breathed. "We'll find it. The Giants know whom to ask to find out where it is. We'll make a Staff of Law. You'll be able to go home. Somehow."

She looked away, as if this were not the answer she desired. But when she spoke, she asked, "Do you think they're going to help us? Seadreamer doesn't want to. I can see it. His Earth-Sight is like what I feel. But it's with him all the time. Distance doesn't make any difference. The Sunbane eats at him all the time. He wants to face it. Fight it. End what's happening to him. And the First trusts him. Do you think you can convince her?"

"Yes." What else could he offer her? He made promises he did not know how to keep because he had nothing else to give. "She isn't going to like it. But I'll find a way."

She nodded as if to herself. For a while she was still, musing privately over the coals like a woman who needed courage and only knew how to look for it alone. Then she said, "I can't go back to the Sunbane." Her whisper was barely audible. "I can't."

Hearing her, Covenant wanted to say, You won't have to. But that was a promise he feared to make. In Andelain, Mhoram had said, *The thing you seek is not what it appears to be. In the end, you must return to the Land.* Not what it appears—? Not the One Tree? The Staff of Law?

That thought took him from Linden's side; he could not face it. He went like a craven back to his blankets and lay there hugging his apprehension until his weariness pulled him back to sleep.

The next morning, while the sunrise was still hidden, lambent and alluring behind the hills, the company climbed into Seareach.

They ascended the slope briskly, in spite of Covenant's grogginess, and stood gazing out into the dawn and the wide region which had once been Saltheart Foamfollower's home. The crisp breeze chilled their faces; and in the taintless light, they saw that autumn had come to the fair land of Seareach. Below them, woods nestled within the curve of the hills: oak, maple, and sycamore anademed in fall-change; Gilden gloriously bedecked. And beyond the woods lay rolling grasslands as luxuriously green as the last glow of summer.

Seeing Seareach for the first time—seeing health and beauty for the first time since he had left Andelain—Covenant felt strangely dry and detached. Essential parts of him were becoming numb. His ring hung heavily on his half-hand, as if, when his two fingers had been amputated, he had also lost his answer to self-doubt. Back at Revelstone, innocent men and women were being slain to feed the Sunbane. While that crime continued, no health in all the world could make a difference to him.

Yet he was vaguely surprised that Sunder and Hollian did not appear pleased by what they saw. They gazed at the autumn as if it were Andelain—a siren-song, seductive and false, concealing madness. They had been taught to feel threatened by the natural loveliness of the Earth. They did not know who they were in such a place. With the Sunbane, Lord Foul had accomplished more than the corruption of nature. He had dispossessed people like the Stonedownors from the simple human capacity to be moved by beauty. Once again, Covenant was forced to think of them as lepers.

But the others were keenly gladdened by the view. Appreciation softened the First's stern countenance; Pitchwife chuckled gently under his breath, as if he could not contain his happiness; Seadreamer's misery melted somewhat, allowing him to smile. The *Haruchai* stiffened slightly, as if in their thoughts they stood to attention out of respect for the fealty and sorrow which had once inhabited Seareach. And Linden gazed into the sunrise as if the autumn offered her palliation for her personal distress. Only Vain showed no reaction. The Demondim-spawn seemed to care for nothing under any sun.

At last, the First broke the silence. "Let us be on our way. My heart has conceived a desire to behold this city which Giants have named The Grieve."

Pitchwife let out a laugh like the cry of a kestrel, strangely lorn and glad. With a lumbering stride, he set off into the morning. Ceer and Hergrom followed. The First also followed. Seadreamer moved like the shifting of a colossus, stiff and stony in his private pain. Sunder scowled apprehensively; Hollian gnawed at her lower lip. Together, they started after the Giants, flanked by Stell and Harn. And Covenant went with them like a man whose spirit had lost all its resilience.

Descending toward the trees, Pitchwife began to sing. His

voice was hoarse, as if he had spent too much of his life singing threnodies; yet his song was as heart-lifting as trumpets. His melody was full of wind and waves, of salt and strain, and of triumph over pain. As clearly as the new day, he sang:

"Let breakers crash against the shore—
let rocks be rimed with sea and weed,
cliffs carven by the storm—
let calm becalm the deeps,
or wind appall the waves, and sting—
and sting—
nothing overweighs the poise of Sea and Stone.
The rocks and water-battery of Home endure.
We are the Giants,
born to live,
and bold for going where the dreaming goes.

"Let world be wide beyond belief,
the ocean be as vast as time—
let journeys end or fail,
seaquests fall in ice or blast,
and wandering be forever. Roam—
and roam—
nothing tarnishes the poise of Sea and Stone.
The hearth and harborage of Home endure.
We are the Giants,
born to sail,
and bold to go wherever dreaming goes."

On his song went, on through the trees and the fall-fire of the leaves, on into poignancy and yearning and the eagerness to hear any tale the world told. It carried the quest forward, lightened Seadreamer's gaze; it eased the discomfort of the Stonedownors like an affirmation against the unknown, gave a spring to the dispassionate strides of the *Haruchai*. Echoing in Covenant's mind like the thronged glory of the trees, it solaced his unambergrised heart for a time, so that he could walk the land which had been Foamfollower's home without faltering.

He had been too long under the Sunbane, too long away from the Land he remembered. His eyes drank at the trees and the grasslands, the scapes and vistas, as if such things ended a basic drought, restored to him the reasons for his quest. Beyond the hills, Seareach became a lush profusion of grapes, like a vineyard gone wild for centuries; and in it birds flocked, beasts made their homes. If he had not lacked Linden's vision, he could have spent days simply renewing his sense of health.

But he was condemned to the surface of what he beheld. As the leagues stretched ahead of him, threescore or more to the coast, his urgency returned. At his back, people were dying to pay for every day of his journey. Yet he could not walk any faster. A crisis was brewing within him. Power; venom; rage. Impossible to live with wild magic. Impossible to live without it. Impossible to keep all the promises he had made. He had no answer. He was as mortal as any leper. His tension was futile. Seeking to delay the time of impact, when the storm born of venom and doubt would hit, he cast around for ways to occupy his mind.

Linden was wrapped up in her efforts to recover from the damage the Sunbane and Sarangrave Flat had done to her. Sunder and Hollian shared an air of discomfiture, as if they no longer knew what they were doing. So Covenant turned to the Giants, to Pitchwife, who was as loquacious as the First was stern.

His misshapen features worked grotesquely as he talked; but his appearance was contradicted by his lucid gaze and irrepressible humor. At the touch of a question, he spoke about the ancient Home of the Giants, about the wide seas of the world, about the wonders and mysteries of roaming. When he became excited, his breathing wheezed in his cramped lungs; but for him, even that difficult sound was a form of communication, an effort to convey something quintessential about himself. His talk was long and full of digressions, Giantish apostrophes to the eternal grandeur of rock and ocean; but gradually he came to speak of the Search, and of the Giants who led it.

Cable Seadreamer's role needed no explanation; his Earth-Sight guided the Search. And his muteness, the extravagant horror which had bereft him of voice, as if the attempt to put what he saw into speech had sealed his throat, only made his claim on the Search more absolute.

But being Seadreamer's brother was not the reason for Grimmand Honninscrave's presence. The Giantclave had selected him primarily for his skill as pilot and captain; he was the Master of the *dromond* Starfare's Gem, and proud in the pride of his ship.

As for the First, she was a Swordmain, one of the few Swordmainnir among the current generation of the Giants, who had maintained for millennia a cadre of such fighters to aid their neighbors and friends at need. She had been chosen because she was known to be as resolute as Stone, as crafty as Sea—and because she had bested every other Swordmain to win a place at the head of the Search.

"But why?" asked Covenant. "Why did she want the job?"

"Why?" Pitchwife grinned. "In good sooth, why should she not? She is a Swordmain, trained for battle. She knows, as do we all, that this wound will grow to consume the Earth unless it is opposed. And she believes that its ill is already felt, even across the land of Home, giving birth to evil seas and blighted crops. And cripples." His eyes glinted merrily, defying Covenant to pity his deformity.

"All right." Covenant swallowed the indignation he usually felt whenever he encountered someone whose happiness seemed to be divorced from the hard fact of pain. "Tell me about yourself. Why were you chosen?"

"Ah, that is no great mystery. Every ship, however proud, must have a pitchwife, and I am an adept, cunning to mend both hawser and shipstone. Also, my lesser stature enables me for work in places where other Giants lack space. And for another reason, better than all others." He lowered his voice and spoke privately to Covenant. "I am husband to the First of the Search."

Involuntarily, Covenant gaped. For an instant, he believed that Pitchwife was jesting ironically. But the Giant's humor was personal. "To me," he whispered, so that the First could not hear him, "she is named Gossamer Glowlimn. I could not bear that she should sail on such a Search without me."

Covenant remained silent, unable to think of any adequate response. *I am husband*— Echoes of Joan ran through him; but when he tried to call up her face, he could find nothing except images of Linden.

During the evening of the quest's third day in Seareach, Linden borrowed Hollian's dirk to cut the splint away from her leg. Her companions watched as she tentatively flexed her knee, then her ankle. Light twinges of pain touched her face, but she ignored them, concentrating on the inner state of her bones and tissues. After a moment, her features relaxed. "It's just stiff. I'll try walking on it tomorrow."

A sigh rustled through the company. "That is good," the First said kindly. Sunder nodded gruff agreement. Hollian stooped to Linden, hugged her. Linden accepted their gladness; but her gaze reached toward Covenant, and her eyes were full of tears for which he had no answer. He could not teach her to distinguish between the good and ill of her health sense.

The next morning, she put weight on her foot, and the bones held. She was not ready to do much walking; so Seadreamer continued to carry her. But the following day she began working to redevelop the strength of her legs, and the day after that she was able to walk at intervals for nearly half the company's march.

By that time, Covenant knew they were nearing the Sea. The terrain had been sloping slowly for days, losing elevation along rumpled hills and wide, wild, hay leas, down fields like terraces cut for Giants. Throngs of grave old woods leaned slightly, as if they were listening to the Sea; and now the crispness of the air had been replaced by moisture and weight, so that every breeze felt like the sighing of the ocean. He could not smell salt yet; but he did not have much time left.

That night, his dreams were troubled by the hurling of breakers. The tumult turned his sleep into a nightmare of butchery, horror made all the more unbearable by vagueness, for he did not know who was being butchered or why, could not perceive any detail except blood, blood everywhere, the blood of innocence and self-judgment, permitting murder. He awoke on the verge of screams, and found that he was drenched by a thunderstorm. He was cold, and could not stop shivering.

After a time, the blue lash and clap of the storm passed, riding a stiff wind out of the east; but the rain continued. Dawn came, shrouded in torrents which soaked the quest until Covenant's bones felt sodden, and even the Giants moved as if they were carrying too much weight. Shouting over the noise, Pitchwife suggested that they find or make shelter to wait out the storm. But Covenant could not wait. Every day of his journey cost the lives of people whose only hope arose from their belief in the Clave; and the Clave was false. He drove his friends into movement with a rage which made the nerves of his right arm ache as if his fingers could feel the hot burden of his ring. The companions went forward like lonely derelicts, separated from each other by the downpour.

And when at last the storm broke, opening a rift of clear sky across the east, there against the horizon stood the lorn stump of *Coercri*'s lighthouse. Upraised like a stonework forearm from which the fist had been cut away, it defied weather and desuetude as if it were the last gravestone of the Unhomed.

Giants who had loved laughter and children and fidelity, and had been slaughtered in their dwellings because they had not chosen to defend themselves.

As the rain hissed away into the west, Covenant could hear waves pounding the base of The Grieve. A line of gray ocean lay beyond the rim of the cliff; and above it, a few hardy terns had already taken flight after the storm, crying like the damned.

He advanced until he could see the dead city.

Its back was toward him; *Coercri* faced the Sea. The Unhomed had honeycombed the sheer cliff above the breakers so that their city confronted the east and hope. Only three entrances marked the rear of The Grieve, three tunnels opening the rock like gullets, forever gaping in granite sorrow over the blow which had reft them of habitation and meaning.

"Thomas Covenant." The First was at his side, with Pitchwife and Seadreamer behind her. "Giantfriend." She held her voice like a broadsword at rest, unthreatening, but ready for combat. "You have spoken of Giants and *jheherrin*; and in our haste, we did not question that which we did not understand. And we have waited in patience for the other tale of which you gave promise. But now we must ask. This place is clearly Giant-wrought—clearly the handiwork of our people. Such craft is the blood and bone of Home to us. About it we could not be mistaken."

Her tone tightened. "But this place which you name The Grieve has been empty for many centuries. And the *jheherrin* of which you spoke are also a tale many centuries old. Yet you are human—more short-lived than any other people of the Earth. How is it possible that you have known Giants?"

Covenant grimaced; he had no room in his heart for that question. "Where I come from," he muttered, "time moves differently. I've never been here before. But I knew Saltheart Foamfollower. Maybe better than I knew myself. Three and a half thousand years ago." Then abruptly the wrench of pain in his chest made him gasp. Three and a half—! It was too much—a gulf so deep it might have no bottom. How could he hope to make restitution across so many years?

Clenching himself to keep from panting, he started down the slope toward the central tunnel, the main entrance to *Coercri*.

The clouds had withdrawn westward, uncovering the sun. It shone almost directly into the stone passage, showed him his way to the cliff-face. He strode the tunnel as if he meant to hurl himself from the edge when he reached it. But Brinn and Hergrom flanked him, knowing what he knew. His companions followed him in silence, hushed as if he were leading them into a graveyard hallowed by old blood. Formally, they entered The Grieve.

At its end, the tunnel gave onto a rampart cut into the eastmost part of the cliff. To the north and south, *Coercri* curved away, as if from the blunt prow of the city. From that vantage, Covenant was able to see all The Grieve outstretched on either hand. It was built vertically, level after level of ramparts down the precipice; and the tiers projected or receded to match the contours of the rock. As a result, the city front for nearly a thousand feet from cliff edge to base had a knuckled aspect, like hands knotted against the weather and the eroding Sea.

This appearance was emphasized by the salt deposits of the centuries. The guardwalls of the lower ramparts wore gray-white knurs as massive as travertine; and even the highest levels were marked like the mottling of caducity, the accumulated habit of grief.

Behind the ramparts, level after level, were doorways into private quarters and public halls, workshops and kitchens, places for songs and stories and Giantclaves. And at the foot of the cliff, several heavy stone piers stood out from the flat base which girdled the city. Most of these had been chewed to ruins; but, near the center of *Coercri*, two piers and the levee between them had endured. Combers rolling in the aftermath of the storm beat up the levee like frustration and obstinance, determined to break the piers, breach the rock, assail *Coercri*, even if the siege took the whole life of the Earth to succeed.

Considering the city, the First spoke as if she did not wish to show that she was moved. "Here is a habitation, in good sooth—a dwelling fit for Giants. Such work our people do not lightly undertake or inconsiderately perform. Perhaps the Giants of this place knew that they were lost to Home. But they were not lost to themselves. They have given pride to all their people." Her voice held a faint shimmer like the glow of hot iron.

And Pitchwife lifted up his head as if he could not contain his wildness, and sang like a cry of recognition across the ages:

> "We are the Giants,
> born to sail,
> and bold to go wherever dreaming goes."

Covenant could not bear to listen. Not lost to themselves. No. Not until the end, until it killed them. He, too, could remember songs. *Now we are Unhomed, bereft of root and kith and kin.* Gripping his passions with both hands to control them, restrain them for a little while yet, he moved away along the rampart.

On the way, he forced himself to look into some of the rooms and halls, like a gesture of duty to the dead.

All the stone of the chambers—chairs, utensils, tables—was intact, though every form of wood or fiber had long since fallen away. But the surfaces were scarred with salt: whorls and swirls across the floors; streaks down the walls, encrustations over the bedframes; spontaneous slow patterns as lovely as frost-work and as corrosive as guilt. Dust or cobwebs could not have articulated more eloquently the emptiness of The Grieve.

Impelled by his private urgency, Covenant returned to the center of the city. With his companions trailing behind him, he took a crooked stairway which descended back into the cliff, then toward the Sea again. The stairs were made for Giants; he had to half-leap down them awkwardly, and every landing jolted his heart. But the daylight had begun to fade, and he was in a hurry. He went down three levels before he looked into more rooms.

The first doorway led to a wide hall large enough for scores of Giants. But the second, some distance farther along the face of the city, was shut. It had been closed for ages; all the cracks and joints around the architrave were sealed by salt.

His instincts ran ahead of his mind. For reasons he could not have named, he barked to Brinn, "Get this open. I want to see what's inside."

Brinn moved to obey; but the salt prevented him from obtaining a grip.

At once, Seadreamer joined him and began scraping the crust away like a man who could not stand closed doors, secrets. Soon, he and Brinn were able to gain a purchase for their fingers along the edge of the stone. With an abrupt wrench, they swung the door outward.

Air, which had been tombed for so long that it no longer held any taint of must or corruption, spilled through the opening.

Within was a private living chamber. For a moment, dimness obscured it. But as Covenant's eyes adjusted, he made out a dark form sitting upright and rigid in a chair beside the hearth.

Mummified by dead air and time and subtle salt, a Giant.

His hands crushed the arms of the chair, perpetuating forever his final agony. Splinters of old stone still jutted between his fingers.

His forehead above his vacant eyesockets was gone. The top of his head was gone. His skull was empty, as if his brain had exploded, tearing away half his cranium.

Hellfire!

"It was as the old tellers have said." Brinn sounded like the dead air. "Thus they were slain by the Giant-Raver. Unresisting in their homes."

Hell and blood!

Trembling, Seadreamer moved forward. "Seadreamer," the First said softly from the doorway, warning him. He did not stop. He touched the dead Giant's hand, tried to unclose those rigid fingers. But the ancient flesh became dust in his grasp and sifted like silence to the floor.

A spasm convulsed his face. For an instant, his eyes glared madly. His fists bunched at the sides of his head, as if he were trying to fight back against the Earth-Sight. Then he whirled and surged toward Covenant as if he meant to wrest the tale of the Unhomed from Covenant by force.

"Giant!"

The First's command struck Seadreamer. He veered aside, lurched to press himself against the wall, struggling for self-mastery.

Shouts that Covenant could not still went on in his head: curses that had no meaning. He forced his way from the room, hastened to continue his descent toward the base of *Coercri*.

He reached the flat headrock of the piers as the terns were settling to roost for the night and the last pink of sunset was fading from the Sea. The waves gathered darkly as they climbed the levee, then broke into froth and phosphorescence against the stone. *Coercri* loomed above him; with the sun behind it, it seemed to impend toward the Sea as if it were about to fall.

He could barely discern the features of his companions. Linden, the Giants, Sunder and Hollian, the *Haruchai*, even Vain—they were night and judgment to him, a faceless jury assembled to witness the crisis of his struggle with the past, with memory and power, and to pronounce doom. He knew what would happen as if he had foreseen it with his guts, though his mind was too lost in passion to recognize anything except his own need. He had made promises— He seemed to hear the First saying before she spoke, "Now, Thomas Covenant. The time has come. At your behest, we have beheld The Grieve. Now we must have the story of our lost kinfolk. There can be neither joy nor decision for us until we have heard the tale."

The water tumbled its rhythm against the levee, echoing her salt pain. He answered without listening to himself, "Start a fire. A big one." He knew what the Giants would do when they heard what they wanted. He knew what he would do.

The *Haruchai* obeyed. With brands they had garnered from Seareach, and Seadreamer's firepot, they started a blaze near the base of the piers, then brought driftwood to stoke the flames. Soon the fire was as tall as Giants, and shadows danced like memories across the ramparts.

Now Covenant could see. Sunder and Hollian held back their apprehension sternly. Linden watched him as if she feared he had fallen over the edge of sanity. The faces of the Giants were suffused with firelight and waiting, with hunger for any anodyne. Reflecting flames, the flat countenances of the *Haruchai* looked inviolate and ready, as pure as the high mountains where they made their homes. And Vain—Vain stood black against the surrounding night, and revealed nothing.

But none of that mattered to Covenant. The uselessness of

his own cursing did not matter. Only the fire held any meaning; only *Coercri*, and the lorn reiteration of the waves. He could see Foamfollower in the flames. Words which he had suppressed for long days of dread and uncertainty came over him like a creed, and he began to speak.

He told what he had learned about the Unhomed, striving to heal their slaughter by relating their story.

Joy is in the ears that hear.

Foamfollower! Did you let your people die because you knew I was going to need you?

The night completed itself about him as he spoke, spared only by stars from being as black as The Grieve. Firelight could not ease the dark of the city or the dark of his heart. Nothing but the surge of the Sea—rise and fall, dirge and mourning—touched him as he offered their story to the Dead.

Fully, formally, omitting nothing, he described how the Giants had come to Seareach through their broken wandering. He told how Damelon had welcomed the Unhomed to the Land and had foretold that their bereavement would end when three sons were born to them, brothers of one birth. And he spoke about the fealty and friendship which had bloomed between the Giants and the Council, giving comfort and succor to both; about the high Giantish gratitude and skill which had formed great Revelstone for the Lords; about the concern which had led Kevin to provide for the safety of the Giants before he kept his mad tryst with Lord Foul and invoked the Ritual of Desecration; about the loyalty which brought the Giants back to the Land after the Desecration, bearing with them the First Ward of Kevin's Lore so that the new Lords could learn the Earthpower anew. These things Covenant detailed as they had been told to him.

But then Saltheart Foamfollower entered his story, riding against the current of the Soulsease toward Revelstone to tell the Lords about the birth of three sons. That had been a time of hope for the Unhomed, a time for the building of new ships and the sharing of gladness. After giving his aid to the Quest for the Staff of Law, Foamfollower had returned to Seareach; and the Giants had begun to prepare for the journey Home.

At first, all had gone well. But forty years later a silence fell over Seareach. The Lords were confronted with the army of the Despiser and the power of the Illearth Stone. Their need was sore, and they did not know what had happened to the

Giants. Therefore Korik's mission was sent to *Coercri* with the Lords Hyrim and Shetra, to give and ask whatever aid was possible.

The few Bloodguard who survived brought back the same tale which Foamfollower later told Covenant.

And he related it now as if it were the unassuageable threnody of the Sea. His eyes were full of firelight, blind to his companions. He heard nothing except the breakers in the levee and his own voice. Deep within himself, he waited for the crisis, knowing it would come, not knowing what form it would take.

For doom had befallen the three brothers: a fate more terrible to the Giants than any mere death or loss of Home. The three had been captured by Lord Foul, emprisoned by the might of the Illearth Stone, mastered by Ravers. They became the mightiest servants of the Despiser. And one of them came to The Grieve.

Foamfollower's words echoed in Covenant. He used them without knowing what they would call forth. "Fidelity," the Giant had said. "Fidelity was our only reply to our extinction. We could not have borne our decline if we had not taken pride.

"So my people were filled with horror when they saw their pride riven—torn from them like rotten sails in the wind. They saw the portent of their hope of Home—the three brothers—changed from fidelity to the most potent ill by one small stroke of the Despiser's evil. Who in the Land could hope to stand against a Giant-Raver? Thus the Unhomed became the means to destroy that to which they had held themselves true. And in horror at the naught of their fidelity, their folly practiced through long centuries of pride, they were transfixed. Their revulsion left no room in them for thought or resistance or choice. Rather than behold the cost of their failure—rather than risk the chance that more of them would be made Soulcrusher's servants—they elected to be slain."

Foamfollower's voice went on in Covenant's mind, giving him words. "They put away their tools."

But a change had come over the night. The air grew taut. The sound of the waves was muffled by the concentration of the atmosphere. Strange forces roused themselves within the city.

"And banked their fires."

The ramparts teemed with shadows, and the shadows began to take form. Light as eldritch and elusive as sea phosphorescence cast rumors of movement up and down the ways of *Coercri*.

"And made ready their homes."

Glimpses which resembled something Covenant had seen before flickered in the rooms and solidified, shedding a pale glow like warm pearls. Tall ghosts of nacre and dismay began to flow along the passages.

"As if in preparation for departure."

The Dead of The Grieve had come to haunt the night.

For one mute moment, he did not comprehend. His companions stood across the fire from him, watching the specters; and their shadows denounced him from the face of *Coercri*. Was it true after all that Foamfollower had deserted his people for Covenant's sake? That Lord Foul's sole reason for destroying the Unhomed was to drive him, Thomas Covenant, into despair?

Then his crisis broke over him at last, and he understood. The Dead had taken on definition as if it were the flesh of life, had drifted like a masque of distress to the places which had been their homes. And there, high on the southmost rampart of The Grieve, came the Giant-Raver to appall them.

He shone a lurid green, and his right fist clenched a steaming image of emerald, dead echo of the Illearth Stone. With a deliberate hunger which belied his swiftness, he approached the nearest Giant. She made no effort to escape or resist. The Raver's fist and Stone passed into her skull, into her mind; and both were torn away with a flash of power.

In silence and rapine, the Giant-Raver moved to his next victim.

The Dead of The Grieve were reenacting their butchery. The flow of their movements, the Giant-Raver's progress from victim to victim, was as stately as a gavotte; and the flash of each reiterated death glared across the waves without noise or end, punctuating heinously the ghost dance of the Unhomed. Damned by the way they had abandoned the meaning of their lives, they could do nothing in the city which was their one great grave except repeat their doom, utter it again and again across the ages whenever *Coercri* held any eyes to behold their misery.

From room to room the Giant-Raver went, meting out his

ancient crime. Soon, a string of emeralds covered the highest rampart as each new blast pierced Covenant's eyes, impaled his vision and his mind like the nails of crucifixion.

And as the masque went on, multiplying its atrocity, the living Giants broke, as he had known they would. His anguish had foreseen it all. *Joy is in the ears that hear.* Yes, but some tales could not be redeemed by the simple courage of the listener, by the willingness of an open heart. Death such as this, death piled cruelly upon death, century after century, required another kind of answer. In their desperation, the living Giants accepted the reply Covenant had provided for them.

Pitchwife led the way. With a sharp wail of aggrievement, he rushed to the bonfire and plunged his arms to the shoulders in among the blazing firewood. Flames slapped his face, bent his head back in a mute howl against the angle of his crippled chest.

Linden cried out. But the *Haruchai* understood, and did not move.

The First joined Pitchwife. Kneeling on the stone, she clamped her hands around a raging log and held it.

Seadreamer did not stop at the edge of the flames. Surging as if the Earth-Sight had deprived him of all restraint, he hurled his whole body into the fire, stood there with the blaze writhing about him like the utterance of his agony.

Caamora: the ritual fire of grief. Only in such savage physical hurt could the Giants find release and relief for the hurting of their souls.

Covenant had been waiting for this, anticipating and dreading it. *Caamora*. Fire. Foamfollower had walked selflessly into the magma of Hotash Slay and had emerged as the Pure One.

The prospect terrified him. But he had no other solution to the venom in his veins, to the power he could not master, had no other answer to the long blame of the past. The Dead repeated their doom in The Grieve above him, damned to die that way forever unless he could find some grace for them. Foamfollower had given his life gladly so that Covenant and the Land could live. Covenant began moving, advancing toward the fire.

Brinn and Hergrom opposed him. But then they saw the hope and ruin in his eyes. They stepped aside.

"Covenant!"

Linden came running toward him. But Cail caught her, held her back.

Heat shouted against Covenant's face like the voice of his destiny; but he did not stop. He could not stop. Entranced and compelled, he rode the mourning of the Sea forward.

Into the fire.

At once, he became wild magic and grief, burning with an intense white flame that no other blaze could touch. Shining like the gem of the *krill*, he strode among the logs and embers to Seadreamer's side. The Giant did not see him, was too far gone in agony to see him. Remembering Foamfollower's pain, Covenant thrust at Seadreamer. Wild magic blasted the Giant from the fire, sent him sprawling across the cold stone.

Slowly, Covenant looked around at his companions. They were distorted by the flames, gazing at him as if he were a ghoul. Linden's appalled stare hurt him. Because he could not reply to her in any other way, he turned to his purpose.

He took hold of the wild magic, shaped it according to his will, so that it became his own ritual, an articulation of compassion and rage for all torment, all loss.

Burning, he opened himself to the surrounding flames.

They rushed to incinerate him; but he was ready. He mastered the bonfire with argence, bent it to his command. Flame and power were projected outward together, so that the blaze lashed tremendously into the night.

He spread his arms to the city, stretched himself as if he yearned to embrace the whole of The Grieve.

In wild magic, white puissance without sound, he shouted: Come! This is the *caamora*! Come and be healed!

And they came. His might and his will interrupted the masque, broke the *geas* which locked the Dead in their weird damnation. Hearing him, they turned as if they had been waiting through all the long ages of their anguish for his call. In throngs and eagerness, they began flowing down the passages of *Coercri*.

Like a river, they swept out onto the headrock of the piers.

Toward the fire.

The Giant-Raver tried to pursue them. But the breaking of their eternal round seemed to break also his hold over them, break the spell of his maleficent glee. His form frayed as he moved, blurred until he was only a tingling green smear of memory across The Grieve—until he faded into the night, and was lost.

And the Dead continued toward the fire.

The *Haruchai* drew back, taking Linden and the Stone-downors with them. Pitchwife and the First went with aching bones to tend Seadreamer.

Vain did not move. He stood in the path of the Dead and watched Covenant's immolation with gaiety in his eyes.

But the Dead passed around him, streamed forward. Need and hope shone through their pearl faces.

Reaching out to them as if they were all one, as if they were only Foamfollower in multiform guise, Covenant took them into his embrace, and wept white fire.

The wild magic struck pain into them, seared them the way a physical conflagration would have seared their bodies. Their forms went rigid, jaws stretched, eyes stared—specters screaming in soul-anguish. But the screaming was also laughter.

And the laughter prevailed.

Covenant could not hold them. They came into his arms, but they had no bodies that he could hug. Nothing filled his embrace; no contact or benison restored him to himself. He might have been alone in the fire.

Yet the laughter stayed with him. It was glad mirth, joy and restitution which Foamfollower would have known how to share. It ran in his ears like the Sea and sustained him until everything else was gone—until his power was spent against the heavens, and the night closed over him like all the waters of the world.

TWENTY-SEVEN: Giantfriend

THE next morning, the *dromond* Starfare's Gem arrived in a gleam of white sails, as if it had been newly created from the sun's reflection on the blue Sea. It hove into sight like a stone castle riding gallantly before the wind, beautifully both swift and massive, matching the grace and strength of the Giants.

Covenant watched its approach from the cliff above *Coercri*.

He sat far enough back from the edge to appease his fear of heights, but close enough to have a good view. Linden, Sunder, and Hollian were with him, though he had only asked for the company of the two Stonedownors. Brinn and Cail, Stell and Harn were there also. And Vain had followed Covenant or Linden up through The Grieve, though his blackness offered no explanation of why he had done so. Only Hergrom and Ceer remained below with the Giants.

Earlier, Sunder had told Covenant how he had been saved when his power failed. Linden had watched him amid the blaze, reading his wild magic, gauging the limits of his endurance. One moment before the white flame had guttered and gone out, she had shouted a warning. Seadreamer had dashed into the bonfire and had emerged on the far side with Covenant in his arms, unharmed. Even Covenant's clothing had not been singed.

In the dawn, he had awakened as if from the first irenic sleep of his life. Sunrise had lain across the headrock of the city, lighting the faces of Linden and the First as they sat regarding him. The First had worn her iron beauty as if behind it lay a deep gentleness. But Linden's gaze was ambiguous, undecided.

In a severe tone, she asked, "Why didn't you tell me what you were going to do?"

"I didn't dare," he replied, giving her the truth. "I was too afraid of it. I couldn't even admit it to myself."

She shifted her position, drawing somewhat away from him. "I thought you'd gone crazy."

He sighed, allowed himself to express at least that much of his loneliness. "Maybe I did. Sometimes it's hard to tell the difference."

She frowned and fell silent, looking away toward the Sunbirth Sea. After a moment, the First roused herself to speak.

"Thomas Covenant," she said, "I know not whether in truth the path of the Search lies with you. I have not seen with my own eyes the Sunbane, nor met in my own person the malice of him whom you name the Despiser, nor felt in my own heart the nature of what must be done. But Pitchwife urges that I trust you. Cable Seadreamer has beheld a vision of healing, when he had learned to believe that no healing remained in all the world. And for myself—" She swallowed thickly. "I would gladly follow a man who can so give peace to the damned.

"Giantfriend," she said, containing her emotion with formality, "the Search will bear you to the land of the *Elohim*. There we believe that knowledge of the One Tree may be gained. If it lies within our doing, we will accompany you to the Tree, hoping for an answer to the peril of the Earth. This we will do in the name of our people, who have been redeemed from their doom."

She passed a hand over her tears and moved away, leaving him eased, as if it were the outcome of his dreams.

But he arose, because there were still things he had to do, needs to be met, responsibilities to be considered. He spoke to the Stonedownors, led them to the upper rim of *Coercri* with Linden, the *Haruchai*, and Vain behind him, sat facing the morning and the Sea and the unknown Earth.

Now he would have liked to be alone with the aftermath of his *caamora*. But he could see the time of his departure from the Land arriving. It sailed the same salt wind which ruffled his hair and beard, and he knew he had no choice. Every day, more lives were shed to feed the Sunbane. The Land's need was a burden he could not carry alone.

For a time, he sat exchanging silence with his companions. But at last he found the will to speak. "Sunder. Hollian." They sat attentively, as if he had become a figure of awe. He felt like a butcher as he said, "I don't want you to come with me."

The eh-Brand's eyes widened as if he had slapped her without warning or cause. Surprise and pain made Sunder snap, "Ur-Lord?"

Covenant winced, fumbled to apologize. "I'm sorry. This is hard to say. I didn't mean it the way it sounded." He took hold of himself. "There's something else I want you to do."

Hollian frowned at him, echoing Sunder's uncertainty.

"It's the Sunbane," he began. "I'm going to leave the Land —try to find the One Tree. So I can replace the Staff of Law. I don't know what else to do. But the Clave—" He swallowed at the anger rising in his throat. "I don't know how long I'm going to be gone, and every day they kill more people. Somebody has to stop them. I want you to do it."

He stared out to Sea, went on speaking as if he feared the reaction of his friends. "I want you to go back to the Upper Land. To the villages—to every Stonedown or Woodhelven you can find. Tell them the truth about the Clave. Convince them. Make them stop surrendering to the Riders. So the Sunbane won't destroy everything before I get back."

"Thomas Covenant." Sunder's fists were clenched as if to hold off outrage. "Have you forgotten Mithil Stonedown? Have you forgotten Stonemight Woodhelven? The people of the Land shed strangers to answer their own need for blood. We will convince no one. We will be slain by the first Stonedown we dare to enter."

"No." Covenant shook his head flatly. He knew what he meant to do, and felt sure of it. "You'll have something that will make them listen to you. And you can use it to defend yourselves if you have to." With both hands, he removed the cloth-wrapped *krill* from under his belt, and extended it toward Sunder.

"Covenant?" The Graveler looked his astonishment at Linden, at Hollian, then back toward Covenant. Linden sat with her eyes downcast, watching the way her fingers touched the stone. But Hollian's face brightened as if in recognition. "The *krill* is yours," Sunder murmured, asking for comprehension. "I am a Graveler—nothing more. Of what use is such a periapt to me?"

Deliberately, Covenant held out his hope. "I think you can attune yourself to it. The way you did to Memla's *rukh*. I think you can use the *krill* the way you use the Sunstone. And if you put the two together, you won't need to shed blood to have power. You can use the *krill* to rouse the *orcrest*. You'll be able to raise water, grow plants, do it all. Without blood. Any village will listen to that. They won't try to kill you. They'll try to keep you.

"And that's not all. This is *power*. Proof that the Sunbane isn't the whole truth. It proves that they have a choice. They don't have to obey the Clave, don't have to let themselves be slaughtered."

With a twitch of his hands, he flung off part of the cloth so that the *krill* shone into the faces of his companions. "Sunder," he implored. "Hollian. Take it. Convince them. We're all responsible—all of us who know the na-Mhoram is a Raver. Don't let the Clave go on killing them." The light of the *krill* filled his orbs; he could not see how his friends responded. "Give me a chance to save them."

For a moment, he feared the Stonedownors would refuse the burden he offered them. But then the *krill* was taken from him. Sunder flipped cloth back over the gem. Carefully, he rewrapped the blade, tucked it away under his leather jerkin. His eyes gleamed like echoes of white fire.

"Thomas Covenant," he said, "ur-Lord and Unbeliever, white gold wielder, I thank you. It is sooth that my heart did not relish this quest across unknown seas and lands. I have no knowledge of such matters and little strength for them. You have Giants with you, and *Haruchai*, and the power of the white ring. I am of no use to you.

"I have learned that the Sunbane is a great evil. But it is an evil which I comprehend and can confront." Hollian's countenance supported his words. Her relief was a glow of gratitude. "I desire to strive somewhat for my people—and to strive against this Clave, which so maligns our lives."

Covenant blinked at the repetitions of silver arcing across his sight. He was too proud of Sunder and Hollian to speak.

They rose to their feet. "Ur-Lord," the Graveler said, "we will do as you ask. If any blow may be struck against Clave and Sunbane by mortals such as we are, we will strike it. You have restored to me the faith of Nassic my father. Be certain of us while we live."

"And be swift," added Hollian, "for we are but two, and the Sunbane is as vast as all the Land."

Covenant had not noticed Stell and Harn unobtrusively leave the cliff; but they returned now, carrying supplies on their backs. Before Covenant or the Stonedownors could speak, Brinn said, "The Sunbane is indeed vast, but you will not meet it alone. The *Haruchai* will not surrender their service. And I say to you that my people also will not suffer the Clave unopposed. Look for aid wherever you go, especially when your way leads within reach of Revelstone."

Sunder swallowed thickly, unable to master his voice. Hollian's eyes reflected the sunshine wetly.

The sight of them standing there in their courage and peril made Covenant's fragile calm ache. "Get going," he said huskily. "We'll be back. Count on it."

In a rush of emotion, Hollian came to him, stooped to grip her arms around his neck and kiss his face. Then she went to Linden. Linden returned her embrace stiffly.

A moment later, the Stonedownors turned away. They left the cliff with Stell and Harn beside them.

Covenant watched them go. The two *Haruchai* moved as if nothing could ever change who they were. But Sunder and Hollian walked like people who had been given the gift of meaning for their lives. They were just ordinary people, pitifully small in comparison to the task they had undertaken; and yet their valor was poignant to behold. As they passed over the ridge where the ruined lighthouse stood, they had their arms around each other.

After a moment, Linden broke the silence. "You did the right thing." Her voice wore severity like a mask. "They've been uncomfortable ever since we left Landsdrop—the Sunbane is the only world they understand. And they've lost everything else. They need to do something personal and important. But you—" She stared at him as if in her eyes he had become an object of fear and desire. "I don't know you. I don't know if you're the strongest man I've ever met, or the sickest. With all that venom in you, you still— I don't know what I'm doing here." Without a pause, as if she were still asking the same question, she said, "Why did you give them the *krill*? I thought you needed it. A weapon against Vain."

Yes, Covenant breathed. And an alternative to wild magic. That's what I thought. But by accepting the *krill*, Sunder and Hollian had made it once more into a tool of hope. "I don't want any more weapons," he murmured to Linden. "I'm already too dangerous."

She held his gaze. The sudden clarity of her expression told him that, of all the things he had ever said to her, this, at least, was one she could comprehend.

Then a shout echoed up the face of *Coercri*. "Giantfriend!" It was Pitchwife's voice. "Come! Starfare's Gem approaches!"

The echoes went on in Covenant's mind after the shout had faded. Giantfriend. He was who he was, a man half crippled by loneliness and responsibility and regret. But he had finally earned the title the First had given him.

The *dromond* came drifting slowly, neatly, toward the piers. Its rigging was full of Giants furling the sails.

Carefully, like a man who did not want to die, Covenant got to his feet. With Linden, Brinn, and Cail, he left the cliff. They went down to meet the ship.

Here ends THE WOUNDED LAND, Book One of
The Second Chronicles of Thomas Covenant.

Glossary

Aimil: daughter of Anest; wife of Sunder

a-Jeroth of the Seven Hells: Lord of wickedness; Clave-name for Lord Foul the Despiser

Akkasri na-Mhoram-cro: a member of the Clave

aliantha: treasure-berries

Amith: a woman of Crystal Stonedown

Andelain, the Hills of: a region of the Land free of the Sunbane

Andelainscion: a region in the Center Plains

Anest: woman of Mithil Stonedown; sister of Kalina

Annoy: a Courser

Atiaran Trell-mate: former woman of Mithil Stonedown; mother of Lena

Aumbrie of the Clave: storeroom for former Lore

Bandsoil Bounds: region north of Soulsease River

Banefire: fire by which the Clave wields the Sunbane

Bannor: former Bloodguard

Berek Halfhand: ancient hero; the Lord-Fatherer

Bloodguard: former servants of the Council of Lords

Boulder Fash: region in the Center Plains

Brannil: man of Stonemight Woodhelven

Brinn: a leader of the *Haruchai*; protector of Covenant

caamora: Giantish ordeal of grief by fire

Cable Seadreamer: a Giant; member of the Search; possessed of the Earth-Sight

Caer-Caveral: Forestal of Andelain; formerly Hile Troy

Caerroil Wildwood: former Forestal of Garroting Deep

Cail: one of the *Haruchai*; protector of Linden

Cavewights: evil earth-delving creatures

Ceer: one of the *Haruchai*

Centerpith Barrens: a region in the Center Plains

Chosen, the: title given to Linden Avery

Clang: a Courser

Clangor: a Courser

Clash: a Courser

Clave, the: the rulers of the Land

Coercri: former home of the Giants in Seareach

Colossus of the Fall, the: ancient stone figure formerly guarding the Upper Land

Consecear Redoin: a region north of the Soulease River

Corruption: *Haruchai* name for Lord Foul

Council of Lords: former rulers of the Land

Courser: a beast made by the Clave by the power of the Sunbane

Croft: Graveler of Crystal Stonedown

Crystal Stonedown: home of Hollian

Damelon Giantfriend: son of Berek; former Lord

Defiles Course: river in the Lower Land

Demondim: spawners of ur-viles and Waynhim

Despite: evil; a name given to the designs of Lord Foul

dhraga: a Waynhim

dhubha: a Waynhim

dhurng: a Waynhim

diamondraught: Giantish liquor

Din: a Courser

drhami: a Waynhim

dromond: a Giantship

Drool Rockworm: former Cavewight

durhisitar: a Waynhim

During Stonedown: home of Hamako

Earthpower, the: the source of all power in the Land

Earthroot: lake under *Melenkurion* Skyweir

Earth-Sight: Giantish power to perceive distant dangers and needs

eh-Brand: one who can use wood to read the Sunbane

Elena: former High Lord; daughter of Lena and Covenant

Elohim: people met by the wandering Giants

Emacrimma's Maw: a region in the Center Plains

Fields of Richloam: a region in the Center Plains

Fire-Lions: fire-flow of Mount Thunder

First Betrayer: Clave-name for Berek Halfhand

First Mark: former leader of the Bloodguard

First of the Search: leader of the Giants

First Ward: primary knowledge left by Kevin

Forestal: a protector of the Forests of the Land

Foul's Creche: the Despiser's former home

Furl Falls: waterfall at Revelstone

Garroting Deep: former forest of the Land

ghohritsar: a Waynhim

ghramin: a Waynhim

Giants: a seafaring people of the Earth

Giantclave: Giantish conference

Giantfriend: title given first to Damelon, later to Thomas Covenant

Giantship: stone sailing vessel made by Giants

Giantway: path made by Giants

Giant Woods: a forest of the Land

Gibbon: the na-Mhoram; leader of the Clave

Gilden: a maplelike tree with golden leaves

Glimmermere: a lake on the upland above Revelstone

Gossamer Glowlimn: a Giant; the First of the Search

Graveler: one who uses stone to wield the Sunbane

graveling: fire-stones

Gravelingas: former master of stone-lore

Gravin Threndor: Mount Thunder

Gray Desert: a region south of the Land

Gray Slayer: Lord Foul the Despiser

Graywightswath: a region north of the Soulsease River

Greshas Slant: a region in the Center Plains

Grieve, The: *Coercri*

Grim, the: a destructive storm sent as a curse by the Clave

Grimmand Honninscrave: a Giant; Master of Starfare's Gem

Grimmerdhore: former forest of the Land

Halfhand: title given to Thomas Covenant and to Berek

Hamako: sole unharmed survivor of the destruction of During Stonedown

Harn: one of the *Haruchai*; protector of Hollian

Haruchai, the: a people who live in the Westron Mountains

Heartthew: a title given to Berek Halfhand

Herem: a Raver; also known as *turiya*

Hergrom: one of the *Haruchai*

High Lord: former leader of the Council of Lords

Hile Troy: a man formerly from Covenant's world who became a Forestal

Hollian: daughter of Amith; eh-Brand of Crystal Stonedown

Home: home of the Giants

Hotash Slay: flow of lava protecting Foul's Creche

hurtloam: a healing mud

Hyrim: a former Lord of the Council

Illearth Stone: green stone, source of evil power
Illender: title given to Thomas Covenant

Jehannum: a Raver; also known as *moksha*
jheherrin: soft ones; living by-products of Foul's misshaping
Jous: a man of Mithil Stonedown; son of Prassan; father of Nassic; inheritor of the Unfettered One's mission

Kalina Nassic-mate: mother of Sunder; daughter of Alloma
Keep of the na-Mhoram: Revelstone
Kevin Landwaster: son of Loric; former Lord; enactor of the Ritual of Desecration
Kevin's Watch: mountain lookout near Mithil Stonedown
Kiril Threndor: Heart of Thunder; chamber of power within Mount Thunder
Korik: former Bloodguard
krill, **the:** knife of power formed by Loric Vilesilencer
Kurash Festillin: a region in the Center Plains

Lake Pelluce: a lake in Andelainscion
Landsdrop: great cliff separating Upper and Lower Lands
Law, the: the natural order
Law of Death, the: the separation of the living and the dead
Lena: daughter of Atiaran; mother of Elena
lianar: wood of power used by an eh-Brand
Lord of wickedness: a-Jeroth
Lord Foul: the Despiser
Lords, the: former rulers of the Land
loremaster: ur-vile leader
Loric Vilesilencer: son of Damelon; former Lord
Lower Land, the: region east of Landsdrop
lurker of the Sarangrave: swamp-monster

Marid: a man of Mithil Stonedown
Master, the: Clave-name for the Creator
master-rukh: iron triangle at Revelstone which feeds and reads all other *rukhs*
Melenkurion Skyweir: a mountain in the Westron Mountains
Memla na-Mhoram-in: a Rider of the Clave
metheglin: a beverage; mead
Mhoram: former High Lord of the Council
mirkfruit: papaya-like fruit with narcoleptic pulp
Mithil Stonedown: a village in the South Plains
moksha: a Raver; also known as Jehannum
Morin: a former First Mark of the Bloodguard

Morinmoss: a former forest of the Land
Mount Thunder: a peak at the center of Landsdrop

na-Mhoram, the: leader of the Clave
na-Mhoram-cro: lowest rank of the Clave
na-Mhoram-in: highest rank of the Clave
na-Mhoram-wist: middle rank of the Clave
Nassic: father of Sunder; son of Jous; inheritor of the Unfettered One's mission
Nelbrin: son of Sunder; "heart's child"

Oath of Peace: former oath by the people of the Land against needless violence
Offin: a former na-Mhoram
One Tree, the: mystic tree from which the Staff of Law was made
orcrest: Sunstone; a stone of power, used by a Graveler

Pitchwife: a Giant; member of the Search; husband of the First of the Search
Prothall: a former High Lord
Prover of Life: title given to Thomas Covenant
Pure One, the: redemptive figure of *jheherrin* legend

Quest for the Staff of Law: former quest which recovered the Staff of Law from Drool Rockworm

Ramen: a people of the Land; tenders of the Ranyhyn
Ranyhyn: the great horses; they formerly lived on the Plains of Ra
Ravers: Lord Foul's three ancient servants
Reader: a member of the Clave who tends and uses the *master-rukh*
Rede, the: knowledge of history and survival promulgated by the Clave
Revelstone: mountain-city of the Clave
rhysh: a community of Waynhim; "stead"
Riddenstretch: a region north of the Soulsease River
Rider: a member of the Clave
Ritual of Desecration: act of despair by which Kevin Landwaster destroyed much of the Land
Riversward: a region north of the Soulsease River
rukh: iron talisman by which a Rider wields power
Runnik: former Bloodguard

sacred enclosure: former Vespers hall at Revelstone
Saltheart Foamfollower: former Giant

samadhi: a Raver; also known as Sheol

Santonin na-Mhoram-in: a Rider of the Clave

Sarangrave Flat: a region of the Lower Land

Search, the: quest of the Giants for the wound in the Earth

Seareach: a region of the Land; formerly inhabited by the Giants

Second Ward: second unit of Kevin's hidden knowledge

Seven Hells, the: a-Jeroth's desmesne; desert, rain, pestilence, fertility, war, savagery, darkness

Seven Wards, the: collection of knowledge hidden by Kevin

Shattered Hills: a region of the Land near Foul's Creche

Sheol: a Raver; also known as *samadhi*

Shetra: a former Lord of the Council

Sivit na-Mhoram-wist: a Rider of the Clave

skest: acid-creatures serving the lurker of the Sarangrave

soft ones: the *jheherrin*

soothreader: a seer

soothtell: ritual of prophecy practiced by the Clave

Soulcrusher: former Giantish name for Lord Foul

Staff of Law, the: a tool of power formed by Berek from the One Tree

Starfare's Gem: Giantship used by the Search

Stell: one of the *Haruchai*; protector of Sunder

Stonedown: a village; formerly, a village based on stone-lore

Stonedownor: inhabitant of a Stonedown

Stonemight, the: a name for a fragment of the Illearth Stone

Stonemight Woodhelven: a village in the South Plains

Sunbane, the: a power arising from the corruption of nature by Lord Foul

Sunbirth Sea: ocean east of the Land

Sunder: son of Nassic; Graveler of Mithil Stonedown

Sun-Sage: one who can affect the progress of the Sunbane

Sunstone: *orcrest*

sur-jheherrin: descendants of the *jheherrin*; inhabitants of Sarangrave Flat

Swarte: a Rider of the Clave

Swordmain/Swordmainnir: a Giant trained as a warrior

test of silence: interrogation technique used by the people of the Land

Third Ward: third unit of Kevin's hidden knowledge

Three Corners of Truth: basic formulation of beliefs promulgated by the Clave thronehall, the: the Despiser's former seat in Foul's Creche

Treacher's Gorge: river-opening into Mount Thunder

treasure-berries: *aliantha*; a nourishing fruit

Trell: father of Lena; former Gravelingas of Mithil Stonedown

Triock: a former man of Mithil Stonedown who loved Lena

Trothgard: a region of the Land

turiya: a Raver; also known as Herem

Unbeliever, the: title given to Thomas Covenant

Unfettered, the: formerly, lore-students freed from conventional responsibilities

Unfettered One, the: founder of a line of men waiting to greet Thomas Covenant's return to the Land

Unhomed, the: the former Giants of Seareach

upland: plateau above Revelstone

Upper Land: region west of Landsdrop

ur-Lord: title given to Thomas Covenant

ur-viles: Demondim-spawn; evil creatures of power

ussusimiel: nourishing melon grown by the people of the Land

Vain: a product of ur-viles' breeding experiments

Vespers: former self-consecration ritual of the Lords

Victuallin Tayne: a region in the Center Plains

Viles: a race of beings which created the Demondim

vitrim: nourishing fluid created by Waynhim

voure: a plant-sap which wards off insects

Vow, the: Bloodguard oath of service to the Lords

vraith: a Waynhim

Waynhim: Demondim-spawn, but opponents of the ur-viles

Weird of the Waynhim, the: Waynhim concept of doom, destiny, or duty

white gold: a metal of power not found in the Land

white gold wielder: title given to Thomas Covenant

Wightwarren: catacombs; home of the Cavewights under Mount Thunder

wild magic: the power of white gold; considered the keystone of the Arch of Time

Windscour: region in the Center Plains

Windshorn Stonedown: a village in the South Plains

Woodhelven: a village; formerly, a village based on wood-lore

Woodhelvennin: inhabitants of a Woodhelven

Wraiths of Andelain: creatures of living light which inhabit Andelain